JOANNA
TROLLOPE

JOANNA TROLLOPE

A VILLAGE AFFAIR
A PASSIONATE MAN
THE RECTOR'S WIFE

DEALERFIELD

This edition first published 1991
Copyright © 1989, 1990, 1991 by Joanna Trollope

The moral right of the author
has been asserted

Bloomsbury Publishing Ltd, 2 Soho Square, London W1V 5DE

A CIP catalogue record for this book
is available from the British Library

Printed in England by Clays Ltd, St Ives plc

A Village
Affair

JOANNA TROLLOPE

FOR LOUISE

CHAPTER ONE

On the day that contracts were exchanged on the house, Alice Jordan put all three children into the car and went to visit it. Natasha made her usual seven-year-old fuss about her seat-belt, and James was crying because he had lost the toy man who rode his toy stunt motorbike, but the baby lay peaceably in his carrycot and was pleased to be joggling gently along while a fascinating pattern of bare branches flickered through the slanting back window of the car on to his round upturned face. Natasha sang 'Ten Green Bottles' to drown James and James amplified his crying to yelling. Alice switched on the car radio and a steady female voice from *Woman's Hour* explained calmly to her how to examine herself for any sinister lumps. Mud flew up from the winter lanes and made a gritty veil across the windscreen. James stopped yelling abruptly and put his thumb in his mouth.

'You are an utter baby,' his sister said to him disdainfully. He began to cry again, messily, round his thumb.

Alice could see his smeary wet red face reflected in the driving mirror. The voice on the wireless said that if you disliked touching yourself, you should get someone else to feel for you. The interviewer said – perfectly reasonably, Alice thought – how would anyone else be able to feel what you could feel, not being, as it were, on the inside of yourself?

'Crying like that,' Natasha said to James, 'makes people think you are a girly.'

James let out a wild squeal and flung his motorbike-clutching fist out sideways at his sister, just able to reach her cheek. Eyes wide with outrage and turned at once upon her mother, Natasha began to cry. In the very back, conscious of an atmosphere he didn't like, Charlie's soft round face gathered itself up in distress. He opened his mouth and screwed his eyes up tight. Alice stopped the car.

1

'The lymph *nodes* – ' said the *Woman's Hour* woman into the racket.

Alice turned her off. She undid her seat-belt and twisted herself around.

'Be quiet!' she shouted. 'You beastly, beastly children. I won't *have* this. You are not to quarrel in the car. How can I drive? Do you want me to drive you into a wall? Because that's what will happen.'

Natasha stopped crying and looked out of the window for walls. There were none, only a hedge and a hilly field and some black and white cows.

She said, 'There aren't any walls.'

Alice ignored her.

'Where did I say we were going?'

'In the car,' James said unsteadily.

His sister looked at him witheringly.

'To our new house.'

'Yes. Don't you *want* to see it?'

'Yes,' Natasha said.

James said nothing. At that moment he didn't want anything except to put his thumb back in, which he dared not do.

'Then,' Alice said, 'nobody will say one single word until we get there. Otherwise you will have to stay in the car while I get out and look at everything. Is that clear?'

She buckled herself in again and started the car. Natasha watched her. She was the only mother Natasha knew who had a pigtail. It was very long. It started high up, almost on top of her head, and ended up half-way down her back. It was fat, too. Usually, she pulled it over one shoulder. Natasha wanted one like it, so did her friend Sophie. Sophie's mother had sort of ordinary hair you couldn't really remember, like mothers usually had. Looking at her mother's pigtail made Natasha suddenly feel affectionate, out of pride.

'I'm sorry,' she said, in a minute voice, because of the ban.

Alice beamed at her quickly, flashing the smile over her shoulder.

'Nearly there.'

Alice had always wanted to live in Pitcombe; everybody did, from

2

miles around, and if a house there was photographed for sale, in *Country Life*, the caption always read, 'In much sought-after village'. It was the kind of village long-term expatriates might fantasise about, a stone village set on the side of a gentle hill, with the church at the top and the pub at the bottom, by a little river, and the big house – baroque – looking down on it all with feudal benevolence. Sir Ralph Unwin, who owned the big house, three thousand acres and two dozen cottages still, was tall and grey-haired and an admirable shot. He drove a Range Rover through the village and waved regally from the elevated driving seat. He allowed Pitcombe Park to be used constantly for functions to raise money for hospices and arthritis research and the church roof, though he drew the line at the local Conservatives. 'I'm a natural cross-bencher,' he would say, knowing he would be admiringly quoted. Alice had only met him once, introduced by John Murray-French from whom they were going to buy the house, and he had said, 'You are more than welcome to Pitcombe, Mrs Jordan, particularly if you have children.'

She had wondered if he was well aware of how charming he was. Lady Unwin was charming too, in that capable, administrative way that women acquire after long practice on councils and committees. Lady Unwin chaired the county's St John's Ambulance Brigade and the local hospice committee and saw it as her duty to attend PCC meetings and NADFAS outings and the village over-sixties jaunts. She had grasped Alice's hand in her own large and flexible one with its pink painted nails and peerless Georgian rings and said, 'Oh my dear, hooray. Just what we need, some new young blood to liven us all up.'

And Sir Ralph, taking his wife by the arm in one of those public displays of proud affection for which he was liked as much as for the independence of his politics, said with a warm smile, 'Don't trust her an inch, Mrs Jordan. She'll have you on every rota and committee in sight, within minutes.'

Everyone round them had laughed. Alice had laughed too. She had liked it. She had felt welcomed and included, almost part of the life that she was quite certain she wanted to live in Pitcombe *for*. When they had heard, at a dinner party, that John Murray-French was selling up, privately, she and Martin had hardly slept for excitement. His was not just a house in Pitcombe, but one of *the* houses in Pitcombe, half-way down the hill, with the beeches of the Park above it and the river three fields below it, at the end of a little cul-de-sac which ran from the main street between pretty, low, haphazard rows of cottages. There was an orchard beyond it, and a paddock where the children could have a pony and, on top of the garage, a wonderful high beamed room with north light where John Murray-French carved the ornamental decoy ducks for which he had become mildly famous and which Alice could use as a studio. She hadn't painted since James was born, more than four years ago. But she would be able to now, she knew it.

She swung the car in off the main street and drove carefully down between the cottages. It was early afternoon and the lane was quite empty except for a crumpled old face at a ground-floor window between a spider plant and a begging china dog in a large green hat. Alice waved and smiled. The face took no notice at all. A black cat on a garden wall didn't even stop washing to watch them go by. At the end of the lane were the two slender weathered stone pillars that announced the entrance to The Grey House. They had stone bobbles on top, smeared with ochre and greenish grey lichen. Beyond them, two clipped deep green rows of hornbeam marched towards the house. Alice stopped the car, suddenly exultant. Everything was going to be all right, it was, it *was*.

'Help yourselves,' John Murray-French had said on the telephone that morning. 'I'll be out but Gwen will be around somewhere supposedly packing books but probably swilling my gin in the broom cupboard. She knows you're coming.' He paused. He was very fond of Alice. So had his son been, but too late, when she was already married. 'I'm so pleased it's you,' he said.

'Oh, John – '

'I've lived here for thirty-five years. Can't believe it. I'd hate it to go to a stranger.'

'I *promise* we'll love it. I mean, we already do. In fact, I think it's the answer – '

'The answer? To what?'

There had been a tiny pause.

'Oh,' she said, in a more matter of fact voice, 'three children, more space, studio for me. You know.'

She let the car creep between the hornbeams. The children,

4

sensing the drama, began to give little squeals of excitement in the back. Natasha had already written, in all her books, partly from pride, partly to prevent James ever claiming them:

This book belongs to:
Natasha Jordan
The Grey House
Pitcombe
Wiltshire

And there it was. Long, low, grey, with its pretty sashed eighteenth-century windows reaching almost to the floors, its heavy panelled door with pediment and lion's-head knocker, its three brick chimneys, its terrace over the valley, sitting so beautifully in its pleasing sweeps of golden gravel and green grass. Sinuous grey arms of wisteria twined up over the pediment and along the façade, and either side of the front door a bay tree grew glossily in a Versailles tub. It was perfect.

Alice climbed out of the car and released the children. They raced down the lawn at once, still squealing, to climb the iron park railing that separated the lawn from the paddock below. Alice opened the back and picked up Charlie. He was very pleased and beat about in the air with his hands and crowed. She went up to the front door and rang the bell. John had said not to bother but she didn't want to alienate Gwen in any way, hoping she would stay and clean the house for her, as she had done for John for a decade.

Gwen opened the door after a very long time, clearly meaning to upstage Alice, but was undone in an instant by the sight of Charlie in his blue padded snowsuit.

'Ah. Bless him. Isn't he lovely? Come in, Mrs Jordan. The Major said you'd be over.'

Alice turned to shout for the children. They were still on the railings.

'I'd leave them,' Gwen said. 'Can't come to no harm. Who's a lovely boy, then?'

Charlie regarded her impassively.

'He's very good,' Alice said, anxious to be friendly. 'The best of the three, really. But he weighs a ton.'

'Would he come to Gwen, then?'

She held out her arms. Charlie allowed himself to be transferred without protest. He examined Gwen's face solemnly for a while and then her pink blouse and her maroon cardigan. Finally, after long scrutiny, he put a single shrimp-like finger on her crystal beads.

'Aren't you gorgeous?' Gwen said to him, quite melted. 'Aren't you and Gwen going to have a nice time, then?'

Alice felt a rush of gratitude towards Charlie.

'Actually, I was going to ask you – '

Gwen turned a beaming face on her.

'I thought you might be. Course I'll help.' She turned her face back to Charlie. 'Gwen's not going to turn down an old heart-throb like you, now, is she. I'll take him into the study, Mrs Jordan, and you just poke about. The Major said to. I'll keep an eye out for the children. Now then,' she said to Charlie, 'I wonder if we could find a biccy?'

Alice said faintly, 'He's only got two teeth. He's only eight months. Perhaps – '

'Who's a big boy?' Gwen said moving off rapidly. 'Who'd have thought it? Eight months – '

The drawing room ran for twenty-five feet along the front of the house to the right of the door; the dining room rather less to the left. Behind them were a study for Martin, a room for a playroom, and a kitchen which opened with a stable door on to a wide brick path and then grass and then the eastward view. The stable door had seized upon Alice's imagination when she had first seen it; she had visualised a summer morning, with the sun streaming in through the opened top half, and herself up a ladder, singing while she stencilled designs her head was full of round the tops of the walls. She could *feel* how happy she would be. The kitchen was rather grim now because John was only concerned with it as a place to open tins in, but she had known the moment she saw it how lovely it could be. Looking at it now, darkly cream painted, shabby linoleum floored, with its scrubbed centre table cluttered with half-empty marmalade jars, and corkscrews and newspapers and ripped-open brown envelopes, she suddenly had a tiny twinge.

It was very tiny, but it was there. It was like a sudden, faint, malicious little draught of cold air on a golden summer day, or a wrong note in a melody, very transient in itself but leaving something unnerving behind it. Alice shook herself, took hold of

6

the comforting end of her plait, and looked sternly at the kitchen. Pale yellow walls, she had settled on that, white woodwork, strip, sand and polish the floor, scented geraniums along the windowsills, dried hops along the ceiling beams, jars of pulses and spices on the dresser, a rocking chair, patchwork cushions, a cat . . . She began, without warning, to cry. It was horrifying. Why was she crying? Huge sobs, like retching, were surging up brokenly inside her and these vast tears were spilling over and she couldn't *see*. She fumbled frantically for a handkerchief, scrabbling in the pockets of her coat and her skirt, up her sleeves, in her bag. She found a crumpled tissue and blew her nose violently. She *never* cried. Strong Alice who hadn't cried since after Charlie which was obviously post-natal. She sat down in one of John's scuffed kitchen chairs and bent her head. She was frightening herself.

Probably she was tired. It had been quite a strain wondering if they really *would* get The Grey House, and Martin wasn't good at this kind of thing and fussed a lot about money and surveys and things like that. She had said to him, trying to encourage him, 'But the *right* things are right, aren't they? I mean, the house *feels* right so I can paint again and make a bit of money at last, and perhaps we could have a pony. It never matters with money in the long run, does it? We always manage. We will now.'

He said crossly, '*I* manage you mean.'

She tried not to feel furious. She tried not to remember that Martin had a private income, even if it wasn't huge, so that money never was a proper problem to them, as it was to other people. They weren't rich, but they weren't uncomfortable either. Martin hated her to talk about his private money; he was very secretive about it. She thought that his pride suffered from knowing he did not earn very much as a country solicitor and probably never would. She told herself he had to pretend he earned all their income, for his own self-esteem. So she waited, looking at his rough, fair head bent over the newspaper, and after a bit she said, 'You see, I think we'll be so happy at The Grey House. That's the element I think is so important.'

They had many such conversations. Sometimes Martin said, 'Aren't you happy here, then?' and sometimes he said, 'Oh I know, I know, I'm just being an ass, you know how I hate thinking about money,' and once he said, 'Thanks a bloody million,' and stamped

7

out. She began to follow him but stopped, and they went to bed that night hardly speaking. That kind of thing was, of course, terribly tiring, far more tiring than digging a whole cabbage patch or painting a ceiling or spending an entire day in London Christmas shopping in the rain. Alice blew her nose again now and stood up. She would go into the drawing room. Nobody could ever want to cry in the drawing room.

But she did. She stood by the fireplace in the lovely long low room with its bookcases, and windows to the terrace, and imagined decorating the Christmas tree in that corner, and doing a vast arrangement of dried flowers in that, and hanging up those marvellous miles of ivory moire curtain that Martin's mother had given her, at all the windows, and she felt worse than she had in the kitchen. She felt despair. At least, she thought it was despair, but she did not think she had ever had a feeling like this in her life with which to compare it. She fled from the drawing room to the dining room, confronted images of herself smiling down the candlelit length of the table across dishes of perfect food, and fled again, upstairs and into the first bedroom she came to.

It was John's. It would be hers and Martin's. It was the room she had dreamed of most, of lying in bed with the view of the valley surging in through those near floor-length windows. She knew where she would put her dressing table, and the little sofa her mother-in-law had given her, and where she would hang her collection of drawings of seated women, a collection she had begun when she was fourteen. She looked at the room now in panic. There was no malevolence in it, nothing in it but its usual graceful, placid charm. The panic was in her. She put her hands to her face. It was burning hot.

In the bathroom John's old pug was curled up in a basket in the bottom of the airing cupboard. The door was open so that he shouldn't feel claustrophobic. He grunted when Alice came in but didn't stir. It was a huge bathroom, with an armchair and a bookcase, ancient club scales, lots of magazines in ragged stacks, a lovely view and several friendly, doggy old dressing gowns hung in a mound on the back of the door. Alice shut the door behind her and locked it. She ran a basin of cool water and splashed her face, then she dried it on John's towel, which smelt attractively male, and sat down in the armchair. Deep breaths, one after the other.

Close eyes. Idiotic Alice, mad Alice, *lucky* Alice. She was still holding John's towel. She buried her face in it. How good male things were when they were impersonal to you: the sound of a strange man's confident stride across a wooden floor, a man behind you at a newspaper kiosk rattling the change in his pocket, the contrast of wrist skin and shirt cuff and jacket sleeve on your neighbour at a dinner party, John's bald old bath towel. She felt better and stood up.

'Never a word of this to anyone,' she said to the pug and went downstairs.

In what would be Martin's study, and was now a fuggy and welcoming burrow where John spent winter evenings, Alice found Charlie sitting on Gwen's knee with her beads round his neck, and Henry Dunne. Henry was Sir Ralph's agent, and although John Murray-French had bought The Grey House from the estate long before Henry's day, it was still regarded as being in the fold. Henry and John's son had been at Eton together and Henry often came in on his way here and there across the estate, to tell him this and that and to describe the hunting days which were his passion and which John, leisurely french-polishing his ducks, didn't seem to mind hearing about, over and over. John's patience meant that when Henry got home he didn't feel the urge to tell Juliet, his wife, all about hunting, which was just as well because it made her scream, literally, with boredom.

Henry thought Alice was wonderful. He thought her beautiful too, with her long dark blue eyes and her astonishing high-plaited hair, but he was rather afraid she might be quite clever. Last New Year's Eve he had hoped she thought him wonderful too because he had boldly kissed her, quite separately from all that lunatic midnight kissing which was always such chaos you might well end up kissing the furniture, and she had seemed to like it. He said, 'Goodnight, my lovely,' to her in a whisper when the party broke up at last and she gave him a long look. But when he saw her next it was in Salisbury, by chance, and she was pushing her baby in a little pram thing and although she smiled at him, she was absolutely composed and even said, 'Wasn't that a lovely party, at the New Year?'

He said, '*You* made it lovely. For me.'

And she smiled at him and shook her head.

9

'Do you mean, Alice, that you didn't – '

'I mean that – '

She stopped. He said, 'What? What? *Tell* me.'

She looked at him again. There was a flicker of fear in her face, he could see it, even a dope like him whom Juliet was always saying had the perceptiveness of a myopic buffalo.

'Please not,' Alice said, and then she had kissed his cheek quickly and pushed her baby into Marks and Spencer.

She seemed only delighted to see him now. She kissed him, said, 'How's Juliet?' and 'Oh, you old ponce,' to Charlie, and sat down beside Gwen.

'The house looks so nice,' she said to Gwen, untruthfully, since she had hardly noticed.

'I do my best. Bit of a business, what with the Major's pipes and the carving and the dogs. But we struggle on, don't we gorgeous?'

Charlie made mewing noises in Alice's direction. She lifted him off Gwen's knee and returned the beads.

'Gwen says she's staying on,' Henry said.

'I know. Isn't it marvellous of her?'

'Four mornings I'll do here. And a day to muck out the Major when he's in his cottage. You should see the place now, walls running with damp – '

Alice stood up, holding Charlie against her shoulder.

'Thank you so much for your kindness, Gwen. It's such a weight off my mind, knowing you'll help me. I ought to go and round up the children now.'

'I'll come with you,' Henry said. 'I only came to leave John the surveyor's report on his cottage.'

Gwen opened the front door for them both. Alice put a hand on it. Her front door. She took her hand away quickly and put it back under Charlie's solidly padded bottom.

'Bye now,' Gwen said. 'Mind how you go. Bye-bye, you lovely boy.'

When the door had shut, Alice said, 'Is she going to drive me mad?'

Henry looked mildly shocked.

'I don't think you'll find anyone else very easily. Everyone is crying out for help and I know for certain Elizabeth Pitt has her eye on Gwen, and so does Sarah Alleyne, except nobody can bear to work for her for more than a month.'

He opened the car boot so that Alice could stow Charlie away in his carrycot.

'We're all thrilled you have got this house, you know. It'll make such a difference to the village.'

Alice straightened up.

'We're so lucky.'

'I'll say. The hordes John has had to beat away don't bear thinking of. He said a chap appeared out of the blue driving a black BMW and offered him four hundred thousand.'

'What has a BMW got to do with it?'

Henry said, faintly nettled, 'He must have come down from the City. *That* sort of money.'

Alice said nothing. She stood quite still and looked at the house. The light was beginning to fade and Gwen had switched on a lamp here and there, coral-coloured rectangles in the soft grey façade. It looked idyllic.

'I'm sick with envy,' Henry said, watching her. 'Me and half Wiltshire.'

Alice turned slowly to face him. She reached out and touched his hand for a second.

'The thing is,' she said, quite calmly, 'that now that I have it, I don't in the least want it.'

And then she burst into tears.

'I don't know what it is,' Martin said into the telephone, keeping his voice down even though Alice was upstairs in the bath. 'She doesn't seem able to tell me. She thinks The Grey House is lovely, she doesn't want to stay here, but she says she is terrified of moving.'

His mother, fifty miles away in Dorset, said, 'Is it the moving itself?'

'Can't be,' Martin said. 'She never minds anything like that. I've never seen her like this.'

'She was very upset for a while after Charlie – '

'That's all over,' Martin said. 'Pronounced A-one four months ago.'

'Have you,' Martin's mother said, 'been quarrelling?'

Too loudly Martin said, '*No.*' Then he said, more ordinarily, 'The odd bicker, I suppose, over what we ought to offer for The Grey House, but not *quarrelling*.'

'Can I speak to her?'

'She's in the bath. She doesn't know I'm ringing you.'

Martin's mother, who loved her daughter-in-law dearly, said with some indignation, 'Behind her back, as if she was unfit to hear? No wonder she cries.'

Martin drooped. It was as it ever was. He couldn't remember a time when he hadn't longed to please his mother, to feel confidential with her, and then to know every time that he had failed. He knew she loved him – but he wasn't ever sure she liked him. It was rather the same with his elder brother Anthony, except that Anthony was tougher and ruder, so that they sparred together. He remembered with customary bewilderment his mother saying to Alice ten years ago, 'I'm glad it's Martin you're marrying, not Anthony. I love Anthony but I know he is really a horrible boy.'

And she meant it. It wasn't a doting mother's joke. Martin wondered uneasily what his mother had said to Alice about him; there was so much she had said to Alice that he would never know.

'Of course talk to her,' he said now, stiffly, 'if you think it'll do any good.'

'Get her to ring me,' Cecily Jordan said, 'when she's out of the bath.'

He sighed and put the receiver down. He was frightfully tired. He had got back from a long day, and everything looked entirely as usual, children in bed, supper ready, Alice in the low slipper chair by the fire in their tiny sitting room, stitching at some tapestry thing until she turned her face up for his greeting kiss and he saw she had been crying. She then cried on and off all through supper. She said, between crying and mouthfuls, that she had an awful feeling of foreboding that it just wasn't going to work. He had said, 'The Grey House, you mean?'

'No – no – not the house exactly, just living there, us living there – '

'But it's the thing you have always wanted!'

'I *know*,' she said, pushing her plate away half-full. 'I know. That's why I am so afraid.'

He tried to jolly her.

12

'You're not afraid of anything! You never have been. You terrify me, skiing.'

'Oh,' Alice said dismissively, 'physical things. Easy. This is something much more alarming, a sort of utterly lost feeling, as if I'd staked everything on something that wasn't there at all.'

Martin began to finish the lasagne she had left.

'I don't understand you,' he said.

He still didn't. Perhaps his mother was right and it was the remains of post-Charlie blues. He felt sorry for her, but at the same time faintly aggrieved that she couldn't behave normally about something she had said she desperately wanted and that he had really had to battle to achieve. He'd had to sell a lot of shares, a *lot*, for The Grey House. He looked round the room, tiny but full of fascinating things and bold stuffs and extraordinary paintings which he wouldn't have chosen himself in a million years but which he found he really liked, now he saw them. Very Alice. He looked into the fire. He felt she was failing him.

When she came down, in a yellow dressing gown with her plait pinned up on top with a comb, he said, trying not to sound surly, 'Ma says would you ring her.'

A kind of light came into Alice's eyes, a look of relief and hope.

'Oh yes,' she said. 'Did she ring?'

'I rang her.'

'Martin, I'm not being deliberately neurotic. I detest feeling like this. If I could stop, I would.'

He got out of his chair and went to kick a log in the fireplace. He thought of his mother's tone to him, on the telephone. He said to Alice, 'Is it me? Is it something to do with me? Are you sick of me?'

Alice gave a little gasp.

'Oh no!'

He grunted.

'Just wondered.'

The wrong note in the melody sang out again, tiny and harsh, in her mind. She went across the room and put her arms round him from behind, laying her cheek against his back.

'You know it isn't that. Haven't I kept telling you that I want The Grey House because I know we'll be happy there?'

'But that doesn't fit in with all this panic.'

13

'Exactly. It's probably some hormone imbalance. That's what I've been thinking about in the bath.'

He turned round and held her. He thought how much more often he needed to make love to her than she wanted to have it made to her. He took a deep breath.

'Go and ring Ma,' he said.

CHAPTER TWO

Before Cecily Jordan had married, she had been, briefly, a Lieder singer. She had gone to Vienna, to train, in 1937, in the teeth of her parents' opposition, and had, at eighteen, fallen wildly in love with music, with Vienna, and with a young Jewish composer and political activist. It was he who introduced her to the pure and lovely solo songs of Schubert and who taught her to vary her performance from lyrical to intensely dramatic, as the Lied required. This he did partly by technical instruction, and partly by taking her to bed and awakening her to a consciousness of her own powers which she found quite natural to express in song.

In the winter of 1939 he made her promise, by threatening never to see her again if she wouldn't comply, to go home at once to England if anything should befall him. He made her write the promise down and sign it. In June 1940, he was arrested while crossing the Ringstrasse, in midday sunlight, and a note from him, containing the written promise, was brought to her while she stood in her sunny, dusty, cluttered room out by the Prater Park, doing her voice exercises.

'To break your promise will make everything infinitely worse for both of us and I should despise, not admire you for it,' her lover wrote. 'The best thing you can do for us now is to take that lovely voice we have made together back to England, and use it as a light in a dark world.'

He did not write that he loved her. Sitting in a series of hideous trains crawling home across Europe, Cecily reflected that he had never said it either. She hadn't noticed, so busy had she been doing the loving for both of them. She arrived in battened-down England in August, numb and almost speechless, and went out to Suffolk to her parents' house, where her mother was relishing the prospect of the privations of wartime, had already sold all her childhood books for salvage and had painted a red line round the bath, four inches

15

from the bottom, as a peculiarly irritating kind of Plimsoll line.

Cecily tried to sing, but she couldn't. War was declared in September but it seemed to her that the news came from very far away and had no direct relevance to her. She slept badly and spent a greater part of each night lying awake reliving Vienna. By day she went for punishing walks and talked a good deal about joining up, which she did not do. Then suddenly, out of the blue, she announced she was going to Canada, to Toronto, to teach singing in a large girls' school. She went for six years. Her parents thought she might marry a Canadian, but she married no one. She returned to England in the grisly winter of 1946 and the following June she married Richard Jordan, whom she had met on the train that she had taken from Southampton after leaving her transatlantic ship.

Richard Jordan was an engineer. He had been in Southampton looking at a bombed site as a possible place for a factory to make drills for wells. He prospered. He and Cecily had two sons in five years and bought a manor house in a wooded valley a mile from the sea beyond Corfe in Dorset. Cecily, who found in due course that she could not naturally enjoy the company of any of the three men in her life, discovered some kind of recompense in the manor's garden. She became a gardener of imagination and then distinction. She wrote books on gardens and was invited to lecture all over England in the sixties and, as her fame spread, all over Eastern America in the seventies.

And then, in 1976, her younger son, Martin, brought Alice home. It was a September day of ripe perfection, the gardens at Dummeridge replete in the late warmth, bursting fallen plums lying stickily in the long grasses, fat things humming and buzzing in the borders. Cecily had been out by the eighteenth-century summerhouse she had discovered derelict in Essex and had transported to Dorset, tying up a heavy double white clematis that obligingly bloomed twice a year, when someone behind her said, quite easily, 'You must be Martin's mother.'

She turned. There was a tall girl standing six feet away. She wore jeans and a blue shirt and her abundant brown hair was tied up behind her head with an Indian scarf.

'I'm Alice Meadows,' the girl said. 'Martin wanted to catch up

16

with the cricket but I said I couldn't bear not to come out here. I hope you don't mind.'

'*Mind,*' Cecily said, 'I should think not.'

She took off her gardening glove and held her hand out to Alice. 'More than welcome, Alice Meadows,' she said.

She had put Alice to sleep in the little south bedroom that she privately thought she would use for herself when Richard was dead. It had a brass bedstead, polished floorboards with rough cream Greek rugs, blue and white toile de Jouy curtains, deep windowsills, and, in a corner, a huge china jardinière out of which a violently healthy plumbago cascaded in a riot of starry pale blue flowers.

'Do you like it?' Cecily said, unnecessarily.

'In every way.'

'It's my favourite room. It has a very nice personality.' She glanced at Alice. 'Are you and Martin serious?'

Alice returned her look, entirely unperturbed. The house and the room and this fascinating, strong-looking woman with her drill gardening shirt and trousers, her beautifully coiffed hair and her ropes of pearls, made her feel that there was nothing to fear or to be decided – it would all be done for her.

'No,' Alice said. 'We have known each other for two weeks. Martin met my brother, playing squash, and my brother brought him home. We have been to the cinema twice and to the pub a bit. You know. And then he asked me here.'

She ran her hand round the fat brass knob on the bed end.

'Do you think,' she said to Cecily, 'that I was wrong to come if I don't mean to be serious?'

'No. Whatever you end up being, you were right to come.'

They went down into the garden again together and Cecily left Alice under a willow at the edge of the lawn while she went to make tea. Alice lay back in an old cane chair whose arms were unravelling in spiny strands, and looked up at the strong blue sky through the fading blond-green fronds of willow and felt – she hunted about in her mind for a word. Happy? Too thin. Content? Too sluggish. Gorgeous? Too self-regarding. But all were right in their way, and so was replete and sleek and blissful, and so was –

Would she, Alice wondered abruptly across her own thoughts, tell Martin's mother about her family? Would she say that to come to this ancient and lovely house, to drowse in this romantic and sensual garden, was an answer to a prayer, the antidote to her own home where the unlovely walls echoed, day in, day out, with her mother's steady complaining? I am ripe for this, Alice told herself, pushing off her shoes with her toes and stretching her bare feet in the sun. I am an absolute sucker for this paradise, I was a pushover even before Martin's mother opened her mouth. She shut her eyes and let the willow dapple its shadow softly across her eyelids. At home now, at 4 Lynford Road, Reading, her mother would be drinking Indian tea out of an ugly mug given away by a garage, while not listening to *Kaleidoscope* or the end of *Afternoon Theatre* on Radio 4, but instead storing up in her mind all the day's grievances which were, indeed, a lifetime's grievances, against her friendly, amiable philandering husband, Alice's father, who was probably, even now, taking a seminar on the Metaphysical Poets at the university and thinking about sex.

She wouldn't leave him. It was one of her complaints to Alice that she wouldn't because she loved him and look how she was treated, how her loyalty was abused. Alice had come to see that it was closer to tyranny than loyalty, even though her father's carryings-on disgusted her. She felt, as she got older, that even her friends weren't safe from him; they all thought him dishy and flirted with him when they came to collect Alice for the cinema or a disco. Alice's mother wanted her to take sides, to defend her, but Alice wouldn't. She thought they were both wrong, and she knew that the moment she had finished art school, she would leave Reading and the hideous house with its charmless contents and her mother's bitter laments and her father's self-indulgence and she would go, like her brothers had, and not come back.

One of her brothers had gone right away, to Los Angeles, where he was a tremendously successful taxi driver. The other had only gone to London, to live happily in a huge disordered flat with six others off Lavender Hill, and do his Law Society exams. It was he who had brought Martin Jordan home – well, not home exactly because passing through was all he could take – on their way to play squash in some tournament in Oxford, and because Alice had been upstairs painting in an absolute fury after the newest student conquest had telephoned quite openly to ask to speak to Professor Meadows, they had taken her to Oxford too. She wouldn't watch them play squash, but went to the Ashmolean instead and looked at

18

the Caernavon marbles, and came away much soothed. Martin Jordan had come down from London four times in two weeks to take Alice out – the last time he had brought flowers for her mother which nobody had done, Alice thought, in twenty years – and then he had telephoned and said he was coming through Reading, on his way to Dummeridge, and that he would collect her. If she'd like to go.

Alice said Reading wasn't on the way to Dorset from London.

'It is,' Martin said, 'if I'm coming to collect you.'

So he had, and they had driven away from Lynford Road and Alice would not look back to wave at her mother because she knew herself to be the cause of a new complaint for daring to go off to enjoy herself while her mother was forced to stay behind and suffer. And here she now was, as long and supple and warm as a stretched-out cat, lying under a willow in a place like heaven, while someone wonderful brought tea which would be, Alice knew, China, in pretty cups, with slices of lemon to float in it and perhaps almond biscuits.

'There,' Cecily said, 'what a contented looking girl.' She put down the tray. 'I hope you like China tea. And Dorothy, who helps me, has made some shortbread.'

Alice said laughing, 'I said almond biscuits in my mind.'

'And China tea?'

'Oh yes – '

Cecily smiled broadly and sat down in a cane chair.

'Martin is still glued to the box.'

'I don't mind. As long as he doesn't want me to be glued too.'

'He says you paint.'

'Yes.'

'Things you see, or things you imagine?'

'Things I see coloured by things I imagine.'

'Lemon?'

'Oh, please – ' She swung herself upright and put her bare feet down on the brisk, warm, late summer grass.

'You don't know,' she said to Cecily with some energy, 'how heavenly this is.'

'I do, you know. Don't forget that I have virtually made it, so I like to take all the credit.'

She held out a shallow eggshelly cup painted with birds of paradise.

'Where I live,' Alice said, taking it reverently, 'everything is as ugly as possible. I think it's my mother's revenge on life for not making her happy.'

'Almost nobody is happy,' Cecily said. 'It's rather that one must devise ways of cheating or eluding *un*happiness. And of course, some people love unhappiness with a passion.'

'My mother just loves it with a grim determination,' said Alice and let out a burst of sudden laughter, 'Oh, oh, I'm mean, *mean* – '

'Yes,' Cecily said, looking at her with great liking, 'you are. Now, you had better tell me all about her and your clever father. I fear you have come into a gravely illiterate household. I believe my husband reads nothing but newspapers and engineering periodicals, Martin reads nothing but colour supplements and his brother Anthony reads nothing at all. What about you?'

Alice put her cup down carefully and lay back again in the cane chair.

'Love stories. I'm mad on love. Do you think it's the answer?'

'Now that,' Cecily said, thinking of her son Martin, 'is something you will have to find out for yourself.'

Even as a baby, a brand new baby, Martin had looked faintly anxious. He was a pretty baby and then a dear little boy and then an attractive bigger boy and finally he emerged as a sturdy, fair, good-looking man. But he still looked anxious. If you were in a good mood, Cecily always thought, you wanted to comfort that anxiety away, but if you were not, his expression resembled the silent reproachful pleading of a dog who has nothing to do all day but beseech you for a walk you haven't time to give it. She loved Martin very much but she didn't want him with her a great deal; she never had. He was undeniably rather dull, but she wouldn't have minded that. It was his want of boldness she found so discouraging, his unadventurousness, his lack of curiosity. Bringing this uncommon girl down was the most enterprising thing he had done in twenty-four years of life. Not only had he brought her down, but he was handling her beautifully. Cecily would have expected him to be too eager, too slavish, but he wasn't. He was quite challenging in fact,

20

and even though Cecily suspected him of being besotted, he gave little hint of it. Alice had the same bold, free manner with him; there were no longing glances or furtive looks. When Anthony came home, later, for dinner the first evening, Alice took almost no notice of him at all even though he was dramatically rude in order to attract her attention. He was so rude that his father, roused from his inner world at the far end of the table, said suddenly, 'Leave the room.'

'Father – '

'Leave the room.'

Anthony turned to his mother.

'Go on,' she said.

'This is barbaric – '

'Leave the room,' Richard Jordan said, and suddenly there was a bull-like threatening look on his face. Anthony got up.

'What will Alice – ' He stopped. They were all watching him. He left.

Cecily seemed quite unmoved.

'I believe a Frenchwoman has written a book describing how she finally got rid of her five sons. I must buy a copy.'

Martin did not try to come to Alice's room that night. She had thought he might and had rather hoped he wouldn't. She had been to bed twice with men before, once when she was seventeen to see what it was like and get the first time over with, and once six months before, driven by a simple physical longing to be made love to. She had, somewhat inevitably, preferred the second time, but neither had been what she was hoping for, which she put down to not being in love with either man. She was quite clear that she wasn't in love with Martin either, and so didn't want sex with him to become some litmus paper test. But she thought, lying there in linen sheets in her charming room while a disgracefully theatrical copper harvest moon hung outside, that she would very much like some good sex. She would like to be taken over by some huge physical force inside herself and feel every atom of her body as a *body*. One of the lecturers at the art school – rather a creep, in fact – had said that good sex made you a better painter. Alice had thought about this and finally had dismissed it as a very sixties view. What about Toulouse Lautrec and Van Gogh for starters? What Alice really wanted to know, she decided, her hands flat on her cotton

21

nightie-clad belly, was what an orgasm really felt like, what it did to you. Then she could stop *wondering*.

She turned on her side, and slid both hands between her thighs. This was the most wonderful place she had ever been to. If Martin asked her to marry him tomorrow, standing perhaps in the creeper-clad stableyard while the white pigeons flew erratically about in the blue air above them, she would say yes. Then she could always come here and, best of all, Cecily would be her mother-in-law. She began to giggle, helplessly, out of happiness and excitement, and Martin, standing in the dark passage outside her door, was very nearly, but not quite, brave enough to come in and ask her what she was up to.

He knew he wanted to marry her. He knew it the moment her brother Josh had pushed open the back bedroom door in that grim house in Reading, and there was Alice in black and red striped tights and a vast blue smock smeared all over with paint and her hair screwed up on top with a paintbrush thrust through it, painting away in a terrible temper. He didn't even look at what she was painting, he was so busy looking at her. He had never seen anyone who looked so – so *vital*. She flung herself at Josh, who seemed equally pleased to see her. And then they had carried her off to Oxford and Martin had felt that his little Mini was absolutely pulsing with interest and life even though Alice didn't say much. She just sat in the back and *existed*, and occasionally he glanced in the driving mirror at her and felt his guts melt. This was *something*.

He found she gave him courage. He could dare with her, conversation with her was a kind of game. He realised, leaving a pub with her ten days later, that he didn't even feel dull or conventional, he felt brilliant. He grew afraid that if he didn't make her his, for ever, that brilliance would go, he would go back to being the dear, ordinary old Martin who fussed about train times and driving conditions and made his mother – however she strove to conceal it – visibly sigh. Asking Alice down to Dummeridge was a brainwave, an absolute corker of an idea, and now here was Alice adoring the house and getting on with his mother like a house on fire. And even his father . . . Anthony had once said, in a rage, that living with their father was like living in a house where the biggest

22

and best room was always locked, and though Martin, by nature both conventional and loyal, was distressed by the image, he recognised the truth of it. His father wasn't exactly dull, he was just ruthlessly private, but he was watching Alice, Martin could see that, and what was more, he liked her. Being Alice – Martin felt himself dissolve at the thought – she didn't appear to notice that Richard was withdrawn. She talked to him, and so he talked back. He smiled at her. The only person she ignored was Anthony and that was Anthony's own stupid fault, all that capering and showing off to attract her attention, trying to impress her by bitching the parents. It was the first time, the first glorious time in Martin's life, that he had scored over Anthony, that he had something Anthony wanted that he couldn't have, that he had found something of real stupendous quality that his father and his mother applauded him for. He was ten feet tall. He was a new, a different man. If he could keep Alice, everything would fall into place from now on, there would be a goal, a future, he would work for *her*.

With stupendous self-control, and guided by a subtlety of instinct he had never experienced before but which he entirely trusted to, he did not propose to Alice for three months. They saw each other every week, and two weekends a month he arrived in Reading with russet or mauve chrysanthemums for Mrs Meadows ('Only get her hideous flowers,' Alice said. 'She despises pretty ones.') and drove Alice down to Dummeridge. He had a half-gun in a local shoot, and sometimes Alice went with him, to beat, and sometimes she stayed at Dummeridge and painted and talked to Cecily. Cecily admired her paintings a good deal and persuaded her into both watercolours and painting pictures of corners of the house. Alice painted a cobwebby window at a turn of the cellar stairs, and a scattering of hens on the old stone mounting block and a corner of the drawing room where a battered little alabaster bust stood on a table shrouded in an Indian shawl against a faded, striped wall covered in miniatures.

At lunchtime they ate eggs and salad and home-made brown bread by the Aga, and Cecily always gave Alice wine – at home there was beer and whisky for her father and sherry for her mother which of course she wouldn't touch for fear of feeling better, but never wine – and they talked as Alice had never talked before.

Cecily even – and it was thirty years since she had mentioned it to anyone – talked about Vienna. The story fired Alice with a yearning passion, not just the love story but the foreignness, and the powerful romance of the voice that blossomed and was then locked away in a box for ever when all the circumstances that had awakened it were wrenched away. Alice had never travelled, except on a school trip to Paris which was chiefly distinguished by interminable and sick-making hours shut up in a bus. The Jordans had all travelled; they took it as a matter of course. Richard travelled constantly, on business; the boys went skiing and both had been on safari in Kenya; Cecily went on her lecture tours and on her own to France and to Italy to look at things, she said, and to eat and drink both literally and metaphorically.

'You should go,' she said to Alice. 'It's criminal that you haven't been to Italy.'

Alice began to think that indeed it was. As the autumn wore on, she became privately very angry when Sunday night came and she had to leave Dummeridge, glimmering away in the firelight in its wealth of old stuffs and books. Lynford Road looked worse on each return, the scuffed carpet tiles in the hall, the uncompromising, harshly shaded ceiling lights, the black and green tiles in the bathroom, the mean proportions that confronted her everywhere, too high, too narrow. She began to long for Martin's Monday call, regular as clockwork, telling her when he was coming down to take her out. His arrivals, invariably punctual, became events of real excitement. Every time she found him standing on the tiled doorstep in Lynford Road, in a tweed jacket she had last seen him wear in the drawing room at Dummeridge and the brogues she could still hear striking the stone flags of the kitchen passage, her feeling of being rescued grew greater and more glamorous.

In the first week of December he arrived to take her out to supper in Marlow. He was wearing a suit and Alice, convinced he would say *something* to her, put on the black dress she had made from a length of jersey from the market, piled her hair high on her head and added some enormous copper earrings a friend at art school had made for an Egyptian exhibition. The restaurant in Marlow had pink napkins and red-shaded lights. Martin made a face.

'Sorry,' he said to Alice.

She wasn't entirely sure why he was apologising; it looked to her just as she would expect a restaurant to look. In any case, she was far too full of anticipation to care if the panelling was phoney or Mantovani was being played whisperingly over the loudspeaker system. Martin ordered everything competently, told her about his week – she hardly listened to him – and then said he had something to tell her and something to ask her. She forced herself to look at him quite, quite straight.

'Tell first,' she said.

'My mother has two commissions for you. Two friends of hers have seen the paintings you have done of Dummeridge, and they want you to paint in their houses. Ma said she has asked a hundred and fifty for you. Each.'

'Each!' Alice said, and went scarlet.

'Well?' He was smiling hugely.

Alice clutched herself.

'It's – it's *wonderful*. So's she. Heavens. *Real* money – '

There was a sudden small hard lump in her throat. She supposed it to be amazement and delight.

'I rang her last night. She really wanted to tell you herself at Christmas, but I made her let me. That's the other thing. The thing I wanted to ask you.'

Alice couldn't look straight this time; she didn't seem able to look anywhere. She looked down instead into her melon and parma ham and Martin said to her bent head, 'Would you come for Christmas? To Dummeridge?'

There was a pause. Oh, Martin thought, you cool, cool customer, don't keep me dangling, don't, don't. Say yes, say yes, say . . .

'Love to,' Alice said. Her voice was warm but not in the least eager. It betrayed nothing of what she was feeling, nothing of the sudden fury that had seized her, a fury against Martin. Ask me, she had screamed at him silently, ask me, *ask* me. And he had said, come for Christmas.

'That's great,' he said. 'They'll all be thrilled, I know it. What about – '

'My parents?'

'Yes – '

'I've spent twenty Christmases with them,' Alice said with a

25

fierceness for which Lynford Road could not be blamed, 'and I think I deserve one off. Granny's coming, anyway.'

They arrived at Dummeridge on Christmas Eve to a house garlanded in green, with pyramids of polished apples and candles and the smoky scent of burning wood.

'So lovely!' Cecily said. 'To have a woman to do it all for.'

From the moment she and Martin got to Dummeridge, Alice was the star of Christmas. She could feel the atmosphere lifting as she entered rooms and knew that everything was being done for her, with an eye on her. She had a fire in her bedroom, and a Christmas stocking of scarlet felt, and wherever she went the eyes of the household were upon her and the hearts of the household were hers. Even Anthony, she noticed, was striving to please. She felt, moving through the lovely rooms, taking the dogs out for windy walks high above the grey winter sea, that this was what she was meant for, that she had somehow come home.

So confident was she, so queenly, that when Martin did propose she felt no elation, no sudden lurch of delight and relief, just a warm acknowledgement of the inevitable. It was Boxing Day and they were racing along Seacombe Cliff, shouting into the wind, when he seized her suddenly, breathless and laughing, and said, 'You will marry me, won't you?'

And she said, laughing back, 'Certainly not!' and ran away from him, and he knew she didn't mean it and chased her and pulled her to the ground and pinned her there, on the cold exciting turf under the racing wild clouds, and made her promise. Then he carried her home to Dummeridge and his father opened champagne and whenever she looked across at Cecily, Alice knew she could have made no other choice. She was loved here.

That night, relaxed and warm and full of power and confidence, she had an orgasm in Martin's arms. He had one rather later. She was a bit confused – the champagne perhaps – as to why she had had one and how much it had to do with what he was doing to her, which wasn't, actually, much at the time, but she felt great triumph that her body had taken her over, as she had been so anxious for it to do. It did occur to her that the release that had happened to her body didn't seem to have overwhelmed her mind at the same time, but she pushed that thought aside, as clearly, if she had had an orgasm with Martin, she must be more in love than she thought, which meant in turn that it would, as a feeling, grow. She slept gratefully in Martin's arms until five, when he gently disentangled himself and went discreetly back to his own room. They met at breakfast in a mood of mutual, and visible, triumph, and Cecily, noting this with inexpressible relief, felt that thirty years of negative life had at last turned a corner.

CHAPTER THREE

They were married, in 1977, by unanimous agreement, at Dummeridge. Alice's mother, quite overwhelmed by Cecily, allowed all decisions to be made for her, including a shopping trip to Bournemouth for her wedding clothes. She returned, saying a little fretfully that she had never cared for green, but she was clearly elated, and refused to describe the trip in order to show her husband and her daughter that she too could have her lovely secrets. Alice didn't care. She went down to Dummeridge every weekend without fail, and made plans – where Martin should look for a job, what kind of house they should seek, where they should go for their honeymoon, what her dress should be made of, what she ought to put on her wedding present list.

'You mean I can actually ask outright for six cream bath sheets and a Spode blue Italian soufflé dish and a dozen wine glasses and a tin-opener?'

'I most certainly do. People expect it.'

'Wowee! Now,' Alice said. 'Let's think what else – '

Martin was offered a job in Salisbury which he took with alacrity, and not long afterwards Alice and Cecily found a cottage on the edge of Wilton, with three bedrooms and a charming elevated fireplace made from an old bread oven, and an apple tree in the garden. It was May and the tree was luscious with blossom. In June, Alice left the art school, packed up her bedroom in Reading and moved down to Dorset. Her mother, truly wounded now, did not even try to stop her because it was so glaringly evident to everyone why she was doing it. Her father, however, did try.

'Are you sure,' he said to her, propping his attractive bulk against the kitchen cupboards and cradling a glass of whisky against his chest, 'that your head hasn't been turned?'

Alice said waspishly, 'Well, that's certainly something *you* would know about.'

28

He laughed. He had always been exasperatingly impossible to annoy.

'Come on, Al. You've only two months more to stick out here. It's a bit rough on us to be so publicly cast aside for the glamorous prosperity of the Jordans even *before* you're married. You look spoiled. We look inadequate.'

'I don't mind how I look,' Alice said, 'and I can't help how you look. The boys have both gone, I've had three years here on my own. At Dummeridge there isn't a permanent atmosphere and I can paint.' A tiny, proud pause. 'I have three more commissions.'

'You might perhaps,' Sam Meadows said unwisely, suddenly struck by the vision of opening the Lynford Road front door to find nobody but his wife inside, 'think of me.'

Alice snorted.

'I see. You'd like me to stay so that there's some sort of buffer state here between you and Mum. Well, bad luck. That's one of the *reasons* I'm going now.'

Sam took a gulp of his drink.

'Frankly, Al, I don't think I could take it on my own.'

'Then you should understand exactly how I feel. Don't *whine*,' Alice said crossly. 'And don't try and make me feel guilty. I'm going, and that's that.'

Her father levered himself upright and came round the kitchen table to put his arm around her and plant a competent, whisky-scented kiss on her head.

'I don't blame you,' he said, 'and you shouldn't blame me for having a go at making you stay.'

'Blame,' Alice said, leaning against him and resentfully acknowledging how good he was at touching women. 'Don't talk about blame. It's a word never used at Dummeridge, and nor is guilt or loyalty or betrayal or any other of the awful emotional claptrap words you and Mum use *all the time*.'

Her father had gone out then, and she had returned to her room to finish packing, and when she came down, her mother was sitting on the brown repp-covered, foam-filled sofa in the sitting room staring into space with her hands gripping one another in her lap. Alice squatted beside her.

'Martin's coming for me at five.'

'I know,' her mother said.

29

'There's not much difference,' Alice said with difficulty, 'between going now and going when I'm married. Honestly, there isn't.'

Silence.

'It isn't – it isn't because I don't – well, it's not that I'm – I'm not fond of you and Dad, it's just the atmosphere here.'

'I see.'

'Nobody asks me to take sides there,' Alice said, pleading. 'I haven't got to think who I'm going to upset every time I open my mouth.'

Elizabeth Meadows continued to stare at nothing.

'I see.' A little pause. 'And is the Jordans' marriage a happy one?'

Alice was rather startled. She had never stopped to consider such a thing, and now that she did it came to her that perhaps it wasn't particularly companionable as a marriage but it was perfectly all *right*, and anyway, they both had their own lives, *that* was the difference.

'They don't want it to be everything in life to them, like you do,' Alice said, making everything worse. 'Cecily has her own career, Richard's very successful – '

'How perfect,' her mother said, as if spitting out broken glass.

Alice sighed. She got up and went over to the french windows that opened into a sad little strip of garden that her mother tended with ferocious tidiness, filling the parallel beds with salvias and African marigolds in regimented rows.

'Look,' she said, 'whatever I do, I can't get it right. Either you're upset or Dad is. So I'm going only a little bit before marriage decently allows me to, where I get it right all the time without even trying.'

Elizabeth said, 'You protest too much. I am not attempting to prevent you,' and then, blessedly, the doorbell rang and it was Martin.

Alice never slept at Lynford Road again. The two months at Dummeridge passed like a happy dream. Richard was away almost all the time, and Cecily was in America for three weeks, and as Martin, taking his final exams, could not be there except weekends, Alice had the house to herself, looked after by Dorothy and as free as air. She slept in a hammock in the garden at midday, and at night wandered about in the pale summer darkness and made herself voluptuous sandwiches filled with cream cheese and dried apricots and chopped walnuts which she sometimes ate sitting quite naked on the moonlit lawn or in the unlit drawing room. She went down to the sea at midnight, with the surprised but politely acquiescent dogs, and swam in the glittering black water, and then walked home barefoot and sat on the Aga, wrapped in a blanket feeling her salty hair dry into long whispering snakes down her back. She meant to paint, but she didn't. She knew she would have to, when Cecily came back, so she spun out her time alone greedily, luxuriously, drifting through the hot hayfields beyond the house, leaning her cheek against walls and trees, lying on her stomach on the lawn with her arm plunged into the goldfish pool watching the light darting in the water and the bubbles of air pour upwards from the hairs on her arm.

She saw Martin off to London on Sunday nights without a pang; indeed, when the sound of the Mini's busy little engine had quite faded away she felt a bubbling up of her spirits, as if she were really free again. This made her go straight to the kitchen and sit down at the huge scrubbed table and write to him very lovingly, telling him how much she looked forward to Friday, and how carefully he must drive. She wrote these letters in all sincerity. When she had written them, she would go down to the sea and swim and swim and swim. Dorothy, finding wet towels on the Aga rail so many early mornings, wondered whether she should say something about the lack of sense in swimming alone in the sea in the middle of the night and decided, looking at Alice, not to. The moment she was married, that freedom would vanish, you never got it again, so even if it was risky, it was worth it, and after all, everything worth having was a risk, one way or another.

Alice had only two visitors besides Martin, while Cecily was away. One was Anthony who arrived unannounced for the night, drank copiously at dinner and tried, in a very practised way, to kiss her afterwards. She said, standing quite rigid in his arms. 'But I don't fancy you at all. I don't find you in the least attractive.'

'Try me,' he said, bending his head.

She bent away.

'In any case,' she said, 'you are only having a go to score off Martin.'

So Anthony dropped his arms and went to bed, and was gone when she woke in the morning.

The other visitor was her future father-in-law, at home for two nights, between journeys. He telephoned her to say he was coming. She said, wanting to be dutiful, 'Is there anything I ought to do? I mean, anything you'd like or usually have – '

No, he said, nothing. She was to take no notice of him; Dorothy could do what had to be done. He would be there for dinner. So she went for a long, aimless, happy walk, spending a great deal of time in an unexpected stream building a dam, and came back about teatime to hear the sound of someone playing the piano. It could only be Cecily. Full of a sudden rush of pleased excitement, she burst into the drawing room crying, 'Oh, I wasn't *expecting* – ' and found that it was Richard.

He stopped and turned round.

'But,' Alice said, 'you don't *play* the piano!'

He smiled.

'I do.'

'But Cecily – '

'I always have. I'm competent but uninspired, as you may imagine. I never play if I think there is anyone in the house.'

She crossed the room slowly, and stood beside him. He had been playing Schubert, too.

'I've really thrown you,' he said, 'haven't I.'

She felt her face grow hot.

'Yes. I thought – ' she paused.

'I know,' he said. 'People do.' He got up from the piano and brushed his hands briskly together as if he were shaking off the disconcerting unfamiliarity. He looked down at her and she wondered if he were very slightly laughing at her, but all he said was, 'You look well. What have you been doing?'

And she said, looking back, 'Absolutely *nothing*.'

He had liked that. He wanted, later, to hear what absolutely nothing involved. She could tell him parts of it, though clearly to tell a man who is about to become your father-in-law that you had lain naked on his drawing room sofa eating sandwiches in the middle of the night was hardly on. She was, to her surprise, sorry when he went away, bound for Heathrow and then the Gulf of Mexico. He hadn't seemed, while he was at Dummeridge, either to take the house away from her – and after all, it *was* his – or to encroach upon her freedom. On the contrary, he seemed to have his

32

own private freedom which tantalised her a little, made her want to know more about him. When he was gone, she found to her intense annoyance that she was just a little lonely, so that when Cecily returned three days later she had the same kind of thankful, over-excited welcome from Alice as from her dogs.

'I shouldn't have left you so long, but this wretched tour was fixed up almost a year ago. Never, never do I wish to have to explain again that it is not possible to make an English spring garden in Selma, Alabama.'

Everything pulled itself together once Cecily had returned. Days and nights went back to their conventional roles, lists were made, letters were written, Alice's wedding dress – ivory chiffon over peach-coloured silk – was finally fitted. Presents arrived by every post, presents from complete strangers and from shops that had never been in Alice's orbit – the General Trading Company in Sloane Street, Harrods, Peter Jones, Thomas Goode, the White House. The dining room at Dummeridge slowly filled up with sheets and china and saucepans and Chinese lamps, things that she, Alice, had chosen and asked for and was now being given. As the piles grew, she discovered that she did not like it, even though she liked the things. It was not that she felt that she was being spoiled, but rather that these bales of towels and pairs of garden shears and boxes of brandy balloons were somehow buying *her*. She tried to say something of this to Cecily, and Cecily, believing her feeling to be the result of the material modesty of her upbringing, said she must simply lie back and lap it up.

'I promise you, people *want* to do this. They would think it most odd if you hadn't a list, and goodness knows you haven't been greedy.'

So Alice wrote her letters obediently and tried to decide constructively about flowers and asparagus rolls and the colour of lining for the marquee which was to be very grand and have french windows in case the day was cool. At night, instead of lying languorously in her linen sheets, Alice lay and worried, worried about details and *little* things and felt that from somewhere a pressure had arisen that was now sitting on her chest and her brow and making it difficult for her to see or breathe.

When her wedding day came, she was in no mood for it. It

happened, of course, the great machine being inexorably in motion, and she went up the aisle most decoratively on her father's manifestly pleased arm, but she felt lonely, all day, and by the end of it she was tearful and exhausted from the effort of seeming as she wished she were feeling.

'She's tired,' Cecily said to Martin privately, tucking them into the car to go away while the guests, unnaturally jolly after champagne drunk unsuitably mid-afternoon, stood on the gravel and cheered. 'Look after her.'

He did his best. She slept most of the way to Athens next day and he was very solicitous and tucked blankets round her and motioned the air hostesses not to bother her with lunch and drinks and duty-free watches. A friend of Cecily's had lent them a villa on Patmos, and they were alone there except for the couple who were caretakers and who were so assiduous in both house and garden that they were quite difficult to elude. They swam and slept and lay in the sun, and Alice drew a bit, and at night Martin made love to her which she didn't mind but didn't seem able to look forward to much, either. What he felt about it she didn't know because they didn't talk about it. They were perfectly companionable and years later, when both of them, separately, tried to remember their honeymoon, neither could, in any detail.

'I think,' Alice was to say to her father-in-law, trying to be truthful and fair, 'I think I was simply *asleep*.'

When they returned, wearing the tan and the faint, pleased air of achievement expected of honeymooners, Alice's parents took the final step of obliterating Lynford Road from her life. They had hardly been home two weeks, and Alice was still in the state of early nesting, where to find the perfect place to hang a washing line gives the keenest pleasure, when her father arrived, quite unannounced. He looked absolutely normal; it was Alice who was astonished. She took him proudly into her little sitting room, sat him down in the only proper armchair they possessed and pointed out various aspects of the room he might admire while she went to make coffee. He said he would rather have a brandy.

'Brandy?' Alice said.

'Yes, brandy.'

'We haven't got any brandy.'

Sam Meadows closed his eyes.

'What have you got?'

'A wine box.'

'Then a glass of wine box, please.'

Alice went out to her kitchen and took one of her new glasses out of her newly painted cupboards and filled it from the wine box. The wine, she noticed irrelevantly, appeared to be being sold by a mustard company. She took the glass back into the sitting room and Sam said, before he even had it in his hand, 'You see, I've come to tell you that I have left your mother.'

Alice, distanced by Apple Tree Cottage and Greece and Dummeridge from her parents' ancient torments, said only, 'For whom?'

'For nobody,' Sam Meadows said. 'For my sanity.'

Alice put the glass of wine in his hand. She said, 'Did you plan this?'

'Oh yes. I'd been planning it for years. I knew I couldn't stay once you were all gone, but on the other hand if I had gone before you might never have been able to leave yourself.' He took a swallow. 'I left the night of your wedding day.'

'You *what* – '

'We drove home from Dummeridge in complete silence. I think the only word either of us uttered was when she said "Mind" passing a bicycle somewhere near Andover. When we got home, she began. Nothing new, just all the usual things, over and over. So I went upstairs and packed a bag – silly really, just like some melodramatic telly thing – and I drove to a university residence where I knew there was an empty room destined for an American postgraduate who had never turned up. I'm still there.'

'But I've *spoken* to you,' Alice said. 'And to Mum. And neither of you ever said – '

'She thinks I'll go back. She thinks thirty years of marriage makes it inevitable.'

Alice looked at her pretty fireplace which she had filled with flowers and leaves.

'You've been an awful husband.'

'I haven't been a *faithful* husband.'

'That's awful. I couldn't stand it.'

Sam finished the wine.

'I wasn't unfaithful in order to hurt your mother.'

'I know that. It's just that she has nothing else.'

'It was that I nearly died of.'

Alice looked at him. She felt both a faint disgust and a mild affection for him, but mostly she felt that none of it had much to do with her.

'What will happen to Mum?'

'I don't know. Of course, I'll give her half of everything. But at the moment she won't discuss anything because she thinks I *must* return. So – ' He looked across at Alice.

'So you want me to go and tell her that you are not coming back and she must think what she wants to do.'

'Yes.'

'All right,' Alice said.

Her father stood up.

'You don't sound much concerned. One way or the other.'

Alice said, with sudden temper, 'You always want such an *emotional* reaction. Well, I haven't one to give you. Or if I have, I mightn't want to show it. Maybe I think you are right to leave and maybe at the same time I think Mum's future looks terrible, but I'm not going to talk to you about it. I'm not going to *wallow*.'

Sam came over to her and put his hands on her upper arms.

'One day,' he said, 'one day when you wake up to real feeling and real pain, one day when you can't have something you long for or you see too late that you have closed the door on something you need, *then* you will understand about communication, and communicating is, after all, the only end of life that makes any sense.'

Alice said indignantly, 'What d'you mean, when I wake up to real feeling?'

Sam dropped his hands.

'Just that.'

When he had gone, Alice went into her kitchen to wash up his wine glass and cried a bit, out of confusion. It seemed a long time until Martin might be home and she was tempted to telephone him but restrained herself, just, and so wasted an afternoon in profitless fidgets around the cottage. When he did arrive, she told him at once, in a clumsy rush, and he came over to her and put his arms round her and said, 'Oh, Allie, I'm so sorry, how awful for you, but really it was inevitable, wasn't it?' And she felt suddenly and

36

wonderfully better. Of course it was inevitable! What else could anyone have expected of that hopelessly ill-assorted pair manacled to one another by law and a perfect graveyard of impossible expectation and broken promises? She leaned against Martin. He said into her hair, 'You've got a new life now, anyway. I mean, they'll just have to get on with it, won't they. You see, you're mine now, aren't you.'

And it seemed then, standing there together, that he was both the answer and the refuge, and so she clung to him and was full of grateful love.

She did, of course, go to see her mother. They sat either side of the kitchen table with their elbows on the worn formica, and Elizabeth said at once, 'I know he won't come back. I have to face having dedicated myself to a man who is quite able simply to remove himself and leave me with the ashes of our life together. My life was his. Now I don't have one.'

'Perhaps,' Alice said, 'he didn't *want* all that dedication.'

She felt sorry for her mother. Her eyes were quite dead, like pebbles, and she was painfully thin.

'There was no way to please him. There was no way to hold him. It was all I wanted, ever, and it was the one thing I couldn't have.' She began to cry, silently. 'I don't want to live any more.'

Alice put her hand out and held her mother's wrist.

'Stop it.'

Elizabeth said, 'You haven't the first idea what I am talking about. You have never felt passionately about anyone in your life. You are so immature.'

Alice took her hand back again. With an immense effort she said, 'I'd like to help. If you'll tell me how.'

'You can't,' her mother said. 'It's nice of you to want to, but you can't. Nobody can except one person and he has finally refused.'

Alice got up and leaned her hands on the table so that she could thrust her face at her mother.

'All right, then. Drown in self-pity if you want to. Refuse help. Keep your stupid melodrama. But just don't forget I offered and you turned me down.'

Elizabeth turned her face away.

'Why should you care?' she said, in the low, bitter voice she had

37

used since Alice arrived. 'There you are, safely married to money and status before you are twenty-one. You're spoiled. The Jordans have seduced you but you'll regret it because nobody, *nobody*, has life *that* easy.'

Alice left the house then, and went for a long and angry walk around the streets where her brothers had done their long-ago paper rounds, and when she returned her mother had made tea and announced, with no preliminary, that she was going to Colchester anyway, to live with her sister.

'So all that scene just now,' Alice said, incredulous and on the verge of tears, 'was for nothing? You *knew*, all along, you were going to live with Aunt Ann?'

'I have nowhere else to go,' her mother said. 'Who would want me?'

'Who indeed,' Alice said to Martin later, dolloping sour cream into baked potatoes for their supper. 'I don't know what to make of her. She's certainly a sensational mother, *that*'s for certain.'

Martin made soothing noises. In his book, parents were not for objective criticism; they should be exempt, somehow, from personal discussion. He hardly knew his mother-in-law, and the unmanageable neurotic bits of her he simply closed his mind to. She had been to university and read law, and that he could encompass quite comfortably, but the rest – best for everyone's sake not to dwell on it. And however much cause she had, he didn't like Allie sounding sarcastic about her. He cut into his potato and cold ham with energy and told Alice about a colleague of his who had a flat in Verbier which he let to friends at reduced rates, and which he had offered to them, in February.

Two weeks later, Elizabeth Meadows left for Colchester and the neat villa of her widowed sister. She took almost nothing with her but her clothes, and left her wedding and engagement rings in a saucer on the kitchen table. Lynford Road was sold, and Sam bought a flat near the university where he could live the kind of life that his greedy, kindly temperament was best suited to. He came to Apple Tree Cottage several times a year, where his benevolent bohemianism made him a great favourite among Alice's new friends who treated him with the same indulgence they might have shown an elderly and affectionate labrador who had suddenly learned to speak. Elizabeth never came. Once a year Alice, with a sinking heart, went to Colchester for a night with the two sisters, and sat miserably in their precisely tidy sitting room while their joint grievance at losing their men occupied the fourth chintz armchair with the strength of a palpable being.

The next three years were – happy. Martin was entirely so, not just in the possession of Alice, but also because he knew – and the knowledge pleased him enormously – his life's major decisions were taken. He had not only taken them, he liked them. His job, which would finally make him a partner, was exactly what he had unambitiously expected, he had a pretty cottage and enough money, and he had Alice. The having of Alice was an incalculable asset, both for what she gave him and for the way in which people saw him, having her. She had taken to plaiting her long hair high on her head on honeymoon, to keep it from tangling like weed in the sea, and now she wore it like that all the time, and people looked at her a good deal. She wore boots and shawls and clothes from India and Peru, while the wives of Martin's colleagues wore navy blue loafers and striped shirts and pearl earrings. She painted borders round the rooms of the cottage, and pictures on the cupboard doors, and gradually people began to want her to paint their cupboards and walls and to do watercolours of corners of their houses that they felt best expressed their personalities, which they then gave to one another for Christmas and anniversaries.

She made curtains for the cottage, great dramatic billowing things that she hung from poles, while her friends turned their own cottages into sprigged milkmaid boxes, and felt, returning to them after supper with Alice and Martin, that they were altogether too timid. Alice learned to cook too, and to garden, and brought to both the eye and the confidence that it is no good wishing for if you are born without. Alice, it was generally agreed, in the rural circles around Salisbury, Alice Jordan had *style*.

And when having style exhausted her, Alice went off, of course, to Dummeridge. For those first three years of her marriage she went two or three times a month, driving down the comfortable southern roads through Cranborne and Wimborne and Wareham to spend a night with Cecily. They were usually alone, but if Richard happened to be there, he made little difference to their aloneness, and Anthony had taken his demanding and difficult personality off to Japan, with an investment company. Cecily was writing a new book on kitchen gardens which was an attempt to revive the ancient potager. A prototype was being laid out at Dummeridge, as complex and orderly as a knot garden, and Alice drew the plan, painting in each red-leaved lettuce, each gooseberry bush trained to grow like a lollipop, each radiating brick path, with the charming stiff precision of a sampler. Cecily had shown her the foreword to the book.

> This book owes so much to other people besides myself. Some of them are dead, like those vegetable heroes of the past, Richard Gardiner and William Lawson. Some are very much alive, and foremost among those is my daughter-in-law, Alice Jordan, whose exquisite plan for my own potager here at Dummeridge you will find as a frontispiece.

'I would take you to America with me, next time,' Cecily said, 'but I don't think it would be quite fair on Martin.'

However, to both of them, a trip to Venice seemed perfectly fair. Martin did not, after all, want to go.

'Honestly,' he said, 'I'm not brilliant at endless churches and pictures of saints. You know me.'

Alice was torn. She felt quite easy at going without him, but at the same time a small disquiet that he didn't *want* to come. This was somehow compounded by the fact that he was so manifestly satisfied at the prospect of his wife and his mother going off to be cultural together. He said this so often and so complacently to people that in the end Alice lost her temper with him and dispensed with her compunction. They had been married almost two years.

Venice filled her with a quite violent excitement. Long after she and Cecily got back – and they were only there for five days – Alice fed herself voluptuous fantasies of living there. She saw herself in a rooftop flat watching the sun sail round behind the belltowers and the domes, a flat with a balcony filled with pots of basil and a warm parapet on which to lean and gaze down into the still, olive-oily green waters of a canal. She saw herself going shopping with a basket, buying aubergines and long, sweet tomatoes from the vegetable boat by the San Barnaba bridge, and fantastic alien fish from the market, and pasta and parmesan cheese from the tiny crammed shops in the lanes of San Polo. In the background of these dreams, she could not disguise from herself, lurked a man. He was shadowy, but extremely satisfactory, and he was not Martin.

Then she became pregnant. She liked it. She was full of energy and aroused everyone's admiration. In their large circle of young couples, some had babies – almost all had dogs – and their mutual stage of marriedness was this possession of a first baby. Alice made no fuss about anything and bore Natasha with ease. Both mother and baby seemed instinctively to know how to handle one another, and Martin, who was not required by Alice to help with nappy-changing or midnight feeds, was deeply envied by colleagues whose wives had pointed out to them that the baby, with all its attendant troublesomeness, was half theirs.

Of course, with Natasha, she could not go so freely and frequently to Dummeridge. So she telephoned, every few days, and once a month Cecily came up to Wilton with armfuls of bounty from the garden and stayed in the third tiny bedroom, and was pleased with everything and enchanted by her granddaughter. She even sang to Natasha sometimes, and Alice and Martin exchanged slightly conspiratorial smiles of accomplishment and pleasure. Alice's friends adored her. They would all pour in for coffee or for lunch round the kitchen table, clutching their babies and their toddlers, if they knew Cecily was there. At Christmas, they gave their mothers copies of Cecily's book which they brought proudly for her to autograph.

It was then that Alice met Alex Murray-French. Alex's father John lived at The Grey House in Pitcombe, a much admired village where all Alice's friends aspired, without much hope, to live. Alex's parents had divorced when he was eight, but The Grey House had been his childhood home, and he chose to return to it a good deal rather than go out to Australia with his mother and stepfather. On one of his visits to his father, he saw a painting of Alice's, a painting she had done for a mutual friend, of a flight of stone steps leading up to an archway and a tangle of creeper. He thought he would like such a painting to send to his mother in Australia, and so he drove to Apple Tree Cottage one afternoon, on the off-chance, and found Alice on the doorstep stripping currants with her baby asleep in a basket beside her under a patchwork quilt.

41

Alex fell in love as suddenly as Martin had done four years before. Alice did not fall back, but she felt she would very much have liked to. He was eager and sympathetic and cultivated. He came constantly, all that autumn, on the pretext of his mother's painting, and Alice basked in his longing and admiration like a cat in the sun. She never flirted with him and he never even tried to kiss her. He told her most eloquently of his feelings, and although she liked to hear him he did not strike an answering chord in her. In the end Martin grew suspicious and angry and Alex took his picture and himself away and left Alice with a real emptiness, a bigger one than she felt was in the least fair.

Martin watched her for a long time after this.

'There was nothing *in* it,' Alice would say. 'He had a crush on me and I didn't have one back. I liked talking to him, that's all.'

Martin knew that, but he still felt sulky about it. He believed her and yet he felt at the same time that that part of her, that differentness in her, that had made him want her so much, was becoming elusive, that he couldn't catch it any more. Instead of feeling that life with her was a lovely chase, he began to feel that she was keeping something back. But because he could not, by temperament, speak of it, he watched her instead, and this made her cross.

Her second pregnancy was quite unlike the first. She felt sick, she was sick, and many days she was so tired that from the moment she dragged herself out of bed in the morning, she was obsessed, all day, with the prospect of getting back into it. James was born with difficulty and didn't seem to like life outside Alice when confronted with it. Cecily dispatched a New Zealand girl, from a London agency, to help Alice, and Apple Tree Cottage strained at the seams under the impact of her capable outdoorsy personality. She certainly worked, and Alice could rest in the afternoons and send Natasha off to nursery school every morning in clean dungarees not laundered by herself, but the privacy of their lives was quite gone. Jennie was only with them for four months, but when she left, in a gale of good will, for a family in Pelham Crescent, she left behind her the constraint between Alice and Martin that they had adapted to encompass her in their lives. Friendly and good-mannered towards one another, they moved through the rituals of Martin's job and Natasha's school runs and James's demands, and supper parties (small), and children's tea parties (large), without somehow either coming together or moving forward.

Alice pretended not to notice that she didn't want to paint. Her friend, Juliet Dunne, whose husband Henry was agent at Pitcombe Park and who was blessed with a sharp tongue and keen percipience, made no bones about pointing this out.

'It's no good *hiding*, Allie. This awful baby business doesn't last long, and if you aren't careful you'll end up like my mother saying why is it every day takes a week. It doesn't matter if you don't *want* to paint. You just have to.'

'I do want to – '

'No you don't. You just want to want to. You won't get real wanting back unless you kick yourself into doing something. Look at our useless husbands. They'll never get anywhere much because they couldn't *make* themselves if you paid them.'

'Why did you marry Henry?'

'Oh,' Juliet said, scraping apricot pudding off her newest baby's chin, 'he was so suitable and so keen and everyone else in my flat was getting married. I quite like him, though.'

'You mean love him.'

'Yuk,' said Juliet.

Alice did try to paint after that, and it bored her so much she was quite alarmed. She took out some things she had done before James was born and they looked to her the desirable achievements of a total stranger, so she put them away again, hurriedly, before they should demoralise her. She had, she told herself, plenty to do in any case and she did it all – a touch of pride here – without any help at all. None of her friends managed their houses and families with no help at all. Cecily was always offering her some, but she said the cottage was too small, and in any case she liked her privacy.

Small things happened. Martin was made a junior partner, Natasha started at a little private school in Salisbury – the children wore checked smocks and had to shake hands, *smiling*, with their teacher each morning – they built on a playroom and another bedroom at the cottage. In the late winter, Alice and Martin went skiing (Alice discovered, rather to her satisfaction, that she liked frightening herself), and in the summer Cecily rented a cottage for them on the north Cornish coast where the children could play on the calm sands of the Camel estuary. Alice began to read, hungrily, novel after novel, carrying lists of them around in her bag along with the purse and cheque books and cash cards and paper handkerchiefs and tubes of Smarties and clean knickers and sticking plasters that formed her daily battle gear. Titles like *And Quiet Flows the Don* stuck in her mind like burrs. She chanted them to herself in the car, while in the back the members of the school run bullied the most tearful, sucked their thumbs and surreptitiously took their knickers off in order to amaze the others with their wicked daring.

When she discovered she was pregnant with Charlie, her first reaction was relief. She felt a great gratitude towards this unexpected baby for mapping out her life for her again and threatening her with its needs. Martin seemed extremely pleased except for taking out, with immense ostentation, an insurance policy against school fees which he appeared to regard, Alice felt, as something he was nobly doing for *her*.

'Ignore him,' Juliet said, 'just fade him out. It's the only way to survive living with a man.'

'But the baby isn't just mine!'

'You try telling any father that. Henry will acknowledge William and Simon when they are captaining the first eleven, and *strictly* not before. If you wanted anything else, you shouldn't have married an Englishman.'

'No one else offered.'

'Allie,' Juliet said, 'just get on with this baby, would you? You'll make a much better job of it than Martin in any case. I despair of myself but I think I envy you.'

Charlie was born, suddenly, a month early, and Alice went into a deep, deep decline. Sunk in the fogs of a profound depression, she was carried off to Dummeridge with the baby where she remained for a month, struggling inch by inch out of the depths into which she had tumbled. Pills, frequent small meals, sleep, confiding conversation and gentle exercise were prescribed as her regime. Martin, thankful to surrender this dismal conundrum to his mother, telephoned nightly for bulletins and was spoiled tenderly by Alice's friends who pitied his male dilemma in the kitchen.

She came home pale and thin and slightly sad, but she was better. Martin was very sweet to her but at the same time anxious she should know that he had suffered too, alone at night with the two elder children and responsible for the morning whirlwind of rejected eggs and lost gumboots. The week Alice returned, Cecily wrote privately to Martin, to the office in Salisbury, and said she thought Alice needed both a change and more support. She suggested a house move and offered to pay for help and for a holiday, a holiday without any of the children, the moment Charlie was weaned.

And then the gods produced The Grey House, out of casual conversation at a dinner party, and presented it to the Jordans on a plate. It was not just the house they offered, but village life, the chance and the need to be part of a proper community, where you couldn't even go to buy stamps, Alice thought excitedly, without meeting several people you knew. There would be a church fête, and a flower rota, and a list for driving old people into Salisbury, or to the hospital, and men from the Park would bring loads of logs in winter, and a Christmas tree, and in the summer she would pityingly watch the neat tourists emerge from the parked Toyotas and peer hopefully – but fruitlessly – down the pretty, sloping street for a tea shop. She would, she knew it, envy no one, long for nothing. In Pitcombe she would feel again what she had felt at Dummeridge ten years ago when she was twenty-one – she would feel she had come home.

CHAPTER FOUR

'Now, the county travelling *library*,' said Miss Pimm with the separating articulateness of Marghanita Laski, 'is a *great* blessing.'

'Tuesdays, did you say?' Alice said, obediently writing it down on her list.

'Tuesday after*noons*. Three to three-*thirty*. The librarian is an excellent vegetable gardener and to be relied upon for *brassicas*.'

'Brassicas', wrote Alice.

James, leaning against Alice, thought, with wonder, that they were discussing underclothes. He had his finger up his nose. He pulled it out and offered it to Miss Pimm.

'Gucky,' he said.

She averted her gaze.

'Mrs Leigh-Brent runs the church *cleaning* rota. And Miss Payne is in charge of the *flowers*. I know Mrs Macaulay would *gratefully* welcome help on Mondays with the community *shop* and of course Mr and Mrs Fanshawe will be happy to register you with the local *Conservative* branch.'

Alice wiped James's nose hard enough with a piece of paper kitchen towel to make him whimper.

'Don't be a disgusting little boy. I don't think I really am a Conservative, but my husband – '

'Not?' said Miss Pimm, swivelling her gaze back.

'No,' Alice said staunchly, remembering Sir Ralph, 'I believe the Park – '

'That,' said Miss Pimm, 'is *quite* different.'

She looked round the kitchen. It looked rather *loud* to her, though considerably cleaner than in Major Murray-French's day. But she did not like being entertained in kitchens, even the kitchens of people newly moved in who might perhaps be forgiven for having nowhere else. When Miss Pimm had brought her mother

46

to Sycamore Cottage fifteen years before, the *first* thing she had done was to make the sitting room respectable for callers. She remembered standing on a chair hammering in nails for the 'Cries of London' above the fireplace, the position they had occupied in all the houses of her life.

Natasha came in through the door to the hall carrying a doll dressed like a teenage fairy, and wearing an expression of faint disgust.

'Charlie's crying and he's pooey,' she said.

Alice stood up.

'Would you forgive me, Miss Pimm?' she said, 'I must just see to the baby.'

Miss Pimm sat on. There was much information yet to impart. She inclined her head.

'I am in no hurry.'

Alice left the room. Natasha came up to the kitchen table and put her gauzy doll down. She looked at Miss Pimm who seemed to have nothing about her that Natasha could admire. The texture of her stockings reminded Natasha of drinking chocolate powder.

'Pretty doll,' said Miss Pimm with extra elaborate articulation, as if speaking to a half-wit.

'She's called Princess Power,' Natasha said. Her voice was proud. 'She's got net petticoats, pink ones.'

She turned the doll upside down to demonstrate and Miss Pimm looked hastily away.

'But,' said James slowly and earnestly, from across the table, 'she hasn't got a willy.'

Panic blotched Miss Pimm's neck with purple patches.

'Have you?' said James.

Natasha hissed at him.

'Shut up.'

'Charlie's,' said James with real sympathy, 'is only little. But it'll probably grow.'

'I'm afraid,' said Natasha to Miss Pimm, 'that in James's class at school they talk about willies *all the time*. But you must just ignore him. Like Mummy does.'

'School!' cried Miss Pimm on a high note of relief. 'And do you like your school?'

'No,' said James. 'I hate everything except being at home.'

47

'He cries every morning,' Natasha said. 'It's so embarrassing. My best friend is called Sophie and she has Princess Power too only *her* petticoats are yellow. I like pink best.'

'Yes!' cried Miss Pimm. 'Yes! Pink!'

Alice came back into the room holding a large baby. Miss Pimm was afraid of babies. Alice sat down and picked up her pencil again, wedging Charlie into the space between her and the table.

'So sorry about that,' Alice said. 'Now, what else was there?'

Miss Pimm wanted to say that a cup of tea was one of the things. It was five past four. She would have liked a cup of tea and a Marie biscuit. She cleared her throat with meaningful thirstiness and said, 'Well, there is our little *Sunday* group.'

Charlie seized Alice's pencil and drew a thick, wild line across her list. Instinctively Miss Pimm's hand shot out to prevent the desecration of neatness, but Alice didn't seem to notice.

'Group of what?'

'Why, *children*.' She looked at Natasha and stretched her mouth into an attempted smile. 'We meet in the church room for songs and stories about *Jesus*.'

'I know about *him*,' Natasha said. 'He gave some people a horrible picnic with bare bread and fish that wasn't *cooked*. And then he walked about all over a lake and made a girl who was dead be alive again. If you ask *me*,' Natasha said darkly, 'I don't believe that bit.'

'Tashie – '

'We have eleven little *members*,' Miss Pimm said hastily. 'And I – ' She paused and then said with quiet pride, 'I play the ukelele.'

They stared at her. To her misery Alice found she didn't even want to laugh. Miss Pimm took their silence as an awestruck tribute to her skills and opened her black notebook in a businesslike way to show she was quite used to such admiration.

'Now, may I tell Miss Payne you would be happy to join the *flower* rota? I believe Mrs *Kendall* lacks a partner. And what about Mondays? The community *shop* is such a boon to our *old* people – '

Go, Alice said to herself in sudden frenzy. Go, go, *go*. I hate you here, you mimsy old spinster, I hate you in my kitchen. *Go*.

'We have unfortunately to share our vicar with King's *Harcourt* and *Barleston* which means mattins only once a month, but he is a *wonderful* man, and we must just be *thankful* – '

48

'C'n I have some crisps?' James said.

'No. Don't interrupt. I am sorry, Miss Pimm, but usually around now I give them – '

Miss Pimm slapped her notebook shut and stood up.

'Naturally. I am sorry to interrupt family *routine*.'

'Oh no,' Alice said, struggling to her feet clutching Charlie, and in a confusion of apology, 'I didn't mean that at all, I only meant – '

'I *came*,' Miss Pimm said, implying by her tone that at least *some* people were still in command of their manners, 'just to *welcome* you to Pitcombe. I make a *point* of it, with newcomers.'

'Yes,' Alice said faintly. 'It's very kind of you and I'm sure when I've sorted myself out a bit – '

'You should *see* upstairs,' Natasha said. 'It's the most utterest chaos.'

Miss Pimm walked to the stable door and lifted the latch. She turned stiffly and gave a little downward jerk of her head.

'Sycamore Cottage. Telephone 204.'

'Thank you – '

'Good afternoon.'

'Goodbye,' Alice said. 'Goodbye – '

The door clicked shut, one half after the other. Alice subsided into her chair.

'Don't cry,' James said anxiously.

'I'm not,' Alice said through a river of tears.

'You are, you *are* – '

Natasha picked up Princess Power.

'I expect you're tired.'

'Yes,' Alice said. 'Yes, I expect I am, I'm sure that's it – '

Charlie's face puckered. James came to lean on her again, his eyes filling with tears.

'Don't do it,' he said. His voice was pleading. 'Don't *do* it.'

But she couldn't stop.

The community shop, Alice discovered, was a large and battered van, owned and driven by Mr Finch, one-time boarding-house keeper and failed poet, who ran Pitcombe Post Office and Village Stores. Twice a week, the shop van trundled out of Pitcombe with its cargo of old age pensions, tins of marrowfat peas and packets of bourbon biscuits, to serve outlying cottages and the smaller satellite

49

villages of Barleston and King's Harcourt. It made thirteen stops in three hours, either outside the cottages of the most infirm, or by the clumps of people standing with clutched purses and plastic carrier bags at designated places along the route.

Mr Finch was very excited to have Alice on board on Monday afternoons. Mrs Macaulay, who was the long-standing other helper on Mondays, despised his artistic sensibilities, believing, as she did, only in good sense and wire-haired dachshunds, which she bred with dedication. 'My girls', she called her bitches. Within the first half-hour of her first Monday, Alice discovered that Mr Finch was misunderstood by his wife who yearned still for their boarding house in Kidderminster which had catered for actors at the Theatre Royal, and that Mr Macaulay had been called to the great dog basket in the sky ten years previously, much lamented by his widow and her girls.

'He was a wonderful man,' Mrs Macaulay said to Alice, as they jolted out of the village, the tins jiggling on their barricaded shelves. 'He could do anything he liked with animals. He inspired perfect trust.'

At the frequent stops, Mr Finch came out of the driver's cab and sat in the doorway of the van at the seat of change. Every time he appeared holding not only his cash box and ledger but also a battered notebook bound in imitation leather which he left nonchalantly on the edge of his little counter, with many a casually pregnant glance thrown in Alice's direction.

'Take no notice,' Mrs Macaulay hissed at Alice, passing her a stack of All-Bran boxes. 'Those are his terrible jingles. Don't give him the chance to mention them.'

At every stop, the van filled rapidly with people, heaving each other up the steps into the interior like an eager crowd of hedgehogs. Alice was stared at.

'Who's 'er?' somebody said from close to the floor.

'Sh, you, Granny. That's the new lady – '

'Who's 'er?'

'Mrs Jordan,' Mrs Macaulay said with great clarity. 'She has just moved into the Major's house at Pitcombe.'

There was a sucking of teeth.

'She won't like that. Miserable 'ouse, that is.'

'But I *do* like it – '

'It's very good of Mrs Jordan to help us,' Mrs Macaulay said, 'because she has three little ones on her hands.'

'Where's me spaghetti hoops, then?'

'Hang on, Gran, they're coming,' and then, turning confidentially to Alice, 'she loves them. She don't need her teeth in to eat them, see.'

At the end of the third stop, Mr Finch laid his hand slowly on his book of poems and looked roguishly at Alice.

'Care for something to read before Barleston, Mrs Jordan?'

Mrs Macaulay was ready for him.

'Sorry, Mr Finch, I've got the cereal section to explain to Mrs Jordan before we get there.'

Mr Finch placed the book flat against his chest, holding it in both hands.

'Are you a reader, Mrs Jordan? I fancy you are.'

'Novels,' Alice said hastily. 'As much fiction as I can get. But you know, with the children – '

Mrs Macaulay tapped her watch.

'Time, Mr Finch, time.'

By the end of the second hour, Alice could gladly have lain down on the lineoleum floor of the van and wept with fatigue. Spring it might be, but the day felt raw and cold, and the depressing contents of the shelves, the tins of butter beans and the packet puddings, only compounded the bleakness. Alice had asked Mr Finch, in his shop the previous week, for an avocado pear, and Mr Finch had made it elaborately plain to her that left to himself his shop would be a profusion of avocado pears, but that the brutish character of his non-poetry reading clientele demanded nothing more *outré* than cabbages.

'I should be only too happy,' Mr Finch said egregiously, hunting in his memory for scraps of Tennyson with which to flatter and impress this delightful newcomer, 'to bring you anything you require on my visits to the wholesaler in Salisbury.'

'Thank you,' Alice said, 'but I'm in Salisbury most days on the school run. It's just that I'd rather use your shop, I mean, I feel I ought – ' She stopped. She had no wish to sound patronising. But Mr Finch had hardly heard her.

' "Why should we only toil," ' cried Mr Finch suddenly. ' "The roof and crown of things?" '

51

Alice looked startled. He leaned over the counter, laying his hand reverently upon a display box of foil-wrapped chocolate biscuits.

' "The Lotus Eaters." '

'Yes,' Alice said.

' "We only toil," ' intoned Mr Finch, ' "who are the first of things, And make perpetual moan, Still from one sorrow to another thrown – " '

The shop door had opened then and in had come Miss Pimm, in quest of a small loaf and a tin of sardines. Alice had seized her chance to flee, and had bought her avocado in Salisbury, later in the day, while picking Natasha up from school.

Now, sitting precariously on her little stool as the van rumbled onwards, she thought again of the avocado.

'If we put – slightly more interesting things on the shelves, do you think we could persuade anyone to buy them?'

'Not a hope,' Mrs Macaulay said. 'Absolutely set in their ways. Same stuff every week, same quantities. See that jar of Mint Imperials? We get through one a fortnight, regular as clockwork. Same with cream crackers.' She glanced at Alice. 'You look tired, dear. I expect it's the move. It really is good of you to join in so quickly.'

Alice said, 'But I always meant to,' and tried not to think of Miss Pimm's visit.

'I mentioned it to her ladyship,' Mrs Macaulay said. 'I said now there's a young woman prepared to pull her weight. Has she called yet?'

'No,' Alice said in some panic, thinking of the disordered rooms she somehow seemed unable to find the energy to disentangle. 'No, she hasn't. Frankly, the house looks so awful – '

'She won't mind that,' Mrs Macaulay said approvingly. 'She isn't one to stand on ceremony. My girls always know when it's her ladyship's car. They give her such a welcome.'

When Alice got home, Gwen, who had consented to look after the children on Monday afternoons until Alice returned, was making them the kind of tea she thought they should have. James was gazing in misery at the thick slice of bread and jam on his plate. The jam was red and he was alarmed by red food. Charlie, on the other hand, was cramming sticky squares of bread into his already packed mouth with the flat of his hand. Natasha, who had decided she would simply wait until Alice's return, had declined to eat anything at all. She sat at the table, neat in her school uniform, and told Gwen about her dancing class where she had been praised for being the flutteriest butterfly.

Alice dropped into a chair.

'It's a killer, that shop,' Gwen said, with satisfaction, putting a mug of thick brown tea in front of Alice.

'Peanut butter,' James pleaded in a hoarse whisper.

'In a minute,' Alice said. 'Just give me a minute. Tashie, why aren't you eating?'

'I was slightly hoping,' Natasha said, with theatrical quietness, 'for Marmite toast.'

'I brought them the jam,' Gwen said proudly. 'My kids used to go mad for strawberry jam.'

'How sweet of you – '

'And look how old gorgeous loves it!'

Charlie's face resembled that of a character in the final scene of a Jacobean revenge tragedy. Sensing them all looking at him, he plunged his gory hands rapturously into his hair. Gwen said fondly, 'Isn't he a card?'

'Gwen,' Alice said, suddenly remembering, 'Mrs Macaulay said today that Lady Unwin might call. And there isn't a civilised corner, except in here, to take her – '

Gwen pursed her lips to indicate that even such a thought had already occurred to *some* people.

'She will, Mrs Jordan. No doubt about it.'

Alice looked up at her.

'Would you help me have a real blitz on the drawing room?'

She looked really, helplessly tired. Even Gwen, who didn't go in for pity, felt sorry for her. She looked what Gwen called pulled down.

'Course I'll help, dear. It'd be a sight easier to clean with all those boxes shifted, in any case. She's a shocker for just popping in, is her ladyship – '

'Peanut butter,' James begged.

'All right,' Alice said standing up and moving slowly to the relevant cupboard.

'Of course,' Gwen said, 'it's all excitement up at the Park with Miss Clodagh coming back.'

Alice began to spread James's bread with peanut butter.

'Thinner, *thinner*.'

'Shut up. Miss Clodagh?'

'The youngest. She's been in America for three years. She always was her parents' favourite. She was a monkey of a child, I can tell you. How can you,' she said to James, 'eat that nasty stuff?'

James gazed at her, chewing, but said nothing.

'I'm being very *patient*,' Natasha pointed out.

'Heavens,' Alice said, 'I might get a whole deputation from the Park – '

The telephone rang. Going to the hall to answer it, Alice said, 'Gwen, could you possibly make some toast for Natasha? I don't like her to touch the grill – '

The telephone was Cecily. She had resolved only to telephone once a week, and then only in the early evening when the children were in bed, because she felt that Alice's state of mind was very fragile just now, and that even if they were all worried sick, they must not let Alice know it. But today Alice had been on her mind so constantly for some reason that she could not restrain herself from ringing up.

'Hello,' Alice said tiredly.

'Darling,' Cecily said, 'you sound absolutely whacked.'

Alice's voice grew warmer, but no more energetic.

'It's the village community shop. I got involved somehow and I've spent three hours in a very cold van selling jars of beetroot to people who told me that I'd hate living here.'

Cecily laughed.

'How funny.'

'It wasn't really,' Alice said. 'It ought to have been. But it wasn't.'

'Then I'm very glad I've rung. Darling, I'm going to be very firm. I *insist* you have some more help, a mother's help, even an au pair girl. You're worn out to start with, and here you are taking on extra things like the shop.'

'I've got help,' Alice said. 'It's sweet of you, but there's Gwen. I've never had so much help – '

She stopped. This was quite true. She had never had so much help and nor had she ever lived in such a muddle. A lump rose in

54

her throat. Sometimes she felt quite paralysed in her inability to sort herself out. She had felt desperate after Martin and Cecily had persuaded her to go to the doctor recently and she had spent two days in the gynae bit of Salisbury hospital while they did tests, and then there had been absolutely nothing wrong with her. Martin had been so pleased. She had felt frantic. If there wasn't something wrong with her, then why did she feel like this?

'You need someone living in,' Cecily said. 'You need a younger Dorothy. I intend to find you one.'

'Please,' Alice said, pleading, 'please, no – '

'But, darling, why on earth not?'

'Because there is nothing the matter with me. You know that. Mr Hobbs said so. I've just got to pull myself together.'

'But why can't you be *helped* to do that?'

'Because,' Alice said on the verge of tears, 'I don't *want* to be. It's so nice of you, but I must get on myself. I'm fine, really I am. Gwen's going to help me with the drawing room and when that's straight I'll feel quite different. I know it.'

There was a pause, at the end of which Cecily sighed.

'Would you consider a compromise?'

Alice sounded wary.

'What – '

'You struggle on for one more month, and if you don't feel any better, will you then let me re-open the subject?'

'All right,' Alice said unwillingly.

'Look, my love, there is no shame in not being able to manage. You have *so* much on your plate – '

'*I* might feel shame,' Alice said.

'Your standards are too high. Is Martin being a help?'

'He's fine. He's awfully busy but he helps a lot at weekends.'

'He's so proud of you.'

Alice squirmed, involuntarily.

'He's doing really well – '

'How are the children?'

'Jammy at present. But fine.'

'I shall have them here in the holidays. I want you and Martin to go away together. I said so two months ago. Shall I ring Verity about your honeymoon house in Patmos?'

'No,' Alice said with too much emphasis.

'Darling – '

'One shouldn't ever try and repeat things – '

'Darling Alice,' Cecily said sadly from Dummeridge, 'how I long to help you and how difficult you make it.'

'Sorry,' Alice said in a whisper. 'Sorry.'

The drawing room was cleared, carpeted, but uncurtained when her ladyship's Volvo, with a brace of handsome springer spaniels penned in the back, drew up outside The Grey House. From her bedroom window, Alice watched Lady Unwin get out, smooth down her pleated skirt, stoop inside the car to bring out a huge hydrangea in a pot and then advance, looking about her, towards the front door. Gwen, who had been washing the stone-flagged hall floor, let her in with alacrity.

'Ah, Gwen. How nice to see you. What a lovely day. Is Mrs Jordan in?'

Gwen showed Lady Unwin into the drawing room.

'Hm,' Lady Unwin said interestedly, putting down the pot, and moving towards the mantelpiece along which Alice's collection of old jugs marched in stout procession. 'Charming.' She turned to smile at Gwen. 'Do tell her I'm here.'

Gwen was sorry that Alice was wearing jeans and an old shirt of Martin's because she was unpacking tea chests, and sorrier still that Alice didn't intend, apparently, to make any changes at all to her appearance. She simply pulled her pigtail over her shoulder and ran downstairs. Lady Unwin, immaculate in a pale grey skirt and soft jersey with handsome pearls, was examining a drawing hung beside the fireplace. She turned and held both hands out to Alice.

'My dear Mrs Jordan. I'm a monster not to come before. Will you forgive me?'

'Oh, of course. I'm afraid we're still in a terrible muddle – '

'Don't speak to me of muddles. My youngest is just back from New York with enough luggage to fill a liner and I am not exaggerating when I tell you that she has spread it over the *entire* house.'

Alice said, 'Would you like a cup of coffee?'

'Thank you so much, but no. I am flying in, literally, on my way to a meeting in Shaftesbury. Look, I've brought this. I've always loved them. It's a lacecap.'

56

'Oh,' Alice said, 'how kind of you – '

'I suppose,' Lady Unwin said, 'you are no relation to Cecily Jordan?'

Alice said, smiling, 'She is my mother-in-law.'

Lady Unwin grasped Alice's hand with warm enthusiasm.

'My dear! What luck. Now *look* – ' She dropped Alice's hand and opened a large, professional handbag from which she took a slim diary. 'Now then. When can you dine with us? Let me see. Saturday fortnight? The eleventh?'

'Lovely,' Alice said faintly. 'Thank you, how kind – '

'And if you are speaking to your mother-in-law, tell her I am a devoted fan. I wonder if she'd *stoop* to talk to our little flower people here? Or perhaps a gardeners' brains trust for the hospice? I must think. Goodbye, my dear – ' She waved a ring-glittering hand around the room. '*Too* pretty.'

People like that, Alice thought, watching her enviously as she climbed swiftly into her car and turned it competently in the drive, people like that don't feel pain. People like Lady Unwin don't get into muddles and feel that their lives are without point and that they don't see the way forward.

'I've got a crush on Lady Unwin,' she said to Juliet Dunne, later, on the telephone. 'I want to be like her when I grow up.'

'Margot?' Juliet said. 'Don't be an ass. Of course you don't. It's an awful life. Luckily she's an old bossy boots so she rather likes it.'

'But she looks as if she's beyond things being able to hurt her. She looks – '

'Allie,' Juliet said firmly, 'if you don't book a holiday for yourself and Martin sharpish, I shall come and do it for you. Oh Lordy, here's Henry, *early*, if you please – Don't,' she said, away from the telephone, 'those are for the children's tea. Allie, dins at the big house will be quite sparky, I promise, and you'll love Clodagh. She's been a frightful headache all her life and has been living with some lawyer in New York for years whom she utterly refused to let Margot and Ralph – What? Oh, Henry says he is a millionaire, the lawyer. Anyway, millionaire or not, she's left him and come home so Margot has gone into her *ultra*-clucking routine. But Clodagh's lovely fun. Allie, I've got to stop and beat Henry up. He's eating all the children's egg sandwiches. Honestly, Allie, Henry is my *cross*.'

*   *   *

'Am I your cross?' Alice said to Martin at supper.

He leaned across the table and patted her but he wasn't giving her his full attention.

'Of course not.'

'If I'm such a burden to myself, I must be a burden to you –'

'You're tired – '

'But that's the effect, not the cause.'

He had his mouth full. Through his fish pie he said, 'Don't agree.' He finished his mouthful and went on. 'You've taken on so much. The village think you're great. Has the rector been?'

'No – '

'He will, then. I saw him in the shop. Seemed nice.'

'He'll only want me to do things.'

'Then say no.'

'But you see,' she said, leaning forward to give him the second helping he always had, 'one of the reasons for living here is to be involved.'

'Not in everything. Not so that you are so tired you can't see straight.'

She said, looking at him hard, 'But I don't think it's that.'

Visibly he flinched. She saw his mind tiptoe away from the turn the conversation was taking, a turn he could not bear. He waved his fork at her.

'Frightfully good, this,' he said.

Two days later, Alice was pushing Charlie in his buggy along the river path. It was a pretty, bright, chill day and there were catkins on the willows and clumps of primroses on the banks. She picked one and gave it to Charlie. He held it respectfully at stiff arm's length and she thought how he was learning because even a few weeks ago he would have tried to eat it.

A man came along the path towards them, a big man in a loose tweed overcoat whom she took to be John Murray-French, and was just raising her arm to wave when she saw he had on a dog collar. When he came nearer, he called, 'Lovely morning!'

'Yes!' she called back.

He said, when he was near enough merely to speak, 'I'm Peter Morris. And you are Mrs Jordan. And I owe you what is known as a pastoral call.'

He was about sixty, vigorous and upright with thick hair and a good colour. He stooped to Charlie who offered him the primrose.

'Thank you, old chap.'

'I know you are awfully busy,' Alice said.

He straightened.

'It's a shocking time of year for dying. They totter on all winter and then, just as it begins to get warmer and lighter, they give up the ghost. It's been one funeral after another. That's why I came out today, to see something *starting* for once.' He looked down at Charlie. 'You're starting, luckily. Is that your only one?'

'He's my third.'

'You don't look old enough. I was going to come and tell you not to let the old biddies bully the life out of you. They will if they can. They do a wonderful job in the village but they know no mercy. Hope you'll be happy here.'

'Oh, we *will* – '

'It's a nice place. And you've a lovely house. I used to go up and play poker with John Murray-French in your house. I expect we'll start again in his cottage when he's settled. Two old bachelors together.' He looked down at Charlie again. 'Never had any children. My wife died before we got round to it.'

'I'm so sorry – '

'So was I. I was a sailor. That is, before the old Admiral up there' – he looked up at the blue sky – 'summoned me aboard. You'll find I speak my mind. If I can't abide something, I say so. And that applies to a large number of bishops. Woolly lot. Why don't they just see what the *Bible* says about things? You know where you are, with the Bible.'

Alice turned the buggy back towards the village.

'I've never really read it. Not since school.'

'Not surprised. People don't. But sixty-five million copies are sold every year, so *someone* reads it. You ought to try.'

'I wouldn't know where to begin.'

'No excuse,' Peter Morris said heartily. He took the handles of the buggy from her and began to push.

'I hear they've got you on the community shop.'

'And the flower rota. But I've jibbed at the Sunday Group.'

'Good for you.'

'But the belonging, I mean, doing things, is part of living here – '

59

'So is getting on with everyone. I always say to newcomers, don't think living in a village is easy. In a town you can pick and choose your friends but a village is like a ship – you have to get on with everyone. Not easy, but not impossible. Hold on old fellow, here come some bumps.'

They emerged on to the broader path below the pub, the Pitcombe Inn. Late daffodils were drooping in the window-boxes and through the partly opened ground-floor windows seeped a stale breath of beer and frying. Peter Morris went on pushing Charlie, past the pub and round the corner up the village street where people hailed him. Alice felt comforted, walking beside him while he pushed and replied briefly to those who greeted him. He stopped at the corner of the lane to The Grey House.

'I'll return the chariot to you.'

'Thank you,' she said. She rather wanted to ask him to come with her.

He said, 'I've bereavement, a broken leg and a bad case of self-pity to see to before lunch, Mrs Jordan. It was nice to meet you.'

He held out his hand and grasped hers.

'Keep smiling,' he said, and put a finger on the end of Charlie's little nose. 'You too, old fellow.'

CHAPTER FIVE

Alice dressed three times for dinner at Pitcome Park, and when she had finished she was more than half-inclined to throw off her final choice and go back to the first one. But there wasn't time, and in any case, Martin was getting impatient. She came downstairs holding the ends of a heavy Turkish necklace of silver and turquoise behind her neck with both hands and asked him to hook it up for her. He was wearing a dinner jacket and looked very sleek and remote. He turned her back to the light in the hall so that he could see, and muttered over the necklace. She stood with her head bent, holding her pigtail away from her neck to help him, looking down at the deep folds of her red skirt and the toes of her embroidered slippers which said 'Made in Jaipur' on ribbons sewn into the insoles.

'There,' he said triumphantly, and gave her shoulder a finishing pat. She let her pigtail fall again, down her back. She had woven it with ribbons for the dinner party and Natasha, who had sat admiringly on the end of her bed watching while she did this, was now sitting on the last step of the stairs trying to achieve the same effect on Princess Power. James sat on the top step crying quietly with his thumb in. He didn't want Alice to go out and he didn't want to be left with Gwen. He said now, removing his thumb just long enough, 'What if there's a baddie?'

Natasha sighed.

'Quite honestly,' she said, plaiting away, 'you watch too much television.'

James loved television. He watched it, clutching a cushion in his arms so that he could bury his head in it if anything on the screen looked as if it might become frightening. But when the television was turned off, the baddies on it seemed to lurk about his imagination much more powerfully than the goodies. He knew Gwen wouldn't be any good at dealing with his fears because she

61

somehow had something to do with the baddies. Only Alice staying at home would be any good.

He stood up.

'Don't go!'

Martin climbed past Natasha up the stairs and knelt below James.

'Now, come on, old boy. We are only going out for a few hours and we are only going to the Park – '

'Don't go! Don't go!' screamed James, staring at his mother past Martin's face.

Gwen came out on to the landing holding Charlie in her arms. He was wearing a yellow sleeping suit and looked like a drowsy duckling. He saw Alice in the hall and yearned out of Gwen's arms down towards her.

'I'll be back so soon,' Alice cried up to her two boys, 'so soon. I'll come in and see you the minute I'm back, I promise – '

'I should just *go*,' Natasha said, not looking up from her task.

'Oh, Tashie – '

James's crying rose to a howl. Martin gave him a despairing look and scrambled back down the staircase to the hall.

'Dear me,' Gwen said, '*what* a silly fuss. Now you've set Charlie off – '

Martin hurried Alice towards the front door, wrapping her coat round her.

'Come on, come on – '

'I *hate* this,' she said unhappily, 'I hate going out when he's so miserable – '

'He only puts it on for you. To try and make you do what he wants.'

'Even so, he *is* frightened – '

Martin said irritably, 'He is frightened of everything.'

He got into the driving seat of the car and leaned across to open the passenger door for Alice.

'He'll be five soon,' Martin said. 'Three years until prep school. He'll have to pull himself together.'

Alice said nothing. There were at least three things she wanted to say, chief amongst them being that she did not think James ought to be sent away to school at eight, but they only had five minutes' time for talk in the car, and they were bound to disagree and then they would arrive at the Park all jangled up and . . .

'Are you sulking?'

'No,' Alice said in as ordinary a voice as she could manage.

'I wish James had a quarter of Tashie's spirit.'

'I expect he wishes it too.'

The Park gates, with their boastful stone triumphs, reared up briefly in the headlights' beam, and vanished past them.

'I say,' Martin said, 'this is rather something.'

'D'you think it will be a huge party?'

'Dunno,' Martin said. He peered ahead. Lights were shining through the dark trees.

'It's *huge* – '

'It sure is.'

Alice thought of the black lace dress discarded on her bed.

'I've got the wrong clothes on – '

'No you haven't. Anyway, it's too late to think that.'

The drive swung round and opened into a floodlit sweep in front of the house; nine bays, ashlar quoins, roof pediment, long sashed windows and, above the front door, the arms of the family, added by a mid-Victorian Unwin who wished the world, or at least that part of it that came to Pitcombe Park, to be in no doubt as to the antiquity of his lineage. Alice leaned forward.

'This is such a *weird* thing to be doing! It's like visits to Rosings in *Pride and Prejudice*. You know, best clothes, best behaviour, kindly patronage – '

'Nonsense,' Martin said tensely.

'But – '

He stopped the car at a respectful distance from the steps to the front door.

'It's a perfectly normal thing to do. And very nice of the Unwins.'

Alice said in a rude voice, 'Well, it isn't normal for *me*.'

Martin said nothing. He got out of the car, shut the door without slamming it and came round to open Alice's door.

'Allie – ' he said, and his voice besought her to be amenable, 'don't let James get to you. He'll be fine, once we've gone.'

'It's nothing to *do* with James – '

The double front doors were opened above them and an oblong

of yellow light fell down the steps. They were instantly silent, like children caught red-handed. Martin put his hand under Alice's elbow, and guided her up the steps. At the top, a small man like an ex-jockey was waiting to open the inner glass doors to the hall. He said, 'Mr and Mrs Jordan,' without a questioning inflexion, and Martin said, 'Evening, Shadwell.'

'How do you *know*?' Alice mouthed at Martin.

He ignored her. Shadwell slipped Alice's coat from her shoulders, murmured, '*This* way, Mrs Jordan,' and went across the hall – it was round, Alice noticed, so did that mean all the doors had to be curved, like bananas? – and opened another double pair, and there was the drawing room and Lady Unwin, swimming forward in a tide of green silk ruffles and ropes of pearls, to envelop them in welcome.

The room was large and grand and there were about a dozen people in it, grouped among the damasked chairs and the tables bearing books and framed photographs and extravagant plants in Chinese bowls. There was also someone particular by the fireplace. Everyone else was dressed as Alice would have expected – indeed, as Lady Unwin would require – in dinner jackets and the kind of silk frock that saleswomen are apt to describe as an investment, but this person looked like the cover drawing for *Struwwelpeter*, which Alice had had to hide from James's fascinated but appalled gaze. All Alice could see, because the person was half-turned away from her, was a wild head of corn-coloured hair and a bizarre costume of black tunic and tights. Whoever it was, Lady Unwin was leaving it until last.

'Alice, dear – may I? – Alice, this is Mrs Fanshawe who lives at Oakridge Farm, simply brilliant with flowers, can't think how she does it, and Major Murray-French you know of course, and the Alleynes from Harcourt House – little ones just the age of yours I think, such fun – and Elizabeth Pitt, Mrs Pitt who is my right *arm* on all these committees, truly I cannot think what I should do without her, and Susie Somerville who is – what are you, Susie? Calling you a travel courier seems so rude when all the tours you take are so *grand*, I simply shouldn't dare to aspire to one, I promise you – and Simon Harleyford who is here for the weekend, so nice to have you, dear – and *Mr* Fanshawe without whom we just wouldn't have our famous summer fêtes, and Clodagh. Clodagh, come over here and say hello to Mrs Jordan.'

The black tunic and tights turned briefly from the small bright pink man she was talking to, said 'Hi' and turned back again.

'I told her,' Lady Unwin said in a stage whisper to Alice, 'I told her to be especially nice to Nigel Pitt because I really *need* him for the hospice. Our present treasurer is threatening to retire, so tiresome but I suppose as he's nearly eighty I shouldn't bully. Come and talk to Susie. She knows everything there is to know about Indian palaces.'

'I don't, actually,' Susie Somerville said, when they were left alone. She was small and leathery and in her forties, dressed in an evening suit of plum-coloured velvet. 'I only know how to get a porter wherever I am and how to change a colostomy bag. Being a courier is murder, sheer murder. Our outfit is so expensive that only the ancient can afford it so I haul these disintegrating old trouts round Baalbek and Leningrad and Udaipur and spend every evening mixing whisky and sodas and Complan. It's a nightmare.'

'Why do you *do* it?' Alice said, laughing.

'Money. They give me vast tips, especially the Yanks who love it that I'm titled. I'd miles rather be married, but I only ever want to marry people who don't want to marry me. So I've got horses as substitute children and a lot of friends and this ghoulish job. D'you ride?'

'No,' Alice said.

'You've got a man,' Susie Somerville said, draining her glass, 'you don't need to.'

Ralph Unwin, in a deep blue smoking jacket and smelling of something masculine and Edwardian, came up to take Alice in to dinner.

'Is Susie trying to shock you?'

'I can't shock anybody any more,' Susie said. She jerked her head towards the fireplace. 'How's Clo, now she's back?'

Ralph Unwin spoke quietly.

'We think she's fine. She won't speak of why she left, so we are simply biding our time.' He glanced at Alice. 'Our daughter, Clodagh. It looked as if she might be going to marry a chap in New York, but she's suddenly come home.' He smiled very faintly. 'Young hearts do mend.'

Susie Somerville and Alice both looked across at the *Struwwelpeter* shock of curls. Alice said suddenly, surprising herself, 'Of course it

65

hurts, but it's better to feel something so strongly that it half-kills when it's over than – '

She stopped.

'Hear, hear,' Susie Somerville said. 'Story of my life. Come on, Ralph. Margot's gesturing like a windmill. Nosebag time.'

In the doorway to the hall, there was polite congestion. Alice found herself next to Clodagh, whose face was difficult to see on account of her hair. Alice could not, out of delicacy, mention New York but she felt she ought to say something.

'We've just moved in to John Murray-French's house.'

'I know,' Clodagh said and moved on to catch up with her mother.

At dinner, Clodagh was next to Martin. When she turned towards him, Alice could see her face, which was neither pretty nor in the least like either of her solidly handsome parents. It was the face of a fox, wide-cheeked and narrow-chinned, except that her mouth was wide too. Because Alice was new to the village she had been put next to her host, and in order that she should not be alarmed by too much social novelty, John Murray-French was on her other side. In front of her was a bone china soup plate edged with gold containing an elegant amount of pale green soup sprinkled with chives.

'Watercress,' John said. 'They grow it further down the Pitt river. Are you liking my house?'

'Enormously.'

'You're too thin.'

'I don't think,' Alice said, leaning so that Shadwell could pour white burgundy over her shoulder into one of the forest of glasses in front of her, 'you know me well enough to say that.'

'It doesn't need intimacy. It needs an aesthetic eye. I don't just know about ducks.'

'Ducks,' Ralph Unwin said. 'Perfect bind. I gather they are coming off the river up the village street again.'

'Does that matter?'

'Only in that someone, sooner or later, slips on what they have left behind, and as they are reckoned to be my ducks, I end up visiting the victim in Salisbury hospital. My dear girl, you haven't any butter.'

Down the table Martin and Clodagh were laughing. She was doing the talking, very animatedly, and Alice could see her excellent, very white teeth. On Martin's other side, Susie Somerville and Mr Fanshawe were having a boastfully comparative conversation about international airports, and opposite Alice a gaunt woman in a grey silk blouse pinned at the neck with a cameo was drinking her soup with admirable neatness.

'You know Elizabeth Pitt, of course,' Ralph Unwin said.

Mrs Pitt leaned forward.

'I know *you*. Two dear little boys and a girl. They look exactly the age of Camilla's three. And you've taken on the dreaded shop.'

Ralph Unwin gave a mock shudder.

'The shop!'

'It's jolly good,' John Murray-French said. 'Has just the kind of food I like. Left to myself I'd live on beans and biscuits and whisky.' He indicated his soup. 'Can't really see the point of vegetables.'

'Are you,' Sir Ralph said to Alice, 'going to start a vegetable garden?'

Alice smiled at him.

'I'm hoping my mother-in-law will do that.'

'Not *Cecily* Jordan!'

'The same – '

'My *dear*,' said Elizabeth Pitt.

'Does Margot know? You won't get a minute's peace – '

'Yes, she does.'

'I *told* you Martin was Cecily's son, you know,' John said. 'It's odd how nobody listens to a word you say unless you are offering them a drink, when they can hear you clear as a bell three fields off.'

Sir Ralph bent his blue gaze directly upon Alice.

'What wonderful luck. Has Martin inherited her talent?'

She looked down the table. Martin was describing something to Clodagh and using his hands to make a box shape in the air. She looked utterly absorbed.

'Not really. I mean, he's very good at keeping a garden tidy, but he hasn't really got her eye.'

'This child's a painter,' John said across her, 'but she won't paint.'

'Won't?'

'I can't, just now,' Alice said unhappily.

67

Sir Ralph put a hand on hers.

'Sort of painter's block?'

'I suppose so – '

'I know!' Elizabeth Pitt said triumphantly. 'Juliet Dunne has a charming one, in her sitting room. Now Juliet,' she said, turning to Sir Ralph, 'has got a brilliant scheme for the hospice garden party – '

Sir Ralph bent towards her. John Murray-French turned away to say to the woman on his far side, 'I gather your trout have got some nasty ailment – '

Alice looked back down the table at Clodagh. She could watch her for a bit now, without distraction. It looked as if she hadn't touched her soup, and she had broken her roll into a hundred pieces and scattered it messily round her place, just like a child. She had very good hands. As far as Alice could see, they were without rings, but her nails were painted scarlet. Her eyes were set slightly on a slant, and even though her hair was light, her brows and lashes were dark. She didn't seem to have on any jewellery except an immense Maltese cross suspended round her neck on a black ribbon, invisible against her black tunic. She was saying something to Martin, looking down, and then she suddenly looked up and caught Alice gazing at her but her expression remained quite unchanged. Alice felt snubbed. She looked towards Sir Ralph and Mrs Pitt, but they were deep in county politics, so she looked instead at all the Unwins on the walls in their gilded plaster frames, regarding the dinner party from beneath their unsuitable, practical twentieth-century picture lights.

When the salmon came, John Murray-French turned back and told her that his son Alex was married, to a French girl whom he had met in Athens. Alice said she was so glad. They ate their salmon talking companionably and Alice tried to be interested in Alex's new job as an investment analyst and at the same time tried to remember the flavour of Alex's brief, ardent interest in her. During pudding – a chocolate roulade or apricot tart – and cheese – Stilton and Blue Vinney – Sir Ralph devoted himself to Alice. He was very charming. He told her of his childhood at Pitcombe, and how two spinster great-aunts had lived in The Grey House then. He told her how his three children had exactly the same nursery rooms as he and his sister had had, which gave Alice the chance to ask a question to which she perfectly well knew the answer.

'And is Clodagh your youngest?'

He immediately looked fond.

'She is. Twenty-six. Of course, she could have been married a dozen times over, but she has impossibly high standards. She's much the brightest of our three. She worked in publishing in New York. Somebody and Row. I'm afraid I'm putty in her hands.'

Alice rather wanted to say that it looked as if Martin was, too. But instead, she said, 'Perhaps she could get a job in English publishing, now she's back.'

'You must forgive a fond old father, but I rather want her here for a bit. Perhaps you could help me devise a scheme to keep her. I know she'd love to see your paintings.'

'Oh no!' Alice said, genuinely alarmed.

'All you creative people, so modest. Now tell me, when are we going to be allowed to meet your mother-in-law?'

When the cheese had been borne away, Lady Unwin rose and swept the women out of the room before her.

'*Strictly* twenty minutes,' she said to Sir Ralph, and then to her charges, 'Clodagh thinks we are absolutely barbaric. Don't you, darling? I suppose Americans wouldn't dream of such a thing.'

Clodagh said, 'The Americans I knew ate in restaurants all the time,' and then she went up to Susie Somerville and said, 'Come on, Sooze. I want a horror story from your latest trip.'

'Braced for it?' Susie Somerville said delightedly, going up the great staircase beside Clodagh. 'Well, you simply won't believe it, but I had an eighty-five-year-old junkie who chose *Samarkand* as the spot to trip out – '

Margot Unwin took Alice's arm.

'My dear, I do hope they looked after you at your end of the table.'

'Beautifully, thank you – '

'Let's find you a loo, my dear, the geography of this house is a nightmare for strangers.'

They went up the stairs together behind Susie and Clodagh, Margot talking all the time, and across an immense landing peopled with giant Chinese jars to one of several panelled doors. Margot thrust it open with her free hand and pushed Alice into the pink warmth beyond.

'Take your time, my dear.'

Alice was suddenly desperately tired. Shut into this baronial bathroom done up in a style Cecily would describe as Pont Street 1955, she could at last look at her watch. It was only ten past ten. There would have to be half an hour without the men, and then half an hour with them, before she could even begin to signal home to Martin across the room. She looked in the mirror. To herself she looked badly put together and amateurish. Perhaps it was time to cut off her pigtail.

Outside the bathroom, Sarah Alleyne was waiting for her. Sarah was fair and expensive looking, and Juliet Dunne had said that she was brilliant on both horses and skis.

'I wondered,' she said now, languidly, to Alice, 'I wondered if we could talk about sharing a school run. My wretched nanny's pregnant and I'm quite stuck, just for now – '

In the drawing room the ladies were gathered, holding cups of black coffee and feigning indifference to a silver dish of chocolates. Neither Clodagh nor Susie Somerville was there. Lady Unwin sat Alice beside her on a little French sofa, and talked about the village. She went through a kind of vivacious inventory of inhabitants, from old Fred Mott who was nearly a hundred through Miss Pimm and Miss Payne to some old thing called Lettice Deverel who played the harp. After twenty minutes, Alice realised that she had not been asked a single question. After twenty-five minutes, the men came in, and after thirty, Susie and Clodagh returned still absorbed in some conversation. Martin was holding both brandy and a cigar, neither of which he normally touched, and he sat down beside the gaunt Mrs Pitt with every show of enthusiasm. Alice realised, with amazement, that he was really enjoying himself.

She could not drag him away until almost midnight, and only then because other people were beginning to look round for Shadwell and their coats and to say, 'Come on, old thing, eight o'clock church tomorrow, don't forget.' Both Unwins kissed Alice goodnight but Clodagh, talking to the Harleyford man whom Alice wondered if Lady Unwin intended to be the next boyfriend, just waved from across the room and called, 'Look at the beams!' to Martin.

'What did she mean?' Alice said in the car.

'She and her brother carved swear words into the beams in the room above our garage, for a dare, when they were little. She couldn't remember what the words were, though.'

He began to laugh.

'Was she nice?' Alice said.

'Good fun,' he said, still laughing. 'Good fun.'

At home they found James asleep in their bed, clutching Alice's nightie. Gwen said she was sorry about it, but he'd been a proper handful. Martin carried him to his own bed, and then drove Gwen home while Alice sat on the floor of James's room and waited for him to sink down into deep oblivion again. She sat with her arms round her knees and her head bent and thought, without enthusiasm, of the dinner party. When Martin came back, she crept out of James's room and went to their bedroom where Martin was chucking his clothes over the back of a chair.

'Did you enjoy it? Did you like tonight?'

He was down to his socks and boxer shorts. He pulled one sock off and dropped it.

'It was terrific,' he said. He pulled off the other sock. 'Wasn't it?'

She went past him to the cupboard where she kept her clothes.

'I think you did rather better than me at dinner.'

'Oh-ho,' he said sounding pleased. He seldom flirted, but he liked to be flirted with. 'D'you think so?'

'I thought she was jolly rude,' Alice said, from half inside the cupboard.

He began to hum. Clodagh had been far from rude to him.

'Give her time – '

'If I can be bothered – '

'Allie,' he said, suddenly serious, 'we can't fall out with the Unwins.'

'Can't?'

'No. You just can't be bolshy.'

He went off to brush his teeth. When he came back, Alice was in her yellow dressing gown, fiercely brushing her hair. When they were first married, he used to love watching her do it; now he got into bed, hardly looking, and punched the pillows into the shape he liked.

'You looked great tonight,' he said absently.

'I felt a mess – '

'Rubbish.' His voice was thickly sleepy.

She went over to the window and parted the curtains to look out. There was a bright hard white moon, and the shadow of the fence lay in a black grid on the silver grass. I would so like to be free, Alice thought involuntarily. I am so tired of myself and the muddle of everything. I wish . . . She stopped.

'Come to bed,' Martin said.

She dropped the curtain and crossed the room to climb in beside him. He turned to roll himself behind her, cupping her breast in his hand. She stiffened, very slightly.

'Okay, okay,' he said. He rolled away. 'Night.'

She reached to turn out her bedside lamp. A silver slice fell through a gap in the curtains.

'Martin. Sorry – '

He grunted.

She turned on her side and lay there, staring into the dim room. Outside an owl called, from across the valley, and after a while another owl answered it from the beeches high above the Park. Then, from down the corridor, but coming nearer at every step, came the sound of James, crying.

'What do you want to go to church for?' Martin said.

They were both slightly hungover, Martin because he had had quite a lot of brandy, and Alice because she couldn't drink much of anything, anyway.

'I feel I'd like to. That's all. It's only an hour and Charlie will be resting. If you could just put the lamb in at half past eleven – '

'I wanted to be in the garden.'

'Then be in it. The children can come outside with you.'

'But the lamb – '

'You come *inside* to do that. It will take you all of two minutes.'

'I don't see why you want to go. You never go to ordinary church.'

'But *I* see,' Alice said, suddenly cross, 'why you *don't* want me to go. It won't do you any harm to have the children for an hour. I want to be somewhere quiet. I want to think.'

'Suppose I want to think?'

'Then you can go to evensong.'

He went out into the garden then, banging both halves of the stable door which failed to latch and bounced open again. Alice had a bad quarter of an hour putting Charlie down for his rest and finding a roasting tin for the lamb and Natasha's other gumboot and persuading James out of his pyjamas and into clothes, so that she had to run to church, which was uphill, and arrived very much out of breath and ill-prepared for calm.

The church was simple and strong and medieval. It had only a nave and a chancel and there was no stained glass in the windows, so that whatever natural light there was came in, uninterrupted. At the west end was a famous Norman font, carved with scenes from the life of John the Baptist ending with his lolling head on a charger, a scene that Miss Payne, who was in charge of the church flowers, liked to screen with a brass jug of golden rod or Michaelmas daisies or delphiniums. Mr Finch, of the shop, was sidesman in charge of books. He pressed *Hymns A & M* into Alice's hands most meaningfully.

She chose a pew at the back. The hassocks had been embroidered by the villagers to celebrate the Queen's Jubilee, each one representing animal or plant or bird life along the Pitt river. Alice knelt carefully on a bunch of kingcups. Ahead of her was a dozen or so backs, of which she recognised a few, and beyond them, Peter Morris in cassock and surplice. Idly she wondered who laundered its snowy folds. The organ began, a little breathlessly, played by Miss Pimm in her Windsmoor Sunday suit. The congregation rose stiffly to its feet.

Holding her prayerbook, Alice thought how much her father admired Cranmer's English. She remembered him giving a sudden impromptu lecture at supper one night on the iniquity of the banal and bloodless language of the modern service book. Pitcombe clearly had turned its thumbs down to the alternative services – what she held, she discovered, was in the still sonorous English of 1928. In the front of her prayerbook was stamped 'The Church of St Peter, Pitcombe' and underneath, in neat elderly script, 'Given in memory of Hilda Bryce, by her loving family'. Did anyone, she wondered, commemorate people that way any more?

She did not really notice what they said or sang, nor did she hear properly what Peter Morris said comfortably for ten minutes, from his pulpit, about St Paul's exhortations to the Romans, on being

73

delivered from the bondage of corruption into the glorious liberty of the children of God. She had said she wanted to think, but she didn't think. She simply sat, and looked at the whitewashed walls and the little monuments in stone and brass lamenting matchless husbands and beloved mothers and sons and observed how the pale sunlight came in and lit up the brass ends of the churchwardens' staffs like tiny flames. And then she knelt with everyone else and read aloud with them the prayer of St Chrysostom.

'Fulfil now, O Lord, the desires and petitions of thy servants, as may be most expedient for them.'

What, she wondered, *were* her desires and petitions, except that she wished to be rid of this preoccupation with the fluctuating graph of her unhappiness? She got up and followed everyone out, and Mrs Macaulay said how nice it was to see her in chuch, and Mr Finch smirked as he took her books, and Peter Morris clasped her hand warmly and told her to remember him to Charlie.

When she got home, they were all sitting round the kitchen table with mugs and the biscuit tin, and Clodagh Unwin was there too. She looked pale, and nothing like as self-possessed as the night before, and she was wearing butter yellow tights, and an enormous grey jersey that came half-way down her thighs, and grey suede boots. The moment Alice came in, Clodagh got up and went across to her, put her hands on Alice's arms and said, 'I came to say sorry. Because I was so horrible last night.'

Alice, startled, said, 'Oh, you weren't – '

'I was,' Clodagh said. 'I was awful. Ma said would I be particularly nice to you, but I was in a temper with her for something that's too boring to mention so I was particularly horrible instead.'

Alice moved away slightly.

'It doesn't matter,' she said. 'You were very nice to Martin.'

He gave a pleased guffaw from the table.

'Oh, *please*,' Clodagh said. Alice gave her a quick glance and saw her eyes were full of tears.

'Don't make so much of it. It doesn't matter. I didn't notice.'

'I don't know,' Clodagh said, with the beginning of a smile, 'if that doesn't make me feel *worse*.'

'Come on, Allie,' Martin said. 'Come *on*. Have some coffee.'

Alice threw her coat over the chair back and reached for an apron on the hook behind the door to the hall.

'I've got to do the potatoes for lunch – '

'I'll do them,' Clodagh said, taking the apron. 'I'm a whizz at potatoes.'

James, who had decided Clodagh was delicious, pulled a chair up to the sink, giggling, so that he could splash about while she peeled. Natasha, who felt a keen desire for Clodagh's boots, stayed by the table to devise a scheme by which she might try them on even if they were going to be too big, which they were, she knew, but all the same . . . Alice, not won over, went to fetch the potatoes from the larder and the peeler from a drawer and a saucepan. She dumped the potatoes in the sink and Clodagh seized her wrist.

'*Please* forgive me,' she said. Her voice was an urgent hiss and her curious grey-gold eyes were bright with intensity.

'You made me feel a fool last night,' Alice said, 'and you're doing it again now. I don't like it. That's all.'

Clodagh dropped her wrist. In a voice so low only Alice could hear it, she said, 'You were the only person last night who *didn't* look a fool.'

Alice went away to find carrots and a bag of frozen peas. When she came back, Martin had gone out again, James and Clodagh were singing and splashing at the sink and Natasha, without being asked, was laying the table, back to front.

'Clodagh's staying,' Natasha said. 'Daddy asked her.'

Clodagh turned round.

'But I won't if you don't want me to.'

'Of course stay. It's very ordinary lunch – '

'You're really kind.'

Natasha stretched up to her mother's ear.

'Oh I so *want* her boots – '

'Aren't they smart.'

Without turning round, Clodagh kicked her boots off backwards. 'Try them.'

Natasha gave a little squeal. James put his arms around Clodagh's waist in case the boots should create a bond between her and Natasha. She dropped a kiss on his head and he looked up at her with passion.

'You've no idea,' Clodagh said, 'how unutterable American

75

children are. We had one that used to come to the apartment loaded with toys and if you admired the smallest thing, he'd say, "Don't touch. Okay?" at the top of his voice.'

James thought this was brilliantly funny.

'Don't touch, okay, don't touch, okay, don't touch, okay – '

'Look – ' Natasha breathed, bending over to admire her feet.

'You look like Puss in Boots.'

'I love them.' She looked up at Clodagh. 'Are they American?'

'Sure thing, baby,' Clodagh said with an American accent, 'Henry Bendel, no less.'

Martin came back with a bottle of wine. He was humming. He kissed Alice's cheek on his way to fetch a corkscrew and then again on his way to fetch the glasses. At the second kiss, she laughed.

'Feeling better?'

'Yes,' she said, surprised.

'I expect church made you feel better,' Natasha said, stroking the boots, 'I think it's supposed to.'

When everyone laughed she looked tremendously pleased and said, in Gwen's phrase, 'Well, this really *is* my day and no mistake.'

Martin poured wine for himself and Clodagh and Alice. Clodagh finished the potatoes and put them on to boil and scooped the peelings out of the sink into the rubbish bin. Alice stared at her.

'Isn't that right?' Clodagh said. She had pushed up the sleeves of her jersey and stood there, shoeless, like a grey and yellow bird.

'It's absolutely right. I just don't associate New York flat dwellers with – '

'Oh,' Clodagh said quickly, smiling at her, 'I always did things like that. I used to scrub floors and stuff as therapy when the whole scene got a bit heavy.'

She came round the table to where Alice was peeling carrots and looked at her intently.

'Hello,' she said.

Alice took a quick swallow of her wine.

'Is this another kind of game? Like last night?'

'No,' Clodagh said. 'I could kill myself for last night.'

Alice's hands were shaking. She put down her wine glass not at all steadily.

'You haven't met my baby.'

'He's so sweet,' Natasha said, still mooning over her feet. 'He's the nicest baby in my class.'

Clodagh dropped her gaze and let Alice go.

'Can we go and find him?'

The children rushed to seize her hands, Natasha shuffling but determined in her boots. They went out of the room and Alice could hear them beginning to clatter, chattering up the uncarpeted stairs. Singing softly, without meaning to, Alice fetched a pan and put her carrots in it, beside the pan of Clodagh's potatoes.

CHAPTER SIX

It was not in the least lost upon Peter Morris that Alice hadn't attended to a word of his sermon; indeed, that she had hardly come to church for any orthodox spiritual purpose at all. This was hardly uncommon. The reasons that brought his congregations to church seemed to him quite as various and tenuous and peculiar as those that kept them away. Folding his stole carefully after the service, Peter decided that Alice had probably come because an hour in church meant you could step off life for a space, stop time. That at least was how she had looked. And no doubt while she sat there, drifting, that decent young husband of hers – good midshipman material – was gardening and minding the children. Peter sighed. The Jordans seemed to him a thoroughly late twentieth-century combination of emotion and imagination on the one hand and Anglo-Saxon aversion to intensity on the other. A polite and lonely alliance.

The village, needless to say, had minutely observed the outward things. Even old Fred Mott, day in day out at his cottage window next door to the post office, had sufficient sight left to say approvingly on Peter Morris's weekly visits, 'That's a fancy piece. *That'll* make 'em all sit up.'

'Who?' Peter said. 'Who'll sit up – '

'All of them old dumps round 'ere. All them old bags.'

His little wet mouth widened into a grin.

'You're an old scoundrel, Fred.'

'Not 'alf what I was when I was young. Not *'alf.*'

It was all very well, of course, to observe that something was troubling Alice, but how to help was inevitably much trickier. When he asked people around the village, the general view was that she was extravagantly blessed among mortals – lovely house, nice husband, dear little children, more than enough money – so that even if she was being helpful in the matter of the shop and the flower rota, that really was no more than her duty, living where she did and having what she had. Rosie Barton, who ran a very successful little computer business in Salisbury with her husband, Gerry, and who had very decided views on the sort of village Pitcombe should be, said, with the seeming deep sympathy that was her stock in trade, that Alice simply had to learn about a village community. Peter had pointed out that Wilton had hardly been an inner city situation to come from, and Rosie said indeed no, but the measure of *involvement* in the village was unique. Peter had said no more. The Barton child, an anxious four-year-old in the care of a succession of au pair girls, seemed never to require from his parents the involvement their business or village life did. And they came to church.

Alice, Peter Morris knew, would have been amazed to find how much she was watched and how much the village knew about her. It had amazed Peter himself, at his first country living in Suffolk, to realise that not a line of washing could go up nor an order of groceries be placed without every item being noticed, and conclusions drawn. When he heard someone in the Pitcombe shop say, 'She keeps the children nice,' he knew that meant that the frequency of lines of socks and knickers blowing in The Grey House orchard had not gone unremarked.

Even with the great Admiral aloft to talk and pray to, Peter Morris was very conscious of his solitariness. He had not really meant to remain a widower so long – his marriage had only managed two years before his wife's cancer had killed her, in four months, start to finish – but he had never found another woman to whom he could talk as comfortably as he had to Mary. He had come very close to it in Suffolk, with a woman who, in the end, decided she could not be a parson's wife, and then, oddly enough, he had found quite recently an excellent friend in Lettice Deverel of Pitcombe. She was over seventy, scholarly, sharp and a Shavian socialist. She kept a harp in her muddled sitting room, and a green Amazon parrot in the kitchen and she had not a minute in the world for airs and graces. In the last three years, Peter Morris had taken to going up the lane from his sturdy early Victorian rectory to her Regency villa at the top of the village when he had a human knot to untie. Even if she said, as she often did, that she knew nothing about backward babies or neurotic spinsters or the male menopause or whatever the current problem was, she was a good sounding board, and simply went on making bread or potting up pelargoniums while he talked himself to some kind of conclusion.

Rose Villa contained an accumulation of a lifetime's energetic curiosity and culture. As a young woman Lettice Deverel had taught in an international school in Switzerland and had learned to ski in brown leather boots – there was a matching brown photograph to prove it. She had then come home to teach with the Workers' Education Authority, and gone on to be librarian of a famous collection on the history of women in England. All her life she had painted, cooked, gardened, written, read, travelled and kept animals and a diary. She played both the piano and the harp. She had always lived alone and had collected a wide and enthusiastic circle of friends. When Peter Morris added himself to the circle, she told him that she was agnostic and that she had never known a priest well before. He said in that case, she was about to learn. She said, meaning it, 'But I won't stand for God being dragged in all the time,' and he had replied, 'Well, He won't mind that as there's nothing He dislikes so much as no reaction at all.'

It had been a good start. Three years later, among a welter of weekly minutiae, they had together been through Clodagh Unwin's defection to America, the death of Miss Pimm's tyrannical but worshipped old mother, a crippling motorbike accident to the brightest boy in the village, cot deaths, Down's Syndrome babies, broken marriages, drunkenness, unemployment, fire, flood and pestilence. Alice Jordan seemed to Lettice Deverel a very minor problem indeed. She went on thumping her dough while she said, 'Of course, you wouldn't trouble yourself about her if she wasn't good-looking.'

'Good morning,' the parrot said from his cage. 'And who's a pretty parrot then?'

'I might,' said Peter Morris, who never minded being found out, 'not trouble myself quite so *much* – '

'She may be a very spoiled young woman, for all we know. And of course spoiled people inevitably become discontented in time.'

'I don't think she's spoiled. I think she may be unhappy, but I don't think it's discontent. It might be disappointment, of course. In her marriage, maybe.'

80

Lettice Deverel had encountered Martin several times in the village; once, outside the shop, she had dropped a bag of flour and he had helped her, most assiduously, to scoop it into the gutter. She gave a faint snort.

'The English public school system – '

'Well?'

' – renders most men incapable of recognising or acknowledging their own states of mind. Makes them emotionally inarticulate.' She poked a floury finger at Peter. 'Makes most of them afraid of women. Drives any of them who go to Winchester quite round the bend.'

'I think Martin Jordan went to Rugby.'

'Stands out a mile off.'

She dumped fat sausages of dough into loaf tins and set them at the back of her ancient Rayburn to rise.

'If you're trying to make me say I think you should go and talk to her, you're out of luck. You leave well alone.'

'Laugh like parrots at a bagpiper,' said the parrot. 'Good morning. Merchant of Venice. Pretty parrot.'

'She's rather a good painter, you see,' Peter said, 'and she won't paint. Or can't paint.'

'Creativity isn't like carpentry.'

Peter Morris stood up.

'Why have you taken against Alice Jordan?'

'I've done no such thing. I've admired her about the village and I've noticed what you have noticed. But I haven't woven sentimental fantasies about her. You leave her be. She's got pride. Now come outside and have a look at the camellia I thought the frost had done for. You never saw such leaders – '

The last week of the spring school holidays was soft and warm, with the sun shining bright and hard through the still bare branches of trees. Pitcombe began to break the winter seal on its doors and windows and pot plants were put out on doorsteps, like invalids, to take a little reviving air. Lettice Deverel washed the blankets on her bed as a gesture to spring cleaning, and started to go for walks again, declining to do so in winter because she said there was no point in walking when you had to keep your eyes on your feet rather than the view. In rubber-soled brogues and grasping a thumb stick, she set off most afternoons at a determined pace and the village, noticing her departures, said to one another, grinning, that spring *must* have come if Miss D. was off again. Fred Mott's grandson, Stuart, who was unemployed and a competition gardener, took advantage of these walks to take a wheelbarrow up to Rose Villa by the field path where he would be less observed, and to help himself to some excellent and well-rotted compost.

Sometimes Lettice went up the hill and round the edge of the Park. Sometimes she went either way along the river path, or across fields by bridleways to King's Harcourt and Barleston. Her favourite walk, however, was to skirt the higher boundary of The Grey House garden and strike east along the hillside, with the river below her and a widening valley view opening out ahead. She noticed, with approval, that the window frames of The Grey House were being painted and that someone had begun to thin out the depressing hedge of mahonias that John Murray-French had simply ignored. There was a new sandpit on the lawn outside the kitchen door, and a tricycle and a pleasingly full washing line. Lettice had never wanted to marry but she was a staunch supporter of family life.

Two fields beyond The Grey House, she could hear children. She dropped down the slope a little so that she could see the river, and there some way below her in the grass sat Alice Jordan and Clodagh Unwin with a basket and a baby, while a girl and a boy were jumping about over the trunk of a fallen willow near-by. It was a very pretty scene. It might have been, Lettice thought, the subject of one of those Victorian narrative paintings on which her artistic teeth had been cut. Alice wore blue and Clodagh was wrapped in a strange cloak of yellow and black. Lettice, who had known Clodagh from a child and believed her to be thoroughly spoiled and the only original child of the Unwin family, considered going down the slope to join them, and to meet Alice Jordan properly. But they looked so complete in themselves that she decided against it, and tramped on above them with her stick in her right hand and her face set determinedly to the eastward view.

'Don't you have any curiosity about me?' Clodagh was saying.

She had been wearing a long string of yellow amber beads under her cloak, and she had taken them off and given them to Charlie

82

who was collapsing them, up and down, up and down, on his knees.

'I'm dying of it,' Alice said, 'but I thought it was generally accepted that no one must ask.'

'Ask *what* – '

'About New York.'

'Jesus,' Clodagh said, 'what *about* New York?'

Alice leaned on one elbow, turning herself towards Charlie and Clodagh.

'Well. I may have got it all wrong, but I understood that a love affair that might have ended in marriage went wrong and you have come home with a broken heart.'

'Broken heart?' Clodagh said. 'Hah! Marriage. *Honestly.*'

Alice waited. Charlie swung the beads from side to side and talked excitedly to them.

'I see,' Clodagh said. 'I'm the poor little jilted fiancée, am I?'

'*I* don't know,' Alice said, 'I don't know anything. And if you want to be mysterious, I never shall.'

There was a pause. Then Clodagh said, 'I don't want to be mysterious. Not to you.'

Alice lay down in the grass and waited. It was ten days since the dinner party at Pitcombe Park, and she had seen Clodagh on eight of them. Clodagh had come down to The Grey House constantly on some pretext or other, bringing with her a tabby kitten and a significant change of atmosphere. It was she who suggested this picnic, just as she had suggested a number of other things – getting the drawing room curtains up, learning songs to her guitar, making fudge, choosing old roses to climb through apple trees – that had made them all feel that life was markedly improved.

'There was a love affair,' Clodagh said, 'and it did end. But I ended it.'

Alice turned her head sideways. She could see the backs of Charlie's and Clodagh's heads against the sky.

'Then even if you're sad, you aren't as sad as you would have been if you had been thrown over.'

Clodagh didn't turn around.

'I'm not sad at all. I'm thankful to be out of it. I was nearly stifled with possessiveness. Couldn't go out without saying where, couldn't telephone without saying who, couldn't buy so much as new socks without being asked who they were meant to impress. And as I was being virtually kept, after I gave up my job, I wasn't in much of a position to object.'

'So he wanted to marry you?'

Clodagh turned round suddenly and lay on her front so that her face was close to Alice's.

'There wasn't any question of marriage.'

'Oh Lord,' Alice said. 'Was he married already?'

Clodagh raised her eyes so that she was looking straight at Alice, only a foot away.

'Alice,' she said, 'he was a woman. That's why.'

Alice thought she had stopped breathing.

'My lover was a woman,' Clodagh said.

Alice sat up.

'So all this millionaire lawyer stuff was just a smokescreen – '

'She was a millionaire. Is, I mean. And she is a lawyer. And she'd have married me like a shot. As it was, she did everything but eat me. So I had to leave.'

'Clodagh – '

Clodagh sat up and put an arm across Alice's shoulders, above Charlie's head.

'Have I shocked you?'

'No,' Alice said. 'Yes. I don't know – ' She turned to look at Clodagh. 'Do you hate men?'

Clodagh began to laugh.

'Oh, Alice – '

'Shut up,' Alice said angrily, twitching her shoulders free.

'Listen,' Clodagh said, 'I like men a lot. I don't sleep with women because I *have* to. I do it because I *choose* to. We all have a choice, you, me, everyone – '

Charlie tipped himself sideways and began to crawl energetically down the grassy slope towards his brother and sister. Alice made as if to follow, but Clodagh held her.

'He's fine. We'll go after him if we need to. We haven't finished.'

'I don't know what to think – '

'Don't try then.'

'Tell me – '

'What?'

84

'Oh, Clodagh, I don't know, I don't – just, tell me – tell me what happened, what's happened to you – '

'Nothing's *happened*. Before I was twenty I slept with boys and girls – girls first of course because of boarding school – and I liked girls better. Nothing happened to me unless you can call the discovery of preferring girls a happening. I've had two proper affairs, one with a writer in London and then this one, with an American lawyer whom I met through my first lover and some libel action over a book of hers. The first affair was really better because we were more equal and I don't like being dominated. If I did, I'd probably like sex with men more. I got stuck in the New York business. I was very bowled over by all the glamour and Concorde and skiing in Aspen and stuff, and by the time that had worn off I was up to my neck, New York job, amazing apartment and this besotted woman. All her friends said she'd kill herself if I left, so I stayed. And then I realised that if I didn't leave, I'd kill *myself*, so I went. And she did try to kill herself but they got her to hospital in time and pumped her stomach and the lover who'd preceded me in her life and always wanted her back anyway has taken her to Florida.'

Natasha came stumbling up the field to say that James had got river *in*side his wellingtons.

'Tell him to take them off and play in bare feet.' Alice was astonished her voice should sound so ordinary.

'And Charlie's eating all kinds of things. We thought we saw him eat a ladybird – '

Clodagh laughed.

'Did he spit it out?'

'No. He sort of crunched it – '

Alice began to get up.

'Perhaps we should go back – '

'No,' Natasha pleaded. 'Please not yet. We're on a voyage. *Please.*'

She went dancing back to the fallen tree. Alice followed her with her eyes, devouringly.

'Did you love her?'

'Of course,' Clodagh said. 'At the beginning. Or at least, I was in love.' She looked at Alice, smiling. 'Are you suggesting I'm only in it for the sex?'

'Of *course* not – '

'Alice,' Clodagh said, and her voice was warmly affectionate, 'you don't know a thing about a thing, do you?'

Alice said nothing.

'A husband, three children but you aren't even awake. You haven't one clue about how wonderful you are, nor how to live – '

Alice's voice was choked with angry tears.

'Don't be *cheap*. Living isn't your jet-setting, sexually indulgent merry-go-round. Living is getting *on* with things, bearing things, making things work – '

'Oh my God,' Clodagh said. She put her hands over her face. After a while she took them away again and said, in the gentlest voice, 'My poor little Alice.'

'I'm not poor. And don't patronise me.'

'Believe me,' Clodagh said, 'that's the last thing I want to do.'

Alice began to rip up single grasses, like tearing hairs out of a head.

'It's *you* who don't know what life is for. You don't live, you just pass the time. You only want to enjoy yourself – '

'Ah,' said Clodagh, quite unperturbed, 'the puritan ethic yet again, I see.' She stretched across and very gently but firmly took hold of Alice's agitated hand. 'Alice. If I'm so wrong and you are so right, why are you so cross and unhappy?'

'I'm not – '

'*Alice.*'

Alice took her hand away and wound her arms round her knees and put her head down on them. She said, muffled, 'I've tried so hard – '

'Too hard, perhaps.'

'You couldn't call my children not living properly – '

'I don't. But you won't have them for ever and you'll *always* have you.'

'Sounds to me like the usual live-for-yourself pseudo-psychological American claptrap – '

Clodagh let a little pause fall and then she stood up so that her voice should come down to Alice from a distance.

'If you aren't happy with yourself, you aren't any use to anyone else. And I should think that should satisfy even your masochistic puritanism.'

And then she went down the slope to the children, who were

delighted to see her and let her come on board their ship and sail over the grassy sea. Above them, in a perfect turmoil of fury and relief and misery and excitement, Alice sat where Clodagh had left her and cried copiously into her folded arms.

When they returned to the house at teatime, Clodagh carrying Charlie and Alice the picnic basket, they found Cecily in the drive, in her car, reading a magazine. Natasha and James were entranced at this and rushed forward with pleased screams but Alice felt, for the disconcerting first time, less pleased than she expected to. She said, 'My mother-in-law,' to Clodagh and went forward behind the children.

Cecily got out of the car all smiles and hugs. She took no notice of Alice's wariness and hugged her too, with her usual warmth, and kissed Charlie and said hello to Clodagh. She had never done this before, never arrived on impulse without warning – it was one of her rules – but then she had never felt so out of touch, so – so *excluded* from Alice's life as she had recently. Even given Alice's precarious state of mind, the telephone had been abnormally silent and when she had, after intense self-examination, tried to ring, there was either no one there or only Gwen who answered the telephone with an affectation that set Cecily's teeth on edge – 'Mrs Jordan's residence' – and was then elaborately, unnecessarily, discreet about Alice's whereabouts.

'Darling, I should have rung – '

'Not at all,' Alice said politely.

Clodagh said, 'I'll go in and put the kettle on,' and went into the house with Charlie on her hip and the others dancing behind her. Cecily watched her go.

'Is she an Unwin from the Park?'

'Yes. The youngest.'

Cecily wanted to say that Clodagh seemed very much at home but stopped herself. She put an arm round Alice.

'It is lovely to see you. I've been longing to see how you were getting on with the house. And I thought, heavens, the holidays are nearly over – '

'We've been so busy,' Alice said. 'I don't know why moving should take up all one's life, but it seems to.'

'And what about some help?'

87

'I'm fine,' Alice said.

'And a holiday?'

'Honestly,' Alice said, and there was an edge of impatience to her voice, 'we don't need one just now.'

'There's Martin,' Cecily said, dropping her arm and catching Alice's tone, 'as well as you.'

Alice began to move towards the house.

'Come in and have tea.'

The kitchen looked undeniably a happy place. There was a blue jug of yellow tulips on the dresser, and on the table James and Natasha were putting out plates and mugs haphazardly on a yellow flowered cloth. Charlie was already in his high chair gnawing on a carrot, and by the window, still in her wizard's cloak, Clodagh was slicing and buttering currant bread. There was a kettle on the Aga and the top half of the stable door was open. In a Windsor armchair by the fire a tabby kitten lay asleep on a blue and white cushion. It was all entirely as it should be and the sight of it caused Cecily's heart to sink like lead.

She had paused, on her way to The Grey House, at the Pitcombe shop and post office. She was not quite sure why she had done this, nor why she had said vivaciously to Mr Finch, 'I am on my way to The Grey House! I am Mr Jordan's mother, you see.'

Mrs Macaulay had been in the shop at the time and so had Stuart Mott's wife, Sally. Mrs Macaulay had beadily taken in Cecily's clothes – very good but my, wouldn't it be a treat to have that much to spend – and Sally Mott, who was tired of having Stuart out of work and under her feet all the time, came boldly forward and said she wondered if Mr Jordan could do with some gardening help because Stuart could probably spare him a bit of time if . . .

Cecily was delighted. The suggestion suited her every wish to help and it gave her a purpose in arriving at The Grey House unannounced and clearly not just passing. She took Sally's telephone number, bought two tins of dog meat – not the brand, Mrs Macaulay noticed, that her girls favoured – and a box of chocolate buttons, and went out of the shop leaving a breath of 'Arpège' behind to daze Mr Finch. He took the washing powder and the packet of aspirin that Mrs Macaulay held out to him and heard his mouth say, 'Will that be all?' While his heart sang Swinburne:

Strong blossoms with perfume of
   manhood, shot out from my spirit as rays.

Now, Cecily put the chocolate buttons down on the table beside
the milk jug. James's eyes bulged with immediate desire and
Charlie, using his carrot as a baton, pointed at them with it and
mewed urgently. Clodagh stopped buttering and with a winglike
swoop of her cloaked arm vanished the box into her pocket.

'After tea.'

'Now, now, *now*,' said James.

'*After* tea.'

'*Now* – '

'*James*,' Alice said, 'you know the rules perfectly well.'

'So sorry,' Cecily said stiffly. She looked round the room.
'You've made this so pretty. And how lovely to have a kitten.'

Natasha slid into a chair next to her grandmother.

'He's called Balloon because of his tummy. Clodagh says he's a
lousy kisser.'

The other side of the table, James began to giggle.

'Personally,' Natasha said, 'I don't kiss him a lot because his
breath is fishy.'

'I'm glad to hear it,' Cecily said.

'There's hens,' James said.

'Hens, darling?'

Alice said, 'We've got a dozen pullets. White Leghorn crossed
with Light Sussex. Clodagh knows about hens and we are learning.'

'They can't do eggs yet,' James said, 'but they can when they're
bigger.'

Cecily eyed Clodagh.

'What a knowledgeable young woman – '

Clodagh put the plate of buttered bread on the table and then
went over to the Aga and said something quietly to Alice who was
making the tea. Alice laughed and said something inaudible back.
They came back to the table together and began in a practised
mutual way to give the children their tea, cutting up Charlie's bread
into little squares, putting honey on James's, pouring milk into
mugs. Alice gave Cecily a cup of tea and sat down beside her.

'Darling,' Cecily said, 'I think I've found you a gardener this
afternoon. Someone called Stuart Mott – '

'He's a rogue,' Clodagh said.

'All gardeners are rogues,' Cecily said, 'more or less.'

'This one's more.'

'But does he know about gardening?'

'I think he must. He's mad about prizes, marrows like hippos, yard-long runner beans. If you lick off all the butter, Charlie Jordan, you will simply have to eat your bread bare.'

Smiling angelically, Charlie laid the bread on his highchair tray and began, with tiny, neat fingers, to pick out the currants. Alice, Cecily noticed, had hardly spoken.

'Darling. Mightn't he be worth a try?'

Alice said slowly, 'I'll suggest it to Martin – '

'I *long* for you to come down to Dummeridge. The potager is having its first real spring and as you were in at its conception – '

'Alice,' Clodagh said, 'are you a *gardener*?'

'You know I'm not – '

'Alice painted the most lovely frontispiece for my book. She was a kind of inspiration – '

'You must beware of my mother,' Clodagh said, stretching over to rescue a sticky knife that had fallen from Natasha's plate. 'She thinks you are a gardening genius but she's quite unscrupulous in bending people to her will. You'll find yourself talking to the Evergreen Club, none of whom can hear a word you say.'

Cecily turned to Alice who was cradling her cup in both hands and drinking dreamily out of it.

'When can you come? Come for the night. Bring everyone, before the end of the holidays.'

'It would be lovely,' Alice said remotely.

'I've started the recorder,' Natasha said to her grandmother. 'I can play "London's Burning" after only two lessons. Will you come and hear me?'

'Yes,' Cecily said unhappily, 'I should love to.'

She got up. Alice said, 'Five minutes only, Tashie.'

Natasha took Cecily's hand and led her out of the room. When the door had closed behind them Cecily had a sudden angry, irrational feeling that everyone in the kitchen was bursting with suppressed laughter the other side of it.

'Do you,' she said to Natasha, despising herself for doing it, 'do you like Clodagh?'

'We adore her,' Natasha said, '*and* I can play the first two lines of "Frère Jacques" too – '

'And does she come here a lot?'

'Oh, every day. And when Mummy was doing the shop she took us on a walk and got us some frog spawn. It is *disgusting*. Of course, a lot of interesting things *are* disgusting. Aren't they?'

'Yes, darling,' Cecily said sadly. 'Yes, I'm afraid that they are.'

When Cecily returned to Dummeridge that night, Richard was at home. She had known he would be and although the knowledge hadn't in any way affected her impulsive drive to Pitcombe, she discovered that she was surprisingly pleased to find him when she got back. He was sitting in the drawing room with an open briefcase and a whisky and soda, and when she stooped to kiss him he said, 'What's the matter?'

'Tired, I think. I've just come back from Pitcombe.'

He went on flipping through papers because it was what she expected of him.

'All well there?'

'Oh yes – '

'Drink?'

'Please – '

He put his briefcase down and went to the drinks tray on the sofa table. He poured a gin and tonic and took it back to her.

'Alice any better?'

'Alice,' Cecily said with some edge, 'was looking fine.' She paused, took a swallow of her drink and then said carelessly, 'There was really no chance to talk to her.'

'No chance?'

'She has a new friend. The youngest child of Pitcombe Park. Seemed very much at home – '

Richard, perceiving at once what was the matter, picked up his papers again and said, 'You should be pleased she has found a friend locally. I thought you were worried she was lonely – '

Cecily got up, rattling the ice in her glass.

'Of course I'm glad.'

Richard said quietly, without looking up, 'Alice had to leave home some day.'

Cecily said angrily, 'Richard, she isn't *well*.'

He said nothing.

'I can't talk to you about it,' Cecily said. 'You can't relate to humankind at all, only to business. I don't suppose you give Alice any thought at all. I don't suppose you ever have.'

He said, in a perfectly ordinary voice, 'How do you know what I think?'

'The evidence of my eyes and ears.'

'I'm a patient man,' Richard said, 'but sometimes you try me to the limit. You don't know what I think because in forty years you have never once asked me.'

Cecily was close to tears. She still stood by her armchair holding her drink because she had meant to walk out on some Parthian shot and go off to the kitchen to grill trout for their dinner.

'Then I'll ask you. I am asking you – '

'What I think about Alice?'

She subsided on to the arm of the chair.

'Yes.'

'My feelings for her are considerable. I am fond of her and I admire her. But I think she has taken a long time to grow up. If she is being awkward now – '

'I didn't say she was being awkward.'

'– if she is disappointing you – '

'I didn't say – '

'Shut up,' Richard said, suddenly angry.

Cecily got up.

'I don't want to hear any more. You haven't a clue. But then you have no idea what women are like or what they need. You never have.'

'Is that so?'

She almost ran to the door.

'I'm going to get supper.' She waved an angry hand at his papers. 'You go back where you belong.'

When the door had shut, Richard sat for a moment and looked ahead of him without seeing anything. Plainly, Alice had in some way defied Cecily, and although he was sorry for Cecily, he was also glad. He sighed and went back to his papers. The considerableness of his feelings for Alice were a self-forbidden luxury.

'Juliet?' Cecily said into the telephone.

It was a quarter to eight. Juliet Dunne had just read the last word of the last bedtime story and had come down to find that the dog had eaten most of the shepherd's pie she had left by the cooker for supper, and then the telephone had rung. So she had answered it with a snarl.

'Oh, Cecily,' Juliet said, 'so sorry to be cross but *really*. Sometimes I hate domestic life so much I am not responsible for my actions. The fucking dog. And, frankly, fucking Henry for needing supper at all. I'd give anything to be a kept woman at this minute.'

Cecily made soothing noises.

'I really rang to talk to you about Alice – '

'Allie? Why, is something – '

'Well, I'm not *sure* – '

'I thought she was looking miles better,' Juliet said. 'I saw her on Tuesday. We had a tots tea party.'

'Do you know Clodagh Unwin?'

'Clo? All my life, practically.'

'She seems,' Cecily said, 'almost to be living there.'

'Whoopee,' Juliet said. 'Best thing in the world. She's the most lovely fun. She'll cheer them all up. Oh Lord, Cecily, here comes Henry. He'll have to have dog food, there isn't anything else. If you'd had daughters, Cecily, would you have encouraged them to get married?'

'Probably not – ' Cecily said, thinking of the briefcase in the drawing room.

'Of course, with sons, I can't wait to be shot of them. But I'm stuck with Henry. Look, I think it's brilliant about Clodagh and Alice and I should think the Unwins are thrilled. They always want Clo to settle down, so a nice dose of happy family life – '

'Is – is she *safe*?'

'Safe?' Juliet said. 'Safe? Clo? Heavens, no. What do you want a safe friend for Alice for? Henry's safe and he bores me to tears, don't you, darling? Cecily, I must go and open his tin of Chum.'

Cecily put the telephone down. Then she went over to the refrigerator and took out the trout that Dorothy had left, ready gutted, on a plate. She looked at their foolish dead fish faces. Tomorrow, she resolved, she would telephone Martin. He was, after all, her son.

CHAPTER SEVEN

Martin Jordan and Henry Dunne met for lunch in the White Hart in Salisbury. Henry had telephoned Martin at his office and said, rather mysteriously, that he had something to discuss and could they meet somewhere that their crowd didn't frequent. Martin said what about the White Hart as it was so large, and so they met there in the foyer, conspicuous in their moleskin trousers and tweed jackets among two busloads of spring tourists, one checking in and one out, in a welter of nylon suitcases and quilted coats in pastel colours.

Henry found them a table in the corner of the bar and went away for two pints of beer and several rounds of prawn sandwiches. When he came back he said, 'I sneaked a look at The Grey House the other day. I must say, you're doing a great job. John's a wonderful fellow, but of course he never much minds how things look.'

Martin was extremely pleased. He had worked tirelessly at weekends in the garden, and was allotting himself four hours' outside painting a week. Alice said 'Oh well done' rather absently to him, quite often, but he didn't feel she quite took in the scale of his achievements, and anyway, he liked other people to appreciate the improvements he was making. He shrugged his shoulders self-deprecatingly.

'Those mahonias had really had it – '

'Awful things. Only worth it for the scent of the flowers in March – '

'Absolutely.'

Henry took a large bite of sandwich, chewed, swallowed, took a pull at his beer and said, in a much more solemn voice, 'Martin, nice as it is to see you, this isn't just a social lunch.'

'I rather gathered that – '

'Fact is, I'm here as Sir Ralph's emissary. To test the water. To put something to you.' He took another bite. 'A proposition.'

94

Martin immediately and wildly thought that Sir Ralph might want to buy back The Grey House. For all the difficulties involved in getting there, now he *was* there he felt extremely possessive about it as well as being conscious that living there added several social cubits to his stature. He put on a soberly considering expression.

'I won't beat about the bush,' Henry said. 'Thing is, Sir Ralph needs a new solicitor. He's decided he must have local advice, particularly for the estate and – this is strictly in confidence – I think he's fallen out with the London lot, naming no names. He wants to change a lot of things – I'll tell you about that later – and he asked me who I would recommend. I suggested your outfit. He thought for a bit and said why not you.'

Martin was scarlet.

'I – I'm not a senior partner – '

'I said that. He said he didn't mind about that, and that one day you would be. Fact is, I think it's your living in The Grey House that's done it. He feels it would be keeping everything in the family, so to speak.'

'I haven't any experience in estate work – '

'I have.'

'I *say*,' Martin said, and beamed.

'Like it?'

'I'll say. That is – if I can do it – '

'Nice piece of business to brandish at your senior partners. I wouldn't like to promise, but it's my guess that estate business will lead to all personal business too in the end, Lady Unwin and all. Pitcombe Park's pet lawyer. Thing is,' he looked at Martin over the rim of his beer glass, 'it'd help me a lot, having you on my side. He can be the devil to handle, used to having his own way. Clodagh takes after him.'

Martin was full of excited generosity.

'She's amazing. She's cheered us all up like anything. Allie's quite different and the children think she's wonderful.'

'That's another thing. You see, the Unwins are pleased as Punch she's taken to you all. Any friend of Clodagh's is likely to be beamed on by them but your family is exactly what they want for her. They were in a frightful state when she got back from the States, made worse, of course, by the fact she wouldn't tell them

95

anything. Margot was all for rushing her off to some frightfully expensive trick cyclist in London to have her head seen to. But life at The Grey House seems to have done the trick for nothing. Sir Ralph said this morning he hadn't seen Clodagh in such good form for years.'

Martin, whose private thoughts about Clodagh were of a guiltily excited kind, said, well, she was the greatest fun . . .

'Oh, she is. But she's a bad girl too. Has those poor old parents running round in circles.' He looked at his watch. 'Can I take it that your answer is at least a preliminary yes?'

Martin said, with enormous self-control, 'You may.'

Henry got up.

'I think the next step is – I mean, before you breathe a word at your office – to see Sir Ralph together. All right by you?'

'Absolutely.'

'Saturday morning? Sorry to cut into gardening time, but it wouldn't interfere with a working week and it's the one morning I have the remotest chance of his undivided attention for three minutes at least – '

Martin rose too.

'Suits me fine.'

They went out into the foyer which was now entirely empty except for an enormously fat woman wedged in an armchair and grasping a Curry's carrier bag on what remained of her knees beyond her stomach. Outside in St John's Street they turned instinctively to one another and shook hands.

'Henry,' Martin said, 'I'm really awfully grateful.'

'Fingers crossed. If it comes off, I'll be the grateful one. See you Saturday.'

And then they separated, two pairs of well-polished brown brogues going purposefully off down the Salisbury pavements among the dawdling shoppers and the pushchairs.

Dutifully, Alice took the children down to Dummeridge for the day. Clodagh had wanted to come, but Alice had said no.

'*Please*. Why not? It's another pair of hands to help with Charlie – '

'I can't explain why not, I just know I couldn't handle it. Clodagh, it's *duty* I'm going for, not particular pleasure.'

96

'What am I going to do all Thursday?'

'Make us an amazing supper to come home to,' Alice said jokingly, but knowing Clodagh would take her seriously.

'Okay then. But I'll have my pound of flesh some other way.'

Alice said happily, 'I know you will.'

At least the children had been pleased about going. Natasha had dressed herself with immense care in fancy white socks and a pink plastic jewellery set, including earrings, which Gwen had given her and which Alice knew would cause Cecily real grief. James had submitted to Alice's desire to compensate for the pink earrings by substituting brown lace-ups for his prized trainers with silver flashes on the heels, and Charlie, promoted from his carrycot to an egg-shaped safety seat in the back of the car, dah-dah'd contentedly to himself while taking off his first shoes and socks and throwing them on the floor.

It was a long drive, but all three were remarkably good. Alice talked to them a lot over her shoulder, because she felt nervous, and because the first thing she was going to have to say was that they couldn't, after all, stay the night. She should have said that at the outset, but she hadn't, and now Cecily would have made up beds and told Dorothy to set up the cot and altogether it was an awful prospect and all her own fault. And then, driving through Wareham, she had thought, with sudden indignation, that she had no idea why she should feel guilty about *Martin's* mother. Martin never seemed to.

Once this had occurred to her, her indignation grew. *She* was the one who made all the running with Dummeridge, and it was a running she had now made for over a decade. Just because she had been so conscientious, they all of course expected her to go *on* being conscientious, so that Martin would have been amazed to be told to remember Cecily's birthday himself, or to bring the children down to see her at Dummeridge. The last mile to the house, the leafy, sun-flecked familiar mile that Alice used to drive with such a joyfully lifting heart, seemed to have lost its charm entirely. She rounded the last curve of the road, went over the little stone bridge that spanned the remains of an ancient moat and pulled up in front of the studded front door with a kind of dread.

The children squealed for release like piglets and went racing into the house shouting for Cecily. Alice followed slowly with

Charlie under one arm and his discarded shoes and socks in her free hand. Natasha and James and Cecily had collided on the stairs and were hugging and chattering, and, watching them, Alice felt small and cold. Charlie stretched out of her arm towards his grandmother, so Alice put him down on the flagged floor and let him stagger across on his soft bare feet, bleating for attention.

'Darling,' Cecily said at last, reaching Alice, 'this is a highlight. I've been looking forward to it so much you can't think. Richard's coming home tonight specially, so you really are honoured. I saw him lurking about with champagne bottles and I've got a salmon trout – '

'Where'm I sleeping?' James said.

'Jimmy James. Where d'you think? In your always bed – '

James, recalled to his own babyhood language, dissolved with pleasure.

'And I,' said Natasha, turning her pink bracelet admiringly on her wrist, 'am in the blue room. Where Mummy used to sleep. In the *golden* bed.'

It was too late. Alice made a feeble last try.

'D'you know, I've done such a dotty thing, I've forgotten all our night things – '

Cecily, jiggling Charlie in her arms, began to laugh.

'Oh darling, how funny! But it couldn't matter less. We'll just have to put Charlie in a hot-water-bottle cover for the night. Won't we.'

The children were visibly happy. Cecily had packed their lunch up in little baskets so that they could elude the tedium of a table and also so that she could have Alice to herself while Dorothy dotingly spooned mashed carrot and liver into Charlie in the kitchen. There were two places laid for lunch in the dining room, either side of a shallow copper bowl containing a brilliant cushion of yellow-green moss studded with scyllas. Cecily helped Alice to a fragrant stew of chicken and cashew nuts, poured her a slender glass of Chablis and said, in the businesslike tone she had promised herself she would use all day, 'Now then. I want to know when you are going to start painting again. No excuses now. Your house is almost straight, the children are settled, the village clearly thinks you are wonderful, so what are you waiting for?'

'Nothing,' Alice said coolly. 'I've started.'

Cecily stared.

'Darling!'

'Two days ago.'

Cecily raised her glass.

'It's wonderful! Here's to you. Tell me all about it, exactly what happened.'

Alice was in no hurry to finish her mouthful. She said deliberately, 'Clodagh locked me into the studio. It was as simple as that. She got the children to help her and they all said I couldn't come out until teatime. At five o'clock, they unlocked the door and stood there with a chocolate cake.'

Her face was faintly glowing. It had all been so extraordinary, she had been taken completely by surprise. It had begun with Gwen coming in during the morning with a painting of a straw hat on a chair by an open french window and saying, 'I hope I'm not speaking out of turn, but this was just lying about in the spare bathroom and I picked it up and thought it was ever so pretty and then I looked and saw – '

Alice was sitting on the edge of the kitchen table sewing name-tapes on James's summer school uniform.

'Yes. I did it.'

'Mrs *Jordan* – '

Clodagh came over from the sink.

'Let me see.'

She turned the painting towards her and examined it.

'Hell's teeth, Alice – '

'I can't do it any more,' Alice said. 'I don't know why, I just can't. I tried and it was hopeless.'

'It's ever so clever,' Gwen said. 'Now my cousin – '

'What d'you mean, hopeless?'

'I mean that I couldn't draw or paint and so I felt rather desperate.'

'When was that?'

'About four years ago – '

'Four years? Now that's odd, because my cousin – '

'Shut up, Gwen,' Clodagh said. She peered at Alice.

'Four years is an age ago. Why don't you try again?'

'I'm afraid to.'

'Just what my cousin – '

'Afraid?' Clodagh said. 'You afraid? This is seriously good, you know, *seriously*.'

And then she had given the painting back to Gwen and gone back to the sink, and when she spoke again it was about a Canadian novelist called Robertson Davies that she said Alice must read.

It was after lunch that it happened. Clodagh and Natasha and James had been giggling away about something and they lured Alice up to the room above the garage on the pretence of needing to find the croquet set, and simply locked her in.

'You can come out,' James had shouted, highly delighted with the whole game, 'when you've painted a picture!'

At first she thought frenziedly that she couldn't, she hadn't any water, or paint rugs, but Clodagh had thought of all that. So in a curious state of being at once both exhilarated and quite calm, she had set up her easel and painted a corner of the dusty window, on whose sill John had left a half-carved duck. A couple of fronds of ivy had pushed their way in and a spider had woven a truly copybook web between the duck's head and the window-frame. She painted very fast and quite absorbedly. When they let her out she was so pleased with herself she was almost sorry they had come. She said now, with a small swagger, 'I always said I'd be able to paint at The Grey House.'

'*Did* you?'

'Oh yes.'

Cecily watched her. She was pleased for Alice but wished very much that it had not been Clodagh who waved the magic wand.

'It all sounds a bit melodramatic to me.'

'It was. But it worked.'

Cecily pulled herself together.

'I'm more pleased than I can say. Not least because it will get all those people off my back who think I can get them an Alice Jordan just by whistling.'

Alice took a swallow of her wine.

'I don't think I want any commissions just yet – '

'Darling, why on earth not? I thought that was the point – '

'I don't want,' Alice said, spacing the words out in a soft, even voice, 'to be beholden to anybody about anything just now. I want to be free to do what I need to do.'

'I don't think I quite understand.'

100

'No.'

'Could you explain?'

'No,' Alice said. 'No. I don't think I could. I just feel it very strongly.'

'Forgive me, darling,' Cecily said sharply, getting up to put a dish of big gleaming South African grapes on the table, 'but you sound like a spoiled adolescent to me.'

'I expect,' Alice said politely, 'that that is because I am not behaving exactly as you would like me to.'

Cecily sat down and pushed the grapes towards Alice.

'I have never tried to influence you in any way.'

Alice said nothing.

'If I have ever given you any kind of guidance – reluctantly, mind you – it is because you asked me for it. When you came here, a gauche girl – ' She stopped.

'Are you going,' Alice said serenely, 'to tell me how much I owe you? It reminds me of conversations long ago with my mother.'

Cecily held her hands together tightly to prevent herself from reaching over and slapping Alice. She closed her eyes for a second and said, 'Don't let's quarrel.'

'I don't want to.'

'No.' She opened them again and gave a small smile. 'Neither of us do.'

Alice rose.

'May I use the telephone? There's something I forgot to tell Clodagh about Martin's supper.'

'What has Clodagh to do with Martin's supper?'

'She offered to get supper for him,' said Alice as if it were the most natural thing in the world, 'because I am here.'

She went away to the kitchen telephone and rang The Grey House. There was no reply. She dialled the Park and Lady Unwin answered and was excessively friendly and said she would fetch Clodagh at once.

'I've lost,' Alice said. 'I've got to stay. Out-manoeuvred.'

'*Alice*,' Clodagh said. 'You're pathetic. How old are you? And I was going to do my Upper East Side Swank Foodie's Fish Curry.'

'Could you do it for Martin?'

'Okay.'

'Clodagh. I'm really sorry.'

'Me too.'

'I'd better go. I'm so grateful.'

'What for? For feeding the family lawyer?'

'*What?*'

'Tee hee,' Clodagh said. 'Serve you right for staying away. See you tomorrow – '

'*What* about the family lawyer?'

'I couldn't *possibly*,' Clodagh said, 'tell you a state secret over the telephone,' and she put the receiver down.

Alice went out into the garden where Cecily and the children were feeding the goldfish with special grains out of a little plastic cylinder.

'I hate him,' James was saying, peering into the water, 'his face is all gobbly – '

'Just like yours, my dear,' Natasha said, tossing her head to feel her earrings swing.

'All well?' Cecily said to Alice.

'Perfectly. She's going to make him a fish curry.'

'I'll make you into a curry!' James shouted excitedly at the pool. 'That's what I'll do! I'll make you into a curry!'

Natasha put her hand in her grandmother's.

'Sometimes, I'm afraid, Charlie eats beetles.'

'Does he, darling?'

Natasha sighed.

'Oh yes. He's a great responsibility. Can we go to the sea?'

It was a long, long afternoon. Alice could not believe the strength of her wishing to be at home. She looked at familiar, beloved Dummeridge in the glory of its spring garden, as if through the wrong end of a telescope, tiny, remote and impersonal. When Richard returned, she kissed him with unusual warmth and Cecily, noticing this, said before she could stop herself, 'And what has he done to deserve all this?'

'She thinks I'm going to open some champagne for her,' Richard said. 'And she's right.'

Dinner was better because Richard was determined, it seemed, to keep things impersonal. He talked about the Middle East, made Cecily talk about her last trip to America – 'Potagers are now sweeping Georgetown like *measles*' – and when the talk inevitably

102

drifted round to the state of things at Pitcombe, he said, 'Guess who rang today.'

Cecily, fetching a wedge of perfect Brie from the sideboard, said, 'Who?' without interest.

'Anthony.'

'Anthony!'

'Coming home,' Richard said. 'Changing continents, changing jobs – '

'Why didn't he ring here? Why didn't he ring me?'

'I expect he will – '

'How odd,' Alice said. 'I haven't seen Anthony for almost ten years. Ten years in the Far East. Before the children – '

'He sent you his love,' Richard said to Alice.

'Me?'

'Dangerous stuff, Anthony's love – '

Cecily said, 'When is all this happening?'

'Soon. A few weeks.'

'I see. My eldest son chooses to come home after a decade at a fortnight's notice and does not seem to think it necessary to inform *me*.'

'He rang me with the facts,' Richard said, pouring more wine. 'I expect he will ring you for analysis and interpretation.'

Cecily drew in her breath, but she said nothing more except, after a pause, 'Darling Alice, tell Richard what's happening to Martin tonight. Too amusing – '

Richard looked at Alice. She took a leisuredly swallow of wine, returned his look and said, without any emphasis, 'He's being fed fish curry by the youngest child of Pitcombe Park.'

Richard's mouth twitched.

'Is he now.'

Alice nodded.

'I promise you.'

'Isn't that,' Richard said measuredly, 'something.'

But Alice couldn't reply because she was suddenly seized with a helpless fit of giggles.

On his way home from the office, Martin stopped at Pitcombe shop to buy seeds and brown garden twine. He was slightly irritated that Cecily had landed him with Stuart Mott who was the kind of gardener whose surface friendliness concealed a sneering contempt for any employer's opinion. If it wasn't for Stuart, Martin would not now be buying carrot and cabbage seed, both of which he considered wasteful to grow and dull to eat. He had meant to start Stuart's employment with the friendly firmness he had heard his father use to junior colleagues on the telephone, but Stuart's faintly curled lip had thrown him off key from the outset. When Cecily had telephoned him the other night with some idiotic objection to Clodagh as a friend of the family, Martin had been so aggrieved with her over her interference about Stuart that he had been quite short with her and the call had ended very coolly on both sides. Of course, being Martin, he had repented of this and had rung back to say sorry and his mother had said she quite understood, they were all clearly rather on edge just now, and no wonder. When she said that, Martin's regret quite evaporated and he wished he hadn't bothered to apologise. Standing in the shop now, spinning a rickety wire rack of seed packets, he felt indignation bubbling comfortably up in him all over again. This was aggravated further by Mr Finch coming stealthily up to him – he knew Martin was no candidate for bursts of lyric poetry – and saying, 'You've an exotic supper to look forward to tonight, Mr Jordan.'

Martin said, without looking up from the printed merits of Nantes Express carrots, 'Have I?'

Lettice Deverel, who disapproved exceedingly of Mr Finch's separate and obnoxious manner to his upper- and working-class customers, and who was half-obscured by a plywood unit of paper plates and doilies, said firmly, 'Mr Jordan's supper is no concern of yours, Mr Finch.'

Mr Finch tiptoed back to his counter and began to make an unnecessary pyramid of nougat bars.

'Miss Clodagh was in this afternoon,' he said in self-justifying tones, 'buying nutmeg and cinnamon. She told me they were to put in Mr Jordan's supper because Mrs Jordan is away taking the children to their grandmother.'

Lettice Deverel emerged and put a packet of sunflower seeds for the parrot down in front of Mr Finch.

'Two wrongs don't make a right, Mr Finch.'

'Seems to me,' Martin said in a jocular voice, coming forward with his seeds, 'that everyone round here knows all about my supper but me.'

'Village life, Mr Jordan,' Lettice Deverel said.

Martin offered Mr Finch a five pound note.

'*Is* Miss Clodagh getting supper for me, then?'

'I couldn't,' said Mr Finch in offended tones, taking the note between finger and thumb, 'possibly say.'

Lettice and Martin emerged into the street together.

'He's a dreadful fellow,' Lettice said, jerking her head backwards, 'but then, running a village shop is enough to addle the sanest wits.'

Martin laughed.

'He's not so bad. Made me rather look forward to my evening.' He bent to open his car door. 'Can I give you a lift?'

Lettice shook her head.

'Thanks, but no. My conscience is burdened by the fruit cake I ate for tea and will only be quieted by a little vigorous exercise.' She looked at Martin with sudden keenness. 'The whole village will know you and Clodagh had dinner together by tomorrow. Take no notice. Tell Clodagh from me that it's time she went off and got herself a proper job. A job where she is *stretched.*'

Martin got into the car and started it and went slowly up the hill. As he passed Lettice, she brandished her thumb stick at him, and a bit further on he passed Stuart Mott talking to Sir Ralph's tractor driver, both of whom gave him a brief, unsmiling nod. When he turned into his own drive, the kitten raced across his path in its usual ritual kamikaze greeting, and there – his insides gave a brief and pleasurable lurch – was Clodagh, taking washing off the line in the orchard beyond. She was wearing jeans and a black jacket embroidered with big, rough, silver stars.

He got out of the car and went to lean on the orchard fence. It was a soft pale early evening and some of the fat buds on the apple trees were beginning to split over the bursting pinkness within. The air, having smelled of cold or mud for months, smelled of damp earth. The hens were muttering about in the grass around Clodagh's feet. Last weekend, she had shown Martin how to measure their progress in coming into their first lay by the number of fingers you could place between the pelvic bone and the breast bone. 'Not yet,' she had said, 'it ought to be four fingers. But coming on.' He bent over the fence to make clucking noises at the hens, of which they sensibly took no notice, and then he said to Clodagh's galaxied back, 'What's going on?'

'Don't sound so thrilled,' Clodagh said, dropping the last garments into the basket at her feet. 'Alice meant to get home but your mother had killed the fatted calf so she couldn't. And you aren't deemed capable of scrambling your own eggs.'

'Wouldn't dream of it,' Martin said, opening the gate for her, 'if you're the alternative.'

'You have very bizarre fish instead.'

'Wonderful.'

He followed her into the house and the kitten joined them, mewing faintly in anticipation of supper. Clodagh stopped and scooped it up and dumped it on the laundry.

'You pig, cat. You've known there was fish in the house, all day, haven't you.'

'The whole village is talking about us. Apparently, you told Mr Finch you were getting supper for me.'

'Yippee,' Clodagh said. 'At least it'll take their minds off Pa's rent rises – '

'Rent rises?'

'I do believe he's putting up cottage rents a whole three pounds a week.' She put the basket down on the kitchen table and picked out the kitten, who began at once to purr like a generator. 'Anyway, you'll know all about that soon, won't you. As our new family lawyer?'

Martin frowned. Spontaneity was one thing, indiscretion quite another. He hadn't even been up to the Park to see Sir Ralph.

'What do you know about that – '

'Quite a bit.'

'I suppose your father talks to you?'

'Yes, he does. But this is different. This was my idea.'

'Your idea? But Henry – '

'Henry suggested your firm. I suggested you. Simple as that.'

Martin was not at all sure if he was pleased about this. Being beholden to Sir Ralph for a benevolent idea was one thing, but to feel you were simply the result of a chance and frivolous notion of Clodagh's was another.

'You're frowning,' Clodagh said.

'You make the whole thing sound so – so off the cuff – '

'It was, rather.'

Martin said stiffly, 'I don't like that.'

106

Clodagh watched him.

'If it had been a man, my father or my brother, you wouldn't mind. It's only because a woman suggested it, you feel insulted.'

'No.'

Clodagh went off to the larder and came back carrying a covered plate and an onion. Martin was still standing rather woodenly by the kitchen table. She put down the plate and the onion and came up to him.

'Just because I thought of you,' she said, 'doesn't mean it's a silly suggestion. Pa wouldn't have taken it up if it were silly, even for me. He was really thrilled. I promise you. You'll see, when you go and talk to him.'

Martin looked at her warily. His gaze was defensive.

'I don't like favours.'

'Martin – '

'I like to earn my way – '

'But you are! Why should anyone offer you this if they didn't think you'd be good at it? And good for us?'

And then Martin, in some confusion of feeling and propelled by an urgency he was suddenly quite unable to control, leaned forward and kissed her. He then put his arms round her and held her very hard against him and bent his head to kiss her again. She said, very quietly, 'No.'

He smiled at her. He thought he was in charge.

'Why no? I want to, you want – '

'Because,' Clodagh said, bending her head away, 'I love Alice. You see.'

He dropped his arms at once and turned away. He could feel his face grow fiery with shame and humiliation. He had broken his own rules.

He mumbled, 'So do I.'

'I know you do.'

'Sorry,' he said. 'Sorry. I don't know what came – '

'Shh,' she said. She came over and took his hand. 'Forget it.'

He thrust his chin out and removed his hand from hers.

'I think I will scramble my own eggs.'

Clodagh sighed.

'As you wish.'

She picked up the plate and the onion and took them back to the larder and returned with a wicker basket of eggs.

'I'll just feed Balloon.'

'It's all right,' Martin said, desperate both for her to go and for a drink.

'Martin,' Clodagh said, and her voice was kind, 'no big deal. It simply didn't happen,' and then she went out through the stable door and after a while he heard her car start up and drive away and then Balloon came and pleaded penetratingly for food.

Later, when he had poured himself a drink and fed the kitten, he went into his study and sat in the spring dusk and was very miserable. He was bitterly ashamed of himself, both for abusing Alice's absence and for choosing someone who, by her own admission, was capable of better loyalty to Alice than her own husband was. He tried to comfort himself by remembering how unresponsive Alice had been recently – it was literally weeks since they had made love – but it was thin comfort and he had no faith in it. He wondered if he was going to be able to face Sir Ralph on Saturday because he felt his folly might be written on his brow for all to see. Not only had he behaved badly, but he had been rebuffed and rebuked. Martin was not a flirtatious man because he didn't have the confidence to be one. He knew he feared rejection and that that fear made him unadventurous, and because he disliked very much being both unconfident and unenterprising and saw no way to remedy either, he sat in the deepening gloom and let his shame stagnate into bitterness. He had far too much whisky while this happened, and then grew maudlin, and wandered about the empty house and forgot his eggs altogether. He went over and over the little incident, foolishly and pointlessly, and finally went to bed in a very bad way indeed, forgetting to lock up downstairs so that Balloon, finding the larder door unsecured, levered his way in and achieved his ambition of three-quarters of a pound of monkfish.

CHAPTER EIGHT

Morning sunshine, coming in through the tall east windows of Pitcombe Park, fell upon the breakfast table, upon a jar of marmalade made by Mrs Shadwell the previous January, upon folded copies of *The Times* and the *Daily Mail* and upon a large biscuit tin bearing a Dymo-stamped label reading 'Her Ladyship's Ryvita'. Her Ladyship was not eating Ryvita. She was drinking a cup of coffee very slowly and trying very hard to concentrate on doing that, rather than on quarrelling with her husband.

The subject was Clodagh. The subject between them in the last six weeks had almost exclusively been Clodagh. At first they had been united in loving anxiety and relief at having her home, and then in approving pleasure over her friendship with The Grey House, but then Sir Ralph had begun to devise schemes to make it possible for Clodagh to remain at home, financial schemes, and what had been a mere crevice of difference between them had widened into a rift.

Margot Unwin loved her youngest daughter with quite as much energy as her husband did, but with more levelness of head. Clodagh's adolescence, a roller-coaster ride of scrapes and truancies and broken-hearted friends who always seemed more loving than loved, had made her mother aware that she needed, in riding parlance, a short rein. Clodagh's elder brother and sister had both been quite safe on longer reigns, being more orthodox, less volatile and much duller, and Sir Ralph had always persisted in believing that Clodagh, left to herself, would emerge as tractable and conventional as young Ralph and Georgia had done. Attempt to coerce Clodagh into anything, he had always maintained, and it's like throwing a lighted match into a barrel of gunpowder; give her all the space she needs and she will come, in her own time, as good as anyone could wish.

'Don't,' Margot Unwin said, 'say gunpowder to me again.'

109

'Sorry,' Sir Ralph said, faintly huffy. He had grown fond of the image, over the years. 'I am only trying to illustrate what I believe.'

'I know what you believe.'

Sir Ralph began to butter toast vigorously.

'And I'm right. Her coming home from America proves I'm right. She couldn't, she found, be as bohemian as she thought she could, so she came home, very sensibly.'

'I don't think,' Margot said, putting down her coffee cup, 'you could call being half-engaged to an immensely successful American lawyer very bohemian. I suppose you mean it was bohemian of them to live together. And it wasn't sense that brought Clodagh home, it was the need of refuge – '

There was a knock and the door opened. Shadwell and two liver and white springer spaniels looked in.

'Mr Dunne's here, sir. And Mr Jordan. I've put them in the library. Mr Dunne said not to hurry as he knows he's early.'

'Thank you, Shadwell.'

The door closed. Sir Ralph rose and shook out his huge napkin like a sail cracking in the wind.

'We'll talk about this later, Margot.'

She did not move, but she said in her most commanding-committee voice, 'You must know, Ralph, that I absolutely disapprove of what you are about to suggest to Henry. It is quite wrong. It is unfair to young Ralph and to Georgina and it will be disastrous for Clodagh. I may not be physically present at the meeting, but my astral self will be.' She paused, and then added, 'Very forcibly.'

And then she picked up the *Daily Mail*, shook it flat and, with the skill of long practice, opened it at Nigel Dempster.

'Who are all those?'

Henry Dunne squinted up at the marble busts along the top of the library bookshelves.

'Roman emperors, I think.'

'Heavens,' Martin said. '*Real?*'

'Oh yes, Grand Tour stuff. This room was done about seventeen-eighty.'

'It's amazing – '

110

'It's lovely,' Henry said, with the carelessness of one quite familiar with amazingness, 'isn't it?'

It was a long room, with three floor-length windows at one end, lined entirely with books. Over the books at one end was pinned a huge map of the estate. By the windows a vast partner's desk was heaped with papers, and parallel to the fireplace an amiable elderly red leather sofa faced a handsome portrait of the Unwin who had made the room and furnished its corners with a marble goddess, a Roman senator and a bronze, after Flaxman, of St Michael slaying Satan. The rest of the room was comfortingly filled with map cases and loaded tables and dog baskets. Here and there enormous hippeastrums reared out of Oriental urns, and turned their majestic striped trumpets to the light. The air of the room smelt of man and dog and polished leather and history. Martin sniffed. This, he thought in the phrase he had once used to himself about Alice, this is *something*.

Sir Ralph and two spaniels came in on a benevolent tide of greeting. He was carrying a file of papers and was followed by Shadwell with a tray of coffee. They sat down round the fire after shaking hands, and the third baronet looked down on them from his place on the overmantel panelling as he had looked down for two hundred years already. Sir Ralph waved an introductory hand towards him.

'Sir John. His elder brother, Ralph, died when only a child. He's the only John Unwin in an unbroken line of Ralphs, back to James I. So you see,' handing Martin a cup, 'you'll be taking on, if you agree, over three hundred of us.'

'Henry did say – '

'Did he? Good. Excellent. I wanted to see you at once but Henry is frightfully cautious. Aren't you, Henry? Insisted on seeing you first. What do you say?'

Martin was afraid that his eagerness was written on his face.

'Well, of course, Sir Ralph, if the idea meets with the approval of my senior partners, I'd be more than happy – '

'I'll make sure they're happy. My dear fellow, of course they'll jump at it. Can't tell you what a difference it will make, having you a stone's throw away.'

Henry, recollecting how he and Juliet were constantly at the mercy of midnight telephone calls about estate business, busied

111

himself with his coffee cup. Martin could discover the job's little hazards for himself.

'The first thing I want to discuss, you see – and this is urgent – is my provision for Clodagh. I know,' Sir Ralph said, waving a dismissive hand at Martin's rising objection of professional inability even to hear the legal problem of someone who was not yet his client, 'you can't tell me anything yet. But I want to tell you. Because it's the first thing I'll want you to deal with.'

He got up and went off for the coffee pot. Behind his back, Henry signalled Martin to smiling acquiescence about anything Sir Ralph might say, however bizarre. He came back and refilled their cups with alarming swoops of his tweed-clad arm.

'Of course, this house and estate go to young Ralph. Goes without saying and I'm only thankful he wants it and doesn't feel he ought to be running a soup kitchen in Stepney or some pop group thing. As to the girls, I've got a couple of farms in trust for them, Georgina's in Wales, Clodagh's not far from here, near Wimborne. They aren't supposed to have them until my death but I want Clodagh to have hers now. I think she needs the income. What do you think? Am I going to have a problem unscrambling the trust? To be honest, Martin, I don't like problems.'

Martin swallowed.

'It's a bit difficult, not knowing anything about – '

'But you must,' Sir Ralph said with energetic friendliness, 'know about trusts. You are a *lawyer*.'

'There are a lot of complications,' Henry said, coming to the rescue. 'And until Martin has seen all the documents – '

'It's an express trust,' Sir Ralph said to Martin.

Martin shifted and put down his coffee cup.

'Usually, if all the beneficiaries of a trust are of age and in agreement, they can put an end to a trust – '

'Excellent!'

'But of course, that may not apply in this case because of other factors I don't know about.'

'What I want, you see,' Sir Ralph said, turning the full charm of his smile upon Martin, 'is to be able to provide Clodagh with enough to live on, without her feeling under pressure to take the wrong kind of job. You have seen enough of Clodagh to agree with me that that must not happen.'

112

Henry, seeing on Martin's face the as yet unspoken question of what was the right kind of job for Clodagh, cleared his throat loudly and frowned.

'Yes,' Martin said lamely, to Sir Ralph.

Sir Ralph went over to the windows.

'Come here and have a look.'

Martin followed.

'See all the new planting? Every tree indigenous. I hate to tell you how many elms we lost and now Henry tells me there's honey rot in the beech hanger. Well, what d'you say?'

He turned and faced Martin.

'My trees, my tenants, my daughter. You and Henry between you, hm? Keep us all in order. Ring Henry later in the week when you have told your partners, and he'll put you in the picture.' He held out his hand and shook Martin's warmly. 'I'm so pleased, so very pleased. Give my love to your pretty wife.'

On the days when Clodagh did the school run, for Alice, Alice painted. She began to paint much bigger, more abstract things, and to think, much more than she ever had before, about colour and light, as well as shapes. When she wasn't painting, or doing things for the children or the house, Clodagh took her round the village, to introduce her to all the cottagers. Clodagh knew everyone. As a child she had made a point of it, partly out of social curiosity and partly out of an appetite for oddness. The village had grown perfectly used to her, so used that she got slapped and shouted at along with their own children. In the village she learned obscene words for parts of the body which she took back to the Park to alarm Georgina with, and scrumped for apples (this was pure affectation for the Park glasshouses yielded white peaches and Black Hamburg grapes) and joined the Bonfire Night gangs that put jumping jacks in village dustbins. Watching the dustbins dance, clattering their lids, had been, she told Alice, one of the purest joys of her life.

In return, the village preferred her to any other Unwin, even though, inconsistently, they would have been shocked to see Sir Ralph or Lady Unwin being as impudently approachable as Clodagh. She had entrée everywhere. Alice, a little self-conscious and anxious not to intrude or patronise, went in her wake in and

113

out of a series of sitting rooms, where the television blethered on unwatched in corners and where old beams and fireplaces had been boxed in with plywood to modernise their old-fashioned short-comings. She drank a good deal of dark tea, listened to endless monologues about health, and helped to wash up in kitchens where potato chips and motorbike parts bubbled companionably away side by side in their pans of oil. In the newer cottages picture windows let in blank blocks of light and fireplace surrounds rose in pyramidal steps dotted with brass animals and ornamental china thimbles. There weren't enough children, Alice noticed, not enough prams in back gardens and tricycles blocking hallways.

'Can't afford it,' Sally Mott told her. 'No one can afford to live here except in a tied cottage. Our Trevor's had to go to Salisbury when he married, same as our Diana did. Pitcombe's going to fill up with outsiders now, once the old ones have gone. Dad's cottage now – '

'I expect we'll sell it to weekenders,' Clodagh said, 'from London. Don't you think?'

'You can laugh – '

'I'm not laughing, Sally. I'm teasing. Lots of employment for all of you, looking after weekenders, so why should you complain?'

Sally Mott had learned a great deal about complaining from Rosie Barton. Rosie's life ran the way Rosie wanted it to and she had been anxious to put some of the village women on their guard about being exploited. Sally was ripe for such views, ripe for grievance. She gave up her job cleaning at the Park soon after Rosie Barton came to the village, and she wasn't going to start again, scrubbing for weekenders, not for anyone, thank *you*.

Lettice Deverel, too, had her views on weekenders. Clodagh took Alice to meet her as well as to drink Nescafé and eat shortbread in the comfortable rectory kitchen. Lettice Deverel said that mud always got the better of phoney weekenders in the end and Peter Morris said they were good for the collection but not really much good for the congregation. When Clodagh and Alice had gone, Peter went up to see Lettice and ask her if she thought Alice wasn't looking very much happier and very much better. Lettice agreed, but she did not sound particularly pleased.

'Sometimes, you give a very good imitation of being a crabbed old spinster – '

'Clodagh Unwin,' Lettice said, 'needs a good *hard* job. She's simply avoiding the issue, queening it over that poor girl.'

'Poor Polly,' said the parrot suddenly. 'Pretty Polly. *Poor* Polly is a sad slut.'

'Why poor?'

Lettice Deverel turned on her kitchen tap and ran water vigorously into a stout black kettle.

'Because two reasons. One, Clodagh is indulging herself. Two, because Alice Jordan is ripe for the picking.'

Peter Morris began to laugh. After a while, having pondered the joke to itself, the parrot joined him.

'So you disapprove of an excellent friendship?'

'I disapprove of people being made fools of.'

'Fool!' the parrot cried with energy. 'Fool! Good morning. Who is a pretty bagpiper, may I ask?'

'Oh dear,' Clodagh said, pushing Charlie up the village street beside Alice, 'Lettice is disapproving of me again. She does it about every three years and she will never tell me why.'

'Perhaps,' Alice said, 'she pays you the compliment of thinking you ought to know why.'

'This time I do know. And what's more, she's ahead of me – '

'What do you *mean*?'

A car drew up beside them and a woman's voice said clearly, 'Mrs Jordan?'

They stopped. The face looking out of the driver's window was brightly made up under careful hair, and surmounted a blue blouse tied at the neck with a bow. Clodagh, behind Alice, hissed faintly.

'Cathy Fanshawe, Mrs Jordan. I've been meaning to come for weeks, but what with one thing and another, I've been so rushed I haven't known whether I'm coming or going. It's the Conservatives – '

Alice stooped to the car window.

'Conservatives?'

'My husband is the local chairman. We're so thrilled you've moved in. Geoffrey said – '

Clodagh gave Alice a sharp dig from behind.

'Mrs Fanshawe, I'm afraid that I'm not really a Conservative – '

'Surely,' Mrs Fanshawe said, thinking of The Grey House and

115

Martin's appearance and the school run to Salisbury in unmistakable uniform, 'you can't think the Liberals are any kind of alternative just now?'

'No,' Alice said, 'I don't. I – '

Clodagh came to stoop beside her.

'She's a babe in arms about politics, I'm afraid. And about most things. Too sad.'

Mrs Fanshawe looked nervous. A well cared-for hand crept up to adjust the bow on her blouse.

'Perhaps your husband – '

'He,' said Clodagh firmly, 'is worse. Much worse. Practically a Communist.'

Alice began to shake.

'So sorry – '

'Perhaps I might just call one evening? With the forms.' She looked directly at Alice. 'We could have a proper chat about it.'

Helplessly, Alice subsided in silent laughter on the pavement. Charlie watched her gravely from his pushchair.

'You see?' Clodagh said to Mrs Fanshawe. 'So sad. Not fit to make an adult decision really. I don't think the Conservatives *could* want her. Do you?'

Pink with indignation, Mrs Fanshawe put her car into gear.

'It's really,' Clodagh said gloomily, 'a hopeless case.'

Alice gave a little yelp. Mrs Fanshawe wound her window up with great speed and let the clutch out too suddenly in her agitation so that the car leaped forward like a kangaroo. Across the street, old Fred Mott watched them from behind his cactus collection; the jerking car, Alice still sitting giggling and helpless on the ground, Clodagh standing above her in an attitude of the profoundest regret. He began to giggle faintly himself.

'What's up with you,' his granddaughter-in-law Sally said, bringing in a bowl of pot noodles from the kitchen.

'Them girls,' Fred said, wheezing. 'Them girls there. Them bad girls.'

Sally looked.

'You don't want to take no notice of them. That's just Miss Clodagh, bullyragging again. That's all.'

Clodagh put her hand under Alice's arm.

116

'Get up, do. *Honestly*. What will people think? First you upset nice Mrs Fanshawe who utterly worships my mother and then you sit on the ground and giggle like a glue-sniffing schoolkid. Charlie's quite shocked.'

'Bah,' Charlie said.

Alice struggled up, wiping her eyes.

'Clodagh, you are absolutely *shameless* – '

'On the contrary. I'm trying to get you off the street and into the privacy of your own home before the whole village thinks you are on the bottle.' She waved across at Fred Mott, chumbling through his pot noodles, and he grinned back and shook his spoon. 'If Sally Mott has seen us, we might as well be tomorrow's headline in the *Sun*.' She began to push Charlie briskly uphill, talking as she went. Weak with spent laughter, Alice followed.

'Stupid,' Sally Mott said, resolving to tell Gwen. 'Too old to behave like kids.'

'I like a bit of fun,' Fred said, letting the noodles dribble down his chin. He glared at Sally. 'I like a gay girl, I do.'

After lunch, Clodagh took Charlie upstairs and put him in his cot and pulled the cord of his musical box so that it began to play 'Edelweiss', over and over, luring him into sleep. Charlie liked his cot. He put his first finger into his mouth, turned on his side and gave himself over to the tinny little tune. Clodagh dropped a kiss on his warm round head, drew the curtains and went down to the kitchen where Alice was putting plates into the dishwasher before she went up to the studio to paint until Natasha and James came home. The room was full of contented post-lunch quiet. Alice shut the dishwasher door and straightened up.

'Don't go,' Clodagh said.

She was standing just inside the doorway to the hall, still holding the doorknob in her hand.

'What, not paint? But I thought – '

'I want,' Clodagh said, 'to talk to you.'

Alice found she was holding her breath. She stayed where she was, by the dishwasher, silhouetted against the window. Clodagh went round the table to the two wooden armchairs by the Aga, lifted Balloon off one, and sat down with him on her knee.

'Come here,' Clodagh said. 'Come here where I can see you.'

Alice came, very slowly. She sat opposite Clodagh, upright and on the alert as if bracing herself for a row.

'What – '

'Wait,' Clodagh said, stroking Balloon.

'What do you mean, wait – '

'Wait until you aren't exuding anxiety and apprehension like a blue flame.' She looked at Alice. 'What are you afraid of?'

'I'm not afraid.'

'Sure?'

'Only – excited afraid – '

'That's all right then.'

There was a pause. It was a silent pause except for Balloon's purring and, far away, a distant aeroplane. It's two o'clock, Alice thought, two o'clock on a Wednesday afternoon . . .

'It's time,' Clodagh said. 'Isn't it.'

'Time? Time for what – '

Clodagh sighed gently.

'Time for me to tell you that I love you. Time for us to begin.'

Alice said nothing. She sat absolutely still and stared at Clodagh. Clodagh picked Balloon off her knee, kissed his nose and put him on the floor. Then she looked back at Alice.

'You know what a spoiled brat I am,' Clodagh said. 'You know how I always want what I want right *now*. Well, by my standards, I've waited for you because I knew it was going to be worth it. I've waited since I saw your reflection in the mirror when you came into the drawing room at home and I felt my stomach turn over. Love at first sight. *Love*, Alice.'

She stood up and crossed the few feet between them and knelt in front of Alice.

'What about you?'

In a slightly strangled voice, Alice said, 'Me?'

'Yes. You. What do you feel about me?'

Alice leaned forward and put her hands either side of Clodagh's face.

'I feel,' Alice said, 'that I hate it when you go out of the room.'

'More,' Clodagh said.

'Everything I do with you is more fun, better, than anything I do with anyone else or by myself. I like myself better. I feel more – more *able*. I'm so happy,' Alice said, putting her arms round

118

Clodagh's neck and burying her face in her hair. 'I'm so happy I feel quite mad.'

Clodagh undid Alice's arms so that she could push her away a little.

'Kiss me.'

Alice bent again.

'No,' Clodagh said, 'on second thoughts, I'll kiss you. I think you need a bit of handling.'

After a considerable time, watched detachedly by the kitten, Clodagh drew away and said, 'Wrong again. You don't need any handling. You just need lots more of the same.'

She stood up.

'Come on.'

'What do you mean?'

'I mean bed.'

Alice gave a tiny gasp.

'Bed!'

Clodagh knelt and undid Alice's shirt and put her hands inside and then, after a few seconds, her mouth. Alice sat with her eyes closed. Relief flooded slowly, heavily through her, relief and release and a sensation of glorious blossoming, like a Japanese paper flower dropped into water and swelling out to become a huge, rich, beautiful bloom. Clodagh turned her face sideways so that her cheek rested on Alice's skin.

'Look at you,' she said, and her voice was as thick as honey, 'look at you. You're like all bloody women. You thought, didn't you, that when two women fall in love, one at least has to have the same sex experience as a man. And that there has to be a woman one, one that behaves as a woman does, with a man. Are you beginning to see? Are you beginning to see that it's so great for us because we know what the other wants because we want it ourselves?' She took her face away and looked up. Alice was in a kind of trance. Clodagh stood up and then bent to take Alice's hands.

'Alice,' she said, 'Alice. Come with me.'

CHAPTER NINE

In June, Anthony Jordan completed the sale of his luxurious, impersonal flat on Tregunter Path, Hong Kong, cleared his office desk, told the girl who had optimistically hoped for four years that he might marry her that he never would, and took a taxi out to Kai Tak airport with ten years' worth of Far Eastern living packed economically into only three suitcases. He told friends that he was exhausted by the climate and the claustrophobia of Hong Kong and that he wanted to try his hand at something other than corporate finance. He did not say that he would otherwise become lumbered with a largely unwanted wife but everyone knew that that was the case, and took sides in the affair, sides that were very largely weighted against Anthony. Enough people had endured his combination of exploitation and exhibitionism to feel nothing but gratitude towards Cathay Pacific for carrying him firmly homewards. When he had gone, Diana McPherson, who had loved him very much despite her better self, found herself asked out a good deal so that people could tell her that it was better to be an old maid for ever than to be married for five minutes to someone like Anthony Jordan.

His father met him at Heathrow. They had met on Richard's travels about once a year, and Anthony had come on infrequent leave, infrequent because he preferred to go to California than to come home. Anthony thought his father was looking well and fit and distinguished and Richard thought Anthony, despite his expensive clothes, was looking slightly dissolute. They took a taxi into Central London to Richard's tiny flat in Bryanston Street, and then went to the Savoy Grill for dinner. Anthony talked a great deal about why he had left Hong Kong and even more about the extraordinary number of alternatives he now had for a job in the City. He said he thought he would like to work for one of the big accepting houses. Richard listened, noticed that Anthony drank too much and ate not enough and then said, gently, that the City was of course a changed place. Anthony said rudely that his father didn't know a thing about the City and Richard sighed because, even if the City had changed, Anthony plainly hadn't.

Only when they were on the way back to Bryanston Street did Anthony ask about his family.

'You must go and see for yourself.'

'Old Martin,' Anthony said, staring out of the taxi window at the seedy muddle of Piccadilly Circus, 'old Martin seems to have done all right.'

'Certainly.'

'More up your and Mother's street, really, what Martin has done – '

'I can only speak for myself and I wouldn't agree with you. As long as you both do what suits you best in life, insofar as that is ever possible, then that's what I want for you, and I should think what your mother wants, too.'

'Very diplomatic.'

Richard said nothing.

'Nice house,' Anthony said and his voice was faintly sneering. 'Lovely wife. Three children. Solid job. Getting on nicely. Pillar of the community. *Good* old Martin.'

'Yes,' Richard said, 'all true.'

'And what you wish I'd done – '

'Not at all,' Richard said in the level, patient voice he used a great deal of the time now, to Cecily, 'unless you wish it yourself.'

Anthony gave a little yelp.

'Bloody *hell* – '

The taxi crossed Oxford Circus and turned left.

'Go and see them,' Richard said again. 'You will really like the children.'

Anthony turned in his seat.

'How would you know? Mother said you hardly ever see them.'

How many middle-class fathers, Richard wondered in a burst of fury, longed passionately sometimes to hit their sons, and envied working-class ones who sensibly just *did*, and thus avoided sleepless nights of emotional torment and pointless days of fruitless negotiations. He took a deep breath.

'I am lucky,' he said, 'in that I have in my life a few people who

121

recognise that I am a human being. I am unlucky in that my family are on the whole not in that number.'

Anthony burst into an exaggerated, cackling laugh.

'Oh it's good to be back! Oh it is! Some things don't change and paternal pomposity is one – '

The taxi stopped. Richard turned to look at Anthony.

'Are you thirty-six?'

'Yes – '

'Thirty-six.' Richard opened the taxi door and climbed out. Anthony heard him sigh and then say to the cab driver, 'Give me forty pence change, would you?'

On the pavement together, when the cab had driven off, Anthony said, 'Why did you ask?'

'I am not,' Richard said, 'going to give you the satisfaction of an honest answer. Nor of a row your first night home. Come on. Bed.'

In the lift, Anthony said, 'I could do with a nightcap – '

'Help yourself.'

'Join me?'

'No thank you. I have to be up at six.'

Grinning, Anthony began to hum, his eyes on his father, and Richard tried to smile back as if they were sharing a joke rather than a mutual animosity.

After a few days in London, Anthony went down to Dummeridge. It was a rare and perfect June afternoon, with a clear and brilliant light, and Anthony congratulated himself on leaving the breathless mists of Hong Kong for weather which behaved as weather was meant to. He had a lot of presents for Cecily, a length of silk, a magnum of pink champagne, an imitation Gucci handbag and a miniature nineteenth-century Korean medicine chest. They had talked every day on the telephone since he had come home, long frivolous conversations that had done much to soothe the soreness in Anthony's heart, a soreness exacerbated by three days in his father's aloof company. *Why* Richard couldn't unbend was beyond Anthony. He was only an engineer after all, however successful. What gave him the right to *judge* all the time, as he undoubtedly did, and then make it very plain indeed if and when he found things wanting. The last three evenings in London, they had, by mutual agreement, gone their separate ways, and Anthony had no idea

122

where his father had been. The flat was as tidy as a ship's cabin. Anthony had a good look round it, a good look, in all the cupboards and drawers, and was surprised to find a photograph of Natasha and James and Charlie on Richard's chest of drawers, and one of himself – quite a recent one, taken on a trip to Manila – and a paperback of Sylvia Plath's poetry beside his bed. Otherwise it was a man's functional flat: clothes, coffee, whisky and aspirin. Anthony could see why his mother never came near it. She called it Father's *other* filing cabinet. She was right.

The lane to Dummeridge was lined with May blossom, thickly pink and white. The grass, Anthony noticed, was not only bright green, but shiny, with the deep gloss of health. He drove the last half-mile slowly, looking at the wooded hills on either side, sniffing for a whiff of the sea and feeling an excited curiosity to discover how he would seem to things at home after all these years and, to a lesser extent, how they would seem to him. The hall door was open as he pullled up, and almost at once Dorothy came hurrying out in a flurry of fond pleasure at seeing him again, and told him that Cecily was out in the garden with Mrs Dunne and the children.

He gave Dorothy a kiss and held her away from him so that he could look at her.

'Totally unchanged.'

She gave a little squeal.

'Rubbish,' she said. 'Nonsense. Cheeky as ever. Go on through, quick. Your mother's panting for a sight of you – '

He went through the hall and caught the familiar scent of polish and flowers and age. The garden door was open and through it he could see a strip of bright green lawn on which a small boy was standing, bent double, and watching Anthony through his legs. Anthony did not much like children. They were, he found, too honest on the whole.

'He's here!' the little boy shrieked, his voice strangled by being upside down. 'He's coming! He's coming!'

He stepped out into the sunlight. Cecily came almost running across the grass and flung herself into his arms. He thought she might be crying. She held him in a tremendous embrace, her face pressed fiercely to his.

'Darling. Darling Ant. Oh, how lovely. You can't think, you simply can't – '

A small, plump young woman with red curls held back by a band was watching them from a group of chairs under the willow tree. The little boy who had called out ran over to her and said with piercing distinctness, 'But you said he was a *boy*. You said he was Mrs Jordan's *boy*. And look, he's only a *man*.'

'Just what I feel,' Juliet Dunne said, laughing and getting up, 'every time Daddy comes home.' She came over to Anthony and Cecily, holding out her hand. 'I'm Juliet. And you are awful Anthony who wouldn't come home and now you have. I've been sort of adopted here, for the summer. Such luck!'

Cecily put out one arm to encircle Juliet so that they were all three linked.

'Anthony, you must take no notice of her. She has a wicked tongue but I put up with her because she makes me laugh.' There was a tiny pause. 'She is a great friend of Alice's.'

'Alice?'

Juliet sighed. She was extremely pretty, like a kitten, with little features grouped close together in a creamy freckled face.

'*So* boring. Allie's got a new friend and won't play with any of her old ones just now.'

Cecily drew them away across the lawn to the willow.

'I'm not awful really,' Anthony said, 'I'm just lonely and misunderstood.'

'I expect,' Juliet said, looking straight at Cecily, 'you had a simply horrible childhood.'

Cecily nodded, laughing.

'Horrible.'

'It *was*,' Anthony insisted. 'Martin was the goodie who could do no wrong. I was the baddie.'

The small boy was trotting beside him. He looked up at disappointing Anthony.

'Mummy likes the baddies on television best.'

'Mummy sounds very promising.'

They sat down in the cane chairs in the speckled, drifting shade.

'Let me look at you,' Cecily said to Anthony.

'I shouldn't. Father didn't like what he saw.'

Juliet said, 'You have bags under your eyes.'

Anthony turned to his mother.

'Is she always like this?'

'I'm afraid so.'

'I feel I've stumbled into a dormitory party – '

'Not quite,' Juliet said. 'It's more like a coven. We're plotting.'

'What?'

'How to get Alice back.'

Cecily said warningly, 'Juliet – '

'Oops. Did I say something I shouldn't have?'

'You might be making too much of too little.'

Anthony scented intrigue.

'What's going on? What is Alice up to?'

'She has thrown herself into village life,' Cecily said. 'That's all. So she hasn't much time for any of us, and we miss her.'

'She used to ring *all* the time,' Juliet said. 'She was the one person I could have a really good complain about Henry to. Your mother's no good at all because she thinks Henry is a dear. I suppose he is really, in rather the same category as a dear old armchair. Or pair of bedsocks.' She began to squeal with laughter. 'You know what's *really* the matter. Allie thinks I'm so funny and I've got no audience just now. Cecily thinks I'm *quite* funny but not nearly as much as she ought to. Oh dear. I suppose I ought to be going.' She looked about her. 'Do you think my luck has turned and I've actually lost two children out of three for good and all?'

Her son, who was clearly used to this kind of thing, said his brothers were in the stableyard.

'Do go and get them, there's a little treasure. Isn't it sad,' turning to Cecily, 'how exactly like his father he looks?'

'She worships Henry,' Cecily said to Anthony.

'I want to know more about Alice.'

'Why do you?'

'I used to fancy Alice – '

Cecily gave a little sigh.

'I know. I used to worry that you were going to make trouble. To spite Martin.'

'I did try – '

'What happened?'

'She froze me out.'

'Oh dear. How tiresome virtue is. There it stands, blocking every

125

path to pleasure. Here come my beastly little children.' She stood up. 'I shouldn't be cross about Allie. She looks as beautiful as the day, so clearly good works suit her.'

Cecily went out to the car and saw Juliet and her boys drive away. When she came back, Anthony was lying in the long cane chair where Alice had lain her first afternoon at Dummeridge, with his eyes shut. He didn't open them when he heard his mother return, he simply said, 'What a rattle.'

'She's sweet.'

'Really. Tell me more about Alice.'

'Why are you so obsessive?'

'I'm not. I'm keenly interested in my brother's family in a most suitable way.'

'You always have a *motive*.'

'Not this time.' He opened his eyes and turned his head towards his mother. 'Tell.'

'There's nothing *to* tell,' Cecily said. 'It is exactly as I said to you just now. She had a bad post-natal breakdown after the last baby, and then a big house move, and now she has taken on a whole load of village responsibilities. She's extremely tired, so that she can't see reason and take a holiday.'

'And her new friend?'

'The youngest daughter of the big house in their village.'

'Isn't that utterly suitable?'

Cecily said flatly, 'Utterly.' She took a breath. 'I want to know about you.'

Anthony shut his eyes again.

'Unemployed.'

'Temporarily?'

'Oh yes. No problem. Quite rich.'

'Also temporarily?'

'Probably. Is Martin rich?'

'No.'

'Comfortable?'

'Yes,' Cecily said doubtfully.

'Rich then. Isn't he too perfect.'

Cecily let a little silence fall, then she said, 'I did rather hope you would bring a wife home with you.'

Anthony yawned.

'I was besieged. Literally. But I didn't seem able to fall in love back. I think I'm still carrying a torch for Alice.'

'You haven't seen Alice for almost ten years. Very useful, supposing yourself to want someone you can't have, so that you need never commit yourself to anyone else.'

'I *did* want her.'

'Only in the same way that you wanted Martin's Meccano and Martin's friend Guy and Martin's diligence over examinations.'

'That's not very flattering to Alice.'

'It's meant,' Cecily said, 'to be not very flattering to you.'

'Oh, me. I've a hide like a rhino.'

'I know.'

'First Father's unpleasant to me and now you are. I shall go to Pitcombe.'

'No,' Cecily said suddenly.

Anthony sat up slowly and put his feet on the grass.

'Why not?'

'Because you are a troublemaker.'

'I don't want to make trouble. I just want someone to be nice to me. Alice will be nice.'

'Alice,' Cecily said, 'has enough to cope with, without you,' and then she gave the game away completely by beginning, with great dignity, to weep.

Anthony could not remember seeing his mother cry before. Indeed, her self-possession had been one of the chief things that had enraged him, as a teenager – *nothing*, it seemed, that you could do or say shook her composure. But she was shaken now. He knew she adored Alice. The main reasons for his own desire for Alice long ago were that his mother adored her, his father liked her a great deal and Martin wanted her. And then of course there were the additional, tantalising reasons of Alice's personality and her fascinating dislike of him. Perhaps Cecily and Alice had quarrelled. Perhaps Cecily was an interfering grandmother. Perhaps Alice's youthful infatuation with Cecily had died and there had grown up instead, as there so often did in such cases, a robust dislike of the former idol. Anthony, turning these interesting speculations over in his mind, was rather inclined to the last view. He thought he would spend a few more days at Dummeridge, or as long as it took for the

127

festal return of the Prodigal Son atmosphere to wear off, and he would make a few calls to contacts in the City – he left a Morgan Grenfell telephone number lying about prominently – and then he would invite himself to Pitcombe. So he made himself very charming to Dorothy, and to the two young men in the garden whom his mother was training, and at meals he tried to elicit more information from Cecily about Pitcombe, information which, he was interested to notice, she seemed peculiarly reluctant to give.

'Anthony!' Alice said into the telephone. She was leaning against the kitchen wall, with Charlie, eating a biscuit, on her hip.

'I want you to ask me to stay.'

'Of *course*. Where are you?'

'Dummeridge.'

'Oh – '

'Exactly. What have you done to my mother?'

'Absolutely nothing.'

'Sure?'

Alice smiled at Clodagh across the kitchen.

'Just a *teeny* bit of independence – '

Anthony laughed.

'I see. Look. When can I come? Nobody is being very kind to me, which is tough when I'm so vastly improved.'

Alice said dreamily, her eyes on Clodagh, 'I'll be kind. I'm kind to everyone just now.'

'Why?'

'Because I'm happy.'

'What, doing the church flowers?'

'Yes.'

'Extraordinary. You do, however, *sound* happy.'

Clodagh bent over James, who was painting a tiny, neurotic picture of a very neat house in one corner of a large piece of paper. He leaned against her and Alice heard him say, '*You* do it.' 'No, Jamie, you.' 'Clo-clo do it,' he said in a loving baby voice, gazing at her.

'Are you listening?' Anthony demanded down the telephone.

'Sort of.'

'If I come on Friday pour le weekend, how would that be? If you're very kind to me, I might have to stay.'

'Do,' Alice said, rubbing her cheek on Charlie's head, 'whatever you like.'

'Is your house lovely?'

'Oh yes,' Alice said. 'It's perfect here. It really is. You'll see.'

She put the telephone down.

'Martin's brother.'

Natasha, who was importantly doing her homework – this term's novelty – looked up from an extremely neat English exercise book to say kindly to her brother, 'Uncle Anthony. Who you have never seen.'

'Nor have you!'

'I *nearly* did. I was more nearly born in time. More nearly than you.'

'Was she?' James whispered up into Clodagh's hair.

' 'Fraid so – '

'Won't I *ever* be the bigger?'

Clodagh kissed him.

'In size, you will be.'

Alice came to the table and sat down with Charlie. She wanted to tell Clodagh about Anthony but Natasha's beady presence made that impossible just now. So she smiled at Clodagh, and Clodagh came round the table and kissed her, and then Charlie, and then Natasha said, 'What about a kiss for good little me doing my homework?'

Clodagh picked her off her chair.

'You're a little Tashie madam, you are – '

Natasha put her arms round her neck.

'I'm going to be like you when I grow up.'

'No. You're going to be like your lovely mother.'

'Can I too?' James said.

Clodagh put Natasha back on her chair.

'Look at you,' she said to Alice.

'Why, what – '

'The cat that got the cream – '

'Oh but I am, I *am* – '

'You are so bloody *beautiful*.'

'Dear me,' Natasha said, 'in front of James.'

'Bloody,' James said softly to his picture, 'bloody, bloody, bloody beautiful.'

Clodagh leaned towards Alice.

'Beautiful.'

'You too.'

'No. I'm a ratface.' She put a finger on Charlie's cheek. 'And Charlie's a moonface.'

'And James,' Natasha said with deadly quietness, 'is a fishface.'

James gave a yelp. Then a car came swooping past the house and there was a chorus of 'Daddy! Daddy!' and Charlie, who had been dozing against Alice like a human teddy bear, became galvanised by the desire to join in.

It was exactly the homecoming Martin wanted. It was the best day he had had at work since the day he had been made a junior partner. He had been summoned in by Nigel Gathorne, the senior partner, to be congratulated, personally, on securing the Unwins as clients for the firm, and to be told, quite plainly, that this, particularly if he made a success of it, would contribute materially to Martin's upward rise. He then gave Martin a glass of fino sherry, a mark of approval all the junior partners recognised as being equivalent to a CBE. He was so genuinely pleased that Martin even managed to put aside all the complications and tribulations that seemed to have dogged his path since his lunch with Henry Dunne at the White Hart. If Nigel Gathorne could offer such warm and *professional* congratulations, then Martin's achievement must be real indeed. Coming out of Nigel's office, he felt he almost owed Clodagh an apology for his petulance over her part in it. Even thinking of her now was possible without an involuntary blush, but of course *she* had made that easy by being so ordinarily friendly to him and such a help with the children and such a good friend to Alice. He had, in his glow of gratitude and achievement, actually had a preliminary look at the Unwin trust papers at once, and really, it wasn't, at first glance, going to be too difficult to unscramble. He visualised a business conversation with Clodagh. It was a happy little fantasy in which he retrieved the self-esteem he had lost in that undignified little scene in the kitchen when Alice was away. At twenty past five, Martin left his office and went back to his car past the Victoria Wine Company so that he could buy a bottle of champagne, which luckily they had on a very reasonable offer indeed.

*   *   *

'You'll be able to handle Georgina,' Clodagh said, admiring the light through her champagne glass. 'Easy peasy.'

They were sitting in the drawing room, to celebrate.

'Is she like you?'

Clodagh avoided looking at Alice.

'Georgina is absolutely straight in every way. She'll be just like Ma, in the end, only quieter. She buys day clothes from Laura Ashley and evening ones from Caroline Charles and shoes from Bally and knickers from M & S. She's a dear.'

Alice said, head back against a chair cushion, eyes half-closed, 'Why don't you go and see her more?'

'Because, for some reason, I really like being at home just now.'

'Never,' Alice said, on the edge of laughter. She turned her head towards Martin. 'Anthony's coming. On Friday.'

Martin pulled a slight face.

'Oh well. It had to happen. How long for?'

'Don't you like him?' Clodagh said, interested. 'Why don't you?'

Alice began. 'He's – ' and Martin, fearing family criticism, said quickly, 'We fought a bit when we were growing up, that's all. He's been in Japan and Hong Kong for almost ten years. He's probably changed a lot.'

'Didn't sound it,' Alice said. 'Sounded exactly the same.'

Clodagh stood up.

'I'm going to read to Tashie. And then you can say what you really think about the Unwins in peace.'

Martin tried not to look priggish.

'I wouldn't say anything behind your back that I wouldn't say to your face.'

'I know,' Clodagh said, and went out of the room, laying a hand lightly on his shoulder, and then on Alice's, as she went.

'I'm so pleased for you,' Alice said to him.

He ducked his head. He looked suddenly as young and vulnerable as James. Alice felt so fond of him. It was only when he wanted to touch her that she . . .

'Allie – '

'Yes?'

'Allie, sorry to sort of mess up the mood, but there's something that's rather been on my mind – '

She took a slow swallow of champagne.

'Tell me.'

'It's, well, it's about us. I mean, we seem to be fine and everything's going really well and – ' He stopped. He loathed this kind of conversation, but a necessity was a necessity. 'Look. It's – about bed. I mean, I may be no great shakes but you don't seem to want me anywhere near you at the moment. I can't remember the last time – weeks, months, I don't know.' He looked at Alice pleadingly. 'Is it me?'

She sat up and put her glass on the floor and folded her hands on her lap. She looked straight at him.

'No,' she said. 'It isn't your fault. That is, it isn't anything you do. Or don't do.'

'Then – '

'It's me,' Alice said. 'I just don't want you to make love to me. I don't in the least want to hurt you but I must be truthful because it's kinder, really, in the end.'

There was a silence and then he said, looking down at his crossed arms resting on his knees, 'D'you think we should get some help? I mean, Marriage Guidance or something – '

Alice said gently, 'I don't want to do that. I want to say sorry, but I won't because I don't want to patronise you. But I don't want to talk to anyone.'

'But will you change?'

'I don't know. I can't tell.'

'So you just want me to wait. Grin and bear it – '

'Yes please. Just for now. Yes – please.'

He got up and walked about a bit and went over to a window and fingered the stiff gleaming billow of the curtains.

'Allie. I've got to ask you this.'

He stopped.

'Ask me then – '

'Will you give me a truthful answer? However much you think it'll hurt me?'

Alice's voice had a little quaver.

'I promise.'

Martin came back to his chair and put his hands on its back and looked at her.

'Is there another man?'

Alice raised her chin and looked at him squarely.

'No,' she said. 'There isn't another man.'

And then Martin gave a long, escaping sigh, and grinned at her and said he thought they had better finish the champagne, didn't she?

CHAPTER TEN

In the Pitcombe Stores, Mr Finch was patiently explaining to his new assistant, Gwen's daughter Michelle, about the arrangement of tinned vegetables on the shelves. It was not that Michelle was stupid, but rather that she wanted to work in Dorothy Perkins, in Salisbury, and they had said she couldn't until she was eighteen, so the village shop was to her no more than a tiresome stopgap at one pound eighty pence an hour. She was elaborately bored, all week, except on Mondays when, this being the show season for Mrs Macaulay and her girls, Mr Finch allowed her to help Mrs Jordan in the travelling shop. Michelle didn't just admire Alice, she really liked her company. When she got home on Mondays, Gwen always wanted to know what Alice had said to Michelle, but Michelle went mulish and wouldn't tell. Her Mrs Jordan, she felt, was different from the one her mother worked for. Her Mrs Jordan talked to her like an equal and lent her books and once gave her a pair of silver earrings like shells so that Michelle had to lock herself in the bathroom and pierce new holes in her ears with a needle stuck into a cork and an ice cube to deaden the lobe.

She said, 'Yeah, okay. Right. Okay,' to Mr Finch but she wasn't really listening. Who cared whether carrots went next to butter beans or peas? She stood and bit her nails and thought about the black leather jacket she'd seen on Saturday that she'd set her heart on.

'There now,' Mr Finch said, 'quite clear I think. Now you just load up from these boxes while I go and give Mrs Finch a hand with the freezer delivery.'

Michelle gave the faintest snigger. Everyone knew Mrs Finch and the freezer delivery driver fancied one another, though why the sight of Mrs Finch with her blue eyelids and purple hair didn't make the freezer man want to crack up Michelle couldn't imagine. He came twice a month, and Mr Finch always shot out to the back to give a hand. Michelle imagined a really good punch-up going on among the fish fingers and ice lollies in the glacial van while Mrs Finch sobbed theatrically into the little lace handkerchiefs she favoured.

When Mr Finch had gone, Michelle began, laboriously, to take the tins out of their cartons and bang them on the shelves. After a few minutes, Miss Pimm came in and scuttled about in pursuit of a ball of string and a packet of custard powder. Long ago, Michelle had briefly been in her Sunday School, manifesting, Miss Pimm was mortified to remember, an unwholesome curiosity in Mary Magdalene and the woman taken in adultery.

'Michelle,' Miss Pimm said, displaying her purchases with exaggerated honesty, 'I believe I owe Mr *Finch* exactly seventy seven *pence* for these two *items*.'

'Right,' Michelle said, getting up without a smile.

She took Miss Pimm's proffered eighty pence over to the till and was an age with the change.

'Three *pence*,' said Miss Pimm.

'I know,' said Michelle. 'I'm not daft.'

Miss Pimm, reddening in her characteristic blotches, opened her mouth to object to being spoken to in such a way and managed no more than a hoarse and humiliating caw. Michelle stared at her. Then the shop door twanged open and Michelle's gaze moved beyond Miss Pimm and lit up. A man's voice said, 'I *am* in Pitcombe. Aren't I?'

Michelle was delighted. She dropped Miss Pimm's change very approximately into her outstretched hand, tossed the wing of hair she liked to let fall into her eyes and said, 'Sorry. This is Las Vegas.'

'Same thing,' Anthony said, coming forward. He looked down at Miss Pimm. She reminded him of a moorhen. He said with great charm to her, 'I'm sure you can help me. I am Martin Jordan's brother. I am looking for The Grey House.'

Frenziedly, Miss Pimm fixed her eyes on his silk paisley tie.

'Yes!' she said. 'Yes!'

Anthony waited. Michelle leaned on the counter and gazed frankly and greedily at him. Miss Pimm raised her troubled eyes to his striped shirt collar. She licked her lips and swallowed.

'Welcome,' she said. 'Welcome to *Pitcombe*.'

The propriety of her own behaviour encouraged her and her eyes moved to Anthony's chin.

'*Up* the village street until you pass, on the *right*, a cottage with an ornamental *well* in the garden. Turn right there, a very *narrow* lane, and The Grey House is *ahead* of you.'

'How very kind,' Anthony said gravely.

His voice was so pleasing, Miss Pimm dared one fleeting glance at his eyes. He was winking at Michelle. Seizing her custard powder and her string, and gobbling to herself faintly in her distress, she scuttled from the shop into the street. Fred Mott watched her unpityingly from his window and then observed that the tall bloke who had just gone in was now coming out and was climbing back into the brand of car the telly ads promised would always get you a sexy bit in a slit skirt. Fred fingered his trousers. Sally had sewn up the slit in his pyjama bottoms. He sniggered. She couldn't sew up the slits in his *mind*.

Anthony drove up the street slowly, Miss Pimm and Michelle quite forgotten. It all looked very pretty and neat, grey stone and bright gardens. Trust Martin not to dare to live anywhere more adventurous than this. By the ornamental well – it was an immense affair with a fretted wooden roof like a Swiss chalet and had a plaster cat creeping along the ridge – he turned right, and beyond the cottages he saw the stone gateposts and the clipped hornbeams and the grey-gold gravel and he said to himself again, *trust* Martin.

He stopped the car outside the very pretty façade. The front door was open. A kitten, past the sweet stage of babyhood and fast approaching a gawky adolescence, was sitting just inside in a patch of sunlight, washing nonchalantly. It took no notice of him.

'Alice!' Anthony called.

There was no reply. He walked into the hall and across it into the kitchen. There was no one there but several people had recently had tea and there was a muddle of mugs and crumby plates. Anthony called again.

In the open doorway to the garden, a small, neat girl appeared.

'Are you Anthony?'

'Yes,' he said. 'And you must be James.'

She sighed. That was the sort of joke James liked. She said severely, 'I am Natasha.'

'I am sorry. Where is your mother?'

'Doing the church flowers. Clodagh's out here. Come and see Clodagh.'

Anthony went out into the garden. There was a sandpit with a very large baby or a very small child in it and a larger child on a little bicycle and a girl in a sort of camouflage boiler suit and a lot of brass jewellery shelling peas into a red enamel pot. She looked up at the sound of footsteps and Anthony thought he had seldom seen anyone look less welcoming.

Clodagh held out a hand.

'You must be Anthony.'

He sat down on the grass beside her. The children all came closer and regarded him. The baby one came very close and poured a cupful of sand over his foot and into his shoe.

'*Charlie*,' Natasha said. She stopped and brushed at the shoe, making clucking noises.

'I gather,' Anthony said, 'that Alice is doing the church flowers. And that you are Clodagh.'

'That's right.'

Anthony took off his shoe and poured the sand out into the grass. Charlie watched interestedly and then took off his own shoe and shook it hopefully.

'Which of you children is which?'

'I'm Natasha. I told you. And that's James and that's Charlie.'

'And I am your uncle.'

'It's so sad,' Natasha said, 'we have three of you and we never see any of you. One is in America.'

'You are seeing me now.'

He looked at Clodagh. He wanted to provoke her.

'Are you the nanny?'

Clodagh wasn't even going to look at him. She went on zipping her thumb along the pea pods so that the peas pattered into the pot.

'No.'

'She's the friend,' James explained.

Clodagh shot him an affectionate look.

'Mummy's friend?'

'All our friend.'

Anthony turned round.

'Bit of all right, here.'

137

Natasha felt a social obligation. She said, 'Shall I show you round?'

'I'd rather you showed me Mummy.'

Clodagh said, 'Take him to the church, Tashie, there's a love.'

'Won't you?'

'No,' Clodagh said. 'I won't.'

Anthony got to his feet.

'Lovely welcome – '

Clodagh said nothing. She was full of loathing.

'Don't I even get any tea?'

Natasha said comfortingly, 'It'll be time for a drink soon. And we ate *all* the chocolate crunchy.' She paused and then she said, 'I could give you a banana, I should think.'

'Certainly,' Clodagh said. 'As many as he can eat.'

Natasha led the way back into the kitchen. She peered into the fruit bowl.

'They're all speckly. Do you mind? I only like them very smooth.'

'I don't really want a banana.'

Natasha looked puzzled. He was a most peculiar uncle. She thought uncles laughed a lot and gave you pound coins and took you for rides in sports cars with the top down. Anthony's car looked very boring. It was even black. She said, 'Shall I take you to the church?'

He sighed and nodded. She led the way out of the house and up the garden to a field path. She told him about her school and about Sophie having to have glasses and about her intense longing to have some too. He nodded a bit but she didn't think he was conversationally very responsive. She asked him if he ever wore glasses and he said 'No', rather crossly, and she began to be disappointed in the role of hostess.

'The church,' she said in a last effort to entertain him, 'smells exactly like my cloakroom at school.'

But he only grunted. They skirted the churchyard wall and Natasha thought of several interesting remarks about the headstones but hadn't the heart to utter them. In silence, they walked up the path to the south porch, and went from the bright warmth outside to the damp cool dimness inside. There were several women dotted around the nave, and dustsheets and trugs of greenery and flowers and pairs of secateurs, and in the aisle a very beautiful woman was sweeping with an almost bald broom. The woman, Anthony recognised with a start, was Alice. Her hair fell in a river down her back from some high-crowned arrangement on her head, and she was wearing something swirling and green. Natasha ran forward and seized the broom, and said, 'Here's Anthony!'

Alice stopped sweeping. She looked up and smiled at him angelically. Then she gave the broom to Natasha and came quickly to Anthony and put her arms round him.

'*Anthony* – '

He held her back. He felt, as he so seldom did, full of a large and happy warmth.

'You look *amazing* – '

She laughed. Then she looked closely at him and said, suddenly sober, 'Oh, poor Ant. I wish you did.'

'Everyone is so horrible to me. Your baby filled my shoe with sand.'

'He didn't mean it!' Natasha cried indignantly, her eyes full of sudden tears. 'He's only little!'

Alice took her arms away from Anthony.

'Don't be an ass, Ant.'

'I *rely* on you to be kind.'

'Are you whining?'

'No. Only pleading.'

She gave him a sideways look.

'If you say so – '

A faint scream came from the west window. On a ladder insecurely poised against the high sill, Miss Payne, as small and round as a blue tit, was losing out to an immense and purposeful white stone vase that she was attempting to fill with cow parsley and iris. Anthony, who liked all diversions for their sakes, sped away from Alice and caught Miss Payne as she tottered, cradling her in his arms like a large pale blue knitted football. He then came back up the aisle with her, as if she were some kind of trophy. She was pink with distressed excitement. The other flower ladies left their assigned corners and crowded round with twitters of concern. Peter Morris, who had been in the vestry screwing up a modest little looking glass so that he could inspect himself before he emerged into the chancel every service, came down into the nave and for a fleeting moment thought Miss Payne was being abducted. Then

Anthony set her gently on the floor and she began, quite helplessly, to giggle. Everybody watched her.

'Of course, nobody her age should even be *asked* to go up that ladder – '

'I've always said we could do with a nice cheerful arrangement of silk flowers up there, no trouble to anyone, only need an occasional shake – '

'You all right, dear?'

'Better sit down, Buntie dear, after a shock like that – '

'Perhaps *next* time, Mrs Jordan, you being so much younger, you could volunteer for the west window?'

'Of course,' Alice said, 'but Buntie wanted to do it.'

Miss Payne nodded violently. Anthony stooped over her.

'Shall I carry you out and lay you down on a nice tombstone to recover?'

She gave a little squeal of delight and horror. Peter Morris moved calmly through the little group and steered Miss Payne to a pew.

'I don't know, Buntie. Cradle-snatching I'd call it.'

Miss Payne began to cry. Peter Morris pulled out what he always called his public handkerchief and handed it to her. Anthony looked at Alice.

'I'd *no* idea doing the church flowers could be such a lark.'

Natasha said in distress, looking at Miss Payne, 'But it's *sad*.'

'Heavens,' Anthony said, '*what* a sentimental little party.' He turned to Alice. 'Wouldn't you like to come home now and pour me a huge welcoming drink?'

'Not much,' Alice said.

'Allie – '

Alice did stern battle with her temper.

'I must finish sweeping up. Tashie will help me. You go and sit in the churchyard and I'll be out in five minutes.'

'All right,' he said reluctantly.

He went down the aisle and Miss Pimm and Mrs Macaulay and Mrs Fanshawe watched him go as if to see him safely off the premises.

'Hold the dustpan steady,' Alice said.

Natasha knelt down and leaned her weight on the dustpan.

'Is sentimental,' she said, looking downwards, 'nice or silly?'

*   *   *

At supper, which they ate in the kitchen with the upper half of the stable door open to the dim summer night, Anthony talked a great deal about the Far East, and, by inference, of the depth and breadth of his experience of life. Alice heard him with affectionate pity and Clodagh with contempt. Martin felt, as Anthony meant him to feel, faintly insecure. He tried, eating his chicken casserole, to tell himself that whereas Anthony had passed ten years, he, Martin had lived them. Anthony had stories; he, Martin, had a wife and children, a house and friends and a solid career. Perhaps, Martin thought, getting up to go round the table with the second bottle of Californian Chardonnay, if Alice would let him make love to her, he would be able to hear anything, absolutely *anything*, Anthony chose to say, with equanimity. He believed Alice when she said she wasn't interested in anyone else. He believed that she loved him – heavens, she was more loving to him and appreciative than she'd been in ages, years even – but there was this bed thing. Suppose she never wanted sex with him again, what the hell would he *do*? It was bad enough now, he sometimes felt quite obsessed by it, thinking about it, wanting it. On top of the physical difficulties there was the siren call of self-pity. Martin knew Alice despised people who were sorry for themselves, but sometimes, after a messy little session alone with himself in the bathroom, he would look at himself in the shaving mirror and say piteously, 'What about *me*?' He got angry with Alice then, and showered himself furiously, muttering abusive things about her into the rushing water. And after that, he felt as he supposed women did after they'd had a good cry, absolutely wrung out and forlorn. He hated the whole business and, try as he might, he couldn't escape the fact that he wasn't the one who had brought it about.

'Don't I get any?' Clodagh said.

Martin came slowly out of his trance.

'And after I've ironed seven shirts of yours today and put new slug pellets round the delphiniums and done the school run?'

He put his hand on her shoulder.

'Sorry. Miles away.'

'Are you thinking about my farm?'

Martin was a poor liar. In a kind of shout, he said, 'Yes, actually.'

Clodagh looked briefly at Anthony.

'Martin is our family lawyer now.'

'How *deeply* respectable.'

Alice said mildly. 'What an old bitch you are.'

'I *needn't* be.'

Clodagh gave a snort. She got up and cleared away the plates and put a blue china bowl of strawberries in the middle of the table. Anthony watched her. He thought that when he next telephoned his mother, he would tell her that he saw exactly why she had reservations about Clodagh as a friend for Alice. He turned to look at Alice. He held his wine glass up to her. She must be sorry for Clodagh.

'Here's to you.'

'Thank you,' she said. But she said it absently. Taking a bowl of strawberries from Clodagh, she said, 'What is your farm like?'

'Lovely.'

'What kind of lovely?'

'A square flint house with brick chimneys and a wonderful Victorian yard. Six hundred acres – '

'Six hundred and thirty,' Martin said.

'It's grown!'

'No. It just wasn't measured properly. I've had it measured. For valuation.'

'Martin,' Clodagh said, putting an enormous strawberry on top of his helping as a reward, 'you are wonderful.'

Anthony said, 'Why don't you live there?'

Alice held her breath.

'It hasn't been mine. When it is, I might.'

'Do you,' Anthony said, leaning forward, 'live here?'

She looked straight at him.

'I live at home. I spend most days here.'

'Why?' Anthony said.

Alice said, without looking up, 'Because we like her to.'

There was a tiny, highly charged pause.

'I see,' Anthony said.

Clodagh said spitefully, 'Do you know how to like people?'

'I know how *not* to like them.'

Martin waved his spoon.

'Pax, you two.'

'We might just, you see,' Clodagh said, embarking on the high

142

wire, 'be about to have a most interesting conversation about love.'

'*Love?*'

Alice looked up. Her eyes were enormous.

'It's the most important thing there is. I always knew it would be.'

Martin, alarmed at this kind of remark being made in public, said quickly, 'Are there any more strawberries?'

It was all the poetry Alice was reading, a sort of sequel to all those novels she used to devour. He shot a glance at her. She was looking at Clodagh but her mind was clearly miles away. Anthony picked up the strawberry bowl.

'There's about six. I'll share them with you.'

He put two in Martin's bowl.

'You don't change, do you?'

'What I don't understand,' Anthony said, 'is why everyone expects me to.'

After supper, Alice put a pot of coffee on the table, and then she and Clodagh moved about in the dimness outside the candlelit circle round the table, clearing up. They were talking together softly, and at the table Martin and Anthony were talking about Dummeridge. After a while, Alice and Clodagh said that they were going to tuck the children in and left the kitchen. When he could hear their feet safely on the stairs Anthony said, 'Come on. Tell me about Clodagh. Why is she here?'

Martin poured a spoonful of brown sugar into his coffee.

'We met her up at the Park. She's been an absolute godsend. A sort of unpaid nanny and companion. It's made all the difference in the world to Alice.'

'Maybe,' Anthony said. 'But is she going to stay for ever?'

'Lord no. She had a bit of a crisis of some kind in the States, so she came home. She'll be off to do something else after the summer. She's that kind.'

'Do you like her?'

Martin flinched a little.

'Of course – '

'When you were younger, you'd have been scared of a girl like that.'

'Well,' Martin said jauntily, 'I'm older, aren't I?'

'Mother doesn't like her.'

'Mother doesn't have to live with her.'

'*Why* doesn't she like her?'

Martin shrugged.

'*I* don't know.'

'You do.'

'Shut up,' Martin said loudly, suddenly angry. 'Shut up, will you?'

'No good losing your temper.'

'I haven't – '

Anthony got up and went over to the open door and lit a cigarette.

'This is quite a place.'

'Yes.'

'Three children. Steady progress up career ladder. Well done.'

Martin said nothing. Anthony came back to the table and dropped into his chair again.

'To be quite honest, I envy you. My future is rather bleak.'

'Surely – '

'Surely what?'

'Surely you can get another money job?'

'Oh sure. But it seems a bit pointless. What *for*? You know.'

Alice and Clodagh were coming back down the stairs. They were laughing.

'I get lonely,' Anthony said, thrusting his face at Martin.

'I'm sorry – '

The kitchen door opened and the women came in. Martin waved the coffee pot in relief.

'Coffee?'

'Lovely,' Alice said, and then to Clodagh, 'It was everything you see, comic *and* pathetic. I wish you'd – ' She stopped. 'Charlie has got out of his cot,' she said to Martin, 'and gone to sleep underneath it.'

'Why didn't you put him back?'

The women looked at one another.

'It seemed pointless,' Alice said. 'And not very kind. We rather admired his enterprise.'

'I won't admire it when he appears in our room at dawn.'

Alice looked deflated.

'I'll put him back then. Later.'

144

Clodagh picked up a bunch of keys from the dresser.

'I ought to go. The drawbridge goes up at eleven.'

Alice moved across towards her. 'I'll come and see you off.'

Anthony was watching. Clodagh, observing this, said lightly, 'No need.'

'I'd like to. You've worked so hard today. Anyway, I must shut up the hens.'

'No,' Clodagh said, and shook her head. 'I did the hens. Before supper.'

She crossed to the stable door and unlatched it.

'Night everyone – '

Alice was gripping the chair back. She saw Clodagh go every night but tonight it was dreadful, heaven knew why. The door closed. She wanted to rush out through the front door and intercept Clodagh's car and get into it with her and just *not* be separated, not be made to be apart, again . . . Instead of doing that, however, she sat down slowly and poured herself some coffee and wished that Anthony wouldn't keep looking at her.

'Brandy?' she said to him.

'Love it – '

Martin got up.

'I'll get it.'

He went out to the dining room.

'Pretty good,' Anthony said. 'For my little brother to find himself the Unwin's lawyer.'

'It was Clodagh's idea.'

'Was it now?'

'Her father is thrilled – '

Martin came back with a bottle.

'Only half an inch I'm afraid.'

He poured brandy into Anthony's empty wine glass. For no reason at all, Alice remembered her father asking for brandy when he came to tell her that he had left her mother and that she hadn't had any then, indeed had never been even part owner of a bottle of spirits in her life. She hadn't been near her mother for a year but she would go now. She and Clodagh would take the children to Colchester to see Elizabeth and perhaps – Alice's heart gave a little lurch – stay in an hotel near-by. And they could go to Reading on the way back and see Sam. Sam would love Clodagh. Perhaps –

perhaps they could stay away for a few days, free, just roaming with the car . . .

She said to Martin, 'I can't think why brandy should make me think of my mother, but really I *must* go and see her.'

'Of course,' Martin said.

'Maybe Clodagh could come and help me with the children – '

'Good idea.'

'Next month – '

Martin stood up, yawning.

'Whenever you like. I'm dropping.' He gestured at Anthony. 'Sleep well. No hurry in the morning.'

'You must feel very proud of him,' Anthony said, when Martin had gone.

'Of course I do.'

'So glad.'

'Anthony,' Alice said, 'enough games for one evening. Time for bed,' and she leaned forward to blow out the candles, and as she did so Anthony found that his long scrutiny of her and of Clodagh had been rewarded and that he had made a most interesting discovery. And so, in order to consider it at leisure, he was quite happy to be shooed upstairs with the remainder of his brandy. The goodnight kiss he gave Alice on the landing was compounded both of admiration and appreciation of the probable complexity of the future.

CHAPTER ELEVEN

On fine afternoons, Lettice Deverel carried the parrot in its cage outside and hung it in an apple tree. It liked this and made bubbling noises of deep appreciation. As long as she was in sight, bent over a nearby border in an ancient Italian straw hat, it continued to bubble contentedly, but if she moved too far away it grew agitated and screamed at her that she was a surly bagpiper. Sometimes she wished she had not confined its education solely to literary references to parrots because now it seemed resistant to learning anything new. Peter Morris had attempted to teach it prayers but it became over-excited and shrieked 'Parrot, parrot, parrot' at him and then cackled with ribald laughter.

Margot Unwin, finding no one in Rose Villa, one warm, still, late afternoon, came round the house into the garden, calling for Lettice. Lettice was at that moment tipping a barrowload of weeds on to her compost heap, but the nearest apple tree remarked conversationally in Lettice's voice, 'Well, Polly, as far as one woman can forgive another, I forgive thee.'

Margot Unwin gave a faint squawk. Lettice appeared with her barrow through a gap in her immense and burgeoning borders. Margot flapped a hand at her.

'I always forget about your wretched bird.'

'Did he say anything improper?'

'Only that he forgave me.'

'Oh,' Lettice said looking pleased, 'that's his bit out of *The Beggar's Opera*. He hardly ever says it. You are much favoured.'

Margot inserted her face sideways under the hat brim and gave Lettice a kiss.

'I need to talk, Lettice.'

'Clodagh?'

'Clodagh.'

147

'Come and sit over here. No, not near the parrot. He always wants to join in and I wouldn't put eavesdropping past him.'

'Why *do* you have a parrot?'

'I like him,' Lettice said, brushing garden bits off a wooden seat. 'He is contrary and amusing and independent. Margot, you look tired.'

'So annoying. But I'm worried.'

Lettice sat on a second chair and removed her hat. Underneath it her grey hair was tied up in a red spotted snuff handkerchief. She wore a rust linen smock over wide blue trousers and elderly espadrilles. Margot Unwin wore a sweeping print frock.

'I shall get us some tea.'

'No, dear. Don't trouble. It's the sympathy I've come for.'

'I doubt there's anything I can *do* – '

'You can listen.'

Lettice had been listening to Margot for thirty years, from the time she had bought Rose Villa and had only been able to spend weekends and holidays there, travelling up and down in the train from Waterloo with her pockets stuffed with sketches of what she would do to the garden. Only young Ralph had been born then and Margot was pregnant with Georgina and very handsome and spirited and impatient with being pregnant at all. There were endless parties up at the Park, weekend parties and shooting parties and tea parties for the children where the guests were accompanied by nannies in Norland uniforms. Margot started by inviting Lettice up as a curiosity, relying on the fact that she would wear breeches or a cloak or clogs and that she would express her decided opinions in a fresh and unconventional way. But then, at one lunch party, Lettice told the table at large that she was not a performing monkey, and went home. Margot followed her. She stood in Lettice's extraordinary and absorbing sitting room in her Belinda Belville dress and the Unwin pearls and said she was sorry. Very sorry. Then she burst into tears and Lettice, who recognised a true if incongruous friend, forgave her.

They had not quarrelled since but Lettice had always, tacitly and tactfully, retained the upper hand. As with Peter Morris, Lettice came to represent a confidante. When Margot Unwin supposed herself out of love with Ralph and very much in love with someone else, when Clodagh ran away from school, when a rampantly

148

attractive and unprincipled Argentinian polo player besieged the defenceless Georgina for months on end, it was to Lettice that Margot came. Perhaps, Lettice sometimes thought, it was simply because their backgrounds were so different that their friendship was so real. Lettice, growing up in an austere academic household in Cambridge, might have come from another planet to that of Margot's adolescent society whirl. But after the apology, Lettice knew an excellent heart beat beneath the Hartnell suits and cashmere jerseys, and, as she grew older, she was inclined to think she valued excellence of heart above all things. She leaned across now and patted Margot's hand.

'I've had half a mind to speak to Clodagh myself. It's time she got on with her life.'

'That's exactly it. And Ralph has made it infinitely worse and has insisted on breaking up the trust so that Georgina and Clodagh get their farms now. Poor George. She doesn't even *want* hers yet but of course she's much too obliging to object. And now Windover becomes Clodagh's and neither she nor her father, it seems to me, have any intention she should do anything other about it than treat it as a giant piggy bank. I'm quite appalled and Ralph is as stubborn as a mule. As for Clodagh – '

Lettice stood up.

'I *am* going to make some tea. Or would you rather have gin?'

'*Much* rather.'

'I won't be a minute. You sit and admire my white delphiniums. All descendents from the ones you gave me.'

'Lettice,' Margot said, 'you are a prop and stay.'

She sat and looked obediently ahead of her and tried to be sensible and not seized with wild envy of Lettice's single blessedness. After a few minutes, Lettice returned with two magnificent gilded Venetian tumblers and a yoghurt pot of pine kernels for the parrot. As she crossed the grass having put these in its cage, it could be heard exulting over its luck.

'It's a nice parrot, really,' Margot said.

'It's a dear parrot. There you are. Now then. It seems that all incentive for Clodagh to do anything enterprising ever again has been removed from her.'

'Exactly.'

'And she is still dancing attendance on those young Jordans?'

Margot took a swallow of her drink.

'Do you know, I was so pleased about that! They are charming, Alice particularly, and those dear little children, and I thought how lovely for Clodagh, how *normal*, how good for her. And now she never goes anywhere else, never wants to do anything else, never wants to see anyone else. I wish them no ill, Lettice, but I wish they had never come. I thought I might try another angle and wheedle Alice's mother-in-law here by getting her to talk to the county WI but she was most peculiar on the telephone. I was unnerved, to be honest. She said she had promised herself to keep quite clear of Alice's territory.'

'Perhaps,' Lettice said, 'you should simply throw Clodagh out.'

'I thought of that. I even said it. She said of course she wouldn't stay for ever and the moment I wanted her to go she would go down to The Grey House or to a farm cottage at Windover. Then she told Ralph about this conversation and we had the most horrible evening. Thank goodness it was Shadwell's night off.'

Lettice pushed the lemon slice in her drink under the surface and watched the bubbles streaming upward.

'Then you must talk to Alice Jordan.'

'Poor girl. She's done nothing wrong except befriend my bad daughter.'

Lettice was silent for a moment, considering how to economise with the truth.

'She is fond of Clodagh. Fond enough it seems only to wish all the best for her. If she sees that hanging about here for too long is bad for Clodagh, she may help to urge her to go. She ought to go – ' She stopped.

Margot looked at her.

'Go on.'

'Young marriages like that,' Lettice said, 'don't need permanent extra adults hanging around them.'

Margot looked indignant.

'Clodagh would never do a thing like that! In any case, Martin Jordan isn't in the least her – '

'All the same – '

There was a pause. It would not be, Margot considered, the first

150

time Clodagh had made mischief; made it not out of malice but purely because she had the power to do so. She stood up.

'I shall talk to Alice Jordan. After the fête.'

'The fête – '

'Saturday, Lettice, and don't you dare to pretend you didn't know about it.'

'Oh I do, I do. That plant stall – '

Margot smoothed down her skirt.

'If we don't make a thousand, I shall suggest we put our herculean efforts into something else. The work is quite appalling.' She looked up at the sky. 'Pray for a fine day.'

'I have never,' Lettice said staunchly, 'prayed in my life.' She stood up and drained her glass. 'But if I *did*,' she said reflectively, 'I'd save it for Clodagh, not the weather.'

'In the old days,' Stuart Mott said, leaning against the shop counter and eyeing Michelle, 'the shop'd always give something for the fête. Dad said.'

Mr Finch disliked Stuart Mott. He disliked all the Motts. He thought them shiftless and dishonest. They were also a plain family. At least the Crudwells, who proliferated in Pitcombe as the Motts did, had some Romany blood and were picturesque to look at, even if their girls were without morals and were constantly being caught up at the army camp at Larkhill. Mr Finch had come to abhor human sexuality. He supposed that his abhorrence was the result of thirty-three years of Mrs Finch. He leaned on the other side of the counter and said to Stuart, 'The old days were different. The village shop got used properly then because nobody had cars to take them into Salisbury. I can't afford to give away so much as a packet of cabbage seeds.'

'Don't need cabbage seeds,' Stuart said, still looking at Michelle. 'Got more'n enough cabbage plants. We'd like a nice box of chocolates for the tombola, though.'

Michelle was friends with Stuart's daughter Carol and she thought Stuart was dirty to keep staring at her like that. She wasn't going to open her mouth and give him the chance to speak to her, though, so she turned round with her back to him and began to rearrange hairslides on a blue card hanging against the shelves where Mr Finch kept what Mrs Finch called toiletries. Along the shelf where the soap and talcum powder stood, Mrs Finch had tacked a swathe of mauve net and an imitation orchid.

'I'll give you a box half-price,' Mr Finch said, 'and bang goes my profit and then some.'

Michelle was going to help Alice and Clodagh on the white elephant stall. They'd asked her themselves. And Martin had made a sort of speed game with pegs on a wooden board which you had to cover with plastic cups, as many as you could in thirty seconds, because Lady Unwin had asked him to. Gwen was doing teas with Sally Mott and Miss Pimm was taking the money for them. Mrs Fanshawe was in charge of the cake stall and at this moment, to judge by the smell, Mrs Finch was in her kitchen in a ruffled nylon apron making her contribution of iced fancies. 'My specials,' she called them. Even Michelle, who could eat four Twix bars at a sitting, wanted to throw up at the sight of all that pink and yellow fondant icing. While she baked, Mrs Finch was working her way through the score of *The Merry Widow*. She had reached the waltz. Stuart Mott pointed to the largest box of chocolates.

'I'll give you two quid for that one.'

Mr Finch lifted down a small box of fudge which said it had been made of clotted cream in a cottage.

'This is my best offer. Sixty pence is all I'm asking.'

With elaborate reluctance, Stuart Mott counted out sixty pence in very small change.

'You helping Mrs Jordan, then,' he said to Michelle's back.

She shrugged.

'Might be.'

'She's taken a fancy to you, hasn't she. I know all about that. Nothing goes on up there that I don't see.'

He picked up the box of fudge. Michelle hadn't turned round and Mr Finch, priggishly mindful of Lettice Deverel's opinion of gossip, turned aside to wipe his bacon slicer.

'That brother's staying on,' Stuart said. 'He's a funny bloke. Nice car. You seeing our Carol later?'

'Dunno –'

Stuart walked over to the door.

'See you Saturday.'

'Goodbye,' Mr Finch said, wiping vigorously.

Michelle said nothing. The one thing her eleven years of

schooling had taught her was that you could be infinitely ruder if you kept your mouth shut.

'If I wasn't here,' Anthony said to Martin, surveying Pitcombe Park just before the fête opened, 'I wouldn't believe this sort of thing still went on.'

Martin was trying to wedge a card table sufficiently steady to hold his game.

'It goes on all over England. Every summer. Thousands and thousands of village fêtes. Can you find me a flat stone?'

They had been allotted a corner of the great grass terrace below the house, under a laburnum tree. To their left Lettice Deverel, in a blue hessian apron with a sort of kangaroo pocket in front for money, was pricing geranium cuttings and courgette plants rooted in old cream cartons at ten pence each. Miss Payne, her helpmeet at the plant stall, was surreptitiously marking most of these down to five pence before arranging them invitingly on a trestle table draped in green dustsheets that had been dyed expressly for this purpose ten years before and which spent three hundred and sixty-four days of the year folded up in Miss Payne's box room.

Beyond the plant stall, an old kitchen table by a magnificent yellow peony bore a depressed collection of second-hand books, mostly paperbacks, the throwouts of the village's collective holiday reading. Mrs Macaulay, who never read anything except *Good Housekeeping* and dachshund breeding handbooks, arranged her stall according to the width of books, so that *War and Peace* and old medical dictionaries lay between hefty doses of improbable espionage and pornography. Mrs Macaulay was, of long experience, realistic about her afternoon and had brought her knitting. She would sell any historical romance she had to Mrs Finch, anything with thighs and breasts on the cover to Stuart Mott and have a terrible time finding anything for the Unwins or the vicar who were all obliged, by tradition, to make a purchase from every stall. Beyond that, she would have plenty of time in her folding chair beside the peony to negotiate the shawl collar of her cardigan jacket.

As close to the house itself as they could get – and laughingly insisting that that was where they had been *put* – Gerry and Rosie Barton set up what they called their community stall. This had involved both of them visiting every cottage in the village for a contribution, explaining, with unfading smiles, that they wanted every person in Pitcombe to feel just a little bit *involved*. Granny Crudwell, interrupted in a Saturday afternoon's wrestling on television, had told them to bugger off. Other people had produced scraps from their gardens and jars from their larders and, in Miss Pimm's case, two mustard cotton crocheted dressing table mats, so that the community stall under its banner 'Your Village Stall!' resembled the kind of nameless detritus people are thankful to leave behind when they move house. Rosie and Gerry were not attending to their stall; they had left their fat and despairing German au pair girl, whose sole aim in life appeared to be the meticulous correctness of her lifeless English, in charge. They themselves were flitting from stall to stall, smiling and encouraging the stallholders and indulging in the little jokes which inferred, no more, that *we*, the village, were somehow in cahoots, and superior cahoots at that, against the Big House, and all that it stood for. Sally Mott and Gwen admired Rosie Barton. At least she didn't give herself airs. There were some people round here, Sally said to Gwen as they filled the Mothers' Union tea urn, who needed to be reminded we were living in the twentieth century. When Rosie had started her Village Wives' group, Sally Mott had been the first to sign up. As she said, living with Stuart and old Fred made you desperate for some area of your life where you could be sure you'd never meet a man.

The tea stall was flanked on one side by Stuart Mott and his tombola, and on the other by the white elephant stall which Alice and Clodagh had taken real trouble over. Every bit of rubbish they had collected had been mended and washed and polished and Alice had made a huge banner to pin on poles above the stall on which a line of elephants, trunk to tail, was dancing. It had been an immense amount of work organising the stall, and Alice had been grateful for it because it had given her something to do with Anthony. Anthony had been staying for over a week now, and he was beginning to get her down. He watched her, all the time, and spoke to her in words that were very affectionate, but neither his look nor his tone matched his words. Clodagh had stayed up at the Park far more while Anthony was around and when she did come to The Grey House, to help with things for the stall, she was sharp and aloof. Alice had tried to corner her to talk about what was happening, and twice she had tried to telephone secretly, but Clodagh had simply said, 'Wait till he's gone, Alice, wait.' But for Alice, who had at last woken up and who was full of appetite and gratitude, this was almost impossible. She resolved she would ask Martin to move Anthony out; after all, Martin didn't want him there, hadn't wanted him at all in the first place, it was *she*, with her overflowing heart, who had said come, do come, *I'll* be nice to you, I'm nice to everyone just now. But he'd brought something nasty with him and he had added to it since he came. Arranging a row of little cut-glass bottles on a piece of white cotton lace, Alice thought she would ask Martin *tonight* to ask Anthony to go. And at the idea her heart simply lifted and she turned to give Clodagh a smile of pure love.

Clodagh put a cardboard box of fivepenny and tenpenny pieces into Michelle's hands.

'Run over to Martin with these, would you? It's his float. Twenty-five pence a go or five for a pound.'

Michelle went off across the lawn in her new white stilettos.

'What a bloody week,' Clodagh said. 'I've missed you. I've never missed anyone so much. When is that bastard going?'

Alice looked quickly at Natasha who was piling their float money into neat categories.

'As soon as possible. I'll ask Martin – '

'He knows. Anthony knows. He knew at once.'

'Knows?'

Mrs Fanshawe was approaching with a paper plate of cupcakes.

'I don't care,' Alice said. 'I don't care if the whole world knows.'

'I've brought these,' Mrs Fanshawe said, 'because you stall ladies always get left out at teatime.'

She put the plate down.

'*Thank* you,' Alice said. A vast relief was bubbling up in her.

Mrs Fanshawe looked quickly over the white elephants.

'Do you know, my grandmother had exactly that vase? I remember it distinctly. You helping Mummy with the change, dear? That's never your baby! He's grown so . . . Must fly, you know how they all fall up on the cake stall the moment they're let in. Must be at my post! Granny Crudwell's made one of her fruit cakes and to tell the truth you can almost smell the brandy from here . . .'

She backed away. Clodagh made her nervous. Alice said softly, 'I'd like to tell *her*. I'd like to tell everyone.'

Over by the pair of Union Jacks wedged in painted oil drums that marked the entrance, Shadwell blew on a whistle. At once a surge of thirty or forty people hurried into the circle of stalls and made purposefully for their particular objects. As the first two possible competitors, a couple of boys of about twelve, approached the game under the laburnum tree, Anthony said casually to Martin, apropos of nothing they had been saying before, 'Of course, Clodagh Unwin is a lesbian.'

Martin said, 'What do you *mean*?' and then the bolder boy held out fifty pence and, when Martin began to explain the rules, said, 'I know. I played it before.'

Martin handed him a stack of plastic cups and set his stopwatch. 'Ready? Rubbish, Anthony. Anyway, how do you know – '

Anthony said nothing. He waited for the boy to score, and then for his shyer friend to score two higher and for their scores to be entered in a notebook, and then he said, 'I know because she is having an affair with Alice.'

There was a silence, and then Martin said with great distinctness, 'Alice is my *wife*.'

'Alice, your wife, and Clodagh Unwin are having an affair.'

A small girl was being helped up towards Martin by her granny. She was holding twenty-five pence. Martin explained the game, very carefully, and between them the granny and the small girl slowly put six cups on the pegs in thirty seconds and then the stopwatch rang and the child began to cry. Her granny, promising treats, took her away with an accusing look at Martin.

He said to Anthony, 'Don't talk such utter, bloody rubbish.'

'It's true.'

'It's a lie. It's a barefaced bloody lie. You've made it up because you're jealous.'

'It's true,' Anthony said. 'You only have to watch and you'll see.'

Sir Ralph, jovial in a Prince of Wales checked suit and a yellow rose in his buttonhole, came up and said he'd better make a fool of himself like everyone else. Martin said that it was jolly good of him, sir. He made a great thing of not understanding the rules and then attracted quite an audience when he actually played, with immense skill and swiftness, topping all three previous scores. He straightened up and clapped Martin on the shoulder.

'I like to outwit a legal brain when I can.'

There was a ripple of polite laughter. Sir Ralph, saying he'd better buy an improper book from Mrs Macaulay, took his small crowd with him. When he was out of earshot, Martin said, 'I want you to go away. Now. Just go. Wherever you are you make trouble, and I don't want you making it here. Just get the hell out, will you, *now* – '

Anthony took a step away.

'You want me to go because then you think you won't have to face the fact that your wife is a dyke.'

Martin fixed his eyes on Sir Ralph's checked back stooping over Mrs Macaulay's bookstall.

'If I wasn't in the Unwins' garden, I'd smash your fucking face in.'

Anthony sighed.

'Smash what you like. It doesn't change facts. No one but you could possibly have lived with such a set-up and not noticed. But then, you only ever *have* seen what you wanted to see.'

Several people were approaching.

Anthony lingered for a second as if contemplating saying more, but then he said, 'Bye,' quite lightly and moved away towards the drive. Martin straightened up and looked at his customers. They seemed to him miles away. Then the first one, Sir Ralph's tractor driver, wearing a T-shirt which said 'If you hate sun and sex . . . don't come to Greece' across the chest, said, 'What do I have to get to beat the boss?'

'A great man,' Martin said, in mild reproof. His voice sounded perfectly ordinary.

'Watch me, then,' the tractor driver said. He held out a pound coin. 'Watch me beat 'im then.'

It was almost completely dark in the drawing room. They had been sitting there for hours while the light faded and the scent of the lilies John Murray-French had planted years before came pouring in through the open windows. There were just Alice and Martin. Clodagh had gone home after the children had been put to bed. She would not stay for supper, she said, they knew where she was if they needed her. They had been silent for ages now, quite silent since Martin had stifled a brief bout of weeping and declined to let Alice comfort him. He had been very polite. He had been polite all evening. Alice wondered if she had ever found him as lovable as she did now. She said to herself, 'He is being wonderful,' and was full of admiration.

'You can't comfort him,' Clodagh said, before she left. 'It's arrogant to think you can.'

He had uttered one cry of reproach. He had turned to her in the half-dark and said, 'How *could* you?' And she knew he meant not only how could you do this to me, but how could you fall for a woman, have sex with a *woman*? So she had leaned forward and said, trying to help him to see what was so crystal clear to her, 'But you see, it wasn't because Clodagh was a woman. It was because Clodagh was Clodagh. Can't you see?'

He'd given a little grunt.

'I like everything I have better because of her,' Alice said, and then, with the idiotic confidence of her happiness, in the midst of it all, added, 'Even you. I like you better because of Clodagh.'

That was when he had cried. Not for long, though. He had blown his nose with great decisiveness and after that they had stayed quiet in their chairs in the deepening darkness. Balloon had come in and made a few enquiring remarks and had jumped on Martin's knee and been thrown off, with quite unfamiliar fury, and so had stalked out again, aggrieved. At long last Martin said, 'What about the children?'

She turned her head towards him.

'What about them?'

'Well – ' He shifted in his chair. 'You and Clodagh, influence and things. You know – '

'No!' she shouted. 'I do *not* know. Clodagh adores them. So do I. We are two loving adults, not aggrieved minority group proselytisers – '

'Shh,' he said, calming her. 'Shh. Sorry. I didn't mean – I mean, I thought – ' He stopped. Then he said more firmly, 'Do they know?'

'They know I love Clodagh and she loves me. They love Clodagh. They don't know about adult love because they are all under eight.'

There was another pause. Then Martin said, 'I could never reach you. Could I? Never. Just at the beginning a bit – '

'Please – '

'I remember thinking, taking you out to dinner once at some fearful joint in Marlow, I'll propose to her, and I was longing to, and then I suddenly realised I had the power to wait, so I did. I was so happy. I suppose it was the only time I had the upper hand.'

'I did love you,' Alice said. 'I do. I do love you.'

'But not *in* love – '

There was a little silence.

'No,' Alice said. 'Not *in* love. Never with anyone.'

'Till – now,' he said painfully.

'Till now.'

He gave a little grunt. Then there was a thump and she realised, from where his voice came from, that he had stood up.

'I'm going to bed.'

'Martin – '

'Don't worry,' he said, forcing a little bark of laughter. 'I'll do the decent thing. I'll sleep in the spare room.'

'You've been so – marvellous – '

'Long way to go yet – '

'Not tonight.'

'No,' he said. 'Not tonight.' And then he went softly across the dark room and opened the door and a faint gleam of light from the landing above illumined him in the doorway.

'Good night,' Alice said. 'Try and sleep.'

'You too.'

The door closed. She put her head back. In a minute she would telephone Clodagh, but for now she would sit there with her eyes shut and think of Martin and of the affection and admiration he aroused in her, which led, inevitably, to her feelings for Clodagh which had made all this possible, all this joy and richness and sadness, all this *life*. Whatever was coming now, Alice told herself, she could manage. Every muscle of her emotions was in condition to comfort and cope and see some way forward. She stretched her arms out in the darkness and flexed her fingers. The bridge – such a bridge – was crossed.

CHAPTER TWELVE

Anthony rang Cecily and told her he was going to Majorca for two weeks; a friend had lent him a villa.

'Where are you ringing from?'

'London.'

'I thought you were at Pitcombe – '

'I was. I left on Saturday. You can have too much village life.'

'Anthony,' Cecily said. 'What have you done?'

'Nothing – '

'Then why are you going to Majorca?'

'Because I'm a natural sponger, as you know, and I'm being given a fortnight's shelter in return for repainting a loggia. Luxury shelter, mind you.'

'I don't doubt it. How was everyone at Pitcombe?'

'Fine,' Anthony said heartily.

There was a pause, and then Cecily said, 'Well, off you go. And mind you *do* paint the loggia.'

'Trust me,' Anthony said and put the receiver down.

Cecily went out into the garden. Her white border was looking spectacular; it had taken eight years to achieve. She had planned it, she remembered, to celebrate Natasha's arrival, her first grandchild. She went down the length of it, stooping and peering, whipping out the odd grass that had seeded itself among the lupin spires, but she wasn't really concentrating. She was thinking about Anthony. About Anthony and Alice and Anthony's going to Majorca. When she had left Vienna, she had thought she would never be caught up, heart and soul, in human things again. She had gone on feeling like that, all through the early years of her marriage, even through Anthony's and Martin's childhoods, and when gardening took her over, it seemed to her quite natural that it should, quite natural that something passionate but platonic should fill up the vacuum she

160

had endured since she left Vienna. But ironically, the gardening had brought her back to a hunger for humanity; it seemed, quite simply, to have led that way. She told herself that it was far too late to reach Richard and that her sons were both, in their separate ways, alien to her – Anthony too unreliable and dangerous, Martin too conventional. And then came Alice, and because of Alice Cecily could make the connection, really make it, not just long to with Martin and Anthony – and she would have with Richard too, if he had allowed her anywhere near him. And now here she was, more than three times the age she had been when she left Vienna, as trapped in the intensity of family feeling as she had ever been in romantic and erotic love. Such feeling was, she discovered, pulling dead tufts off an artemesia, quite as intense and obsessive as her earlier passion had been. She could scarcely credit the number of wakeful nights and restless days that those very people she had resigned herself to being unsuited for – a natural accident, she would say – had caused her.

At the end of the white border there was a bower. It was made of golden hops trained around an arched trellis and it contained a stone seat with a back like an acanthus leaf. It had been photographed – twining gold-green fronds, lichened stone, clumps of grey-leaved, white-flowered rock rose – for a dozen books on English gardens. Even now, on a grey day without the brilliance of blue sky behind the brilliance of the hop leaves, it was a satisfaction to look at. Cecily stood in front of it for some time, and considered how long it was since she had had a really creative idea. It was almost as if you could pour your creativity into people or into your work but seldom into both. There simply wasn't *enough* for both. Men knew that. Men didn't even try to cover both. She could weep, she thought, standing there in front of her acanthus seat, she could simply weep at the frustration of this division, this unwanted intrusion into the wholeness of herself . . .

'Telephone!'

She turned. Dorothy was standing at the far end of the border flapping a duster. She began to walk quickly back.

'So sorry!' Dorothy said, 'but it sounds urgent. The vicar from Pitcombe – he says – '

'The *vicar* – '

'Yes. A Mr Morris – '

Cecily ran. In the hall, the telephone receiver lay beside a luminous white hydrangea in a Chinese bowl.

'Mr Morris?'

'Ah,' Peter said. 'I'm so glad to speak to you. Nobody's hurt. You must understand that. All your family are unhurt. But I think you should come. I think they need you. I think your son would like you to come.'

'What's happened?'

Peter Morris said carefully, 'There has been an emotional upset.'

'What sort? What do you mean?'

'Could you come? It would be easier to explain to you, if you came – '

It would not, really, and he knew it. It would never be easy to explain but it was always worse on the telephone, when one was unable to see the other person's face. He screwed his own face up at the reproduction on his study wall of Carpaccio's St Jerome at his desk with the little dog badgering him silently from the floor nearby, and said, 'Everybody is well and being cared for, but your family needs your support.'

'I'll come,' she said. 'I'll be two hours.'

'Come to the vicarage. Come to me first.'

'Yes,' she said. 'Yes.' And he could hear her voice falter.

He put the telephone down and looked at the chair where she would be sitting when he told her that her daughter-in-law and Clodagh Unwin had become lovers and appeared to have no intention of ceasing to be lovers. He would have to tell her how Alice had come to him the night before, in a very bad way indeed, and asserted that her husband had tried to rape her. Rape, she had said, over and over. 'He tried to force me. He's mad, he's *mad* – '

He had sat her down in the rectory kitchen and made tea. Alice told him how good Martin had been initially, how accepting, and then how he had suddenly changed and come bellowing at her, accusing Clodagh of trying to fob him off with being the Unwins' lawyer as compensation for taking Alice, and how he had flung her on the floor and wrenched at her clothes and his own and been uncontrollably violent and savage, shouting all the time and weeping, and how James had come in and that of course had stopped things. Then Martin had locked himself in the spare room and could be heard sobbing there, and Alice had rung Clodagh who came down from the Park to help her comfort James, and she had left them together and come here because they needed a doctor, she thought, and more than a doctor probably, she didn't know, she could hardly think . . . The mug of tea in her hand was jerking uncontrollably and tea was splashing down on to her skirt, great hot splashes she hardly seemed to notice, so Peter took away the mug and sat and watched her until he thought she might be able to tell him again, more slowly, what had happened.

'He kept roaring,' Alice said. 'He kept roaring at me, "You're a lesbian, do you hear me, you're a *lesbian*" – '

'But you are. If what you tell me of you and Clodagh is true, you are.'

'And is that so wrong?'

'Yes,' Peter Morris said. 'It is very wrong.'

She gazed at him. Her mass of hair was loose and wild.

'But it made everything better, happier – '

'No,' Peter said. 'That is an illusion. It was a selfish, short-term pleasure. There is nothing good in a pleasure which inevitably creates innocent victims.'

'And if I was a victim before?'

'Free will,' Peter said. 'Always a choice, all your life.'

'I'm not bad,' Alice said, weeping suddenly, 'I'm not a wicked woman.'

'I know that. Goodness, essential goodness, does not guarantee anyone against wrongdoing.'

'It isn't wrong! How can love be *wrong*?'

'In itself, it can't. It is what you do with it.'

He had then telephoned the doctor at King's Harcourt and had walked Alice home through the Sunday twilight to The Grey House where there was silence behind the spare room door and in the kitchen a subdued, uneasy quiet while Clodagh read to James, and Natasha at the table filled in the diagrams in a dot-to-dot book. James was on Clodagh's knee, but when Peter and Alice came in she set him on the floor and came across to Alice and put her arm round her. Peter could not look at them. He went over to the table and admired what Natasha was doing.

'They don't, of course, look *real*,' Natasha said, drawing on. 'Because of all the corners.'

James went across to Alice and Clodagh, his thumb in his mouth, and leaned against them. He was in his pyjamas. Alice stooped to lift him and he put his arms round her neck and stuck his bare foot sideways so that Clodagh could hold it.

'Dr Milligan is coming,' Alice said. 'He will give Daddy something to help him sleep.'

'When I had chicken pox,' Clodagh said, 'when I was little, Dr Milligan gave me a biro and told me to draw round every spot I could find. It took a whole day.'

James chuckled, his face in Alice's shoulder.

'I shall go upstairs,' Peter said. 'I shall go up and wait for the doctor.'

Alice carried James back to the Aga and sat down with him on her knee. Clodagh stayed where she was.

'Alice – '

'Yes?'

'You're not wavering? What did Peter say to you – '

'That what we have is wrong.'

Clodagh snorted.

'I hope you took no notice.'

'I must take notice. But it does not mean, if I take notice, that my mind is changed.'

Natasha looked up and watched Clodagh.

'And your heart?' Clodagh said. Her head was high. She was wearing a brief, pale grey dress and she stood upright in it, a narrow shaft under her cloud of hair.

'Of all people,' Alice said, 'you know about my heart.'

Clodagh came forward suddenly and leaned on the table. She said urgently to Alice, 'It's real you know. *Real*. It isn't just *pour épater le bourgeoisie*.'

'I know.'

Clodagh put her hand on Natasha's.

'It isn't selfish. It's giving. It folds in other people. It's what's best in women – '

'Clodagh,' Alice said, 'I know.'

Tears were running down Clodagh's face. She took no notice of them and they dripped on to the table.

'You *must* know it,' Clodagh said. 'Everyone must. They must see that it is as strong and real as ordinary love. I never knew that before but now I do. Oh, *Alice* – '

They were all watching her. James had taken his thumb out. Alice stretched out a hand.

'Clodagh. Clodagh, why all this, why worry – '

'Because of the centre line,' Clodagh cried out, letting go Natasha's hand and covering her wet face with her own. 'Because of that. Because I'm afraid of it, because I'm afraid it will pull you back, it will, it *will* – '

Natasha got hurriedly off her chair and came to her mother. Alice took her hand. She sat upright in her chair, holding her children, and although her face was quite drained by fatigue, she said in a voice of great calm, 'You needn't be afraid.'

Clodagh took her hands away from her face and went over to the roll of kitchen paper on the dresser and tore off a strip and blew her nose ferociously.

'Alice. Oh my precious Alice. You are such an innocent – '

And then the doctor had come. He had gone upstairs with Peter Morris to Martin, who, bruised to his very depths by his own behaviour as well as by the bitter discoveries of the last twenty-four hours, had conducted himself with the passive courtesy of a well-brought-up schoolboy, and had been helped into pyjamas and into bed, and given an injection to help him to sleep. Outside on the landing, with a weary distaste, Peter Morris explained the circumstances to Dr Milligan and then the two men went down to the kitchen and found that Clodagh had gone and that Alice was sitting at the table playing hangman with her children.

Dr Milligan said he would call again tomorrow but he thought Martin should be taken away for a while.

'So that,' he said to Alice, 'you can put your house in order.'

Alice said nothing. She stared at the spot on the table where the hanging lamp made a neat circle of apricot light.

'It isn't "F",' Natasha said. 'Only four more wrong and I've hanged you.'

Alice felt the two men looking down at her, big, grey-haired men in a late Sunday comfortableness of clothes. She heard Clodagh in her mind, Clodagh saying to her, laughingly, 'Why should men despise you? Honestly, you're a walking stereotype. Do women despise gay men? Alice, Alice – '

She looked up with difficulty.

'I will ring your mother-in-law in the morning,' Peter Morris said.

'Oh – '

'Yes,' he said firmly.

Doctor Milligan moved away towards the door.

'I'd get those children to bed if I were you. And yourself.' He opened the stable door. 'Rain,' he said, and went out into it.

Peter Morris came round the table and laid a brief passing hand on each child's head.

'You can always ring me – '

'Yes.'

'Martin will sleep all night.'

'Yes.'

'Get to bed now.'

When he had gone, Natasha said, sighing, 'It was all Uncle Anthony, wasn't it?'

'Well, partly – '

'Will Daddy be better in the morning?'

'A bit better.'

'Who's doing the school run?'

Alice thought.

'Mrs Alleyne.'

James's lip trembled.

'No – '

'It's her turn – '

'I want Clodagh – '

'Yes. Yes. I know.'

She stood up and took James's hand.

'Come on. Bed.'

He trailed after her, dragging on her hand. They went slowly up the stairs, past the eloquently closed spare room door, and along the passage to James's room where his bed awaited him under a fly-past of model aeroplanes. He looked very small and fragile in bed. The sight of the back of his neck filled Alice with panic. She kissed him quickly for fear she might cry before she was out of the room, and for once he did not beseech her to stay, but put his forbidden thumb in and turned docilely on his side.

In her room next door, Natasha was settling Princess Power into her pink plastic castle for the night. Without turning, she said, 'Should I say goodnight to Daddy?'

'I think he is fast asleep. Have you put out your ballet things, for tomorrow?'

Natasha nodded. Tomorrow, Alice thought. Monday, ballet class, community shop, Clodagh to see to the children at teatime, Martin awake again, Cecily coming, Gwen coming, everyone beginning to know. And before that, this night to get through. She went over to Natasha and kissed her.

'The moment she's organised, Tashie, you hop in. I'll come in later, when I've had a bath.'

'I wish,' Natasha said, 'that I could have her Power Chariot too.'

'Perhaps, for your birthday – '

Natasha began to talk, softly and intimately, into the pinkly mirrored throne room. Alice went out and closed the door. Then she listened at all the other doors, even, after a struggle, at the spare room door, and then she went along to her own bedroom and took her shoes off and lay down on her bed. She did not turn the light on. She simply lay there in the pale darkness and stared up into it, and outside, in the summer night, the rain pattered down on to the hard, dry ground.

'What are you telling me?' Cecily said, but she didn't really mean it. She knew.

Peter Morris said nothing more. He got up and went over to the window and looked out at his damp garden.

'And the doctor?'

'He went to The Grey House this morning. He thinks you should take Martin home with you for a few days. He needs looking after.' He turned from the window. 'The results of shock, you see. What might, a century ago, have been called a brainstorm.'

Cecily had her eyes closed.

'This whole business is grotesque.'

'But it is happening.'

She opened her eyes and spread her arms out to his study walls.

'But here – '

'In Pitcombe?'

'Yes.'

'Humanity is no different. It's just that the setting is prettier than, say, Solihull. And no crowds to hide in.'

Cecily said with a kind of stiff shyness, 'It must seem absurd to you, but I have never encountered such – such a – a situation before.'

'Nor I,' Peter said. 'Men yes. But not women. It is quite different, with women.'

Cecily shut her eyes again.

'No doubt – '

Peter Morris crossed the room and laid his hand on her arm.

'We must go round to The Grey House.'

'The children – '

'They are at school.'

'Not the baby.'

'The baby is where he should be,' Peter said. 'With his mother.'

Cecily allowed herself to be helped from the chair and guided from the house. The village street was empty except for Stuart Mott trimming the two green moustaches of privet that separated Miss Pimm's harsh little front garden from the pavement. He looked up when he saw them coming and gave a tossing nod of his head to show that he couldn't possibly relinquish the handles of his shears to wave. He knew who Cecily was. It looked, from the way she was walking, as if she had some bad news to break at The Grey House. Perhaps Mr Jordan's father had died or something had happened to that brother. Miss Pimm, dusting her dead mother's bureau in the front first-floor room, saw them too, and remembered that she had seen Peter Morris walking Alice along like that, as if sheltering an invalid, only the night before. Miss Pimm picked up her mother's inflexible photograph. The night of her mother's fatal stroke, she had gone straight to the rectory, just run there, even before she telephoned the surgery. It was the only time in her life she had ever tasted brandy.

'Is – is it known,' Cecily said, 'in the village?'

'Not yet.'

'Must it be?'

'It can't be stopped – '

'Why should not Alice go,' Cecily said, suddenly angry and turning upon Peter. 'Why must it be poor Martin – '

'The children.'

'Yes – '

'My feeling is that Martin and Alice must heal separately before they come together again to heal their marriage.'

Cecily snorted.

'Their marriage! My dear Mr Morris, that is surely over – '

'Not at all.'

He gripped her arm to cross the street.

'Such a betrayal,' Cecily said, thinking not solely of Martin.

'No worse, I think, than conventional adultery. Both are sins. Neither need destroy a marriage, given sufficient support.'

In the lane leading to The Grey House they met first the milk float and then a pick-up truck bearing Martin's heavy-duty lawn mower away for repair. In the last cottage garden, a rubber sheet blew on the washing line beside several pairs of immense pyjamas. At the gateway, Peter Morris took Cecily's arm more firmly and led her across the front of the house and round to the stable door to the kitchen. The top half was open and inside, in jeans and a checked shirt, very pale and with extremely neat hair, Martin sat at the table with the newspaper before him.

He looked up when their figures darkened the doorway, and then stood up, and said, 'Hello, Mother,' and came over and opened the door and kissed her cheek. Then he said, 'Good morning, Peter,' and stood back, politely, as if there was nothing more he could do.

Cecily put her arms round him. He stood and allowed her to. Then he said, 'Would you like some coffee? I expect there is some.'

'Darling,' Cecily said. 'Darling.'

'Please,' Martin said. He put her arms away.

'I've come to take you home, darling. I've come to take you home with me for a while – '

'I should like that,' Martin said.

'My car is at the rectory – '

She looked round the room.

'Where is Alice?'

Martin said carefully, 'Alice is taking Charlie for a walk in his pushchair. She would be glad for me to be at Dummeridge.'

Cecily gave a savage little yelp.

'I am *sure* she would!'

Martin's face immediately creased with distress and Peter Morris came forward and took his arm.

'Of course she would. She wants to see you better. We all do.'

'Heaven knows what Milligan gave me last night,' Martin said. 'I feel as if I'd been hit with a sledgehammer.' He put his hand to his face. 'I tried to ring the office. Alice said – '

Cecily put her arm around him.

'Don't worry about those things. Don't worry about anything. We'll take care of them.'

'My bag,' Martin said. 'I packed my bag – '

Peter went upstairs to look for it. On the landing, he found Gwen, bundling sheets into a pillowcase for the laundry.

'That's his mother come then?'

'Yes – '

Gwen believed clergymen had a threefold social duty to baptise, marry and bury and no business to step beyond it.

'I suppose you got her to come?'

'I am looking for Mr Jordan's bag – '

'If you'd wanted to be useful,' Gwen said, pushing in sheets patterned with Paddington Bear, 'You'd have sent Clodagh packing weeks ago.' She jerked her head towards an open door. 'You'll find Mr Jordan's bag in there.'

'Gwen. Gwen, I hope you'll stay. At least until Mr Jordan gets back – '

'Depends,' Gwen said, 'on what I'm asked to do. Doesn't it.'

Peter said with some asperity, 'I don't seem to remember you having any moral difficulties with Major Murray-French's girl-friends.'

Gwen gathered up the bursting pillowcase.

'That was different, wasn't it? That was *normal*.' She moved towards the stairs. 'If I stay, it'll be because of the kids. You can't despise the kids, can you?'

Alice, on the river path with Charlie, saw Cecily's car go down the village street, cross the bridge and climb easily up the opposite hill, southward. She could see two heads in it. When it had disappeared, she put Charlie into his pushchair with his drooping bunch of buttercups, and pushed him resolutely up the street, talking to him animatedly. Cathy Fanshawe, coming out of the shop, saw her and ran across to say breathlessly that the fête had made nine hundred and fifty-one pounds, would you believe it? Alice said how wonderful. Cathy thanked her profusely for her stall and ran back

170

again to her car. Soon Cathy Fanshawe would know why Martin had been taken away by his mother.

In the kitchen at The Grey House, Clodagh was frying a sausage for Charlie's lunch. Gwen had pointedly gone home. Clodagh too had waited until Cecily's car had pulled away from the rectory. She had had nothing to do all morning but wait. She had meant to speak to her mother, but Margot had gone up to London early for a dental appointment and lunch at the Parrot Club. The speaking would have to happen that evening or else Margot would hear, distortedly, from the village, and Clodagh wished her to know that she, Clodagh, would be leaving quite soon, and taking Alice and the children with her, to Windover. She had said nothing of this to Alice. She was waiting until she and Alice were alone.

When Alice came in, she put Charlie into his highchair and then went over to Clodagh and held her. Neither of them said anything. Charlie, looking for something he could reach, found the telephone cable and pulled it, so that the receiver clattered off and Alice had to come to its rescue.

'Awful *boy*.'

Charlie beamed.

'I am a coward,' Alice said. 'I couldn't face Cecily.'

'There are quite a lot of cowards around here,' Clodagh said, turning the sausage, 'and you ain't one.'

She put the sausage in Charlie's dish, with a chopped-up tomato, took it over to him, and cut it up.

'Nah,' Charlie said.

'It's all you're getting.'

He blipped the pieces of sausage with his spoon. Clodagh put her hand on Alice's shoulder.

'Sandwich?'

'No thanks. Nothing. Not hungry.'

'Alice,' Clodagh said, 'this is no moment to have the vapours. We are just beginning to get somewhere.'

Alice smiled. She picked up Clodagh's hand and laid her cheek on it.

'It's not the vapours. It's lack of sleep and lots to think about. And anyway, I must go. Shop day.'

Clodagh opened the door.

'I'll be here when you get back. We all will. Waiting for you.'

171

They stood and looked at each other. Then Alice leaned forward and kissed her and went out into the garden towards the drive.

The Community Shop was standing as usual in the yard behind the post office. Also as usual, Mr Finch was standing on some aluminium steps washing the windscreen with a plastic bucket in one hand and a sponge in the other. The back doors of the van were open, and what was not usual was that Mrs Finch, in a frilled floral blouse, was inside stocking up the shelves. Mrs Finch prided herself on having no manual part in the business though she kept an eagle eye on the books, and if she was minding the shop when a customer wanted potatoes she would pull on rubber gloves before she touched them and make it very plain, with deprecating remarks and smiles, how unaccustomed she was to this aspect of what she called the commercial world.

Alice went up the steps into the van.

'Hello, Mrs Finch. No Michelle?'

Mrs Finch paused, holding two bottles of vinegar.

'No, Mrs Jordan. No Michelle.'

'Is she ill? She was fine on Saturday – '

'She is quite well. She is serving in the shop.'

'I see,' said Alice, who didn't. 'Well, let me do that. I know you don't like it – '

'Mrs Jordan,' said Mrs Finch, clasping her bottles, 'I am not one to flinch.'

She took a breath. She had rehearsed this to herself several times, ever since Gwen's astonishing visit to the shop shortly after midday. She put the bottles in their allotted place and turned towards Alice with her hands folded against her sunray pleated skirt.

'Mrs Jordan, I am sure you will not misunderstand me. I am also sure you will understand why I must, out of delicacy, say this to you, rather than allow Mr Finch to. Michelle will not be on the van with you this afternoon because her mother has requested that she shall not be.'

Alice began to laugh.

'Don't be *idiotic* – '

Mrs Finch watched her.

'I've lived a bit, Mrs Jordan. There isn't much I haven't seen. I'm not one to judge. But I'll tell you that in not judging, I am very rare. Very rare indeed.'

172

CHAPTER THIRTEEN

'**Y**ou will not,' Sir Ralph said, banging his fist into his open palm, 'stay here one more hour. You will not. You will leave Pitcombe.'

His face was scarlet. Margot and Lettice Deverel, who had been summoned from a peaceable kitchen supper with the parrot, both endeavoured to speak, but he brandished his arms at them, commanding them silence.

'I put all my faith in you. All my faith. And you have betrayed me and perverted all the decency of your upbringing – '

'Ralph,' Margot cried. 'Ralph. Don't be so exaggerated. It doesn't help. Clodagh is still Clodagh.'

'Of all people,' Sir Ralph said. 'Of all my treasured people.'

Clodagh was sitting very upright on a small sofa in her father's library. She had gone to her mother soon after her return from London about seven o'clock and it was now after ten. Mrs Shadwell had as usual left a cold supper in the kitchen but nobody had been near it. It seemed, when she had begun upon it, that there was far more for Clodagh to tell her parents than she had supposed, particularly as she had had to repeat many things and explain many more. The separateness of her intimate life, which she had come to believe was inviolable, seemed not to be so; the purity of her independence was, before her eyes, being trodden all over by violent distress and abhorrence. Margot had not, whatever her feelings, said one unkind word. Her father had made it plain that her sexual tastes revolted and bemused him and that he was personally outraged that she should have sought to gratify them in Pitcombe. She had tried to explain about love, and it was his reaction to that that had sent her mother to the telephone for Lettice Deverel.

Sir Ralph had always been fond of Lettice. Privately he admired her brain and strength of personality, and publicly he called her, with affection, our jolly old bohemian. When Lettice came into the room, still in her gardening trousers, he held his hands out to her piteously and said, 'What are we to do? Oh, my dear, what is to become of us?'

Lettice had taken his hands and kissed him, and then gone over to kiss Clodagh, before saying, 'We are not going to lose our heads.'

'You don't understand – '

'My dear Ralph, I do. I understand you all.'

He had been calmer then, and while Lettice talked to him Clodagh had sat with her head bent and attempted to quiet her own storm of rage by thinking of Alice. No one should say a word against Alice, she was resolved upon that. But then her father did, he could not help himself; he cried out that Alice must have persuaded his daughter and Clodagh screamed with fury at him and then he said she must leave Pitcombe within the hour. It was melodramatic, crude, stupid, oh all those things and worse, but it was human and, most of all, it was *happening*.

'There is no end to the horror,' Sir Ralph said. 'It will be round the village like wildfire, round the county. The reputation of centuries – '

'Ralph,' Lettice said warningly.

'It *will*,' he insisted.

'It will be a nine days' wonder. What *do* you suppose goes on inside some of your own cottages? In intimate matters,' Lettice said, placing a hand on each of her trousered knees, 'your tenants are infinitely more experienced than you.'

He glared at her.

'How dare you.'

She was unperturbed.

'It will be a nine days' wonder. Seven if Clodagh goes quickly.'

Margot made a little mewing sound of misery.

'We are both going,' Clodagh said. 'Alice and me. We will go together.'

'I hope not.'

'Alice has *children*,' Margot said.

'They come too.'

'I hope not,' Lettice said again. She looked at Clodagh. 'That should not be the future. There *is* no future in that. The future lies in you using your able head for the first time in your life. It wouldn't hurt you – ' She paused. 'It wouldn't hurt you to learn to be alone.'

Clodagh turned her head away.

'You may have been spoiled,' Lettice said. 'There's no call to spoil yourself.'

Clodagh's teeth were clenched.

'I'm thinking of Alice.'

'Are you? And her children no doubt. How will they fare, brought up as they have been, if you take them to Dorset and expect local society to accept you both as an ordinary couple? Rural society can't do it. Maybe city society can, though I doubt it does. I believe it to be thin, sham stuff. And what has their father done, beyond be a man? A dull man perhaps, an unexciting, inhibited man, but no brute. Just a man. Live with that, will you? World well lost for love, eh?' Lettice leaned forward and prodded the air towards Clodagh. 'If Alice was a free woman, I'd say off with the pair of you and good luck to you. Shut up, Ralph. But she's not and I can't say it.'

Clodagh felt not only anger now but fear. She couldn't delude herself that Lettice was a conventional, orthodox, right-wing old puritan, however hard she tried, and if *Lettice* said they couldn't because of the children . . . She tossed her head. Nonsense. Of course they could. The battle would just be bloodier. She said so.

'I shall never have your children at my knee,' Sir Ralph said suddenly, ignoring her remark.

Margot, even in the emotional state she was in, could not look at Lettice.

'If that's what's worrying you,' Clodagh said brutally, 'I can easily bear a man for *that* – '

Sir Ralph gave a little cry. Margot got out of her chair and came across to slap Clodagh's hand.

'Behave yourself!'

'Bed,' Lettice said, getting up.

'Well, certainly no more of *this* – '

Clodagh got up too and went swiftly over to the door. It was huge and panelled and painted white, and as she stood against it for a moment before she opened it she looked to Margot as she had looked before she was twelve, when the mischief of her childhood turned into the waywardness of her adolescence.

175

'You are *not*,' said Lettice, watching Margot, 'going to start asking yourself where you went wrong.'

Clodagh went up the dim stairs without putting the lights on. The air was deep misty blue, but not dark. On the landing the enormous Chinese ginger jars that had come home with an adventuring eighteenth-century Unwin gleamed like fat-bellied barbaric gods. There were eight of them, on rosewood plinths, and as a child Clodagh had named each one. Now she went past them as if they were strangers, past the little Chippendale sofa where she had posed, every birthday, for a photograph, past the naïve painting of pigs she had always said she would *kill* Georgina for (and Georgina had half-believed her), past the icon of St Nicholas she had once believed could see her conscience, past the cabinet of fans and the cabinet of snuff-boxes, past her mother's bedroom door and off the plushy broadloom overlaid with Afghan rugs of the main landing, on to the haircord of the old nursery passage and her bedroom which looked south towards the beeches, the beeches which hid Alice from her view.

She knelt on the window seat and looked hard down through the beeches. Alice was there. Alice, who needed her. Alice whom she had rescued. That had been the most exhilarating discovery of Clodagh's life, that discovery that Alice didn't believe, deep down, in her own value. When that became plain to Clodagh, when she saw that however different, however stylish Alice *looked*, she didn't have real faith in herself, she even doubted the worth of what she *was*, out here in the demanding conventionality of country life – then Clodagh had felt real intoxication coming on. *She* could wave the wand. She could do for Alice what Alice couldn't quite do for herself.

And she had done it. Alice was changed, but then, so was she. She laid her cheek against the smooth wood of the folded shutters. She needed Alice now. She hadn't meant to; in fact, having never needed anyone, only wanted them, briefly, it hadn't occurred to her that needing might happen. The thought of not having Alice made her want to scream and scream, hysterically, and break things. Nobody should make her bear such pain. Alice was *hers*. She would woo her again, a second time. She had wooed her to be hers, now she would woo her to be hers for ever, to come away with her.

She leaned forward so that her forehead rested on the window-

176

pane. It was nearly as dark as it would get. If she went and stood in front of St Nicholas now, and stared at his intractable dark Byzantine face, she would be able to look at him without a tremor. She had done a good thing. After a quarter of a century of doubtful goodness, Clodagh had no doubt that now she was on the right track. She had made an unhappy woman happy, and the happiness had spread all round her, to her children, to her friends, to the village. As for Martin – well, that was a slight casualty, but one outweighed by all the benefits. Clodagh's mind went rapidly over Martin, a small thing taken in proportion to the whole. In any case, he had, consciously or unconsciously, damaged Alice. And it was Clodagh who had healed her.

She left the window and went over to her bed and put on the lamp beside it. A moth with a pale furry head and black pin-dotted wings immediately began to bang senselessly about inside the shade. Clodagh watched it. Then she spread out her hands in the glow of the lamplight and looked at them. On the wedding finger, she wore the silver band Alice had given her. She had given Alice a ring too, a ring as fine as a thread, and Alice had slipped it on her own wedding finger, under the ring Martin had given her. They had not spoken at all during that little ceremony, just sat, touching hands, across Alice's kitchen table one afternoon while Charlie, on the floor, rattled a wooden spoon inside a plastic mug and shouted at it. That was how it had always been, so unstagey, so strong and unsentimental, so *real*. And that was how it would always be.

'I'm so sorry,' Alice said, 'I don't quite understand. Will you come in?'

Rosie Barton said she would love to. She followed Alice across the hall and into the kitchen and Alice could feel her eagerness at her back, like an electric fire.

'Coffee?' Alice said.

'I'd *love* it. What a morning!'

She sat herself down at the table which still bore the children's breakfast bowls and leaned on her folded arms and said with immense solicitousness, 'How *are* you?'

Alice had her back to her, putting the kettle on the Aga. She said, 'I'm all right, thank you.'

177

Rosie said, '*Alice –* '

Alice turned. Rosie was not smiling but her whole face and attitude exuded sympathy.

'Look,' Rosie said, spreading her hands on the table. 'Look, I know we don't know each other very well, but I hope we can rapidly put that right.' She smiled. 'I'd like to. We'd like to. Alice, I've come to offer you our support, mine and Gerry's. I don't want you to be in any doubt about it.'

Alice put her hands behind her back and gripped the Aga rail. God, why wasn't Clodagh here? But she was taking the school run into Salisbury, because she had said she would be better able to brazen it out with Sarah Alleyne than Alice.

'I'm afraid,' Rosie Barton said, and her voice was very kind, 'I'm afraid a place like Pitcombe has some very archaic attitudes. They can't be changed overnight, but we won't give up because of that, I can promise you. But Gerry and I were worried that you might feel quite isolated. We feel it is always such a help to know you are not alone.'

Alice went over to the dresser and took down two mugs. Then she put coffee into the glass filter jug and poured boiling water on to it, and put it, and the mugs, on the table among the cereal boxes and jam jars.

'You don't have to say anything,' Rosie said. 'I can imagine how you feel.'

Alice said as gently as she could that she didn't think so. Rosie took no notice of this but began to describe the many gay friends she and Gerry had, had always had, and how much they valued them and what sweet people they were. In fact, their youngest's godfather was gay and he was a wonderful person and had been in a stable relationship for years.

'Gerry and I,' she said, 'regard it as perfectly natural.'

Alice pushed the plunger of the coffee pot down, very slowly.

'Then you are wrong. It isn't natural but it's as strong as if it were. For some people, it is stronger *and* preferable to what is natural.'

'*Exactly,*' said Rosie Barton.

Alice poured coffee.

'It's kind of you to want to help, but I don't think you can. And I don't think we want help – '

'But the village – '

'I know,' Alice said. She had yet to brave the shop, but today Gwen had said that she would not come to the house if Alice and Clodagh were in it together. Alice had laughed at her absurdity and Gwen had become very huffy, and Alice had suddenly seen that she was about to cry, and that she was in a real confusion of prejudice and affection, and been sorry, and said so.

'I'm afraid,' Rosie said, spooning brown sugar into her mug, 'that people *are* talking.'

'Of course they are. But they won't talk for long.'

Rosie looked disappointed, but she said bravely, 'Well, that's a wonderful attitude.'

'Not really. It's more a sort of recognition.'

'And your husband?'

Alice stared at her.

'This really is none of your business.'

'I'm so sorry, I was only trying to help – '

'I've told you,' Alice said, 'you can't, and I don't want it.'

Rosie stood up.

'Alice, I know you're upset. Who wouldn't be? I could kick myself, I've come far too soon. But I must tell you this. I do have experience of campaigns. A *lot* of experience. And you can't run them alone, it simply isn't possible. So in a week or two, just remember we are there. Anything we can do, anything – '

'I am not a campaign,' Alice said. 'We are not. We never will be. We are people.'

'Yes, of *course*.'

Rosie began to move towards the kitchen door. Her mind was already forming the profoundly understanding things she would say to Gerry about Alice. It was, of course, the fault of the village. The sheer weight of intolerance and narrow-mindedness was enough to drive anyone on to the defensive. From the doorway, she gave Alice a little smile and wave.

'We're always there. Don't forget.'

'Give me the whole village baying for blood,' Alice said later to Clodagh, 'the whole of Wiltshire if you like. Anything, anybody, rather than one more minute of Rosie Barton's sympathetic understanding.'

Then she made sick noises, and the children, who were eating tea

179

in a desultory way, were enchanted by her and enthusiastically joined in.

Miss Payne was so fond of Alice. Doing the church flowers with Alice had been such fun after all those years of Cathy Fanshawe and her passion for silk flowers when there were lovely real things in the garden, even if they didn't last and shed petals three days after they were done. When Miss Payne heard about Alice and Clodagh she had been desperately upset and had had to take her angina pills again after not having to take them for seven months. Of course, Miss Pimm wouldn't speak of it at all but just went round the village looking like the spinster aunt in a Giles cartoon, the one in a permanent state of shock. Buntie Payne wasn't shocked so much as made utterly miserable. Every time she thought of Alice – and try as she might, she *kept* thinking of Alice – she thought of those little children and Alice being so sweet to her over some broken delphiniums, and all that Alice and Martin had done to the house, and the life of the village. That made her cry and then she had to put another tiny white tablet under her tongue, and *make* herself sit still.

But when she sat still she had even more time to think, and then she thought about love which, in her virgin state, was very much more interesting and real to her than sex had ever been. She had never really loved a man beyond members of her own family, but she had loved – did love – women all right. Feeling the tablet fizzing away beneath her tongue, she asked herself what on earth she would do without her sister Marjorie, even if she did live in Taunton, and her friend Phyllis who lived at King's Harcourt and whom she saw at least twice a week. She had said something of this to Lettice Deverel whom she had met on the field path that ran parallel to the village street behind the cottages, and Lettice had said, 'It's one of the curses of our age. Sex has driven out friendship.'

Buntie Payne had said, did she mean the sixties and the permissive society, and Lettice had said well, partly, but the rot had begun with the Bloomsbury Group, much earlier.

'The moment self-indulgence gets into the hands of the intellectuals,' Lettice said, 'society is in for sailing in a rudderless ship. It is now considered bourgeois to control yourself.'

Buntie hadn't really known what she was talking about, but being seized by a sudden spasm of bewildered, unhappy sympathy for Alice, cried out, 'They mustn't make it hard for her!'

And Lettice said that you couldn't stop them; all you could do was not join them.

'Hypocrisy being, as it is, a national pastime – '

Buntie didn't need telling that. She had heard Sally Mott and Janet Crudwell airing their opinion of Alice in the village shop only the day after Janet's two eldest had been brought back by the military police from Lark Hill Camp at three in the morning. Buntie, choosing onions one by one, had been seized with indignation, and when Sally and Janet had left the shop and she had been handing her bag of onions to Mr Finch she had heard herself demand, 'So. A hunger for love or a greed for money. Where do *you* stand on that?'

But Mr Finch, whose imaginative capacities had recently been so stretched he could summon up neither opinion nor poetry, had simply goggled at her, and said, 'Pardon?'

'It's awful of me,' Juliet Dunne said to Henry, holding her face in both hands, 'but the whole thing absolutely turns me up.'

Henry was filleting a kipper with extreme precision.

'I really don't want to talk about it – '

'No, darling, but you never *want* to talk about anything in the least personal. Looking back, I can't quite remember how you conveyed to me that you wanted to marry me. Did I set you a questionnaire?'

Henry buttered toast in silence.

'The thing is, I've simply got to talk to you because I have to get all this off my chest and you are all I have, by way of audience. *Please* stop crunching.'

Henry put his toast down with an air of obliging martyrdom.

'How can you *eat*?'

He looked at his forbidden toast.

'With great difficulty.'

'*Henry*,' Juliet said, and began to cry again.

She had cried quite a lot of the night, and the previous evening. It wasn't that Henry wasn't sorry for her, because he was, but he was having rather a bad time with his own feelings and until he had got to grips with them, he hadn't much energy to spare for Juliet.

'Aren't you revolted?' Juliet said between sobs.

Henry sneaked a morsel of kipper. He was revolted; less so than if Alice and Clodagh had been two men, but revolted all the same. And puzzled, intensely puzzled. And somehow let down, almost betrayed, almost – heavens, almost *humiliated*.

Juliet blew her nose.

'It's incredibly reactionary of me, I'm sure, but it's the truth. It turns everything upside down. It makes such a nonsense of everything we were brought up to. I *hate* it. I feel sick and I feel lost.'

Henry picked up his toast again with one hand and reached out to pat Juliet with the other.

'I've known Clodagh all my life,' Juliet said. 'I can't *believe* it. All my life and she's been like this. And Alice. I *loved* Alice. There was no one else I could complain to like I could to Alice – '

'She isn't dead,' Henry pointed out.

'How can *anything*,' Juliet said, getting up to fetch the coffee percolator, 'be the same again after this?'

'Not the *same* – '

'Trust goes,' Juliet said. 'Once that goes, you've had it. That's why I couldn't possibly stay married to you if you slept with anyone else. I'd never trust you again so we'd have nothing to build on any more.'

Henry looked down at his plate and thought of Alice, and how he felt about Alice. And now here was Juliet talking as if Alice had deceived her personally and in so doing had destroyed the vital trust in a friendship.

'Alice is your girlfriend,' Henry said, 'not your husband.'

Juliet began to pour coffee, unsteadily, mopping at her nose with a tissue.

'She was special to me.' She stopped pouring. 'At the moment, I hate Clodagh. *Hate* her.'

'Shouldn't do that – '

'Well I *do*.'

Henry pushed his plate away.

'That's not going to help Alice.'

'She doesn't *want* help – '

'How do you know?'

182

'Rosie Barton went to see her and got very short shrift – '

'And when did you and Rosie Barton ever see eye to eye about anything?'

Juliet hid her face behind her coffee mug.

'Henry. The truth is I don't know what I'd say to Alice because I don't know what I *feel* – '

'Why don't you just ring and say you're still friends?'

'But *are* we?' Juliet cried. '*Are* we? I mean, can we be after this?'

Henry stood up and began to rattle the change softly in his trouser pockets. He said, 'I'm going to see Martin.'

Juliet stared.

'What'll you *say* to him?'

'Dunno. Nothing probably, nothing much.'

'*Poor* Martin – '

'Yes.'

He went round the table to Juliet and she leaned tiredly against him.

'You're behaving much better than I am,' Juliet said. 'But then you always have. Haven't you.'

He put his arms round her and stooped to kiss the top of her head.

'No,' Henry said.

Martin had several visitors from Pitcombe besides Henry. Sir Ralph Unwin came, and so did John Murray-French and Peter Morris. Only Sir Ralph spoke of Alice and Clodagh directly, but that was more, Martin could see, because he was literally exploding with his own feelings than because he thought it best to be straightforward with Martin. Martin was thrown, but he didn't blame Sir Ralph for letting go any more than he blamed Henry or John or Peter for not letting go. He himself behaved with great control while they were there. Only when they were gone, and Cecily was safely in her study or in the garden, did he give way to the consuming and inarticulate rage that possessed him. At night it took the form of hideous dreams, dreams of violence and savagery and killing that sometimes had in them people he had not thought about for years like the prefect at school who had told him how pretty he was and who had then – because Martin had been afraid and disinclined to do what he wanted – instituted a campaign of brilliantly subtle mental cruelty.

The rage was more exhausting than anything Martin had ever known. It fed on everybody, everything, and it refused to subject itself to reason. It boiled in him like some seething, evil broth, and whether he controlled it or gave vent to it out on the cliffs with his mother's dogs, he felt no better. Sometimes he thought he would burst, and often he wished he would, trapped as he was in this boiling cauldron. Cecily would say to him sorrowfully that she wished he could let go. If only she knew! He suspected that if he let go entirely, he would die, and most days, for a spell at least, he wished for that. He imagined the cool, quiet, dark state of nothingness because, when it came to the crunch of thinking about Heaven, he discovered that he didn't want to believe there was one. He could not bear the thought of any further existence, in whatever form. The most desirable state was nothingness, just not to be. That seemed to him the only state in which there could be no torment.

The only crumb of comfort – the smallest crumb – came from the oddest quarter, from his father. When Richard came home from a journey to Australia, Martin saw at once, and to his amazement, that Richard perceived his rage. Richard made much less fuss of him than Cecily but he was, for all that, much more tender. He made Martin feel that he was not a broken child but a fellow man. Martin heard him, one morning, saying to Cecily in a voice of great anger, 'For God's sake, will you allow him his *dignity*?'

He could not hear Cecily's reply. He was sure she made one because she never let accusations just stand, she always had to defend herself. She looked old and tired just now. So, Martin thought, looking in the shaving mirror each morning, did he. He avoided looking at himself except for shaving because somehow the sight of his face made him desperate for his children, for Charlie particularly, in his cheerful baby simplicity. And he couldn't think of them because that led back to Alice, to himself and Alice, man and woman, and then, of course, the path of thought went downwards suddenly into the roaring cavern of his anguish and his rage.

Richard cancelled a follow-up trip to Australia because of Martin.

Instead he told Martin they were going to pull down a stone shed that had once held a primitive pump engine, and use the stones to repair the wall at the far end of the famous potager. In the fields beyond, the fields that ran up between the woods towards the sea, they were harvesting, early. The huge combine, like a vast ship, went calmly up and down the golden slopes leaving behind it the shorn earth and the great rolled bales. At midday, there was always an hour of quiet and the odd bold rabbit would streak across the fields and vanish into the sanctuary of the woods. The air smelled of burned earth and dust because, although the sun rarely came out, it sailed imprisoned behind a steady veil of cloud which kept the land heavy and warm and quiet. Martin and Richard worked mostly in silence. Martin said once, 'I'd forgotten how good you are at this sort of thing.'

And Richard, turning a piece of stone in his hands to see how it would fit, said, 'So had I. I sometimes think I've quite a lot of talents I didn't exercise. Usually through my own fault.'

When the wall was finished, Martin said he wanted to return to work. Cecily grew very agitated and said how could he, where would he live, who would look after him, was he going to divorce Alice? He said he didn't know about divorce, in fact he didn't know about anything much, just now, except that he wanted to stop feeling an invalidish freak and go back to work. He would live, he said, with the Dunnes. Henry and Juliet had invited him for as long as he wanted.

'But I shall have nothing left,' Cecily said later, fiercely, to Richard.

'There's me – '

'You! You need nobody. You never have.'

'I am made up,' Richard said, 'of exactly the same human components of need as you.'

And he went away then, and by some instinct went up to the old playroom in the attic and found Martin there, with a tumbler of whisky, weeping without restraint because he had thought nobody would hear him.

CHAPTER FOURTEEN

Most days one of the children asked when Martin would be better enough to come home. Usually Alice said, soon. Once a week Juliet came over and picked them up and took them home with her so that they could see Martin, and the night after these visits James usually wet his bed. It was the school holidays and the days yawned for occupation. Alice devised a list of duties, and Natasha's was to go down to the shop. She liked this because all down the street people stopped and talked to her and asked her how she was and Mrs Finch would come out of the back part of the shop and give her sweets and sometimes a kiss pungent with Coty's 'L'Aimant'. The rest of the day she did not like so much. The feeling in the house was peculiar, without her father, and she missed school, and Sophie, who had been taken to Corfu by her family. She spent a lot of time in her bedroom, drawing a wardrobe for Princess Power, and she wrote a huge notice saying 'Private – Keep out' which she stuck on her door, four feet from the floor so that James could not possibly avoid seeing it. Behind the closed door, besides drawing, she spent a good deal of time painting her toenails with Clodagh's scarlet polish.

When Cecily telephoned to suggest that she and Martin and Dorothy take the children to Cornwall – as usual, she said with emphasis – Natasha thought it quite extraordinary that Alice wasn't coming. James, in floods of tears, said he wouldn't go without Alice. Natasha said why couldn't they *all* go, Alice and Martin and Clodagh and everybody, and Alice said it was difficult to explain but she was desperately tired in the complicated way that happened to grown-ups sometimes and she had to be by herself for a bit.

'So Clodagh can come,' said Natasha.

'Well – '

'Clodagh isn't tired.'

186

'Clodagh can't come. Clodagh has got something else to do that she can't *not* do.'

'I'll ask her to come,' Natasha said. 'We can show her the witches' rock.'

James's eyes bulged at the memory of it.

'I can't come,' Clodagh said. 'I'd love to. But I can't. I've got to plan my future, you see. I've got to find a job.'

Natasha said then at least a holiday would make Daddy completely better and he could come home afterwards. Then she burst into tears. Alice, trying to hold her, said, 'I do promise you that when you come back, everything will be sorted out.'

But Natasha would not be held and shouted, 'I *hate* you!' and rushed out into the garden and picked up Charlie's sandpit spade and hurled it so that it sailed up into the air, far further and harder than she had meant, and came down through the greenhouse roof. Then she stood and sreamed with panic at what she had done. James, standing in the kitchen doorway and watching her, began to pee helplessly into his shorts.

Cecily came to collect the children herself. She thought Alice looked awful, but she would have been even angrier if Alice had not looked awful. Indeed, she looked so awful that Cecily would almost have liked to say or do something affectionate but Alice, though perfectly polite, made such a gesture quite impossible. Together, they put the children's bags into the boot of the car, and then strapped in Charlie's car seat, and Charlie into his car seat, and urged Natasha and James to get in beside him. Nobody was quite crying but everybody almost was.

'Bring me some shells,' Alice said through the car window.

'Mummy – ' James mouthed at her, not daring to speak for fear of letting out his sobs.

'You might find a starfish – '

Cecily put the car into gear.

'I'm sure we will. And James is old enough for the smallest surfboard now – '

'James! Isn't that lovely?'

The car slid forward. Three faces turned her way, crumpling, and Cecily's free hand waved from the driver's window. Alice made herself stand there and wave back until the car was gone between the hornbeams and then she turned and went back into the empty house.

'If we were city women,' Alice said slowly, 'we'd have a completely different life. It's being country women that makes it so difficult – '

She stopped. City or country made no difference to Clodagh. Clodagh was Clodagh wherever she was.

'Difficult for me, I mean. Even if I moved to a city, I'd still be a country woman now. I'd still feel visible.'

'You're visible because you're you.'

'I'm *too* visible just now – '

There had been a nasty little moment in the shop that morning, a moment when Cathy Fanshawe had ignored Alice's greeting and turned effusively to speak to Stuart Mott who was buying cigarettes and staring at Alice with a look of such repulsive interest that she had felt quite sick. When she came out of the shop, Michelle had darted up to her, out of the shop yard, and had clutched her convulsively and wordlessly, but it wasn't enough to undo the silent insults of Cathy Fanshawe and Stuart Mott. Going up the street, slowly, with her head as high as she could get it, she thought that even the cottage façades looked as if they had taken stands, were holding their breath until she was past.

'You must get away,' Clodagh said.

They were lying in the orchard under the old Russet Egremont where Clodagh had suggested they plant a Paul's Himalayan Musk which would spread through the gnarled branches like a cascade of late blossom . . .

'No,' Alice said slowly.

'Yes. *Yes!*'

Clodagh rolled on her side and propped her head on her hand. She put out her free hand and ran a forefinger down Alice's profile.

'Come with me. We'll go down to Windover. We'll start a new life there together, you and me and the children. I'll get a job. You'll paint. *Alice* – '

Alice turned her head to look at Clodagh.

'Windover will be just the same as here.'

'No. *No.* Here everyone knew you as a married woman. There we'll arrive as two women, you and me, no past. We can do it. We can do anything we want.' She pushed her face close to Alice's.

'You don't need money. I've got that. You don't need anything, you just need to come. I love you. Do you hear me? I *love* you.'

Alice just went on looking. After a long time, it seemed to Clodagh, she said, 'And I love you. More than I think I have ever loved anyone.'

'Then come, then *come* – '

Alice turned back to look at the sky. She pulled a long grass from its sheath beside her and put the juicy end between her teeth.

'Loving you makes all decisions much more difficult. Loving anybody does – '

Clodagh snorted.

'You sound like Lettice – '

Lettice had stopped Clodagh the other day, coming down from the Park, and had taken her by the shoulders and said, very fiercely indeed, 'If you love Alice Jordan, my girl, you have to let her go.' Clodagh had been amazed. She still was. She liked Lettice a lot but some of her opinions had got stuck in some kind of timewarp. Throw away the best thing that had ever happened to her? Deliberately? Causing heartbreak all round? Honestly.

Alice was frowning.

'Alice,' Clodagh said softly, to win back her attention.

'Mm?'

'Look at me – '

Alice turned.

'I'm looking – '

'Tell me why you love me.'

Alice smiled, a slow, lazy smile.

'I love your gaiety. And your freedom of spirit. And your arrogance and strength and mad courage. And I love your love for me.'

After some time, Clodagh said, 'We don't have to go to Windover. I can sell it. It's worth millions, I should think. We'll go abroad. We can go anywhere. What about the South of France?'

'Lovely,' Alice said, but her mind had slipped into neutral once more.

'You have to come with me, you know. You'd only be half a person without me. Like I'd be, without you.'

'I know.'

'Then when shall we go?'

Alice sat up and pulled her plait over her shoulder and began to pick grass seeds out of it.

'You must go.'

'Shut up!' Clodagh shouted in panic, springing up.

'Calm down,' Alice said. 'I just mean for a bit. I must be absolutely alone, for a bit – '

Clodagh stooped to seize her shoulders.

'You won't go and see Martin, promise – '

'Martin is in Cornwall.'

'Or Juliet. Or my mother. Or – '

'*Clodagh* – '

'Promise!' Clodagh screamed.

Alice slapped her.

'Shut *up*!'

'Sorry,' Clodagh said, crying. 'Oh God, Alice. Oh my *God*!'

She fell on her knees beside Alice.

'I'll kill myself if you leave me.'

Alice put her hands over her face.

'Think what we've shared,' Clodagh said. 'Think what we do together. No one else can do that for you, no one. Only me. We'll go to France. We'll have a house in the sun, we'll all go naked in the sun. We'll have a garden with lavender and thyme and a terrace over a valley. We'll never have to be apart, nights and days together, days and nights. The children will be bilingual, brown as nuts and bilingual. We'll make love when we want to, quite free, in sunlight and moonlight, and you'll come so alive you'll wonder you ever called it life before – '

Alice's hands were shaking. From behind them she said, 'Be fair.'

'*Fair*?'

Alice put her hands in her lap and held them tightly.

'I expect you think I am deeply bourgeois but I can't come to paradise dishonestly – '

'Dishonest? What the hell's dishonest about us? It's being so bloody *honest* that's half-killing you!'

'Clodagh,' Alice said. 'Clodagh. I can't think while you're here.'

'I'm terrified of your thinking – '

'What would *you* do,' Alice said, 'if you had three children?' She looked at Clodagh squarely. 'And a husband.'

190

'It's excuses,' Clodagh said at once. 'All excuses – '

'Call it whatever names you like. Nothing changes what *is*, what I have in my path that you don't have in yours.'

Clodagh grew excited again.

'I see, I see. You're going to be the sacrificial lamb, nobly giving up the best happiness you'll ever be offered – '

'I didn't say anything about giving up anything. I have thought about sacrifice and I'll think some more. You could think about it too. You could think about a good deal, and stop shouting at me.'

'Alice,' Clodagh said, 'I'm scared as hell.'

Alice put out a hand and took Clodagh's.

'I remember the day you told me your lover in New York was a woman. We were down in the river meadow and the children had made a boat out of a log and you were wearing your wizard's cloak. I shan't ever forget that conversation. I shan't ever forget that I suddenly could see the powers and freedoms that might be mine. "We all have a choice," you told me. "You, me, everyone." Well, you had chosen, and then I did. Nobody made us, we chose. And now here we are with the results of our choice and we have to choose again – '

'I can't *believe* what I'm hearing!'

'Yes you can. You know it's true. "If you can't stand the heat, stay out of the kitchen," you said to me.'

Clodagh snatched her hand away.

'But you won't stay in the kitchen *with* me!'

'I didn't say that. I haven't decided anything. But we must be apart for a bit. I don't want it but I can't think at all while there are emotional demands all over me, yours, the children's, anyone's. It isn't just the *now*, you see, it's the future too. Things never stand still, do they.' She looked at Clodagh. 'You ought to think about your own future too. For your own sake.'

Clodagh stood up. She was wearing a peculiar patchwork skirt with long handkerchief points to the hem, which brushed against Alice's bare arm. Alice looked with love at the triangle of red and yellow cotton lying against her skin.

'Just a week,' Alice said.

'I'll go to London.'

'Yes.'

'Who knows' – defiantly – 'who I may meet?'

191

Alice said nothing. Clodagh moved away to lean on the apple tree trunk.

'Wouldn't you care?'

'Of course – '

'Would it make you angry?'

'No.'

'Sad?'

'Very.'

'Alice – Alice, why don't you resent anyone for anything, damn and blast you?'

'I do.'

'You *don't* – '

'I do. I just can't resent anyone for something I've done – '

'Go to hell!' Clodagh shouted. She swirled from the tree in her gypsy rags. 'Priggish, conventional, bloody bourgeois! I'm going, I'm *going* and you'll never know where!'

And then she ran from the orchard and across the lawn by the sandpit and Alice heard her car start up and roar furiously round the house and down the drive. Then Balloon came, dancing through the long grass, to remind Alice that, crisis or no crisis, a cat would like his supper.

When the Unwins heard that Clodagh was going to London, they both tried desperately to stop her.

'But you *wanted* me to go. In fact you *ordered* me – '

'Not to London.'

'Why not to London, for God's sake?'

They could not answer her. They could not utter what they had newly learned about London. Clodagh watched them struggle for a while and then she said, 'You mean that you think I'm going to London to cruise.'

Even she was sorry. She looked at the *utter* misery on their faces, their self-confident, prosperous, genial faces, and was sorry.

'I'm not,' she said, and her voice was softer. 'I'm not interested. It's one of the things you don't understand. But I must get away from here, I must be somewhere anonymous. I might,' she said, trying to make small amends, 'I might see about a job.'

Margot drove her to Salisbury station and they listened to the car radio on the way, to an adaptation of an Arnold Bennett novel, and there was a scene between an overbearing mother and a defiant daughter longing for independence, and neither Margot nor Clodagh could turn it off for fear of tacitly admitting that it had any particular significance to either of them. It was market day in Salisbury and it was trying to rain, warm, thin, summer rain that made the roads feel greasy. The spire of the cathedral rose imperturbably into the grey clouds and tourists carrying National Trust carrier bags spilled off the narrow pavements in search of lavatories and Marks and Spencer and Mompesson House. Margot gazed at their apparent ordinariness with passionate envy and Clodagh with energetic scorn. At the station, Clodagh bought a single ticket.

'Oh darling, not a return?'

'No,' Clodagh said. 'Not because I'm not coming back. But because in my present mood I just wouldn't like the feeling.'

They were ten minutes early for the train.

'Don't wait – '

'I want to.'

'Ma,' Clodagh said, 'please don't wait.'

'I can't bear to see you so unhappy,' Margot said, her own face ravaged by wretchedness.

'It's pretty hateful – '

'Oh, Clodagh – '

'*No*,' Clodagh said. 'Don't start. If it makes it easier, just pretend I'm in love with a man.'

A flash of anger braced Margot.

'I will certainly *not* stay, to be spoken to like that.'

Clodagh watched her go, upright in a summer dress of cream linen, watched her stop to speak to an elderly porter who had helped with Unwin school trunks for fifteen years, watched her smile goodbye to him and go out past the folded iron gates to the station yard, back to her car, back to Pitcombe, where Alice was.

When she got to London, she took a taxi to Highgate, to the flat of the woman writer who had been her first real lover. The writer had a new lover, another writer, and they made Clodagh extremely welcome and were most sympathetic about her pain and her fears. It was comforting to be in their flat, to be in a room where the atmosphere was full of acceptance and understanding. She talked far too much and they were very patient. During supper, one of them said, very gently, that she didn't think promiscuity would be the answer, and Clodagh said probably not and that was almost the worst part of it, not being able to *affect* Alice just now.

'I feel,' she said, 'that I'm the one that's given her the confidence to behave like this. So can you see why I feel so frantic?'

They could. They made her camomile tea and put her to bed in a little, comfortable back bedroom with a copy of *Sinister Wisdom* that one of them had brought back recently from America. Then they told her to try and sleep, and went out, and Clodagh could hear them moving about, clearing up, talking companionably to one another, and she looked at the room with its blue and white cotton curtains and its brass lamp and the rough white Greek rug on the floor, and she was so consumed with longing and envy that she turned her face into her pillow and cried and cried as if her heart would break.

In her kitchen, Juliet Dunne pretended to make watercress soup. She chopped shallots and made stock from a cube and hummed a bit but it wasn't any use. She'd only started because she'd met this very tired bunch of watercress lurking in the fridge behind the walnut oil and the Mister Men yoghurts, and she'd thought she'd just do something with it as a distraction from thinking of Martin and Alice sitting eight feet apart on her terrace supposedly having a talk. She had always happily regarded the roles of wife and mother as the absolute pits, but they were knocked into a cocked hat by the role of mediating friend. It was *awful*. Offer the participants a drink and they both say no, thank you, just Perrier, ask them where they'd like to sit and they say anywhere, it doesn't matter; say, trying to make a joke, look, I'll come and break it up in ten minutes and they look mortally offended. So you shove them out on to the terrace and say *do* look at my Whisky Mac rose, don't you think it's almost as disgusting as the drink, and they ignore you and sit down, sighing, a long way from one another as if they suspected a contagion. So you hop about a bit, being inane, and then you say oh my God something in the oven, and rush into the kitchen for another bloody cry and then you think, must *do* something, can't just sit here and wait, so you find some practically fossilised watercress and think, aha, I'll make *soup*. But all you really want to do is go on bawling, in between tiptoeing to the window and looking out at their unhappy, separate backs. I *hate* being fond of people, Juliet thought, stirring her dissolving stock cube with a knife handle, I simply hate it. I'd much rather loathe them, like I loathe Clodagh. At least you know where you are, with loathing.

After twenty minutes or so, Alice came and stood in the kitchen doorway.

'Martin's gone for a walk. It's so kind of you to have him.'

Juliet had her back to Alice, stirring her soup.

'You know I'm not kind.'

'And it was kind to have us both here – '

'Shut up,' Juliet said. 'Stop mouthing crappy platitudes at me.' She turned round. 'Did you get anywhere?'

'No.' Alice paused and then she said, 'He wants me to apologise, I think. He wants it to be all my fault.'

Juliet said nothing. She took the soup off the cooker and peered at it.

'Henry'll never eat this. Looks like pond slime.'

Alice said, 'I'll go home now. But thank you.'

Juliet banged her saucepan down.

'What the hell *do* you expect from him? What has he done, poor brute, except be the boring old Englishman he's always been – the one you married?'

'It isn't as simple as that – '

'Simple? You bet your life it isn't simple.' She came across the kitchen, holding the wooden soup spoon. 'Allie. Allie, how *could* you?'

Alice looked at her.

'How could you treat Martin like this? How could you be so absolutely normal all these years and then suddenly – God, Allie, have you fallen off your trolley?'

'In order to even begin to understand,' Alice said, 'you have to want to.'

'And what about *you* trying to understand Martin?'

'I do.'

'You *do*?'

'Understanding unfortunately doesn't mean I can wave a wand and put everything right, but it does mean that I'm trying to take everyone into account.'

Juliet marched back to the cooker.

'*Too* good of you.'

Alice left. As she went out of the Dunnes' house, she could see Juliet's little boys on a climbing frame across the lawn. She got into her car. On the floor there were bits of Lego, and a cassette tape of *Charlie and the Chocolate Factory* and a bangle of Clodagh's, purple and gold, that Natasha had borrowed to take to school and awe Sophie with. There were also rather a lot of sweet papers.

'I want you to be more slutty,' Clodagh had said to her. 'My beautiful, sexy, slutty Alice. I want you to let your elastic go. Life to the senses, death to sense.'

Alice started the car, and drove slowly down the drive to the lane. The heavy August green of the countryside weighted the land right down. Some days, when it was still, you felt the fields could not breathe. Gross weeds lined the lanes, tangling on the verges. Alice thought she felt like it looked, exhausted, weighed down, ripe for harvest. She put her hand up for her pigtail, and held it as she drove, one hand on it, the other on the steering wheel.

As she came into The Grey House the telephone was ringing. An immense happy certainty seized her. It would be Clodagh. Clodagh had been away a week and it would be so like her to ring now, in the early evening, so that Alice didn't have another whole night to get through, wondering where she was. She took her time, confidently, getting to the telephone, and when she picked up the receiver, she was smiling.

'Hello?'

'Alice,' Richard said.

'*Richard* – '

'I won't ask how you are because you can't be other than awful.'

'Yes.'

'I'd like to see you.'

She closed her eyes. Tearless for so long now, she could feel the floodgates weakening.

'Alice?'

'Yes. Yes, I'm here – '

'I'd like to see you. Would you like to see me?'

'*Yes.*'

'Come to London. I'd come to Pitcombe except that I don't want to be curtain-twitching fodder. Come before the children get back. Have you heard from them?'

196

'Postcards – '

'I'll see you on Tuesday,' Richard said. 'Come to the flat. We'll have lunch.'

'Yes,' Alice said, crying.

'Come on, love. Come on – '

'Don't be kind to me, it's hopeless – '

He laughed.

'I'll see you on Tuesday,' he said.

It was mattins on Sunday morning. The sun was out, and the clumps of hollyhocks by the lych gate were jubilant with their papery trumpets. Mattins was preferred by the Protestant *habitués* of Pitcombe because the hour was civilised and there was no delicate dilemma as to whether one should eat, or not, before communion, and if *not*, in Miss Payne's case, risk the humiliation of breakfastless internal rumblings in all the quietest and most holy moments. Once she had been compelled to go out of the church entirely and suffer an agony of blushes by a table tomb in the churchyard.

August was usually a poor month for congregations because of holidays, but this particular Sunday seemed to fall between the end of Europe and the beginning of Scotland in the Pitcombe holiday calendar. The narrow nave, decorated with immense white phlox sent down from Pitcombe Park, intermingled with royal blue artificial delphiniums provided by Cathy Fanshawe – 'Good God,' Henry Dunne said, hunting for hassocks, 'is it Lifeboat week?' – filled satisfactorily with people, red-faced from harvest and Cornwall, brown-faced from Umbria and Tenerife. Miss Pimm, in a brown print, with tremulous bare arms, sat at the organ. The choir, a mixed bag of Motts and Crudwells and the reluctant Barton child who was required, by his parents, to *participate*, sat below her, picking their noses and whispering.

Rosie and Gerry Barton sat in the front pews on the right, opposite the Unwin pew. The Bartons were smiling, the Unwins were attempting to. Behind the Unwins, the Dunnes formed a loyal cohort, Henry in a blazer with his old regimental buttons, Juliet in a blue flowered frock, their boys – whom Henry intended to hold in half-nelsons for most of the service – in identical T-shirts and shorts. Buntie Payne sat across the aisle from them and smiled at

197

the children, which emboldened them to make grisly faces. Down the rest of the aisle, scattered in twos and threes, sat the Fanshawes, a local farmer, John Murray-French with his cricket-watching panama on the pew beside him, several visitors, Michelle and her friend Carol, a new family who had modestly chosen a back pew, and old Fred Mott, in his wheelchair, wheeled up by Mr Finch who believed him to be an absolute test case for the promise of universal redemption. He sat wheezing a little, fingering his trousers and loudly sucking on Fishermen's Friends.

Peter Morris came out of the vestry in the green stole of Trinity and looked pleasedly at the church. He went down the aisle greeting people, and then up to the choir to say a few admonishing words. He often thought he would have forgiven them a great deal if they had been able to sing at all. Then he went back into the vestry for a few private moments, moments in which he was always surprised at how easily and earnestly prayer came, and went back into the church and saw Alice Jordan, sitting alone and very upright two pews behind the Dunnes. She was staring straight ahead. Instead of embarking upon the bidding prayer, Peter went down the aisle to her and said, in the resounding silence, 'How nice to see you, Alice,' to which she said thank you. He then went back to the chancel step, opened his arms wide and began.

Alice, kneeling, sitting, rising, told herself she must get through it. She said the Lord's Prayer, but she did not say the General Confession or join in the hymns which everyone else seemed to sing with a kind of exaggerated gusto. It occurred to her that the atmosphere was like the one she imagined prevailing in doomed aircraft, tremendous stoicism tussling silently with incipient hysteria. Sir Ralph, as churchwarden and sidesman, came round with the collection bag during 'Lead me, Heavenly Father, lead me' and Alice dropped in her coins without looking at him. During the sermon, the little Dunne boys, who had known her all their lives, twisted round to beam broadly at her, and were cuffed back into place by their father. It was only at the end that her courage faltered, and in the last hymn she slipped quickly out of her pew so that Buntie Payne, who had been planning to kiss her in front of everyone, turned eagerly to do so after the Peace and cried in a voice loud with disappointment, 'Oh, it's too bad! Really it is! She's gone!'

CHAPTER FIFTEEN

'I was going to take you out,' Richard said, 'but then I thought that the moment either of us managed to say something we really wanted to say there'd be a waiter asking if we wanted pepper on our salads. So I went to Selfridges Food Hall and got this.'

Alice looked down at the coffee table in the little sitting room of Richard's flat. On it was a bottle of wine, a plastic envelope of smoked salmon, brown bread and a lemon.

She said, 'Are you going to grill me?'

'Heavens no. Why should I do that?'

'Because you are Martin's father.'

He picked up the bottle of wine and went to find a corkscrew.

'I'm a human being too. I'd have to be a pretty unpleasant one to drag you all the way to London just to tick you off.'

He disappeared for a moment into the tiny kitchen, reappearing with wine glasses.

'You mustn't be defensive.'

Alice threw her head up.

'I don't want to be. But I keep feeling driven into it.'

It had been so lovely in the train, coming up, being nobody. And the Tube had been even better, jammed in with people, all strangers.

'London's a luxury,' Alice said, accepting a glass of wine, 'after Pitcombe.'

'Yes,' he said. 'Yes, it would be.'

He put a hand on her arm and steered her into an armchair.

'Are you hungry?'

'Not terribly.'

'Drink up then. We've got all day.'

'But the office – '

'It can wait.'

'Martin said you had built a wall together – '

'You *saw* him?'

'Yes,' Alice said. 'At Juliet's. It didn't really work.'

'No,' Richard said. 'It wouldn't have. Poor boy.'

Alice said nothing.

'Poor boy,' Richard said again. 'Poor boy. He's been misinformed, somehow, all his life. He wouldn't begin to understand. He's in a rage of not understanding.'

'I don't blame him,' Alice said. 'I wouldn't have understood either. Before Clodagh.'

'Talk to me,' Richard said. He leaned forward and poured more wine into Alice's glass. 'Talk to me.'

'No – '

'Yes. I may be one of the few people who can help. I love Martin.' He paused. 'I love you. I think I understand Martin. I would like to understand you.'

'I don't want this,' Alice said. 'I don't want my marriage kindly mended.'

'I don't want to mend it.'

'You *don't*?'

'No,' Richard said. 'But I want a resolution. For him, for you, for my grandchildren.' He looked at Alice. 'Talk to me, about Clodagh.'

'I can't – '

'Why not?'

'Because you're a man.'

'Alice,' Richard said, 'I don't think you know very much about men, or you wouldn't say such a thing. Do you trust me?'

She thought.

'I don't know – '

'Pay me the compliment of knowing that I will believe you and probably understand what you tell me.'

Alice got up. She walked round the little room fiddling with things, an ashtray on a sideboard, a marble egg on a wooden stand, a foolish adult toy made of a heap of magnetic paper clips on a black glass base. Then she came back to her chair and sat down.

'What makes it so difficult is that the love between women has *always* been belittled. Hasn't it? Down the ages. Treated as something at best foolish, like – like a kind of silly harmless hobby.'

She put her wine glass down and picked up the lemon, rolling it in her hands and sniffing it.

'But what I feel – and I may never fall in love again – is that what Clodagh has given me has enriched me. It hasn't impoverished anything about me, hasn't taken anything *from* me, if you see what I mean. It's grown me up. It's enabled me to love everyone else in my life properly, and as far as I can see only another woman would do for that instructive kind of love because only another woman could see I needed it and could understand about the children and self and the permanent balancing act of motherhood and self. Only another woman,' Alice said firmly, 'could understand and – and *supply.*'

Richard slid off his chair on to his knees beside the coffee table and began to make competent sandwiches.

'If you want to know,' Alice said, rolling the lemon, 'bed isn't the most significant thing. At least, after the beginning it wasn't. I think sex is more important for Clodagh than for me. If I'm honest. But what I love, what I'm terrified of doing without again, is the life force. A kind of elixir. Do you see?'

He nodded, peeling salmon off cellophane strips.

'You can't imagine how much fun we have. You can't conceive of how differently I see myself, because of her. It's a kind of revelation.'

Richard took the lemon away from her, cut it and began to squeeze the juice on to his sandwiches.

'I was so lonely,' Alice said. 'I don't blame Martin. He didn't know what to do about me, and I didn't know what to do about me either. But Clodagh did. I woke up. When I looked back at getting married and honeymooning and then being married, I think I was simply asleep. I must have been. Twelve years, dawdling about in a kind of half-life.'

Richard put two sandwiches on a plate and balanced it on her knee. 'Eat up.'

Alice looked at the plate, then at him.

'Do I make sense to you?'

'Yes.'

'Can you imagine what I mean?'

'Of course. I've felt something like it. But in my case it was for the opposite sex, rather than my own.'

201

'Who was it?'

'Cecily, of course,' Richard said.

'*Cecily!*'

'Yes.'

Alice took an unenthusiastic bite of sandwich.

'You talk,' she said. 'You talk now.'

There was a little pause, then Richard said, with great carefulness, 'If you had had a confident, loving man make love to you, this would never have happened. You'll think that's just common or garden male arrogance. It isn't. There's a world of difference between making love and having sex. I was never able to make love to Cecily as I wished to because her mind was quite closed to me. The summit of her emotional life was Vienna and she would never allow anything to approach it in case it proved only an illusion and the giant, secret romance of her life crumbled to dust.'

He stopped, and rose to fill Alice's glass. She waited, watching him.

'But I could have loved her, if she'd let me. At the risk of sounding incestuous, I could have loved you, because, like Clodagh, I know what you are like and what you like.'

He looked at Alice.

'I'm not jealous of Clodagh. I'm only sorry that you should be put through this hoop for her, socially. I understand exactly what you say about loneliness. I've had a mistress for years – fifteen to be exact – because I'm a tender man and a passionate man and Cecily can't let herself allow me to be either. It doesn't suit her to acknowledge that I *like* women.'

'Martin – ' Alice said.

'Cecily never brought the boys up to like women. She didn't try. They are both afraid of women. I didn't try either. I didn't see until too late. In that respect, I am quite as much to blame as she is.'

Alice reached over to take Richard's hand.

'So sad,' Alice said. 'So sad. You are actually exactly the right man for her.'

He smiled.

'Oh, I know that. I've known that for forty years.'

Alice bent her head.

'Forty years! The things people live with – '

'Sometimes you have to. If you don't at heart want anything else.'

'But a *mistress* – '

'Would a string of call girls be better?'

Alice looked up.

'You mean – ?'

'Yes.'

'*Jesus*,' Alice said, with Clodagh's intonation.

'I haven't been allowed to make love to Cecily for almost twenty years.'

'But you *still* – '

'Yes, I still.'

'Wouldn't you like to have stopped? Loving her, I mean – '

'Only very theoretically. And occasionally. Perhaps I'm just immensely pigheaded and won't admit to failure. Perhaps it's love.'

Alice flung herself back in her chair.

'*Love*,' she said.

Later, when he was driving her to Paddington, Richard said quite casually that he would like to buy her a little flat or house in Salisbury, to be near the children's school. He said it would be a secret between the two of them. He said it would have no strings. She could have it for a month or a year or however long she wanted it for. She felt quite bewildered by the offer and said, looking away from him, 'But why?' and he said for the children first and for her and Martin second.

'*Martin?*'

'If you have some independence, he won't feel so threatened or resentful. It will make the next step easier. He cannot bear the thought that the law will require him to give money to a woman he believes has betrayed him. If you don't need so much from him, that's one less battle. One less battle is good for the children.'

'But you can't, why should you – '

'Mind your own business,' Richard said. 'Just let me know when you know.'

In the train, tiredness fell upon Alice like a hammer blow. She put her head back on the orange tweed headrest with which British Rail sought to cosset its passengers, and closed her eyes. Through her mind a procession of people moved, Clodagh and her children and Martin, her parents, her parents-in-law, Clodagh's parents, all spinning slowly by, their faces seeming to wheel up out of a soft darkness and then melt away again into it. I am the link, Alice thought. All these people, through me, have their future. It's a horrible power, but it's real. And it's mine. Even if I don't want it, it's mine. Things aren't going to happen to me now because I have to make the next things happen. I have to choose. I am far beyond any point I ever was before and there's nothing to shield me now. I am in a high, bare, painful place . . .

'Excuse me,' a voice said next to her, 'but am I on the right train to make a connection for Didcot Parkway?'

Elizabeth Meadows opened the door of her sister's house in Colchester and found Richard Jordan there. She was so astonished that she almost shut the door again in fright. He said, smiling, 'I wondered if you would have forgotten what I looked like.'

'Yes,' she said, 'No – '

From the through sitting room where she was polishing the brass fire-irons, Elizabeth's sister Ann called, 'Who is it? I wish you'd shut the door.'

'Come in,' Elizabeth said.

He followed her into the cream painted hall where a Swiss cheese-plant sat exactly in the centre of an otherwise empty table, and then into the sitting room. Ann Barlow was wearing cotton gloves to protect her hands from the brass cleaning wadding and a flowered pinafore with a big front pocket on which 'Breakages!' was embroidered in royal blue stranded cotton. She scrambled to her feet, frowning. If there was one thing she hated more than an unexpected caller, it was an unexpected *man* caller.

'You remember Richard Jordan. Alice's father-in-law – '

In Ann Barlow's mind, the Jordans were entangled with the breakdown of her sister's marriage. She pulled off a glove and held out an indifferent hand, making ritual noises about coffee which Richard said untruthfully that he would love. He was directed towards a flowered armchair from which he could see a regimented garden and a white painted seat and a line of washing hung up in strict order of size. Elizabeth did not know what to do with him. She resented him fiercely both for coming and for looking so at ease now he was here. She sat opposite him and stared at his well-shod feet and resolved that she would not help him conversationally.

He did not seem to mind her unfriendliness. He told her that James had learned to swim in Cornwall, which she remained inflexible about since Alice hadn't seen fit to tell her they were going to Cornwall in the first place. He admired the delphiniums and said Cecily was opposed heart and soul to the notion of the new pink ones. He remarked on the beastliness of the A12, to which Elizabeth managed to reply that she didn't drive any more, and then Ann came in with a tray of coffee and there was the usual fuss – Elizabeth despised Ann's houseproudness as deeply suburban – with little tables and spoons and plates to catch biscuit crumbs. When the fuss had subsided, Richard began to talk very differently. He said he was here without Alice's knowledge or permission but she had enough to cope with just now and he had made a unilateral decision to come that he would probably be punished for. He then said, with a calm Elizabeth found horrible, that Alice and Martin had separated because Alice had had a love affair with a woman, and that Alice was at the moment trying to determine her future and Martin was trying to recover from a breakdown. He then said, unwisely, that he hoped they would not be too harsh on anyone. At this point, Ann Barlow put down her coffee cup and left the room.

'I hope,' Richard said, 'that I have not shocked your sister.'

'Of course you have.'

'And you? Have I shocked you?'

'Nothing,' Elizabeth said angrily, 'nothing really shocks me.' She gave Richard the first proper look she had awarded him. 'You are a meddler,' she said. 'And I doubt your motives.'

He shrugged.

'I hoped to smooth Alice and Martin's path – '

She snorted.

'I'm not a fool. Prurient is the word that springs to mind. Prurient is how I should describe your action in coming here.'

He lowered his head. She thought his colour was darkening.

'Heaven knows,' Elizabeth said, 'heaven knows what your motives are, what they have ever been.'

He kept his head down.

'Could they not be,' he said into his chest, 'could they not be altruistic?'

'Impersonally, of course they could be. In your case, I doubt it. I resent your coming. I resent your crude translation of my daughter to me. I resent your possessive attitude to grandchildren who are as much mine as yours. I resent your patronage. I resent the divisions you have, as a family, made in mine.'

He got up, abruptly, clumsily.

'I had better go.'

She said nothing. He was beside himself with rage.

'I shall tell Alice of this – '

'You are wrong to suppose she will have any sympathy for you. Much less gratitude.'

He wanted to shout at her that he saw exactly why Sam Meadows had left her, why Alice had seen in Cecily the mother Elizabeth had declined to be. He began, but she went past him to open the sitting room door and then the front door and he found himself outside, beside a bed of stout begonias, bellowing to himself in the quiet residential road, almost before he had said a quarter of it. There was nothing for it but to drive back to London.

Two days later, Alice received two letters at The Grey House. One was from her mother.

'I had a call from your father-in-law,' Elizabeth wrote, 'in the course of which I learned a great deal more about him than about you. Perhaps you will write. Perhaps you will even come and see me. Do not be afraid of coming, because I would not try to counsel you.'

It was signed, 'With love from your mother, Elizabeth.' The other letter was no more than a postcard. It was undated and unsigned, and it simply said, in Clodagh's wild black writing, 'Women need men like fish need bicycles.'

That was all. The next day the children came home and Alice realised, holding them with great relief and love, that in the fortnight they had been away she had come to no decision at all.

'What are you doing?' James said. He was holding a plastic ray gun and half a biscuit.

'Writing to Grandpa.'

'Can I too?'

'Yes, but not on this paper. On your own bit of paper.'

James put the ray gun down on Alice's letter. He did that all the time now, putting his spoon on her plate, his book across her newspaper, his toothbrush into her mouth.

'Jamie – '

He put his hand on the gun. Silently he dared her to move it away.

'I can't write – '

He raised his other hand and pushed the bitten biscuit at her mouth.

'*Darling*. Don't – '

'Eat it!'

'No, Jamie, no, it's all licky – '

He jabbed it against her lower lip and it broke.

'You broke my biscuit.'

'You broke it. Being silly. Move your gun so I can write.'

He kept his hand on the gun and screwed his foot round on the piece of biscuit that had fallen on to the floor until it was a brown powder.

'*There.*'

Alice took no notice. He threw another bit down and did the same thing. Alice gripped the table edge and her pen and glared at what she had written.

'After thinking it over and over, I know I must decline your offer. The price – the price of having to rely on you – is too high. I can't do it. You are too protective, somehow, too *administering*. I couldn't breathe. I don't really know if I trust you.'

She thought, I should be saying this, not writing it, but if I say it he will argue with me and try to persuade me otherwise. And I may say, like last time, all kinds of things that I should not have said.

'Gun,' said James loudly. 'Gun, gun, *gun*.'

He pushed it roughly into her pen-holding hand and hurt her. She held the hurt hand in the other, tense with pain and fury, and he watched her.

'Gun,' he said again, but with less confidence.

'Go away,' Alice said. 'Go away until I have written my letter. Go and play with Tashie.'

He shook his head, but he was chastened by the red mark on her hand. He crept under the table and lay down and put his cheek on Alice's foot, and after a while she could feel tears running into her sandal. She moved her toes, so that he could feel them, and with an immense effort picked up her pen again.

'I can't,' she wrote to Richard, 'be the cure-all for your frustrations. I don't want that ever again, the prison of gratefulness. I *am* grateful, but I'd rather be it from a distance, on equal terms.'

She felt James's hand on her other foot.

'Jamie? You're a bit tickly – '

He giggled, faintly.

'You trapped me,' Alice wrote, 'didn't you. You trapped me into talking. I'd rather not think why you wanted to do that and I'd rather not think why you want to help me. But what has happened to me has moved me out of the objective case into the subjective case so that I am not available for anyone else's plans just now.'

She signed the letter, 'With love from Alice'. When it was licked up and stamped, by James, they put Charlie into his pushchair and found Natasha, who was arranging her Cornish shells into an interminable exhibition all around the upstairs windowsills, and went down to the post. On the way they met Lettice Deverel who was very kind and ordinary and invited them to tea to meet the parrot. When they got home, Alice made cheese sandwiches for lunch and they ate them in the garden while the children talked about all the things they would do when Daddy and Clodagh came home again.

'Have you seen her?' Clodagh demanded.

Lettice held the telephone at a little distance from her ear.

'Yes. Yes, I have.'

'And? *And?*'

'We didn't speak of you, if that's what you mean.'

'How did she look?'

'A little tired. That's all.'

'Lettice,' Clodagh shouted. 'Lettice. How can you be so awful to me?'

There was a little silence. The parrot, across the kitchen, clucked approvingly at a grape it held.

'I used to think,' Lettice said, 'I used to think that you had promise and originality. And courage. Now I don't know. I'm more depressed by this episode than I can tell you. You seem to me like some kind of Hedda Gabler, all style and shallow selfishness.'

In London, sitting on her fortunate friends' sofa, Clodagh began to cry.

'Except you have a heart,' Lettice went on. 'I know that because I can see it's been touched. Oh, Clodagh dear, I do beg you to *make* something of your life.'

'No!' said the parrot. 'No. No. No. *Not* pretty.'

It threw the grape stalk out of its cage.

'I can't give this up,' Clodagh said. 'I can't. I'll die.'

'On the contrary, you will live much better.'

'Is she missing me? Does she look as if she's missing me?'

'Don't ask me idiotic questions. Ask me how your poor parents are.'

'Well?'

'Much in need of hearing from you. You should have rung them, not me.'

'I couldn't ask them about Alice.'

'You shouldn't be asking anyone.'

'What about the children then? Did they mention me?'

'No. We only spoke of the parrot.'

'Oh, *parrot*,' said the parrot. 'Dear parrot. Dear me.'

Clodagh's voice grew small.

'I *long* to come down.'

'I dare say – '

'But I'm not crawling to *anyone* – '

'If you don't get off your bottom, Clodagh Unwin,' Lettice said, 'and make an independent decision, you'll find that Alice will probably have made them all for you.'

'What d'you mean? What's going on? What did Alice – '

'I mean nothing, except that Alice has three children and no money of her own and can't fiddle-faddle around like you can.'

'Has Martin been around?'

'No. He's living with a friend in Salisbury.'

'I'm coming down, damn what everyone thinks – '

'Think!' Lettice cried. 'Think! *You* try a little thinking.'

The parrot hooked its beak into the wires of its cage and began to haul itself up to the top. When it got there, it hung upside down for a bit and then it said, with great calm, 'Damn *and* blast.' Lettice began to laugh. Delighted, it joined in, and Clodagh, hearing what appeared to be a roomful of merriment in Pitcombe, put the telephone down, in despair.

Martin was just waiting. He had stopped talking to anyone about Alice, particularly to Cecily. He had a very comfortable room in a friend's house on the edge of the Close in Salisbury, and he was working hard, and seeing his children once a week when Alice left them for him at The Grey House and went out, and he was making sure he played tennis a good deal and golf a bit, and he had accepted an invitation to stalk in Sutherland in October. He was making quiet plans to sell The Grey House. Whatever happened next, they couldn't possibly stay there.

Cornwall had restored him in some measure, certainly as to how he stood with his children. He liked being with them but was amazed at how much they needed done for them, how insatiable and helpless they were. Except for the brief time over Charlie's birth, he had never been responsible for them, a thing he didn't like but was perfectly prepared to do, if he had to. He felt perfectly prepared for a lot of things. That was the trouble, really, feeling like that. Nothing seemed violently upsetting any more or impossible to face or to be worth very much angst of any kind. When he tried to think what really *mattered* now, he couldn't. So he thought he would just get on with each day, as unremarkably and pleasantly as he could, and wait. In any case, if he waited, in the end it would be Alice who had to do something. And that would be only just. Wouldn't it?

CHAPTER SIXTEEN

On Friday nights, Sam Meadows went to Sainsbury's. He had grown rather to like the expedition because the store was full of people who had just finished work and who were full of a pre-weekend relief and excitement. As the years of his lone living went on, he found to his amusement that he was making sure he had no teaching commitments early on Friday evenings to get in the way of going to Sainsbury's. He also noticed how he was beginning to buy the same things, whisky and white bread and black cherry jam and pasta and jars of *pesto*, and how he would make for the same check-out because there was such a dear little woman on the till, who ducked her head at him, bursting with half-hidden smiles.

Since he had left Elizabeth, a good many women had tried quite hard to live with him. He had let two of them begin but they had both had over-clear ideas about how life should be lived, and had been unable to keep those ideas to themselves. The only woman he had wanted, in ten years, to come and do whatever she liked with his life as long as she came, hadn't wanted to. She liked his bed, but preferred her own life outside it. Because of this, Sam had continued to love her and had stopped collecting his pupils like an array of Barbie dolls. They still flirted with him, particularly if essays were late, but these days he could just let them. In any case, the university now had a ferocious female Committee Against Sexual Harassment.

Sam had five years to go before he retired. When he retired, he thought he would go and live in Wales, preferably in a fishing community, and write a book on the power of language that would become an indispensable text book in schools. When he had done that, he would write fools' guides to the Bible and classical literature because he was still so exasperated, after thirty years of teaching, to find that clever modern students of literature were so ignorant of both that they couldn't get through a line of Milton

211

without having to look up the references. After that, he thought he would probably die, and be buried in an austere Welsh hillside under the wheeling gulls. He didn't really want a headstone but he did want something to indicate that he had meant to be a poet, so that posterity should know that inside his apparently phlegmatic, idle, pleasure-seeking bulk, quite a lot of striving had gone on.

Standing in the Sainsbury's queue one August Friday, he was offered most of a very small, very wet dolly mixture by a gregarious baby in the child seat of the next trolley. He accepted it gratefully and ate it. It tasted of scented soap and reminded him of the sweets of his childhood. The baby reminded him of Charlie. Or rather, not of how Charlie looked, because Sam had only seen him once when he was too new to look like anything, but more that Charlie existed, that Sam *had* a baby grandson. In the early spring, Alice had sent Sam photographs of The Grey House and had said that it would all be ready for him, when he came for his annual summer visit. After that, he had heard nothing. He hadn't minded or noticed much, because he presumed that she had been too busy, and because he had been busy himself, but now, standing in the queue and smiling at the strange baby (it was not a pretty baby, it had a high domed forehead and its chin was glossy with dribble, but the gift of the dolly mixture had been true generosity in one so young), he thought that perhaps Alice's silence was beginning to have a flavour of oddness. Half the summer vacation had gone and she had not even telephoned. No more had he, he wasn't blaming her, but now that he thought about her, he found that he wanted to see her and his grandchildren. By the time he had got his groceries to the car, he wanted to see them very much indeed.

When he got home, he put the grocery boxes on the kitchen table beside the remains of a very good lunch of Scotch eggs and Guinness, and went to the telephone. Alice answered it with a kind of breathless eagerness, but when she heard who it was she became constrained.

'What's up?' Sam said.

There was a silence.

'Come on,' Sam said. 'Come on, Allie. Is something wrong?'

'A great deal has happened – '

'Are you all right?'

'Oh yes. Perfectly.'

212

'And the children?'

'Fine. Absolutely fine.'

'Don't fool around with me,' Sam said. 'I am your non-interfering father. I also smell a rat.'

'Martin isn't here any more – '

'Allie – '

'I fell in love with someone. Martin's living in Salisbury.'

Sam pressed the receiver against his skull until it hurt, and closed his eyes.

'I'll come – '

'Please. You don't have to. I really am managing. There's a lot to be decided, but I'm doing it, bit by bit.'

'Where's this other fellow? Is he with you?'

'It isn't a fellow,' Alice said. 'She's a girl.'

Slowly Sam raised a clenched fist and knocked his knuckles on his forehead, bang, bang, rhythmically.

'A girl.'

'Yes.'

A kind of groan.

'Allie – '

'I can't possibly explain over the telephone. Nor can I convince you how all right I am. Sad, of course, but all right.'

'The children, how are the children – '

'They miss Martin and they miss Clodagh – that's her name, Clodagh – but we are getting by, getting on – '

'You thought I was Clodagh, telephoning – '

'Yes,' Alice said. 'I did. We haven't communicated at all for three weeks.'

'I'll come down tomorrow.'

There was a little pause and then Alice said, 'I'd like that.'

'Hold on there,' Sam said. 'Hold on.'

He was close to tears.

'I'm holding,' Alice said. 'I promise you I'm not going to fall off anything.'

'I'll be with you by teatime. No, earlier, lunchtime. I'll be with you by lunchtime.'

He put the telephone down. It was quite silent in his kitchen except for a bluebottle that had got into one of the grocery cartons and was fizzing about noisily against the cellophane packets of

213

pasta. Sam went over to the box, pulled out his new bottle of whisky and took it into his bedroom, holding it against him with both arms. Then he lay down on his bed, still holding the bottle, and began to cry and cry, like a baby.

Mr Finch was unpacking New Zealand apples from nests of blue tissue paper. It was the sort of job Michelle should have done, but Michelle had handed in her notice because she said she didn't like his attitude to Mrs Jordan. She must have said something similar to her mother, because she had then left Pitcombe and gone to live with her married sister in Poole, and Gwen was buying twice as many Silk Cut as usual and wearing a face like a boot. One of the Crudwells, Heather, who wore black stonewashed jeans so tight you wondered how she had got her feet through, had offered to come and help instead. But Mr Finch was frightened both of her sexuality and her light-fingeredness, and had declined. So she had brought two friends into the shop to laugh at him with her, and he had been very miserable. Even Mrs Finch, whose sympathy for him had run out long ago on account of his want of style, had been sorry for him.

'It's Alice Jordan's fault. Without all that business, this would never have happened.'

She said that a lot now, in between reminding him that she had never, being a woman of experience, been one to judge. In Mr Finch's view, almost everyone judged. It seemed to him that he was probably the only person who didn't, and that was not because he had no opinion but because he was so entirely bewildered. The *strangeness* of the affair paralysed him, he had never come across anything like it. The element that really shook Mr Finch was the combination of emotional and sexual unorthodoxy and – you could see this plainly on Alice Jordan's face – the *reality* of it. The thing was actual *and* stupefying. However much of a good face Alice put upon things, it was all too evident that with Clodagh away she was suffering real pain, the pain of having new, vital, tender roots ripped up at just the moment they began to take hold and grow. It frequently occurred to Mr Finch that he understood far more about poetry than about life, because life was often just too peculiar to take in.

A very few people felt as he did. He knew that because of the things they were doing. He'd heard that Mrs Macaulay had been up to The Grey House to offer Alice a puppy, a free puppy. Gwen had

214

told him that, contemptuous of Mrs Macaulay and disgusted with Alice, who had declined the puppy and then gone into the downstairs lavatory and cried her eyes out. Buntie Payne, though prone to immediate distress if Alice's name was mentioned in the shop, had flown like an enraged kitten at Sally Mott who had remarked, for Mrs Finch's benefit, that villages were too small to cope with bad influences.

'Don't you use the word bad of Alice Jordan!' Miss Payne had cried.

Sally Mott had banged out of the shop and Miss Payne had had to sit down to weep and be given a glass of water and to explain, over and over again, how strongly she felt but how she couldn't quite describe what it was that she felt so strongly about.

The pub, where Mr Finch allowed himself a weekly pint, was simpler in its approach, perhaps because fewer women went to it. In the lounge bar the subject was hardly mentioned, and in the public, led by Stuart Mott, there was briefly considerable crudity and then, with the football season starting up, loss of interest. As for the church – well, here Mr Finch's frail faith, born out of a love of ritual and a powerful wish that something, some day, might come out of regular church attendance, was very disappointed. He had hoped for a sermon on sin, full of words like evil and phrases like wrong-doing, not because he wished to see Alice condemned, but because he wanted a stout moral rail upon which to put his own hand. What he had got was a sermon on St Barnabas and another on inner city renewal. The strange part, thought Mr Finch, gazing fixedly at a single apple he held in his hand, was that a business like this, an upset like this Alice Jordan–Clodagh Unwin thing, was that it drove you in on yourself for hours and hours of self-examination. The firm ground you thought you stood on suddenly began to heave and shudder and give way. Mr Finch put the apple on the rack with its fellows and frowned at it.

Behind him, Sam cleared his throat.

'I was wondering if you could direct me to The Grey House?'

Mr Finch turned slowly. Sam was wearing a crumpled blue shirt and a red spotted handkerchief knotted round his throat, and had an air of comfortable bohemianism that filled Mr Finch with envy. He hoped it was not immediately visible that his own trousers were made of polyester.

215

'I shall be only too pleased – '

He took Sam out on to the pavement and pointed up the hill.

'Go straight up until you come to the cottage with the well in the garden – the well is purely ornamental – and turn right there. The gates of The Grey House are directly ahead.'

He waited for Sam to tell him who he was and why he was going to The Grey House, but Sam merely said thank you and climbed back into his car – the interior, Mr Finch noted with admiration, was chaos – and drove off as he had been directed. Forlornly, Mr Finch went back into the shop, reflecting that it was the lot of those who worked in service industries to be, for the most part, entirely invisible to those they served.

Alice, who had never been a demonstrative child in the least, seemed to want Sam to hold her; so he did. He held her for a long time in her bright kitchen while she neither cried nor said much beyond that she was pleased to see him and that she had had no idea that coming alive would be so hard. For the rest of the time she just had her arms round his solid trunk and her cheek on his chest. He was deeply touched by this. After many minutes she sighed and withdrew slowly and went to fetch a bottle of cider from the larder. While she was away, he leaned on the bottom half of the stable door and watched a pram under an apple tree which was rocking violently and intermittently. There was washing hanging out and a half-grown cat asleep in the sun and a trug of lettuces beside it. One of the things about humankind that had never ceased to amaze Sam was that in most cases, whatever the drama, life went on. Emotions and psyches were torn to ribbons, healths and minds were broken, lives were crushed, but on, on, went the relentless business of keeping the machine going, meal after meal, washing and sweeping and going to bed. Perhaps, he thought, turning to accept his glass of cider, it was the treadmill that stopped you going mad. Perhaps the need to do the laundry saved your sanity.

'Maybe I should have told you,' Alice said, sitting on the corner of the table, 'but I didn't tell anyone. I didn't want to. I felt so free. You know, there's been *years* of ought to's and have to's and suddenly there was pure, clear, strong *want* to. It was such a relief. There simply was no choice.'

She looked at Sam.

216

'Society isn't necessarily right about what's good for you.'

He drank.

'It's right,' he said, 'about what's good for most people. But not for everyone. It's the majority that makes the rules and then we call it society. A woman colleague of mine says she resents society for making divorce so easy. That's a circular resentment. She ends up, most likely, with herself.'

'You always do, don't you. That's the great battle, learning to live with yourself – '

'I don't think,' Sam said, looking at her, 'that it's a battle that ought ever to be won.'

'I hurt,' Alice said. 'I hurt all over. I don't think that there's an inch of me that doesn't hurt, inside or out. Every tiny bit of feeling hurts, loving most of all, which is the one thing I want to do, must do – '

Sam stopped leaning on the door and went across to Alice and held her pigtail at the base of her neck. She leaned her head back against his hand for a moment, and then she leaned it against him.

'I'm going to quote you something.'

'Poetry?'

'George Eliot.'

'I only ever,' Alice said mournfully, 'read *The Mill on the Floss*.'

'This is *Adam Bede*.'

She turned her face into his shirt front.

'Tell me.'

' "We get accustomed," ' Sam said into the space of kitchen above her head, ' "to mental as well as bodily pain, without, for all that, losing our sensibility to it: It becomes a habit of our lives and we cease to imagine a condition of perfect ease as possible for us. Desire is chastened into submission, and we are contented with our day when we have been able to bear our grief in silence and act as if we were not suffering. For it is at such periods that the sense of our lives having visible and invisible relations beyond any of which our present or prospective self is the centre, grows like a muscle that we are obliged to lean on and exert." '

Then it was quiet. It was quiet for a long time and neither of them moved until a small commotion could be heard in the hall, and then the kitchen door opened and there, with James squealing joyously in her arms, stood Clodagh.

★　　★　　★

217

'You know why I've come back,' Clodagh said later while they were getting supper. 'Don't you?'

'Yes.'

'I think I'll remind you all the same. I've come back to collect you. You and the children. I'm selling everything. We can go anywhere.'

Alice went on slicing mushrooms. Upstairs Sam was reading *Winnie-the-Pooh* to Natasha and James, giving Australian accents to Kanga and Roo. It was a great success. Shrieks of pleasure filtered occasionally downstairs. Charlie, in his sleeping suit, was in his highchair in the kitchen eating raspberries with his fingers. Balloon, replete with supper, slept against the Aga. Outside the open stable door, the late summer countryside lazed in a syrupy sunset.

'Don't stonewall me,' Clodagh said. 'That's what you did when I went away. You said you must think. I've been away nearly a month and it's been a nightmare. Have you had a nightmare?'

'Yes,' Alice said. She slid the mushrooms into a casserole. 'I was silly to think I'd find any peace. There was no one but it was rampageously unpeaceful. I felt that I was in one of those little mechanical revolving machines used for stone polishing. Except that I seemed to be the one stone that wouldn't polish.'

'You needed me,' Clodagh said.

There was a little pause and then Alice said, 'I *wanted* you.'

'*Needed.*'

'I looked need up in the dictionary,' Alice said. 'It said it was a state that required relief. That seemed rather feeble.'

Clodagh put her hands on Alice's shoulders and turned her.

'If you don't have me, you'll stop living.'

'So you keep saying.'

Clodagh's eyes were bright with tears.

'Alice. Oh, Alice, have a little *pity* – '

She took her hands away.

'You can't imagine what it was like in London. Eleanor and Ruth were so kind but they have each other. Ma and Pa are trying to be kind, even Pa, but they haven't a clue. Loving you has stopped me belonging anywhere because I'm not fit for anyone else but you. You've ruined me for other people. I don't want anything any more but to make you happy. And your children. I'd do anything for your children.'

218

She looked across at Charlie who had fitted a raspberry on his finger like a thimble and was regarding it with wonder.

'I adore Charlie,' Clodagh said.

She sat down on a kitchen chair and bent herself round her knees.

'I hate whining like this. But it's so important. I want to *give* to you and the children. I know I'll be better if I do, a better person. I thought, while I was in London, that I'd like to work for you all. I was so happy when I thought of that.'

Alice came to sit next to her. She put a hand out and stroked her wild head, and thought, as she had thought before, that when Clodagh was distressed she became like an exotic broken bird with tattered, gorgeous plumage and splintered frail bones showing through.

'Clodagh.'

There was silence.

'Clodagh, I didn't want to say this now but we seem to have got to the point where I have to because there isn't anything else we can say with this between us. I'm not coming away with you. If it's any comfort, I'm not going back to Martin either. I expect you'll accuse me of being pompous, but I've made those decisions because it wouldn't be honest to live with either of you. Desire doesn't come into it. What does come into it is all the emotional leftovers I'd have to tow into either relationship and which I'd never be free of. It's no good blaming anyone and it would be worse to lug blame around with me.'

After some time, Clodagh raised her face and glared at Alice.

'I sometimes wonder if you even *have* a heart – '

Alice got up and went over to Charlie, lifting him out of his highchair. She said over her shoulder, 'I can't keep saying I love you. It loses value if I keep saying it, like some silly jingle. But I do. If you're in the pain you say you're in, you should be able to imagine how I feel too. I'm scared stiff of being without you. But I have to be.' She put her face briefly into Charlie's neck. 'I'm not telling you the way I wanted to but I suppose that's inevitable. I'll probably make an awful mess of telling Martin too.'

Clodagh was crying. Seeing her, Charlie's face began to crumple up.

'You see,' Alice said, 'we've got to stop this. We've got to stop all this not sleeping, and crying, and giving each other such agony – '

'*Your* way!' Clodagh shrieked. '*Your* bloody way!'

Alice had a sudden spurt of temper.

'How you hate it, don't you, when you can't have yours!'

Charlie began to wail. Clucking at him, Alice took him out of the kitchen and up the stairs. From Natasha's room came the sound of Rabbit explaining something officiously to Tigger who wasn't listening. Alice carried Charlie into his cot where he settled at once into the private oblivious contentment that lived there. She pulled the string of his musical box which began to play 'Edelweiss' unevenly. Suppose, she thought, bending over Charlie while he sucked ferociously on his fingers, suppose that instead of coming down and attempting to storm her way to success, Clodagh had come to tell Alice that it was over and that she, Clodagh, had found someone new? What then? Would that have been easier? She straightened up. Easier, but worse. Once you had stopped letting things happen and started to make them happen, you couldn't go back . . . Clodagh had known that all her life, which was why she was in such anguish now, powerless, rudderless.

In a sudden rush of pity, Alice ran back downstairs to the kitchen, but of course Clodagh was gone, leaving all the knives and forks on the table crossed over one another in a childish gesture of love and anger.

'So you want a divorce,' Martin said.

'Yes.'

'I ought to tell you that I feel pretty bitter.'

'Yes. I know.'

'I'm not to blame.'

'It all,' Alice said, 'goes too deep for blame. Or apology.'

'I don't see it that way.'

'I know. I know you don't. You think that if I were to grovel and apologise abjectly you would suddenly feel better, everything would be all right. Well it wouldn't and nor would you because *nothing's* that simple and this particularly isn't.'

Martin had taken a flat overlooking the river. He had been most insistent that Alice should meet him there, whether to assert his independence, or to demonstrate the sad impersonality of his life now, she could not guess. It was a sunny flat, on the first floor of a

substantial Regency house, furnished inappropriately in early
Habitat. They sat in two foam-filled chairs covered in chocolate
brown corduroy and watched the river and a family of swans with
three beige, black-beaked, adolescent cygnets.

'You can't get away from the fact that I'm the victim,' Martin
said.

'You speak as if I set out to hurt you. To *punish* you. As if I acted
out of malice – '

'You did,' Martin said. 'I bored you. I disappointed you.'

Alice said nothing.

'I expect you wished you had never married me.'

Still she said nothing.

'You shouldn't have married anyone, anyway,' he went on,
goading. 'Should you. You have to face that now, whatever else you
refuse to see.'

She looked steadfastly at the swans.

'I don't expect a judge will be very keen on giving you care and
control of the children.'

Alice said, 'Why must you insist that I am your enemy?'

'You are. You humiliated me the worst way a woman could
humiliate a man. It's your doing.'

'Would you have preferred me to have slept with another man,
thereby showing you up as an inadequate lover?'

'Yes,' Martin said. 'No,' and put his head in his hands.

'Stop thinking about sex. It isn't really about sex. At least, sex is
only a part.'

'I can't – '

'I don't want a divorce so that I can live with Clodagh. I want a
divorce because I'm not going to live with anyone. If you think
you'll feel better by making it all difficult, I can't stop you. You
have heaps of people on your side. But I'm not going to help make
it a battle. I'd rather be your friend than your enemy. I'd rather be
– Clodagh's friend than her enemy. But I won't for all that pretend
I regret what has happened because it wouldn't be true.'

'You must be mad.'

'I expect it's easier to think that.'

'Easier!'

'If you tell everyone I'm mad then you don't have to consider
what I am or what I've done seriously. You don't have to

221

acknowledge that I'm part of the human pattern. You don't even have to begin to look for anything good.'

She stood up.

'I must go. I'm lecturing. I seem to have an awful tendency to lecture at the moment.'

He gazed at her. He didn't want her to go and did not know how to make her stay.

'I'll see the children on Saturday – '

'Of course.'

'How much do they know?'

'What you would expect,' Alice said, 'at their age. They just want everything to be normal again.'

'And who's fault is that?' Martin cried out, unable to stop himself. 'Who's fault is that, that it isn't?'

When Alice had gone, he went to his bathroom at the back of the flat and watched her walk across what had been the old kitchen yard of the house, to her car. Well, his car really; he'd bought it, after all. She was wearing a huge, full, long denim skirt and a red shirt and a suede waistcoat and her plait fell down her back as straight as an arrow. He leaned his forehead on the glass. She opened the car door and climbed in, folding her skirt in after her, and shut the door. Martin closed his eyes. A sense of loss, a terrifying, savage sense of no longer having something that had been his alone, engulfed him in a black flood of bereavement.

Sam, sitting in the garden of The Grey House with a copy of the *Times Literary Supplement*, was half-supervising his grandchildren. This occupation struck him as being rather like invigilating public examinations, except that the children did not fix him with the anguished, reproachful stares of candidates immobilised by exam nerves or inadequate revision. Instead they seemed absorbed in some extraordinary ritual under a car rug hung between kitchen chairs and only came out intermittently to make him solemn offerings of daisy heads on a tiny plate which Charlie seemed eager to eat. Sam let him. The Elizabethan kitchen, after all, had made excellent use of violets and marigolds.

His presence in the house for the last few days had given it a solidity. Rituals had formed at once around him, as grandfather and as man, little tendrils of the instinct for security reaching out to

222

cling to him. He liked it. He thought he liked it a great deal more than he remembered liking fatherhood, which had come at a time in his life when he wasn't ready for it. His grandchildren interested him a lot; he was struck by the dignity of Charlie's babyhood. He was sorry to think that his children had not interested him very much, a sign, he thought now, of his immaturity then. He saw the realistic female certainties in Natasha and the romantic male agonies in James and he now saw in his daughter, Alice, a mixture of both, as he supposed they ought to exist, in adults who were adults. He also saw, to his delight, that he had a role. The family came to him. They came, Alice had said – and she had said this sadly – in a way they had not come to Martin.

'He is too young,' Sam had said. 'Just as I was. He is still too full of self.'

She had been determined to go and see Martin. Sam had said it would achieve nothing and she replied that it wouldn't *now*, but that it might make some little difference, later. When she came back, Sam had a plan to put to her. They would all live together. With whatever her share of the proceeds of The Grey House came to and whatever he could get for his flat, they would put together and buy a house near Reading, for the five of them. He envisaged a ménage of security and individual freedom. If, when the dust had settled, Clodagh wanted to visit them, well, he wasn't going to object. And Martin could of course come and go as he wished.

Charlie came crawling over the grass and hauled himself upright on Sam's trouser leg.

'Hello, old man.'

Charlie beamed. Sam thought of his journeys to Sainsbury's and how in future he would put Charlie in the child seat of the trolley. He lifted Charlie on to his knee.

'How about living with your grandfather then?'

Charlie examined a shirt button intently.

'We could have a dog.'

From the drive came the sound of Alice's horn, announcing her arrival home. Holding Charlie, Sam stood up and, calling the children to him, led them all round to the garage to greet her.

223

CHAPTER SEVENTEEN

The cottage was undeniably ugly. It was built of yellowish brick under a blue slate roof and stood in a long garden that ran down to the lane, a tangled garden with aggressive great clumps of delphinium and hollyhock and ornamental sea kale. There was also an apple tree groaning with fruit; it was clearly in the habit of being so prolific because one long, low, laden branch was propped up on a stout wooden stake driven into the ground.

The cottage was uncompromising as well as ugly. It had four rooms upstairs and two downstairs, and in a narrow wing running out at the back, a bathroom above a depressing kitchen. The previous owners had believed very much in hardboard. It was nailed over fireplaces and panelled doors and bannisters and beams, and had then been painted in either mauve or apricot emulsion to blend in with the surrounding walls. In the sitting room there was a fireplace of faintly iridescent tiles and below every tap in the house stains spread in green and brown tongues.

Two miles further up the valley there had been a pretty cottage for sale. It was built of stone and the interior was beamed and friendly. There had been great pressure on Alice to choose it because even if many of those exerting pressure didn't much, at the moment, care where she lived, they wanted the children to live somewhere attractive. But Alice had been adamant. She had been adamant about a lot of things and choosing East Cottage rather than the pretty stone one was one of them. The others were that she would live alone and that she would not, because of the children and their schools, leave the Salisbury area. She would move to the other side of the city, but she and Martin would have to risk meeting by mistake now and then. She was also adamant that he and the children should see a great deal of each other.

Natasha was disgusted with East Cottage. Her bedroom was the size of a cupboard and smelled of mushrooms. The walls were

224

papered with fawn bobbly stuff and there was a grey bit on the ceiling that looked squashy. Alice said the room would be absolutely transformed, just you wait, but Natasha didn't want to wait, any more than she had wanted to leave Pitcombe. She told Alice quite often that she hated her and was confused and miserable to find that she felt no better after saying it, so she said it again, louder, to see if that worked. Even school didn't seem the same, with no Grey House to go home to, and Sophie wouldn't be friends this term, so Natasha turned to Charlotte Chambers who was slow and charmless but who had a swimming pool at home and a huge drawing room with a white carpet. The sitting room at East Cottage had no carpet at all, just a piece of rush matting. Alice said that room was going to be wonderful too, just you wait, so Natasha had gone to stay for a whole weekend with Charlotte Chambers, to punish Alice. But the punishment had gone wrong because Natasha had been so homesick. She came home on Monday night, after school, and she shouted, 'I hate this house!' and then she cried and cried and clung to Alice. Alice said to her, 'I know it's hard to feel it, but every day we are going forward.'

'But I want to go *back*.'

'That's the saddest thing to do. Nothing is ever as good as you thought it was. Because *you* change. You see the old things with changed eyes and they *aren't* the same.'

Lettice Deverel came to tea. She came bumping up their stony drive in her old car with the parrot in its cage on the back seat. It was not a good passenger and had screamed most of the way but was pleased to be stationary and accepted a slice of apple with goodish grace. Lettice said that it would probably live for about sixty years more than she would, and that she must find a very kind, interesting person who would look after it when she was dead. James, mesmerised by the parrot's self-possession and humour and little grey blue claw holding the apple, went into a fantasy of being considered sufficiently kind and interesting. He gazed ardently at Lettice, to make her notice.

'Margot Unwin would like to see you,' Lettice said to Alice.

'Lord – '

'She needs to. It's very pathetic to see someone so capable so sad and confused. And of course she cannot talk to Ralph because she *wants* to understand and he cannot bring himself to.'

'Do you mean she wants me to *explain* – '

'I think so.'

'Lord,' Alice said again.

'She wants you to go to the Park.' Lettice looked at Alice. 'I'm afraid Clodagh is going back to America.'

Alice said in a low voice, 'I thought she would.'

'I hope it's just a passing impulse.'

'To be made a fuss of, do you mean, to be comforted?'

'She has never been hurt before, you see.'

Alice looked at her children.

'I think it's worse to leave being first hurt until you are grown up.'

'You never know,' Lettice said. 'You never know in life, which is good experience and which is damage. Do you?'

After tea, they went out of the cottage to the long shed where Alice was making a studio. Her easel was already set up and there was a trestle table with a workmanlike array of paints and bottles and jam jars of brushes.

'I shall keep myself,' Alice said. 'Martin is keeping the children, but I shall keep myself. And about time too, I can't help thinking.' She picked up a drawing. 'Peter Morris has commissioned a painting of Pitcombe Church. The interior. So I'll have to sneak back to do that.'

'Don't you *sneak* anywhere,' Lettice said. She took the sketch and looked at it. 'What is this horrible cottage for? A hair shirt?'

'It isn't horrible. It's real. You wait until I've finished with it. You see – oddly enough – it's easier to bear things here. It feels *mine*. Partly because it isn't what's expected of me, I suppose. That isn't defiance, just the best way to go forward – '

She stopped. Lettice eyed her.

'Will you be lonely?'

'No,' Alice said. She took the sketch from Lettice and propped it on the easel. 'Are you?'

'No.'

'Then you see – '

'Yes,' Lettice said, thinking of the sufficiency she had made for herself. 'Yes. Of course I see.'

Sam came most weekends. He was an enormous asset, not only

emotionally, but also because he proved to be very capable with tools. He was delighted with himself, over this.

'If you'd told me, ten years ago, to re-hang a door, I'd have gone *straight* to the pub. But look at this. Go on, push it. See? Smooth as silk. Come on, Jamie, pick up my hammer. What use is an apprentice if he won't even carry my clobber?'

He was entirely unresentful that Alice had declined to set up house with him, and as the weeks wore on he came to think that she had been quite right and that he very much liked his new double life, single in Reading, family at East Cottage. He began, too, to feel first pity and then affection for Clodagh. Without Clodagh, he would not have had these enriching and complementing roles. He made a list of winter projects for East Cottage – 'Replace gutters where necessary – Clear wilderness behind shed – Start log pile – Replace all lavatory glass with plain, etc. etc.' – which he tacked up in the kitchen so that Elizabeth, who came, astonishingly, for two nights, was drawn back and back to it, to read it over and over as if she couldn't believe her eyes.

The children thought her peculiar, but peaceful, because she did not attempt to be affectionate. She seemed to like East Cottage and professed herself quite prepared to paint window frames, which she then did patiently for forty-eight hours. She declined, to Alice's relief, to have any kind of conversation even approaching a heart-to-heart, and only said, while they were washing up once and the kitchen was noisy with the children, 'Well, you've taken a very long time to work yourself through all that nonsense, and you chose a very strange way out, but you've done it. And that's a great deal.'

When she left, she said she was going to work for the Citizens' Advice Bureau and had taken a flat in central Colchester.

'I should have done it ten years ago. Ann is a very ennervating companion. But I'm doing it now, just in time. Don't come and see me, it's a dreadful journey. I shall come and see you.'

When she had gone, James said, 'Was that really a granny?'

'Yes!'

'Oh,' he said, 'I thought she was a school lady.'

From Cecily and Richard, Alice heard nothing. Cecily saw the children when they were with Martin, and they would return to

227

East Cottage with new jerseys and bars of chocolate and books. This enraged Alice.

'It shouldn't,' Sam said. 'They are just the sad symbols of frustrated power.'

'I loved her so much,' Alice said. 'And now I can hardly bear to think of her. She wanted to eat me up.'

'Didn't Clodagh?'

Alice looked deeply distressed.

'Oh,' she said, 'Don't – '

Sam was sorry.

'I didn't mean they were the same. In any way. Oh, Allie – '

But she wouldn't speak of it any more and after a while Sam heard her, in her bedroom, crying.

'Why is Mummy crying?' Natasha said.

'Because she is missing Clodagh.'

Natasha nodded.

'Sometimes,' she said, 'that makes me cry, too.'

East Cottage was half a mile out of a village. It was an odd village, without a shop or a pub, and the church only had a service every three weeks. The priest, a young, cadaverous, scowling man, who was deeply frustrated to find himself with five rural churches instead of the inner city parish he had wanted, came to see Alice and sat drinking mug after mug of tea while he told her how useless he felt. He'd had some sort of breakdown – he would not, mysteriously, be precise – and this living was supposed to be his stepping stone back to his *real* calling. He was called Mark Murphy. Alice liked him. On his second visit – he came for supper and ate as voraciously as he had drunk tea – she told him, as a kind of test, about Clodagh, and he said, 'Love's terrifyingly hard to come by, isn't it? You have to grab it when you get the chance.'

His vicarage was a small, unappealing modern house in a neighbouring village which he said had the soul of a shoebox. He took to coming on Saturdays sometimes, to help Sam with clearing the garden, and when Sam asked him if he shouldn't be at home with his family, he said there wasn't one to be at home with, because his wife had left him two years ago and had gone home to Newcastle with their baby.

'I'm sorry,' Sam said.

'Yes,' Mark Murphy said, and sighed. 'So am I. She said she had no idea that the other woman in a priest's life might turn out to be God.'

Sometimes, in the lane going down to the main road to Salisbury, Alice passed a fair girl driving a dented Citroën with the back full of children. They had passed each other indifferently several times and then, by mutual consent, began to smile and wave. The girl left a note in the wooden mail box at Alice's gate.

'I'm Priscilla Mayne,' the note said. 'I live half a mile the other side of the village in the Victorian ruin that looks like a squat. No telephone yet. Come and see me when you feel like it.'

Alice thought she would feel like it very soon. When a postcard came from Anthony – she put it in the Rayburn at once – and one from John Murray-French which said, 'The new Grey House people are decent and dull. Don't lose touch,' she felt in some peculiar way that the possibilities in the as yet unknown Priscilla Mayne had somehow much more reality than her past, known though it was. Sam told her that this was the stuff of freedom, and that she must learn to drink whisky.

'Why?' she said laughing.

'Robert Burns. "Freedom and whisky gang tegither." Actually, freedom is headier than whisky but why not celebrate one with the other?'

It was almost Christmas before Juliet came to East Cottage. She came on a wet day when the cottage, still in a state of raw upheaval, presented its most lowering aspect, and Alice came upon her standing by her car and staring at the mountainous, sodden bonfire of Sam's clearance schemes.

'*Allie* – '

Alice seized her arm.

'Come in. Come in out of the rain. I've just made some unsuccessful bread.'

In the kitchen, Juliet burst into tears.

'Allie, it's all so *awful* – '

'No. No, it isn't. I like it here.'

'I don't *mean* here. I mean life in Pitcombe.'

'Don't be silly. We can't have left that big a hole – '

Juliet said, sniffing, 'You've left *heaps* of holes. Great black ones.

People are falling in all over the place. I've been in one for *months*. That's why I didn't come.'

'Isn't everyone making rather a meal of it?'

'Of *course* they are. Villages just do. Martin's seeing someone called Sophie. I cannot *tell* you how suitable she is. She drives a Mini and has a King Charles spaniel. Allie, I really hate you.'

'Yes,' Alice said.

'I do. How could you leave us all in the lurch like this? Henry's got so pompous I think I'll have to knife him. It's only kind. I'm calling him Eustace in the mean time so I expect he'll knife me first. Allie,' Juliet said, bursting into fresh tears, 'it's such a relief to see you even if I think your behaviour so detestable that I can't think how it *can* be.'

Alice poured them both a glass of wine.

'I'm doing the school run,' Juliet said. 'I really shouldn't. Blubbing and booze makes me quite incapable of anything except *more* blubbing and booze. Are you pleased to see me?'

'Tremendously.'

'Have you got new friends?'

'One. And I'm planning another.'

'Don't like them too much – '

'That's not very kind.'

'I don't want to be kind,' Juliet said, 'I want to punish you like mad.'

Alice took Juliet all over the cottage and explained what she was going to do with it. Juliet said it hardly seemed worth it.

'It isn't just a cottage,' Alice said.

Juliet said too right, it wasn't. They got Charlie up from his rest and took him down to the kitchen, and he sat in his highchair, damp with sleep, and yawned at his lunch. Alice gave Juliet more wine and made omelettes and they talked about Cecily and Martin and the Unwins, and when Juliet said she really must go, really, truly, she came and put her arms round Alice and kissed her, a thing she had almost never done, and then she drove away in the rain, waving and waving.

When she had gone, Alice took Charlie into the sitting room and put him on the floor with his cars and the garage she had made him out of a grocery carton. Then she brought in coal and wood and newspapers to light a fire before the children came back from school, and knelt by Charlie, blowing at the kindling. When it had flared up comfortably, she sat back on her heels and watched the flames and Charlie crawled into her lap and offered her a police car. She put her arms round him and laid her cheek on his warm head. Even as she sat there, holding Charlie, Clodagh was somewhere above her, above those relentless grey clouds, flying alone to New York. Alice shut her eyes. Clodagh. To be remembered always with pain and thankfulness.

A
Passionate
Man

JOANNA TROLLOPE

FOR TOBIT

CHAPTER ONE

O ld Mrs Mossop always put her teeth in for the doctor. She did not accord this honour to the vicar because the vicar was too much in earnest, and physically unprepossessing with it. But the doctor had sex appeal and to that Mrs Mossop responded, never mind being over eighty and in the process of dying slowly from a secondary cancer. So when the doctor's mud-splashed car pulled up outside her cottage – she was always on watch from her chair by the window – she would fish about in the tumbler on her windowsill where her teeth swam, and slot them into place.

This little ritual was never lost upon the doctor.

'All the better to eat me with, I see.'

Granny Mossop gave a high laugh.

'Spit you out again sharpish!'

Archie Logan smiled. He was very fond of Granny Mossop and he found her fierce gallantry in the face of her slow inexorable dying extremely moving. The room in which she sat smelled like a mouse's nest, crammed in every corner with cuckoo-clock furniture and ornaments and crocheted mats. Over the fusty muddle the great grey face of the television set presided calmly. Granny Mossop only turned it on to watch boxing and football and disasters on the news. She didn't mind blood, she told Dr Logan. Her father had been a gamekeeper. She'd grown up with blood.

He put his bag down on a fat armchair full of knitted cushions and rummaged in it. He had to toss questions nonchalantly at her or she would say, 'That'd be telling,' and they would get nowhere.

'Holding on to what you eat?' he said, his back to her.

1

'More or less. Don't fancy much.'

'I hope your daughter's looking after you.'

Granny Mossop snorted.

'Indian muck'n rubbish. I won't touch it.'

He bent over her to begin his examination. She was as small as a sparrow. While he was occupied, she peered into his thick hair and observed a scattering of grey hairs.

'You forty yet?'

'No,' Dr Logan said equably, listening to her heart.

'I didn' have a grey hair till I were fifty-three.'

'Ah. But you are made of sterner stuff than me. Back pain?'

She hated confessing, so she said nothing.

'Back pain,' he said, stating it.

He straightened up to write something down, dwarfing the little room and the littler woman.

'I'm going to give you something to slow the machinery up a bit.' He had said 'bowels' to her once and her response was so strong that now he resorted to euphemism.

She tossed her head.

'That all you can do for me?'

He surveyed her with affection.

'I could always shoot you.'

She loved that. She flung her head back with delight.

'You'd miss! You'd miss!'

'If you lose any more weight, you'll probably be right.'

She ducked her head suddenly and spat her teeth out into her cupped hand. It was his signal to go. When she'd had enough, she made it very plain and, in Archie Logan's view, her dignity and independence came even before the pace of her dying. Her teeth fell with a splash into the tumbler.

'I'll give the prescription to Sharon. She can pick it up with the next Indian take-away.' He shut his case and looked over towards her. 'I'll be in again on Friday.'

She snorted again faintly. He let himself out, stooping through the low doorway that led directly into the cottage's front garden where the lank remnants of a runner-bean row flapped above an empty rabbit hutch. Over the fence in the next-door garden, Granny Mossop's grandchildren's impudent modern washing blew

2

on a yellow nylon line. Her daughter Sharon had taken out the little cottage windows of her front room and replaced them with a single bleak sheet of plate glass, so that the room behind gaped exposed and defenceless to the public view. Archie Logan could see a half-adult boy in jeans and black leather jacket slumped in a chair in front of the television. How long, Archie wondered, slamming the cottage gate with vehemence, how long since that boy had been in to see his grandmother?

He looked up at the October sky. The sun was just beginning to go down behind some dramatic streaks of grape-coloured cloud and, for no reason that he could think of, Archie Logan was suddenly and poignantly reminded of a holiday he and Liza had had years before, an autumn holiday in Tuscany, when they had been caught in a thunderstorm at Bagni di Lucca, all among the rocks and the river and the chestnut trees. They had been drenched, soaked to the skin, and, while stumbling back to their car, had been accosted by a courteous man with an umbrella who had taken them back to his immense and battered Edwardian villa and given them baths and malt whisky. Archie could see Liza now, wrapped in her host's mothy old camel-hair dressing gown, sitting on a club fender with her bare feet held up off the marble floor, sticking her tongue down into her whisky glass. 'The Tuscan winter rains,' their host had said in his beautiful English, 'can be long and terrible.'

The thought of Liza made Archie think he would go home before evening surgery. Liza would be at home because Wednesday was her whole day off from Bradley Hall School, where she taught part time. And Mikey would be back from school and he would see Imogen before she was put to bed. And there might be a letter from Thomas, a letter to heal the wound of his first letter from boarding school.

'I don't see why I have to be here,' Thomas had written. 'It's awful. I liked going to school in Winchester and then coming home for bed. I don't like going to bed here. It's when I cry.'

Archie got into his car and banged the door shut with unnecessary violence. He drove off at great speed, and old Mrs Mossop, who had been waiting for his farewell wave –

although she planned to ignore it – drooped a little in her solitary chair.

Liza Logan, her red curls tied up in a Black Watch tartan ribbon, was sitting at the kitchen table hearing her second son's reading practice. Across the table Imogen, who was three, drew uneven suns and stars on the cover of the current parish magazine with a black wax crayon. In the utility room off the kitchen, Sally, a local farmer's daughter who looked after Imogen while Liza was teaching, and did a lot else besides, was pulling out of the tumble dryer an avalanche of socks crackling with static. A liver and white spaniel, sprawled on a blanket in a corner, was the only creature to rise politely when Archie entered and wag its feathered tail in greeting.

'It's Daddy,' Imogen said to her mother helpfully.

Liza raised her face for Archie's kiss.

'So it is.'

Archie kissed her mouth. He always kissed her mouth, however casual the kiss. It had been her mouth with its faintly swollen bee-stung lower lip that had first drawn him like a magnet, across a room at a party, to peer at her with desire and fascination. The party had been to celebrate Liza's engagement to someone else and Archie had been taken along by a mutual friend who disliked walking into parties alone. The morning after the party, Archie had begun to lay seige to Liza and within ten days he had captured her from Hugo Grant-Jones and, instead of a sapphire surrounded by very bright new diamonds, Liza was wearing a battered old half-hoop of garnets that had belonged to Archie's dead mother.

'Five stones,' Archie said, sliding the ring on to her finger. 'For five words: Will you be my wife. Will you?'

'Oh yes,' Liza said, and then without meaning to, 'yes *please*.'

It had been like 'Young Lochinvar'. Fosters, Fenwicks and Musgraves, in the form of Liza's outraged family and friends, unleashed a torrent of disapproval and pressure and objection. Archie put Liza into his car and drove her to Argyllshire where his father had a house on the shore of Loch Fyne, a house without a telephone, and kept Liza there for two rapturous weeks. Then he brought her back south, and married her.

4

'When I come home,' he said to her now, his mouth still almost on hers, 'why don't you get up and wag your tail?'

'Oh, I do. In my mind. You see, Mikey had just got to this perfectly riveting bit about what a kestrel gives its young for breakfast, and not even the entrance of – '

'Mice,' Mikey said suddenly. 'Kestrels eat mice. They like bloody things.'

'Tho', said Imogen who had a lisp, 'do I.'

Archie went round to look at her drawing.

'Black stars. How very sophisticated.'

Imogen looked at him pityingly.

'The yellow ith broken.'

'Of course. I've just been to see Granny Mossop. Not a word of her condition will I breathe to higher authority or it will be hospitalisation for her at the double and she will die of a broken heart before her liver does it. Her fucking, bloody daughter – '

'*Archie* – '

'Sorry. Her selfish and heartless daughter brings her garbage from the Star of Agra take-away which her poor old guts can't even begin to cope with. Can you imagine?'

'I'll make her a milk pud.'

'You're an angel. But she won't thank you.'

Liza raised her face to him.

'But you will.'

He bent again.

'Oh, I will – '

'Fucking,' said Imogen conversationally to Mikey.

'Shhh,' he said delightedly.

Sally came out of the utility room with a plastic laundry basket heaped with folded clothes under one arm. Mikey plucked at her as she passed.

'Did you hear what Daddy said?'

Sally, whose home-life vocabulary was comfortably thick with obscenities, said she had.

Archie said, 'Sorry, Sal.'

'It's all the same to me,' Sally said, picking Imogen up deftly with her free arm. 'What you say about Sharon Vinney.'

Imogen put her arms around Sally's neck.

5

'I thaid fucking.'

'I heard you,' Sally said without interest. 'And if I hear you say it again, I'll smack your bottom. Come on, bath time.'

'*Not* hair wash – '

'Imo,' Archie said, 'won't you blow me a kiss?'

But the nightmare of probable hair wash had gripped Imogen's mind and she could not hear him. When the door had closed behind them both, Imogen could be heard still pleading urgently as she was carried up the stairs.

'Even if Sally wasn't a tower of strength,' Liza said, 'I'd employ her simply to wash Imogen's hair. Archie, your father rang.'

He gave her, at once, his complete attention. As she often remarked to friends, and to her sister Clare who was the only one of her family she ever really saw, she had never known a father and son as close as Archie and Andrew Logan. At first, she had loved it because she had felt taken into a powerful, impregnable male citadel as a precious captive. They had both brooded over her with exciting possessiveness. She had been transformed from being just the third daughter of a Haslemere accountant into someone particular and valuable. But of course, in time, she had grown used to that transformation and now the bond between father and son seemed to her rather more exclusive than inclusive, and to have about it an air of male self-sufficiency which, try as she might, she could not help resenting. She sometimes thought that if Archie had not retained his power to stir her so, she would not have minded his adoration of his father so much.

'What did he want? Isn't he coming on Sunday?'

'Oh, he's coming. But he wants to bring someone.'

'Of course,' Archie said comfortably. 'Maurice Crawford. It's about the new series – '

'No,' Liza said, shutting up Mikey's reading book, and rising. 'It's a woman.'

'A woman! Good God.'

Liza began collecting up the mugs and plates on the table.

'She is called Marina de Breton. He sounded quite excited.'

'Marina de Breton – '

'Yes.'

'What a deeply affected name.'

6

'She can't help that. She's the widow of a Louisiana cotton king or something.'

'American!'

'No,' Liza said. 'Greek. Or Italian.' She put the mugs on the draining board and came over to Archie. 'Darling. Don't look so thunderous.'

'I'm not – '

'You look,' Mikey said encouragingly, 'just simply bloody livid.'

'Dad doesn't *have* women.'

'You don't know he has this one. He only wants to bring her to lunch, for goodness' sake.'

'You said he sounded excited – '

'Archie,' Liza said exasperatedly, 'don't make so much of so little.'

He would do this, cling obstinately and exaggeratedly to a mere shadow of an idea and make a whole imaginary mountain of it in no time, and it was one of the things about him that drove her mad. Others were his untidiness and the impulsiveness that throbbed in him as steadily and regularly as a second heartbeat. Perhaps he'd inherited all these disordered qualities from his Welsh mother, because Sir Andrew Logan certainly hadn't passed them on.

'You're being a fool,' Liza said to Archie. Mikey was watching them both with troubled interest. 'Your father says may he bring one harmless woman to lunch and you behave as if she was a – a – ' She broke off, at a loss for an analogy.

'A wicked witch,' Mikey said, and then added, because his suggestion had fallen into a complete silence, 'I expect.'

Archie shrugged.

'Sorry.'

'Anyway,' Liza said, 'even if she is someone special, you ought to be pleased. For him, I mean.'

Archie looked at the clock above the cooker.

'Lord. It's ten to six. Liza, I've a few calls to make after surgery so half-past eight, maybe – '

'Maybe.'

He took her arm and pulled her to him so that he could kiss her,

7

and while he was doing it, it occurred to Liza that if Sir Andrew really did feel something particular for this de Breton person then she could have Archie back all to herself. Thinking this, she responded to his kiss with enthusiasm.

'Wonder bird,' he said to her and, stooping to kiss Mikey as he passed, went whistling out to his car.

In the waiting room of the local health centre, a couple of dozen people sat about on green-painted chairs among the rubber plants and the low tables for magazines which were exactly the right height for toddlers to create mayhem on. It was a new health centre, with swooping roofs like a Swiss chalet, and immense windows to the floor which, at night, patients avoided sitting next to. Cork notice boards afforded plenty of space for exhortations about obesity, alcohol abuse, Aids and drug addiction, and, behind sliding panels of pine and glass, the receptionists and pharmacist sat like bank clerks.

When Archie came through, at a run, there was an affectionate murmuring. Dr Logan was always late, always, but then he was never too busy to see you and always had a smile and he was wonderful with children and the old people. The health visitors and district nurses were keenly conscious that the place had a different atmosphere on Dr Logan's days off, less energetic, less, well, less fun, really. He came in for a good deal of tolerant, maternal cluckings, except from the pharmacist who was clever and sharp and divorced and who cherished for him much stronger feelings than those of amused affection, and therefore kept herself aloof from him and was rigorously courteous when they spoke. When Archie and his rush of apology had disappeared through the double doors at the far end of the waiting room, the senior nurse on duty went off after him with quiet officiousness, to check that the slats of his venetian blind were discreetly pulled vertical and that the examining couch was suitably shrouded in a clean, disposable paper sheet.

'There we are, Doctor. Everything all right?'

He was hastily riffling through the buff packs of patients' notes on his desk.

'Yes,' he said absently. 'Thank you.'

8

'I've put out a clean roll of towel by the basin. And fresh soap. And I moved the disposable gloves nearer the bin. Seemed more logical.'

'Don't move things,' Archie pleaded. He looked up at her. She was a suburban little woman who was determined to reform the muddle and mess of this country practice into something altogether more trim.

'I only thought – '

'I know.' He flapped some notes at her. 'Not your fault. But I can only work in chaos. Ask my wife.'

Nurse Dillon allowed herself a little smile to show that she was not in the least disappointed that she had failed to please him. He had mud on his shoes, she noted. She looked at it penetratingly for a second and then went away to summon the first patient.

Archie liked taking surgeries. Long ago, long before Liza, he had had a raven-haired girlfriend who had demanded to know if he was going to be a doctor because he liked bodies. Yes, he said, he did like bodies, and, after a pause, he had added that he particularly liked women's bodies. This had given the raven-haired girlfriend the perfect opening for a great deal of predictable abuse which he came to see was an attempt to make him admit that he liked her body better than any other. He did, for a week or two – or perhaps it was really her lustrous waterfall of black hair that was so weirdly erotic – but then he became repelled by the rapacity of her character and her body ceased to interest him. But the bodies of the sick were another matter, a matter of extraordinary interest: how and why this delicate, complex and individual human machine should develop strains and faults, and how those, in turn, were dependent upon the fuel of personality. He wasn't like his father, who preferred the seclusion of laboratory and operating theatre, and he grew impatient with manuals and books. What he liked was the listening and the touching, the sense of exploration and sometimes discovery that made even the prospect of old Fred Durfield, hobbling in now in a perfect gale of grievance against the arthritis that was gradually doubling him up like a series of human paper clips, an absorbing one.

'You're no use,' Fred said. 'Them damn tablets i'n't no use. I'm goin' to die as crippled as my father before me.'

9

He thumped a transparent brown plastic bottle down on Archie's desk. It was almost full.

'How many of these have you taken, Fred?'

'No more'n a couple. Didn't do no good.'

Archie began to explain patiently the mechanics of a course of medicine, knowing that Fred would neither listen to nor heed him. Fred's mother, seventy years before, had fed him her own rural fatalism along with his childhood porridge, a fatalism that ran in a black stream through so many of Archie's villager patients. He wasn't sure, however, that he did not prefer it to the helpless rag-doll surrender to ill health and state medicine of another section of his patients, an almost greedy abandonment of self-sufficiency to an endless cycle of pills and self-neglect. A permanent state of not being quite well became as natural and necessary to them as breathing. Children, on the other hand, could only be what they were, well or ill, and among the middle- and upper-class patients there prevailed an ostensible impatience with ill health, a desire to be seen to make light of anything the matter.

Diana Jago, who occupied the best house in Archie's village, and who now sailed in after Fred Durfield, began by kissing Archie as if they were at a cocktail party and went on to say with throwaway nonchalance, 'Too boring, but it's my wretched foot, that poisoned thing, simply won't go away,' and then rushed straight on to ask about Archie's children.

Put Diana Jago in hospital, he thought, examining her big and handsome foot, and she'd be demanding at once to know why, in this day and age, the food was still so disgusting.

'Do you know, I don't think it's poisoned. I think it's gout.'

'Archie. Don't be *idiotic*. Gout – '

'Could be. Long-term side effect of the diuretic you take.'

'But I'm a woman. And I never drink port.'

'I'm afraid neither have anything to do with it.'

'Archie,' Diana Jago said firmly, settling her domed velvet hairband more securely on her sleek corn-coloured head, 'do not be an ass. How do I go home and tell Simon I have *gout*? He will simply crack up. I'll never hear the end of it.'

But she was enchanted at the ludicrousness of the possibility.

Archie could hear her at meets – she looked mouth-watering on horseback, particularly in the severe sartorial glamour required for hunting – calling penetratingly across to her friends, 'You haven't heard, too utterly laughable, but I have gout, I tell you, no, I'm not making it up – it's total agony, I can tell you – but, yes, *gout* – '

He prescribed her Naprosyn, was kissed again, promised to bring Liza to supper soon and exchanged her breezy, attractive presence for a small boy who had fallen off a shed roof.

'What on earth were you doing up there?'

But the boy, who had been hiding from his stepfather and who knew that further trouble awaited him for doing to his arm whatever he had done, merely looked at the floor and said, 'Nothing.'

Only when he came out of the surgery did Archie think again about his father. Their bond was both strong, and of long standing, because the Welsh girl whom Andrew Logan had found when on a walking holiday in Betws-y-Coed and had persuaded to come to Glasgow with him, and to marry him there, had been killed in a car smash on the A80 going out to Garnkirk to look at a dining-room table – golden mahogany, the advertisement had said, not red, and about 1820 – advertised for sale in the *Glasgow Herald*. Archie had been a baby, in a carrycot in the back of the car, from which he had been plucked by a policeman, with no more than bruises. His mother had died at once, from the impact of crashing into a van which had stopped in front of her without warning. She had broken her neck.

She had been married to Andrew Logan for three years, and, if he had ever opened his heart to anyone, she was the only possible person. He took her body back to her family in the Vale of Conway, and endured with difficulty the emotional Celtic fervour of her burial service. Then he resigned from his job at the Glasgow Royal Infirmary, sold his flat in Park Terrace, and brought his baby son south to London and a narrow Georgian house in Islington, convenient for public transport to the Middlesex Hospital. Once settled, he gave himself over to his boy and to his work on the secondary circulation of the heart.

11

Odd, Archie thought now, turning the car out of the health centre car-park and into the dark lanes of the Hampshire countryside, odd to think that his father's work on the heart had made him an international figure while leaving, quite literally, his own heart untouched. Sir Andrew had lived now for almost forty years without a woman. Archie's childhood had featured a number of housekeepers of whom only one, a strong-minded widow with a passion for Pre-Raphaelite painting, could he recall with either affection or distinction. She had taken him once, by train, to the city gallery in Birmingham to show him the wealth of her enthusiasm, and he had adored the paintings with a kind of adolescent lust, and been badly thrown by his father's disapproval of the whole expedition.

'Great painting,' Andrew Logan had said to his son, 'really great painting, is without self-indulgence.'

He thought that, Archie came to learn, about life, too. Great lives, however visionary, must be underpinned by diligence and self-denial. Extravagance of feeling or behaviour would only dissipate those precious energies that were there precisely to enable a man to make his life of value. It was often hard for Archie, in whom a powerful sensual appetite had been planted along with a measure of wayward emotional and mental powers which he sometimes suspected owed their being to the more eloquent and excitable air of the Vale of Conway. Archie had ardour; his father, as far as he could possibly perceive, had not. His father had instead balance and judgement and, in addition, honour and a most effective compassion, a compassion that achieved results for its objects.

But no woman. My lifetime almost, Archie thought, flicking up his headlight beam so that distant objects, trees and bushes, seemed suddenly to leap out at him. And his father was so sweet to Liza, had been so from the beginning, from that first meeting at the Savoy Grill, where he always liked to eat, where they kept him a secluded table and where he was looked after by a waiter of great experience who owned a cigar cutter once given to him by Winston Churchill. They had sat Liza between them and persuaded her to eat the first oysters of her life and, at the end of dinner, Andrew Logan had picked up Liza's little hand, and kissed it and said, 'I'm a grim old stick, but you'll find me very steadfast.' She

12

had adored it. Adored him. He had made a point, from the beginning, of including her in every way in his love for Archie. Indeed, he spoiled her. He seemed to like it. When Liza sometimes got angry now and declared furiously that grown men, real *mature* men, grew out of this nursery dependence on their fathers, she never accused Andrew of favouring Archie, because, even in a temper, she knew it wasn't true.

And when the bizarre chance happened, and it was discovered that all the inhibitions Andrew Logan had before people simply fell away before the television cameras, Liza was quite as proud as Archie. That first series of *Meeting Medicine*, when half the nation, it seemed, stayed in on Tuesday nights to watch those quirky, humorous, fascinating explanations of their bodies to themselves, had had them both rejoicing, quite spontaneously.

Very occasionally, as his father's fame grew and he was photographed in groups that invariably included lovely women, Archie would say to Liza, 'D'you think he has a secret girlfriend?'

And Liza usually said, 'God, I hope not. I'd be so jealous.'

But now, faced with the possibility that he had indeed found a woman, Liza didn't seem to mind. You should be pleased, she'd said, pleased for your father.

'Well,' Archie said out loud, turning the car into a curved drive in front of a solid stone house thickly moustached in pyracantha, 'I'm not pleased. Not pleased at all.'

From an upper window a curtain moved and the anxious figure of the patient's wife peered down into the drive.

'In fact,' Archie said to his car as he slammed the door behind him, 'I'm bloody miserable. So there.'

13

CHAPTER TWO

T he doctor's house was not a pretty building. It was a Victorian brick villa of great solidity, with double bay windows in front whose sashes rose and fell with reliable and weighty efficiency. The house was set on the edge of the village of Stoke Stratton in a wide, shallow trout-stream valley sloping down through the gentle chalky hills to Winchester. Stoke Stratton, a miscellaneous village architecturally, straggled along a minor road parallel to the Stoke river, with path-like lanes running down from it to the water's edge. Other lanes wandered away from the road and the river towards the northern lip of the valley, and on one of these less desirable lanes – the best houses were of course close to the river – Beeches House was set on a gentle bank.

In front of the house a rough lawn dotted with the paraphernalia of children's amusements – a climbing frame, a sandpit, a swing suspended from an immense cherry tree that flowered profusely and pinkly in spring – stretched down to the lane and was separated from it by a post-and-rail fence, patchy with brilliant moulds. Behind the house, and beside it, was a semicircle of beech trees, through which could be glimpsed the fields of plough and pasture rising to the modest skyline. The right-hand sweep of trees also served to screen their only neighbour, a cream stucco bungalow set in a regimented garden, inhabited by a middle-aged couple who lived in terror of being asked to be involved in anything. It was really on account of the beeches that Liza and Archie had bought the house.

Inside, the house had a sturdy, pleasant and practical feel that Archie told Liza was inescapably bourgeois. It was, of course, but it was to Liza a very much more acceptable variety of bourgeois

14

than the refined sort – fringed lampshades and Dralon upholstery – that had permeated the house in Haslemere. Her mother disliked colour, indeed she was alarmed by visual strength of any kind, and Liza's childhood had taken place against a dim background of muted pinks and blues and little lamps and midget ornaments. After that, Beeches House seemed to her to have an exciting and masculine strength, and its position, in open country on two sides, to be properly uncompromising. She had only driven Archie down the residential road where she had grown up – her parents felt they were making some kind of moral stand by refusing to welcome him to The Lilacs – and he had said that he had no idea that families lived in such places, not really lived. And Liza, adoring him, reduced to rubble when he kissed her, said he was right: they couldn't.

They were married five years before they bought Beeches House. Before that, Archie was working as a junior hospital doctor in London and they lived in the basement of Andrew's house in Islington. Then he sold it, to move into a mansion flat near Victoria Station which he said reminded him of Glasgow, and Archie, who had by now decided that general practice was where his inclination lay, found a job with a rural practice in Hampshire, and Beeches House. They brought Thomas to it as a baby, and from it Liza went twice to the maternity unit in Winchester, to give birth to Mikey and then to Imogen. For family holidays, they packed the children into the car and drove up to Argyllshire, to the little house Sir Andrew had bought when he left Glasgow, on the shoreline of Loch Fyne going down to Inveraray. The view from the house was directly across the water to a romantic castle-like mansion designed by Sir Robert Lorimer and backed by a famous pinetum and rearing purplish hills. Liza could never drive there without remembering the sheer glory of her first arrival, literally carried off by Archie and then wooed by him with unblinking intensity, both in bed and out, until, feeling herself to be his treasure, she knew herself also to be his slave.

Beeches House was the first house of her own that Liza had ever decorated. Her taste, strive as she might against it, tended perilously towards the tidy, so that after eight years Beeches House inside had an unresolved air as Liza's matching curtains and cushions and penchant for crisp cottons strove to hold at bay Archie's relentless acquisition of anything that caught his eye, the more peculiar the better. Birds of prey in glass cases, ancient fowling pieces, a Victorian sledge, threadbare rugs, immense jardinières, huge reproductions of Turner sunsets and Rossetti women, a fifties pinball machine adorned with cone-breasted girls in pedal-pushers, a rug made from a polar bear, old polo sticks and fishing rods, jugs and jars and antique medicine bottles, rioted triumphantly across Liza's stripped and waxed floors and leaned drunkenly against her clean pale walls. Although irritated by the mess they made, she admired them, because they represented a wholeheartedness she was afraid she did not possess (briefly, when she first met Archie, she had hoped otherwise), but she did not know what to do with them beyond dust and polish and neatly glue back bits of broken moulding. So she left them mostly where they were – trying not to adjust the angles to something more conventional – and thus Diana Jago, coming to supper for the first time, met a suit of armour in the sitting room and a stuffed badger in the downstairs lavatory, and went shouting off to tell her friends that the new doctor couple were an absolute find.

It was Diana Jago who had organised Liza's job at Bradley Hall School. Liza had read French and Spanish at the University of East Anglia, and had then been to a teacher training college outside Cambridge – it was, indeed, at a party in Cambridge that she had met her first fiancé, Hugo Grant-Jones, who had had all the impeccable credentials of a family house in Sussex, a low golf handicap and a fledgling career in a big City accepting house, that had so endeared him to Liza's parents. When Liza and Archie were first married she taught for a dispiriting year in a North London comprehensive school – she concluded she was literally too small to make any impression on thirty fourteen year olds whose every energy was channelled into defeating her – and then got herself a post in a modern languages department of a London girls' day school, where she was extremely happy. She taught until Thomas was born, and then the move came, and two more babies, and it was only when Imogen was almost two that Liza began to feel that she needed to claw back some part of herself and her life that was not devoted to the sustaining of Archie and the children. She also thought she would like some money of her own. Archie was as open as the day about money and perfectly prepared to give her anything she asked for, provided he had it, but oddly, this very generosity put a constraint upon her capacity to ask for much. She found herself accounting to him painstakingly for expenditure, explanations that were perfectly incomprehensible to him because he both trusted her and was not much interested in the first place.

So when Diana Jago came in one day unannounced, as she liked to do, leaving a magnificent bay gelding tethered to Liza's garage wall – 'No, no, don't fuss, he's fine, it'll give him time to repent over quite appalling behaviour yesterday, *and* in public' – and asked, as she always did, if there was anything she could pick up for Liza in Winchester, Liza said, 'Well, yes, actually. A job.'

'Mrs Dr Logan dear, what do you mean? The checkout at Sainsbury's?'

'No,' Liza said, heating milk for coffee. 'A teaching job. I am a qualified teacher and I want to go back to it.'

'And what,' Diana said, 'does our revered physician have to say to that?'

'All for it.'

'I'd no idea. That you taught, I mean. I thought you were simply an all-singing, all-dancing housewife. Brilliant cook. You should hear the carry-on from Simon when we've been to dinner here. I just say to him, come *on*, darling, the nags don't complain so why should you? What do you teach?'

'French mostly, but Spanish if I'm asked.'

'Olè,' said Diana Jago.

Two days later, she rang Liza to say she'd been shopping for a job as requested and she'd got one.

'You don't mean it!'

'Interview all ready and palpitating for you. Bradley Hall. I've known the Hampoles since I was a child and, although they are madder than hatters, it's not a bad school. At least the children are told how to hold their knives properly and get walloped if they call the lavatory the toilet. June Hampole's waiting for you to ring her.'

'Oh,' Liza said. 'Oh, I'm so grateful – '

'Well, don't be. After one term there, you will probably be

17

cursing my name for even thinking of it. Our two went before they boarded and it didn't seem to do them any harm. Must fly. I've got an appointment in London to have my fangs seen to. Curses, curses.'

Bradley Hall School was housed in an immense eighteenth-century barrack in decayed parkland some seven or eight miles from Winchester. The Hampole family were Catholic, either extremely devout or flamboyantly lapsed, and Bradley Hall had been their home for over a hundred years. It was built in a hollow square around a central courtyard, where a powerfully virile stone Pan rose out of a dry and crumbling fountain basin, and possessed a ballroom, a shattered orangery, a chapel and, in the grounds, an eerie domed ice-house roofed in grass.

It was June Hampole who, twenty-five years before, had decided to start a preparatory school – for both sexes – in the house, in order to enable her and her only unmarried brother to go on living at Bradley Hall. She was rewarded for this enterprise by discovering that she liked children very much indeed and also found them interesting. Her brother Dan was intermittently quite useful over the financial business of the school, but only intermittently, since bad behaviour of an exotic and eighteenth-century kind took up most of his energies. The one thing she could be grateful for was that his unorthodox ideas for pleasure did not include little boys.

Liza, arriving for her interview with Imogen sitting solidly on her hip, was shown into a most desirable room, a small, west-facing panelled room through whose immense floor-length windows the teatime sun was pouring uninhibitedly. The room was in chaos. Books, papers, folders and files were stacked haphazardly on pieces of furniture whose elegance and quality were quite unmistakable. Dirty cups and glasses stood about among plants in pots crying out for water and, in front of the lovely fireplace, two great basset hounds slumbered ponderously. When June Hampole came in, her appearance had exactly the same air of patrician disorder as her room, and in her greying curly hair two flowers of winter jasmine had caught themselves up, like yellow stars.

Liza had liked her at once. June had taken Imogen from her –

18

'What a stout little party' – and settled down for the interview with Imogen on her knee, to whom she gave some marvellous sliding old ivory toy for amusement. She seemed only anxious that Liza should be happy working at Bradley Hall.

'Order, you see, just doesn't seem to come to me naturally. I really do intend to employ you for French, but suppose Mrs West were ill, I might have to shunt you on to Common Entrance English sometimes. Would Latin terrify you? Or mathematics?'

'Yes,' said Liza. 'Particularly maths. I learned long before it was taught as a kind of logical exercise.'

'So fascinating,' June Hampole said, spreading out one of Imogen's fat hands, 'modern maths. What will you do with this little person if you come here?'

'I'll find someone – '

'Sally Carter,' June said. 'That's who you need! And she must get away from home a bit. Her father manages our farm and he uses Sally as slave labour. Shall I speak to her?'

'This is extraordinary,' Liza said. 'No sooner do I express a wish for a job than I am surrounded by people arranging it all for me.'

'We are *avid* for you,' June Hampole said. She reached for a tarnished silver box and took out of it a piece of shortbread, which she gave to Imogen. The basset hounds, scenting food from the depths of sleep, roused themselves and lumbered over to fix Imogen with lugubrious glares of envy and loathing. Imogen ate her biscuit unperturbed.

It was fixed that Liza should teach French to the three top forms – aged roughly ten to twelve – on two mornings and two afternoons of each week. In her absence at home, Sally Carter looked after Imogen – who rapidly became devoted to her because she was perfectly prepared to sing and play the same baby rhymes and games in endless repetition – and cleaned bits of the house. Liza was shy at first of suggesting she might clean lavatories or the kitchen floor, but Sally said the only thing in the house she'd rather die than do was touch anything fragile or precious, like Liza's Bohemian glass pitchers which stood on the drawing-room mantelpiece. After a few weeks, Sally said she'd come half of Liza's day off, too, and keep the ironing up together, and Liza perceived that the job was a refuge to her as much as anything, and was pleased to agree.

Bradley Hall School was not arduous employment. The classes, never over twenty in number, were composed of children whose upbringing had encouraged discipline of behaviour and outspokenness of mind. None of them were outstandingly clever and the intense parental ambition which Liza remembered from her London teaching days was almost wholly absent. A decent competence was expected, sufficient to get the boys into the right preparatory school before the right public school, and the girls into senior schools which could be trusted not to be exaggeratedly intellectual.

'Daddy says,' one ten year old said cheerfully to Liza, surveying a French pronoun exercise almost obliterated in red ink, 'that there's really no hope for me because I'm as utterly thick as him.'

Outside the classroom – Liza taught in a great white drawing room, floored in parquet and furnished entirely with scabrous desks and chairs – the school's eccentricity was manifest. Morning assemblies took place in the chapel before an altar and reredos crowned by a macabre and agonised crucifix brought back from Spain by a nineteenth-century Hampole. The figure on the crucifix, in order to defuse its possible nightmarish effects on the smaller children, was known in the school as Albert. Several pupils went on to their next schools with the conviction that Jesus and Albert were inextricable and interchangeable.

Lunch was eaten at the relatively watertight end of the orangery. June Hampole would have liked the food to be vegetarian, but, faced with relentlessly carnivorous parents, most of whom shot and fished with regularity and competence, she compromised by providing the children with mounds of organically-grown vegetables to accompany their sausages and stews. The atmosphere at meals was that of an enormous, excitable family, the younger children being offhandedly helped by the older – 'For heaven's sake, Matthew, open your stupid mouth' – and the staff member at each table keeping up a proper flow of conversation – 'Now what is it that makes you think a dog has a conscience?' Breaks were taken in various areas of the park, and running about screaming was encouraged in order to ensure the tranquillity of the ensuing afternoon: 'Come on, Melissa, haven't heard a really good bellow out of you all week!' Uniform consisted of stout pairs of blue or red drill dungarees worn over home clothes – a great impediment, the junior class teachers discovered, to getting to the lavatory on time – and a blue parka with a quilted lining which was worn indoors as well as out during the winter owing to the volatile temperament of the school boiler. Liza's classes, sitting blowing on their fingers in the glacial drawing room, resembled a Peking assembly line on a winter morning.

The staff room, which Liza grew to relish, had been the gun room of Bradley Hall. Square and darkly panelled with wooden pegged gun racks still in place around the walls, it boasted a cavernous fireplace and a gathering of elderly and welcoming armchairs. On a trestle table under one window stood an electric kettle on a tin tray, and an array of coffee jars and biscuit tins and heavy white mugs, once the property of the local British Legion hut. The room was never dusted or tidied up and you could always rely on finding someone in it to talk to.

Bradley Hall School depended on part-timers. Men and women of all ages who had had, at some point in their lives, some mild brush with teaching, pedalled or drove to Bradley Hall several times a week to teach everything from Greek to the French horn. 'None of them are exactly mad,' Liza said to Archie, 'but most of them are pretty odd.' There were three teaching constants: Mrs West, who taught English formidably well along outmoded and grammatical lines; Commander Haythorne, who ran the so-called science department with fierce practicality ('First thing I do is teach a girl how to change a plug'); and Blaise O'Hanlon. Blaise O'Hanlon was June Hampole's nephew. His Hampole mother had married an Irishman of formidable charm and waywardness, and, when their only son had emerged unsteadily from Trinity College, Dublin, had decided that, if he were not to embark upon the same improvident and wearisome path as his father, he needed a little English stiffening. So she sent him to his aunt June at Bradley Hall, to teach history from a violently Irish standpoint and to supervise soccer, cricket, the school choir and the boiler.

Blaise O'Hanlon told Liza during the second week of her employment that she would save his life.

'You're lovely,' he said to her, making mugs of coffee for them

21

both in the staff room. 'I have fantasies about you at night already.' He splashed boiling water from the kettle approximately at its targets. 'It's your mouth. How am I supposed to keep myself off your mouth?'

Liza had laughed. Blaise O'Hanlon was twenty-two. She was thirty-four and quite in control. She took her coffee mug and went to talk to Commander Haythorne. Blaise followed her.

'You'll never,' he said to Commander Haythorne, 'you'll never be keeping this woman from me.'

He hadn't stopped. In the four terms Liza had been at Bradley Hall, Blaise O'Hanlon had never ceased to tell her that she was all he wanted or needed. She had been, by turns, flattered and exasperated. He never tried to touch her and he never spoke to her amorously in front of the children. In the end, she began to feel it was simply a stupid, childish, sexless game, yet if one of her half-days went by without seeing him, she noticed. She would not let herself think she minded, but she noticed. She told Archie, occasionally, things Blaise had said or done, and he laughed. He did not laugh complacently, but with the unselfconsciousness of a man who, being faithful to his wife because he wants to be, assumes the same voluntary fidelity in her.

Sometimes, driving to school along lanes whose seasonal changes were very vivid to Liza – brought up, as she had been, to think of 'outside' consisting only of a controlled garden – the pleasure of her life struck her forcibly. She liked the shape of it, the small and manageable degree of independence she now had; she liked her country life and in it, her new authority as teacher of the children of so many people who were not only Archie's patients – 'Good Lord, you Logans, you simply *run* our lives, do you realise?' – but guests at the same parties, members of the same local committees, users of the same shops and services. Catching sight of herself in the driving mirror, she thought she even looked better because of it: less puppy plumpness, more interesting.

The only cloud was Thomas. Liza was afraid that Thomas was the last kind of child who should have been sent away to school. She had been in two minds about it all along and she still was. It was Sir Andrew who had suggested he board to prepare him better for public school, and it was Sir Andrew who was paying. All discussions about it were deeply unsatisfactory, largely because Archie, whose paternal instincts were wholly against the project, was equally at the mercy of filial instincts which made him incapable of overriding his father. They found a school in the New Forest, a jolly-looking place with Labradors in the headmaster's study, and plenty of family photographs and balding teddy bears in the dormitories.

Thomas, white-faced, said he liked it. He went to stay for a night to do some entrance tests and came home saying he liked it. He boasted about it at his day school in Winchester, starting most sentences with, 'When I go to Pinemount . . . ' and then occasionally, in the last holidays before he departed, had terrible weeping rages for no reason, and twice, to his unutterable chagrin, wet his bed.

Archie said to him when they were alone cleaning the .22 rifle Archie kept for shooting rabbits, 'Look, you don't have to go to Pinemount, you know. Nobody's forcing you. Grandpa thought you might like the chance, but a chance is all it is.'

'I want to,' Thomas said.

'Sure?'

'Yes.'

'There'd be no shame in changing your mind. We'd say at school that we'd changed ours, not you yours.'

'I don't want to change my mind.'

Liza and Archie took him down to Pinemount together. It looked reassuringly old-fashioned and friendly. Thomas walked away from them holding his old blue stuffed rabbit at arm's length as if he didn't like to be too closely associated with either it or them. There was tea for new boys and their parents which was, Archie said later, the most purgatorial social experience invented by man, and after it, they left Thomas and a few others in the care of an amiable man called George Barnes, who said, for the boys' benefit, that the sooner they could get rid of the parents and get down to business the better.

Liza cried most of the way home and, just the Winchester side of Romsey, Archie had to stop the car because he was crying, too,

23

and couldn't see. He wanted to say to Liza that he felt he had somehow failed both her and Thomas, but he did not say it because she would then have had the added burden of feeling she must comfort him.

After a bit, she blew her nose with resolution and said, 'Thomas would think we were pathetic.'

'He's probably not even thinking about us any more – '

'No.'

'It couldn't possibly be a happier sort of school.'

'Oh no.'

'Liza – ?'

'Yes.'

'One mustn't confuse one's own misery with someone else's imagined misery.'

She said nothing. Archie started the car.

'Except,' he said, 'it's imagining his possible misery that creates one's own.'

Thomas was not allowed to write home for ten days. There were all kinds of sound, humane, teacherly reasons for this. When his first letter came, it was in atrocious babyish writing and contained all the resentful unhappiness they had hoped to cheat fate of, by imagining the worst beforehand.

'Why can Mikey and Imogen be at home,' Thomas wrote, entirely forgetting his own choice and resolve, 'and not me?'

At the bottom of the sheet, he had drawn a picture of himself and the blue rabbit and underneath he had written 'We are sad'. Liza took the letter to June Hampole, who read it with the serious attention she gave anything to do with children.

'He can't bear to blame himself for having got his expectations wrong so he *has* to blame you. But it will pass. I promise. Reality will block out his expectations and he will accept that. Poor Liza,' said June Hampole, putting an arm round her shoulders. 'The little fiends are so brilliant at putting the boot in.'

Privately, Liza thought she might put her own boot in. Just a small boot. She would produce Thomas's letter at lunch on Sunday, and show it to her father-in-law, in front of Marina de Breton. It was not so much that she wanted to make Sir Andrew unhappy, as to elicit from either him or Archie – and preferably Archie –

an admission that Archie's bond to his family came before that to his father.

In the car, going to school, she practised saying, 'Archie wouldn't have agreed to Thomas's going away if the suggestion hadn't been yours.'

She thought she could say this very smilingly, in front of a stranger. She felt suddenly happy and certain, driving between the hawthorn hedges with half-bare trees marching across the fields beyond them, against a translucent sky streaked dove-grey and pale-blue. Perhaps she could begin to move things as she wanted, perhaps her power – which she would never abuse, she was certain of that – was just beginning to spread fledgling wings. Perhaps the time was quietly coming when she would not be the dependent one, the cherished childlike one, and would move from the outer circle of their life, where she presently wheeled gently with the children, into the steering, driving heart of it.

She drove into the old stableyard of Bradley Hall, and parked her car beside the wire-wheeled Alvis that Dan Hampole drove to Winchester station *en route* for London and his arcane pleasures. A double file of small boys in football boots was jiggling up and down outside a doorway, and, in front of them, Blaise O'Hanlon, his untidy Irish glamour accentuated by a frayed tweed jacket of dashing cut and an immense, dirty yellow muffler, was talking and tossing a soccer ball from hand to hand. As Liza pulled up, he sent a boy to open her car door for her.

'"L'absence est à l'amour,"' said Blaise to her as she passed him, '"ce qu'est au feu le vent; il éteint le petit, il allume le grand."' Please identify the quotation.'

But she went by him, laughing. There was no need to obey.

CHAPTER THREE

Archie, on duty on Saturday night, and called out to violent stomach pains just before midnight, and to a stroke which had smitten someone's houseguest just before dawn, slept until ten o'clock on Sunday morning. It then seemed fair to Liza to send Mikey up with a mug of tea and Imogen behind him with as much Sunday newsprint as she could manage. Archie pulled them into bed with him, but Imogen said she must take off her shoes, and struggled out again.

'Just thocks,' she said reprovingly to Mikey, climbing back in. Her hair, which grew in the same soft curls as her mother's, had been tied high on the back of her head with a ribbon woven with edelweiss. She wore a Shetland jersey under a triangular pinafore of green corduroy and she smelled of baby soap and Marmite. Archie put his face into the duckling nape of her neck and breathed in deeply.

'Nah-nah-nah-nah-nah,' said Imogen, holding a newspaper upside down and pretending to read it. 'Nah-nah-nah.'

'What's Mummy doing?' Archie said between slow kisses.

'You thcratch,' Imogen said, leaning forward. She twisted round and pushed his unshaven face away. He caught her fingers in his mouth.

'Doing lunch,' Mikey said. He offered Archie a photograph of an immense black American boxer. 'Would he beat you up?'

'Only if you were very annoying.'

'Now,' said Imogen, 'my finger'th wet.'

'Lick mine then,' Mikey said kindly.

'Bite,' Archie said, snapping his teeth. 'Bite, bite, *bite*. What have you been doing to those fingers?'

Mikey held up a hand piebald with purple stains.

26

'The felt-tip leaked. I was doing a picture for Grandpa.'

'What of?'

'A kestrel. With a mouse.'

'The mouse hath blood,' Imogen said with satisfaction.

'Grandpa is bringing a friend, you know.'

'Mummy thaid – '

'It's a lady,' Mikey said, running his purple finger round Mike Tyson's great gloved fist. 'She's called Mrs de Breton. Imogen drew her some flowers.'

'Did you, darling? What sort of flowers?'

'Black,' said Imogen.

Archie drank his tea.

'What is Mummy making for lunch?'

'She cut the bone out of the meat,' Mikey said. 'With a big knife. And then she put a whole lot of junk in.'

'What sort of junk?'

'Apricots and those little yellow nut things – '

'And rithe,' said Imogen. 'Black rithe.'

'Black rice?'

'She said it was wild,' Mikey said, lying back on the pillows. 'Looked pretty tame to me.'

Archie lay back beside him.

'Michael Logan, you have filthy ears.'

Mikey wriggled sideways so that his face was almost touching his father's.

'Clare's coming to lunch, too. She rang up and said she'd got the bad blues so Mummy said come to lunch.'

Imogen stood up unsteadily in bed, releasing a rush of cold air across Archie, and began to jump.

'Don't,' said Archie.

Imogen fell over.

'Just one'th – '

'No.'

He caught her and held her against his chest.

'No,' she said, her voice rising in protest. 'No, no, no – '

The door opened and Liza came in wearing a plastic apron which said across the front 'A Good Mother Makes a Happy Home'. She held out a jar of honey.

27

'I can't get the top off.'

Mikey seized the jar.

'Why d'you want honey?'

'To smear on the lamb.'

Imogen began to scramble out of bed.

'I do it – '

Archie took the jar away from Mikey and unscrewed the top.

'I gather Clare's coming.'

'Yes,' Liza said, stopping herself just before she said sorry. 'She sounded miserable.'

Archie swung his legs out of bed and stood up.

'Sometimes I think I'm getting compassion fatigue over Clare.'

'She *is* unhappy – '

'She loves being unhappy.'

'Archie,' Liza said. 'If, as we are, you are lucky enough to be happy, it really is the least you can do to include people in your life who are unhappy.'

Archie bent and kissed her.

'What a priggish little popsicle you are.'

'You only say that because you know I'm right.'

'Now then,' Mikey said, rolling himself up in the duvet, 'no argy-bargy.'

Liza put her hand on the door.

'It's a quarter to eleven. Your father is coming at twelve and the fire isn't lit and I don't know which wine.'

'Why are you cross?'

'I'm not cross. I'm just cooking Sunday lunch for seven and a rice pudding for Granny Mossop, having been up since a quarter to eight and done the children and the dog.'

Archie pulled on a blue towelling robe.

'Well, I'm cross.'

Mikey, encased in wadding like a human Swiss roll, sat up.

'Why?'

'Because,' Archie said, 'I don't want Mrs de Breton to come to lunch.'

'*Archie*,' Liza said.

'Why not?' Mikey said.

'Because.'

'How can you be so *stupid* in front of the children?'

'Easily,' Archie said, and went off to the bathroom.

When Sir Andrew's city-clean Rover stopped in the drive, it was the children and the spaniel who ran out to greet him. He opened the driver's door and Mikey and Imogen scrambled up to kiss him while the spaniel bounced barking on the gravel.

Marina de Breton, who had scarcely seen the English countryside before and who was charmed by the rolling slopes of the Hampshire hills, said, 'Well, Andrew, this *is* a welcome and no mistake.'

Mikey looked at her. She seemed to him very golden. From his perch on the doorsill of the car, he surveyed her gravely across his grandfather.

'Marina,' Sir Andrew said. 'This is Imogen. And this is Mikey. And you two, this is Mrs de Breton.'

'Yeth,' said Imogen.

'Hello,' Marina said, smiling. 'I am very pleased to meet you.'

She had an American voice, like television. When she said 'very', she sounded just like television. Mikey gaped. Even her clothes were golden.

'Could you please let us out? Mikey, go round and open Mrs de Breton's door. Come on, Imogen. Hop off.'

Mikey trotted round the Rover bonnet and opened the passenger door. Marina de Breton rose out of the car like a swan.

'Thank you,' she said.

Her soft suede sleeve lightly brushed Mikey's face. He wished he had not written 'For Grandpa' on the kestrel picture, so that he might have given it to Mrs de Breton. To his amazement, she took his hand. At six, he hated to have his hand held, but now he led Marina de Breton towards the house.

'Mummy,' he said, feeling a sudden and uncharacteristic obligation to be hostly, 'has put wild rice inside the lamb.'

'My,' said Marina de Breton, '*wild* rice. That's Indian rice. Indians harvest that rice in boats. It's very rare.'

'Red Indians?'

'Of course,' Marina said. 'What other Indians would they be that poled their boats along the lakeshore looking for wild rice?'

29

What, indeed. Leading her carefully up the steps to the front door, Mikey fell deep into first love. In the hall, his parents were waiting.

'This,' Mikey said, 'is my mother and my father.'

Marina held out her free hand.

'Who I am charmed to meet.'

Liza took Marina's hand in both hers in a futile attempt to convey that, if it hadn't been for Archie, she too would have rushed out eagerly to greet her. Archie, amiable, equable, affectionate Archie, had abruptly thrown a fit of childish perversity and refused to leave the house when the Rover slid up the lane. And Liza, rather than risk a row at the moment of Sir Andrew's arrival which would then poison the air with furious and exaggerated insults, chose, against her better judgement, to stay with Archie. She made this decision on the second of observing, quite suddenly, real misery beneath Archie's defiance. He had glanced at her only for a moment, but that glance was full of unhappiness.

So she said, 'Truly, I don't know what you are afraid of,' and then she had stayed beside him in the hall for some minutes, and they neither of them spoke, and Liza felt very foolish. So, to make up for all this complexity, she greeted Marina de Breton with warmth.

Archie took her hand with unexceptionable courtesy, and then, as was his wont, put his arm round his father's shoulders and kissed him. Liza had never got used to this. She despised the terrified physical inhibition of her own family, yet was startled every time to see those scorned barriers broken down. And to kiss Sir Andrew, so spare, so Scots, so buttoned up in many ways, seemed a double audacity. But he responded to Archie. He always had.

His father looked, Archie thought in bewilderment, extremely well. He wore a suit of Prince of Wales check, and a yellow waistcoat, and his lean, upright figure seemed to have an uncommon elasticity. When he stooped to pick up Imogen, and swing her into his arms – usually he waited until he was sitting down before he lifted her on to his knee – Archie wondered if this youthful display of grandfatherly playfulness was for the benefit of Marina de Breton.

Marina said she would adore some sherry if she could have some ice in it. Archie said she could have anything she wanted in it. She looked straight at him, smiling.

'Like a nice little chili,' she said.

'Imogen,' Liza said quickly, 'leave Grandpa's moustache alone.'

'Grandpa doesn't mind,' Sir Andrew said through Imogen's investigating fingers.

'Tickly,' Imogen said.

'Too right,' said Marina de Breton.

Liza made a hasty sweeping gesture with one arm.

'Do please sit down – '

'I think,' Marina said, settling gracefully into a low chair, in supple folds of caramel suede, 'that this is a charming room. Mikey, who is that character in the corner?'

Mikey looked towards the suit of armour.

'That's Sir Bedevere.'

'I found him,' Archie said, coming in with a tray of glasses, 'in a mystic lake.'

'Complete with mystic sword?'

'No,' Liza said, chattering. 'No. In a cellar, actually. The cellar of the house of one of Archie's patients. He'd gone down to find a bottle of wine, as instructed, and there this thing was, covered in rust, lying on an old mattress. And Colonel Chambers said he could have it. So he put it in the car with its great metal feet hanging out of the tailgate and we went at it with wire wool; boxes and boxes – ' She stopped.

'When you are the right size,' Marina said to Mikey, 'you must try him on.'

Mikey's eyes bulged.

'Me, too,' said Imogen.

'You're a *girl* – '

'Marina,' Sir Andrew said serenely to Liza, 'is an art historian.'

'Andrew,' Marina said with equal composure, 'I am nothing of the sort. I did a six-month course on the decorative arts in New York and I spent a summer at I Tatti. I'm no art historian.'

Liza stood up.

'Would you excuse me a moment? I must just peer into the oven – '

'I shall come and peer with you,' Marina said.

31

'You can't.' Liza was genuinely horrified. 'Not wearing that – '

Marina rose. 'I most certainly can. I want to see every inch of this delightful house.'

Followed by Mikey, they left the drawing room.

'I wanted to take you all *out* to lunch,' Marina said. 'I didn't want you going to all this trouble. But Andrew was adamant. I feel I should just have been more adamant still.'

Liza opened the kitchen door and a rich waft of roasting meat came out to meet them.

'It's so nice of you, but really, I don't mind. I'm quite used to it and my sister Clare is coming. She's divorced and she gets a bit depressed, living on her own. Now, stay right over there while I open the oven door. Mikey, guard Mrs de Breton. I'm so worried about her beautiful suit.'

Mikey herded Marina against the kitchen dresser and spread his arms wide to defend her from the menace of flying fat.

She said, laughing, 'Oh, this is just adorable. I love the whole thing.'

Liza put the roasting tin on the table and began to baste the meat.

'You did all that?' Marina said.

'Oh yes. I quite like cooking – '

'So do I,' Mikey said.

'Mikey is a whizz at pancakes.'

'If I was very nice to you, Mikey, would you someday make me pancakes?'

Mikey nodded vehemently.

'And you have an elder brother?'

'He's at boarding school,' Mikey said, dropping his arms but not moving away. 'He cries there.'

Marina looked at Liza.

'He cries?'

Liza said unhappily, 'It was so kind of Andrew to send him. And I'm sure he'll be fine. But he's taking a bit of time to settle down.'

'It was Andrew's idea?'

'It was a kind one. It was to get Thomas used to the idea of being away at public school.'

'And what,' Marina said, taking a slow sip of her sherry, 'do you think?'

Liza put the lamb back in the oven.

'I didn't want him to go,' she said with her back to Marina.

'And did you say that?'

'Sort of – '

'My dear Liza. This isn't fair of me at all. It's none of my business. But I'd have felt just as you feel. Mikey, would you know where there was more ice for my drink?'

When he had sped off, Marina said, 'Would you like me to speak to Andrew?'

Liza was startled. She thought of Thomas's letter which she had intended to produce in front of Marina. It now seemed a shabby little scheme, and in her shame she said, too abruptly, 'Oh no – '

Marina went over to the sink and looked through the window at the leaf-strewn lawn and the half-bare beeches and the pale autumn pastureland rising to the pale autumn sky.

'What a lot you achieve,' she said to Liza, over her shoulder.

No one had ever said anything of this kind to Liza.

'Do I?'

Marina turned round.

'Husband, house, children, garden, teaching, cooking. I'm bowled over – '

Mikey came back with an ice tray.

'Clare's come. Imo's being stupid and jumping on the sofa.'

'Isn't Daddy stopping her?'

'He's talking to Grandpa.'

Liza ran back to the drawing room. Imogen had fallen off the sofa and was crying in Clare's arms. Over by the bay window, which overlooked the lane, Archie and his father were deep in conversation.

Liza took Imogen from her sister and put her firmly on the floor.

'Looks like you had a lovely welcome – '

Clare was taller and thinner than Liza, with large anxious eyes and hair drawn back into a black velvet bow on the nape of her neck.

'They're talking about cot deaths.'

'How cheerful. How are you?'

Clare made a balancing movement with her hand.

'So-so.'

'Clare,' Liza said, 'this is Marina de Breton.'

'I am afraid', Marina said, taking Clare's hand and smiling, 'that they are talking about cot deaths because of me.'

Politely the sisters waited to be enlightened.

'My late husband left a trust to be used for the promotion of humanity's understanding of itself. Mostly it goes on schemes for schools and colleges, and some educational scholarships. But I saw the last series of *Meeting Medicine* and just *knew* that's where Louis would have wanted his money put. And his youngest daughter lost a baby that way, so the only condition I made to Andrew was that at least one programme – '

Clare's eyes were immense with sympathy.

'Your grandchild?'

Marina raised her eyebrows.

'No, indeed. Louis de Breton changed wives like other men change their shirts. This daughter was a child of his second marriage. His funeral was bizarre. The front pews of the church were solid with his widows, *solid*. Children and grandchildren as far as the eye could see.' She winked at Liza. 'I wore scarlet. And a hat as big as a wheel.'

They stared at her. Archie, turning from the window, caught them at it, gazing, silent, his wife, his sister-in-law and his second son. Only Imogen, doing unsuccessful headstands on the sofa cushions, was outside the spell.

'Darling,' Archie said, 'shall I carve?'

Sir Andrew was enormously happy. He looked about the dining-room table and felt a rich pleasure in everyone round it and everything on it. To him, each person, each dish, each glass and fork, seemed to have an extraordinary value and vitality, reflecting his own sudden and miraculous sense of not just being alive, which he was used to, but of living, down to each last nerve end, which he was not. He had been disconcerted, even embarrassed, by this uncharacteristic exuberance at first, had been afraid he was going to make a fool of himself, and, in the process, destroy the sober

34

esteem in which, he knew perfectly well, the world held him. But his confidence had grown with the realisation that he was not, as he had feared, a victim of elderly and absurd folly, but, rather, one of the chosen; a man – a little late in the day, perhaps – chosen to have his half-empty cup suddenly filled until it brimmed and spilled. All over his mind and body and heart, doors, long shut, some never even opened previously, were swinging wide. Looking down at his plate of lamb and vegetables, Sir Andrew was shaken with a shudder of unquestionable ecstasy at the recollection of being in bed wih Marina de Breton.

'Oh dear,' Lisa said anxiously. 'Are you cold? I'll get an electric fire. The radiator in here never works properly – '

'I'm not cold in the least,' Sir Andrew said, turning upon her a radiant smile.

She said in amazement, 'You look so happy!'

'I am.'

She blushed. He did not. He continued, with great dignity, to look unabashed and radiant.

'Liza,' he said teasingly, 'have I shocked you?'

'Not shocked – '

'Your stiff old Scots pa-in-law shouldn't fling his cap over windmills, eh?'

'Don't,' she said.

He was laughing gently. Suddenly furious with him for not having the decency to be self-conscious, she looked away and briefly caught Archie's eye across the table. He raised one eyebrow.

'More peath,' Imogen said, beside her mother. 'Heapth and *heapth* more peath.'

'Only when you have eaten everything else.'

'This,' Marina said to Archie, 'is some of the best lamb I have eaten in my life. And being Greek, I do know about lamb.'

'Greek?'

'Greek. I only put the accent on for customs officials and traffic wardens and inattentive shop assistants and anyone else tiresome. I left Athens when I was three. I had charming and unsatisfactory parents who thought New York was simply waiting for them with bated breath, which of course it was not. I do believe outrage and disappointment killed my mother. She was an early dope

35

fiend, in the days when it was still chic. Ikons and cocaine and Fortuny evening dresses – the last word in dated debauchery. Poor Mamma.'

'You are making it up,' Archie said.

'My dear. It is far too outrageous for that.'

She gave him a quick glance. He was looking away from her, towards Clare on his other side.

'Do you believe her?' Archie demanded.

Clare, whose susceptibility to male physical charms, even the familiar ones of her sister's husband, always threw her into confusion, said, 'I – I think so.'

Marina burst out laughing.

'That's adorable!'

Archie took Clare's hand.

'Don't be bullied – '

'You see,' Clare said, gathering courage from his grasp, 'Liza and I had such an unutterably boring upbringing that we can never believe it when other people tell us how fascinating theirs was. I used to pray and pray to be kidnapped and then, lo and behold, Liza was. By Archie. So unfair.'

'And did nobody kidnap you later?'

'Oh yes,' Clare said, looking down. 'Robin did. But having me wasn't as exciting as chasing me. So he went off to chase someone else.'

'That's too bad,' Marina said. 'I hope she made him perfectly miserable.'

'She does. But he likes it. I suppose it's a sort of permanent chase.'

Marina turned to Archie.

'And are you a chaser?'

'No.'

'With all these women patients Andrew tells me of, feigning illness like crazy for two seconds of your undivided attention?'

'Even,' Archie said composedly, 'with all of them.'

He stood up to carve second helpings. It looked to him as if Marina was going to throw him another challenge, so he said deliberately, 'I like being married.'

'You and your father,' Marina said, 'are remarkable men.'

She turned to Mikey, diligently eating beside her.

'And will you be a doctor, too?'

'I'm going to be a cook.'

'A cook?'

'And live here always,' Mikey said.

'You are a very unusual boy. Boys commonly can't wait to leave home. I have eleven stepgrandsons in America and they leave home all the time.'

Mikey thought about this. He thought about his bedroom and the picture of Superman over his bed and the torch he had under his pillow to flash signals on the ceiling with, after his light had been turned off. And he thought of Thomas.

'If I leave, you see, I mightn't like it so much.'

'So,' Marina said, 'will you bring your wife back to live here, too?'

'I don't want a wife. I want a dog.'

'I'm not sure that's quite the same,' Clare said quickly.

Marina waved a hand.

'He's on to something, you know. Louis de Breton's dogs had a much better time than his wives. Archie, if you were going to offer me more of that sensational lamb, I shall save you the trouble and say yes please. And I never have second helpings. Never in this world. Do I, Andrew?'

And she looked across the table at him and together, wrapped in some intimate and delightful joke, they began to laugh.

Much later, Liza said she and Clare would do the washing up, and why didn't Archie make a bonfire? Sir Andrew had driven Marina de Breton away with mysterious indications of pressing things to be done in London, and Archie had not uttered since their departure which inhibited Liza from saying all the things she was bursting with. When she suggested a bonfire, Archie just nodded and collected up his children and the spaniel and old newspapers and matches and went out into the dying afternoon. From the kitchen window, Liza watched him with a mixture of sympathy and exasperation. Clare, struck by the effortless glamour of his appearance in tall Wellington boots and an immense and dishevelled Aran jersey, felt his evident dejection to be almost tragic.

Archie himself was chiefly consumed with self-disgust. His own view of love was founded upon generosity, and, while he was well aware that clumsiness and pure maleness often prevented him from fine-tuning this outlook, his every basic instinct in love was bent upon giving. A colleague of his, whose wife had become entirely swallowed up by her Open University course in psychology, had said fretfully once to Archie, 'In my view, the least she *owes* me is a decent dinner at night.' Archie had been both struck and shocked by this. Obligation did not come into his emotional scheme of things – responsibility, yes, contributions from both sides, certainly, but never a feeling of being beholden, of being in someone's debt. Looking at Imogen now, picking up spiky beech nut shells and putting them into a broken flowerpot, made him realise the extent of her dignity and, even at three, her separate valuable power to love without abasing herself or compromising herself. He, her father, wished to give her emotional space. He wanted her love, but he wanted it freely given. He wanted his father's love in the same way, and he had always had it. He had it now. His father had, today, been demonstrably affectionate. But he had also shown that he was full of another kind of love, full of it. Archie plunged his fork into a mound of garden rubbish and flung it to the top of the bonfire.

'Jealous bastard,' he said to himself. 'Childish, shameful, jealous bastard.'

Thick, unecologically sound, blue-grey smoke uncurled itself slowly into the air and filled Archie's eyes with the blessed excuse for tears. Mikey came drifting up through the gauzy air and held out his closed fists.

'What have you got?' Archie said, smearing his jersey sleeve across his eyes.

Mikey opened his fists and revealed a pound coin in each.

'One for me and one for Imo. I'm holding on to hers because she thought it was chocolate.'

'From Grandpa?'

'No,' Mikey said. 'From Mrs de Breton.'

Archie looked unhappily down at the fat golden coins.

'Did you like her?'

'Of course,' Mikey said.

38

'Why?'

Mikey looked away, his face contorted with the impossibility of describing his susceptibility to her charm.

He said uncertainly, after a while, 'I liked her ear-rings.'

Archie held his arms out.

'Come and give your old da a hug.'

He lifted Mikey up so that his rubber-booted toes bumped against his knees. Mikey put his arms out stiffly behind Archie's head, still gripping the money.

'I'm going to save up for a guinea-pig. One of the ones with whirly bits in its fur.' He bent his head back to look into his father's face. 'You can share it if you like.'

'He's wonderful with the children, isn't he?' Clare said, rinsing wine glasses at the kitchen sink and gazing out of the window. 'Perhaps if I'd had a baby, Robin wouldn't have left.'

'He would, you know. He'd have left just the same and it would be worse for you, now, with a baby.'

'Nothing could be worse,' Clare said.

Liza was stretching plastic film over leftover helpings of lunch.

'Clare, you are not to talk like this – '

'I swore I wouldn't,' Clare said. 'I absolutely swore. But listening to Marina at lunch made me so depressed and sick of myself. I mean, you simply can't imagine her letting life get her down, can you? I thought she was amazing. And she looked so wonderful. How old do you think she is?'

Liza, who was full of the same envious admiration of Marina, said she supposed about her mid-fifties.

'But she was so sexy. Wasn't she? I mean, you and I will never be that sexy. We never have been. Have we?'

Liza was impelled to say that she thought Archie found her sexy, but stopped herself in the nick of time because it struck her that, whatever he felt, she didn't feel herself to be sexy. She picked up a cloth and began to dry the glasses Clare had washed.

She said in a very sensible voice, 'She's much more exotic than us. And sort of international. And rich. Being rich is supposed to be very sexy.'

'And all that suede, and gold jewellery. And her wonderful

39

shoes. I bet they were Italian. Liza, did you notice Andrew could hardly keep his hands off her?'

'Of course I noticed.'

'Is that what's the matter with Archie?'

Liza began to put the polished wine glasses on a tray.

'Well, it is a bit unhinging – '

'Telling me,' Clare said. 'She filled me with dissatisfaction. You're so lucky, she might become your mother-in-law and give you lunch at the Connaught and lovely presents. She looks that sort of person. Robin's mother can't see anything wrong with Robin. It has to be my fault he left. That's what she thinks.'

'Marina understood about Thomas,' Liza said. 'She offered to speak to Andrew and my first reaction was to say no, but I wonder – '

Privately, Liza thought there were other things Marina might understand about, too. 'The first of many meetings,' Marina had said to Liza before she was driven away. And she had smiled. There had been an edge of female complicity to that smile.

'I'm taking a rice pudding down the lane to old Mrs Mossop,' Liza said. 'Want to come?'

'Not really. But I don't want to go home either.'

'Clare,' Liza said warningly. She opened the bottom oven door and took out a Pyrex dish.

'I'm three years older than you,' Clare said. 'And we might almost be different generations. Look at you. All this domestic bliss and a job and village life – '

Liza wrapped a clean dishcloth round the Pyrex dish.

'Hold that.'

On the way down the hall, they passed through a lingering breath of Marina's scent and stopped to sniff.

'Honestly,' Clare said. 'It's like having a crush at school.'

Liza began to giggle.

'Aren't we idiotic?'

'No, no, I love it; I love this carried away feeling – '

'Me, too.'

'Think of what life is like for Andrew, I mean, just think – '

'I know. I simply didn't know where to look at lunch.' Liza

opened the front door. 'Do you think they just drove straight back to London to go to bed?'

'Yes,' Clare said, 'of course they did. And left us all here, years younger, simply green with envy – '

'Speak for yourself!'

'Can you,' Clare said, stepping carefully down the drive because of carrying the pudding, 'can you talk to Archie about it?'

Liza thought.

'No,' she said, 'I don't think I can. Not about that.'

'But I thought you talked about everything. Sex and everything – '

'But not Andrew and sex.'

'No,' Clare said, 'perhaps not. But will Archie think about it?'

'Yes,' Liza said slowly. 'I don't see how he can help it,' and then she took the pudding from her sister and went away with it down the lane to old Mrs Mossop's cottage, and found her there, alone in her darkening room, watching the empty Sunday lane.

'When I want charity,' Granny Mossop said, 'I'll ask for it.'

But she grew cross when Liza offered to remove the pudding and, when the sisters peered back in through the window as they left, she was hunting for spoons.

CHAPTER FOUR

O n Monday morning, Liza accused Archie of behaving like a child. She did this over breakfast, causing Mikey to weep and remember he had not done his violin practice, and Imogen to refuse, flatly, even to look at her breakfast. They were all late and a faint disheartening drizzle was misting the kitchen windows. Archie, whose provocative crime had been to remark that the sitting room still smelled like Harrods, got up in silence, kissed his children, and went off to his car. Liza was impressed to find that she felt buoyed up by indignation rather than borne down by tears, as was her wont in such situations, and merely said to Imogen as Archie's car could be heard revving in the garage, 'Eat that up when you are told.'

The car went down the drive and Imogen picked up her cereal bowl and held it upside down over the floor.

Driving down the lane towards the village, Archie wrenched his mind on to the day ahead. Surgery, visits, an hour or two at the local cottage hospital (saved from the great central state crushing machine only by relentless local effort), a practice meeting, more visits and evening surgery. The practice meeting would, he knew, be about the installation of computers at the health centre. Intellectually he was all for this but emotionally he rebelled. One of his colleagues had described him as a refugee from an A. J. Cronin novel which Archie thought, on the whole, pretty accurate. He also knew, without complacency, that diagnostically and in human terms he was the best doctor in the practice. His colleagues, with varying degrees of good and bad grace, knew this, too, and would in consequence emphasise their own additional roles as, for instance, anaesthetists at local hospitals. Archie had no wish to be anything other than a rural general practitioner and, when it was pointed out to him that he was bound to get the fidgets at forty, he said he was planning a really big break-out then, so as not to disappoint them. The pharmacist at the health centre had overheard him say this once, and had endured several terrible nights subsequently, plagued by impossible fantasies of which she was later ashamed.

Because he was early, on account of the incident at breakfast, Archie paused at Stoke Stratton post office. This was run by Mrs Betts, a formidable widow from a Southampton suburb, who used it as a power-base from which to shape and control the village. She was secretary to the Women's Institute, founder of the rambling club and organiser of the village fête. She had also revived a gardeners' group and was Clerk to the Parish Council. Tall, solid and handsome, Mrs Betts had brought to Stoke Stratton a very clear idea of what English village life should be like and a strong determination to impose this vision on the few hundred people who came to buy stamps at one end of her shop and throat lozenges, birthday cards and potting compost at the other. Progress, in Mrs Betts's view, meant power in the hands of the bourgeoisie and the neatening of sloppy agricultural ways. On her counter stood a homemade advertisement enticing her customers to sign a petition asking the local farmer not to drive his tractors down the main street of the village. As the farm lay above Beeches House, and the lane leading to it was usually liberally strewn with succulent chunks of mud, Mrs Betts was very pleased to see Archie as an early customer.

He asked for a dozen first-class stamps, some brown envelopes and a packet of peppermints.

'And you'll sign my petition, Dr Logan.'

'Sorry, Mrs Betts. No go. I've no objection to mud.'

'Come now, Dr Logan. Think of Mrs Logan. I saw her and her sister coming down your lane yesterday with the greatest difficulty.'

'It's a natural hazard of country life – '

'Only because no one has thought to do anything about it. Where would we be if we all just accepted things? Dr Logan, there are seven old footpaths now open again round this village thanks to me and my ramblers.'

43

Archie folded his stamps and slid them into his wallet.

'Richard Prior is a good neighbour to me, Mrs Betts. I'm not going to provoke him and I don't mind his mud.'

Mrs Betts laid her large capable hands on the counter.

'Dr Logan, it's you professional people who must take the lead. It's not like the old days when there was a squire to turn to. It's up to people like you and Mr Jago now to preserve our heritage.'

Archie gave her an enormous smile.

'Do you know, I think mud *is* part of our heritage.'

In the road outside, the Vicar was parking his car behind Archie's. Colin Jenkins was a narrow, pale man in his thirties with a passion for committee work, who was to be seen driving into Winchester for diocesan meetings of one sort or another far more often than around his parish. On the rare occasions when he and Archie had coincided at a sickbed, Archie had felt strongly that, should the patient die, Colin Jenkins would regard his soul as one more convert to the egalitarian and socialist bureaucracy which was his evident notion of the hereafter.

'You can't talk to him,' an unhappy patient of Archie's had once said. 'When my son was killed, I couldn't talk to him at all. If I'd tried, I'd only have got an anti-government tirade.'

This morning, Archie was in no mood for Colin Jenkins. As the Vicar slid out of his car, Archie gave a preoccupied smile and wave intended to indicate his hurry, and climbed into his own. Reflected in his mirror, he saw Colin standing in the road, looking after him, a figure at once self-satisfied and forlorn. Archie put his foot down. He suddenly wanted a telephone.

He rang from his room at the health centre.

'Sorry,' Sally Carter said, 'Mrs Logan's gone. She went twenty minutes ago. If you ring the school, you might get her before lessons.'

He rang Bradley Hall. The school secretary, a kind, confused woman with a sweet telephone manner and an aptitude for muddling bills, said Liza was in prayers.

'I'm so sorry. They've just gone in, only just. I can hear them singing "When A Knight Won His Spurs". Shall I ask Mrs Logan to ring you when she comes out?'

'No,' Archie said. 'No, thank you. It isn't urgent. It can wait.'

'But I'll tell her you rang – '

'No,' he said again. 'No. Don't bother.' And then he put the receiver down and wondered what on earth had impelled him to say no, and not just once, but twice. A dull misery collected in his throat and settled there. He cleared it decisively once or twice, but to no avail. He leaned forward and pressed his intercom button.

'Mrs Hargreaves for Dr Logan, please. Mrs Hargreaves.'

Liza sang enthusiastically. All around her the children, who liked the hymn and its clear images of storybook chivalry, sang with equal fervour. Above the altar, Albert on his tortured cross seemed to be wincing at the jovial atmosphere of folksy Protestantism in which he found himself, an atmosphere June Hampole was careful to encourage so that no enraged father could possibly accuse her of Popery. Looking across at Liza singing innocently of the death of dragons, June observed how well she looked, how happy. Liza Logan, June Hampole thought, shuffling through her pockets for the prayer she had chosen and now seemed to have mislaid, was a prime example of middle-class excellence, an unshakeable rock of competence and decency and endeavour. As she grew older, her experience would give her authority and she might well, June thought, surprise herself by her own strength. June found her piece of paper and went up to the lectern below the altar.

'Let us pray.'

The children rumbled to their knees on the floor of the chapel. June put on her spectacles and unfolded the paper.

'Dog biscuits,' the piece of paper said. 'Blankets from dry cleaners, gin, telephone tennis court people for resurfacing estimate.'

'Today,' June said, 'we are going to pray to St Antony of Padua. He liked pigs and he is the patron saint of lost things. I am tempted to rename the lost property cupboard The Cave of St Antony. Close your eyes and pray for something you have lost. I have lost this morning's prayer.'

And I, Liza thought, putting a restraining hand on the restive small boy beside her, have lost something, too. Something I did not much want. I have lost some of my inadequacy. The small boy twisted himself free and hissed in a stage whisper that he had lost his recorder.

'We'll find it after prayers,' Liza said softly, sure that she would.

'Now,' he said. '*Now* – '

'No. After prayers.'

He subsided against her and put his thumb in his mouth. She put her arm round him and thought of his parents, a tough self-confident pair who ran a small racing stable and were friends of Simon and Diana Jago. Her arm round their child, Liza reflected that today she could cope with them too with perfect assurance.

'Our Father,' June Hampole said. 'Which art in heaven, Hallowed be Thy name – '

The familiar rhythms rolled round Liza: the daily bread and the trespasses, the temptation and the forgiveness. From now on, she would forgive Archie, she would be very understanding about his attitude to Marina, she would make a huge imaginative effort to put herself in his shoes. This was difficult since she could not imagine caring much, one way or the other, if her own father produced a substitute for her mother, but not, she told herself, impossible.

'Amen,' said June Hampole and the staff and children with emphasis.

They rose, whispering, to their feet.

'No talking!' Commander Haythorne bellowed.

They began to shove each other instead until the neat lines of children bulged and swerved like serpents.

'No pushing!' shouted Commander Haythorne.

'Isn't this,' Blaise O'Hanlon said, materialising at Liza's side, 'just your best moment of the day?'

'I always rather want to join in – '

'Exactly. We are doing break duty together. I have engineered it with Gaelic cunning. What is your first lesson?'

'A passage from *Lettres de mon Moulin* with the sixth form.'

'Isn't that dreadfully advanced? Why aren't they allowed *Madame Bonnard Va au Marché*?'

'My *recorder* – ' a voice pleaded, three feet from the floor.

'Justin, I'm coming to look for your recorder. Because sometimes I simply can't bear her. Little dollops of Daudet and Fournier and Verlaine keep me sane and stretch their tiny minds.'

Two girls flattened themselves elaborately against the frame of the chapel doors to let Liza and Blaise go through.

'Thank you, Sophie. And Tamsin.'

'What I'd really like,' Blaise said as they emerged into the school hall floored in forbidding, gleaming squares of black-and-white marble, 'is to be in your class and be ticked off by you.'

'Go away,' Liza said. 'Go away and don't be creepy.' But she was smiling.

In the lost property cupboard Justin's recorder lay where Liza had visualised it, in a box among other recorders, hockey sticks, pens, pencils and a butterfly net – the principle at Bradley Hall being to sort lost objects according to shape rather than category.

'There,' she said. 'What did I tell you?'

He blew into it experimentally to see if it remembered him.

'What do you say?'

He glared. He was at an age when manners seemed almost an hypocrisy.

'Thank you,' he said, but he was scowling. Then he went scuffing off down the passage, tooting intermittently, and Liza withdrew to the drawing room.

The sixth form liked their Daudet, after the initial and ritual complaints. For most of them, their only contact with the French was quarrelsome little episodes in queues for ski lifts in the Trois Vallées and thus they were incredulous of Daudet.

'Are you sure he was French?' one of them said.

'Absolutely.'

At break time, Liza made them all zip up their parkas before they lined up with the rest of the school in the orangery for milk and a biscuit and were subsequently released into the damp grey air. Herding them towards the old orchard – where they were not permitted to eat the apples since a seven year old had bitten inadvertently on a sleeping wasp – Liza was joined by Blaise O'Hanlon, wearing round his neck the whistle he used for football coaching. He simply walked beside her, saying nothing but listening to what she was saying to the children around her.

47

'Our baby's come home. Mummy brought it. It's got no hair and red feet.'

'I expect you had red feet when you were that little.'

'Mrs Logan, Simon's got my Snoopy and when I tried to get it he done bashed me in – '

'Simon – '

The toy came whirling through the air.

'Stupid Snoopy, stupid, stupid, stupid – '

'What is your baby's name?'

'Oh, it doesn't have a name. It's just a baby.'

'Our baby's called Oliver – '

'We had one but it grew up and now it's Naomi – '

'Snoopy's got a poo-face – '

'Mrs Logan, Simon said poo – '

The crowd jostled its way through the orchard gate and dispersed to race about and scream in obedience to expectations. Liza and Blaise strolled to a central position and waited for someone to fall off something or be knocked over, and Liza, in addition, waited for Blaise to flirt with her. He did not. He said, instead, rather sadly, that he had been homesick for Ireland all weekend and couldn't seem to stop thinking about it.

'Not Dublin so much, as the West. My father has a house in Connemara. I kept wanting to be in that house by the peat fire with proper Irish rain outside, not this milksop stuff.'

'Well, why don't you go? At half-term. Why don't you fly to Shannon and go?'

'I might,' Blaise said, and looked straight at her.

Two boys, in pursuit of a battered Bramley apple they were using as a football, came careering past, missed their footing in the slippery grass, collided and cannoned into Liza. She staggered back, off balance, and was caught deftly by Blaise.

He said, 'You idiotic, clumsy little sods,' and restored Liza gently upright. Then he did not take his arms away.

She said, 'Oh, thank you, Blaise, but really I'm fine.'

He said, 'Me, too,' still holding her.

She twisted to look in his face and it wore a new and serious expression. He made a tiny movement and, realising that he was about to kiss her in the midst of a hundred and eighty-three

48

children, she made a sudden and determined effort and broke free.

'*Blaise.*'

He said nothing. He merely gave her a long, hard look and then moved away, blowing his whistle to round up their charges. Liza felt breathless and strangely daring, a feeling not unlike the one she had experienced at breakfast when she told Archie he was behaving like a child. The two boys with the apple came up and said, looking at their feet, that they were sorry.

'It's all right,' Liza said. 'You slipped.'

They gaped.

'Didn't you?'

They nodded.

'Well, then. Off you go. End of break.'

They cantered off, howling. Liza thought of Mikey doing the same thing on his well-ordered Winchester playground. Then she thought of Thomas.

'What is it?' Blaise said, coming up.

Her eyes were huge.

'Thomas.'

'May I comfort you?'

'I – I don't think you'd better.'

He took her hand. She removed it.

'No.'

He sighed.

'Do you think I'm different today?'

Liza shot him a glance.

'A little gloomier – '

'The thing is,' Blaise said, 'that serious lust has turned into serious love. I'm in real pain.'

'Nonsense.'

'Liza – '

'Come on,' she said repressively, but her heart was very light. 'Come on. We have to get this lot unbooted and into class.'

Driving home after lunch, Liza stopped in the village to buy a postal order for a set of rubber dinosaurs Mikey had saved up for, from the back of a cereal packet. He had taught Imogen a dinosaur song that began 'Hocus, pocus, I'm a diplodocus' which she sang

49

with the relentless repetitiveness of the Chinese water torture. When Thomas had had his dinosaur phase – as inevitable a part of childhood, it seemed, as losing milk teeth – he had suffered nightmares about a *Tyrannosaurus rex* which he could see circling in the beech trees on windy nights, clashing its leathery wings and gnashing its terrible teeth.

Mrs Betts liked Liza. She approved of her clean, pretty appearance, the deference she showed to senior Women's Institute members, and her suitable, socially responsible job. Liza, in her turn, tried not to be put off by Mrs Betts's refinement, bossiness and mauve mohair jerseys (today's had a pie-frill collar and three glass buttons) and to remember that Mrs Betts encouraged the kind of village community rallying that Colin Jenkins's wife declined to do.

'Now, Mrs Logan,' Mrs Betts said with an arch smile. 'I know you're not going to fail me.'

'I hope not,' Liza said.

Mrs Betts made a flourishing movement towards her anti-mud notice, and her coloured glass bracelets chinked together playfully.

'Naughty Dr Logan wouldn't sign this morning. Said he wasn't upset by Mr Prior and he didn't mind mud. All very well for you, I said, but what about poor Mrs Logan, visiting the old people down the lane that looks more like a field? To be perfectly honest, Mrs Logan, Mr Prior is taking more and more liberties with this village. I hear a nasty rumour that he wants to sell off the field next to your house for development. People like that have to be stopped early on, Mrs Logan. And that's where my petition comes in.'

Liza, who didn't in the least mind about the mud, but was alarmed at the threat of development, said, 'Are you sure about that? About the field next to us?'

Mrs Betts leaned forward.

'Between you and me, I've a friend on the local planning committee and he,' she paused so that Liza could draw interesting inference from the pronoun, inference flattering to Mrs Betts, 'gave me to understand that an application has been submitted by Mr Prior. No more than a hint, mind you. Just giving me fair warning.'

50

'When did you hear this?'

'Saturday night.'

Liza thought of Mrs Betts and her friend in the lounge bar of The Keeper's Arms, the pub in King's Stoke, their neighbouring village. It had wall-bracket lights, shaded in red imitation silk, and fake-tapestry cushions, and kept a range of country wines which proclaimed themselves to be made from elderflowers, and wheat and whortleberries. She could imagine Mrs Betts saying, 'Mine's a small port, please.'

'Oh dear,' Liza said. 'Have you told anyone?'

'Just yourself and Mrs Jago when she popped in for a "Get well" card. I would have mentioned it to Dr Logan but he was in such a rush – '

'Surgery,' Liza said appeasingly.

'Of course, Mrs Logan.'

Liza looked at the anti-mud petition. The Jagos hadn't signed nor had old Mrs Mossop's family, but everyone else down her lane had spelled themselves out in capital letters. Mrs Betts held out a menacing pen.

'Thank you, Mrs Logan. Such a help to have your support.'

Uncertainly, Liza signed. Mrs Betts pushed the postal order across the counter.

'I don't know who imagines we have a quiet life in the country, Mrs Logan. In my view, you can't let up for a minute – '

The door from the road opened and admitted a decisive-looking woman in a waxed cotton jacket and corduroy trousers tucked into shapely rubber riding boots. Mrs Betts smoothed her mohair bosom and braced herself.

'Good afternoon, Mrs Prior.'

Liza gathered up her postal order in panic. Her signature on the petition seemed twice the size of anyone else's.

'Hello, Susan. What a dreary day. Would you forgive me? I must dash. Imogen – '

The door banged behind her. Susan Prior glanced after her, glanced back at the counter, took in the petition and moved to the far end of the shop to examine, apparently, a rack of birthday cards.

'It is quite beyond me,' she said carelessly, her back to Mrs

51

Betts, 'why people with the mentality of garden gnomes ever want to live in villages in the first place.'

At home, Sally was vacuuming the sitting-room carpet and Imogen was rushing at corners with a flamingo-pink feather duster.

'Thpiders, thpiders!'

Sally switched off the machine.

'There's two telephone messages on the kitchen table. And Mrs Mitchell says she'll bring Mikey back as she's got to go into Winchester anyway.'

Imogen dropped the feather duster with a scream. A real spider, small but stout of heart, was advancing up the bamboo handle.

Sally said, 'Don't be silly, Imogen. Spiders are nice. Come and help me put him outside.'

Imogen scuttled behind Liza and buried her face in her skirt.

'Oh, Imo, what a cowardy – '

Sally carried the duster to the window and shook the spider out into the air. With Imogen still glued to her skirt, Liza hobbled away to the kitchen and discovered that one of the telephone messages was from Marina: 'Mrs de Breton says she will ring again later.' Good, Liza thought, attempting to detach Imogen with one hand while carrying the kettle with the other. Imogen, in order to show that this was a game, not a spider panic, would not be detached, however, but dragged herself behind Liza, clutching her skirt.

'Don't, darling.'

Imogen clung harder.

'Imogen, let go.'

Gripping the folds of brushed cotton in limpet hands, Imogen buried her face and shoved it hard against Liza's thigh.

'Stop it, Imogen. Let go and don't be such a stupid baby.'

Imogen pretended she could not hear. She breathed a hot damp patch through the fabric against Liza's thigh. The telephone rang. Dragging Imogen crossly behind her, Liza limped across the room.

'Hello?'

'Liza? My dear. It's Marina. I have to thank you for possibly the best Sunday ever. I detest Sundays but yesterday I adored.'

'We adored having you.'

52

Imogen opened her mouth wide, braced her teeth against Liza's skirt and bit as hard as she could.

'Ow – '

'My dear,' Marina said in alarm. 'What is happening?'

'My horrible little daughter. Wait a moment – '

Liza put down the receiver, seized Imogen and ran with her out of the room. Imogen was bawling now, her face scarlet and furious.

'Stay out there,' Liza said. 'Stay out, you beastly little girl.'

She shut the kitchen door and wedged a chair-back under the handle.

'I'm so sorry,' she said to Marina. 'Imogen suddenly bit me. I suppose it's her revenge for my going out to work.'

'Imogen? That angelic baby?'

'Not angelic,' Liza said. 'An angelic-looking fiend.'

Imogen was crashing some object on the far side of the door.

'Stop it!' Liza shouted.

There was a pause while Imogen considered the effect she was having, and then the crashing began again.

'Excuse me,' Liza said desperately.

She put down the telephone, moved the chair, opened the door and seized Imogen, running with her down the hall towards Sally. As she ran, Imogen tried to bite her again.

'Sally, I'm on the phone and she's being frightful – '

Sally, with whom Imogen was seldom frightful, put down her duster and took the child from Liza.

'Heading for a smacked bottom, I see.'

Liza ran back to the telephone.

'Hello? Oh, I'm so sorry – '

'What would you say', Marina said, 'to a day in London with me? Lunch, and perhaps an exhibition. Or a movie. I'd come down to you, but I'm sure it would be better for you to come up to me. I just feel – ' She paused and then said with great warmth, 'I just feel you and I have a great deal to say to one another.'

'I'd love it,' Liza said, smiling into the telephone.

'Would you?'

'Oh yes – '

'Then,' said Marina, 'go get your diary. Right now. And we'll

53

make a date.' She paused again, and then she said, 'It's time you had someone spoil you.'

Archie did not come in until twenty past ten. He had telephoned to say he would be late, and so Liza had eaten her share of supper after she had put the children to bed, and put the rest in a low oven for Archie. Then she took her marking in by the sitting-room fire and corrected seventeen dictées and fourteen comprehensions. When those were done and stowed efficiently away in the red canvas bag she used for school books, she made herself a mug of coffee and settled down to think what she would wear to go to London and have lunch with Marina. She had reached the guiltily excited conclusion that she had nothing suitable, and must therefore go shopping, when Archie came in, having organised an emergency ambulance to take a child with suspected meningitis into Winchester hospital. Having announced this, he pulled Liza out of her chair into his arms and said he was sorry about this morning. Liza said so was she. Then Archie kissed her and said he was starving, so Liza went away to the kitchen and returned with his supper on a tray.

Archie said, 'Why are you looking so pleased with yourself?'

'Am I?'

'Yes. Something nice happened?'

Liza thought of Blaise and of Marina.

'No. The reverse really. Imogen was ghastly while I was on the telephone and Mrs Betts told me Richard wants to build on the field next to us. Scared me, rather.'

'Why?' Archie said with his mouth full.

'*Why?*'

'It wouldn't affect us. We've got the trees between us.'

'*Archie* – '

He cut a canyon in his potato and wedged in a piece of butter.

'I've no objection to Richard making a bit of cash. And why shouldn't more people have the chance to live in the country?'

'Archie, it would ruin living here. Horrible little houses and horrible suburban people keeping themselves to themselves – '

'You little snob,' Archie said without heat.

She was pink with indignation.

54

'I'm not! How dare you? How can you be so obstinate? It would be awful to have the field built over. It – it would devalue the house – '

'I don't think so.'

'Archie,' Liza cried, standing up. 'Why don't you care?'

'I do,' he said. 'But not about this sort of thing. I care about people.'

She shouted, 'You are so bloody pleased with yourself.'

He put his knife and fork down and looked at her.

'You know I'm not.'

'Yes, you are. You are! Well, I'm sick of it. I'm sick of doing everything *you* think is right. I'm sick of being treated like a child. I'm sick of you being so patronising and I'm sick of doing every damn blasted thing to please you all the time!' She paused for an angry breath and then she shouted, 'And I'm spending the day with Marina next week. In *London*.' And then she rushed out of the room.

When she had gone, Archie took two more increasingly unenthusiastic bites of supper and put the tray on the floor. He sat with his elbows on his knees and stared at the rug between his feet, half-thinking about Liza and half-wondering why these curious shapes and patterns should occur so naturally to the Afghan mind. After a moment or two the spaniel, who was called Nelson after an enthusiasm of Thomas's, inspired by seeing the Admiral's tiny embroidered swinging cot aboard the *Victory*, pushed the door open and began to take a powerful discreet interest in the remains on Archie's plate.

'Leave it,' Archie said.

Nelson sat down two feet from the tray and longed for it with every fibre of his being. Archie picked the tray up and carried it out to the kitchen, pausing on his return to listen up the stairwell. There was silence. Part of Archie had hoped for the excuse of hearing Liza crying, but there was no sound of any kind. He went to the telephone and rang Winchester hospital and was told that his child patient was about to have its lumbar puncture. He said he would ring back in an hour. Then he went back to the kitchen and made a mug of coffee and carried it back to the sitting room.

As he crossed the hall, the bathroom door above him shut with decision.

He turned on the television, and then he turned it off again. He read the leader and letters page of the newspaper without absorbing any of it. He drank his coffee. He had a conversation with Nelson and disentangled several burs from his extravagant ears. Then he leaped up, crossed the room and bounded up the stairs two at a time, bursting into their bedroom to find Liza sitting up composedly in bed with her hair brushed, reading an article on the Church of England's neglect of the successful, in a Sunday paper. She did not look up.

'Liza,' Archie said.

'Mm?'

He sat on the edge of the bed.

'What is it?'

She looked at him briefly, then returned to her paper.

'I explained. Downstairs.'

'But it isn't true. I don't patronise you. I depend on you.'

She looked up again.

'You make me,' she said, 'feel limited and suburban and narrow. I might be all those things and I might, too, be fighting like anything against them.' She shook the paper slightly. 'It would be nice to be given a bit of credit now and then.'

'But I don't think these things. I don't think the same way as you about this development, but I can't see what that has to do with all these accusations.'

'That's exactly what I mean,' Liza said.

He put his hand out to her.

'Liza.'

'No,' she said. 'Just because you have the upper hand in bed – '

'But you like me to have the upper hand in bed – '

She turned her face away.

'Perhaps you shouldn't take so much for granted.'

He stood up.

'Jesus,' he said. 'This conversation might be happening in Hebrew for all I understand it.'

Liza said nothing. He lifted his fists and beat them lightly against his temples.

'Can you tell me, very simply, what we are talking about?'

Liza laid down the paper and folded her hands on it.

'You and me. Your attitude to me. Your assumptions about me. My self-knowledge telling me that many of those assumptions are unfair.

'I see,' Archie said. He walked slowly round the bed, thinking, and came to a halt, looking down on Liza.

'And all this grew out of my not sharing your abhorrence at the prospect of new houses in the field next door?'

Liza bent her head.

'Oh God. Archie, you are so obtuse – '

He waited. She offered no further explanation.

After some moments he said, 'Clearly,' and then he went downstairs to telephone the children's ward at Winchester hospital once more.

CHAPTER FIVE

Marina de Breton took great trouble over Liza's day in London. She explained to Sir Andrew that it was sheer self-indulgence, plotting a treat for someone sufficiently unspoiled to appreciate one. All her stepgrandchildren, a Kennedyesque brood of talent, instability and unceasing problems, had grown up so accustomed to the cushioning effect of the de Breton fortune that they were immune to the luxury of being imaginatively indulged. It had not taken her long to realise that her best gift to them was a brusquely humorous refusal to treat them as moneyed little stars, and an accompanying insistence on speaking to them as if they were both unremarkable and tiresome. This approach had won her a surprising amount of affection, but it did not allow her natural generosity much room for manoeuvre.

She was the only one of Louis de Breton's wives whom he had not divorced and she knew perfectly well that she owed this dubious distinction purely to the fact that he had died before he got round to it. She was quite clear in her own mind as to why she had married him which was that like some gifted, exhausted, moneyless Edith Wharton heroine she was absolutely sick of the brave struggle of managing on her own. Clever but inadequately educated, without family in America after the early deaths of both her improvident parents, she had married once, very young, a law student who had abandoned her a year later for the fellow student who was about to bear his baby. After that, she moved precariously from job to job, usually fund raising for, or promoting, small orchestras and ballet companies, or organising minor exhibitions in out-of-the-way New York galleries, the unsteady pattern of this being given brief respites by a series of lovers, all of whom she

58

managed to retain as friends after their return to their wives or the discovery of another mistress.

Louis de Breton arrived as a most unlikely fortieth birthday present. Large and overbearing, with all the outward mannerisms of a Tennessee Williams bully-boy, he came to a gallery opening Marina had organised because his oldest granddaughter had contributed the sculpture that stood in the centre of the main room, an angular column of rusting spears and pikes entitled *Woman With Two Horses* and priced at ten thousand dollars. Marina, dressed in narrow black with a scarlet matador jacket she had made herself from a *Vogue* pattern, offered a glass of champagne to the burly man in a tuxedo standing in front of the sculpture. He looked at the champagne and said did she have any bourbon.

Then he waved a hand at *Woman With Two Horses* and said, 'Is this garbage?'

'Yes,' Marina said. 'I am afraid it is.'

'Overpriced garbage?'

'That, too.'

'My granddaughter made it.'

'In that case,' Marina said, 'I sincerely regret that it is garbage.'

Louis de Breton bellowed with laughter. Armed with his bourbon, he went round the gallery repeating Marina's remark, particularly to the sculptor's mother, his daughter-in-law, who, he told Marina later, was a scheming bitch. Next day he sent Marina a coffin-sized box of orchids and asked her to dine with him. She agreed, on condition that he never sent her orchids again. So he sent her roses and lilies and stephanotis in pots and branches of forced lilac and posies of violets every day for six weeks. And then he married her.

She was not in the least in love with him. She found him excellent company, generous, domineering and selfish. His physical appetites were both large and fickle, and he had never troubled to control his temper. For the first year he was willing, and at times even eager, to be both companion and confidant, but, if ever, unlike Scheherazade, her capacity to entertain him brilliantly and with novelty flagged even a little, he grew morose and then took himself off in search of more dissolute pleasures. Marina did not suffer too badly. In her mind, she had made a form of bargain

59

with Louis de Breton, and was well aware that she had deliberately made her bed and must now lie on it. So, as far as possible, she relished her security, got to know as many of his exaggerated family as she could, enrolled herself in art history courses and took herself travelling. On the whole she declined to allow herself to feel lonely.

After eight years of this curious life, Louis de Breton died of a heart attack, and Marina could then confront the fact that he had wished to leave her for a Filipino beauty queen. The immense and infinitely complex will took almost four years to disentangle as past wives and mistresses emerged from the woodwork in a seemingly endless stream of claim and counterclaim, but Louis de Breton's wishes for his fifth and last wife were one of the few unequivocal elements in it. Marina was left with a substantial apartment on the Upper East Side, a sizeable income, and the administration of the Louis de Breton Foundation, which its founder had originally set up as a tax dodge but had then become irrationally fond of and had wished to be used for its true purpose. It became, for Marina, her first real career. It brought her occupation, preoccupation and a chance to exercise both her administrative skills and her long-unrequired benevolence. Then, in quest of Sir Andrew Logan, it brought her to London.

She telephoned him and asked him to dine with her. He said he would be delighted, and suggested the Savoy Grill. They met at eight, drank a glass of champagne together and dined at Sir Andrew's usual table. They talked of everything except the purpose of the dinner which had been for Marina to suggest the funding of a *Meeting Medicine* series. When the bill was brought, Sir Andrew deftly removed it to his side of the table and extracted his cheque book.

'If you are going to behave like this,' Marina said, 'you will make talking business impossible.'

'Exactly.'

'Then please give that check to me.'

'If I give the bill to you,' said Andrew Logan, who had never made such a remark to a woman in his life before, 'then I shall not have a clear conscience about taking you to bed.'

She had blushed.

He finished writing the cheque, capped his fountain pen, put it away in an inside pocket and looked at her over his half-moon spectacles.

'Is there anywhere else you would prefer?'

She shook her head. She was speechless. He rose from the table, came round to move back her chair and offered her his arm.

'Then we should waste no more time.'

He had needed, as Marina put it to herself, a good deal of relaxing. But once relaxed, he had, in one of Louis de Breton's phrases, moved a mountain or two. Marina had arrived in London in late August and two months later she was still there. As far as she could see, there was no incentive to return to East 62nd Street and every incentive to remain in London. She moved out of her room in the Connaught and took a small serviced flat off Eaton Square where she and Andrew Logan conducted an infinitely pleasurable love affair, only interrupted by his work and visits to his flat in Victoria to take the telephone messages on his answering machine.

When he proposed marriage to her, he did it with none of the assurance with which he had first proposed bed. It had been a most unhelpful time of day, just after breakfast, and it was plain that he had not meant to say anything so momentous, but she had inadvertently alarmed him, as she took away the coffee pot, by saying casually that she thought she ought to go back to New York and see how things stood.

He seized the coffee pot from her and then, still clutching it absurdly, said, 'You would not go for long – '

She looked surprised.

'No,' she said. 'I shouldn't think so.'

'And you would come back.'

'Andrew – '

'I must tell you that I could not bear it if you did not come back. I should not know how to live any more. Don't go, Marina. Don't leave me. Marry me. I beg of you, marry me.'

She reached out and gently took the coffee pot out of his hands and set it on the kitchen counter. It was a tiny kitchen, as efficient and flexible as a ship's galley, with scarcely space for two people to pass. So Marina hardly needed to move a step to put her arms round Andrew Logan.

'Of course I'll marry you.'

'You will?'

His eyes were closed.

'I'm afraid,' she said, 'that I've assumed I was going to for at least the last month.'

He began to laugh. He said, 'Thank God. Oh, thank God,' and then he said he must take her down to Hampshire and introduce her to Archie.

'But not as your fiancée.'

'Not?'

'No,' Marina said. 'One shock at a time.'

Privately, she thought she would tell Liza first. Even, remembering the rumblings of emotional thunder she had heard in Archie's presence, ask Liza how to break the news. There was a strong possibility of a particular bond between herself and Liza, a chance of the kind of intimate female friendship that enriches all the other relationships the participants have. Marina thought, with wonder, that she was about to be very blessed, and, when she thought that, it made her cry. Andrew Logan, who had shrunk from women's tears all his life, adored it when she cried.

'You're nothing short of a miracle for Andrew,' Liza said, spearing a radicchio leaf out of her salad. 'It's written all over him. I've never seen him like this. I thought he was a dear, right from the start, but such a buttoned-up Scot. You know. And now – ' She put the radicchio into her mouth and waved her fork. 'Now he's absolutely illuminated.'

Marina said, 'It's quite miraculous for me, too.'

Liza, full of excellent gnocchi and Soave and a beautiful morning of watercolours in a Cork Street gallery and taxi rides and being given a green cashmere jersey that Marina said was entirely made for Liza and which she insisted on buying ('Well, if you won't take it now, I shall simply wait and give it to you at Christmas'), said generously, 'I do hope you will marry,' and then blushed.

'Oh, we will,' Marina said. 'As soon as we can tell everyone.'

'Archie?'

'Archie.'

Liza picked up her wine glass and held it by the rim and looked down into it.

'It isn't personal, you know,' she said. 'It isn't you. It's anyone. It's having his father all to himself, all his life, and no mother.'

Marina said, 'I wouldn't dream of mothering him. Or depriving him of his father in any way that is his.'

'I know. I don't think it has anything to do with logic.'

'Of course not.'

Liza looked up.

'He's frightfully emotional, you see. He takes things to heart so much. When he loves people, he really loves them.'

She could feel silly, faintly tipsy tears pricking at the thought of Archie's loving-heartedness.

'I can see all that,' Marina said.

Liza bent her head. She was filled at once with remorse at her recent behaviour towards Archie and a simultaneous and sudden recollection of Blaise O'Hanlon saying to her, 'I'm in real pain.' Marina watched her.

'What is it?'

Liza said, 'Oh. Oh, nothing really. Just some stupid cross-purposes – '

'Your little boy?'

'Thomas? Partly. And other things.' Liza raised her head and said boldly, 'Sometimes, I feel so inadequate. Archie's so – so wholehearted, he lives so generously, he – ' She made a little negative gesture. 'He's such a thorough human being, if you know what I mean. And then I feel that I can't measure up to the size of him. I am so much bolder away from him; I feel so much more confident. It's almost as if he is – ' She stopped, and after a tiny pause said more firmly, 'I know he isn't judging me. I don't mean *that*.'

Marina made a competent sign to a waiter for coffee.

'What I don't see,' she said, 'is why you should want to be like him. Why you aren't pleased and proud to be yourself.'

Liza said, flattered, and thus without complete conviction, 'England is absolutely full of girls like me.'

Marina said, laughing, 'Don't be absurd,' and reached out and took Liza's hand. 'I think maybe you just need your husband to

63

yourself. Maybe it's time Archie was weaned off his father.'

'Espresso,' the waiter said, in caricature Italian, putting a tiny cup in front of each of them.

'It isn't that they aren't both kind to me,' Liza said earnestly. 'It's more – ' She paused, anxious to be quite fair and entirely honest. 'It's more that Archie feels his father understands everything about him so instinctively and, vice versa, that he doesn't really need to try completely to understand me.'

Marina drank her coffee and wondered what it really was that Liza was trying to say. She knew from long experience what it was like to live with someone who baffled you, or denied you access to vital areas of themselves, and perhaps there were parts of Archie he had never transferred from his father's guardianship to his wife's. Perhaps, too, those things were in better hands with Andrew than with Liza? But Liza, Marina thought, watching her unwrap an almond biscuit from its tissue paper, wasn't greedy; she just wanted what most humans wanted, to be loved and also to be acknowledged.

Although she perfectly well knew the answer to her next question, Marina leaned forward a little and said, 'Do you think all this would be helped if I were to marry Andrew?'

Liza nodded vehemently.

'Good,' Marina said. 'So do I.'

'Does he talk about Archie much?'

'Not an abnormal amount.'

Liza said with a tiny pride, 'I was engaged to someone else when he met me.'

'I know. I heard. He bore you off.' Andrew had also said, 'I was so relieved it was little Liza. Archie had had such a turbulent love life, violent enthusiasms followed by violent antipathies, everything from shop-girl waifs of seventeen to a terrifying divorcee of forty-four who prowled about after Archie simply growling with lust – ' Marina smiled at Liza. 'Andrew was so pleased it was you.' She leaned across the table again. 'Now, my dear, we are going to a movie in a darling little movie theatre I have discovered full of armchairs. And then I shall make you promise solemnly to come and see me again soon. And then I shall let you go home.'

'It's been *perfect*,' Liza said. She picked up the sleek carrier bag that held her new jersey and peered inside with a little sigh of contentment. 'Should I tell Archie?'

'About my marrying his father? No. No, I don't think so. Wouldn't you think it only right that his father should do that?'

Archie had resolved that he would not allow Liza's day with Marina to become an issue. If she wanted to make a private mystery of it, he would let her, and would simply hope that whatever grievance it was that she had against him would become either clear to him, or evaporate. So he asked her about the practicalities of the day, envied the acclaimed French film she had seen, said, 'Oh, Liza, it makes me think of Lucca,' when she mentioned the gnocchi, and admired the jersey which was, as he said, a dozen cuts above any jersey that had ever entered Beeches House before. Then he kissed her, said, 'I'm so glad it was fun,' and went away to read C.S. Lewis to Mikey, leaving Liza in the kitchen feeling at once slightly superior and mildly frustrated.

When he came down, they had supper together and the telephone did not, for once, ring at all. They talked about incidents in the practice and incidents at Bradley Hall and not about Marina or Andrew or the threatened development. While Archie was peeling an apple, the telephone did ring at last, unable to contain itself, but it was not a patient for Archie, but Chrissie Jenkins, the Vicar's wife, for Liza, who wanted to know if Liza would stand in for her at Sunday School this week, as her mother at Lymington was ill and she had to go down there for the day. Liza, thinking of the restaurant at lunchtime, the shop where Marina had bought her jersey, the luxurious plushy darkness of the cinema, and contrasting all these with Stoke Stratton village hall on a Sunday morning, and Lynne Tyler playing the sad, damp piano with several vital notes missing, said yes, without much grace.

'I wouldn't ask,' Chrissie Jenkins said, whose whole life was dedicated to getting other people to do parish work in order to show the world that she was married to Colin and not to God, 'if it wasn't a bit of an emergency. She relies on me, you see, being a trained nurse.'

'No, it's fine,' Liza said.

65

'We're doing the miracles this term. I expect little Imogen's told you. It's the feeding of the five thousand this week, and we were going to act it out. Lynne says she'll bring brown bread cut into fish shapes, and will you bring white? And a little basket or two – '

'Yes,' Liza said. 'Yes.'

'Thank you ever so much,' Chrissie said. 'I know how you like to do your bit.'

'Cow,' Liza said, putting the telephone down.

It rang again at once, and this time it was Cyril Vinney, old Mrs Mossop's son-in-law, to say his sciatica was so bad he didn't know how he was going to make it through the night.

'And the awful thing is,' Archie said, collecting his bag, 'that I wouldn't much care if he didn't.'

Stoke Stratton village hall had been built just after the war. It was a wooden-framed hut, gloomily creosoted, with metal window frames painted municipal-green. It consisted of one oblong room from whose ceiling hung, alternately, ineffective electric heating bars and unenthusiastic lighting strips, and, at one end, a grim little kitchen and a pair of institutional lavatories. The Women's Institute, at the instigation of Mrs Betts, had made flowered curtains for the windows and contributed a square of orange-and-brown-speckled carpet which swam, isolated, at one end of the polished wooden floor. But for all its charmlessness, Stoke Stratton was proud to have a village hall. Not only were the functions in it twice or thrice weekly – badminton, old-time dancing, Young Wives, Evergreen Club, Mother and Toddler Group, Poetry Circle, Ramblers' Club, Village Preservation Society, Gardeners' Club, jumble sales, Christmas fayres, harvest suppers, P C C meetings, Youth Group discos – but Stoke Stratton graciously rented it to neighbouring King's Stoke and Lower Stoke, neither of whom boasted such an amenity.

On Sunday mornings, Colin Jenkins turned the heaters on, on his way back from early communion, so that by the time the Sunday School assembled, they could only just see their breaths before them. It was the only Sunday School in the three villages, and provided a blessed child-free hour on Sunday mornings for parents who could be bothered to deliver and collect. Liza, armed with half a loaf – 'Shouldn't it be pitta?' Archie had asked unhelpfully – and several small bread baskets, arrived to find a dozen little children sitting at a trestle table colouring in simplistic pictures of the raising of Jairus's daughter. Imogen, who knew the form, ran to battle her way into a place at the table and corner the crayons she wanted, but Mikey hung back and said he thought he'd just watch.

'But why? Why don't you join in?'

He put his face babyishly into Liza's side.

'I don't want to.'

Lynne Tyler, a valiant and friendly woman whose husband was Richard Prior's cowman, came out of one of the lavatories holding by the hand a shrew-faced child clutching a blue plastic handbag.

'We do this all morning,' Lynne said to Liza. 'In and out. She won't go alone and she won't do anything when I take her.'

'Can't you ignore her?'

'Last time I did, we had a disaster. Now come on, Kirsty. You sit down and do your drawing.'

'Wanna wee –'

'No, you don't,' Liza said, lifting her firmly on to the bench next to Imogen. Imogen clamped a hand on the nearest pile of crayons.

'Mine,' Imogen said.

Kirsty began to cry.

Liza said, 'Let's just start. Mikey, let go. Do you usually start with a prayer?'

'Oh no,' Lynne said, almost shocked at such a pedestrian idea. 'We have a little song. Don't we? Imogen, you tell Mummy what we sing.'

Imogen fixed Liza with an implacable stare.

'"Jethuth,"' said Imogen clearly, '"wanth me for a thunbeam."'

'There now,' Lynne said, and went to the piano.

All the children climbed off the benches and clustered round her, all except Kirsty, who sat where she was and watched a trickle of pee run from under her skirt on to the floor. Sighing, Liza went to the kitchen for a bucket and a cloth.

'Jesus wants me for a sunbeam,' the children sang unevenly.

67

'Jesus wants me for a star. I am Jesus's little rainbow. Shining, shining from afar.'

They subsided raggedly on to the Women's Institute carpet.

'Hands together, eyes closed,' Lynne said, swivelling on the piano.

'We pray for our homes and our families. Sit still, Adam. And for our mummies and our daddies and our brothers and our sisters – '

'And our dog.'

'And our dog, Stephen. We thank you for the lovely countryside. And our food and drink. And all our friends. And we ask you to look after everyone we know who isn't well. And now,' said Lynne, 'Imogen and Mikey's mother is going to tell you the story.'

'Wanna wee,' Kirsty said loudly.

Lynne got up patiently, but Liza seized Kirsty and dumped her on the bucket she had brought from the kitchen.

'You can sit there and pee to your heart's content.'

Kirsty hit Liza with her handbag. Lynne looked deeply shocked at the whole episode.

'Is she a Vinney?'

'Yes,' Lynne said.

'That explains it then,' Liza said heartlessly. 'Don't worry. I'll face any music there is. Don't move,' she said to Kirsty. 'Until I say.'

Kirsty subsided slowly down into the bucket until she was doubled up. Then she began to howl. At this moment, the door at the end of the hall opened and Blaise O'Hanlon came in. Everybody stared, particularly Liza.

'Hello,' Blaise said. 'Hello, kiddiwinks. Hello, Liza.' He held a hand out to Lynne. 'Hello.'

'What are you doing here?'

'I came with a message from June,' Blaise said. 'About Tuesday. Dan has ploughed up the telephone cable with the rotavator so she couldn't ring. I went to your house and your nice doctor husband said you were here with loaves and fishes. Why is that child in a bucket?'

'It's the best place for her,' Liza said.

Blaise went over and pulled Kirsty upright.

'You are very unattractive,' he said to her with enormous charm. 'And you smell like a fishing smack. But I don't see why you should be condemned to a bucket.'

Kirsty gazed up at him with rapture.

'This is Mr O'Hanlon,' Liza said to Lynne. 'He teaches at Bradley Hall School.'

Lynne smiled at him, partly out of natural friendliness and partly because he had been kind to Kirsty.

'What message?' Liza said.

Blaise was wandering about among the children.

'I'll tell you afterwards. Mayn't I stay and help? I say, are you Mikey? I remember you from a football match. You run like the wind.'

Mikey blushed and nodded vigorously.

'We'd be only too pleased if you'd stay, Mr O'Hanlon,' Lynne said. 'Now, hands up who's going to be Jesus.'

'I'll be Jesus,' Blaise said. 'And then I can get this lot organised. Now, come on. I'll have you, and you, and you over there in green trousers, as disciples, and the poor bucket child can be the boy who brought the fishes. And the rest of you can be the multitude. Who can tell me what a multitude is?'

'I'm so sorry,' Liza said to Lynne, 'I really am. He's being impossible.'

'Oh no. No, he isn't. You can see he's a born teacher. I think it's lovely he wants to help.'

Liza went over to a grey plastic chair and sat down, half indignant, half enchanted. In a matter of moments, Blaise had the multitude seated on the carpet – 'Now don't go near the edge because it is the sea and you will drown' – and was standing before them with his arms outspread and the disciples jostling each other to be the ones completely next to him.

'It had been a long, hot day,' Blaise said, half an eye on Liza. 'And you lot in the crowd had been wandering about after Jesus all day without a *thing* to eat or a *drop* to drink – '

Lynne tiptoed round to sit next to Liza.

'He has a real gift, hasn't he?' she whispered. 'And he's ever so young.'

'He's ever so naughty,' Liza said with emphasis.

'Sweet face – '

'And then one of the disciples – it'd better be you, Green Trousers – said, "Master, there's a boy here with two loaves and five fishes." Or was it five loaves and two fishes? Can't remember. Doesn't matter. And then you, little Miss Bucket, come up – come on, come here – and show me and all the others what you have got in your basket.'

Kirsty held up her basket so high that nobody could see.

'Can't see, can't see,' complained the multitude.

'If you are tiresome, Miss Bucket,' Blaise said, 'I shall deprive you of your starring role and dump you back in the chorus.'

Kirsty knelt on the carpet and put her basket on the floor and the multitude crowded round and pawed it and spilled the loaves and the fishes.

'Pick it all up,' Blaise said. 'Or I shall go away and leave you unprotected from frightening Mrs Logan.'

'Poor little Kirsty,' Lynne said. 'It's lovely to see someone take notice of her.'

'And of course all the disciples said there won't be anything like enough for five thousand people and Jesus said just you *wait*. Now, Green Trousers, you take a basket, and Mikey another, and little Ginger Specs, you have this one, and take them round the multitude – and do you know, there was heaps and heaps, the baskets were always full and everyone ate so much they had to lie on the ground groaning like you do at Christmas. Oh dear, Miss Bucket, what are you snivelling about now?'

Kirsty held out a diamond-shaped slice of brown bread.

'I don't like fish – '

'Brilliant!' Blaise said. He spun round on Liza. 'Hear that? Amazing. Oh, the power that is mine – '

Liza got up.

'Which I'm now going to take away. Go and sit down and let Lynne and me finish in peace – '

'I'm sure you're very welcome,' Lynne said loudly, rising too and determined to show Blaise some Christian courtesy. 'Very welcome to stay, indeed. Isn't he?' she said to the children who all chorused enthusiastically in agreement. 'Shall we teach him our butterfly song? Come along, Imogen. You show Mr O'Hanlon the movements we do.'

She went over to the piano and struck a chord.

'If I were a butterfly, I'd thank you, Lord, for giving me wings. And if I were a robin in a tree, I'd thank you, Lord, that I could sing – '

Waving his wings and opening and shutting his beak, Blaise O'Hanlon smiled in triumph at Liza over Imogen's energetic head.

'Well,' Liza said later, in the lane, 'what was the message?'

'What message?'

'The message you came with so urgently from June who cannot telephone because Dan has inadvertently ploughed up the cable.'

'There isn't one. And actually, the telephone cable at Bradley Hall is overhead and a very unsightly thing it is too.'

Liza stopped walking.

'Then what is this pantomime all about?'

'I wanted to see you. I couldn't wait until Tuesday. I had to see you. I had to see where you lived.'

'We live at Beeches House,' Mikey said helpfully.

'I know that now,' Blaise said. 'But I didn't before and I longed to. So I came.'

Grasping Imogen's hand tightly, Liza began to walk very fast up the lane. Blaise and Mikey ran to keep up with her.

'I can't think about anything else,' Blaise hissed.

Imogen began to grizzle and drag backwards.

'Imo, come on. Blaise, I can't have this kind of conversation here. I can't have this kind of conversation anyway, I mean. Imogen, I shall spank you.'

Imogen wrested her hand free and flumped down on the road. Blaise dropped back and picked her up.

'I won't embarrass you,' he said, hurrying after Liza with his burden. 'I won't hang around. I just had to have a sight of you, that's all. Couldn't you just say one nice thing to me to keep me going until Tuesday?'

Liza said nothing.

'It does seem a bit hard,' Blaise said, panting slightly. 'You could spare me a crumb, really you could.'

Liza said, 'You're making a fool of me – '

'No,' Blaise said. 'No.'

He stopped and set Imogen abruptly on her feet.

'Look at me.'

Liza halted and slowly turned to face him six feet away.

'You're not just lovely,' Blaise said almost diffidently, 'but you're different. You're special. And the thing that turns my heart over is that you don't realise that you are.' He put a hand on Imogen's head. 'If you only knew the power that is yours.'

Liza gazed.

After a moment, Blaise sighed and took his hand away from Imogen and said to Mikey, 'I ought to go, you know. Would you like to look at my car before I do? It's a Morgan and although I terribly disapprove of showing off, I must tell you that it has wire wheels.'

CHAPTER SIX

Stratton Farm lay a few hundred yards up the lane from Beeches House. The farmhouse was an amiable building on to whose Tudor and Jacobean ramblings a prosperous eighteenth-century owner had slapped a graceful Georgian façade. It was constructed of comfortable pinkish brick under a mellowed tiled roof, and, at a respectful distance from it, across a space of admirably kept garden, lay the farmyard and the stables. The whole looked thriving and unpretentious, a working farm whose owner's chief interests lay in horses and herbaceous borders. Even the pig unit – highly successful and the reason for the briskly authoritative columns that Richard Prior contributed to country magazines – was hidden behind a line of stalwart Victorian barns, and veiled in Virginia creeper.

The Priors had lived at Stratton Farm all their married life. The house and four hundred acres had been a joint wedding present from Richard's father and uncle, whose sole descendant he was. Twenty-five years later, the acreage had grown to over seven hundred, and pigs had brought Richard prosperity. Susan Prior had borne him two laconic sons and was an admired horsewoman and trainer of gun dogs. Richard, a lean, lounging man, was renowned for his lack of sentiment. 'If it doesn't work,' he would say candidly at parochial church council meetings, of motions whose inspiration owed more to emotion than pragmatism, 'then scrap it.'

The Priors' social moral code was essentially Whiggish. Their farm workers lived in sound cottages and were expected to return good labour for fair treatment. The Priors could always be relied upon in a crisis and equally to be very plainspoken about any kind

73

of dishonesty or slacking. This paternalistic attitude spread to their view of the village. 'I don't mind a few city ponces like you,' Richard often said to Simon Jago, who was a senior merchant banker. 'But only a few. Villages are for villagers.'

'Mr Prior,' Mrs Betts of the post office would confide to her planning officer friend on Saturday nights, 'lacks what I call common courtesy. He may have been born a gentleman but I'm afraid you'd often never know it. Quite frankly, I wouldn't address a dog in the way Mr Prior sometimes speaks to the Vicar.'

'Frightful woman,' Richard Prior said of Mrs Betts. 'And as for Jenkins, you could wring him out. No wonder the Church of England is going to the dogs, full of lefty wimps like him.'

When he submitted his planning application for developing the field below Beeches House, Richard Prior knew exactly what his motives were. Half of them were businesslike – the best economic use for an awkward field that had never proved successful for grazing or planting – and the other half were social. Watching the Stoke villages fill up with weekenders and commuters to Southampton and retired people had disturbed him greatly. The miscellaneous cottages, which had once sat realistically and appeal-ingly in gardens where cabbages, dahlias, washing, hens and motorbike spares jostled for space among the nettles, were increas-ingly being bijoued up into Hansel and Gretel dwellings, gleaming with new paint and fresh thatch and sprouting incongruous carriage lamps and fanciful name-plates. The gardens, fenced, hedged, trimmed up and squared off, were disciplined into anonymity, the flowerbeds dug so assiduously as to resemble chocolate-cake crumbs.

And with the refinement came price rises. Children born in Stoke Stratton cottages and wishing, in turn, to raise their own children there, were driven by the cost of it to the faceless housing estates on the edges of Winchester and Southampton. Old Mrs Mossop and her Vinney children only remained where they were because Richard Prior owned the cottages and would not turn them out in Mrs Mossop's lifetime on account of her dead husband who had worked tirelessly at Stratton Farm all Richard's time there, refusing to take any holiday that did not coincide with those dictated by the Church calendar. Even when Granny Mossop died,

Richard did not plan to turn the Vinneys out. He was well aware that their shiftless, expedient way of life was as much a part of the village as old Mr Mossop's obdurate industry had been; all he would actually draw the line at was employing a Vinney.

Indeed, in his view, the Vinneys and the Mossops, the Carters and the Durfields, and all the other village families whose ancestors lay in Stoke Stratton churchyard, should all be able to remain living among their roots. It was, in his opinion, both right and natural. To this end, he proposed to build on the controversial field one substantial house which would make a fine profit, and, at the opposite end, half a dozen simple, two-bedroomed cottages to be let to young couples who had not been born more than ten miles from the village.

'It's the only way,' he said to Archie Logan, 'to keep this village going and to defeat the electric lawn mower brigade.'

They were sitting at the kitchen table at Beeches House, with Richard's plans spread out on the table between them, weighted at the corners with tumblers, and a jug of water and a bottle of whisky.

'I'm afraid it'll mean a bit of mess and noise for you for a year,' Richard said without adjusting his tone to apology. 'But we'll try and minimise that.'

Archie bent over the plans. He was doing his best to ignore Liza, who sat at the other end of the table, sewing name tapes on to Mikey's new games clothes, and pointedly not saying anything. Richard, who was used to living in a household where people only spoke if they had something constructive to say, was perfectly used to silence and saw nothing sinister in Liza's. She sewed with little quick jabbing stitches, occasionally pausing to give the plans and Archie a look of contempt.

The plans showed the big house at the Beeches House end of the field, and cottages clustered at the far end. A belt of trees would screen the one from the other, and all they would share would be the access entrance from the lane. The big house would have an acre of garden and a pleasant, unremarkable view across fields and hedges to the church tower and some jumbled village roofs. The cottages would each have an oblong of garden at the back and a communal space of grass between them for their children to play on together.

75

Archie said he thought it all looked jolly good. Liza thought it looked horrible. The big house would attract people of the mentality she had grown up with, and now thoroughly despised, and the cottages would blare rock music all weekends and their inhabitants would hang their washing out permanently and let their children scream like a school playground. She did not wish to say any of this in front of Archie or Richard, both of whom would think her very uncharitable and small-mindedly snobbish, and both of whom she might resentfully think were right. So she sat and sewed and thought, as she did a great deal, of Blaise O'Hanlon, and, as she did only slightly less, of Marina.

It was, quite literally, spell-binding to have someone so in love with her. She was quite sure she was not in love back but she was absolutely fascinated by Blaise's feelings. She went over and over them with wonder and, when she looked in the mirror to brush her hair or put on her ear-rings, she tried to see herself as Blaise saw her, tried to see both the freshness and the mystery he said she had. Her consciousness of his infatuation – she was determined to label it sensibly so – made her feel different physically: elated, shining-eyed, powerful. And everything Marina had said to her confirmed these sensations. 'I don't see,' Marina had said to her, 'why you aren't pleased and proud to be yourself.'

'Mrs Betts,' Richard Prior said to Archie, 'is forming a Stoke Stratton Preservation Society.'

Archie made a face.

'She's a powerful lobbyist,' Richard went on. 'She'll rally all her ramblers, you know. I just have to make sure I've got quality and leave quantity to her. I thought I'd start with you and Simon Jago. And I might succeed with the Vicar on sociological grounds.'

'I'll see Simon,' Archie said. 'I don't think Simon will be any problem.' He looked at Liza. 'Do you, darling?'

She gave him a blank look. He raised his eyebrows and shrugged, but said nothing. If Liza wished to score off him – as she so often seemed to, just now – then he would not give her the satisfaction of doing it in front of Richard Prior.

Liza raised her sewing to her mouth and bit off a thread, saying between her teeth as she did so, 'I don't suppose Simon Jago would

76

disapprove of any money-making scheme.' She emphasised the 'money'.

Richard Prior looked at her briefly, and without admiration. Then he said to Archie, 'I thought we'd plant a hedge the far side of your beeches, to give you a bit of cover. And I'll stick up some hurdles until it's grown.' He stood up and put his tumbler down on the part of the plan where the cottages would stand. 'I'll leave these with you for now to ruminate over.'

'I'll ring you,' Archie said. 'I'll ring you when I've had a think.'

Richard Prior went to the outside door, the steel rims to his brogue heels ringing on the floor.

'Good man.' He nodded minimally at Liza. 'Thanks for the dram.'

'Why,' Liza said when the door had closed behind him, 'why do you have to be so wet? Why agree? He's heaps rich enough. Why help him to be richer?'

'That isn't the point.'

'Oh. Really.'

'No,' Archie said. 'No. The point is what he is trying to do for the village.'

'But he doesn't have to live with the results! He won't have a Vinney-type slum on his doorstep! It's easy to be so noble from the safe distance of Stratton Farm.'

Archie began to fold up the plans with elaborate carefulness.

'The cottages,' he said in the level voice he used in practice meetings when he was, as he usually was, in a minority, 'the cottages will be at least a hundred yards away. There will be our belt of beeches, a new hedge, a new house and garden, and a new stand of trees between them and us.'

Liza said, 'Don't speak to me in that awful voice.'

'I don't know how to speak to you,' Archie said.

Liza took a breath. How to tell him, how to reach his true understanding and tell him that she had come to the end of a particular road on the map of their marriage, the road along which he had so far led her – lovingly, generously, but led her – by the hand. She had drawn level with him now and sometimes she wanted to step off the road for a moment and be alone. And she wanted him to recognise this, to recognise that things did not

77

always stay as they always had been, that needs changed and so did capabilities. Liza wanted Archie to recognise *her*.

She said, in as gentle a voice as she could manage, 'You speak to me as if my point of view couldn't possibly have the validity of yours because I'm me and you are you and all that that implies. Why can't you speak to me with the courteous interest you speak with to other people?'

Archie said, 'I was under the impression that I was being perfectly polite. And of course I am interested in what you think. I just don't think you have thought far enough or widely enough.'

'And I,' said Liza, 'think you are a pompous prig.'

He waited, out of hope and long experience, for her to cry. If she cried, then he could go round the table, and kneel by her chair and hold her and kiss her bee-stung mouth and comfort her. Comforting her was a way of getting close to her and Archie relied upon being close to her. But Liza didn't cry. She did not even look remotely as if she might. She folded the last pair of marked socks into a tube, put them neatly beside the others on the pile of shorts and shirts and rose to carry them to a chair by the door, ready to go upstairs.

Then she walked back to the oven, opened the door and said to Archie without turning round, 'Perhaps you would lay the table. It's fish pie and salad, so we only need forks.'

'I love your fish pie,' Archie said.

He began to open drawers and cupboards in search of glasses and forks and plates, and then to put them on the table with uncharacteristic precision. Lining up a fork parallel to a plate, he said, 'Liza – '

'Yes?' she said, without turning from the stove.

'I don't quite know how to put this, but I haven't changed. I love you and I esteem you, as I always have. None of that has changed.'

She came forward to the table with the fish pie between her hands, swaddled in a cloth. The top was golden-brown and speckled with parsley.

'Oh yes,' Liza said lightly. 'I know that. In fact, it's part of the trouble. It's me who's changed. That's the difference, now.'

★

Even though they were brother and sister, it was rare for June and Dan Hampole to eat together at night. For one thing, June preferred a tray on her knee in her sitting room with the basset hounds and absolutely anything that happened to be on television, while Dan, having spent such days as he did spend at Bradley Hall, drifting about tinkering and fiddling with the electrics and the plants in the conservatory, wanted the evening to be something of an occasion. And for another, June liked eggs and baked beans and toast and anything else she could eat without looking at it, and these tastes offended Dan. He liked to take a great deal of trouble over complicated food, and then, having donned an elderly black velvet dressing gown that made him look like a decadent prior, to eat it at a proper table with wine and candles and conversation. As the Hampoles had been brought up to regard cleanliness as suburban rather than godly, these stately evenings of Dan's, smeared with candle-grease and spilled wine, resembled Miss Havisham's mouldering wedding breakfast. The food was always excellent but it was imperative that no non-Hampole observed the extreme casualness with which Dan cooked it in a kitchen where cats roamed unchecked across the table tops and mice grew stout and brazen in the unswept corners. Once a month or so, spurred on by something particularly successful he had achieved with a rabbit or a partridge, Dan would invade June's study and say, 'Tonight's a night, old duck,' and she would reluctantly abandon her burrow and pin some of her mother's brooches on her jerseys and cardigans, and join Dan in what was originally the dining room but was now given over to history lessons.

Since Blaise's arrival, world history had taken on a wild and romantic aspect, with a strong bias in favour of bloodshed and Irish struggles. The long wall that faced the windows had been stripped of its pictures – these were now hanging densely in Dan's private apartments – and made into a giant pinboard for pictures and posters of great battles with the Battle of the Boyne in prime position in the centre.

Spooning an orange and port sauce over June's partridge, Dan waved at the wall above him and said, 'You'll have to speak to him, you know.'

June, who was thinking how comical it was to be sitting at a

79

Regency snap-top table in a sea of pupils' desks, before a great branched candelabra and a decanter of claret, said rather absently, 'Speak to whom?'

'To Blaise.'

'Why must I speak to Blaise? He's being very peaceable just now. How inky this room smells.'

'He's being very peaceable because he is up to something.'

'But you're always up to something and I never speak to you, although I often think I should.' Dan put a glistening plateful down in front of her. 'Oh, poor little bird. I do wish partridges didn't mate for life. Out there, there will be a sorrowing widower.'

'Oh no, there won't because here he is. June, the things I get up to, I get up to miles away from Bradley Hall. Blaise is getting up to his thing right under your dear but unobservant nose.'

June stared.

'What thing?'

Dan settled himself opposite her and flourished open a huge and dingy napkin.

'Darling June, Blaise is trying to persuade little Mrs Logan to fall in love with him.'

'Nonsense.'

'Not nonsense. Fact.'

'Perfect nonsense. She is an irreproachable wife and mother and she has far too much sense. Anyway, Blaise is very annoying and not at all seductive.'

Dan said, with his mouth full, 'You are not Mrs Logan. You are his exasperated aunt.'

'I think this is all mischief. I expect he has a crush and it will wear off, like all crushes. In any case, what evidence have you?'

'My eyes,' Dan said, in the voice of Long John Silver. 'I saw her swoon in the orchard and be clasped in his arms.'

'*Swoon?*'

'She was knocked flying by some rampaging little toads. But she stayed swooning for far longer than was decent and eluded being kissed by a hair's breadth. And he hangs about for her and whispers to her and writes her torrid letters.'

'Dan,' June said, putting down her knife and fork. 'How do you know that?'

'Because I went to his room on Sunday morning when he had mysteriously vanished, and not to Mass, in search of my field glasses which he had borrowed and not returned, and there on his table lay a letter, which I read, in which he told Mrs Logan that he knew he was in love because he wished for her happiness even more than his own and that this had never happened to him before.'

'Bosh,' June said.

'Too true.'

June thought for a moment, chewing, and then she said, 'Of course, it's very isolated here for a boy used to a city, so I suppose you can't blame him for daydreaming. But I absolutely refuse to believe that Liza Logan encourages him in any way. She might be kind to him but she wouldn't let him take a single liberty. I am quite sure of that.'

'I think,' Dan said, spooning up his gravy with loud slurps, 'I think you should ask her if Blaise is being a nuisance. And see if she blushes.'

'I'll do no such thing! She is a valued member of staff and I wouldn't insult her. But I will keep an eye on Blaise. Can't you take him up to London with you sometimes?'

'The whole point about London,' Dan said weightily, 'as you well know, is that nobody knows where I go or what I do. Blaise tagging along would be a nightmare.'

'Where is he now?' June said suddenly.

'Gone to the pub. He's a great hit at the pub. Why? Did you fear he'd gone to moon about under Mrs Logan's windows?'

'Certainly not.'

'I'd keep an eye,' Dan said, tipping the decanter to pour wine inaccurately into both their glasses. 'It's your school and your staff and all that, but I'd keep an eye, if I were you. Young men can be so – so *rapacious*.'

On one of her days off school, while Sally oversaw Mikey's homework and put Imogen to bed, and Archie was still doing evening calls, Liza went round to see Diana and Simon Jago. She did not tell Archie she was doing this and she did not yet know what she would say when he discovered she had been, but neither consideration deflected her. Diana Jago was a friend, a true friend, and Simon, inaccessible behind his carapace of English public-school blandness, was always very gallant to her, and she did not doubt her welcome.

The Jagos lived at Stoke Stratton House: pink brick and long sash windows and porticoed porch in the best eighteenth-century tradition. Inside, it was furnished and decorated with expensive confidence, particularly at the windows, which were hung with heavy silks and chintzes under elaborate pelmets of swags and tails. Diana's horsiness gave way indoors to a penchant for great splendour and great whimsicality so that in the drawing room, nestling in the rich folds of the yellow silk curtains, crouched a family of American porcelain frogs as big as small cats, their backs patterned with daisies.

Diana Jago did not take Liza into the drawing room but into a small red sitting room with a sophisticated carpet and an immense fire. In front of this, Simon sat in an armchair with the newspaper and a drink, and, when Liza came in, he got up and said, 'I say, my reward for coming home early,' and kissed her with a blast of gin and British Rail.

'She's come to bend our ears,' Diana said. 'You start on him,' she said to Liza, 'and I'll get you a glass of wine.'

Liza sat on the club fender.

She said to Simon, 'It's about Richard Prior and his development.'

'Ah,' Simon said. 'Then it depends upon which way my ear is to be bent.'

'Away from letting him build.'

Simon took a gulp of drink.

'Good girl.'

'Heavens,' Liza said. 'I thought I'd have to argue.'

'So did we,' Diana said, coming back into the room with a glass of white wine and a dish of peanuts. 'Here. That do? Liza, I had a smallish dust-up with the divine Archibald in the surgery this morning because he's all in favour, so I assumed you'd be too.'

'No,' said Liza, very decidedly.

'Can't understand it,' Simon said. 'Hybrid piggies keep the Priors more than comfortable and the village is quite big enough as it is. And if he's going to build cottages on the cheap, they'll be frightful to look at. Probably look like the piggeries.'

Liza turned her glass slowly round.

'I thought you'd be *pro* it for the same reason as Archie is. I see what he means about helping the village young, but I think the price is too high.'

'It's the thin end of a very nasty wedge,' Diana said, sitting on the arm of Simon's chair. 'Next thing you know, we'll be a suburb of Winchester. It drives me witless to have to agree with Mrs Betts, but I do. Got a cigarette?'

'No,' Simon said. 'Buy your own.'

'I do. And then you smoke them. Liza, I hate to quarrel with the blessed Doc, but I simply have to. Think who'll get those cottages. Probably that hopeless Durfield boy the Army threw out for drugs, and a dreaded Vinney or two. The whole thing is all too easy for Richard, stuck up there at the farm out of sight, sound and smell.'

'That's what I said to Archie,' Liza said.

'Christ,' said Diana, kicking a slumbering Labrador by the fire. 'If you're going to fart like that, for God's sake go and do it in your basket.'

The dog sighed but did not stir.

Simon said, 'I fear the whole thing might be rather unpleasant. Feelings running high and so on. Liza, have the other half.'

She shook her head.

'I must go back and grill a chop.'

'More than I'll get – '

'Too right,' Diana said.

Liza stood up.

'I wish you'd ask us to dinner again soon,' Simon said. 'It's the only decent food I get. Correction. It's the only food I get.'

'Take no notice,' Diana said, ushering Liza towards the door. 'Nobody got a paunch like that on a starvation diet. Give Archie my love. I thought he looked a bit crestfallen this morning.'

When Liza got back, Archie was in the kitchen, on the telephone.

'Look, darling, it's only until Sunday. We'll see you on Sunday.

83

And if you're in the rugger team and second in French, it really cannot be the end of the world.'

There was silence, and then a faint cheeping began, the far end of the telephone line. Liza mouthed, 'Thomas?' and made a movement to take the receiver, but Archie motioned her away.

'What do you mean, picking on you? Oh. Yes, that is rather horrible, but if you are having a dormitory fight, you do get a bit bashed up; it isn't necessarily deliberate. Are you sure? I mean, are you sure someone has taken him and you haven't just lost him? I see. Look, we'll be down on Sunday and we'll see Mr Rigby. Yes. Yes, Mummy is here. All right, darling. Chin up. Bye, Thomas – '

Archie passed the receiver to Liza.

'Darling? Thomas – '

'Someone's stolen Blue Rabbit. I know I didn't lose him. He's always on my bed. And then they got me on the dorm floor and pulled my hair and when I went to cry in bed Rabbit wasn't there and they laughed. Mummy,' Thomas said, his voice catching in his throat, 'I really am trying to bear it, but bits of it, I can't.'

'Oh, darling – '

'I've only got one more 10p. If it goes pip-pip, will you ring back?'

'Thomas, love, we'll be seeing you in three days – '

'That's so long – '

'Look. I won't ring you, but we will ring Mr Rigby. How's that?'

'No!' Thomas shouted.

'But if you feel bullied – '

'No! No, you mustn't!'

The telephone pips began, and over them Liza called, 'Only till Sunday, darling. Only till Sunday!' and heard Thomas saying urgently, 'Don't go, don't go, don't go – '

She turned to Archie.

'Should we ring back?'

He opened his mouth to say he thought that ringing Thomas's form master would be more constructive, when the telephone rang again and Liza snatched it up.

'Thomas?'

84

'I'm afraid not,' Sir Andrew said. 'Only your old pa-in-law.'

'Andrew!'

'Do Thomas and I sound so alike?'

'We've just had Thomas on the telephone in rather a state, and then his money ran out and I thought he had found another ten pence and rung again. How are you?'

'Extraordinarily well.'

'I'm so glad. Would you like Archie? He's actually right here.'

Archie came over to the telephone with uncharacteristic reluctance.

'Dad?'

'I'm sorry about Thomas. Is it something serious?'

'Impossible to tell, particularly over the telephone. But unnerving enough.'

'Of course. Poor little fellow. Archie, I shall be in Winchester next Monday. Could you have lunch with me?'

'Lunch?' Archie said in amazement.

'Yes. Lunch. Don't you eat lunch?'

'Of course I do. But why are you asking me to have lunch with you in Winchester? Why not here?'

'Archie,' Andrew said patiently. 'Will you have lunch with me in Winchester on Monday?'

'Yes,' Archie said. 'Of course I will – '

'And you see Thomas on Sunday?'

'Yes – '

'Then you will be able to tell me what is the matter and what you have been able to do, won't you? What about the hotel in the Close, about one? I'll see you in the bar.'

'Dad – ' Archie said.

'Love to Liza. And the little ones. I'll see you on Monday, and I'll write to Thomas.'

Archie put the telephone down and turned to Liza.

'What is going on?'

She was standing by the table, leaning against it with one hip. She was wearing jeans, a blue shirt and a cream wool jersey, and she looked about sixteen. She put a hand out to Archie.

'Nothing sinister – '

85

'He's getting married. That's it, isn't it? He wants to marry Mrs de Breton and he is taking me out to lunch to tell me so.'

He stopped. Liza waited. After a little while, she came away from the table and put her arms round him. He did not respond.

She said gently, 'Be sensible. What could be better for him? Why should he live alone? Why shouldn't he be in love? It's so unreasonable to be so resentful.'

He looked down at her, but not in the least as if he was seeing what he looked at.

'It's the unreasonable things,' he said, 'that wrench your very guts.'

CHAPTER SEVEN

'I spent a good deal of your childhood,' Sir Andrew said, pouring Chablis, 'trying to get married again. I was lonely, certainly, but I was also convinced that you needed a woman about. A woman to relate to. The trouble was that I couldn't find her.'

Archie, sliding his knife along the backbone of a Dover sole, said nothing.

'And then, after a while, I stopped trying. I suppose it is the usual human ability to adapt to what one has, or hasn't, got. If you cease to look at women simply as potential wives, and instead look at them as women, the field obviously becomes much broader. Yet, at the same time, the emotions involved become much shallower, rather as talking requires much shallower breathing than singing. For long stretches of time, I simply did not sing.'

He picked up his glass.

'While you were at home or at university, this state of affairs did not seem significant. Indeed, it was not significant. Though anxious not to be a preoccupation to you, I lived a very satisfactory emotional life with you and through you. As you got older, and started to manifest characteristics quite unlike my own, that satisfaction grew deeper. But nobody can, or should, live vicariously through another, particularly not parents. When you fell in love and married, it was with my absolute blessing, but for all that, it reminded me, for the first time in a long time, that I had my own life to live. It was not easy. I was out of the habit.'

He paused, took a swallow of wine and then said, 'Are you going to sit there in silence, chewing, until the end of lunch?'

Archie sighed.

'I am listening.'

'Good. Do you have any comments so far? Does what I am saying seem to ring true and to chime with what you remember?'

'I don't remember any women,' Archie said.

The waiter, who had recognised Sir Andrew, came up with an air of elaborate discretion and put a dish of potatoes at his elbow. Sir Andrew said, 'Thank you,' and then to Archie, as if the waiter had already moved away, 'I seldom brought any home. If I'd met a woman that I had loved enough to propose to, I should have.'

'And now you have.'

'And now I have.'

Archie moved his glass of water slightly so that the ice cubes in it clattered together.

'You have never talked like this before. Not remotely. You have never talked about feelings.'

'I know.'

'I thought that you didn't like it. I thought you were contemptuous of people who talked about their feelings.'

'I am contemptuous,' Sir Andrew said, 'of people who can't face bearing painful feelings and try to off-load them on to others. And I think that the people one discusses one's feelings with should be few, and dear, and the occasions upon which one does it, seldom.'

'And this is one.'

'Yes. And you are one of the two people in my life that I would, or could, talk to in this way. The other is, of course, Marina.'

'Of course.'

Sir Andrew pushed the dish of potatoes across to Archie.

'I want you to understand me, Archie. I want you to understand both the kind of life I have lived and the kind of life I have found. And, in return, I very much want to understand you. I want to understand your reluctance.'

'I'm not sure,' Archie said, 'that I understand it myself.'

'Sometimes, you know,' his father said with this astounding new ease of his, 'I was so envious of you and Liza. Not of you having her, love her as I do, but of what you had together. Now I am on the brink of such a relationship myself. Do you think that somehow wrong?'

'No.'

'And do you think it, in some instinctive way, disloyal to your mother?'

'No.'

'And do you very much dislike Marina?'

Archie coloured.

'I hardly know her.'

'And your every vibration indicates to me that you neither wish nor intend to.'

Archie hunched over his plate. After some seconds he said, 'You are wrong to suppose that.'

'Then help me,' Sir Andrew said.

Archie pushed his plate aside. He said with difficulty, 'I have – always had you. And then I had Liza. Between you, you know me. You know that, despite outward appearances and some very strong convictions, I am not as confident as I seem.'

He stopped.

'And?'

'I don't seem to have men friends,' Archie said. 'I mean, I get on with the members of the practice all right, but I don't need them, I don't want to do jolly boys' things with them.' He broke off and then he said directly, 'I am afraid of losing you.'

'How can you lose me?'

Archie began to marshal the stray forks and spoons around his place mat. He was simultaneously stricken by feeling something painful, something enormous and nameless, and by knowing that what he was about to say was but a slim excuse for the truth.

'You'll belong to – someone else,' Archie said, boiling with shame.

The next table, who had also observed Sir Andrew and were pretending they had not, were startled to hear him say with vehemence, 'How? How will I? How can Marina's husband cease to be Archie's father when both he and she are bent upon family bonds? How,' said Sir Andrew, growing angry, 'how can you say such foolish, childish things?'

Archie shook his head wordlessly. The waiter came up and began to slide plates and dishes off the table.

'What is the matter with you?' Sir Andrew said, when he had

gone. 'How can you object to a situation which will only affect you for the better, because I shall be happy, but will also avoid your having to look after me when I start falling to bits?'

Archie looked up. His father, who had always looked the same to him, restrained, well cared for, controlled, but always, chiefly, his father, now looked different. The outward things were all the same: moustache, shirt-cuffs, breast-pocket handkerchief, were all as precise as usual, but beyond them there was an unfamiliar energy, a new vitality. Gazing at his father, Archie perceived that he suddenly looked not just happy, but blazingly male. Deep in Archie, a profound longing stirred like a long unsatisfied hunger. He bent his head. Tears were pushing behind his eyes.

He said gruffly, 'I'm so sorry.'

Sir Andrew put a hand out across the table.

'You'll see. Give it a few months and you'll see how you will benefit. You can't fail to. You know better than I how generous love makes one.'

Archie nodded. He grasped his father's hand. The waiter, appearing with a trolley laden with undesirable puddings, was entirely unnerved by this and crashed his cheesecakes into the neighbouring table.

'In any case,' Sir Andrew said, taking no notice and smiling at his son, 'what makes you think I could do without you?'

The cathedral was full of Monday afternoon quiet. By several pillars, the flower ladies were assiduously topping up the water levels in great pyramids of chrysanthemums and the odd subdued autumn tourist drifted round the nave in gentle quest of Jane Austen's memorial. In a side aisle, dwarfed by a baroque monument, a College boy, illicitly away from the sportsfield, was having a tense and unsatisfactory conversation with a girl in black suede thigh boots whose stance alone indicated her desire to get away. As Archie passed them on his way to the choir, she gave him a pleading glance.

The choir stalls were quite empty, except for a solitary man in a mackintosh gazing at William Rufus's tomb. Archie climbed up to the back row on the south side and subsided against the screen to give himself a satisfactory view of the royal chests of the Saxon kings of England. He stared at them for a long time. A woman came up to join the man in the mackintosh.

'Can't be the real thing. Not *the* William Rufus. Must be a copy.'

'It's real,' the man said. 'That's the whole point. It's him.'

'Doesn't seem possible.'

'That's the point,' the man said again. 'It is possible. It's real history.'

The woman straightened up.

'Can't take it in.' She moved away a little. 'Coming for a coffee?'

'In a minute. I'll follow you. I'll only be a minute.'

When she had gone, he leaned forward and laid a hand on the tomb. His eyes were closed. Then he opened them and saw Archie watching him. He smiled. And then he took his hand off William Rufus and put it in his pocket and went slowly out of the choir as if he were reluctant to leave it. As he went into the north aisle, he turned for a second and Archie raised his hand. For a moment, the man remained, looking back, and then he moved slowly away down the north aisle and Archie's hand fell back into his lap.

What, he wondered, was he going to do? How had it come about that he, Archie Logan, liked and loved all his life, should now feel himself to be wandering alone in some darkling place? And, what was worse, a darkling place with no map. He had always had a map. He had always known, with a benign, unpushy certainty, where he was going; he had been conscious, ducking into Granny Mossop's low doorway, that she was truly worth more to him than his father's public glories ever could be. Even now, he knew he did not want those glories, and he knew that, at least, with an energy that was familiar to him.

But, despite that energy, he felt helpless. All around him, those people, those precious people, who had wheeled like planets round his central earth, seemed to have changed. His father, Liza, even Thomas – stoutly declaring on his Sunday visit that they must forget his wound-up telephone call from school – all seemed to him to have found maps of their own, maps that led them away from him and into territory where he was reluctant to follow. In Liza's case, would she even allow him to follow wherever she was going? And, if she beckoned to him, could he come and be the led rather than the leader?

He slid forward until his knees were resting on the low carpeted bench in front of him. He was willing, he told himself, to be taught. He was willing to change. That was not the problem. What was the problem was the sense of being immobilised, as if the understanding of being alive, which had always come to him as naturally as breathing, had suddenly vanished. If he was his own patient, he thought, laying his head on his folded arms, he would tell himself that he was profoundly depressed. But he could not do that, somehow. What was there to depress him? Thomas was not being bullied. His father was, as he said, not removing himself, only adding to himself. Liza had every right to remind him that she was changing and developing; indeed, it shamed him to think she had had to point it out. She had also pointed out, and so had his father, that he was behaving like a child. Was that it? Was some childhood spectre of a lost mother and a thus doubly precious father stealing out of the past and his subconscious to haunt him now? Or was it just being about to be forty? Or was it both, everything?

In the choir stalls below him, a woman slipped into a pew and knelt and bent her head. She had brown hair, held back above her ears with combs, and a dark-blue overcoat whose folds crumpled softly over the pew behind her. She could have been any age between thirty and fifty. Was she, too, Archie wondered, down some cul-de-sac without any idea of how to turn round? Or perhaps her husband had run off with her best friend; or she had a child in hospital; or she had found another man and wanted to be comforted into feeling easy about it. She turned her face a little, towards the altar, and Archie could see that she was in her forties and that she looked quite composed. Perhaps she had just come in to say thank you. Archie reflected with some despair that he had much to be grateful for, but that he simply did not seem able to reach that gratitude. He knew it but he could not feel it. He could feel nothing except that he was trapped, and full of longing.

He stood up. Dim, respectful lights were being switched on down the aisles. The woman in the dark-blue coat rose from her knees, smoothed and shook herself into place and set off towards the west door with the air of a person with the right amount of purpose. William Rufus was sinking into shadows. Why, Archie said to himself, why am I not at peace?

Crossing the Close back to the hotel car-park, Archie was intercepted by his sister-in-law, Clare. She worked for the city archivist, a job she claimed any filing clerk could do. She was wearing a grey flannel skirt and a navy-blue blazer, and was carrying a shopping basket containing files and a tin of cat food.

She said, 'Oh, Archie!' in the breathless way she usually greeted people, and he kissed her and asked her how she was.

She said, 'Oh, you know. Dusty and depressed.'

'Don't always be depressed, Clare.'

'I know. It's so boring for everyone, isn't it? Have you got time for a cup of tea?'

'Not really. I've been playing truant for lunch.'

She drooped.

'Walk back to the car with me,' Archie said. 'I'll drive you home.' He took her basket. 'You and the medieval records.'

'Saxon, actually. It's amazing how fascinating it ought to be and how boring it is.'

'What would you like to do instead?'

He began to move away and she took a few quick steps to keep up with him.

'I think Liza's life looks pretty good.'

'I'm not sure she'd agree with you.'

'Archie?'

'Country doctor's wife,' Archie said a little wildly. 'Village life. Three children. Local job. I suppose it must seem a bit confining sometimes.'

Clare said nothing. A small nausea of apprehension knotted her stomach. Did Archie know about Blaise O'Hanlon? Clare herself did not know from Liza, who had not even hinted at him, but from Blaise, in person. Blaise had turned up at her house one evening the previous week and told her, almost before introductions were over, that he must talk to her about Liza.

'There's nobody else, you see. And I must talk. I knew you existed because Liza told me, and I thought you would talk to me.

93

I can't talk to Liza because she is so adorably resolute, so please, please can I talk to you?'

He had stayed to supper. Whisking up a soufflé, Clare reflected that it was probably a year since she had cooked for a man, and it was absolutely typical that when she did it was for a man who was not in love with her, but with her sister. He ate ravenously and was full of praise.

'Oh, this is so delicious. Are you sure there's no more? Not even crumby little edge bits? Wouldn't it be easy if you could be Liza?'

She believed in his love completely. She could not bring herself not to. But even Clare could see that for Liza Blaise was no match for Archie. To Clare, Liza and Archie had one of those rare relationships where mutual roots seemed tangled round each other.

She said to Blaise, 'There isn't any hope, you know.'

'Then I'll make there be some.'

'You mustn't be so destructive,' Clare said, excited in spite of her better sense.

'I only want to give,' Blaise said, finishing the wine. 'And I need her. Need is so different from want.'

Clare was alarmed.

'What are you planning?'

'Persuasion,' he said. 'A long, loving campaign of persuasion. I want to persuade her to see how different she is. She has no idea. She's like the Sleeping Beauty.'

'And is Archie the thorny hedge?'

'Archie?' Blaise said, briefly bemused. 'What about Archie?'

'She's married to him. He's her husband.'

Blaise looked directly at Clare.

'He doesn't see her as I see her.'

'You don't know that! You don't know her at all!'

'I do,' Blaise said. 'I knew her at once.'

'Reverting to me,' Clare said now to Archie. 'Do you think I'm emotionally retarded because I always want what I can't have? Or at least, I think I do.'

They had arrived in the car-park. Struggling to find the right key and to open the passenger door for Clare and to stow her basket on the confusion of the back seat gave Archie a few moments

94

to wrestle with the memory of the jealous longing that had stricken him during lunch with his father.

When he at last answered Clare, he could say with some cheerfulness, 'Heavens, no. It's only another form of words for striving. If we all liked the status quo, think what a plodding life we'd lead. It's – ' He paused, and then said with more seriousness, 'It's the – dissatisfaction and the hunger that keeps us exploring.'

He started the car and slid it out from the ranks of other cars into the narrow street leading away from the city centre.

Clare said, 'I think that sounds very insecure.'

'Of course it does. It is.'

'Robin was like that. Always exploring. His wasn't striving, it was just self-indulgence.'

Archie said, changing gear to swing steeply uphill towards the prison, 'That's another thing altogether. That's a fear born of getting to know someone and realising that they know you.'

'I thought that was love,' Clare said.

'It is. At least, it's part of love.'

'Then – '

'Clare,' Archie said, fighting with conflicting messages from his head and his guts. 'I don't think I can quite cope with this topic at three-thirty on a Monday afternoon in heavy traffic.'

'Sorry,' Clare said at once. 'Sorry.' She pressed herself back into her seat. 'I only ask you things because you look as if you know.'

Archie said with vehemence, 'I know nothing.'

Clare's house, a narrow Victorian end-of-terrace house, stood on the edge of a rough little green below the prison. A low wall and a square of paving divided it from the road in front, and a brick path led up to the door. Archie followed Clare, carrying her basket, and waited while she put the key into the lock and turned it and swung the door open to reveal a narrow hall and a narrower table bearing a letter rack and a china dish for keys and an arrangement of dried flowers.

Clare said, 'Are you sure about tea?'

'Quite sure. But thank you.'

'Give my love to Liza.'

'Of course.'

'And thank you for the lift.'

He bent and kissed her cheek. She smelled of L'Air du Temps. Liza used to wear it once. Sweet, schoolgirl scent; the scent, Archie had once said teasingly to Liza, of tennis-club socials in Haslemere. Liza had never worn it since. Clare waited until Archie had walked down her path and closed her gate after him, and then she shut the door and walked along the hall to the kitchen which looked, dispiritingly, exactly as she knew it would, since she had been the last person in it.

Archie drove out of Winchester, endeavouring to fix his mind resolutely on nothing at all but the remainder of his professional day. What was to be gained by letting his mind slip back into that turbulence which seemed, all at once, to freeze him and to churn him up? Better by far to think of things he could affect than things he was powerless to affect. Better, but impossible. Impossible to keep his imagination and thoughts in check, just as it would be impossible to go home to Liza and say, Look, I don't know what is the matter with me but it's acute, and can you help? He had never said such a thing to Liza. He would feel, he told himself, that it was letting her down, to saddle her with his misery. What could she do, poor girl? We all survive, he told himself, on a mixture of self-knowledge and self-image, a balancing act of how things are and how we wish they were. But what, oh what, Archie thought, gripping the wheel, is it that I am so ardently wishing for?

He drove the car into the health centre car-park and brought it efficiently to rest in the rectangle marked out by painted lines and 'Dr Logan' lettered neatly on the tarmac. There was an hour before surgery, an hour with his dictating machine and then letters to consultants about ruptured Achilles tendons and chronic back pain, malfunctioning livers and nasal washes. He spread his hands out across the steering wheel. They might, at that moment, have been the hands of a stranger. Could it be . . . ?

Someone tapped on the driver's window. The pharmacist was mouthing through the glass at him. He wound the window down.

'Dr Logan. Thank goodness you've come. There's no doctor here, they are all out on call, and Mr Barrett has just been brought

96

in by his daughter. Why she did not take him to hospital I can't imagine. It looks to me like a heart attack. Could you – '

Archie seized his bag from the back seat and flung the door open, almost knocking her over.

'Coming,' he said. 'Coming.'

Blessed emergency, blessed Mr Barrett. Leaving the car door swinging wide, Archie leaped out and ran. The pharmacist closed it behind him gently, and then leaned against it for a moment, and dreamed.

'Thing,' Imogen said commandingly.

She lay on her tummy in the bath in a flotilla of plastic boats and dolls.

'Look,' Liza said, kneeling by the bath with a soapy sponge. 'I've been singing to you for hours.'

Imogen rolled over and lay luxuriously on one elbow.

'Daddy come. Daddy thing.'

'Daddy is doing surgery.'

'Thally thing.'

'Sally has gone home with a headache. I expect you gave her a headache by screaming.'

Imogen considered this. She had screamed at teatime when Liza's appearance from school had put paid to her plan of playing with the telephone while Sally was occupied with the ironing. Once, she had randomly dialled a number and a woman had answered, so now she dialled and dialled, when she thought no one was noticing, and whispered fiercely, 'Hello, lady, hello, lady, hello, lady,' into the receiver. She loved it.

'Not headache,' Imogen said defiantly, rolling over again.

Liza gazed at her perfect little bottom.

'You are an awful child, Imogen.'

'Mummy thing.'

Liza got up from her knees.

'No. No more singing.'

In her skirt pocket lay a letter from Blaise. She had not opened it. Half of her thought she would throw it away unopened; a quarter of her thought she would read it the moment Imogen and Mikey were safely in bed, and the last quarter of her thought she would simply carry it about, unread, like a little phial of magic whose potency vanishes when opened.

Mikey, undressed down to his socks, appeared in the doorway.

'Daddy's come.'

'He's doing surgery. He won't be back for hours.'

'I am back,' Archie said. 'It wasn't my night. I forgot.'

He stopped to kiss her, and then lower for Imogen, dipping his tie in the bath water.

'Thing,' Imogen said.

'Thing yourself,' Archie said, and picked up Mikey. 'If you're going to be a success with the girls, M. Logan, you must always take your socks off first, not last.'

'Why?'

'So as not to look ludicrous. Don't fiddle with your willy.'

Mikey lay back against his father's shoulder, and closed his eyes.

'Willy likes it.'

'How was lunch?' Liza said.

'It was what I thought it would be. He is getting married.'

'Who?' Mikey said.

'Grandpa.'

Imogen stood up in the bath and flapped her arms for attention.

'Out, out, out, out, out – '

'So?' Liza said.

Archie looked at her.

'Out!' shouted Imogen.

Liza stooped to lift her out into a bath towel.

Archie said to her back, 'He was very affectionate.'

'Of course he was,' Liza said, towelling.

Archie peeled off Mikey's socks and lowered him into the bath.

'It's cold,' Mikey said. 'I don't want this doll thing. Or this.' He began to throw toys out of the bath.

'Stop it!' Liza said.

A purple plastic hippopotamus hit Imogen's leg and fell on to Liza's foot.

'Ow!' Imogen shrieked. 'Ow! Ow! Ow!'

'Shut up. It didn't hurt. If your father was affectionate, why are you looking like that?'

'Ow,' Imogen sobbed, clutching her leg theatrically.

'Like what?'

'Gloomy.'

'And,' Mikey said, 'I don't want this stupid crocodile.' He picked it up and hurled it over his shoulder. It struck Archie in the groin.

'There's no point,' Archie said. 'There's just no point.'

He stooped over the bath and gripped Mikey's arm.

'Stop that at once.'

Imogen bounced upright on Liza's knee and made the letter in her pocket crackle faintly.

'No point in what?'

'Trying to talk to you. Trying to explain.'

Liza began to pull Imogen's nightie over her head.

'Bath time isn't the perfect moment, certainly – '

'Not pink one!' Imogen shouted from inside the folds of brushed cotton. 'Not pink! Not pink!'

Archie, heedless of his sodden tie and his jacket cuffs, began to soap his son. I'm lonely, he wanted to say to Liza. I'm lonely and I'm ashamed of it. Come back, Liza. Come back where I can reach you.

Mikey squealed.

'Don't tickle!'

'I have to. Your feet are so disgusting. Why do you have such disgusting feet?'

'They are sweet feet,' Mikey said stoutly.

'Now they are. They weren't two minutes ago.' He turned to look over his shoulder. 'Liza?'

She was buttoning the last of the buttons up Imogen's back. The nightie, to Imogen's disappointment, was blue.

'Yes?'

'Hello.'

She smiled at him. It was a kind smile but not a loving, surrendering smile.

'Hello.'

'Forget it,' Archie said. 'I'm being an ass. Just forget it. I won't mention it again.'

'I do understand,' Liza said, standing up with Imogen in her

99

arms. 'It's just the difference between mountains and molehills. That you have to see, I mean.'

Archie turned away and looked down at Mikey.

'Precisely,' he said. Precisely, he thought. Except that our definitions of mountains and molehills are in exactly opposite proportion to one another.

Mikey reared up out of the bath and put wet arms round his father's neck.

'I just did a fart,' he said and collapsed into peals of laughter.

CHAPTER EIGHT

His first wedding ceremony, Sir Andrew recalled, had been a pawky Scottish business. A red sandstone Glasgow church, a scattering of pursy Logan aunts, an apprehensive collection of Welsh relations of the bride's, bemused by the lack of spontaneity and singing, drizzle, and the burden of the participants' double dose of virginity, had made it a day not to be remembered. He had felt so responsible for it all, so much the engineer, so much the one who must create any happiness or security they might hope for, that he had been quite bowed down by his burdens. What a bridegroom, he thought forty years later, what a grim and corseted prospect for a girl! Poor little Gwyneth. Poor, bewildered Gwyneth, trying to find some path through to me, and I couldn't help her because I didn't know the way myself. All I could do was be loyal and hardworking and let her buy things for the house, things after things: cookers and chairs and vases and rugs and pictures. I hope they comforted her. I hope, he thought, tying a silver-grey tie on the morning of his second wedding, I hope she has forgiven me. If she can see me now, I earnestly hope she will understand why this morning, my second wedding morning, I want to sing and sing. If she has kept her sense of humour in Paradise, perhaps she will only remind me that I can't and never could. She sang like a bird; it was agony for her to hear me try. So I stopped. But today I shall start again. To celebrate this day, I shall open my mouth to myself in my dressing-room mirror, now, and I shall sing 'Jerusalem'. I shall even sing the second verse twice.

★

101

Marina lay in her bath. It was her last bath in this bath. Today she would give up the flat and move in with Sir Andrew until such time as she could find them a pretty house, with a garden; a house, she hoped, somewhere near Campden Hill. On the morning of her wedding to Louis de Breton she had showered in her minute, cardboard-walled apartment, then been married, wedding-break-fasted and carried aboard an aeroplane for the Caribbean, all before eleven in the morning. It was eleven now and she was still in the bath, independent rather than dependent, choosing not chosen, a possessor rather than possessed. The dignity I have this morning, she thought, surveying her painted toenails pushing above the bubbles of the bath essence, is the result of the indignity I had that other morning. I so disapprove of marrying for money, but I did it. I should have been punished for it, and I have been rewarded. Here I am, about to dress myself in clothes I have paid for myself to go off and marry my perfect companion. That strikes me as a gorgeous combination. That satisfies me through and through. I am my own mistress where I should be, and his mistress where I should be. If I never have such a bath again, Marina told herself, drawing out the bath plug with her toes, I shall always remember this one with grati-tude. I shall always remember that, for twenty minutes, an hour before I married Andrew Logan, I felt that the balance of my life was perfect. I control the things that are natural and proper for me to control, and I am at his disposal for the rest.

'Thank you,' she said out loud, climbing out of the bath and picking up a towel. 'Thank you very much indeed. And I mean it. Cross my heart and hope to die, I mean it.'

Because it was the first weekend of the Christmas holidays, Thomas was at home for the wedding. He wore his school suit. It was grey flannel and poorly proportioned and he didn't care for its associations, but he saw, after a term's acquaintance with the proprieties, that it was the correct thing for him to wear to his grandfather's wedding. Without being asked, he added his school tie and black school shoes. He thought Mikey, wearing sandals and a new jersey instead of a jacket, looked very wrong. Imogen, in a plaid smock frock with a white lawn collar, looked like a tartan robin. A tartan robin who would steal the show. Thomas

102

hoped she would not get over-excited and out of control. Boarding school had suggested to him that to be conspicuous was pretty terrible. Imogen, with her penchant for screams and somersaults, could do with a dose of boarding school. Now that he was away from it, Thomas could look at his tie in the mirror with something approaching pride. It was a badge, after all, a badge that separated him from younger boys like Mikey, who had to wear sandals and who could not tie a tie properly. The envy with which Thomas had thought of Mikey while he was at school turned to pity now he was away from it. Mikey was so young, such a pest. When Mikey had said, 'Anyway, you don't know Mrs de Breton and I do, she gave me a pound,' Thomas had been full of rage, but it had soon turned to pity. In a proper suit and a school tie, he, Thomas, could hold his own against Mikey with Mrs de Breton. He had spoken to her on the phone. She had said, 'Next to marrying your grandfather, the best thing about my wedding day will be meeting you, Thomas. And you must call me Marina.' He had kept that a secret. After a term at school, he had got good at keeping secrets. His head was full of them. And because he was only nine, his privacy was a consolation to him, a refuge, and not yet a lonely burden.

Liza had a new suit for the wedding. It had a velvet collar and cuffs, and gunmetal buttons like regimental buttons, and it fitted her like a glove. It had been very expensive. Liza had wanted a dress, a dress with a full skirt and then, perhaps, a jacket that would go with it, and afterwards with lots of other things. But Diana Jago, who had been shopping with her, had said, 'Come on, come on – what do you want to look like? A country doctor's wife?' It had been fun, shopping with Diana; far more fun than shopping with Clare, who had expected to be asked and had been aggrieved when she wasn't. Diana whirled through shops like Marina did, saying, 'Don't touch that, too dire for words,' and, 'Put that straight back, common *and* boring,' while the assistants loved her and stopped making hopeless suggestions. And here Liza was in her curvy little suit, and a small hat with no brim and a feeling that today would cement the new dimension she was developing. It was giving her such strength, this dimension.

Blaise's letter lay, still unopened, in the kitchen drawer where she kept the cellophane circles for jars of jam, and freezer bags, and the icing set – a kitchen drawer, not even a romantic drawer full of underclothes or handkerchiefs. At the end of term, Liza had said to him, 'Happy Christmas,' and kissed his cheek in full view of Mrs West and June Hampole, and had then done the same to Commander Haythorne. That was three days ago. Turning slowly in front of the mirror, Liza thought that he would probably telephone soon.

Archie, hosing mud off the car to make it more suitable for London, resolved to stand no nonsense from himself today. He had kept his word to Liza and had not referred to the forthcoming wedding again, and had endeavoured to look as he wished he felt. He had bought a silk Paisley tie. He had not only taken his one good suit to the dry cleaners but had collected it, too. It hung upstairs now, waiting for him, to be worn to his father's wedding. In a drawer or a cupboard somewhere, he had a photograph of his father's wedding to his mother. He hadn't looked at it for years, but he remembered it as both poignant and dismal, as amateur a business as today's promised to be polished. The spaniel came out of the house and stood looking despondently at the car. How do dogs always know, Archie thought; how much do they suffer from these huge instincts that dominate them so?

'Nelson,' he said. 'We will not be long, and when we come back it will all be over. For me, it will be like a headache lifting. I'm sure of it.' The spaniel sighed. 'Don't sigh,' Archie said. 'It's catching.' He splashed a last sweep of water across the windscreen and turned off the tap. Liza was calling. 'Coming,' he shouted. 'Coming.'

Accept things, people said; don't break the rules. But who, except the unhappy, should ever want to do otherwise?

The Register Office was full of flowers and smelt of furniture polish. The registrar had a perfect haircut and an irreproachable suit. Archie, Liza and the children stood in a row slightly to Sir Andrew's right, and behind Marina was one of Louis de Breton's grandsons, who had flown over from America especially, and the woman from whom she had rented her flat, who made an exhausting point of never doing business without friendship. The grandson wore a pink carnation as big as a small cauliflower in the lapel of a plaid wool jacket, and the muscles of his jaw flickered faintly over the chewing gum inside. Liza thought it was perfectly sweet of him to come. She planned to make her thought very plain to him over lunch. She felt excited, standing there behind these two people sounding so positive in their promises, excited with a breath of anticipation as if a hidden door was about to open and she, in her new chic suit, could just slip through. Who knows, she thought, admiring Marina's graceful back, who knows what may happen now?

Even Imogen was being good. There was enough to look at, enough amusement to be gained from standing on a chair seat (usually forbidden), which made her taller than Mikey, to distract her. There was also her father, just beside and half behind her. She could feel her father going up for ever towards the ceiling and all the way down to the floor. If she jiggled too much his hand came down on her like a clamp, but, when she tossed a glance at him, he wasn't even looking at her as she expected, he was looking straight ahead out of a window criss-crossed with little black lines. She beamed at him, waiting for his response. Then she shut her eyes and opened them up at him very, very slowly. He never moved. Nobody was looking at her; not Mikey, not Thomas; nobody. Imogen bent her gaze and stared down over the gathered curve of her front to the just-visible toes of her patent-leather shoes. In their shine, she thought she could see the ears of her hair ribbon. She leaned forward, a little bit, a little bit. 'Stand up,' Archie hissed. Imogen leaned a fraction more and fell forward with a crash.

Archie had seized her and was hurrying her from the room almost before she had breath enough to scream. The scream burst from her as she and Archie burst out on to the pavement.

'Stop it,' Archie said. 'Stop it. You aren't hurt.'

'Knee,' Imogen wailed. 'Knee. Knee.'

They inspected both.

'Not a mark,' Archie said. 'You are a hellkitten.'

'Bang,' Imogen said, still sobbing. 'Bang knee.'

'I told you to stand upright. If you had done what you were told, you would not have fallen.'

He set her on her feet.

'Kith knee,' Imogen said hopefully.

'No,' Archie said. 'You kiss me for causing all this trouble.'

Imogen rubbed her wet face against his hand.

'Is that a kiss?'

She nodded, curls and ribbons bobbing.

'Good now,' Imogen said doubtfully.

'Are you sure?'

He stooped to pick her up again.

'Imo,' he said. 'I love you.'

She regarded him. She put her thumb in.

'Blow nose,' he said, fumbling for a handkerchief.

'Isn't it odd to think that one day you'll have an awful Imogen of your own?'

She leaned into the handkerchief and snorted. He carried her up the steps and in through the double doors, past the waiting room and in, once more, to the room where his father was being married. Had been married, in fact. They were all kissing each other and shaking the registrar by the hand. They were laughing. It was over. I want to go home, Archie thought, clutching Imogen, I want to drive out of London, away from all this – this cold, urban competence. I want to go home.

Lunch was very glamorous. It was in a hotel, with velvet armchairs for everyone, even the children, and tablecloths that came right down to the floor, and napkins so big, Mikey discovered, that he could cover himself completely with his from his head as far as his knees. He let its starched folds slide down until he could see over the top, until he could see Thomas sitting between Marina and the young American. ('Hi, you guys,' he had said to them. 'We're all in it together now.') Thomas's ears were red. Thomas was excited.

'Sit up,' Archie said.

Imogen was next to Liza, on an extra cushion. Liza was not paying her much attention because she was being nice to Marshall, Marina's stepgrandson. He was in law school. He had had a narcotics problem but he was all straightened out now, he said.

106

He thought Marina was a great lady, the kind of lady, he said, who was rare in our country. He said that a good deal, 'in our country . . . ' His clear blue eyes were blank and mad.

'Hi, sweetheart,' he said to Imogen, craning round Liza.

She turned her head away flirtatiously.

'She's in deep disgrace,' Liza said. 'She disturbed the wedding.'

'You don't have to pay attention to weddings,' Marshall said. 'They come and go. In my family they have them all the time.'

'Have you had one?'

'I'm celibate,' Marshall said seriously. 'Since Aids.'

'But that doesn't prevent you marrying.'

'I can't test for sexual compatibility. Not any more, since Aids.' He looked at the smoked salmon on his plate. 'Does this have chemical colouring?'

Miriam Bliss, who owned Marina's flat, told Archie that there was no profession she admired as much as medicine.

'People only say that,' Archie said, 'when they have been lucky enough not to have to test our limitations.'

'But you see, you and your father,' Miriam went on, ignoring him, 'represent medicine's private and public faces between you. That's what I find so thrilling. Don't you agree? I mean, here you are, the hands-on GP, and there's your father, an absolute laboratory wizard. And we couldn't do without either, could we? So fascinating.'

Archie leaned his chin on his hand and looked at her.

'Is property owning fascinating?'

She coloured.

'Are you making fun of me?'

'No,' he said. 'But I fidget when people begin on the fascination of medicine. They get reverent. I can't bear it.'

'But, my dear,' said Miriam Bliss, recovering herself, 'there is a magic to medicine; you can't deny it. You aren't just engineers, you are engineers with hearts. Don't you agree? And in this caring age – '

'It isn't,' Archie said, craning towards her as a plate of duck-breast slices, fanned out in a shiny pool of russet sauce, was put before him. 'It isn't caring. We have compassion instead of religion, but it's a social compassion. It's guilt.'

Miriam Bliss said to herself that for such an attractive, articulate man he was strangely difficult to talk to.

'Guilt?'

'Over losing God and finding Mammon.'

'Is this chicken?' Mikey hissed.

'No. It's duck.'

'Duck!' He paused. 'Do I like duck?'

From across the table, Thomas said clearly, 'When I went out to lunch with Fanshawe we had duck his father had shot.'

Mikey began to eat voraciously.

'Adorable children,' said Miriam Bliss.

'I adore them,' Archie said. 'I don't really expect anyone else to.'

'Marina does. My dear, you should hear her talk about them.' She looked at Imogen who was eating matchsticks of carrot with her fingers. 'Divine. Really divine.'

'Am I what you expected me to be?' Marina said to Thomas.

He thought not. He had been expecting someone more granny-ish, with grey hair and boring shoes.

He said aloud, 'I didn't think you'd laugh so much.'

'I used not to. It's what happens when you are happy.'

'Sometimes,' Thomas said, 'I laugh when I'm frightened.'

'People, I mean grown-up people, make the great mistake of thinking that being very young is amusing. It isn't. I remember, as a child, being mostly excited or afraid. Do you feel that way?'

Thomas nodded.

Marina said, 'If you had your eyes closed, would you know you were eating duck, not chicken?'

'Not really.'

'I don't know,' Marina said. 'These fancy places. Think that they can get away with anything. What is your absolutely best food?'

'Baked potatoes,' Thomas said.

'With sour cream and crispy bacon bits and chives?'

'I've never,' Thomas said truthfully, 'had them like that.'

'I'd rather have a baked potato right now, wouldn't you? Look at Imogen. She's flirting with the waiter.'

'Don't look,' Thomas said. 'It makes her worse.'

'Do we dare give her a mouthful of champagne with pudding?'

'Champagne!'

'Certainly.'

'I've never had champagne,' said Thomas with glowing ears.

'I don't expect you have been to a wedding before. There's usually champagne at weddings. Look.' She held out her left hand to Thomas and showed him a thin band of pale, shiny gold. 'I'm married to Grandpa now. I am your stepgrandmother.'

She bent and kissed him.

'And I'm so pleased about that.'

The champagne came in a bottle as tall as Imogen. She stood up on her chair and squealed. Then a cake came, a frothing white meringue cake with a silver vase of white freesias on it.

'You are so sentimental,' Sir Andrew said to Marina. 'How could you order such a fearful thing?'

'For Imogen. And she loves it. Look at her.'

A waiter lifted off the vase of freesias, and put it down in front of Marina. Then he removed a single flower and went round the table and threaded it into Imogen's hair ribbon. Rapturously, she lifted her skirts to stuff them into her mouth and revealed her ruffled petticoat. From the next table came a round of applause.

Marina cut the cake with an immense silver scimitar. It was pale inside, speckled with glacé fruits. The children watched with intense interest. Archie watched Marina. In a moment he would have to propose a toast to the health and happiness of his father and stepmother. It seemed superfluous. They were both way beyond needing the gentle benison of others' good wishes.

The waiter was filling tall glasses from the extraordinary bottle. Mikey counted. There was one for him. Imogen poked her finger into the soft sweet mess of her cake and then sucked it loudly. Marshall de Breton told Liza that he didn't eat sugar any more. Liza was tired of being kind to him and said that there was sugar in champagne.

'Natural sugar,' Marshall said reprovingly.

'Only a sip,' Liza said to the waiter putting a glass in front of Imogen.

'All!' Imogen shouted, leaning forward. 'All! All!'

Archie pushed her glass out of reach. With one hand holding

109

Imogen hard against the back of her chair, Archie raised his own glass with the other.

'Could you all listen? For just one moment?'

He rose to his feet, holding the glass.

'Will you all join me in wishing Marina and my father a long, happy, healthy life together.'

There was a cheer. Tables round theirs took up the cheer. Everybody stood up, holding their glasses high. Imogen jumped and squealed. All round the table, people turned to each other to hug and kiss. Archie kissed Miriam Bliss and then moved round her to put his arms about his father. Sir Andrew's eyes were full of tears.

'God bless,' Archie said, kissing his cheek. 'All blessings. Really. Truly.'

He let his father go. Marina was stooping over Thomas, saying, 'I'm so glad you like it. It's so sophisticated to like champagne.' Archie put a hand on her shoulder. She straightened and turned to him.

'Archie. Dear Archie – '

He took her in his arms.

'Marina.'

'I'll do everything in my power to make him happy. I don't want to change any of the good things – '

Archie felt tears rising. He said, 'Marina,' again and then he bent his head and kissed her on the mouth.

It was a soft night, for December. Archie put Nelson on to his lead, pulled on Wellingtons, and went off into the damp sweet air that still smelled of autumn over winter.

'There you are,' Liza had said to him when they got home. 'You've lived through it. Haven't you? And really, it wasn't such a big deal, was it? It was just a lovely wedding.'

Archie had smiled. Liza had taken off her suit and was standing there in just her petticoat, rounded and sweet. She came over and kissed him, such a kind little kiss with just the smallest, faintest edge of condescension.

'Silly Archie.'

'When I have feelings,' Archie said, taking her wrists for one

110

last try, 'they are very real to me. And strong. The fact that they look trivial from the outside doesn't alter that, nor does any effort I might make to hide them.'

She sighed. She said, 'I know all that.'

He let go.

'No, my darling. You hear me and you dismiss it.'

'Don't quarrel,' she said pleadingly. 'Not after such a lovely day. You were sweet today. You were lovely to Marina.'

He said, 'I want to make love to you.'

She started laughing.

'Oh-ho. All this romance is so catching – '

'Come here.'

She skipped sideways.

'Let me just see if Thomas is asleep – '

When she came back, he was naked. She let him undress her, which they both liked, and then she waited to be kissed, as she usually was, all over. But tonight Archie was perfunctory in his kissing. Not only that, he was rough. 'Ow,' Liza said once or twice, sounding like Imogen. 'Don't. You're hurting.' He came very fast, not waiting for her. And when he had come, he did not say in her ear as he usually did, More, more, more. He simply lay with his face buried in the pillow beside her neck for a few moments, and then he levered himself up, and out of her and said, 'I'm sorry. That wasn't exactly a masterpiece of finesse.'

'It's a bit much,' Liza said, 'to take your anger out on me.'

'Yes. I'm really sorry. I did want you. I do.'

Liza rolled sideways off the bed.

'I'm going to have a bath.'

Archie stood up.

'I'll take Nelson out. It's my Sunday on tomorrow.'

'It's dark. He's been out – '

'I want to,' Archie said, struggling into clothes. Liza gave him a quick glance and pulled on her dressing gown.

'How awkward you can make our lives when you try,' she said.

For a split second, he thought he might hit her. He held his breath. She gave him a tiny, fleeting look of triumph, as if she had guessed, and went off to the bathroom. Archie went downstairs

111

and took a courteously astonished Nelson out into the dark.

He crossed the lawn and went through a gap in the hedge to the field where Richard Prior planned to build his houses. The darkness gradually resolved itself into greater and lesser densities, trees and bushes, and through them the lights of far houses, and the bungalow next door where the Pinkneys crouched in terror of being involved. Nelson strained at the lead, the night being loud with the scent of rabbits.

'Sorry, old boy,' Archie said. 'If I let you go, you'll be gone for hours.'

A pheasant rose whirring out of the darkness ahead.

'Painted foreign hen,' Archie said to Nelson. 'Take no notice.'

They crossed the space where the big house might stand, Archie stumbling in the rough grass. It irritated Liza that he would never take a torch, but he said he preferred to stumble; a torch spoiled the darkness. Nelson made little hopeful darts here and there, stirring up the scents of earth and leaf. The dark air lay softly on Archie's grateful face. Above him, a blurred moon hung among pale stars and from all around came the faint settling-down cluckings and twitchings of hedgerow life. He lifted his face, eyes closed.

I must go back, he thought. I must go back and apologise properly. For behaving like a brute. Why did I? Why did I want to be violent? I did want to. I felt fierce and hungry. Liza seemed too small, too sweet for what I wanted. What happened? Why should I be like that? It's over, today is over; I was dreading it but it seemed to pass me at a distance and now it's over. I should have taken Liza to bed, laughing; I should have been full of relief. God, Archie thought, opening his eyes, my God, how I detest people who take themselves so seriously. Am I having a severe sense of humour failure? Am I going mad?

'Am I going mad?' he said to Nelson.

He turned towards home. A light shone in the kitchen and above it another from their bedroom, and beside that the landing. While he watched, Liza came to the bedroom window and drew the curtains across. Typical, she would be thinking, typical of us to draw them only after we have made love. That kind of abandonment always used to make her laugh; she loved to be lured

112

into carelessness. 'Let go,' he would say to her. 'Go on. Trust me. Let go.' Perhaps she hadn't really liked it, only the idea of it. Perhaps it was in her nature to keep something back, not to chuck herself off cliffs with him as he wanted her to do, as he could do himself. Perhaps, Archie thought, moving unevenly towards his house, perhaps taking life in great gulps as he had always done was wrong because it tore roughly at the edges of other people's more delicate lives. Maybe he was paying for past greed with present misery.

'Do you suppose,' he said to the spaniel as they pushed through the hedge, 'that this is a kind of growing up?'

Liza was rummaging in a kitchen drawer. She had a fistful of jampot covers in one hand. She did not look up as Archie and Nelson came in.

'Do you really want to make jam now?'

'No,' Liza said calmly. 'I'm looking for a letter. A letter from a friend.'

Archie said, 'I am genuinely sorry I behaved like a rugger scrum just now.'

She turned. Her face was clean of make-up and her hair was pinned on top of her head with a plastic clip.

'Oh, Archie – '

'I mean it.'

'I know. Please don't start all over again. I know. It doesn't matter.'

She put the jampot covers back in the drawer and pushed it shut.

'I just wish you wouldn't make such a meal of everything. It all has to be a big issue with you, doesn't it? Everything has to be a big deal.'

'Some weeks ago,' Archie said, 'you complained that I didn't make a big enough deal of you. That I belittled you. What is it that you really mean?'

Liza put her hands over her ears.

'No more – '

'Talk to me,' Archie shouted. 'Talk to me. Please.'

Nelson crept to his basket. Liza took her hands away and put

113

them in her dressing-gown pocket. The letter met her fingers.
'No, darling,' she said. 'No more talking. Not now.'
And then she smiled at him again, and went up to bed.

CHAPTER NINE

The Stoke Stratton Preservation Society had its first meeting the week before Christmas. It took place in the village hall, decorated since late November with tired paper streamers, an unenthusiastic Christmas tree and drawings, done by the Sunday School, of Baby Jesus, mostly coloured bright pink with yellow hair.

Simon Jago was chairman, Mrs Betts secretary and prime mover. Mrs Betts had stationed Sharon Vinney – seasonally out of work from the local watercress beds – in the shop-end of the post office to give herself time for Society paperwork. The night before the meeting she had arranged chairs in rows in the village hall, each one bearing a fact sheet on the development and, on a table for the committee, in front of them, a scarlet poinsettia in a pot, a carafe of water and several glasses. Behind the table stood a blackboard with a map of the field pinned to it.

Now, dressed in a knitted frock of lilac wool with a scalloped hem and a tie-neck, Mrs Betts stood inside the village hall door, and welcomed people in. She wore pearl and diamante ear-rings and was very gracious.

'I can't stand,' Diana Jago whispered to Liza as they came in together, 'being in the same boat as her.'

'She's loving it,' Liza said.

Mrs Betts shook their hands warmly.

'So good to know people are really prepared to stand up and be counted!' She turned to Archie. 'Well, Dr Logan, I never expected to see you here.'

Archie smiled at her.

'I am a man of infinite surprises, Mrs Betts.'

115

He went past her to the back row of seats, and chose one. Diana and Liza, with Diana making mock-furious faces at him, went past him, up to the front, and sat in a prominent place. After a while, Richard and Susan Prior came in, and went to sit either side of Archie.

'Mrs Logan,' Mrs Betts said, bustling up. 'Mrs Logan. I really must protest. This is not a public inquiry. This is a private meeting for like-minded people. I really cannot have Dr Logan and Mr Prior making difficulties.'

'Oh, I don't think they will. I'm sure they are just here as observers – '

'Would you be so good as to make sure of it? I really haven't gone to all this trouble to have my efforts undermined.'

Liza went pink.

'Mrs Betts, I can't possibly – '

'Have a word,' Mrs Betts said. 'Just a little word. Please, dear.'

Diana stood up.

'I'll come with you.'

They walked to the back of the hall.

Diana said easily to Archie, 'Old Ma Betts is worried about barracking from the back row.'

'I'm here to listen,' Richard Prior said.

'That's what we said.'

'Do you think,' Susan Prior said to Liza, 'that it's a good idea to run errands for that woman?'

'I wasn't. I simply – '

'It's all of a piece, of course,' Susan went on, across her. 'All of a piece with you worrying about the class of neighbour you might get.'

Liza gave a little gasp. She looked at Archie. He should defend her! But he merely said, 'Trading insults won't help anyone.'

'Archie!' Liza said.

'I can't sit with you,' Archie said helplessly, 'because you are the opposition.'

Liza was close to tears.

'But she – '

'Is a rude cow,' Richard Prior said. 'Always has been.' He looked

116

up at Diana. 'I came to hear you, actually, Mrs J. Are you as good on your feet as you are in the saddle?'

'One squeak out of you,' Diana said, 'and I'll ask for you to be ejected. All three of you. Come on, Liza. Back to the front with me.'

Liza was glaring at Archie. His face registered nothing.

'See you later,' he said to her.

'He should have stuck up for me,' she cried to Diana, following her back up the hall. 'Why did he let Susan snub me?'

'She didn't snub you.'

'She did! She said I was suburban.'

Diana turned and looked at Liza.

'No. No, she didn't.'

'She implied it – '

'Liza,' Diana said, pushing her down into her chair, 'Liza, look. You and Archie don't agree over this. You can't expect him to rush to your defence when you say things he believes are wrong. You *do* mind about your neighbours. So would I in your position. Well, out with it, then. Say yes, Susan, I do care who lives next to me and it's all very well for you to sneer, living half a mile from anyone. Fight back – '

Mrs Betts stepped forward from the table, ear-rings sending forth whiskers of rainbow light, and cleared her throat.

'Ladies and gentlemen, I must first say how thrilled I am – ' She glanced behind her. 'We are, to see so many of you this evening. I think I may safely say that such a number indicates the strength of feeling that this proposal has aroused. Mr Jago will outline the development plans for us, and then what I – we – would like is to hear points from the floor.'

How could he, Liza thought, how could he let her be so rude to me? And in front of Diana. My view is just as valid as his. I know it is. In fact, it's more so because he isn't thinking of me and the children and our quality of life, and I am. He's just following out some impersonal social principle. And he's doing his usual things. Liza's a darling, she imitated Archie to herself, but she has no brain. He doesn't look at me, Liza wailed silently, he doesn't see me, and yet he demands that I look at him, that I corkscrew

117

myself into understanding his adolescent self-absorption, his unreasonableness . . .

'What I want to know is,' Cyril Vinney said, heaving himself and his beer gut roughly upright, 'what these houses are going to cost?'

'Mr Vinney, that is not perhaps relevant – '

'A million quid!' someone shouted from the back. 'That's what that field's worth, as a site! A million quid!'

'Half,' Richard Prior called without heat.

'I'm not moving,' Cyril Vinney said, 'until I get an answer to my question.'

Why do I bother, Liza thought, watching Simon Jago attempt to talk Cyril Vinney down. Why do I care what Archie thinks? 'You have such power,' Blaise had written. 'It's the power of someone both mysterious and honest. What a combination! I admire you so. Can't you see?'

Archie was saying, 'I do think we should get off the question of money, and on to the question of the preservation of village life.'

'Tell that to old Prior!' Cyril Vinney shouted.

Simon Jago said that he would like all remarks addressed to the chair.

There were some sentences in Liza's letter from Blaise that she knew by heart, even though she had only read it a few times. I deserve this, she told herself; I deserve to be recognised for myself at last. Archie doesn't see me for what I am, he only sees me in relation to himself. 'You are changing me,' Blaise had written. 'I am different, I have a different vision because of you.' Liza looked down at her lap. Simon Jago was explaining how the field in question was the end of a long green corridor running out from Winchester, and, if it disappeared, the remaining strip could then be considered an infill all the way to the industrial estates on the edge of the city. 'That field,' said Simon, 'may not look like much to you. But to planners and developers it is a last bastion, a bastion they want demolished.'

Archie, at the back, stirred uneasily. He did not in the least want to continue sitting next to Susan Prior, but he felt both that Richard was right and that to move seats now would create more rifts than

118

ever. He glanced at the back of Liza's head. It looked extremely indignant. He could not blame her, and yet he felt, with a sinking heart, that she was not handling her opinion well, that she might humiliate herself. He also felt, almost above anything, that he had not moved because he could not. An alarming inertia, the inertia that seemed to lie in wait for him these days like a migraine, filled his mind and limbs with lead. His glance strayed back to Liza. She couldn't help him, could she? Or wouldn't she? He must not think about it. He must divert his mind.

Between Liza and Archie, in the crowd, sat the Vicar, Colin Jenkins, who ostentatiously expressed no opinion on the development, but who was quite unable to resist a meeting. Archie's roving thoughts swooped down on him like a bird of prey. Colin's wife was out on night duty, no doubt, bent upon her relentless task of asserting her independence from Colin's spiritual master. Archie thought He probably got entered on Chrissie Jenkins's kitchen calendar on a weekly basis, along with nursing shifts and parish meetings. Pop God in for ten minutes between the Thursday Club for young mums and a trip to Tesco, and that's Him dealt with until the weekend.

Mrs Betts was handing out forms. They were forms for enrolment in the Society. She swept deliberately past Archie and the Priors.

'May I have one?' Archie said. 'I'd like to see – '

'Never too late for a change of heart,' Mrs Betts said.

Susan Prior leaned to look at the form with him.

'I'm sorry if I upset your wife.'

'Would you say so to her?'

Susan got up and walked to the front of the hall. Everyone was standing now, Liza with the Jagos, and Susan said to her, without preamble, 'I'm sorry if you thought I was rude.'

'You were rude,' Diana Jago said.

'I don't have to agree with you,' Liza said, wishing she had not said it the moment it was out and then, making matters worse, 'I am perfectly entitled to my own opinion.'

Susan looked at her.

'So you are,' she said, and moved away.

Simon Jago put a hand under Liza's elbow.

119

'Forget it.'

'She always sounds so sneering – '

'No, no. Just blunt. Calls a spade a spade.'

Liza said, 'I'd better find Archie – '

'Of course.'

'Thank you. Thank you for standing up for me.'

She pushed through the disorderly crowd of chairs and people.

'Poor little thing,' Diana said, watching her go. 'I don't suppose she's ever said boo to Archie before.'

'Come on. Archie wouldn't be hard on her. Not Archie . . . '

'Every marriage,' Diana said surprisingly, 'has its own balance. It's a natural balance. Liza's tried to tip theirs a bit, that's all.'

'Good God. Has she? Why?'

'Search me. I just know – '

'Forty-seven members,' Mrs Betts said triumphantly, steaming up to them. 'And eleven more promises. Now, Mr Jago, we really can get started.'

There was a crush to get out of the hall. In it, Liza lost Archie and found herself next to Colin Jenkins who said he hoped she didn't mind him saying so but he was a bit concerned about the fire hazard of the Sunday School carrying real candles at their crib blessing service.

'Twelve children,' Liza said. 'Or fourteen. A dozen little candles. Parents all round. I'm sure it will be perfectly safe.'

'There ought to be a code of practice about these things,' Colin said. 'Then we'd know where we were.'

Liza stared. Ahead of her in the crowd she glimpsed Archie, head and shoulders above the rest. She saw Sharon Vinney pluck at him as he passed, and mouth something, and she saw Archie bend swiftly towards her and then, as if she had hit him, jerk away from her and shove his way forward into the night outside.

'Excuse me,' Liza said to Colin Jenkins and began to press forward herself. She had to pass very close to Sharon Vinney who wore a quilted skiing jacket and swinging ear-rings in the form of crucifixes.

'You can tell him,' Sharon said loudly to Liza as she went by,

120

giving out a blast of fried food and old cigarette, 'you can tell him that I'm not the only one. The whole village thinks the same. The whole place – '

In the lane outside, Liza could find no Archie. She called him, self-conscious at the sound of her voice and his name. After a while, Mrs Pinkney from the bungalow crept up and said she had seen Archie walking away a few moments ago, in the direction of home.

'Quite fast, Mrs Logan. I think he thought you were ahead of him. At least, I wouldn't like to be definite, but I think – '

Liza set off, running. At the Beeches Lane turning, she caught Archie up.

'I'm here!' she called. 'Archie! Wait!'

He took several more strides before he halted.

'Mrs Pinkney said you thought I'd gone – '

'No,' Archie said.

'But why did you rush off, then? Why didn't you wait? It's dark, Archie, it's a dark night – '

'Sorry,' he said. 'Sorry.'

His voice sounded half strangled.

'Was it Sharon? I came rushing out after you, just in case, and here you are stampeding off and just leaving me – ' She broke off. She couldn't see his face. She took a deep breath and said loudly, 'Well, whatever she said to you, you bloody well deserve!'

Archie began to walk again. She hurried to keep up with him.

'What, Archie, what is it, what did she say? What – '

'She said,' Archie shouted, 'she said I was neglecting her mother and that I was not fit to be a doctor.'

Liza drew a huge breath.

'But that's nonsense. Take no notice. You know it isn't true – '

Archie swung round in the lane, almost on the spot where Blaise had said, 'If you only knew the power that is yours,' and gripped Liza's shoulders.

'It is not nonsense. It is true.'

Oh, my God, Liza thought, I can't stand any more of this. It's always been bad, Archie's violent over-reaction to things, but this

121

autumn it's got really out of control. And I haven't got the energy to humour him any more, really I haven't. She drew a breath.

'Sharon Vinney,' said Liza in the level, quiet voice she used in class, 'is a mischief-maker. You've said it yourself, often. There's nothing she likes better than a bit of trouble to stir. And it isn't as if she does anything for her mother herself. She expects the Health Service to do it all. She expects you to do everything she won't. I'm sorry I shouted,' Liza said with great kindness. 'Really I am. But you mustn't be a silly Archie.'

He drew his breath in sharply. Liza tried to take his hand in the darkness and found his fist was clenched.

'Archie, please – '

'I'm hungry,' he said. 'I'm terribly hungry,' and began to walk away once more, up the lane, leaving her no alternative but to follow.

'I don't know what's the matter,' Liza said to her sister on the telephone. 'It's like living with some mad stranger. He sat miles away from me at the meeting. Then he just let Susan Prior be frightfully insulting without even attempting to defend me. And then he took some stupid village remark to heart and rushed off home leaving me to follow on my own. In the dark.'

Clare, whose genuine sympathy was not unmixed with a small pleasure at Liza's dismay, settled herself more comfortably by the telephone and said, 'Does he know about Blaise, do you suppose?'

There was a brief, complete silence.

'How do you know about Blaise?'

'From Blaise.'

'What?'

'He came here,' Clare said, while the pleasure grew and began to dwarf the sympathy. 'He came here because he was desperate for someone to talk to.'

'I don't believe it!'

'It's true. Of course,' Clare said, ignoring the huge excitement she had felt when Blaise described his love for Liza, 'I didn't encourage him at all. I mean, I'm sure he's as much in love with the *idea* of being in love as he is with you. I'm sure you see that.'

Liza said nothing.

'After all,' Clare said, sensing a tiny triumph, 'he can't hold a candle to Archie. And it's just a crush, really, isn't it, a schoolboy crush?'

Liza took a deep breath.

'Archie knows nothing about Blaise, because there is nothing to know.'

Clare's triumph began to deflate.

'Liza – '

'I can't help Blaise's feelings. I can help my own and they are under perfect control. I don't need you to point out what the matter with Blaise is.'

'No,' Clare said, drooping.

'You're as bad as Archie,' Liza said, gathering strength. 'You imagine all kinds of awful things that couldn't possibly happen. Do you really think I would risk all I've got for something so silly?'

'No,' Clare said.

'Let's stop talking about it,' Liza said, generous at the approach of victory. 'I tell you why I really rang. It's about Christmas. Will you come and have Christmas Day here? Please. We'd love it.'

Typical, Clare thought miserably, putting down the telephone. I have the upper hand for the first time in ten years and I lose it in three sentences. Not just that, but Liza's right. She was justified in being cross. Who, in their right minds, would risk Archie for Blaise? She got up and went along the hall to her sitting room. On the table in the window she had put a neat, small Christmas tree, carefully decorated in gold and silver and scarlet. Archie would laugh at that tree. He'd think it half-hearted, inhibited. No wonder Liza had strength, living with someone of such appetites. It gave you confidence, being with Archie. Her tree had no confidence, poor thing, sitting neatly on its table, obediently glowing with symmetrical fairy lights. She leaned against the wall and looked at it.

'Sorry,' Clare said to her Christmas tree.

★

123

On Christmas Eve, Sir Andrew and Marina telephoned from Kenya. They were in the last week of their honeymoon. The children, dressed for bed, had a minute or two each on the telephone to them. Imogen was very excited.

'Hello, lady, hello, lady, hello, lady,' Imogen shouted to Africa. From Africa, Archie could hear his father laugh.

It was paradise, they said. They were at Malindi and had been on safari. Marina was beside herself about the birds. They had been on a private safari and had been given breakfast out in the bush, breakfast with napkins and Cooper's Oxford marmalade and eggs and bacon cooked on a bonfire.

'But no *Times*,' Sir Andrew said. 'All that was missing was *The Times*.'

'Are you brown?' Liza asked. 'Are you brown as nuts?'

'As cornflakes – '

'Oh! Oh, it sounds so marvellous!'

'It is,' Sir Andrew said. He was laughing. 'It is. Her ladyship shot a guinea fowl. Lovely shot. We'll bring the cape back, for salmon flies. For Archie.'

'Can you hear that boom–crash?' Marina asked, coming on the line to Thomas. 'Can you hear? That's the Indian Ocean. I'll bring you shells – '

'Yes,' Thomas said, cramming his ear to the receiver. 'Yes.'

'Happy Christmas, darling. Give them all a hug from us. A big Christmas hug.'

It was quiet and dull when they put the receiver down.

Mikey said sadly, 'They saw a lion.'

Christmas seemed suddenly commonplace, beside a lion.

Liza said, 'Everything she touches becomes special, doesn't it? You can't have ordinariness, not with Marina – '

'Sh – ' Archie said.

She flashed him a look of irritation.

'Not *still* – '

He crossed to the kitchen door.

'I've got a few calls, I won't be long.'

'Granny Mossop?' Liza said unkindly, to punish him for his persistent unacceptance of Marina.

Archie paused, his hand on the doorknob. He seemed about to

124

say something noisy, but then he changed his mind and said in a perfectly normal voice, 'I sent Granny Mossop into hospital two days ago.'

'Oh, good, good – '

'Not good,' Archie said. 'She won't speak to me. Or the nurses.' He looked at the children. 'Into bed, you lot. Or You Know Who'll never come.'

Abruptly, Imogen remembered.

'Chrithmath!'

She went scuttling up the stairs, squealing like a piglet.

Colin Jenkins disliked Christmas. At Christmas and Easter, he was quite unable to control the parish, which took the bit between its teeth and plunged into the festivals with a lavishness which Colin felt was both wrong in itself and mainly attributable to the materialism of the present government. Chrissie had, as usual, declared the over-excitement of the parish not to be her responsibility.

'Sorry, dear, but it really isn't my business. I've done my organising. I did it in November. What with Mother and the hospital, I've got my work cut out as it is. You should just put your foot down. Really you should.'

The interior of the church was flagrant proof that he had not. It was crammed with as much decoration as it could hold: window-sills furred with pine branches, pillars wound with ribbons, pedestals in every corner bearing explosive arrangements of greenery and scarlet silk poinsettias, six inches across, bought by Mrs Betts from her wholesalers in Southampton. From the chancel arch a gold cardboard star spun on a chain of tinsel, and, below the lectern, illuminated by miniature electric light bulbs rigged up by Lynne Tyler's husband, stood the Sunday School crib, the cast only lacking the three kings, who lay in a shoebox in the vestry, awaiting Twelfth Night.

It not only irritated Colin to see the church turned into some ceremonial garden centre, but also to see it full of people who never came to church otherwise. They'd come at Christmas because it was quite jolly; they would telephone for wedding or funeral or christening arrangements in the faintly imperious manner of people booking holidays; they were full of inflexible theories about the

125

way vicars – and, even more, vicars' wives – should live their lives, but any suggestion that they might use the church for its regular and intended purpose caused indignation and resentment. When he was a young man, Colin had once been so stirred by a speech given by Bishop Trevor Huddlestone that he had, for at least a month, determined to become a missionary. Christmas at Stoke Stratton made him regret with particular energy his failure to keep that resolve.

He expressed his disapproval by refusing to dress up for Christmas. They could have him simply in a surplice and black stole, and, if he stuck out like a sore thumb in all the gaudy nonsense, so much the better. Maybe that would get the message home. The church, of course, was packed, from the Jagos in the front pew with their two languid daughters tossing sweeps of blonded brown hair from their faces, to Lynne and Robbie Tyler at the back with their brood of children and a clutch of aunts and grans. Mrs Betts, who believed God to be primarily the President of the Women's Institute, wore a fancy tweed coat with a matching hat, and was accompanied by a daughter and a son-in-law so suitable in dress and demeanour that they might have been designed for her, as fashion accessories.

About halfway down, sandwiched between pews full of Christmas strangers staying in the village, Liza, Archie and Clare had penned the children between them. Archie was not on call again until Boxing Day, but his morning of Christmas freedom had begun at ten past four when Imogen had appeared, covered in chocolate and strenuously wishing to play post offices. By nine o'clock, the day had felt already done to death, and when Clare appeared at ten-thirty, in time for church, both Liza and Archie had fallen upon her like castaways sighting a sail. Clare, who could not help drawing comfort from other people's misfortunes, was heartened at the sight of them and began to feel a dim glow of appropriate enthusiasm. Anything, after all, was better than waking alone to a silent city that was bound to be full, just bound to be, of blissful couples in bed together, opening stockings crammed with sentimental, intimate jokes.

Liza was wearing a cream jersey that Clare knew, after she had hugged her, was cashmere. It was from Marina. So was the

126

beautiful brown snake belt she had on, and the computer games for the boys and the princess dressing-up clothes for Imogen and – what for Archie?

'A rod,' he said, gesturing towards it. 'A trout rod.'

'But it's a beauty!'

'Yes,' he said flatly. 'Far too much.'

Liza seized Clare's arm and mouthed silence. In the kitchen, alone for a moment, she had shown Clare a tiny box with a garnet-and-pearl pin in it, a heart on a golden bar.

'Who's it from?'

'Shhh. Guess.'

'No,' Clare said, eyes enormous.

'Yes. Silly ass. I shall give it straight back.'

'It's awfully pretty.'

Liza put the box back in the kitchen drawer. The card that had come with the box lay under the drawer's lining paper.

'What did Archie give you?'

'A picture. A Victorian watercolour of the Stoke river.'

'It sounds lovely!'

'It's sweet,' Liza said, thinking of the garnet pin.

Archie had been very kind to Clare. He had made her coffee and talked to her all the way down to church and given her Thomas to sit next to. Above the carols, and the readings, delivered at top-speed in an incomprehensible scream by the older members of the Sunday School, Clare could hear Imogen's intermittent grizzling. She was not the only one. Dotted around the congregation, the child victims of Christmas hype whined and fidgeted. Clare, without responsibility for any of them and pleased to be in this comfortable, celebratory, unspiritual gathering, briefly felt quite happy.

But for all that, she could not help perceiving that Archie was not. Finely tuned as she was to notice every quiver on the seismograph of her own feelings, Clare had become morbidly sensitive to atmosphere. Archie was smiling certainly. He sang the carols, admonished Mikey for wriggling, glanced with affection at Liza, at his children, at Clare. But he was not happy. Just below the surface, Clare thought, lay some trouble, manifesting itself in glimmers of tension and defensiveness. She worried that it was

Blaise. It was not reasonable to worry about Blaise, she told herself, but instinctively it was not to be avoided. Liza had said someone in the village had upset Archie. Could it be that? Or could it be that Liza's new little manner with him, a kind of condescending little manner, thinly masking a sizeable impatience at his attitude to his father's marriage, was affecting him more deeply than anyone suspected? Oh dear, Clare thought, how awful, how interesting, how consoling. Should she say anything about Blaise? Heavens! Should she?

Thomas seized his *Songs of Praise* and riffled through it officiously.

'"Hark the Herald",' he hissed. 'There you are. Seventy-four.'

Two days before the New Year, Sir Andrew and Marina came home. They had had a horrible flight, they said, delayed and rough, and Sir Andrew was feeling a bit battered by it, but all they needed was a good night's sleep and they would be down, as planned, on New Year's Eve.

Archie was on duty throughout the New Year. When Liza had suggested asking his father and Marina, he had said do, yes, do, with unexceptionable enthusiasm, but of course I shall be in and out a lot. That did not seem to Liza to matter. Indeed, it might be easier to have only his intermittent presence for the first staying visit. She, on the other hand, was excited about it. She and Sally cleaned the spare room, and she put on new white linen pillowcases and sheets with embroidered hems. She made lists of meals and, as she did it, imagined how warm Marina would be in her praise of them.

Early on the morning of New Year's Eve, the telephone rang. Liza, thinking it would be a patient, picked it up preparing to say that Dr Logan was already at the health centre.

'Liza – '

'Marina!'

'My dear,' Marina said. 'Liza. I've called – I'm so sorry, but I've called – '

Her voice sounded light and faint.

'Marina,' Liza said alarmed. 'What is it, what has happened?'

'Forgive me. It's a little difficult. One moment – '

There was a pause.

Then Marina said, 'Liza. Dear. I'm afraid I have to tell you that Andrew is dead.'

CHAPTER TEN

Stuart Campbell, senior partner in the practice, was very delicate with Archie. He had met Sir Andrew himself a couple of
times, and had felt admiration for him both professionally and
privately. He also felt that Archie could have gone much further
and faster in his own career if only he had chosen to, and had
said to his wife, once or twice, that Sir Andrew's fame inhibited
his son. So, while he wished to condole most seriously with
Archie, he also felt his junior partner's life might now begin
to blossom. Archie, after all, he repeatedly told colleagues
exasperated by Archie's impulsiveness or forgetfulness, had the
human touch.

Dr Campbell's habits were stately. He was in his late fifties and
enjoyed the image of an old-fashioned rural general practitioner,
invariably tweed suited, comfortable in farm kitchens, regarding
the weather from the exclusive point of view of a fisherman. Grey
summer days, to Stuart Campbell, were good days, because they
cast no shadows on the water. When he spoke to his colleagues,
he liked to summon them magisterially into his own room at the
health centre and speak to them, very genially of course, from the
far side of his desk. The other doctors sat the same side of their
desks as their patients. They said it inspired confidence. Stuart
Campbell said it did precisely the reverse.

He did not, however, summon Archie to him, but went instead
to find him after surgery. Archie was scribbling notes in his
immense black hand but stopped as Stuart came in, and instinctively rose, like a schoolboy. Stuart waved a hand.

'My dear fellow – '

He put the hand on Archie's shoulder.

'You have all my sympathy. Betty's, too. A great shock.'

Archie, though drawn, looked perfectly composed.

'Thank you.'

'Wonderful life,' Stuart Campbell said, removing his hand. 'Wonderful to know how much you've done in life, how much you've given. I feel very privileged to have met him.'

'Thank you,' Archie said. 'Thank you for coming in.'

'My dear boy. It's the very least – And of course if there's anything at all that any of us can do, here, you've only to say the word.'

Archie gave a small sigh.

'There's very little to do, actually. Being my father, everything is in apple-pie order.'

'If you want more time off – '

'No,' Archie said quickly. 'No thank you. I shan't want that.'

'I thought perhaps your stepmother might like – '

Archie looked down.

'She's a very independent woman.' He looked up again and gave a little smile. 'I'm sure she'll make her own decisions.'

'Yes. Yes, of course.'

He paused. Then he put his hands in his trouser pockets and said, 'Coronary, I suppose?'

'Complete occlusion. No previous symptoms beyond tiredness after a long flight the day before.'

'Archie,' Stuart Campbell said with more energy. 'Archie, don't hold out.' He took his hands out of his trouser pockets and gripped Archie's arm. 'Sometimes, as you know as well as I do, it's easier to let go in front of someone whom you do not have to protect, like your wife. And I'd understand, my dear fellow, heavens, I would.'

Archie gazed at him.

'I'm a clumsy fool,' Stuart said. 'Spoken far too soon. Betty always says I've the tact of a rhino.'

'No,' Archie said. 'You could not be kinder. Really. And I'm so grateful. But I'm all right. Very sad, of course, but perfectly all right.'

131

'I don't like it,' Stuart Campbell said later to his wife. 'I don't like the look of him.'

Betty Campbell, who considered Archie a man oversized in every direction, said she thought it was a mercy he hadn't broken down. It never helped for a man to weep, anyway. Stuart was about to protest, and then recollected that Betty and her partner had lost at their weekly bridge four, and refrained. When her next remark turned out to be, 'And don't you go meddling. There's no one like doctors for interfering,' he was glad he had.

The next day, in the post office, he met Liza. She was looking pretty but subdued and the elder boy was with her. Stuart waited until they had bought the stamps and writing paper they had come in for – Mrs Betts, heavy with genteel condolence, served Liza as if she were an invalid – and then he ushered her back into the lane to say, 'I do hope you'll let me know if there's anything we can do. We can fill in for Archie between us, you know. And there's always such a mountain of paperwork at such times.'

Liza turned to him gratefully. Large, easy, unthreatening men like Stuart Campbell brought out all that was sweetest and most female in her.

'You are so kind. But I don't think he wants anything to be different. It's his way of coping. And his stepmother is amazing: so brave, so competent.' She looked up at Stuart. 'They had only been married three weeks. A month ago on Friday. I can't bear it.'

Thomas, beside her, was again apprehensive, and then certain, that he would cry. He shuffled sideways and glared into the bare twigs of the hedge, where litter had blown and hung like grimy rags. The tears rose and the rags blurred and quivered.

'You must ring me,' Stuart said, 'if you're at all worried. About anything. It wasn't – a usual relationship.'

'No.'

'So very close. Most fathers and sons get on, all right. But not like that.'

'Perhaps,' Liza began and then glanced at Thomas's shaking

132

back, and stopped. She went over and put her arms round him.
'Darling.'

'Perhaps,' Stuart said, understanding her.

She looked at him over Thomas's head.

'It's this quiet, quiet sadness. So out of character.'

Whose quiet sadness? Thomas thought, calming down a little.
And what was out of character? Characters were people in plays.
Cartoon ones were Mickey Mouse. He snuffled a bit against Liza's
shoulder and felt descend upon him the terrible weariness that
followed the bouts of weeping.

'The one thing I've learned from doctoring,' Stuart said, 'is
that the exceptions exceed the rules. A hundredfold. And trauma
invariably creates exceptions.'

'I'm keeping a close watch –'

'I've no doubt of it, my dear. Just let me know if you notice
anything disturbing.'

Thomas disengaged himself and rubbed his face vigorously with
his anorak sleeve. Stuart put a brief hand on his head.

'Well, your father has plenty of people to comfort him, that's
for sure.'

'But the trouble is,' Thomas said, 'that we're the ones who need
comforting. And Marina.'

Marina. At any mention of her name, they felt filled with awe and
pity and love. At least, Liza and Thomas did, and so, in his
unformed gawky way, did Mikey. She had wanted them all
to come to London; she had wanted them all to be as close to
Sir Andrew – the last living second of Sir Andrew – as she could
get them. So Liza had left Imogen with Sally for the day –
'Come too!' Imogen had bellowed, but not for long, with Sally
there – and they had driven up to London on New Year's Eve
and found Marina in the Victoria mansion flat, alone in the sitting
room full of towering Edwardian furniture brought down from
Scotland.

She did not weep although she had plainly wept earlier. She
held each one of them hard, and then Archie and Liza had gone
into the big, gaunt bedroom where Sir Andrew lay, in new blue
pyjamas, wearing an inscrutable expression, neither happy nor

133

sad, merely absent. Liza had never seen anyone dead before and was a little afraid of that, but very much more afraid of what the sight of his dead father might do to Archie. But it seemed to do very little. He was, after all, more than accustomed to it. He simply stooped and kissed his father's forehead, and so Liza thought she had better do so, too. The flesh was soft and cool; remote but not particularly dead. She took Archie's hand, but he did not grip hers, merely let their palms lie together. He longed for Liza to cry. She did not because it did not seem necessary; there was no reality for her at that actual, real moment of standing by the body, looking down into that familiar, dead face.

When they came out, Marina and the boys were sitting on the sofa close together.

'Would you like to see Grandpa?' Archie said.

Mikey flung himself back into the sofa cushions.

'No.'

'Thomas?'

'A bit,' Thomas said.

Marina took his hand.

'From the doorway?'

He nodded. He stood up and Archie took his hand and led him along the passage to the bedroom. Thomas halted in the passage and looked through the open door into the bedroom, and saw his grandfather lying very neatly, with bare feet. The bareness of his feet shocked Thomas deeply. It was improper, rude to leave his feet bare.

He said roughly, 'He ought to have his slippers on.'

'Yes,' Archie said. 'Of course he should.'

Thomas pointed.

'They're there.'

Archie went across to the chest of drawers, which bore exactly the boxes and brushes he remembered from boyhood, and picked up the slippers. Thomas did not move. Then he went over to the bed and fitted the slippers on to his father's feet.

'There,' he said. 'Do you think that is more suitable?'

He turned. Thomas had gone. He was back in the sitting room, saying to Mikey in a voice harsh with boasting and bafflement, 'He only looks asleep.'

Mikey hid his face in the sofa cushions.

Thomas said to Liza in an incompetent whisper, 'Let's go home. I want to go home.'

'Of course you should,' Marina said. 'Of course. But you'll be glad you came.'

Liza began to pick up her handbag and look for Mikey's jacket.

Marina said to Archie, 'We'll talk tomorrow. It's all under control today.'

'Yes,' he said. He went out of the sitting room and back to his father. Marina, after a moment, followed him.

'I rang Maurice Crawford. He came at once. He is doing the certificate.'

Archie was stooping over his father.

'I'll go,' Marina said. She craved his questions.

'You don't have to.'

'But you might want to be alone – '

'Too late,' he said.

'He died in my arms,' she said. 'Literally. He wasn't alone for a split second at the end. Maurice says he will have known nothing, just a stab of pain and then – ' She stopped and put her hand to her face. 'I'm so sorry. I forgot you were a doctor.'

'Not at all,' Archie said. He straightened up.

'I said we could talk tomorrow. But of course we could now, if that's what you want – '

'No,' Archie said. 'No, thank you.'

'I don't want to do anything except the way you want it.'

'Thank you.'

He came up to her and gestured that she should precede him back to the sitting room. She hesitated, briefly overwhelmed with a longing to be comforted, on the very edge of flinging herself into his arms. But nothing whatever in his face or manner invited that.

So she simply said again, 'I'll do things just the way you want,' and walked ahead of him.

Liza could see they had not communicated. Archie went across to Mikey and lifted him into his arms.

'Could I have a hamburger?' Mikey whispered urgently. 'A London one?'

Liza put her arms around Marina.

'Would you like me to come up and stay? It would be so easy, with the holidays, and Sally. And I'd love to be with you. If you'd like it.'

'Dear,' Marina said, shaking her head. 'Dear Liza. I'll tell you the minute I need anyone. There's no one I'd rather have than you. But there's so much to do just now and I'm best alone for a bit. I'm used to being alone. More used – more used than not.'

They drove home almost in silence, pausing only to buy the boys two monsterburgers in white cardboard boxes, and two drinks in lidded cups as big as buckets. Once or twice, Liza put her hand on Archie's, on the steering wheel, and he gave a cursory pat with his other one, but apart from that she gazed out of the window at the charmless suburbs and then at the lifeless winter landscape that edged the motorway. In the back seat, heartened by food, the boys tussled mildly together and forgot the morning.

Colin Jenkins paid a pastoral visit. He had done this once before, on arrival in place of his mild, scholarly predecessor who had been an honorary canon of the cathedral and had retired into the heart of the city. On that first visit, Liza had made coffee and talked to him a little awkwardly in the sitting room round the bump that was to be Imogen. He had not met Archie until they had coincided at a hospital bed and he had known, with a small resentment, that Archie had had the upper hand at that meeting. Now, emboldened by the passing of time, Colin rather imagined that the ball, at this interview, would be in his court. It was not supremacy over Archie that he wanted, he told himself, but a chance to fulfil his proper role. He, the unbereaved, would be the stronger, the one able to give.

He called in the evening. Archie opened the door wearing jeans and a dark-blue fisherman's jersey. He had no shoes on, only thick white seaman's socks, and the absence of shoes was, for some reason, disconcerting. He led Colin into the sitting room where there was a fire in front of which Nelson lay on his side. Liza was watching television, but, when Colin came in, she got up and

136

switched it off, and there was the sudden extreme silence that the banishment of television leaves.

'I've called to offer you both my very great sympathy. And to tell you that I shall pray for you. And your father.'

Archie said nothing. Liza guided Colin to a chair.

'We opened some wine. Will you have some?'

'Oh no. No, thank you.'

'Coffee?'

'I couldn't put you to the trouble,' Colin said. 'I only came for a moment or two. I thought . . . ' He looked at them both, Liza back on the sofa, Archie still standing up. 'I thought we might say a prayer together.'

'Good God,' Archie said.

'It is,' Colin said firmly, as if proffering an unwanted indigestion tablet, 'very comforting.'

'I'm sure,' Liza began, 'for some people – '

'But you are Christians. You are churchgoers. You are part of the Christian family.'

Liza looked at Archie.

After a pause he said, without much grace, 'I may be a religious man – I may have a deep religious sense – but I am not at all sure there is a God. Not your God, in any case.'

Colin smiled. It was his smile of patient understanding.

'But if you are religious, then surely that implies belief in God?'

Archie sat down on the arm of the sofa and put his head in his hands.

'I don't think – ' Liza said.

'Christ,' Archie shouted across her, raising his head. 'Christ! Don't you even know what religion means? Are you so hidebound by your colourless bureaucratic orthodoxy that religion only means to you this frightful modern Church with its doggerel hymns and playschool prayers?' He got up. 'Religion, Colin, is an awakened sense of some great controlling force, an awareness that above or beyond there is not just a freedom but a fulfilment. And this awareness of power and possibility makes us strive ever onwards, morally, emotionally, spiritually. What on earth has such a concept to do with the dreary pen-pushing second-rate God you want to offer me?'

137

And he left the room.

Liza said, 'Oh, Colin, I'm so sorry, you must forgive him. He's terribly upset, he – '

'Of course,' Colin said, all indulgence. 'It's only to be expected. Quite understandable. And I gather they were particularly close. It's a hard blow.'

Liza nodded. She was torn between pity for Archie and fury with him, while at the same time realising that his speech to Colin was the longest and most eloquent he had made since Andrew died.

'Perhaps,' Colin said, 'you and I might pray together now. For Archie, as well as for his father?'

Liza looked at him helplessly. What alternative, but to agree, had Archie left her? Colin Jenkins, victorious, smiled and closed his eyes.

'Oh, God, our Father – '

'How could you?' Liza cried. 'How could you be so rude to him?'

Archie shrugged.

'It was absolutely gratuitous! He's an annoying little man but he meant well, and he was only doing his job!'

'It was insulting,' Archie said, rolling away from her in bed. 'It was insulting to be spoken to like that.'

Liza took a deep breath. She was sitting up against the pillows. She folded her hands in front of her on the duvet. The thing to do was to keep very, very calm.

'I see. So your grief is special and more awful than anyone else's. Just as your love for your father was special and greater than anyone else's. No one is fit to help you because you are in this special category. Diana Jago comes to see you and you just stare at her. Richard Prior, of all people, comes to see you and you look at him like a dog that's been kicked and will never trust people again.'

Archie lay listening, his eyes open.

'It's the same old thing, isn't it? It's the same old arrogance. It doesn't occur to you, does it, what hell Marina is going through or what a nightmare she had? You won't lift a finger to comfort

138

her. Oh no. She took away Archie's daddy so she must be punished. How long are you going to keep this up? How long? Because people will get sick of your self-indulgence, and the first of them will be me.'

Archie did not stir. She looked across at his exposed shoulder and the back of his head.

She said in her most Mrs Logan-of-Bradley-Hall-School voice, 'And the children are not going to the funeral.'

There was silence. It lasted half a minute and then Archie said, 'Yes, they are.'

'Mikey and Imogen are too young. And Thomas doesn't want to.'

Archie rolled over.

'He does.'

'No,' Liza said. 'He's had bad dreams ever since you took him in to see Andrew the day he died. He's had them most nights.'

'He hasn't said anything about them to me – '

'He probably knows there's little point in saying anything to you just now. It's like living with someone deaf and blind.'

By his side, Archie's fists were clenched.

'Have you quite finished?'

'I think so,' Liza said.

Archie got out of bed.

'Where are you going?'

'To the spare room.'

'I see,' Liza said. 'Melodrama to the end.'

Dizzy with rage and misery, Archie banged the door behind him. When he opened the spare-room door, he realised he could not sleep there. It was still waiting for Andrew and Marina, the high white pillows piled up, untouched, virgin. Choking with tears, he stumbled downstairs and cast himself on the sitting-room sofa. Alone in their bedroom, Liza slid neatly down under the duvet, turned on her side and cried and cried as if her heart would break. On the landing, crouched against the banisters, Thomas shivered in his pyjamas and listened.

★

139

Thomas thought St Stephen's Church in Rochester Row was horrible. It was a sad, dead colour and everything about it seemed too tall and sharp and most unfriendly. The street was horrible, too, grim and red, like a menacing great passage. Why on earth his grandfather's funeral had to happen in such an awful place was incomprehensible.

It was frightening being so few of them, just him and Archie and Liza and Marina one side and a few old men in dark suits the other. Archie had said there would be a huge memorial service later, which would be very cheerful because it would be all about the marvellous things Grandpa had done, but Thomas might not be able to come to that, because of school. He wished he hadn't come to this. He'd said yes partly to please Archie and partly to spite Mikey, and he regretted both of those reasons now, sitting between Liza and Marina in the gloomy dark with the almost unbearable sight of Grandpa's coffin there, in front of them, on a chrome trolley with rubber wheels. The trolley and the wheels offended Thomas the way his grandfather's bare feet had done.

He thought it unlikely he would cry any more. He thought he must have cried himself right out. He was sick of crying. The only thing to do was not to think about Grandpa, and not to think about going back to school, either – the other black beast that lurked about waiting for his mind to lie idle for a second. He seized his prayer book. He would count all the 'e's on one page. Liza's hand came down and turned the pages back to the correct place and ran a pointing finger along the current line of prayer. Thomas waited until she had taken her hand away and then he closed the prayer book with enormous carefulness and put it in front of him, on the polished wooden ledge. He would have nothing to do with it.

The undertaker's men came up the aisle. There were six of them. They were not all the same size and they were not pleasing to look at. Slight quivering beside him told Thomas that Liza had begun to cry. He leaned forward imperceptibly, and out of the side of his eyes saw that his father's eyes were full of spilling tears that he was doing nothing about, just letting them brim and fall. It was terrible. The undertaker's men undid some little bolts, lifted the coffin on to their shoulders and made a wide sweep in front of the brass rods of the rood screen; then Thomas realised that they were going to walk away down the aisle. Carrying Grandpa. They were carrying the coffin away. Where? To do what . . . ? A vast black mushroom ballooned up inside Thomas's head and shoved at his skull and his tongue and the backs of his eyes.

Marina's hand appeared. It took his, very hard. Then her face followed it.

'Look up there,' Marina said. 'Go on. Look up.'

Her other hand was pointing.

'Where?' Thomas said, battling with the mushroom.

'Up there. Look up there.'

Above the choir stalls, Thomas could dimly see a faraway roof. It looked blue. It glimmered.

'Stars,' Marina said. 'Just look at that. Hundreds and hundreds of golden stars.'

January had laid its repressive hand on Stoke Stratton. It had not sent snow, but frost; frost and pearl-grey skies to brood over dark trees and dun grass. In the garden at Beeches House, only a brave eleagnus had any colour. If people had to die, Liza thought miserably, why did they do it at a time of year that seemed quite to have lost hope? She knelt on the floor of Thomas's bedroom, in front of his school trunk, with the Pinemount uniform list on the floor beside her, and a pencil to tick off the endless columns of socks and shirts and soccer boots. Thomas, who was supposed to be helping, was slumped on the sofa downstairs in front of a video of *Superman*. She had neither the heart nor the energy to rout him out. They were all worn out with each other, tired of death. Pinemount might at least be a change for Thomas, a place where death and all its ramifying complications were swiftly swamped by timetables and sport.

She put her face down into the trunk. It smelled poignantly of detergent and boy. She, too, longed for term to begin, partly because she so much needed a structure once more, and partly because she wanted Blaise O'Hanlon's admiration back, an admiration that she had, magnificent in her sternness, told him

141

he must desist from, when he had telephoned from Dublin two days before Christmas. She wanted it, she told herself, because living with Archie was so lonely just now; lonely and complicated. It was complicated because he could fill her with frustrated fury, as he did the night Colin Jenkins came, and then, as at the funeral, with real pity: he had turned to her, in that beastly church, and put his arm round her and drawn her to him, and that, for all its sweetness, was more confusing than anything.

She straightened up. She must not think about it. She must think about marked hairbrushes and spare name tapes and towels with loops on them, for swimming. On Thomas's bed, above the opened trunk lid, Blue Rabbit lay propped against the pillow and watched her lugubriously out of his brown embroidered eyes. Perhaps, Liza thought, picking up the list once more, perhaps now that Andrew was dead, the idea of Pinemount might die, too? But she would have to talk to Archie, and at the moment how could anyone, anywhere, talk to Archie?

'Old rubbish,' Granny Mossop muttered.

She lay on her side in a high hard bed in the geriatric ward and mumbled her lips about. She was so thin now that her bed had had to be padded up for her, and, because of the constant accidents of her condition, she was padded, too, a bundle of alien white hospital swaddlings out of which her little brown hands and arms crept like twigs.

'You are not old rubbish,' Archie said. He sat on a chair by her bed and leaned so he could see her. 'You are not here because you are rubbish, but because you couldn't manage at home any more.'

'Could,' she said.

Her teeth floated upside down in a jar of pink fluid on the bedside trolley. Without them, her mouth sucked and fluttered, collapsing in on itself. Archie put a hand on hers.

'Sharon was worried – '

'Ha!'

He dared not ask if Sharon had been in to see her mother. Granny Mossop twitched her hand free. She gestured feebly at the ward.

142

'Old fools.'

She was difficult to hear. He bent closer. She smelled of cloth and age and illness. They were afraid jaundice was setting in. She would smell worse then.

'I'll be back,' Archie said. 'I'll be back in a few days.'

'Ha,' she said again, with less emphasis.

'I will. I promise you.'

He did not want to leave her. He stood up and waited for a moment, looking down on her wasted, nut-like face and uneven tussocks of white hair. I am afraid, he thought, I am afraid that if I leave her she will die, and if I am not here when she dies, then I will never know.

He went down the polished corridors of the hospital, past screens and pairs of double doors and a mystifying complexity of green signs sending the scarcely hopeful sick down the labyrinths to a chance of cure. A good many of the staff knew him because he was a faithful visitor of practice patients, and some of them stopped him and said how sorry, how very sorry they were about Sir Andrew and how much he would be missed. Thank you, he said, yes, how nice of you; no, we had the funeral quickly because it was what he wished, and there will be a memorial service later.

'It's harder, if you're a doctor,' a staff nurse he had known for years said to him. 'People don't think that. They think that because you know, you understand and so it's easier. But it's the reverse really, isn't it? It's knowing why that makes accepting so hard.'

'And unfinished business,' Archie said.

He went out to find his car. He had no desire to get into it and less to drive back to the health centre. He unlocked the door, and climbed into the driver's seat and sat for a while looking at, but not seeing, a brisk, inflexible shrub planted against an unlovely brick wall. Thomas would be getting to Pinemount now, driven by Liza with Diana Jago, whose spirits could be relied upon to remain buoyant and infectious. Was second term better than first? Or was it worse because there were no optimistic apprehensions left, you only knew the worst? He started the car. What was worst or best any more? Where was there anything but plateau? 'I

143

remember thinking one morning,' a woman patient afflicted with profound menopausal depression had once said to Archie, 'I thought: Is this all there is?' He turned the car into the traffic. God, Archie thought. Is it?

CHAPTER ELEVEN

The distinguishing feature of spring terms at Bradley Hall School was that the temperature outside the building felt considerably higher than that inside. The boiler thundered dully away in its basement, pouring heat into the brick walls that surrounded it and only managing to send a tepid trickle through the immense old toast-rack radiators that stood so optimistically under every window. The first day of term was usually spent twisting old newspapers into sausages that could be crammed into the frames of the huge, beautiful eighteenth-century windows that now shook in the winter winds like loose teeth.

The first assembly was always rather festive, chiefly because June Hampole was so genuinely pleased to see the children back. Beaming at them over an enveloping muffler, she told them that the school cat had had seven kittens – two toms, she said, and three queens, and two that seemed, however hard she peered, quite androgynous – and that the forsythia was bravely out in the central courtyard and that everyone was to wear gloves for lessons until they were told they might take them off.

'The children cannot write in gloves,' Mrs West called clearly.

'All the better. They are at the most receptive age for learning by heart.'

Liza, laughing, allowed Blaise to catch her eye. He looked older, a little thinner, and his air of dishevelled bohemian glamour was even more pronounced. He had said nothing to her yet, merely looked. Liza was wearing the green jersey Marina had given her.

'You must all sit very close to one another,' June Hampole said. 'But there is to be no touching. No silly touching, that is. And we will pause every ten minutes or so, and do a minute's jumping.'

145

Mrs West, a professional of forty years' experience, winced faintly. Her English classes would proceed in the orthodox manner they always did. She had brought an electric fan heater with her. Jumping would not even be considered. Liza, happy for the first day in weeks, wanted to laugh out loud at the thought of jumping. Her classes could jump to their verbs. The whole assembly was laughing.

'No laughing!' Commander Haythorne barked.

June Hampole, thoughtfully chewing the earpiece of her spectacles, said they would have a closing prayer. She had not looked one out; she merely thought she would invent one on the spot.

'Dear Father,' she said musingly, and paused. 'Dear Father.' The children, heads bowed, waited. 'Dear Father, this term is like the year, a new page. Which we are going to write on. With great kindness to one another and no fibs and no bullying. Our pens,' said June Hampole gathering speed, 'shall be our loving hearts as well as our desire to do well and to make our parents proud of us. And . . . ' She paused again. 'And. And Amen, I think.'

'Amen,' the children chorused loudly.

In the crowd pushing out of the chapel, Liza waited for Blaise's voice at her shoulder. She did not hear it. She was carried out into the hall and surrounded by children wishing to tell her about Christmas presents and skiing holidays and how they thought they had a sort of pain. Across their heads, she saw Blaise herding his first football lesson down the dark passage that led to the fearsome and beetle-infested changing rooms. He did not glance at her. He had not, of course, Liza told herself, noticed she was there.

She turned sternly upon her first classful and said, 'Now that's quite enough attempts to deflect me. In you go. And we'll get the jumping over at the beginning.'

She did not see Blaise at break. She sat beside Commander Haythorne on the accommodating leather sofa in the staff room and he offered her a ginger biscuit out of his particular tin, and told her about his Christmas in Wales, and Liza was a very animated listener in case Blaise should come in and think for one instant that she was waiting for him. He did not come in. She ate her biscuit and Commander Haythorne described the majesty of the seas at Marlow Sands in winter and the atrociousness of his daughter-in-

146

law's housekeeping skills, and her high delight in the day dimmed a little and admitted itself to be troubled.

The morning wore on, and lunchtime came, an Outward Bound exercise in the orangery where the frost still iced the glass inside, and steam rose from the mounds of potatoes and cabbage in exaggerated clouds. Liza seated herself at the head of her usual table and after a while Blaise came in with a troop of boys, and passed her, saying, 'It's murderous out there. The ground's like iron. Am I liable if they break their little legs?'

His voice was easy and conversational. It was the voice he used for everybody. He then stopped by Mrs West and said something quite prolonged to her and made her laugh. Liza turned brightly to the child beside her, a plain and eager girl of eleven who never seemed aware that her determination to sit next to members of staff at meals did not endear her to her contemporaries.

'Well, Laura. Was Christmas all it should be?'

'Mrs Logan, it was brilliant. Granny came and so did my other grandfather and we went carol singing and Mummy didn't have a headache, not once, and I had champagne and the dog was sick but not on Granny, luckily, and on Boxing Day – '

But he looked at me in prayers, Liza thought. It wasn't an ordinary look, either. He's just being careful, he's not arousing suspicion. I must play the same game, of course I must.

'I really, really hate cabbage. It's my worst thing. Do I have to eat it, Mrs Logan? Do I really, really have to eat this cabbage?'

'Simon, I think you should eat two bites. To do you good. Then you can leave the rest.'

'But I'll be sick. I promise.'

'Eat it with something. Eat it with a bit of sausage.'

'I love cabbage,' Laura said.

'Then,' said Simon, looking at her with pure contempt, 'you can eat mine.'

The afternoon was long. The chill of the day had settled down into real, penetrating cold, and the novelty of a new term had worn off in the face of universal recollection of what school was like. Liza's classes dozed and fiddled, sucking their gloved fingers and then trying to poke woolly filaments off each other's tongues with pencil ends. They were bored with French, bored with trying to

147

concentrate after a month's freedom. At twenty to four, the first cars appeared and the mothers got out of them to stamp about on the drive and bellow at each other about the hell of the weather and the double hell of Christmas. When the last bell went, a gasp of relief ran round the class like a gust of wind. Banging their desks and scraping their chairs, they stampeded past Liza back into their real lives.

She went slowly out to her car. She, too, was extremely cold, and fumbled to get the door open with rigid fingers. In the glove compartment lay the garnet pin. She had planned to return it to Blaise and she had planned exactly what she would say. She looked about her. Mrs West was backing her car out carefully from the corner she always used, and the part-time mathematics teacher, who found Bradley Hall's unorthodoxy quite bewildering, was loading piles of exercise books into her boot. Prep already! The first day . . . There was no one else. No Blaise. Liza waited a little. The mathematics teacher and Mrs West drove slowly past her and turned towards the main gates. Liza started the engine. She backed her car and turned it, switching the fan and the heater on to full so that the interior roared like a train in a tunnel. She drove out on to the main drive and turned for home. Across the lawn, and halfway across the adjacent field, a man was walking, away from the school. He wore Blaise's yellow muffler.

There was a notice on the door of Stoke Stratton post office. 'Appeal!' it said sternly. 'Don't give in! Lobby all officials!' It was written in thick black ink on one of the large sheets of blossom-pink paper Mrs Betts favoured for her edicts.

'What's happened?' Liza said.

Because of the cold, Mrs Betts was encased in a home-knitted Aran cardigan which gave her the contours and solidity of a hot-water cylinder.

'We shall not give up,' Mrs Betts said. 'I shall go to the House of Lords if necessary.'

Sharon Vinney, intermittently dusting the postcard rack, gave an audible snort.

'What is it?' Liza said. 'Is it the field?'

'He,' said Mrs Betts with deadly emphasis, 'he thinks he has got planning permission.'

'He has,' Sharon said. 'It's final. It'll make all the difference to our Trevor. He'll be first on the list. Somewhere for him and Heather to set up home at last.'

Trevor Vinney, a pale, resentful young man who worked, without enthusiasm, as a mechanic at a Winchester garage, had a small dark girlfriend and a smaller darker baby. The girlfriend spent a good deal of the day sitting in the village bus shelter, with the baby beside her in a pushchair, smoking cigarettes she rolled herself and staring at passing traffic with an angry longing.

'Your new neighbours, dear,' Mrs Betts said to Liza. She raised her eyebrows almost to her richly tinted hairline.

Liza said, 'But that's so quick. I mean, we only heard about it two months ago – '

Mrs Betts leaned forward.

'Quite frankly, Mrs Logan, it isn't all as it should be. Something's been going on.'

Sharon stopped dusting. She put her hands on her hips and waited. Mrs Betts lowered her voice.

'I intend to find out. My friend – '

'You'll find nothing on Mr Prior,' Sharon said clearly. 'He's straight, is Mr Prior. Dad worked for him since he came and he said he was a right bugger but he was straight.'

Mrs Betts adjusted the cuffs of her cardigan.

'Don't use bad language in the shop, please, Sharon.'

Sharon glared. Then she turned and went to the far end of the shop where blue packets of aspirin and yellow bottles of disinfectant and scarlet boxes of sticking plaster comprised what Mrs Betts called 'my first-aid corner'.

'I can say what I like to her,' Mrs Betts confided to Liza. 'I pay her the basic industrial wage and I mind her terrible manners for her. She won't leave. Oh no. I'd have to sack her. Where else would she find a job which meant she knew all the gossip in the village before anyone else?'

Liza glanced down the shop.

'Trevor Vinney – '

'Precisely. There really is no time to be lost. Do you think Dr Logan might come round to our point of view now that reality is staring him in the face?'

149

'I don't know,' Liza said. 'I'll try.'

She was suddenly oppressed by fatigue and dull despair. This day had promised so much and had failed in everything. The granting of planning permission for the field was merely the last dreary straw.

'May I have five pounds' worth of first-class stamps?'

'Mrs Logan,' Mrs Betts said. 'I really have no wish whatsoever to intrude upon your and Dr Logan's personal grief, but there is no time to be lost. Letters, you know, appeals to our MP. Now, Mrs Logan, *now*.'

Liza looked up at her as she slid the stamps over the counter. Her powdered face was smiling, but absolutely implacable. No wonder Mr Betts had run away. Rumour said he had run a long way away, too, to Australia, and not for another woman at that. He had simply fled.

In the kitchen, Sally was giving tea to the children. She had made them sandwiches, whose crusts she had not cut off, and poured out mugs of milk. On the way from the garage, Liza could see through the kitchen window that they were eating and drinking with perfect docility. When she entered, however, Imogen immediately shouted, 'Not milk! Not milk! Juith! Juith!' and Mikey squirmed off his chair and said he didn't want to eat his crusts.

'How can you stand them?' Liza said to Sally.

Sally said, with truth, that they didn't do this to her. She got up, retrieved Mikey, took Imogen's mug away from her and put a teapot down in front of Liza.

'Mr Prior's got his permission.'

'Thank you, Sally. Yes. I heard. In the post office.' She poured out tea and then, cradling the mug in her hands, looked out of the kitchen window into the dark and doomed field beyond.

'Seems a shame,' Sally said.

'I know.'

'Mrs Jago's been in. Left you a letter. She said – '

Mikey put a crust between his teeth and then blew it to the far side of the table. Imogen immediately did the same.

'I can't stand it,' Liza said.

Sally reached over and took both the children's plates away.

150

'Fine. End of tea. No biscuits.'

'Bithcuit!' Imogen wailed.

Sally scraped the sandwich remains into Nelson's supper dish.

'Too late.'

'No! No!'

'Yes,' Sally said. 'Perhaps you'll remember next time.'

'I'm hungry,' Mikey said.

'I expect you are.'

Liza said, 'Sally, I'd propose to you if I wasn't already married.'

'It's always easier if the kids aren't yours.'

Liza thought of Bradley Hall. Immediately, she wished she had not. She looked at the dresser drawer where her letter and card lay hidden. Did Blaise . . .

'Bithcuit,' Imogen whined, leaning against her.

'No. You were silly with your sandwich. Remember?'

'Pleath. Pleath bithcuit – '

Sally stooped to pick her up.

'Come on, madam. And you, Mikey.'

'Whaffor?'

'I'll give you what for. Just come.'

'Sally. Thank you so much – '

'Mrs Jago said would you ring her – '

'Yes. Yes, of course. It'll be about the field.'

'Can't imagine anything worse,' Sally said, shuddering, 'than having all those Vinneys and Durfields next door.'

She opened the kitchen door and an icy blast from the hall bounced in.

'Cold,' Imogen said at once. 'It'th cold.'

'How would you know?' Sally said, bearing her away. 'How would you know inside all that podge?'

When the door had closed, Liza opened Diana's letter:

Too awful that Richard should get his wretched permission. And simply *whizzed* through – we had to wait nine months for permission to change the garage roof from flat to hipped. Can you ring me? Love, D.

Liza dialled. She imagined the telephone ringing out in Diana's large, warm kitchen where cooking took second place to feeding the dogs. It rang and rang. Liza counted to twenty rings and then she put the receiver down.

Cutting through the lanes from the main road to Basingstoke, Diana Jago passed an unremarkable car unremarkably parked in a gateway. This was a common occurrence. Travelling salesmen, particularly, criss-crossing England on their private network of routes and shortcuts, were often to be found parked in gateways, either eating sandwiches and gazing glassily at the field beyond, or asleep against their head rests with their mouths open. It was only when Diana was twenty yards past this car that she realised that the man in it had been neither eating nor sleeping. He had been staring in front of him in a most unnatural way. He was also Archie Logan.

Diana's kindness, which was genuine, was not of a sensitive, delicate kind. The moment the message about Archie sitting staring in a closed car had travelled from her eyes to her brain, she braked, put her car into reverse and shot back to the gateway. Then she got out into the fierce grey air, and knocked on the window six inches from Archie's face. He wound it down. His expression was quite without surprise.

'What are you doing? Are you all right?'

'I was thinking.'

'So I saw. But you don't look the thing at all. You look frightful. Are you ill?'

'No,' Archie said.

Diana thought for a moment.

'Wind the window up,' she said.

Obediently, he wound it. She came quickly round the car and opened the passenger door.

'Now, look,' she said, getting in. 'It's like a fridge in here. Whatever's the matter won't be helped by freezing. Not even grief. Start the engine at least and we'll get the huffer huffing – '

Archie shook his head.

'No. No.'

Diana took his hand.

'Archie – '

He looked away from her, out of the car window, but he did not remove his hand.

'Archie, dear. Would it help to talk?'

There was a silence.

After a while, without turning his head, Archie said, 'I'm so angry.'

'Yes,' Diana said. 'So should I be in your place. A perfectly wonderful life like your father's cut off quite needlessly while all kinds of utterly useless, intolerable people go on and on – '

'No,' said Archie. 'Not that.'

He turned his head to her.

'Not that. Not his dying. About how he died.'

'But I thought – I thought it was a coronary.'

'It was.'

Archie took his hand away and put it, with his other one, on the steering wheel.

Staring straight ahead out of the windscreen, he said, 'She did it. She caused it. They were in bed, they – '

'Archie!' Diana said. 'Stop it! Stop it at once – '

'I wasn't there!' he shouted, turning to her. 'Don't you see? I wasn't with him and if I'd been with him when he died, I'd have understood. As a doctor, as a man, there's something that I won't ever know now, that I would have known. Death is so important, so significant, perhaps it is even the key to life, it inspires awe and peace all at once. I know all that. Intellectually, I know all that. But I don't know it in my heart and soul, I don't feel it. If I'd been with my father, I would have felt it, I would have known for ever more what that stupendous, suspended time is like when everything is suddenly clear, comprehensible. That moment of death, that extraordinary, precious moment after death – '

He stopped.

Diana said gently, 'But you couldn't be there. You were his son, not his wife. It isn't reasonable to think you should have been there. And if he did die while they – while they – ' She paused while endless impossibly improper terms thronged unusably through her brain. 'Well, what could be better? What better last moment could there be for any man?'

153

'He wasn't that sort of man,' Archie said. 'He wasn't impulsive, he was orderly. He liked preparedness. He was made to be different, he was changed. It killed him – '

'But he probably liked it. People do. He was released, perhaps. I mean . . . ' Diana said, floundering. 'I often think that when I break my neck hunting, as I'm bound to do because I'm such a perfect fool, Simon'll marry someone quite different and he'll become different and probably quite happy. Not too happy, mind you, or I'll haunt him. But it isn't necessarily miserable, making a change. I mean, your father probably felt thirty-five again.'

'She didn't even tell me first,' Archie said.

'Who? What? I thought Marina rang Liza at once – '

'Liza was not my father's son. What right had Marina to tell anyone before she told me? She didn't even try to tell me. She didn't even ask Liza where I was. She just left a message. Hah!' Archie lifted his hands and pressed his palms to his temples. 'It might have been school-run arrangements. Dear Archie, your stepmother rang to say your father's dead.'

'But it wasn't like that. Liza came straight down to the surgery, she came to find you – '

Archie dropped his hands.

'I'm not blaming Liza.'

'It seems to me,' Diana said, 'that you are determined to blame somebody.'

'Only myself.'

'Well, it doesn't sound like that.'

'No,' he said, glancing at her. 'No, it doesn't, does it? Home you go, Mrs Jago. Enough humouring of impossible men for one afternoon.'

'You aren't impossible. It's just this damned grief. So unpredictable.'

'It's more,' Archie said. 'More than grief. That's what's so damnable, really.'

Diana put her hand on the door.

'Will you be all right? Are you safe to drive?'

'Perfectly. I shall go straight back to the health centre and be a good little doctor.'

'I'm not patronising you, you know – '

He leaned across and briefly kissed her cheek.

'I know. You are a kind woman, an excellent friend and a knockout on a horse.'

She got out of the car and closed the door carefully. Archie watched her climb into her own car and start it. She waved to him briefly, put the car into gear, pulled out of the gateway and drove off, her hand involuntarily on her cheek where he had kissed her.

'More thtory,' Imogen said.

She lay under her flower-patterned duvet with her hair brushed and her thumb poised for plugging in.

'No,' Liza said. 'You've had your story. Why do you always ask me things you know I must refuse so that I am forced to say no all the time?' She leaned forward and kissed Imogen's bath-scented cheek. 'You make me into a nag and it isn't fair because I'm not.'

'Thall I love you?' Imogen said unfairly, putting her arms round Liza's neck.

'I'd rather be loved than exploited,' Liza said, thinking not only of Imogen.

'Kith, kith, kith,' said Imogen, rubbing her face against Liza's and then, after a minimal pause, 'More thtory.'

'You're outrageous. No. No more story. I'm going to read to Mikey and then I'm going to telephone Mrs Jago. Let go.'

Imogen released her arms and put her thumb in. Then she turned on her side and closed her eyes and shut Liza out of her life.

'Sleep well, darling.'

Imogen said nothing.

Mikey was sitting up in bed with his dinosaur book. He had brushed neither his hair nor his teeth, and, despite his bath, still smelled of grey wool and school and socks. He gnashed his teeth at Liza.

'I'm a pterodactyl.'

'Must you be?'

'This is my big jaw. And my wing stuck to my finger.'

'I'd like to read *The Lion, The Witch and The Wardrobe*.'

Mikey flung himself back on his pillow.

'That's a girls' book.'

155

'It most certainly is not.'

'There are no guns in it.'

'Nor are there,' Liza said quickly, 'in dinosaur books.'

Mikey sat up again.

'But there are teeth.'

'They didn't all have teeth. Some of them had beaks.'

Mikey seized his book and began to riffle urgently through it.

'No, no, listen – '

'Mikey,' Liza said. 'I spent all today with children. I've had enough of children. I don't know why I bother to argue with you, really I don't. If you won't let me read something civilised, I'm not reading at all.'

'You read to Imogen,' Mikey said sternly. 'You read her *Thomas Goes to the Doctor* and you said you would never ever read her that again and you did.'

'But there's nothing to read in your dinosaur book. It's all pictures, and very bad pictures at that.'

'You hold the book,' Mikey said, consolidating victory, 'and I will talk to you about the pictures.'

'They win all the time,' Liza said on the telephone to Diana Jago. 'They argue on and on and then they win.'

'Don't argue back – '

'I know. I get caught up before I know where I am.'

'It's the penalty of having clever children. Ours were so dense it was no problem to outwit them. Liza, I wanted to talk to you about this field.'

'Yes. It's awful. I'd no idea it was happening so fast.'

'I want to twist your arm,' Diana said. 'Simon thinks you'd have a great effect if you went to see the Chief Planning Officer in person, as a representative of the family most affected.'

'It's too late! He's got planning permission – '

'Outline. The developer has yet to consolidate it. If he gets it, then we can't appeal. We have got to make sure he doesn't.'

'Why me?' Liza said, shutting her eyes.

'Because you are pretty and appealing.'

'Thanks a million!'

'Will you?'

I'm too tired, Liza wanted to say. I'm too worn down with

156

Archie and the children and Andrew dying, I'm too disappointed in today, I'm full of frustration . . .

'All right.'

'Excellent,' Diana said. 'The Chief Weasel is called Derek Mullins. Quick as you can. Richard's talking to a developer already, the man who built those nasty little objects on the King's Stoke crossroads. And Liza – '

'Yes,' she said, leaning against the kitchen wall.

'Don't be too hard on Archie.'

'What?'

'He's taken quite a knock – '

'Don't you start,' Liza cried, springing upright. 'Don't you start telling me how precious and special his grief is and how there was never a father and son like those two. I don't want to hear another word. All that distinguished their relationship, if you ask me, was that Andrew spoiled Archie rotten!'

'I didn't so much touch a raw nerve,' Diana said later to Simon over supper, 'as tread heavily on one. She simply flew at me – '

'What is this?' Simon said, prodding at his plate.

'Liver.'

'Are you sure?'

'Yup.'

'Will she go and see Mullins?'

'Reluctantly. Things aren't good there.'

'They'll be worse if she doesn't go and see Mullins.'

'I'm not given,' Diana said, 'to feeling sorry for people. I don't care for it much and I loathe people for being sorry for me. But I am sorry for the Logans. Aren't you?'

Simon put his fork down.

'Tell you something. If I have to eat this liver, I'll be very sorry for myself indeed.'

'Suit yourself,' Diana said. 'I don't care and the dogs'll be thrilled.' She looked at her plate. 'Do you know, I think you're right. It does look pretty filthy. Shall I make a cheese sandwich?'

Archie came in just before nine and Liza, with a faint air of martyrdom, gave him supper. He thought, as he ate it, that however delicious it was – which it was – it was soured by the

157

resentful dutifulness with which it was seasoned, and that he would very much have preferred to have opened his own tin of soup, which came without much flavour, admittedly, but also without emotional strings.

While he ate his goulash – Liza had not, even on the first day of the new term, forgotten the sour cream – she sat the other side of the kitchen table and flicked through the newspaper. She had a mug of camomile tea. Archie had a glass of wine; Liza had declined one. Archie could not tell her about his encounter with Diana Jago and Liza could not describe her disappointing day nor her powerful desire not to go and see the Chief Planning Officer. Neither of them could mention Marina and speculate about Andrew's will because Archie had said he could face nothing of the kind just now and Liza had declared she could not face Archie's attitude. So he ate and she rustled and each struggled to endure the misery of their several solitudes. The telephone rang as Archie was finishing and a woman from Lower Stoke said her husband had just broken the fish tank while cleaning it out and had cut his hands and was pouring blood like a river. Archie gave her instructions and said he'd be right over.

'Why can't people ever, ever manage to stay in one piece for a single hour?' Liza said, looking up from the paper.

'The surprising thing,' Archie said, 'is that so many of them do. All their blessed lives.'

Then he kissed Liza's hair and went out into the black darkness. She put his plate and glass into the dishwasher, let Nelson out, laid breakfast, retrieved Nelson, toured the ground floor shutting and locking and switching off, and then went upstairs to run herself a bath.

Archie was away for almost an hour. Liza heard his car, and then a familiar sequence of doors and footsteps and then he appeared in their bedroom doorway and looked at her.

'Was it serious?' she said, glad of something she could ask him.

'Yes,' he said. 'Yes. He'd caught a vein. He's gone into Winchester to be stitched.' He paused. 'I'm just going to write a letter.'

'A letter?'

Archie never wrote letters.

'Yes. A letter. I won't be long.'

'To Thomas?'

'No,' Archie said. 'Not to Thomas. To Marina.'

Liza turned towards him, delighted.

'Oh!' she cried. 'Oh, Archie! I'm so glad!'

CHAPTER TWELVE

The flat in Victoria was not an agreeable place to be. Sir Andrew had bought it out of a mild nostalgia for the tall red sandstone houses of his Glasgow youth, because it was on the first floor of such a building. But he had had little aesthetic eye for his surroundings, and, since the building was heavy with competent Edwardian stonework and joinery, he had been satisfied, untroubled by the gaunt height of the rooms and windows. He had observed the solidity with pleasure and was impervious to the atmosphere.

The atmosphere added to Marina's suffering. The flat faced west, so that the only sunlight was the tired low light of late-winter afternoons, which came filtering through gauze curtains with difficulty and fell unenthusiastically upon the surfaces of the heavy, alien furniture that had belonged to her long-dead, never-known parents-in-law. There were almost no pictures, merely a handful of dim sepia drawings of buildings and a mountainous landscape or two, purple with heather. The books were numerous and entirely factual except, Marina discovered, for one Alistair Mac-Lean novel, a paperback, lurking embarrassedly at the end of a shelf of august political biography. She took it out, before Morley's *Life of Gladstone* crushed it utterly, and thought how it added to her sudden isolation to realise that this man, whom she had loved so much, clearly never read fiction. If she hadn't known that, what else had she not known?

She had too much time to speculate about such things; too much time while she simply waited. It was unlike her to wait, unlike her not to act and begin to push life, however wretched it might be, forward again. But she could not act. She attempted to do all kinds of things to force herself to act, like making inventories of all Andrew's possessions, or having an estate agent round to value the flat or even, on one particularly bad day, to buy herself an air ticket back to New York which was clearly, she told herself, what she must do. But she could not bear, in the end, to do any of those things. She could not bear to do anything that seemed to separate her from Andrew. She could tell herself, a thousand times a day, that he was dead and gone, gone for ever, but she simply could not bring herself to perform a deed that proved the reality of that insupportable fact.

She understood, she thought, why Archie was so stone silent. He had not been in touch since the funeral and she guessed that he, too, was in the cold-turkey state of suffering before grief becomes assimilable. Sometimes she talked to Liza on the telephone, but she didn't like to do that too often until she had recovered something of her self-possession. Her pride, as well as her heart, was tormented by grief. So, while she waited for herself, she also waited for Archie. The flat would be his, so would the contents, so would all Sir Andrew's money, and the Scottish cottage she had never seen; she had no doubts as to all that happening, eventually, when she could come to life a little again. In the meantime, all she could manage to do was wait. I'm just waiting, she told herself, over and over again, I'm just waiting for something to happen.

At Bradley Hall School, influenza arrived with the first snow. It was unsatisfactory snow, thin and wet and disobliging about being moulded, but the flu was much more wholehearted. The classrooms thinned out dramatically; Dan Hampole took to his bed with a bottle of whisky, a kettle and a brown paper bag of lemons, and then Mrs West, usually dauntless in the face of child-spread infections, telephoned to say she could not even raise her head from the pillow.

'I'll do extra,' Liza said to June Hampole. 'Sally won't mind coming in more often for a while. I'll take some of the English classes.'

The garnet pin still lay in the glove compartment of the car, and Blaise O'Hanlon had as yet been no more than polite and friendly.

'I'd like to be here more,' Liza said truthfully. 'I'd like to help. It's sad at home just now.'

161

June Hampole said it would be a godsend, just for a week or two.

'Fine,' Archie said that night. 'Do. We're all better busy, just now.'

More snow fell, snow with greater purpose. The garden at Beeches House disappeared under its uniform white blanket and Imogen became imperious to be out in it for hours at a time, mesmerised by her own tracks and, even more, by the faint arrow-headed ones sketched out by birds. Sally came every day without complaint, and Archie and Liza left, often at the same time in the morning, their car tyres creaking up the hard-packed lane. The house grew tidy and a little impersonal in Liza's long absences so that when she returned to it after dark on the short winter days it felt pleasurably unfamiliar, as if the domestic responsibility was no longer all, heavily, hers. Just now, that suited her. Her romantic imagination, thirsty for relief from Archie and his father's death, was quite taken up in persuading Blaise O'Hanlon that he need not obey her stern instructions to behave himself to the letter. In such a frame of mind, it was a relief to leave so much domestic administration to Sally.

It was Sally who took the call from Pinemount. She had put Imogen and Mikey to bed and was coming downstairs with her arms efficiently full of the next morning's dirty laundry, when the telephone rang. A pleasant man's voice asked to speak to Dr or Mrs Logan and, when Sally said neither of them were back yet, the man said his name was George Barnes, from Pinemount, and that he would ring later. Sally wrote the message down and left it where she usually left messages, and cleared up the kitchen until Liza, bright eyed from the cold and a most enigmatic and exciting encounter, came in from school.

Liza did not look at the messages. Recently she had felt reluctant to, as if they represented in some measure the ordinary shackles of life that part of her at least had managed to shed. She felt a strong disinclination to discover, each evening, that the garage could not service her car the day she wanted; that Chrissie Jenkins had put her on the new Sunday School rota for the third Sunday of each month until the summer and that Mikey's school runs would be disrupted for six weeks because of parental skiing holidays.

162

Her inclination instead, that evening, was to go upstairs and look at herself in the mirror in the bathroom where the light was bright and truthful. She wanted to see if she looked different, now that Blaise had kissed her. Or, to be absolutely accurate, now that she had kissed Blaise. She had, at last, after many of the most delicate manoeuvrings, found Blaise alone in his classroom after school, and had attempted to return the pin to him. He had said no. He had been very flustered.

'No,' he said. 'No. Really. It was for you. You must have it.'

She put the box down on his desk. His evident confusion excited her and made her feel both strong and controlling.

'I can't take it. It was absolutely sweet of you, but it's out of the question.'

His face darkened. He looked away from her, at the poster of the Battle of the Boyne where the ragged Irish troops had the faces of gypsy angels.

'Blaise – '

'You don't understand – '

'Oh, but I do,' Liza said. 'I do. Look. I'll show you that I do.'

And then she had put her arms around his neck, and kissed him.

'There,' said Liza, smiling. 'There.'

And she had walked out of the room and the school and left him standing there with the little box lying before him. She had climbed into her car, and laughed, simply laughed out loud at the adventure she was having, at her power. Hadn't Blaise said she had power? And now, looking at herself in the bathroom mirror, she wanted to laugh again.

Downstairs, a door banged and Nelson barked, too late as always. There was a pause and Liza began, without hurry, to brush her hair. Archie came upstairs, holding the list of telephone messages.

'Did you see this?'

Liza watched him in the mirror. She waited for him to kiss her.

'No. What is it?'

'George Barnes rang from Pinemount. Why didn't you ring back?'

'Because I didn't see it.'

'But you were back before me.'

163

'Only just. I haven't done anything yet. I haven't even been in to see the children.'

Archie said, 'I'll ring. I'll ring now.'

'He's probably got flu, poor boy.'

'Do you want to ring, then?'

'No,' Liza said. 'No. You do it.'

She put down her hairbrush. A tiny shame nibbled at the corner of her pleasure.

'Thomas – '

'You go and kiss the little ones,' Archie said. 'I'll telephone.'

Imogen lay asleep on her back in a welter of stuffed animals and open books, illuminated by the dim glow from her toadstool nightlight. She never woke at night except if her toadstool was switched off, when she would wake instantly and roar with rage. Liza piled the toys and books at the foot of the bed, and settled the quilt around Imogen's stout small body. Imogen opened her eyes.

'Hello, lady.'

Liza stooped to kiss her.

'Night night, darling. Go back to sleep.'

But Imogen had never left it. Mikey, on the other hand, lay full of ploys to keep Liza upstairs. He put an arm like a clamp about her neck.

'I hurt myself at school and I didn't cry.'

'Oh, Mikey. What kind of hurt?'

'My head. On the locker door. Can you write a note saying I mustn't have school fish? Please. Please, please, please. Donovan doesn't have to have fish – '

'No. No, I couldn't.'

She began to disengage herself.

'I'm sick of Sally putting me to bed,' Mikey said. 'Why does she have to? It's so boring, always Sally. I'll never learn to read with Sally, only with you.'

'It's only for a little while – '

She stood up.

'Where's Daddy? I heard him. Don't go yet, don't go. If I have to have school fish, I'll be sick on the floor – '

Liza fled downstairs.

164

'I see,' Archie was saying into the telephone. 'Yes. Thank you so much. If you're sure – ' He listened a little. 'We'll talk about it and I'll ring you back. Yes. All right then. Goodnight.'

'What?' Liza said at once.

Archie turned round and leaned on the back of a kitchen chair.

'Thomas has been having nightmares. He has walked in his sleep on two or three occasions. They don't seem at all worried. George Barnes said he simply thought we ought to know.'

'Nightmares!'

'About his grandfather,' Archie said. 'George Barnes wanted to know exactly what happened.'

'Like your insisting he saw the body and went to the funeral.'

'I told him Thomas had done both.'

'I bet you didn't tell him you – '

'Shut up,' Archie said. He took his hands away from the chair. 'I'm going down to Pinemount.'

'Why?'

'I want to see Thomas.'

'But George said they were coping, that there was no need – '

'Liza,' Archie said, 'I need to see Thomas.'

'You won't help, you can't, you're too emotional. You just want the drama of it; it's all a part of this great drama of yours you won't let go of – '

Archie lunged forward and seized her wrist.

'No.'

Her eyes were full of alarm.

'I thought it was going to get better,' she said. 'Since you wrote to Marina.'

He let her go.

'That has nothing to do with this. Will you come with me? I'll go tomorrow, I've a half-day.'

'I can't. I'm teaching.'

'Cut it.'

'No,' Liza said. 'I can't. And anyway, I don't think either of us should go.' She paused and then she said, 'It isn't fair. Trust the professionals. Your father always said so.'

'Please yourself,' Archie said. He looked at her. There was

165

something in her he couldn't even recognise. 'I'll go, all the same. I'll go tomorrow.'

The New Forest struggled patchily through the snow with clumps and tufts of bush and bracken. It looked, Archie thought, driving through it, forlorn and shabby with its snow mantle disintegrating messily into smudged blots, a landscape very suited to his mood. It was a relief to have to concentrate upon driving, with the great lorries on their way to Bournemouth and Poole hurling up filthy plumes of slush that made it sometimes impossible to see. It was even more of a relief to have something to do that satisfied him; to have a proper mission.

He had supposed, after he had written to Marina, that he would feel better. He had supposed that it would release him. It had been a dreadful letter. He had written it after brooding on it for days, and then reread it the next morning, and still sent it. An excited horror filled him at the recollection of it, at the memory of the accusations with which he had crammed it. He had been sure that, if he exorcised himself of all the anger and bitter unhappiness he felt, then he would be free again to return to the Archie he had once been, the one he remembered as being both content and purposeful. The satisfaction of being a doctor would return, as would his delight and comprehension of Liza. His isolation would at last be over.

But it was not. The letter was sent and silence followed its sending. He became absolutely neurotic about the post arriving, wrenched apart by both longing for a reaction and dreading one. And in the midst of his divided feelings was a very strong consciousness that the letter had changed nothing, only added to his confusion and his sense of being paralysed. Rather than set him free, his bonds were even tighter. He, who had always supposed himself to be courageous, was terribly afraid.

The grey road, blurred with greyer slush, bore relentlessly on between the stretches of unremarkable Forest – what a poor thing William Rufus would think his Forest had dwindled to – and bungalows, and petrol stations with red plastic canopies and spinning signs advertising videos. How ugly, how temporary, what an utter, utter waste of being alive, of having chances. Why did people opt for the second rate? Was he doing that? Was he letting his life slide and drift into some decent, dreary stagnation?

The sign for Pinemount's village appeared trimly on the left-hand verge. Thomas. Archie braked sharply and turned down a lane into sudden countryside.

Thomas said he would like toasted tea cakes and a banana milk shake. The Wimborne tea shop was almost empty, furnished in immemorial tea-shop style of wheelback chairs and dim checked tablecloths and imitation horse brasses hanging on straps against walls of cream embossed paper. It smelled of dust and butter. Thomas, who looked perfectly normal, was mildly excited to be allowed out with his father for an hour and regarded the tea shop as the most appropriate place to be. He said Bristow's parents always gave Bristow tea here which was why he knew banana was the best kind of milk shake to have.

Archie said, 'Darling. What about these bad dreams?'

Thomas looked embarrassed.

'Who told you?'

'Mr Barnes.'

'Mr Barnes,' Thomas said. 'He's so interfering.'

'Not at all. He's kind. He was worried about you.'

Thomas took a bite.

'Once I woke up on the stairs.' His voice was awed. 'It was amazing.'

'Could you tell me about the dreams?'

'Not really.'

'Mr Barnes seemed to think they were about Grandpa.'

Thomas looked down.

'I don't know what they were about.'

'But you told Mr Barnes that they were about Grandpa.'

'I told Matron,' Thomas said, chewing. 'She kept asking and asking.'

'Darling Thomas. Do try and tell me. So I can help you. Do you think about Grandpa?'

'A bit.'

'Does it worry you?'

167

Thomas put down his tea cake. He said loudly, 'I don't like Mummy crying. Or you. Why do you?'

'We're very sad,' Archie said, too quickly. 'Because of Grandpa.'

Thomas looked at him.

'No.'

'Darling – '

Thomas said in the same loud flat voice, 'Rackenshaw's parents are divorced. So are Harris's. I don't want you to. I don't *want* it.'

Archie put his arms round Thomas.

'Darling Thomas, don't be an ass. What on earth put such a thing in your mind?'

Thomas was in tears. He put his damp and buttery face into Archie's shoulder.

'You might. You quarrel. And then Grandpa isn't here now.'

'You are in a muddle, aren't you?' Archie said, trying to keep his shaking voice light. 'Such a muddle. It sometimes happens, you know, when something awfully sad happens, like Grandpa dying, that people get a bit short-tempered, because of being so sad, and one of the deeply unfair things about life is that you get crossest with the people you love the most, that's all . . . '

Thomas pulled away and picked up his milk shake.

'I don't want to talk about it.'

'But if you don't talk about it, the bad dreams might go on.'

'No, they won't.'

'How can you be sure?'

'They just won't.'

'Thomas,' Archie said, 'are you making all this up?'

'No,' Thomas shouted, going scarlet.

'I have to ask you things, you see, to try and make it better.'

'I want to go back to Pinemount.'

Archie leaned forward.

'Is it better this term? Do you like it now?'

'I just want to go back,' Thomas said. He turned half away from Archie. 'Thank you for tea.'

Archie was close to tears.

'Darling Thomas. Listen just one moment. Mummy and I are not getting a divorce. Absolutely not. And, although Grandpa isn't here with us in body any more, we needn't be afraid of that.

168

We must remember him and enjoy remembering him. He would want that, wouldn't he?'

'Mr Barnes said you can't see God but He's everywhere,' Thomas said, still turned away. 'But I don't believe him. If I wasn't here, there'd just be a space.' He got hurriedly off his chair. 'I'll miss prep, Daddy.'

Archie stood up.

'But you'll remember what I said. No need for worry. No need at all.'

Thomas glanced at him and then moved towards the door to the street.

When Archie had paid the bill, and joined him there, Thomas said, 'Why didn't Mummy come?'

June Hampole sat on the end of her brother's bed. He had made himself very comfortable, with an old ponyskin car rug, two of the kitchen cats and a portable wireless. June had rather thought he was sufficiently recovered to get up, but Dan said the convalescent period was the time when one had to be particularly careful and that he was pleased to announce that the idea of two eggs baked with cream, sea salt, black pepper and unsalted butter had become increasingly preoccupying as the afternoon wore on.

'I'll try,' June Hampole said. She looked out of the window at the early black February evening and said, 'Oh, dear Dan, you were right and I simply don't know what to do.'

'Ah,' he said.

'It's Blaise and Liza Logan.'

'Now,' Dan said, settling back into his pillows. 'Now I am surprised. I thought that would be over. I thought Blaise returned to school looking like someone who has emerged thankfully from an obsession.'

'No,' June said. 'I saw them.'

'Did you pounce?'

'No – '

'Damn,' Dan said. 'Damn this flu. I'd have pounced. You'd better tell me.'

'I really don't want to. It's so pathetic, somehow, so banal. They were in the courtyard by her car, and they were kissing.'

169

'Where were you?'

'In the little sick room making sure that poor Edward Milligan who always has something the matter, and who, I am sure, is about to get flu, hadn't been forgotten up there. I looked out of the window. Not for anything particular, just because one does look out of windows. And there they were. Kissing. And – '

'And?'

'Oh, Dan,' June said. 'Liza Logan looked so much as if she were liking it.'

'Ha!' Dan said. 'Of course, Blaise is very personable.'

'Don't be frivolous, it's so unhelpful. What should I do?'

'On reflection, nothing.'

'Nothing! But last term you were advising me to have a word with Liza – '

'That was last term,' Dan said. 'I think the situation was different then. I think the balance has shifted. Do you know anything about Blaise's Christmas holidays?'

June picked up one of the cats and tried to settle it on her knee.

'No. Only that it was fun, he said. I've really hardly seen him, what with the new term, and flu.' The cat strained itself out of her grasp and returned to its ponyskin hollow. 'It's so silly, but I really feel I want to cry. She's such a dear, such a good, reliable teacher, so popular. That bloody boy, Dan, that blasted, bloody boy!'

Dan leaned out of his nest and took his sister's hand.

'Don't cry, Juney. It's not worth it. Really it isn't. Don't think about it and don't do anything. It'll be over in a minute, no bones broken. And now what about my eggs? Butter in first – '

The kitchen was dark and cold, and when June switched on the light there was a lot of scuttling. The kitchen cats, who had followed her down, began to wail for supper, leaping on to every surface she approached in order to be able to nag her more effectively. She couldn't think, getting out eggs and butter and the little coddling dish she knew Dan would want, why she should feel so upset. But she did. She almost felt betrayed and as if she had been made a fool of, although there was no logic to that, she knew. She got down on her hands and knees to light the reluctant oven while the cats screamed and pushed their hard greedy heads at her hands. If only Liza had not looked so eager – no, not exactly eager, more persistent. Every line of her body, even inside a winter coat, had looked tenacious, and her hands had been behind Blaise's head in a most decided way. The oven spluttered, belched out a blast of raw gas, and produced a small grudging row of blue flames. If Liza is humiliated, June thought, if Liza humiliates herself, I shall feel it so keenly. And what other outcome, with that charming, feckless boy, can there possibly be?

Sally Carter, giving Imogen lunch in the kitchen after a morning of nursery school, saw the van draw up in the field gateway a hundred yards down the lane. She left Imogen picking up single peas with her fingers, and went to stand by the sink so that she could see properly. There were three men, wearing the sludge-coloured outdoor jackets you got so sick of in winter, and two of them went round to the back of the van and opened it and took out bundles of stakes made of raw, yellow new wood. The third man had a plan which he unfolded into the wind, and stood studying it while its edges flapped like sails. When the other two joined him, he doubled the plan up into a manageable size and began to point towards Beeches House. Then all three of them began to cross the field. The surveyors have come, Sally thought. The appeal's failed. Mr Prior's found a developer.

'Finished,' Imogen said. She leaned back in her chair and closed her eyes in triumph.

Sally took a carton of yoghurt out of the refrigerator. It was the last one. In fact, the fridge was almost empty. Mrs Logan didn't seem to be concentrating.

'No,' said Imogen.

'It's all there is.'

They looked at each other. Imogen said conspiratorially, 'Rai-thinth – '

'I don't see why you shouldn't,' Sally said.

She took a jar of raisins out of a cupboard and put a handful of them on a saucer. Imogen sighed with pleasure. The telephone rang.

'Is Dr Logan there, please?'

'I'm afraid not,' Sally said. 'He's out doing calls just now.'

'I know. I just rang the surgery. I hoped he might have called in at home.'

The caller sounded American. Sally said, 'Is that Lady Logan?'

'Yes,' Marina said. 'I'm so sorry. I should have said so at once.'

'Is it urgent?' Sally said, slightly hoping for a little drama in a long afternoon alone with Imogen.

'In a way,' Marina said. Her voice was hesitant. 'Don't worry. I'll try the surgery a little later. Is Mrs Logan there?'

'No,' Sally said. 'She's teaching full time just now.'

'Oh. Oh, I didn't know. And Imogen. Is Imogen there?'

Sally carried Imogen to the telephone.

'I've got raithinth,' Imogen said. 'Heapth of raithinth.'

'Darling,' Marina said. Her voice shook.

'Thally gave them to me.'

The line went dead. Imogen gave the receiver back to Sally.

'Gone,' she said.

In London, Marina sat by her telephone and wept. The urge to speak to Archie had been so violent, and not being able to gratify it, and then her disappointment and simultaneous relief, in addition to the unexpected poignancy of hearing Imogen, were all too much. She could hear herself crying, great tearing, deafening sobs; could the people in the next flat hear her, even through these redoubtable walls? She had tried to make something happen, and it had refused her, and now, for these terrible moments at least, everything was worse than ever.

She had been going to say to Archie that she understood. She had been going to try to refrain from telling him that his letter had caused her several days and nights of anguish, and only tell him instead that he must attempt to teach himself to see that they were on the same side, that their pain and loss were in many ways the same, that they might even help each other. She had vowed to think about this for a week or so, and maybe write it to Archie in a very carefully judged letter, but the urge to speak to him, to tell him in her own voice, to hear him, had come upon her with such strength that she had seized the telephone idiotically, all at once, in the middle of a working day. And she had had the impression, when she had rung the health centre, that Archie had actually been

172

there and had refused to take her call. On my own, Marina thought, loathing her self-pity. That's all that's come out of this. On my own again.

CHAPTER THIRTEEN

When Archie went back to the hospital later in the day, the curtains were pulled round old Mrs Mossop's bed. In the morning, in response to a call from the hospital, he had taken Sharon Vinney in to see her mother, who was in a coma and lay, fathoms down in herself, like a tiny beaked primeval bird.

Sharon had cried and cried. The features of her coarse handsome face became quite blurred with crying. She sat shaking with tears by the hospital bed, begging Archie not to leave her alone there.

'But you might prefer to be alone,' Archie said. 'It might do you more good. So that you can talk to her privately.'

Sharon shook her head. Her stiffly bleached hair hardly stirred.

'It's too late. It's too late for that.'

'It isn't too late for you,' Archie said.

'I can't stay here. Honest I can't. I need a cigarette – '

Archie stooped over the bed. Granny Mossop's breathing was so shallow it hardly stirred the impersonal white folds of her hospital nightgown. Why, in God's name, was she not granted the dignity of her own? He looked at Sharon.

'Why isn't she in her own nightgown?'

Sharon fled. Following, Archie caught up with her in the car-park. She was drawing furiously on a cigarette.

'I don't want to hear anything from you,' Sharon said. 'As a doctor you're stuck in the Dark Ages. All talk, you are. All talk and no tablets.' She glared at him with reddened eyes. 'Talk to Mum! She's dead, isn't she, as far as I can see. She's gone.'

'No,' Archie said. 'But she will probably die today.'

Sharon began to weep again.

'No thanks to you!'

Archie drove her home in silence. She snuffled intermittently and blew her nose on crumpled paper tissues.

When he dropped her in front of her cottage, Archie said, 'Would you like to go back this evening? Because I'll take you, if Cyril's busy.'

Sharon struggled out of the car and stood for a moment looking across the lane at the unfriendly winter fields.

'What's the use?' she said. 'What's the bloody use?'

Archie went back alone. He took evening surgery, and then he paid two home visits and then he drove to Winchester. The geriatric ward, dim except for one or two pools of light over patients' beds, was quite quiet. Archie parted the curtains by old Mrs Mossop's bed and went in.

She looked much as she had that morning. He felt no urge at all to examine her, merely a wish to sit down by the side of the bed and hold her hand. He slid a forefinger up the inside of her wrist. Her pulse was barely perceptible. He rested his elbows on his knees and enclosed her hand in his.

He sat there for a long time, in the gentle quiet. A nurse put her head in at one moment, and tried to catch his eye, but he did not see her. He did not think much, he merely let his mind bob and drift at will in the queer, sweet peace of being alone with the last minutes of Granny Mossop's life. And, when the end came and she died with no commotion, he did not stir for some moments. He did not want to. He wanted simply to go on sitting there, in that strange suspended time that had no measure, and breathe in the momentousness of her little, silent ceasing to be.

He did not let go her hand. In the feel of it lay all the significance and simplicity of that moment, all comprehension of this end of life which seemed at once quite familiar and yet huge with awe. He did not want to let go. He wanted this curious time that was no time to go on and on until he could be sure what it was he had learned, until he could articulate it as well as feel. There was no hurry to let go. There was nothing else to do. This time was the only thing that mattered and it was quite outside human things, worldly things. Archie bent his head until his forehead rested on his hands that held Granny Mossop's hand. Here was the still centre of everything that turned and whirled.

175

The curtain rings rattled faintly on their rails. Slowly, Archie raised his head. The night sister was looking in on him.

'He's a one-off,' she said to a staff nurse later over a cup of tea. 'You'd have thought she was his own mother. Wonder what he did it for?'

'I have something to tell you,' Archie said.

Liza was marking comprehension exercises on the kitchen table. She wore a new polo-necked jersey and she had tied her hair back, as Clare did, with a black velvet ribbon. It made her look less sweet, more sophisticated. She put the forefinger of her left hand on the line of an exercise book to mark her place, and waited.

Archie pulled out a kitchen chair opposite Liza and sat down. Some early forced daffodils stood in a blue-and-white jug between them and Archie pushed them aside so that he could see her.

'Two things, actually.' He paused. 'Granny Mossop died. An hour ago. She was quite unconscious before she died.'

Liza said, 'Oh, I'm sorry. I'm so sorry.'

'Yes.'

'Does Sharon know?'

'Yes. I think she is still determined that her mother's cancer was my fault.'

'But you know, don't you, Archie, that that's just a cover-up for her own guilt.'

'I don't know what I know,' Archie said in a voice of peculiar gentleness. 'I just know I was glad to be there, glad to be with her, when she died.'

'You were there!'

'Yes. I've just come from the hospital.'

Liza put her hand across the table.

'There can't be many doctors like you.'

'It was chance. Chance that I was there. A lucky, lucky chance.'

'How Sharon will abuse you for doing what she failed to do!'

'I don't mind,' Archie said. 'I don't mind any more.'

Liza pushed away the open exercise book.

'And what was the other thing? The second thing?'

'Marina,' Archie said.

'Marina!'

176

'I wrote her a terrible letter.'

'But I thought – '

'I know. I let you think it. But it was not a letter of sympathy, it was one of blind rage. I accused her of killing my father with her demands and depriving me of understanding his death.'

'Oh, Archie,' Liza said.

'Yes.'

She put her hands over her face.

'How could you – '

'I could easily. Then. But not now.'

She took her hands away and looked at him.

'What are you going to do about it? Poor Marina, it's unthinkable – '

'I – I must speak to her. She tried to telephone and I wouldn't take the call.'

'You must go and see her,' Liza said with energy. 'You must go up to London at once and see her. And – ' She shut her eyes. 'Archie. What can you say?'

'I shall have to hope,' Archie said, 'that I'll know when I get there.'

Liza got up and went to fiddle with things on the dresser: two oranges in the fruit bowl; a ragged pile of opened, unanswered letters; a pair of sunglasses with one lens missing that Imogen liked to wear, her face turned to the ceiling so that they wouldn't fall off.

'You scare me,' Liza said. 'You really do. Your reaction to some things seems so unhinged, you're so obsessive, so relentless.' She looked round at him, swinging the sunglasses from one hand. 'It doesn't seem to make sense, the way you behave. One minute you're being really imaginative and sweet with Granny Mossop; the next you're writing horrible letters to poor Marina. And Thomas. What did you say to Thomas? I wish I'd stopped you going. I don't trust you, Archie. I can't. You make it impossible for me to trust you. Suppose everybody felt they could just let go, like you do? How do you think we all feel, living with someone so unpredictable, so immature?'

Archie, gazing at the hard yellow of the infant daffodils, said nothing.

'I don't know what I feel any more,' Liza said. 'I really don't. I'm worn out by you.'

Archie raised his face.

'Is it really all my fault? All of it?'

'I don't want a row,' Liza said.

'So I may not defend myself?'

She came back to the table and began to rearrange the books on it.

'I really must finish these. And it's late.'

She held her breath. It was such a risk she was taking, such a test of her power. Archie pushed his chair back and stood up. She waited for him to lunge at her, seize her wrist, grab her shoulders, even kiss her. But he did not. He simply stood for a moment looking quite impenetrable and not at her, and then he went out of the kitchen and she heard his steps going along the polished boards of the hall, and then up the stairs to bed.

Archie reached London in the early afternoon. It was a sudden, soft, fair day, a false herald of spring, and his overcoat, a doughty tweed affair acquired ten years before in Inveraray, felt a cumbersome nuisance. He took it off and slung it round his shoulders and decided, in order to postpone his arrival in Victoria, to walk from Waterloo, across the river. Marina did not, after all, know that he was coming. He had told Liza that he had telephoned, because she had asked him, but he hadn't. He did not know why he hadn't, he had just felt unable to. It might well be that Marina would be out, and he did not know what he would do then. He did not know, in fact, what he was going to do at all except go there, and see her. And, for some reason he could not fathom, the prospect of seeing her filled him with all kinds of feelings, but not with dread. It did not cross his mind that she might refuse to see him.

It had not crossed Marina's mind, either, that he might come. She had resolved that her next move was to be some sinking of pride and then to speak to Liza; no, not speak to her, ask her. Ask her advice as to what she should do next, about Archie. She would dearly have liked to ask what she should do next about the rest of her life, too, but her pride, so carefully nurtured over more than half a century, drew the line at some things, and showing herself

178

too vulnerable and helpless before Liza was one of them. She was, in fact, sitting by the window in the quiet dead time of mid-afternoon, making a list of things she might say to Liza, and trying out ways of saying them, when her intercom down to the building's front door rang imperiously. Going to answer it, and supposing it to be the young man from the estate agency who had said he might be round on Thursday but more likely Friday, she discovered that it was Archie.

He did not take the lift. She stood on the landing by her front door and watched his head come up the stairs, steadily round and round the lift shaft. He was wearing a big coat, like a cloak, with the collar turned up around his neck, and his hair, Marina thought, had grown longer and looked very thick. As he came up the last flight, she took a pair of large spectacles framed in pale tortoiseshell out of her jacket pocket, and put them on. He stopped two steps below her.

'I've never seen you in glasses.'

'I only wear them,' Marina said, 'when I want to see particularly well.'

She led the way back into the flat, into the sitting room where Mikey had hidden in the sofa cushions and declined to look at his dead grandfather.

Archie pulled his coat off his shoulders and said, 'I've no business to ask you to help me, but I've no idea how to begin.'

'I wish I smoked,' Marina said. 'It's so useful for such moments as these. Les mauvais quarts d'heure are one thing, les mauvais moments quite another and almost worse. Why did you come at such an impossible time of day? What can I offer you at three in the afternoon? Too late for lunch, too early for a Martini.'

'Is it?'

'Is that what you want? A Martini?'

'No,' Archie said. 'No. I don't want anything.'

'In that case,' said Marina, sitting down at one end of the sofa and turning her spectacles on him, 'why have you come?'

Archie put his coat down on an armchair and crossed to sit the other end of the sofa.

'You know why.'

'I'd like you to explain, however.'

179

He looked at her. He spread his hands.

'It's so odd,' Marina said. 'I've been so sorry for you, so desperately sorry, even to the point of feeling I should apologise to you for marrying your father, for being there when Andrew died, for making – yes, goddammit – for making Andrew so happy. But now you are here I don't feel abject at all. Nor contrite. I feel very strong and pretty determined. So you tell me, Archie Logan, all that's been going on and see if you can't make a better fist of it than you have done up to now.'

Archie put his head back into the cushions. He felt weirdly at ease.

'Liza thinks – at least I think she thinks – that I am having a very tiresome, extreme form of male menopause.'

'And?'

'And I expect she is right.'

'That's a cop-out,' Marina said. She smiled. She had not smiled for days. Archie turned his head sideways to look at her.

'Shall I tell you how I feel?'

'I think you'd better,' Marina said. 'I think it will relieve both our minds.'

Archie said, 'I despise people who do this.'

Marina waited.

'I don't know much about Dante,' Archie said. 'Except for that lovely picture, and one other thing. It was something to do with being banished from Florence for trying to rule with justice and finding himself wandering alone in the countryside, in a dark wood, without companions or possessions or a map. I seem to remember that that was a metaphor for how he felt inside, as if he had lost the centre line, after fighting for it, and was completely at sea. Didn't know where he was going or what he was looking for. Just felt a great tearing yearning for what he had lost and also for something more, something that would illumine the rest of life and give it vitality.'

He stopped.

After a while Marina said, 'There is an interesting theory about such crises. They are thought to affect creative people particularly and I would class you as creative. The theory is that at this half-way point in life a crisis does occur, a crisis such as Dante

180

had, and what it represents is the first confrontation with death, now that half one's life may be presumed to be over. And that prospect of death paralyses the victim – he sees death as a kind of helplessness. Sometimes it paralyses him almost literally. Look at poor Rossini.' She looked sideways at Archie. 'Do you buy my theory?'

'Oh yes,' he said. 'I buy it. But I think it is only part of the trouble.' He looked about him. 'Poor Marina. What a horrible room this is.'

'I've had too much time to think that. Also to think how incongruously redolent of Andrew it is.'

'Sell it,' Archie said. 'Just sell it.'

'I began. But I feel it's yours.'

He turned his head again.

Marina said, 'I know he left it to me. I know that. But I don't need it, I don't want it. I can't recognise him here.'

Archie gazed at her. Then he turned his head away from her, very slowly, and said in a voice thick with tears, 'I was with a brave old patient when she died three nights ago. I was there all the time, and afterwards. I've been at plenty of deaths but I've never understood a death before, not like that, not suddenly knowing death. I can't remember it now, but I knew then and I'll know for ever that I knew. That's one reason I've come. I thought I could only know such a thing with my father. I thought you had deprived me of that. That's why I wrote – one of the reasons I wrote.'

'I know,' Marina said. 'You made yourself perfectly plain.'

He whipped his head round and leaned sideways to seize her wrist.

'I'm so sorry. Oh, my God, Marina, I'm so sorry.'

'Dammit,' Marina said. 'Dammit. Do *not* make me cry.'

'Please cry – '

She bent forward over his hand.

'I didn't know one could be in such pain as this. I didn't know what it was like to miss someone so much. I'm just ripped to pieces, Archie, and I can't stand it and can't stand your seeing it.'

She took her hand away from his and fished in a pocket for a handkerchief and blew her nose fiercely.

181

'I like it,' Archie said.

She shook her head.

'We weren't talking about me. We were talking about you. You said Dante's dark wood was part of the trouble. What was the rest?'

He leaned forward and put his elbows on his knees and stared down at the carpet.

Then he said without looking at her, 'I want you.'

He raised his head and stared across the room at a formidable Edwardian chiffonier, its fretted doors lined with leaf-green silk.

'I was jealous of my father. I still am. And, now that he is not here, and like you I am shaken to the core with missing him, I want you more than ever.'

There was a little pause, and then Marina said, 'Now, you look here. Just you look at me. I'm almost old enough to be your mother, I'm a granny in specs.'

He turned his head and looked at her over his shoulder. She had not moved from her sofa corner.

'Marina,' he said.

He stood up and stooped over her, taking her hands and pulling her to her feet. Then he took off her spectacles and laid them on a nearby lamp table.

'Archie – '

'Shhh,' he said.

He put his arms around her and held her hard against him and kissed her hair and her neck. Then, like someone at the top of a helter-skelter, Archie took his steadying hands away from the sides and let himself go.

'I want you,' Archie said to Marina, and bent to kiss her mouth.

He caught the last train from Waterloo to Winchester. It was sleepy and seedy, full of tired yawning people with unbrushed hair, and the aisles and tables were strewn with used paper cups and discarded evening papers. It seemed to Archie a glorious train. It appeared to have a reality, an energy quite disproportionate to its appearance and purpose. He found a seat in an empty quartet of four and threw himself into it, pressing his face to the dark glass to see his extraordinary, illuminated countenance reflected there.

182

It had been so hard to leave her. He had hardly managed it, probably would not have done if she had not ordered a taxi and locked herself in the bathroom. He had stood in the passage outside the locked door, dressing slowly, and laughing, calling out to her, perfectly idiotic with happiness and fulfilment. She had come out at the end when the taxi came, in a white towelling robe with her hair on her shoulders, and he had seized her.

'I can't go, I can't, not now, not after this – '

But he had gone, because she had made him go, walking down the stairs as he had come up them, wrapped in his big coat, except that going down he looked up at her, all the way, and she leaned on the banisters and looked down, all the time, for the very last glimpse of him. In the taxi he had wanted to laugh. Dark, bright streets went by, Parliament Square, Big Ben, the oily glitter of the river, the way he had walked only that afternoon, before he had made his discovery.

This discovery, he thought lying back in the train, was what he had been seeking, this revelation of quite another dimension to himself, almost as if he had only been alive in part before. Marina had not wanted him to be serious, too intense. She had tried to tease him.

'But you're a mere boy, that's all that's the matter with you. Experience is all. Take it from me. From one who knows.'

Oh, and she did, she did. Archie closed his eyes, but, even with them closed, his head seemed to be brilliant with light.

Liza woke when he came in.

'It's after midnight.'

'I know. I'm so sorry. I should have telephoned.'

He sat down to unlace his shoes.

'How did it go?' Liza said. 'Was it all right? Did you take her out to supper?'

'We had supper, yes.'

He stood up and began to pull off his tie.

'But it was all right?'

'Yes. Yes, it was fine. I'll tell you in the morning.'

'Did she understand? Has she forgiven you?'

183

'Oh yes,' he said, throwing his shirt down on the floor. 'She's forgiven me.'

Liza wriggled down into bed again.

'You don't deserve it.'

'I know.'

'Thank God that's over, then,' Liza said, half muffled by her pillows.

'And you? Did you have a good day?'

'Oh yes,' she said. She sounded as if she were smiling. I'm a swine, Archie thought, I'm an utter, bloody swine.

'I'm just going to have a shower,' he said.

'Leave it. Leave it until the morning.'

'No. No, I can't do that. You go back to sleep.'

Mikey's speedboats still lay cluttered round the bath plug. Archie stepped in among them, and turned on the shower, hurtling cold needles, deliberately too cold. He wanted to sing and to weep. Whatever he had done, whatever came now, he had never felt so absolutely alive before.

In the morning, Liza did not seem much interested in the details. She wanted to know how Marina had looked and if she had reprimanded Archie, but she did not want to know how he had explained himself. Archie told her that he thought Marina had been wearing trousers and a pale jersey and, as far as he could recall, a checked jacket, but he wasn't sure.

'And ear-rings?' Mikey said, eating Coco-Pops.

Archie couldn't remember. He did remember about the spectacles, but they now seemed to him so intimate that he didn't mention them. Liza asked several times if Marina had been angry with him.

'No,' he said, 'not angry. Just firm and a bit crisp.'

'Did she mention your letter?'

'No. I did. I said sorry.'

'So I should hope,' Liza said. 'No, Mikey. Those are already covered with sugar.'

She pushed the sugar bowl away across the table.

'Is this full-time teaching going on much longer?' Archie said. He shamed himself, but he could not help planning.

Liza said, 'One more week.' And, because she did not want her face to betray anything, leant across and said, 'Don't *do* that,' to Imogen who was voluptuously licking honey and butter off a strip of toast. Then she summoned up a shred of defiance and said, 'Why? It doesn't affect you, does it?'

'Of course not.'

They looked at each other, seeing nothing.

'Not nithe,' said Imogen, putting down her bald toast.

'Who's fault is that? You eat it, anyway.'

Liza got up and began to assemble her school bag and car keys.

'Hurry up, Mikey. My run today.'

'Can I sit in the front?'

'No. You can't sit in the front until you are twelve, as well you know. Where's Sally? It's almost ten past. Imogen, eat that toast.'

Archie picked it up and held it in front of her.

'Come on, now. A bite for your nose. And one for your ears – '

His well-being felt to him as if it were gleaming on his skin, like a healthy dog's coat.

'Not ear'th.'

'Neck, then.'

'No. *Bottom*,' said Imogen and shrieked with rapture.

'OK,' said Archie, laughing too, longing to laugh. 'A bite for your bottom.'

Liza said, 'Oh, Archie, for heaven's sake don't encourage her.'

'It's only a game. Isn't it, Imo? A silly toast game.'

Liza looked out of the window. Sally, on her bicycle, was coming down the lane, her scarlet muffler a splash of colour against the tired late-winter landscape.

'There's Sally. Now, Mikey, up to brush your teeth.'

'And one for your knee and one for your left big toe and look, it's gone.'

Archie leaned sideways and kissed Imogen's packed cheek.

'Honestly,' Liza said. 'You do seem happy.'

'You don't sound very thrilled – '

Liza took a dark-blue jacket off a hook on the door and struggled into it.

185

'Of course I am. If it lasts. I suppose your conscience is clear, that's why.'

'No,' Archie said. 'No. My conscience is not clear at all.'

Liza shouted through the doorway.

'Come on, Mikey! Come on – ' She turned on Archie. 'Look, you've said sorry to Marina; that's over, so please, please can we not have a big deal about that, too?'

'Certainly,' Archie said.

Sally opened the door and came in. It struck her that, in some indefinable way, the atmosphere was not only better than usual, but exhilarating, like the first autumn morning of frost.

Before he went down to the surgery, Archie took Imogen and Nelson out into the field where the yellow wooden stakes now stood everywhere in the rough grass. He had not seen Richard Prior for several weeks, and Mrs Betts's impotent fury at the prospect of defeat had caused him to buy his stamps at any post office he passed, rather than endure her tirades at Stoke Stratton. The last time he had been in, she had dropped his change into his palm so that she need not contaminate herself by touching a traitor, and he had felt a dull rage at her stupidity and obstinacy. Now he felt gentler. In fact, watching Imogen weave in and out of the line of stakes that represented the bigger house's front wall, Archie was sorry he had been rude to Mrs Betts, and even sorrier that he had opposed Liza, had belittled her objections. It was too late, for any practical purpose, to be sorry, with the stakes so menacingly there, and the developer's board up loudly by the gate, but it wasn't too late to say sorry to Liza for more intangible things. And yet, he thought, caught breathless by a sudden wild leaping of his heart, if he started saying sorry to Liza now, where in heaven's name would it all end?

Diana Jago, on her handsome hunter, hailed him from the gateway. Imogen and Nelson began to race across, squealing and barking. The horse displayed admirable indifference.

'Sorry,' Archie called, running up. 'So sorry – '

'It's excellent training,' Diana said. 'I reckon if a horse is Imogen-proof, it's bombproof. Hey, Imo?'

Imogen climbed up two bars of the gate and pushed her face

through, blowing at the horse. Diana looked down at Archie.

'You look better.'

'Do I?'

'I've been worried stiff about you. Frightful bore. I hate worrying. And the lovely Liza looks less peaky.' She waved her crop at the field. 'I think you are unspeakable to back this. Really I do.'

'I wish I hadn't upset Liza.'

'Good,' Diana said. 'Excellent. Marriage is a pain in the neck but it ought at least to give you someone to hang in there with. I say,' she leaned down a little. 'The tom-toms tell me not a Vinney was there when poor old Granny died. But you were. Lynne Tyler said you went specially – '

'No, no. Chance – '

'Don't believe you.'

She smiled down at him with affection.

'You've got a rare old daddy, Imogen.'

Archie looked down.

'Bottom,' Imogen said.

She got off the gate.

'Bottom toast!' she shouted, and ran away shrilling across the field.

CHAPTER FOURTEEN

'Look,' Stuart Campbell said, leaning on his desk, 'look. I know you have been through a deeply distressing time, but I'm afraid I must gently point out to you that life must go on.'

Archie, standing just inside the door with his hands in his pockets, said nothing.

'It's six weeks since your father died. I wouldn't presume to put a time limit on grief, nor to dictate anyone's personal reaction, but I'm afraid there is a general feeling in the practice that you are beginning to exploit everyone's sympathy.' He pushed a piece of paper with Archie's large hand on it across the desk. 'I got your note. You say you can't attend the practice meeting because of a patient's funeral. Archie, you haven't attended the last two meetings and, although I applaud your human conscientiousness in wishing to go to Mrs Mossop's funeral, I cannot help, at the same time, feeling that you have your priorities wrong.' He looked at Archie weightily and said, 'Our duty, I should not have to remind you, is to the living, not to the dead. Indeed, and this is something you may have forgotten in the last six weeks: if we allow the dead to preoccupy us too much, we cannot help but penalise the living.'

Archie said, 'I know.'

'Well, then.'

'It's a particular funeral. My reasons are very private and in some way tied up with my father's death. I am aware everyone's been carrying me recently and it won't go on.'

Stuart Campbell sighed. He rolled a pencil across Archie's note. 'Can't your wife go?'

'No,' Archie said. 'She's working.'

She had also refused to go. He had asked her, the day before,

188

but she had refused even to consider it. 'But Bradley Hall is utter chaos,' Archie had said. 'You're always complaining about it, how the timetable is only made to be ignored. Why can't you change with someone?' Liza had shaken her head. 'Because I can't and I don't want to.'

Stuart got up and went to the window and stood there, gazing out and chinking the change in his pocket.

'Archie, I admire you. You know that. You've been the perfect makeweight in this practice, a standing reminder of our human commitment. But I seem to spend too much time defending you just now, making allowances.' He turned round. 'We are the premier practice in this area now, I hardly need remind you. We get a lot of applicants. We can't carry anyone for too long.'

'Six weeks?' Archie said, with some show of spirit.

'But it isn't six weeks, is it, Archie? It's longer. Much longer. Isn't it? When did you – '

He stopped. Then he said, 'I think you had better come to the meeting.'

Stoke Stratton church was surprisingly full, not just with its own villagers, but with people from the neighbouring villages who had been to school with Granny Mossop or had helped her look after the land girls when Stoke Stratton House – now so expensively Jagoed – had been requisitioned in the war. Richard and Susan Prior, whose habits over such things were meticulous, occupied the second pew. Archie, coming in a little late, elected to join them.

'Good man,' Susan said.

The coffin was as small as a child's. It stood on an iron trestle and was almost obliterated by an immense cross of yellow and white chrysanthemums tied with purple ribbons with which Sharon Vinney had attempted to assuage her complex and miserable feelings. She sat in the front pew opposite the Priors, in a new black-and-white jacket and skirt, attended by Cyril and her straggling brood of children and hangers-on, all dressed with extreme care, and almost all in tears. The chancel step overflowed with their flowers, extravagant, inappropriate bouquets, stiffly wired

189

and beribboned, which would later be piled into the hearse and driven away to the crematorium with the tiny coffin. There was not a tribute among them, Archie thought, that Granny Mossop would have spared her contempt.

Even Chrissie Jenkins had come. Granny Mossop had been, after all, as she explained noisily to everyone, their oldest parishioner. She sat in front of the Priors, a dark coat open over her nurse's uniform to make the greater commitments of her life visible to everyone. She turned to smile at Archie, a conspiratorial smile that conveyed her consciousness of the obligation that busy professionals like themselves had to perform those little personal services in life that make all the difference. Archie, who found her a woman of singular unattractiveness, would normally have returned her smile with no more than a nod; but today, with his whole being overflowing with gratitude for being alive, he smiled back. In a moment, on his knees with his eyes closed against the riot of spray carnations and hothouse purple iris, he could, after all, think about Marina.

Colin Jenkins stepped forward. His face bore the marks of inner conflict. An ardent supporter of the new democratic services, with a deep distrust of the English of Cranmer's prayer book, he was forced today, at Granny Mossop's wish, to speak over her coffin the language of archaic and unjustified privilege. He could not even be sure she had not left such a wish just to spite him.

'"I am the resurrection and the life,"' Colin Jenkins said without enthusiasm, '"saith the Lord. He that believeth in me, though he were dead, yet shall he live; and whosoever liveth and believeth in me shall never die."'

Archie hid his face in his hands. How could it be that such life, such intensity of life, should come out of death? And did he care how it had come? No, that did not matter at all. All that mattered was that it had come. And it had.

In the junior cloakrooms at Bradley Hall, Blaise and Liza were doing after-school duty. Once every departing child had been paired off with the relevant coat, bag, and toy brought to show Mrs Simpson who ran the kindergarten class, the duty consisted of a dilatory clearance of the detritus of boots and shoes left stranded on the concrete floor. The cloakrooms, made out of Bradley Hall's onetime coal and wood stores, were lit by bluish-mauve neon strips and provided as glamorous a setting for an assignation as a public lavatory. Blaise went along the aisles between the rows of pegs screwed into frames of red-varnished pitch-pine, kicking the shoes into lockers with dull fury.

'Next week,' Liza said from the adjacent aisle where she was painstakingly trying to find mates for stray boots, 'next week, I go back to part time.'

'Jesus,' Blaise said, kicking. 'Jesus, Jesus.'

'It's probably just as well,' Liza said provocatively.

'For what?'

'You know. You know perfectly well.'

Blaise put his hands on a pitch-pine bar and swung his head and shoulders through the dangling shoebags at Liza.

'I'm sick of all this. I've had enough. I'm going mad, raving mad.'

'But we've seen each other every day, I've even – '

'Kisses,' Blaise said derisively. 'Rotten little kisses. Cock-teasing kisses.'

Liza stood up, still holding a gumboot.

'I'm exhausted,' Blaise said. 'You exhaust me. It's all games, isn't it? Little girly games.'

Liza began to tremble slightly. The blue shadows thrown down by the light made Blaise's face skull-like in its intensity.

'No.'

'Look,' Blaise said. 'I'm sick of being played with. It's a particularly horrible sort of tease, what you're doing. Last full day, you say to me all smug and prissy: No more treats. Had that. Back to hubby now.'

'Shut up,' Liza said.

Blaise took his hands off the beam and vanished from sight.

'Go home,' his voice said. 'Just go home to hubby and the kiddiwinks and bloody well leave me be.'

Liza put down the gumboot and went round to the adjoining aisle. Blaise glared at her.

Liza said, 'You started all this. Remember? Never leaving me alone, letters and phone calls and badger, badger, badger. Now you can't get what you want – '

'What do I want?'

191

There was a small highly charged silence. Later, looking back, Liza recognised that silence as the last moment of her fantasy, the final seconds of the extravagant illusion with which she had fed herself for so many months.

She said, proudly, fatally, 'You want me to go to bed with you.'

And Blaise, suddenly exchanging petulance for vengeance, said, 'Not any more.'

She looked at him. He looked back, his chin slightly raised.

'What?'

'You blew that,' Blaise said fretfully. 'Weeks ago. Stringing me along. Games, games, all the time – '

'But just now, you said – '

'Oh, that's habit. I got in a muddle. I got so confused and exhausted I couldn't remember where I'd got to. And anyway, you seemed to expect it.' His voice grew accusing. 'You've been expecting it all term, haven't you? Talk about the boot being on the other foot! Well, you're too late.'

Liza felt for the top of the lockers and sat down on them. Shoebags bumped round her, redolent of rubber and old sock.

'Just now,' she said, 'just now, you said being so near and yet so far was driving you mad – '

'I didn't mean it,' Blaise said. 'I didn't mean that. I mean having you darting me pregnant glances, lying in wait for me – '

Liza put her hands over her ears.

'But you kissed me! You said – '

'Of course I kissed you. You kissed me. I could hardly spit you out, could I?'

Liza looked up at him. His face was black against the bluish light.

'You're loathsome,' she said. Her voice shook hopelessly. 'And you're mad.'

Blaise said, 'Anyway, there's a girl in Dublin – '

'Coward.'

'I met her at Christmas. She's my age.'

'Go away!' Liza screamed. 'Go on, get out, go away – '

The door at the far end of the cloakroom opened and let in an oblong of yellow light.

June Hampole called, 'Who's there? Who's shouting?'

They emerged sheepishly into the brighter light.

192

'Oh, Liza,' June Hampole said. 'Oh dear.' She looked at them both. 'How sordid.'

'Not any more,' Blaise said angrily. 'Nothing any more. Nothing.' He tried to push past June into the lit passage beyond. She put up an arm and stopped him.

'I think we'd better talk,' June said. 'Don't you?' She looked at Liza and sighed. 'Please come to my study, both of you.' She turned and began to walk back towards the school hall, Blaise following. He did not even glance at Liza. There was nothing for her to do but bring up the rear.

'I couldn't go home,' Liza said. Her face was blotched with crying. 'I simply couldn't face it.'

'No,' Clare said. 'No. Of course not.'

'I've made such a fool of myself – '

'No,' Clare said kindly. 'You allowed someone else to make a fool of you.'

'No!' Liza shouted.

There were empty coffee mugs on Clare's kitchen table and a pink sea of used paper handkerchiefs.

'I'll never get over it.'

'Of course you will.'

'I can't believe I could have let it get that far. I can't believe I was so stupid. How can I face anyone after this?'

'No one knows,' Clare said. 'Do they?'

'I wish I hadn't come,' Liza cried, seizing another handkerchief. 'I wish I hadn't told you!'

Clare, magnanimous in rare moral superiority, merely said, 'I shan't tell anyone, and I'm sure June Hampole won't.'

'I shouldn't have come out! I simply didn't think, I was so churned up. I should have stayed inside, shouldn't I?'

'Blaise would have split on you.'

Liza looked at her sister.

'Can you believe how he's behaved?'

Clare thought, as she always thought, of Robin.

'Oh yes. Easily.'

'Months and months of besieging me, a year or more,

193

never letting up! And he came round here! Didn't he? He came round and declared undying love, didn't he, Clare, didn't he – '

Clare got up and took the kettle over to the sink to fill it.

'I don't want any more coffee. Haven't you got any brandy?'

'I've got sherry,' Clare said repressively.

'Sherry, then. Clare – '

'Yes?' Clare said, putting down the kettle and opening a cupboard where her still-intact sets of wedding present glasses stood in shining rows.

'Please, Clare. Don't tell Archie. He mustn't know. Not ever. Please, please, don't tell Archie.'

Clare put two small glasses engraved with partridges on the table.

'Of course I won't.' She put a bottle of sherry beside the glasses. 'He may just know already, mind you.'

'Did you tell him? Have you? What did you say, what – '

'I haven't said anything,' Clare said. 'To anyone.'

She filled the partridge glasses and pushed one towards Liza.

Liza said angrily, 'You fancy Archie, don't you?'

Clare said nothing.

'Sorry,' Liza said.

'As a matter of fact,' Clare said, 'I'm going out to dinner tomorrow night.' She paused. 'To Chewton Glen.'

Liza gazed at her.

'A solicitor in Old Jewry,' Clare said. 'I've known him by sight for ages.'

Liza swallowed her sherry.

'I ought to go.' She looked into her empty glass. 'Clare. I'm so sorry. I don't think I've ever behaved worse in my life.'

Clare touched her arm.

'It isn't all your fault.'

'It is,' Liza said, getting up and peering under the table for her bag. 'It is. And, even if it wasn't, I couldn't have handled it worse.'

She straightened up, clutching her bag.

'I hope you have a lovely dinner. With your solicitor.'

Clare thought of him.

'Well, the food'll be all right, anyway.'

194

Liza leaned forward and kissed her cheek.

'Bye. And thank you – '

'Drive carefully,' Clare said. 'And ring me. If you want anything.'

Thomas stood in the call box. It was a new one, made entirely of toughened glass, and he was afraid that each passing car might contain a master from Pinemount on his way to the Goat and Compasses for his evening drink. They all went there, every night, and got pie-eyed. Bristow said their breaths afterwards were like methylated spirits and that his parents would take him away if they knew that the whole staff got pie-eyed every single night at the Goat and Compasses.

The call box was, of course, out of bounds. You could make calls home from school, if you got a signed chit from your div. master and Matron timed you, standing by the telephone in the sick-room passage, listening to absolutely every word. If every member of the staff craved drink at the Goat and Compasses obsessively, so Matron craved information. She didn't like a single thing to happen she didn't know about. Rackenshaw timed her to see how long she could last before asking where the pretty photo of his mother was, and she had managed two days. Rackenshaw told her he'd put it in the dustbin, but it was under his mattress all the time. Rackenshaw took it out at night and looked at it under the bedclothes with his torch which he kept hidden in his sponge bag.

Thomas didn't want Matron to know anything any more. She had been horribly kind to him when his grandfather died and Bristow had said that was mostly because his grandfather had been famous. Thomas didn't want anybody to be kind. He didn't want anybody to know that he was scared of going to sleep, because of the dreams. He had devised all kinds of minor tortures for himself to stay awake, the most successful of which was quite simple and merely involved sitting up in bed in the dark dormitory, cold and alone and determined. He nearly always fell asleep in the end, but could now goad himself awake again before sleep tipped him over the last edge down into the black pit where the mad dreams waited for him, dreams where everything was grotesquely large or small, and imbued with panic.

195

Thomas had three ten-pence pieces. He had quite a lot more money, saved from the holidays, hidden in little amounts in various places in his locker and his tuck box and his desk in the div. room. They were given twenty pence each Sunday for church collection – it went on the bill, Bristow said – and Thomas had, luckily, been given his as two ten-pence pieces the last three Sundays, so he had put one in the church collection, and saved the other. He put one in the telephone now, and dialled Beeches House. It was cold in the telephone box and the plastic receiver was even colder against his ear.

'Hello,' Liza said. She didn't sound normal.

'Mummy – '

'Thomas! Thomas, darling, where are you – '

'At school,' Thomas said.

'Darling. Are you all right?'

'Sort of.'

'It's visiting Sunday, on Sunday. Not long – '

'Your voice sounds funny.'

'Does it?' Liza said. 'I expect I've got a cold. From school.'

'Are you crying?'

'Of course not,' Liza said, closing her red eyes.

'Where's Daddy? Can I speak to Daddy?'

'He's in London,' Liza said. 'He's helping Marina sort things out. Grandpa's things.'

'Has he gone for long?'

'No. No, I'm sure he hasn't.'

'Mummy,' Thomas said, dissolving. 'Mummy.'

'It's two days until Sunday. Only two. Don't cry, darling, please don't – '

In the dark call box, Thomas cried silently, opening his mouth as wide as he could to prevent sobs getting out. He pressed another coin into the machine.

'Darling?' Liza called anxiously. 'Thomas?'

'I sneezed,' Thomas said thickly. 'Why are you crying?'

'I'm not. I'm not, I promise you. I'm fine. Listen, Imogen's got a new game. She plugged all the little holes in the telephone with sunflower seeds. Isn't she awful?'

Thomas giggled weakly, obediently.

'And Mikey and that dreadful Sam he so dotes on scribbled all over each other's faces with magic marker and Sally scrubbed him and scrubbed him but he still looks all scribbly. I hope he'll be clean by Sunday. Thomas?'

'Yes,' Thomas said, pressing his tired wet face to the glass wall.

'Better now? A bit better?'

'Yes,' Thomas said dully.

'Listen, you think about your awful brother and sister. You tell Bristow. And only tonight and one more night, and we'll be down to see you. That's all.'

'Bye,' Thomas said.

He put the receiver back in its cradle and pushed open the door. It was raining softly, the kind of quiet insistent rain Thomas associated with Scotland. He would get back to school wet. Matron would notice. Grizzling drearily to himself, Thomas set off along the verge at a trot, back towards Pinemount.

They stood together in the corridor of the flat. Archie leant his shoulders against the front door, his arms folded as if he were preventing Marina from getting out. She stood close to him. She wore her spectacles.

'I mean it,' Marina said.

He looked down at her. He was quite unable to look anywhere else.

'The last time,' she said. 'I should not have allowed it again.'

'Ah,' he said. His voice was lazy with satisfaction. 'So you wish I had not come. You wish we had not made love.'

'I can't wish that,' Marina said.

'Tell me.'

'Stop it,' she said. 'Don't seduce me. Don't bully.'

He unfolded his arms and reached out for her. She stepped neatly back, out of his range.

'Archie. I meant what I said. You – '

'I'm listening.'

'I adore sex with you.'

'Again.'

'But you are not mine to have. Sex with you isn't for me.' She looked up at him. 'I'm not a marriage wrecker. Maybe I'm not

197

even for marriage, maybe I'm too realistic. I'm certainly too realistic to destroy a family.'

'So what becomes of me?'

'You're a grown man. You decide. And go catch your train. You should have left hours ago, you'll miss it – '

'Do you suppose,' Archie said, not listening, 'do you suppose that I am likely to give you up the moment I find you? Do you really think, after all that battling through the fog, I'm going to go back into it? Are you? Do you want to feel as you did a week ago?'

'Never again,' Marina said.

He took his shoulders away from the door and stood upright.

'I'm not a marriage wrecker either.'

'But you cannot have both – '

'I can,' Archie said. 'I have.'

She looked up at him, through her spectacles.

'But I won't let you. Don't for a moment mistake what I want. But I've lived long enough not to believe in melodrama any longer. Nor in the staying power of deception. Truth always works its way to the surface somehow. Wives have a nose for truth.'

Archie stepped forward and put his arms around her.

'Go catch your train.'

'In a minute.'

He took off her spectacles and put them in his jacket pocket.

'I don't believe you can stop any more than I can.'

He kissed her.

He said, laughing a little, 'I know just how women feel.'

She stiffened.

'How can you know such a thing?'

'You see?' Archie said, delightedly holding her away from him. 'You see? Instant outrage. Women have the monopoly on feelings, don't they? Women are the ones whose lives are limited by frustration, burdened by society's refusal to let them fulfil themselves, women are the ones trapped by stereotype. Right? That's it, isn't it? I'm not allowed inside that sacred personal life, am I, because I'm a man. I've got my work, I'm the breadwinner, that must satisfy me. But I've got it, whether you like it or not. I've broken into the circle where emotional life colours everything, conditions

198

everything.' He pressed Marina against him. 'Everything is better because of you. Everything. I'm richer, stronger. I found you. I discovered myself. If this is what women have been battling for all these years, I'm with them, all the way.'

'How you do talk,' Marina said.

He laughed.

'I do, don't I? I can, now. That's another thing, isn't it, talking? Women think men can't talk, won't talk. Reticence is some sort of male plot to frustrate them of their emotional dues. What about men – '

'Archie,' Marina said. 'Beloved, beautiful Archie. Go home. Go *home.*'

She could hear him laughing, all the way down the stairwell, and when he reached the street door she heard him yell out, wild and exultant. 'Marina!' Archie shouted, 'Marina!' and his voice came spiralling back up to her. 'Marina!'

CHAPTER FIFTEEN

Dan Hampole said gently, 'There was no need for this, you know.'

He held Liza's letter out to her. They were standing in June's study, the three of them, and some pale, uncertain spring sunlight was falling through the tall windows and lying pointedly on all the dust.

Liza blushed.

'My dear,' Dan said. 'What harm came of it? What harm to the school?'

'Much more harm,' June said, fidgeting with her cardigan buttons, 'much more harm if you were to resign. Blaise will go at the end of the summer, anyway. It was all planned.'

Liza looked down. She had been compelled to write that letter. It was the only expiation she could think of, the only source of even the faintest consolation. If she had felt lonely before, all those months, she had felt doubly so, all weekend. Everything in her, accustomed over long years, had cried out to confide in Archie, to be comforted by Archie. Her secret weighed upon her like an albatross. Writing the letter had, briefly, lightened that burden. She, who had for so long jealously cherished her private fantasy, now longed for frankness. Values that had temporarily seemed an imposition on her freedom had acquired a sudden, fierce poignancy. Thomas, on Sunday, had at intervals appeared too vulnerable to be borne.

'Can't he leave?' she had begged Archie. 'Can't he leave now, and come home?'

'We'll talk about it,' Archie said. They were in the car, in the discouraging Sunday-evening dark, driving home. Mikey and

Imogen, subdued by the day, were quiet on the back seat. 'We'll talk. Really. When we're alone.'

Liza said now, 'I don't know what happened. I wish I could explain. I seemed – to get disorientated, somehow, blown off course . . . '

'It's over,' June said. She hated confessions. 'Don't tell me,' she would say to transgressing children. 'I don't want to know. All I want to know is that you are sorry.' She looked at Liza. 'Closed chapter. Really. All forgotten.'

Liza shook her head.

'Not that.'

Dan took her arm.

'Come on,' he said. 'No more tears.'

He led her out through the hall and on to the terrace where three William Kent urns sprouted bleached stalks from last summer like wispy hair.

'In my experience,' Dan said, 'normal people don't do daft things quite arbitrarily. I do, of course, all the time, but then I am not normal, by normal standards.' He took her arm. 'You are normal.'

'I know,' Liza said in despair.

'Don't you despise it.'

'It's so dull,' Liza said, 'being orthodox.'

'My dear, without the status quo, the whole contraption would fall apart at the centre.'

'It's easy for you to say that!' Liza cried. 'You can disregard it, you don't feel it's up to you to push it along. I'm tied to it. I was brought up to it. People like me can't have adventure, don't dare. We don't feel consumed by the huge things, only by the little ones, petty ones, mean ones – '

'What a dear you are,' Dan Hampole said, patting her hand.

'It isn't enough.'

She looked away from him. The great stone slabs of the terrace were cracked here and there, and furred with aubretia and weeds.

'I love my husband, you see,' Liza said.

'I don't doubt it.'

'You haven't met him – '

'I know of him. Everyone round here knows of him.'

Liza said sadly, 'He knows how to live, you see.' She remembered a phrase of Archie's. 'Big bites. Life in big bites.'

Dan Hampole gave her hand another pat and let it go.

'I shouldn't tell him, all the same.'

'Oh, I won't, I couldn't – '

'It's one of the few things I've learned, keeping mum.' He looked at Liza. 'Don't say a word and don't give young O'Hanlon an inch.'

Liza gazed at him.

'You had your reasons,' Dan said. 'Nothing's for nothing with good girls like you.'

She drove home slowly in the quiet, sad afternoon. Good girl, Dan Hampole had said, a good girl like you. But her kind of goodness had no virtue in it, she thought; it was merely an absence of badness. Really good people, blazingly good people, were often impossible to live with, fascinating, relentless in their advancement of good. Look at St Francis. I'm not good, Liza thought unhappily, I'm just decent. Marina contradicted me when I said England was full of girls like me, but she didn't really know; her judgements are made with her own vision of style and strength. I look different to her because I'm English, that's all. I'm not different; I'm just a fool.

She stopped the car in the village. Diana Jago was standing by the letter box, tearing stamps off a long strip and sticking them on to a pile of letters with a thump of her fist. She wore tight blue jeans and riding boots and a quilted waistcoat and a silk headscarf.

'You Logans,' Diana said. 'Completely gone to earth. Thought you'd emigrated. Where have you been?'

'Working,' Liza said. She got out of the car and leaned against it.

'You look worn out,' Diana said.

'Thanks so much – '

Diana pushed the last letter into the box.

'There we go. The last of the final demands. Simon appears perfectly able to run a bank and totally, utterly incapable of making anything but a hash of his domestic finances.'

'I thought bankers like Simon had their secretaries do that.'

202

'I don't let his secretary do anything outside the office. I've learned the hard way. Come back for a cup of tea.'

'I shouldn't – '

'Ring from my house. Just half an hour.'

'Oh, Diana,' Liza said. Tears rose and spilled. 'I was going to buy a ball of string, would you believe, and freezer bags – '

'Don't cry,' Diana said. 'You'll start me off and Ma Betts will see. Don't, Liza. Come on, get in my car. You can't drive if you're blubbing. We'll pick your car up later.'

'We keep crying,' Liza said, bundled up on Diana's front seat. 'All of us. Archie, me, Thomas. It's frightful. At least when Imogen cries, it's only temper.'

Diana swung her car off the road and down the lane towards the river.

'You're so kind.'

'Nonsense.'

'Diana,' Liza said, 'have you ever made a really awful fool of yourself?'

'Yup,' Diana said. She turned the car into her smoothly gravelled drive and stopped it by the white front door guarded by two stone lions bearing shields.

'And?'

'And nothing. It's just something you have to live with.'

Liza followed Diana across the hall, hushed by its depth of carpet, and into the kitchen. It was stencilled in blue on yellow, with complicated, unsuitable urban curtains, and on the table lay a sprawling pile of tack.

'Always clean it in here, in the winter,' Diana said. 'Much warmer.' She reached for a roll of paper towel, spun off several feet of it and threw it at Liza. 'Now blow your nose.' The sound of the Jago Labradors, penned in their outdoor kennel, came penetratingly through the closed windows. Diana banged on the nearest one. 'Shut up! Bloody dogs. Sit over there, it's the only comfortable chair. Chuck the cat off.'

Liza lifted an enormous square tabby off a cushion in a Windsor armchair and sat down, settling the cat on her knee.

'These deaths knock you for six, you know,' Diana said, getting a catering-sized box of extra-strong tea bags out of a cupboard. 'I wouldn't be surprised if it's worse for Archie precisely because he thought he was so used to it, and could cope.'

'It got full of complications,' Liza said. 'Complications and crossed wires.' She turned her face away from Diana and looked at the yellow wall beside her where a circle of blue-and-white Spanish pottery plates hung like a childish clock. 'I didn't see,' Liza said. 'I was so busy with myself. I've always been so used to him being in charge, of himself as well as us. I never thought to look. I was fed up with him. I got carried away by something else.'

Diana put tea bags and boiling water into thick mugs painted with crude lemons. After a few seconds, she fished the tea bags out with a spoon and flicked them approximately in the direction of the sink. One fell short, on to the floor. Diana took no notice. She carried the mugs over to Liza and then went across to the refrigerator and got out a bottle of milk.

'Milk?'

'Please.'

'Look,' Diana said, sloshing it into the mugs, 'I think Archie feels pretty much the same as you.'

Liza turned her head back quickly.

'Does he?'

'I think he'd agree with you about crossed wires. I know he's having second thoughts about Richard's repulsive plan. Here. Drink that nasty brew. If we were in your kitchen, it'd be Lapsang Suchong and a homemade cake – '

'Don't you believe it. Diana – '

'Yes.'

'Diana, d'you really think Archie feels as I do?'

'I think he feels,' Diana said, remembering Archie's glowing face in the field a week before, 'I think he feels that you haven't been communicating particularly well recently, and he'd like to put that right.'

Liza said, leaning forward, 'There's Thomas, you see. We have to do something about Thomas. He looks awful, so strained. But while it was all tied up in Archie's mind with Andrew and Andrew's wishes, it seemed hopeless even to talk about it. Perhaps now – '

'As Nanny used to say, grasp the nettle.'

'Yes,' Liza said. She was smiling. 'Of course.'

She reached across the table and put her mug down.

'Come on, cat.'

She stood up.

'Go for it,' Diana said.

Archie was standing in the kitchen, propped against the dresser and reading the local paper. He was humming. Something about him made Liza a little doubtful as to how she should begin. She got carrots and onions out of the cupboard and put them on a wooden board on the draining board and began to chop. She chopped the carrots into tiny dice and the onion into wafery rings.

Then, without turning round, she said uncertainly, 'Archie – '

'Yes.'

She looked at her reflection in the night-black glass of the window above the sink. She couldn't see her expression, only her outline, and beyond that, against the lines of plates and jugs on the dresser, Archie, ankles crossed, reading the paper.

'Archie. I want to say sorry.'

He didn't look up.

'What for?'

She battled to keep her voice steady.

'For the way I've behaved. About Andrew. About extra working. About us.'

He looked up. She could see his face, tiny and clear, in the black window.

'That's all right,' he said easily.

'No.'

She turned round. He looked absolutely unperturbed.

'I feel awful about it,' Liza said. Her chest was bursting with the desire to be free of her shame. 'I'm so sorry. I've been horrible.'

He didn't move. He said, smiling, 'No, you haven't. It's been a bit rocky for everyone. I've been a pain, too.'

She bent her head. It was as impossible to stop tears as it was to stop breathing. Perhaps she shouldn't stop them, perhaps they would, as they invariably did, bring him over, bring him to her, make him put his arms round her, hold her.

205

'Archie,' Liza sobbed.

'Don't cry,' he said kindly, from across the room.

She put her hands up to her eyes. They smelled of onion. They made the tears worse.

'I've refused to listen,' Liza said. 'I've refused to talk. I've belittled you.'

Archie put the paper down.

'Look,' he said. 'It doesn't matter. I said so. A lot of the things you said have been quite justified. I'm sorry, too.'

He was still smiling, a kind, impersonal smile.

Liza said, desperate to reach him, 'And there's Thomas – '

'I know.'

'You said we could talk, when we're alone.'

'Do you really think this is the moment, with you in tears?'

'Archie!' Liza cried. She ran across the kitchen and flung her arms about him, pressing herself against his side. Against her hip, in his jacket pocket, something snapped sharply.

'Oh, God,' Liza said. 'What's that?'

'It doesn't matter – '

She dropped her arms and put one hand into his pocket. She brought out half a pair of pale tortoiseshell spectacles, broken cleanly across the bridge.

'Dior,' Liza said. 'Christian Dior.' She did not look up at Archie. 'Marina's glasses.'

Neither of them moved. Liza gazed down at the broken spectacles.

'Why?' said Liza, sick with a sudden new fear. 'Why should Marina's glasses be in your pocket?'

He lay awake, long after she had exhausted herself into sleep. It wasn't a good sleep, he could tell, because she gasped and drew shuddering little breaths and every so often her feet moved convulsively, or her arms. He had made love to her. She had wanted him to, begged him to, but it had not been a success for either of them and it had left her weeping worse than ever, beside herself with weeping.

It was both strange and horrible. Strange because she had not uttered one angry word, and horrible because she had seemed alien to him, pitiable, but not significant, not central. He had tried not to be rough with her, but then had been afraid that, if he were not rough, if he did not goad himself on with a spur of violence, he would not be able to climax and he did not know how he would deal with her, if that happened. As it was, he had dealt with her very badly. He had hurt her, all over. There was not an inch of her body and mind he had not hurt. He could hardly comprehend the damage he had done.

He stared into the darkness. There was no wind, only the faint far sound of owls and across that, cutting sharply now and then, the imperious scream of a vixen wanting a mate. It must have been three o'clock. Perhaps even later. They had talked until almost one, on and on, round and round.

'I don't understand,' Liza said over and over again. 'I don't understand about sex. Not like that. Not when you've known it with love, for making children. Didn't you think of me?'

He had not, while he was with Marina. Before Marina, he had thought of her so much, but then he had been almost a different person then, another man.

'Don't work it out,' he'd said. 'Don't even try. There isn't logic, there isn't a pattern. The changes are like the shifting shapes desert sand gets blown into by the wind. I wasn't deliberate. I'm not now. You weren't.'

'But Marina. Why Marina?'

'Oh, Liza,' Archie said, shaking his head. 'You know why Marina. You know that yourself.'

There had been a long, long silence then, which she had broken by saying flatly, 'You see, I thought she was mine.'

Then she turned on him.

'Is that why? Is that why you chose her? Because she loved me?'

'No,' he said truthfully. 'It never crossed my mind.'

A double betrayal, Liza had said, repeating it again and again, a double betrayal. Both of you. I can't believe it, I can't believe this has happened, but it has, hasn't it, it has.

'Could I have stopped it? If I'd been looking – '

'I don't know.'

'Will you stop it now? Will you? Did you mean to go on, if I hadn't broken her glasses?'

'Yes,' he said.

'You meant to keep it secret.'

'I meant not to tell you.'

'But now? What now?'

'I don't know,' he said.

'But why can't you stop? Why, why – '

'Because,' he said, 'I am afraid to.'

I am afraid, he thought now. I am afraid of doing without this, now I have found it. He rolled on to his side, away from Liza, clenching his fists between his thighs. It was a different kind of fear to any he had known before, involving neither heart nor muscle, but more the possible death of the spirit, the loss of light. What had Liza said to him, all those months ago? 'It's me that's changed.' She did seem to have changed. She had been sharper with him, more impatient, superior. And then tonight none of those things; just abject, pitiful, childlike.

The door opened six inches. A head came round it three feet from the floor.

'My toadthtool'th gone out – '

Archie raised himself on one elbow.

'Imo – '

'It went ping,' Imogen hissed, coming in further.

'Shhh. You'll wake Mummy.'

He slid out of bed and pushed Imogen out of the room.

'Where are your pyjamath?' Imogen demanded. She looked at his nakedness with reproof.

'I'll get a new bulb. Get back into bed.'

He padded down to the kitchen. The vegetables still lay forlornly on the chopping board, the newspaper on the table. Three twenty-five, the clock said inexorably. He found a miniature bulb in the cupboard – Liza did not forget things, run out of things – and carried it upstairs to Imogen. She was not in bed. She stood beside him until the toadstool glowed again in the dark room, and then she climbed in and lay there looking up at him with Liza's face framed in Liza's red curls.

'Put your pyjamath on,' Imogen said, and turned on her side, plugging in her thumb.

208

Liza woke in the dawn. There was no natural light, but a yellow glow came in dully from the landing. Someone had not shut the door. Swimming wretchedly to the unwelcome surface, Liza cast a glance at Archie. He was asleep, turned away from her, and for some reason he had put on his only pair of pyjamas, pyjamas they had bought once while staying in a country hotel in Scotland where the lavatory was half a league down public passages from their bedroom. Why on earth had he put them on? Liza could only suppose, pulling her aching body out of bed, that he had put them on to make himself yet more separate from her.

Everything ached, inside and out. She found her dressing gown and the espadrilles she used as slippers and went out on to the landing. A small metal aeroplane lay against a skirting board and over the banisters hung Mikey's school tie, needing mending, spewing a pale woolly tongue of lining out of its split sheath. She picked it up and put it in her dressing-gown pocket and went slowly downstairs, her espadrilles slapping roughly against her heels.

In the kitchen, Nelson stirred in his basket out of token politeness. She filled the kettle and put it on, scraped the cut vegetables into the rubbish bin – oh, my God, she thought in despair, isn't it just typical of me that I should think, even on a morning like this, that I ought to use the bloody things for making stock? – folded up the newspaper and put it, with all the other newspapers whose life was not yet exhausted, in a square willow basket. The half of Marina's spectacles lay under the newspaper. Liza picked it up and ran a finger over the tiny golden CD on the earpiece. Then she carried it across the room and dropped it through the swing lid of the rubbish bin, on to the carrots and the onions. Last night – she stopped. She would not, at this fatal low-ebb hour before life began again, allow herself to think of last night.

But what else was there to think of? Last night stood there, mammoth, immovable, blocking her path to any other thought. What was to be gained by refusing to confront not only the fact that Archie had been to bed with Marina, and that he had wanted it and she had allowed it, but also that Marina had real power, the power of her personality and her sexuality which could make such a difference to Archie? And when those facts had been confronted, Liza thought, spooning China tea into a pot and adding boiling water from the kettle, then she had to go on, resolutely, and face the additional fact that Marina's power did exist and that the power Blaise O'Hanlon had tried to persuade her she had did not. Marina, schooled by her interesting, unsatisfactory upbringing and her peculiar, unhelpful life, had made something of herself. She did not, as Liza did, see herself always comparatively, and mostly at a disadvantage.

She looked down at the teapot. Heavens, what is the matter with me? Why do I go on making tea in teapots with loose tea when my whole world is falling apart? Why am I such a slave to ritual, to the show of things? Why don't I go and find the brandy or break the glass cases of Archie's stuffed fish or, like the girl jilted by a major newspaper editor, hack the crotch out of all his trousers? Because I'm normal, as Dan said; because I'm designed not to rock boats and, when I try, when I have a dash at it and try, I make a complete and utter mess of it and a fool of myself into the bargain. And I end up whining like my sister Clare.

I want to die, Liza thought, staring out of the window at the dull silver line of new morning that lay along the distant hedge of the doomed field. I just want to die. I don't want to bear this, I don't want to live through bearing this. And I don't even yet know what I have to bear, what Archie will do. What had he said last night? 'Domestic dramas,' he had said at one moment with distaste. 'These domestic dramas – ' She felt quite impotent with angry misery, remembering that. That was what life was, that was what afflicted everyone. How typical of Archie to believe that his life could be lived on a more thrilling level, for higher stakes, how typical of his exaggerated, greedy appetites for things. And yet, and yet, he knew how to lift his eyes from the ground, he wasn't afraid to push forward, he wasn't alarmed by mad people or bad people or sick and revolting people. Had he turned that vast tenderness of his upon Marina? Had he? Oh, the vicious pain of it, if he had.

The sky was now metallic-grey, and life outside the window, in the hedges and the beech trees, was beginning to clear its throat.

Liza found her sewing basket, and took Mikey's tie out of her pocket and began, with small, precise stitches, to confine the lining inside the tube again. M. A. Logan, said the name tape on the tie, in red capitals. Michael Andrew Logan. And Thomas was Thomas Andrew Archibald Logan. Liza's father's name was Brian. It had not occurred to either Liza or Archie to christen either of the boys Brian. They were Logan boys; Liza had felt it to be so, wished it to be so. She wanted Andrew back with a sudden hopeless fierceness, she wanted his sweet affection for her, his Scottish uprightness, his sense of order. If he had not died, none of this would have happened. Or would it? Was something stirring deep in Archie long before Andrew had even married Marina? And, at the same time, had she begun to want something more, to spread her wings, to seem different to herself, and to Archie?

She got up, rolling the tie round her hand and returning it to her pocket. Never had the prospect of a day seemed more distasteful to her, more alarming. She had no idea as to how she should behave, no inclination to adopt one kind of attitude rather than another. Feet thumped overhead. She glanced at the clock. Ten to seven; the alarm had gone off, Archie was going to shave. Slowly, slowly, Liza began to open cupboards and drawers and lay the table for breakfast, bowls and spoons and mugs and plates, boxes of cereal, jars of honey and yeast spread. Nelson got out of his basket and shook himself vehemently, slapping his ears against his head like leather sails. A voice came down through the ceiling, a muffled, steady voice. Archie had turned on the weather forecast, in the bathroom, as he always did, so that he should afterwards hear the news. Then there were thumps and a squeal and quick feet tore along the landing. She must go up, before Mikey put on yesterday's socks again, and give him his mended tie. On it went, on and on. Was that what she and Archie had wanted in their several ways, just to get off the treadmill for a while? Oh, shut up, Liza told herself angrily, shut up, shut up, excuses, excuses.

She went out of the kitchen. The quick feet raced back along the landing.

'Mikey!' Liza shouted. 'Mikey! I hope you're dressing – '

A grey wool foot appeared between the banister bars.

211

'I've lost my tie.'

'No,' she said. 'No. I've got it here. I mended it.'

The foot disappeared.

'Drat you,' Mikey said. 'Drat you. I didn't want it mended.'

CHAPTER SIXTEEN

I t seemed to Thomas a perfectly possible plan. Even if it wasn't, he was going to try it, because it had become necessary. You could, it seemed, signal and signal and the right people took no notice, while the wrong ones noticed every detail and made an embarrassing fuss and so drove you to hide the signals. Matron was a wrong person, the number-one wrong person, and Mr Barnes wasn't much better. Kindness, Thomas had decided, was an awful thing to be saddled with. It made you look like a baby and then, on top of that, you had to say thank you for it.

He had gathered all his money together from all his hidey-holes and hidden it under Blue Rabbit's skin, pushing the coins in through a split in his side seam. There was nearly six pounds. This seemed to him a significant amount and quite enough to get him to London by bus. He had considered the train, but it was very expensive, and there would probably be a difficulty at the ticket office over selling a ticket to someone who, though tall for his age, was definitely only a boy on his own. The national buses, on the other hand, with their red, white and blue livery, ran from Poole and Bournemouth to London for only a few pounds. Thomas had seen them, on his journeys to school, and the fares were painted on the back, in scarlet letters. Return, it said, four pounds fifty. Thomas only needed to go one way and in any case was only a child, so perhaps it would only cost him a pound. He had to get to Bournemouth, of course, but he thought he could do that, on local buses, one into Wimborne, another down to Bournemouth. If he did that at a carefully chosen time of day, when the buses were full of state-school children going home, he thought he could just mix in, not be noticed. And when he got to London – and this moment shone in his mind like a little, bright lantern – he would telephone Marina. And then, in some way which she would achieve, it would all be over.

'Grown-up people,' Marina had said to Thomas without the faintest trace of condescension, 'make the mistake of thinking that life for the very young is amusing. It isn't.'

For Thomas, that moment at his grandfather's wedding lunch had been a revelation. It was not simply that Marina had known and understood the great perils of Thomas's life, but that her understanding and her manner had abruptly inspired him with absolute trust. He knew she knew and that she would tell no one. She had not laboured her point, she had gone on at once to mock the pretension of the hotel and, in so doing, had sealed her and Thomas's little secret nugget of sympathy. She had said her own childhood had been either exciting or alarming. Thomas felt that in his, the two sensations overlapped so often that he hardly knew which was which. The dreams of recent weeks appeared to him as the perfectly natural result of fear and thrill, and thus, even if dreaded, not to be wondered at. He would be able to describe them to Marina and she would not try to belittle them with disgusting baby comfort. 'Don't worry,' people had said – Matron, Mr Barnes, even Archie. 'Don't worry,' as if Thomas could be seduced out of his troubles with a kiss and a sweetie, like Imogen. Marina wouldn't do that. She would, instead, Thomas was sure of it, help him to attack the monster instead of pretending it wasn't there.

The certainty of this, of her ability to help him, made the business of getting to her relatively unalarming. The best moment for getting out of school was after afternoon games, with the showers and changing rooms full of confusion and yelling, and half the masters guzzling tea in the staff room. The hoard of money was prised out of Blue Rabbit and hidden at the back of his football-boot locker, ready to be transferred, at the last minute, to his shorts pocket, just before he initiated his plan. Then, he would embark on a deception to give him time to slip away while everyone else surged avidly in to tea. Thomas planned to complain of a painful foot, and be sent up to see Matron, and then do a quick U-turn in the locker-room corridor, skid out through the courtyard door and have a good half hour's start before anyone noticed he was not in prep.

'I can't see anything,' said John Thorne, who had taken football that afternoon. He was holding Thomas's foot.

'I know,' Thomas said. 'It feels deep inside. Sort of squashed. I expect it happened when I fell over.'

'Did you fall over?'

'Yes,' Thomas said. 'Trying to get the ball from Rigby. Ow,' he added, as John Thorne turned his foot.

'But you weren't anywhere near Rigby.'

'I meant Bennet,' Thomas said.

'Stand up,' John Thorne said. 'Now up on your toes.'

'Ouch,' Thomas said. 'Ow. That really hurts.'

'You'd better see Matron.'

'Yes, sir.'

'Be quick.'

'Mr Thorne – '

Thomas had planned this.

'Yes.'

'Would you keep a bun for me? In tea – '

'All right,' John Thorne said. He thought Logan looked rotten. 'It'll make you hurry.'

In seconds Thomas, his money clutched hard against his thigh, was through the courtyard and into the laurustinus hedge that bordered Pinemount's drive. He looked back fleetingly. Nobody. It was a great temptation to run easily on the drive, but he dared not risk it. He must stay inside the hedge, stumbling a bit, scaring himself with snapping twigs, until he reached the gate, and could dodge out into the lane and then behind the left-hand field hedge. It seemed to take a long time, blundering down the hedge, and so intent was he upon it that he did not for a while hear the even, running adult feet coming down the drive behind him.

'Logan,' John Thorne called. 'Logan, stop running.'

He stopped at once.

'What is all this? Where are you going?'

Thomas began to shake terribly.

215

'To my grandmother. In London – '

John Thorne, who was young and kind and clumsy, came off the drive into the hedge and put his hand on Thomas.

'Sorry, Logan. No go. Sorry.'

Tears began to pour down Thomas's face. He put an arm up, across his eyes.

'Please, please – '

'I heard your money chinking,' John Thorne said, 'when I told you to stand up. That's how I knew. Look. Don't be afraid. I'll come with you to Mr Barnes. Don't be afraid.'

Thomas looked up at him through a sliding screen of tears. Afraid? Why should he be afraid of Mr Barnes? Why did no one ever see what the really frightening things were?

'Sir,' Thomas said obediently.

John Thorne took his arm. He would have liked to put his own arm round Thomas's shoulders but was doubtful about walking back to school in such an embrace.

'Come on, old boy. Come on. We'll get you sorted out.'

'I don't want that,' Thomas said. 'I don't want it. I just want to see my grandmother.'

'We'll tell Mr Barnes that. Shall we?'

'Yes,' Thomas said dully. He remembered suddenly, 'Not my mother and father. Not them. My grandmother.' His voice was urgent. 'It must be her!'

The sick-room door opened.

'Thomas,' said George Barnes, who never called boys by their Christian names. 'Thomas, here they are.'

He looked up. Matron had put him to bed, for some reason, but he wouldn't lie down, he simply sat there in his pyjamas and looked without seeing much at Rackenshaw's newest *Dungeons and Dragons* magazine, kindly lent as a restorative.

'Darling,' Liza said.

Thomas saw she had been crying again.

George Barnes said, 'I'll leave you together – '

The door closed with elaborate softness.

Archie came over and sat on the edge of the bed and looked at Thomas. Thomas looked down at the dragons.

216

'Can you tell us? Can you tell us why you tried to run away?'

'Why didn't you ring? Why didn't you, darling? I'd have come and collected you at once, you know I would – '

'You wouldn't,' Thomas said. 'You didn't.'

Liza was fumbling for a handkerchief. Archie took out his and handed it to her.

'We can take you home now,' Archie said. He longed to hold Thomas but every vibe of Thomas's held him off. 'For ever, if you like.'

Desolation filled Thomas.

'Not come back to Pinemount?'

'Not if it gives you nightmares. Not if you need to be at home.'

Thomas said clearly, 'I need Marina.'

Nobody said anything. Sensing a powerful advantage, Thomas said rudely, 'I can't talk to you.'

'Darling – '

'I'm not a baby!' Thomas shouted. He was so angry with them. Why were they so blind and stupid and unable to see? How could they have all their horrible secrets and be all upset and not tell him the truth about why they were upset and then pretend they didn't know what they'd done? He turned round and lay down with his face in the pillow.

'Come on,' Archie said gently. 'Come on, darling. We are going home now.'

'We needn't talk about it at all. We needn't talk about anything you don't want to.'

Fatigue was stealing upon Thomas, the opiating fatigue of emotion, too much fear. He sighed and stirred a little. Archie bent over him and lifted his long, thin, reluctant body out of the bed-clothes.

'Come on, old boy. Give us a bit of a hand – '

They took off his pyjamas and dressed him like a doll, vest and pants and socks and shirt and shorts – silent shorts; where was his money – and jersey?

'Where is my money?'

'Here,' Archie said. 'Mr Barnes gave it to me.'

'It's mine!'

217

'Take it, then.'

Elaborately, maddeningly, Thomas counted his money and put it in his pocket. They might be able to lift him bodily out of bed, but they couldn't lift his mind out and dress it and take it tamely home. Liza wanted to hug him, so he let her, but it only made her cry again.

They went down the main staircase together, Archie and Liza holding Thomas as if he was an invalid. He resented this but could not summon up one ounce of physical resistance. Mr Barnes came up, and then Mrs Barnes appeared and so did Matron, and there was a lot of bustling about and officiousness and then he was put on to the back seat of the car where they made a nest for him with cushions and rugs. The car smelled familiar and Archie's black doctor's case was on the floor behind the front seat. Thomas lay down. Liza bent over him, tucking the rug round, murmuring. He heard them both get in and the click of the seat belts and then the engine started and made the car throb underneath him. He put his hand into his pocket and held the money. Then he slept.

They drove in silence. There was, if they spoke, only one subject and if they even dipped a toe in that ocean they would be at once sucked in and whirled about in cataracts and waterspouts. Liza knew Archie had telephoned Marina to say – she had to believe this – that they would never see each other alone again, but she also knew he had not wanted, in any way, to make such a call. He had been reluctant to elaborate the reasons for this to Liza – 'Don't ask me, don't keep asking me for answers you then say you can't bear to hear' – but she knew what they were. He was not simply averse to looking at life ahead without Marina, he was also afraid to.

'But you can't mean it! You must be exaggerating. How can you be that deep in, in two evenings?'

'Don't ask me,' Archie said, meaning it literally.

'But I must and you must tell me; you owe it to me to tell me – '

He had looked away from her.

'If something comes to you as a revelation, a discovery, at the end of a long journey, it can happen in seconds, you can recognise it in an instant.'

'Rubbish!' Liza had shouted angrily. 'Absolute rubbish. What value has anything so selfish beside twelve years of marriage and three children?'

'It is quite separate.'

It was the separateness that gave Liza such pain, a complicated, many-headed pain, because for so many months, separateness was exactly what she had craved and now it was the last thing she wanted. But had she – oh, these wearisome analyses, she thought, leaning her head back in the dark car – had she instinctively sought comfort from Blaise's admiration because Archie had withdrawn himself in some way that her subconscious self had recognised and reacted to? Was she in part responsible for Archie's turning to – no, headlong rushing at was more accurate – Marina, because she had been self-absorbed and had allowed herself to believe the enchantments Blaise had spun about her? Did Thomas's troubles all stem from his sensitive unhappy perceptions of tension between them . . .

'Don't,' Archie said abruptly.

'Don't what?'

'Don't keep looking for something to blame. Or someone.'

'There must be some kind of explanation, some reason. Life isn't so arbitrary – '

'People are.'

Liza thought of Dan Hampole. Without the people who trudged along shoring up the status quo, he'd said, the whole contraption would fall apart at the centre.

She said cautiously, 'Unhappy people?'

He sighed. He said, 'Oh yes.'

She waited, staring fixedly at the red tail-lights of the car in front.

'It's those who are unhappy who break the rules,' Archie said. His voice was very quiet and she had to lean sideways to hear him. 'And it's those rule-breakers who test the rules to see if they still hold good, and who push out the boundaries. Without them there would be fewer new horizons.'

He waited for her to accuse him of making excuses, of trying to glamorise something hackneyed and squalid, but she didn't.

219

She didn't say anything. They drove for a long way again in silence and on the back seat Thomas turned in his sleep and snuffled slightly. Poor Thomas. Poor troubled, muddled Thomas, already beginning to make the fatal human mistake of taking himself too seriously. When George Barnes had rung and described, in soothing, measured tones, Thomas's abortive attempt to run away, Archie had waited then, as well, for Liza to accuse him of involving the innocent in his seedy trails, of creating confusion and upheaval in blameless lives of order and regularity. But she had not done that then, either. She had been very frightened for Thomas, and about him, but she hadn't turned on Archie.

He glanced at her. Her face was turned away from him, towards the blank black banks of the Winchester bypass.

'How is Liza?' Marina had said on the telephone.

'Shattered.'

'Of course.'

Archie had been about to say that there was something withdrawn in her, too, something unexpected and private, but Marina forestalled him.

'I shall come down and see her, of course.'

His heart had leapt.

'You will?'

'Of course.'

'Then I shall see you.'

'Archie – '

'Can you imagine how I am to go on, how – '

'Stop that!' Marina commanded, from London.

'Don't you feel it? Doesn't it mean anything to you?'

She had put the receiver down, cut him off. She had left him as she had left him several times before, desperate for more, for revelations and displays of dependence she would not give.

'Are you in bed with me,' he had demanded, 'because you are missing my father?'

She had looked at him without expression.

'That is none of your business,' she said.

She had said that to him, too, when he had asked what she would say to Liza. He longed for her to come down to Stoke Stratton, longed for it fiercely, and dreaded it, too. What a bond women had. What power. And yet, looking quickly again at Liza, he knew he had power now, too, power over her as he had had when they first met and he had borne her away to Scotland. The difference now was that he was not sure he wanted it any more and he was very sure he did not know how to use it.

He swung the car up Beeches Lane, flicking up the headlamp beams. They caught, at once, the huge gleaming developer's board by the field gate. It was painted cream, with a wreath of daisies and poppies and ears of corn around the border, and, in the left-hand corner, a fatuous tabby cat lifted a paw towards the lettering. 'Home At Last', it ran. 'Beeches Lawn, a luxury four-bedroomed house of distinction'. And underneath, in smaller letters, 'Beeches Close. Starter homes of character'. Beyond the board, in the field, an immense pile of bricks loomed like a factory, and straw from their packing blew about in the dark air and scratched against the windscreen.

'Richard's putting those on the open market,' Liza said.

'What?'

'I heard in the post office. He's offered them at twenty-five thousand with mortgage help to anyone under thirty-five born in the Strattons. There's only been one taker. The rest are muttering about the money.'

'Prefer to sulk in rented cottages – '

'Yes,' Liza said.

Archie said awkwardly, 'I'm sorry about that, all that – '

She wanted to laugh.

'That!'

'Yes,' he said.

'Oh, Archie. As if any of that mattered now!'

From the back seat, Thomas rose, instinctively wakened by the approach of home. He was unable to prevent feeling pleased.

'I'm hungry,' Thomas said.

Clare was not impulsive. Or rather, she was afflicted by impulsive feelings which she was afraid to implement in case she could not carry off the consequences. But, emboldened by her dinner at Chewton Glen – her solicitor, though hardly prepossessing to look at, had turned out to be a good companion and more than easy with the wine list – and a further invitation to a point-to-point at Hackwood Park, Clare thought she would simply drive out to Stoke Stratton, without telephoning first.

Liza had not telephoned since she had sobbed all over Clare's kitchen. That episode had left Clare feeling quite indulgent and, at the same time, less dissatisfied with her own life, a state of affairs rather assisted by the solicitor. Being early March, the evenings were growing lighter, and, if she left her office dead on five, she could be in Stoke Stratton before half-past, while the children were still up and could prevent her visit looking, in any way, too tremendously enquiring. She was fond of the children in a bleak, half-hearted way, but she believed them to be spoiled, particularly Imogen, and was too apt to see them as part of the list of assets that Liza possessed and she did not.

She arrived, as she had estimated, at twenty-five past five. Archie's car was gone, but Liza's was parked in the drive with the tailgate up and a box of groceries inside, waiting to be carried into the house. Clare made a quick mental check of what the box contained – packs of white lavatory paper (Archie, Clare knew, had taught Liza to despise pink or blue, or, worst of all, peach), tins of dog food, cereals, an immense bottle of liquid detergent of a size no single person ever aspired to, rafts of fruit yoghurts, loaves, nets of oranges – before picking it up and carrying it round to the kitchen door.

'Yoohoo,' Clare said, pushing the door open with her knee. 'Delivery man!'

Liza was standing at the kitchen table, laying sausages for the children's supper on a baking sheet. She had not taken off her jacket since coming in from school, and looked tired and drawn.

'Oh!' she said. 'Clare. Oh, how nice of you – '

'I met it sitting there, on my way in.'

She put the box down on the table and kissed her sister.

'I went to Sainsbury's,' Liza said. 'I forgot that box.'

The door from the hall was pushed open and Thomas, in a Batman sweatshirt, came in with half a model aeroplane.

'Thomas!'

'Hello,' Thomas said indifferently.

222

'You're back early. It isn't the end of term, is it?'

'He wasn't well,' Liza said, opening the oven door and banging the baking sheet inside. 'Were you?'

Clare and Thomas kissed without fervour.

'You look fine now.'

'Mikey's hidden the glue – '

'He's a lot better. Aren't you, darling?'

'Will you make him find it?'

'Thomas, not now. Clare's just come.'

'Please, please – '

'Five minutes,' Liza said. 'Five minutes' peace.'

'Mum – '

'Thomas,' Liza said, raising her voice, 'go away or I'll never help you find your glue.'

The door banged behind him sulkily.

'What was the matter?' Clare said.

'Tea?' Liza said, unbuttoning her jacket. 'Coffee? Whisky?'

'Tea would be lovely.'

'I'm going to have whisky,' Liza said.

'But you never drink whisky.'

'I do now.'

Clare said, 'Liza, what's going on?'

Liza said nothing. She took off her jacket and hung it behind the door and put tumblers on the table and a half-full whisky bottle.

'I almost never drink this,' Clare said.

'Nor me. But this is no moment for almost never anything.'

'Liza – ' Clare said pleadingly.

Liza looked mutinous. She poured whisky into the tumblers and then ran water into a green jug embossed with vine leaves (Clare remembered Archie bringing that jug home, from a junk shop somewhere) and put it on the table.

Then she put her hands to her face and said, 'Archie's been to bed with Marina and Thomas tried to run away from school.'

Clare sat there. She stared at the whisky in the glasses.

Liza said, 'I'm OK, though,' and burst into tears.

Clare went round the table and put her arms around her sister.

223

Liza, who was always rounded and pleasantly resilient to touch, felt bony and awkward.

'Marina,' Liza sobbed. 'I can't bear that it's Marina.'

'Is it over?'

'I think so. But he doesn't want it to be.'

Clare took one arm away and used it to pour water into the whisky glasses.

'Here,' she said to Liza.

'I didn't mean to tell you,' Liza said, blowing her nose. 'I don't want anyone to know, not anyone. Certainly nobody here; not the village.'

'But they needn't.'

Liza took the tumbler and gulped.

'Oh, Clare – '

'Poor Liza. Poor little you.'

'Oh no,' Liza said, looking at Clare. 'Oh, not that. You know that's not true.'

'Have you told him, told Archie about you and Blaise?'

'Heavens, no – '

'Don't you think you should?'

Liza sat down on a kitchen chair and said, spacing the words as if she were spitting them out, 'I could not bear him to know.'

'But he has told you – '

'No. I found out. I put my arms round him and bust her glasses. They were in his pocket, after – '

'So then he told you?'

'Yes.

'Everything.'

'Oh yes.'

Clare thought about Marina. She remembered saying to Liza, of Marina, 'You and I will never be that sexy. We never have been.' They had been stunned by Marina; they'd got frightfully over-excited about her and pretended they were at school, high on a crush on a prefect. And Archie had been so rude that day, sulky and prickly with hardly-veiled insults. Archie. Clare grew hot thinking about him. Faithful, strong-minded, protective Archie, in bed with his stepmother, his widowed stepmother. It

224

was the stuff of Sophocles, not the stuff of a doctor in Stoke Stratton, a country doctor.

She said in a voice choked with bewilderment, 'Will you part?'

'I – I don't think so.' Liza took a swallow and pulled a faint face. 'I don't know. I don't know if he can go back or come back or whatever it is.'

'But the children – ' Clare lowered her voice. 'Is that what was the matter with Thomas?'

'Partly. And partly Andrew dying and partly, would you believe it, being convinced that, if he saw Marina, everything would be all right.' Liza raised her tired face to Clare's. 'To be honest, I don't really know what's the matter with Thomas. I only know parts of it. He's very angry with us. But he's slept better the last two nights. And he's eating. Archie – ' She bit her lip. 'Archie told him yesterday that relationships were two-way traffic systems and he wasn't too young to realise that. Rich, really, coming from him.'

'But what have you had to complain of, up to now?'

Liza sighed.

'How do you mend trust?'

'Aren't you breaking it, too, keeping your secret?'

'I'm ashamed,' Liza said.

Clare stood up.

'That's something else altogether.'

'What a mess,' Liza said, draining her glass. 'What a mess.'

The door opened. Thomas had added a baseball cap adorned with a golden bat to his ensemble. He hissed at his mother.

'Glue. Glue. Glue.'

'Coming.'

A muffled roaring came through the open door.

'That's Imogen,' Thomas said. 'We zipped her into a sleeping bag. She wanted it, till she was zipped up and then she didn't.'

Liza moved towards the door.

'At least with Imogen around we can't see ourselves as tragic – ' She paused in the doorway. 'One day,' she said, looking back at Clare, 'one day we'll have a whole conversation which doesn't even mention us. I promise.'

Clare backed her car out of the drive and turned it away from Winchester. The solicitor had said he would telephone between six-thirty and seven, but she was confident enough to think it quite a good thing if she were not there, as well as being certain he would try later. She drove through Stoke Stratton, past the post office outside which Mrs Betts was talking to the postwoman, a stout, highly made-up woman in a bursting dark-blue uniform, who shared many of Mrs Betts's aims and prejudices. As Clare drove by, Mrs Betts peered in the fading light to see who it was. It was a severe temptation to wind down the window and call helpfully, 'Dr Logan's sister-in-law!'

'Dr Logan's sister-in-law,' Mrs Betts informed the postwoman.

The health centre car-park was full, it being the middle of surgery. Clare parked on the edge and went in to the cheerful, heartless waiting room where people sat with the despondency induced by waiting.

'I wonder if I could see Dr Logan? I'm not a patient, I'm his sister-in-law.'

Her voice carried clearly round the room. The receptionist said that, if she would care to wait, Dr Logan might be free after all his patients.

'Could you tell him? Could you tell him I'm here?'

The receptionist looked as if this was a well-nigh intolerable request.

'After the next patient.'

'I may see him?'

The receptionist looked affronted.

'Oh no. Certainly not. After the next patient, I will tell him you are here.'

Clare drifted over to a chair beneath a threatening plant with fibrous stems and hideous shining dark leaves, fingered like crude hands. Magazines on yachts and country life and children's board books entitled *Miffy Goes Skating* and *Watch Me Jump!* lay in a ragged heap on the table in front of her. Beside her, a neat old man dabbed forlornly at a streaming eye and opposite, an obese young mother, her tyres of flesh pushing against fancy pink knitting, placidly fed a vast baby out of a bag of onion-flavoured crisps. Their smell hung in the air, fried and synthetic.

It was a long wait. Clare read *Watch Me Jump!* which seemed to encourage the kind of exhibitionism Imogen favoured, and then a long, earnest article on the few remaining untouched Saxon meadows of England. The old man disappeared obediently towards Dr Campbell's disembodied voice over the intercom, and then Archie, unseen, asked tiredly for Tracy Durfield. The great pink-knitted girl crushed the crisp bag into the carpet tiles with her foot and, heaving the baby into her arms, shambled towards the door to the surgeries. Clare picked up *Miffy Goes Skating*. Miffy turned out idiotically to be a rabbit.

It was almost an hour before Archie came to the glass doors, and pushed one open and said, 'Clare.'

She stood up. He looked no better than Liza.

'How good of you – '

'Why?'

'It's good of you to come,' Archie said. 'Whatever for. It's good to see you.'

He led the way into his surgery and offered her a chair by a pinboard which bore riotous drawings by Mikey and Imogen among height and weight charts and exhortations to avoid animal fats but cleave unto olive oil. He then sat down in his own chair and leaned his elbows on his knees.

'I suppose you've been with Liza?'

'Yes. But she didn't ask me to come. She doesn't know I'm here.'

'Ah,' Archie said. He looked at her. 'So have you come to say to me what I would expect, in these circumstances, a loyal sister to say?'

'I hope I'm loyal,' Clare said. 'I don't know. But I think I'm right.'

She paused. Archie waited, polite and weary.

'I've got something to tell you,' Clare said.

When Clare had gone, Archie sat at his desk for a long time and drew on his scrap pad a huge stylised sun with rays like sword blades. He gave the sun heavy-lidded eyes and a sleepy, lazy smile. He wrote 'Liza' beside it, several times. Clare had said Liza was too ashamed to speak to him of her non-affair with the young

227

Irishman at Bradley Hall. What do you mean, Archie said, what is there to be ashamed of? And Clare had stumblingly said something about loyalty and Archie had perceived that Liza had humiliated herself, because the affair was never consummated, had come to nothing, had been no more than a brief colliding of two separate fantasies.

'You won't be angry with her, will you?' Clare had said.

'Oh no,' he said. 'No. I wouldn't dream of it.'

He felt no anger. He felt nothing but a dim pity, a mild incredulity that Liza could have been so willing to be deluded. He thought he might have met the man once, on a Sunday morning, when he had come to Beeches House looking for Liza, and he had seemed like a delightful undergraduate, eager and charming, polite; not a threat, not someone of substance.

Archie got up to lock his surgery door. Then he went back to his drawing of the sun and looked at it and felt a stab of pain for Liza, pain about her, pain on her behalf. Then he reached for the telephone and dialled Marina.

'I knew it would be you. I told you not to call – '

'Marina,' Archie said, leaning against the clean grey wall of his surgery. 'I am desperate to see you.'

She said nothing. He could not even hear her breathing.

'Just once. Just once more. I must know, I must fully understand, I must get something of you so deep in me that, even if we never see each other again, I will have that, I will never lose the richness you have given me; the gate will never swing shut again – '

He paused. There was another silence and then she said, 'My dear, you mistake me. You mistake the gate.'

'Never in this world – '

'I may have woken you up,' Marina said more strongly, 'but I am not the answer. You have to be your own answer.'

'Do I mean nothing to you?' Archie said stupidly.

'Holy shit,' Marina shouted furiously. 'What kind of garbage question is that?'

Archie straightened up.

'Quite right. Sorry. I'm consumed by wanting to see you, be with you.'

'It wouldn't help. There's nothing that will help either of us

228

right now. When you can face that, you'll have taken the first step through your gate.'

'Aren't you afraid?' Archie said. 'Aren't you afraid of the future?'

'I'm appalled at it. But I'm not afraid. Maybe I'd prefer fear to horror. What a choice!' She paused and then she said, 'I'm going to see Liza.'

'Why?'

'Unfinished business. Something I want to give her.'

'Of course,' Archie said, closing his eyes. 'I regret saying why – '

'Why do you Logans have to be such decent men? It's a killer to – '

'To what?'

'I was unwisely going to say self-control.'

Archie began to laugh. His eyes were filling with tears.

'We would rather be ruined than changed,' Marina said.

'What?'

'I'm quoting. W. H. Auden: "We would rather be ruined than changed, / We would rather die in our dread / Than climb the cross of the moment / And let our illusions die".'

Archie said, 'But you aren't my illusion.'

'No, my dear, I am not. I am your cross of the moment.'

'Marina – '

'You pay heed to Mr Auden, Archie,' Marina said. 'There's no glamour to being ruined. Only a man would be romantic enough to think there was.'

'I don't want to change.'

'There you go,' her voice suddenly sharpened. 'And now I'm going, Archie. I'm going back to America.'

He gripped the telephone.

'When, when – '

'In a week.'

He turned his face and pressed his forehead to the wall. Then, without another word, he took the telephone receiver away from his ear and replaced it quietly on the handset. Almost at once, someone began knocking on his surgery door.

'Dr Logan? Dr Logan? Mrs Durfield is on the telephone. Could you – ?'

229

CHAPTER SEVENTEEN

'Exposed!' proclaimed the banner in Stoke Stratton post office. Beneath it, pasted to a sheet of blossom-pink card was a cutting from the local paper. Richard Prior, claimed the cutting, had swindled his village. Those starter cottages he had declared he would insist upon building, and for which he had gained initial planning permission, had proved a smoke screen. They were being advertised as three-bedroomed cottage homes now, with country kitchens, and integral garages, priced at three times the amount he had promised to pin them to. 'Nobody wanted them,' Farmer Prior contends. But who has he asked? Not a single villager in Stoke Stratton. 'It's a plot,' a long-standing resident, Cyril Vinney, told the *Chronicle*. 'It's a dirty trick.'

Cyril Vinney, Marina thought, standing outside the post office, wrapping her coat hard round herself against the wind. Cyril Vinney, dirty tricks, swindles, this dreadful little shop, all part of English village life, all far more part of it now than Anne Hathaway or Gilbert White. She had stopped there because she was early and her visit was enough of a burden to inflict upon Liza without being early, too. She had gone into the post office, and Mrs Betts, spying her cashmere coat, had instantly evolved a new and repulsive manner, at once familiar and egregious.

'Lady Logan. What a very unseasonal day. How can I help you?'

'I'd like some candy for the children,' Marina said.

Mrs Betts began to put jars on the counter, folksy imitation old-fashioned jars containing humbugs and toffee and aniseed balls.

'I'm afraid the children have no aesthetic taste,' Marina said. 'They like garbage.'

230

Mrs Betts gave a little laugh. Charm bracelets shaking deprecatingly, she pointed out packets of snakes and spiders made of scented jelly and a jar of brilliant balls marked 'House of Horror Gobstoppers'.

'Perfect,' Marina said.

'Staying long?' Mrs Betts said.

'No,' Marina said. 'Only a flying visit.'

'Another time, then,' Mrs Betts suggested. 'The village is charming in spring. The daffodils, you know.'

It seemed the moment to seal her own fate.

'This spring,' Marina said, 'I shall be looking at American daffodils.'

Mrs Betts rolled her eyes with mock rapture at the heady, impossible notion of foreign travel.

'A spring holiday – '

'No,' Marina said. 'Home.'

Carefully sealing up the paper bags of sweets, Mrs Betts pushed her luck.

'Oh, Lady Logan, how I understand. When Mr Betts was taken, I felt I could not endure Southampton a moment longer – '

Marina snapped two pound coins down on the counter.

'Is that sufficient?'

Mrs Betts was, momentarily, thrown. She gave Marina her change in silence and then hurried to open the street door. It was only when she was outside that Marina observed the banner. 'Exposed!' Horrible word, cruel, suggestive of defenceless things abandoned, precious things laid bare, secrets branded with slurs of squalor and shame. She was still holding the paper bags. What disgusting things she had bought! Their sweet, clamorous, offensive smell rose even in the cold air. There was a litter bin close by. Above it, another of Mrs Betts's hand-lettered signs read 'In here please. And help us to win the Michelmersh Cup!' Marina dropped the paper bags into the bin and moved away to her car. With luck, Mrs Betts would find them later.

Liza waited in the hall.

'Will you stay and see her?' she said to Archie. 'Do you want to?'

'No,' he said. 'I won't.'

'Perhaps you should – '

'For whose sake? Yours?'

'No.'

'Then not,' Archie said.

He was kind to her, kind and polite. He had told her, the night before, with the same gentle courtesy, that Clare had been to see him and had relayed to him the story of Blaise O'Hanlon's infatuation with Liza. She had waited in longing and dread for a reaction. There was none. It didn't matter, he had said, don't worry, poor Liza, stupid overexcited boy. He had sounded as if the whole affair, which had cost her so dear, had really very little importance, and scarcely any significance for him. It had been the most gigantic anti-climax, and had left her seething with frustration.

'I can't touch you,' she had cried out to him, 'can I? I can't, I can't – '

'Wait,' he said. 'Wait.'

'How long? How long have I got to wait? I've been waiting months, years.'

He said, 'There's so much to confront, you see.'

And then he wouldn't speak again. Asking him if he meant to see Marina when she came was a way of forcing him to speak, goading him, trying to get through. And yet again, he was elusive. I'd stay for your sake if you want it, he said. How could that help? How could it possibly help to be in the same room as Marina and Archie and imagine . . .

She had sent Thomas down to the gate. Imogen was not yet back from nursery school. It was a relief to ask Thomas to do something that he would actually do just now, because ever since he had come back from Pinemount he had been naughty, rude and disobedient, not at all the biddable, sensitive Thomas she was used to.

'You can't make me,' he'd said to Archie when requested to stop drumming on the table at breakfast with a couple of spoons, 'can you?'

'I'm not sufficiently interested to try,' Archie said.

Thomas drummed louder. Archie got up and went out into the

232

garden and Liza saw him standing by the hedge looking at the poor field, the poor about-to-be desecrated field. Thomas drummed on, his eyes on Liza. After a few moments, she went out, too, and upstairs, and sat on the edge of their unmade bed and stared at the mark on the blue-and-white wallpaper where Mikey had once thrown a toy tractor. In the kitchen, Thomas put the spoons down, and snivelled.

Now, he swung on the gate. Liza could see him, swinging, as was strictly forbidden, on the end away from the hinge. At least his presence would ease seeing Marina. She had almost died, hearing Marina on the telephone calmly saying that she wanted to come down, that she wanted to see her, Liza. 'Yes,' she had said blankly. 'Yes. Thursday. No, I don't teach that day. Yes.' And it was arranged, settled, and here she was, jagged with nerves in the hall, waiting, as she and Archie had once waited for Andrew and Marina to come.

Marina drove Sir Andrew's Rover. She stopped it in the gateway and Thomas flung himself off the gate and into the passenger seat. They paused there a moment, and Liza, peering through the narrow windows beside the front door, could see that they were talking, talking with animation. Then Marina brought the car up the drive and stopped it and climbed out. She wore a camel-hair coat and her hair was loose. She waited for Thomas and then she came up to the house, and he opened the door for her and she walked in and said, 'My dear Liza.'

Liza stared.

'It is so generous of you to let me come.'

'You made me,' Liza said.

Marina took off her coat and draped it over the newel post of the banisters.

'I had to.'

'Thomas,' Liza said. 'Will you go and fetch the bottle of wine from the fridge, and two glasses and a corkscrew?'

She went ahead of Marina into the sitting room.

'I don't know why you've come,' Liza said. 'You can't do anything for my peace of mind and I'm not much interested in yours.'

233

She sat down on the sofa. Marina went across to the window and looked out, and then she came back and sat beside Liza.

'But I hope I *can* do something for you.'

Thomas came in, carrying the bottle and glasses on a tray. Suddenly he was not an asset but a hindrance.

Marina said, before Liza could invent a ploy, 'Thomas, you may go and play in Grandpa's car as long as you absolutely promise not to touch the brake.'

'He isn't allowed – ' Liza began, nettled at a more inventive authority than her own.

'Today he is. For fifteen minutes.'

Thomas, glowing, ready to lie on the drive for fifteen minutes if she asked him to, went dancing out, slamming the front door behind him.

'Look,' Marina said. Her voice was not at all steady. 'I'm not going to apologise. What I did – we did – is too complex for that. Apology isn't adequate, doesn't cover enough. And I'm not going to make excuses. It's all too deep, too complicated, too enormous.'

Liza wound the spiral of the corkscrew down into the cork of the wine bottle and pulled.

'I'm not interested,' she said again.

She poured the wine. It was white and cold, unsuitable for the day, appropriate to her feelings.

'No.'

'How could you do such a thing to me?'

'I don't know,' Marina said. 'I do not know.'

'And I suppose you think you'll feel better by saying you wish you never had?'

Marina stared at her.

'Liza, we shouldn't get started on all that.'

'You mean, please can we evade confronting what you've done?'

'Liza – '

'I'm so angry,' Liza said. 'I'm boiling with anger. It's such a relief to be angry.'

She held out a glass of wine. Marina took it by the stem.

'Have you tried being angry with Archie?'

'That is no business of yours.'

'Quite right,' Marina said more briskly, sitting up, tasting her wine. 'It is not. Archie is no business of mine in any way. I never thought to take anything that wasn't mine, never thought even to want it. Pain and grief can scramble your rational mind – '

'Oh, I know,' Liza said. 'I know. Don't expect sympathy from me. I'm a woman, remember? So are you. We had a bond. Did you think of that, as you climbed into bed with Archie, did you think of me?'

Marina took a swallow of wine. Liza's anger, so righteous, so justified, gave her such strength, but even in that strength she could not be expected to see where wings might briefly take you, forbidden great healing wings.

'No,' Marina said.

'I think you had better go back to London. I don't want you here, in my house, on my sofa.'

'I'm going back to America. I'm going at the weekend.' She stood up and put her unfinished wine glass on the mantelpiece among Liza's jugs. 'I'm leaving everything, the flat, my share of Andrew's money, everything. I've seen my solicitor. It's all in order. It's all yours. I've left it to you.'

'Suppose I don't want it?'

'You may give it to the children.'

She looked down at Liza.

'I've left Archie something, too.'

Liza looked away.

'I saw Maurice Crawford. They want to make the new series of *Meeting Medicine*, quite soon, this summer. They want Archie to take Andrew's place.'

Liza said woodenly, 'I'll tell him.'

The door opened. Thomas said, delighted, 'I turned on everything.'

'And then off again?'

'And on and off and on and then off – '

'Then please go and open the gate for me, like a kind boy.'

Liza burst into tears.

'I don't want you to go. I don't want you to go like this. Why did this awful mess have to happen?'

'Don't ask,' Marina said, putting her arms round Liza. 'Don't ask. I guess we'll never know.'

'But what about me and Archie? What will happen to us? What have you done to us?'

Marina dropped her arms.

'He loves you,' Marina said. 'He never stopped. What happened was no part of that.'

'Go away!' Liza cried. 'Go away!'

Marina went slowly out into the hall and took her coat off the banisters. She stood, holding it like a limp body.

'What you and Archie have,' she said to Liza across the space between them, 'won't be the same, certainly. But it won't be worse, either. It may well be better. Liza?'

'Yes – '

'Take the money. Take the flat. It's the best possible thing I can do for you. It has more value than financial, more value to you. It will help you, it will give you strength, a position of strength. My dear Liza, it will give you just the right, the healthy amount of independence. It will make you more of a partner with Archie, believe me.'

Then she put on her coat and walked slowly across the hall and out of the house.

Archie's journey home was impeded by an earth-mover. Huge and ponderous and improbably painted the colour of egg yolk, it moved up the Stoke Stratton road with an air of majesty, its great hopper peering before it like a proboscis. Behind it, traffic could only crawl until it swung, almost with an air of triumph, into the field where it would soon begin to tear at the turf and expose the poor, raw entrails of the earth. As Archie turned into his own drive, he could see Thomas by the hedge, staring at the digger. Archie sounded his horn and Thomas came running.

'Did you see?'

'The digger? Yes, I did.'

'I don't want it,' Thomas said. 'I don't want it in our field. If there keep on being little new houses, it won't be country.'

'I know. I thought they would be a different kind of house.'

He got out of the car. Thomas looked pale and tired.

'Marina came.'

'Did she?'

'Mummy cried.'

Archie looked down at him.

'Stop her!' Thomas shouted. 'Stop all this horrible stuff!'

'Yes,' Archie said. He put his hand out to Thomas. 'Will you come in with me?'

Thomas said, on the edge of tears, 'Marina's going back to America – '

'Yes,' Archie said. 'She wants to. It's where she lived before Grandpa.'

'But I can't see her in America!'

'Why not? When you're older, you can fly to see her.'

'I don't expect you'll let me,' Thomas said, cheated of defiance.

'I expect we will. If Mummy agrees. Come on. Come in and find her with me.'

She was in the sitting room, sitting. Just sitting and staring. Archie went in and sat down next to her and Thomas stood in the doorway and glared at them.

'Liza,' Archie said.

He took her hand.

'I suppose you're waiting to hear what she looked like and what she said.'

'She said I could play with her car,' Thomas said loudly. Archie turned to him.

'Thomas, would you go and find Sally and the others? Just for a little while?'

'Why?' Thomas said. 'Why? Why does it always have to be bloody secrets?'

'It won't be. It will all stop. But I have to talk to Mummy.'

Thomas gave the sitting-room door a shattering slam and pounded down the hall. Then there was the second slam. Then there was a singing silence.

'Liza,' Archie said. 'I am so sorry.'

She turned to him. Her face was sore with tears.

'Don't start. Don't start that – '

'I want to stay married to you. I want us to go on.'

'But,' Liza whispered, 'you want her – '

'You're my wife,' Archie said. He took her hand.

Liza said, 'She's giving me the flat. And the money Andrew left her.'

'Then I suppose you can leave me if you want to.'

'I don't want to. But – '

'But?'

She looked down.

'I don't want you to stay because it's the decent thing. Or because of the children. I only want us to go on if we want to, us, you and me.'

'I do want that.'

'But you said you were afraid of losing a dimension you had found.'

'I am afraid.'

Liza stood up and put her hand on the mantelpiece where Marina's glass still stood. She touched it.

'I am afraid to live a little life,' Archie said, 'when I might live a much greater one.'

'That's how I feel,' Liza said. 'That's it exactly. That's how I feel all the time, trapped in littleness.' She turned away from him and hid her face.

'I was in an awful place,' Archie said, behind her. 'In my mind, and my feelings. It was all tangled up with my father and with you. I can't explain it, but Marina appeared to be the answer. She unlocked all the cages, turned the lights on, let me out. How valid that was, I don't know. I don't expect I'll ever know, but it was how it seemed. She was absolutely central to everything that was obsessing me. I thought she was the answer. I believed she understood. I still think that, that she understands, but the rest I can't be sure of.'

Liza did not take her hand off Marina's glass.

'I can't go back,' Archie said. 'That I am sure of. I don't think you can, either. We have to go on.'

Liza said, almost dreamily, 'Harness your dimensions to something else?'

'Oh, Liza.'

She half-turned.

'Marina has spoken to Maurice Crawford. They want you to take Andrew's place for the new series of *Meeting Medicine*. Could that fit your new dimension?'

'Never in this world,' Archie said.

He stood up, too, and came close to her.

'I'd hate it. I'd hate to try and do what he did.'

'Burned your fingers – '

'Don't.'

'Well, then,' she said. 'What are you going to do?'

He hesitated.

'I don't know. Literally. Today Stuart Campbell asked me to look for another practice. Take your time, he said. Nothing personal, old fellow. We need to alter the balance here a bit, expand, maybe look for people with hospital attachments, sure you understand, old boy, best for you probably in the long run if you're honest, quiet country practice, maybe, try Norfolk or the Dales, marvellous country for the children – '

She put her arms round him.

'You wouldn't think,' Archie said thickly, holding her, 'you wouldn't think I could mess that up, too, would you? You wouldn't think, looking at me, that I was such a superlative cocker-up of everything, would you? Give it to Archie Logan, if it's worth anything, give it to Archie and watch him make a complete balls of it, fuck it right up, people, jobs, relationships, you name it, he'll wreck it for you in a flash. No one to touch him for it.'

'Oh,' Liza said with some spirit. 'Oh really. How you do exaggerate.'

'I always have – '

'I know,' she said. 'I know. It drives me mad.'

'You're smiling – '

'I'm not. I'm grimacing.'

The door opened abruptly.

'Yuk,' said Mikey at the top of his voice. 'Kissing.'

239

CHAPTER EIGHTEEN

'I assure you,' Mrs Betts said, laying a hand upon her bosom, 'I assure you it's true. I heard it from Mrs Logan herself.'

Diana Jago declined to react. The post office was quite full, and its atmosphere had become highly attentive.

'As true as I am standing here,' Mrs Betts said, lifting her chins so that her voice might carry, 'Dr and Mrs Logan are being driven out by Mr Prior. His activities have made it impossible for them to continue at Beeches House. They are forced to sell it to the developer. I hope,' Mrs Betts said penetratingly, her eyes upon Trevor Vinney's girlfriend listlessly choosing sweets, 'I hope those who didn't have the courage or the decency to put in for those houses, having whined for them, now realise the consequences.'

The girlfriend took no notice. She hadn't hoped for a house; she had given up hoping for anything much when early, unwanted motherhood had made it very plain to her that hope of any kind was not for her.

'I think that's quite uncalled for,' Chrissie Jenkins said clearly. She held a card in a cellophane envelope with 'In Deepest Sympathy' printed in silver across a wreath of flowers. 'Dr and Mrs Logan are going on account of the children, for little Thomas. He has to have – ' She paused. 'He has to have a special school.'

'Mrs Logan made no mention of that to me – '

'I expect she doesn't want it known.'

'So tell the whole post office – '

'They're going,' Sharon Vinney said, taking her not-daughter-in-law's sad little handful of cash, 'because they've come into money. That's why. They can do better than Stoke Stratton now. Don't you give them nuts to the baby.'

Diana Jago changed her mind about a reel of adhesive tape and a bottle of disinfectant and put them back on the shelves. She went out, past them all, and shut the shop door with emphasis.

'Poor Mrs Jago,' Mrs Betts said. 'I'm sorry for her, really I am. Always supposed herself such a friend of Mrs Logan's and has Mrs Logan confided her plans to her? Not a bit. You can understand her being upset, can't you?'

Diana drove her car at tremendous speed to Beeches House. It was the first day of the spring holidays and on the front lawn an assembly of stepladders and upturned chairs and blankets proclaimed that Thomas and Mikey were making a camp, the acceptable male version of playing houses. Sally Carter was on the grass behind the house hanging up washing while Imogen sat beside her in a plastic laundry basket and clipped pegs in a toothlike fringe down the front of her duffel coat.

'Is Mrs Logan in?'

'No,' Sally said, going on pegging. 'She's gone to Winchester.'

'To get a lorry,' Imogen said.

'A lorry?'

'For Thcotland.'

Diana crouched down beside the laundry basket.

'Why do you need a lorry for Scotland?'

'To put my bed in,' Imogen said. 'And the wheelbarrow and the thofa.'

Diana straightened up.

'Sally. What is going on?'

'They are going back to Scotland – '

'Back?'

'Dr Logan was born in Scotland.'

'Where the hell are they going?'

'Glasgow,' Sally said. She picked up a blue shirt of Archie's. 'I'm going, too. I'm going to look after the children and do a secretarial course.'

'The hell you are,' Diana said. 'The village is buzzing with rumours and here you all are calmly planning to go to Scotland – '

Imogen began to scramble out of the basket.

241

'Mummy'th come – '

Liza got out of the car. She saw Diana and waved, and then stooped back inside for an armful of brochures and a green folder.

'Look,' Diana said, running down to her. 'Look. I may not be exactly family, but I am a mate. Right? What is going on?'

'I was going to tell you,' Liza said. 'Really. When everything was settled – '

'What everything?'

'This house, where we'd go, Archie – '

'Archie?'

Liza looked at her with great directness.

'He's resigned.'

Diana stared.

'Resigned? From the practice? Whatever for?'

'We need a new start,' Liza said firmly.

Diana leaned forward.

'Look. Are you OK? You and him?'

Liza began to walk towards the house.

'Oh yes.'

'Liza – '

'Diana,' Liza said. 'I don't want talk. I don't want speculation. I don't want to be discussed as if we were a problem family.'

'You don't want to face facts,' Diana said.

Liza stopped walking.

'Oh, but I have.'

Her face was suddenly suffused with something Diana could not fathom.

'And now I'm going on. We're going on.'

'But are you all right?'

Liza nodded.

'We are going to live in Scotland. We're selling everything.'

'But Glasgow – '

Liza looked down.

'Yes.'

Diana whispered, 'What happened?'

'Everything.'

'Oh, Liza. Poor Liza. Poor Archie. What will Archie do?'

242

'I don't know. We don't know.'

'He'll still be a doctor, of course – '

'I don't know.' She looked straight at Diana. 'It doesn't matter. It doesn't seem to matter.'

'Because of money?'

'Only partly. Something else – something more – about living for living. I've got to learn – ' She paused and then she said, 'It was me who said Scotland.'

'Good for you.'

'And I went to see the developer about selling this. I've given my notice in, at Bradley Hall.'

Diana leaned forward and kissed her cheek.

'Go for it,' Diana said. 'Just go for it. And this time, get it.'

Archie stood on the pale polished stone floor, a step above William Rufus. He had his back to the altar and before him the great vault of the nave rushed away towards the west window. At his feet, William Rufus lay modestly under his greenish pitch of lead, gleaming from the touch of millions of interested, speculating hands. Archie stood with his own hands behind his back and looked at the spires of wood and the arches of stone and remembered that other day when he had come in to William Rufus, bringing with him the shackels of his longing and his confusion.

They were still with him, but they no longer manacled him. He could still feel with real pain, feel all those past sensations; he could roll before his spiritual and sensual memories the death of his father, Marina's lovemaking, and the dying of Granny Mossop which now seemed to him no less than some kind of gift. He looked down at William Rufus. Nine hundred years dead and still remembered, if more for the manner of his dying than his living, as proof, if proof were needed, that the human heart possesses a muscle as elastic as it is enduring, as unpredictable in its behaviour as it is reliable in its need for reassurance.

'Pompous ass,' Archie said to himself.

He stepped down between the choir stalls and laid his hand briefly, with affection, on the tomb. Then he went quickly down the centre aisle and through the west door out into the sunlight of the Close. As he went up the steps, a stocky cleric came down

243

them, an affable-looking man reading a letter. He glanced up and caught Archie's eye. He looked vaguely familiar. Archie stopped walking.

'Hello!' the clergyman said heartily.

He held out his hand. Archie took it.

'Good to see you!'

'And you.'

'Haven't seen you for so long. How is everything?'

'Fine now,' Archie said. 'I think.'

'Good! Good!' He peered at Archie. 'And how's that boy of yours?'

'I think he'll be fine now, too – '

'Splendid bowler. Always thought that.'

'Sorry?' Archie said.

'Your boy. Splendid bowler.'

'He's only had one term of cricket – '

'One term?'

'He's nine,' Archie said. 'I think you've got the wrong chap – '

'Have I? Surely not. You're the musician, aren't you, the cellist, boy at the College, College boy – '

'I'm a doctor,' Archie said. 'I was a GP out in the Strattons.'

The clergyman slapped his forehead.

'Good Lord. Are you? Heavens! Frightfully sorry – '

They both began to laugh, backing away from one another.

'Yes. Never had a boy here, though of course one always hopes – '

'Of course, my word, yes, how stupid of me, how stupid – '

'Not at all, doesn't matter, really – '

Archie reached the top of the steps.

'Quite funny, really – '

'Absolutely!' the clergyman called. 'Absolutely! I just mixed you up with everybody else. Absurd!'

He vanished into the cathedral. Archie began to laugh. Mixed up. Mixed up with everybody else! The irony was perfect, perfect in every aspect.

He flung his arms up in appreciation towards the heavens and then, regarded with some apprehension by an elderly woman in

244

a mushroom felt beret with a shopping basket on wheels, began to run, still laughing, over the shabby grass, back towards his car.

The Rector's
Wife

JOANNA TROLLOPE

FOR ANTONIA

CHAPTER ONE

As usual, there were five of them on the village green, waiting for the school bus. Also as usual, they began to talk differently as Mrs Bouverie approached, louder, more self-consciously, and the younger two, in their all-weather uniform of jeans, and bare feet thrust into stiletto-heeled shoes, put their cigarettes behind their backs. It was, Mrs Bouverie thought, as if she were a headmistress. But she was worse than a headmistress; she was the Rector's wife.

Every weekday afternoon in termtime, the school bus from Woodborough stopped at Loxford village green and decanted nine children. The reception committee of mothers was always waiting, partly out of maternal duty, but mostly because those ten minutes on the village green filled the same gossiping function as ten minutes at the village pump had for earlier generations. When the children clattered, yelling, down the bus steps, their mothers regarded them with a mixture of disgust and pride, as if amazed anew each afternoon that they had managed to produce children of such spectacular offensiveness.

The last child – and the oldest – was always Flora Bouverie, who came trailing down the bus steps burdened with splitting carrier bags and fragile, half-made artefacts, peering about her blindly for her mother. She took her glasses off, every journey, because, if she did not, they were taken off for her and thrown out of the bus window into a hedge. Mrs Bouverie knew this, and she also knew that the Loxford mothers despised her for meeting a child of ten. If she had said, But I meet her as miserable compensation for enduring Woodborough Junior which is quite the wrong school for her, they would have despised her even more.

'Intolerable,' Flora said, dropping her bags on her mother's feet.

She scrabbled about in her duffel-coat pockets until she found her glasses. 'I hate this coat. I look like a train spotter.'

Anna Bouverie thought with revulsion of the bags of jumble lurking in the Rectory garage. 'I know. But the alternatives are even worse.'

Flora put on her glasses. She looked up at her mother with eyes enlarged and blurred by the lenses.

'What does cretinous mean?'

'Literally, mentally defective.'

Flora looked round at the village children swirling, screaming, across the green, like gulls round the ships of their mothers. 'Exactly!' Flora shouted after them.

One mother turned back. She worked most nights in the pub, and was the self-appointed keeper-up of the village spirits, relentless in her jollity.

'See you tomorrow, Mrs B! Don't be late!'

They all cackled with guilty laughter.

'What does she mean?' Flora said, staring after her.

'I'm usually late for the bus. I have to run. They watch me running. That's all.'

'Frankly,' Flora said, stooping for her burdens, 'I think it's intolerable.'

'You're full of huge new words – '

'English,' Flora said briefly. 'We had to find six words out of a newspaper. We always do everything out of a newspaper for English.' She paused. 'I found flatulence. It means burping – and the other one.'

'Farting,' Anna said. Woodborough Junior's familiarity with rich obscenities had overlaid Flora's natural vocabulary with an anxious and reacting gentility.

'Yes,' Flora said, looking away.

Anna bent to disentangle a bag or two from Flora's fingers.

'Come on. Tea. It's starting to rain.'

Ominous little gusts of wind were digging playfully in the nearby litter bin and scattering crisp packets about. They blew damp draughts against Anna and Flora's faces and veiled Flora's spectacles with infant specks of rain. The mothers and children were out of sight now, reduced to no more than faint yelps from among the council houses built on rising ground above the green, and there was no one else about, and would not be, until the men began to come home at dusk.

'Why,' said Flora, in the dead and hopeless tone of one who has uttered a particular, heartfelt question over and over, to no avail, 'why does school have to be so horrible?'

Loxford church was medieval, with a square tower and a Norman tympanum over the south door of the Harrowing of Hell. Loxford Old Rectory was Georgian, built of the same blond stone as the church, and it sat behind grand double gates whose posts were boastfully crowned with new stone eagles. Loxford New Rectory was redbrick and had been built in the early sixties. It had, Anna Bouverie's mother said, all the quiet charm of a bus shelter.

Its redeeming feature was its setting. It had been built on a piece of glebe land behind the church, with a narrow drive running up beside the churchyard wall, separating it from the lane, isolating it from other houses. Its front windows looked towards the church, and its back ones over farmland to a series of gentle green hills, the furthest one crowned with a low, dark copse, like a pool of spilled ink. When Peter and Anna had come for interview, Anna had looked at the hills with hunger, and not at the cramped kitchen or the meanly proportioned sitting-room, and had urged Peter to accept. 'Oh, we must,' she had pleaded. 'You must. Please.'

He had been doubtful. He was doubtful about being sole incumbent in five parishes – he had visualised a team ministry – and even more doubtful about the rural ministry in itself. Did he . . . Was he . . .

'While you are waiting for God to write it down for you in capital letters,' Anna had shouted finally, exasperated out of all diplomacy, 'I shall decide for you both. We are going to Loxford.'

To Loxford. Loxford with Quindale, Church End, New End and Snead. After six years in a Birmingham slum parish, Anna thought, you became desperate not to have a front doorstep strewn with down-and-outs and to have a back garden littered with worms, not discarded syringes and used condoms. Six years! Six years of bringing up Charlotte and Luke with chicken wire tacked across inside their bedroom window, and a security system worthy of Alcatraz so that the parishioners who needed to get to you never could. Flora had been conceived the minute they reached Loxford, out of sheer relief. Anna supposed that she should then have had another baby, to keep Flora company, but had found that she felt as unlike having another baby as she had once felt like it.

Walking up the drive beside the churchyard wall, Anna said, 'What happened to Marie? I thought she was your friend.'

'She went to Germany,' Flora said, stopping to peer at the wall, where moss was beginning to swell into new plump spring cushions. 'With her father. He's a corporal.'

Half Flora's school were Army children. They lived briefly in the great camps round and about, and then vanished. Flora envied them because all the things she craved in life they could buy cheaply in the NAAFI. They seemed to take money for granted. Flora, accustomed to a life of bare sufficiency, knew differently.

She put down a bag and dislodged a green dome of moss.

'Look – '

Flora had always dawdled. Toddler walks with her had been a superhuman test of patience as she squatted by every puddle, slowly stirring the water with sticks, and picked up myriads of stones, tenderly brushing them free of earth and inserting them with infinite laboriousness into pockets already grinding with pebbles. She roared with fury if helped or hurried.

'It really is raining now,' Anna said.

Flora must be fed, the sitting-room fire lit, the dining-room tidied for tonight's Parochial Church Council meeting, supper organised. And then, there was her translation. Paid by the page, Anna translated German and French technical books into English. It was dreary work, but it was private. Peter had discovered that his five villages would not like him to have a working wife.

'You will find,' Colonel Richardson of Quindale House had said, not unsympathetically, 'that it would cause a lot of resentment. A lot. Particularly among those who don't go to church – ' he eyed Peter – 'but might?'

Peter did not repeat this to Anna. There would have been no point; she would simply have laughed. Her natural vivacity, her particular charm, had led her too often into thinking that people would be drawn into seeing things her way, with disastrous results. At least, Peter had found them disastrous, and he would find them so again if Anna chose to try and charm Colonel Richardson out of his opinion of working clergy wives. So, to avoid this, Peter merely said that, for the moment, he'd appreciate it a lot if she'd keep working a bit quiet. She had taught in a language school in Birmingham three mornings a week, a language school with a crèche, run by an enlightened Belgian woman, where Charlotte and Luke had gone until they were old enough for school. She said to Peter, 'Teaching is very quiet. Isn't it?'

'No,' he said. 'Not invisible enough.'

They had been in Loxford six months then. She was happily pregnant and still sustained by the hills. She saw the advertisement for a technical translator in the newspaper. It was easy to learn the vocabulary, as easy as it was dull. So strange, she sometimes thought, to have all this engineering knowledge in three languages and still be so unable to apply a single word of it that she could scarcely change a plug without helpful diagrams. In order to make a weekly sum of money even dimly visible to the naked eye, she had to translate fifty pages a week, a drudgery she tried to regard as ineluctable as brushing her teeth or washing the kitchen floor. A decade of it now, ten years at two and a half thousand pages a year. Best not to think of it, in case her temper slipped out of gear and, as once she had done, she threw a bowl of apples at Peter. She had missed; the bowl had broken. It was a blue-and-white pottery bowl Peter's mother, Kitty, had brought back from a timeshare holiday with a friend in southern Spain. The apples had rolled everywhere, gathering bruises and fluff. She had found one months later under the vegetable rack, shrunk to the size of a nut, dark wizened brown, and smelling of cider.

'Where's Daddy?' Flora said, setting her moss down carefully on the kitchen table.

'Gone to see the Bishop.'

'Wowee,' said Flora. She pressed the moss and watched a trickle of earthy water ooze out of it. 'Why?'

Slicing bread, Anna said untruthfully, 'I honestly don't know.'

The Bishop had been to Woodborough Junior once, to take prayers. Flora, unwisely, told her class he would wear a purple robe and a great cross round his neck and a huge ring like a winegum. He arrived in a dark suit and a black shirt buttoned down over his dog collar and kept his hands folded so that nobody could see if he had on a ring at all, let alone one like a winegum. It had been a humiliating day for Flora and she bore the Bishop a grudge in consequence.

'Would you like cheese in your sandwich?'

'What I would really like,' said Flora, knowing there wasn't any, 'is chocolate hazelnut spread.'

Recognising the game, Anna waited.

'Or black cherry jam. Swiss jam.'

Silence.

'Or smoked salmon,' Flora said inventively, never having had any.

'Or cheese.'

'OK,' Flora said, 'cheese.'

'Cheese, please. I can't think why I'm making this sandwich for you. Why aren't you making it yourself?'

Flora stuck out her hands and her lower lip.

'Search me.'

'Flora,' Anna said, 'have you got prep?'

Flora put her hands over her ears and began to jump about all over the kitchen.

'Shut up, shut up, shut up, shut up – '

Again, Anna waited. She watched Flora with exasperation and pity. Charlotte and Luke had managed school perfectly well, had made friends, had slipped effortlessly in and out of all the required fads and fashions. Charlotte had gone on to university; Luke was now at sixth-form college. Flora was different. She was cleverer

6

than either of them, more elusive, more fragile. She said some-times, of school, 'But I can't make the right conversation,' and it was true. Something uncompromising in Flora prevented her from understanding where she went wrong. Her frustrated jump-ing, which sent her thick, straight, dark hair – Anna's hair – flying up and down like dog's ears, was no more than a maddened ex-pression of how she felt when reminded of school, of a world where she was doomed to remain odd.

Anna put the sandwich on a plate, and then put the plate on the table, beside the moss.

Flora stopped abruptly, and said, 'I forgot my flute.'

'Does it matter?'

'Yes!' Flora said on a rising note. 'It's my lesson tomorrow, I must practise – '

The telephone rang.

'I'm so sorry,' Anna said into the receiver, 'Mr Bouverie is out just now. He should be back by six; could you – oh. Oh, I see. Are you sure he said he would call? All right, I'll tell him. Mrs Simms, 7 New End. Goodbye.'

She put the receiver down.

'Daddy apparently forgot to go and see Mr Simms in Wood-borough General.'

The telephone rang again.

'No,' Anna said, 'Mr Bouverie isn't back yet.'

Flora came up close and mouthed, 'My flu-u-u-te. My flu-u-u-u-te.'

'A wedding in May. I'm afraid he has his diary with him. Could you call back? Before seven-thirty, he has a meeting. No,' Anna said, 'no. He won't mind that you aren't churchgoers.'

'He will, actually,' she said when she had put the receiver back. 'He will, but he can't.'

'My flute – '

'Flora,' Anna said, pushing her fringe off her forehead, 'I can do nothing about your flute. Daddy has the car. And now I have to do an hour's work.'

Flora turned away and cast herself, face down, across the table, narrowly missing the sandwich.

'It's the end of the world,' she said. 'It's intolerable.'

7

She kicked one of her bags. Very slowly, its side seam split open and a flute rolled quietly out on to the floor.

Anna worked at a little table in their bedroom. It was an Oriental table, donated by her mother who was an actress of the old school and given to lavishness of gesture. The table was made of bamboo, lacquered scarlet, and the top was painted with gilded peonies. It bore its load of textbooks incongruously, and a typewriter that a parishioner had given Anna, a weekender who worked on a London newspaper, and who had sworn, positively, that she had outgrown the thing, didn't need it. 'Chuck it in a jumble sale,' she had said to Anna, trying to make it easier to accept.

'I've got pride,' Anna had replied, taking it, 'but no false pride. Thank you very much indeed.'

It was electric. It produced smooth, bland sheets of text that Anna's publishers greatly preferred to the characterful efforts of her previous old portable. She sat down in front of it and looked at the half-page she had typed that morning. She thought of Peter. He would by now have left the Bishop, would be crossing the Close to find his car, would know what lay ahead for them both. She looked out of the window and saw the brown strip of plough, and then the line of willows marking the river, and then the green slopes rising, dotted now with the first sheep of the year. In a month, she thought, in just a month, I might be looking at quite a different view. And what is more, I might never ever have to look at German again except on a menu in a restaurant on the Rhine where we might go, like other people do, for a real holiday instead of borrowing mildewed cottages and cardboard holiday-houses from people to whom we then have to be disproportion-ately grateful. She looked up at the bedroom ceiling, where a pale stain recalled a burst pipe nearly fifteen months ago. Through that ceiling, and through the roof above it, lived God, omniscient, omnipresent God. 'You try living your adult life on nine thousand a year,' she said to Him, and bent, with a sigh, to her typewriter. The telephone rang.

★

8

Luke Bouverie missed the last bus out of Woodborough to Loxford, so he thumbed a lift. This happened most nights and he had grown to think that it was an easier and more interesting way of travelling, particularly as his looks and his load of schoolbooks and his thinness caused people to stop. They were mostly local people, often men from the villages who worked in Woodborough. Only once, last autumn, had there been an unnerving lift, a well-dressed man in a Mercedes, who had wanted Luke to drive on towards Devon with him, had offered him dinner and a night at a hotel, had put his hand high up on Luke's thigh, and been altogether menacing. Luke, who had a reputation for staying cool, had panicked. He had heard himself squeak in a long-outgrown pre-pubertal voice, 'You be careful, my dad's a vicar!' and the car had stopped and the man had sworn at him viciously, using some phrases Luke later regretted not remembering, and Luke found himself shaking on the dark verge a mile out of Snead. He had had to walk home, three and a half miles, but luckily his parents were out, at some deanery get-together, and Trish Pardoe, who helped in the shop, was babysitting Flora. Trish never asked questions; she was only interested in telling you things. That night, she'd said, 'If you'd come out the Quindale way you'd never've got through; it's flooded right across the road from Briar Farm to the old water tower, three feet deep, burst water main,' and Luke had said, 'Yeah,' and gone out to the kitchen to raid the fridge.

This evening, his lift was Mike Vinson who worked as an electrician for a firm in Woodborough and ran the Loxford cricket team. He and his wife had so done-over a cottage on the green that its original simplicity had been quite obliterated in an orgy of DIY neo-Georgian. Mike Vinson had a respect for the church. He never darkened its doors, but he thought it was the proper place for weddings and christenings and funerals, and he was always prepared to rig up lights for the annual parish nativity play, with a dimming spotlight to beam sentimentally on the Virgin Mary. He would say, casually, to his wife later that night that he had given young Luke Bouverie a lift home. 'Nice lad,' he would say. 'Nice manners.' He would go to bed with a small satisfaction at having given a lift to the Rector's son.

9

Luke said, 'I'm hopeless. I always miss the bus.'

'You'll be driving soon,' Mike said. 'Own car, and all. Change your life.'

'Yes,' Luke said, suddenly miserable. He had practised in the car, but there was no money for lessons and as for a car of his own! Even the family car had come from some Church-loan scheme. The application form for a driving test had lain, unfilled in, in the muddle on his bedroom table since his seventeenth birthday. Anna had promised him lessons – when they knew. Knew what? 'Just wait,' she said, smiling. 'Not long now.'

'And what'll you do with your life?' Mike said. 'Vicar like your dad?'

Loyalty just prevented Luke from saying, 'No fear!' He said, 'I want to do art.'

Mike tried to imagine it, and failed.

'Stage sets,' Luke said, to help him. 'Theatre design.'

Mike nodded. He had no vocabulary to ask what he felt were appropriate questions. 'Nice boy,' he planned to say to Sheila later, 'artistic, too. Interested in drama.' Sheila liked drama. When he had found her, on holiday in Bournemouth, she had been very keen on amateur theatricals. She'd stopped for him, though. He didn't like the thought of her kissing other men, even in *Show Boat*.

'Father approve?'

'I think so,' Luke said.

'And your Mum?'

Mike's voice was elaborate with nonchalance. In his view – a strictly private view aired neither to Sheila nor to the lounge bar of The Coach and Horses in Quindale – Anna Bouverie was, well, something; not just a looker, but something more, something –

'She's all for it.'

Mike took a grip on himself. 'Been here a long time – '

'Yes, since I was seven.'

'What happens,' said Mike, abruptly interested, 'what happens to vicars? I mean, do you get to climb the ladder?'

'What?'

'Chances of promotion. That's what I mean. Where does your dad go from here?'

Luke thought.

'Well, he's rural dean, so I suppose the next thing is arch-deacon.'

Mike slapped the wheel.

'He'll be a bishop one day! What d'you reckon?'

'I don't know,' Luke said. His whole soul had been so given over to dreams of leaving Loxford recently that he was startled to think his father might share them. 'He's happy here,' Luke said stoutly. He did not want his parents to leave Loxford; just him to leave. He wanted them to be where he could visualise them.

The Loxford sign gleamed briefly from the black hedgerows.

'Lovely village,' Mike Vinson said, 'smashing. I grew up in Harlesden. You don't know you're born, growing up here.'

Courteously, he drove to the far end of the green and let Luke out by the church.

'Really kind of you,' Luke said, getting out. 'Thank you.'

He turned up the drive. The Rectory's windows glowed behind drawn curtains. His father couldn't be home yet because he would have turned half the lights off again. Some evenings, his parents almost seemed to circle round after one another, his mother turning lights on, his father switching them off. 'It's the tiniest luxury,' his mother would say and his father would reply, without looking at her, 'No, it isn't. It's provocation.' Luke thought that, as his father plainly was not home yet, he would use his absence to do a little preliminary softening up of his mother, about plans for the summer.

She was in the kitchen. She was wearing the huge red skirt she had made out of some curtains someone had sent to the jumble, and a black polo-necked jersey, and she had tied her hair up with the Indian scarf Luke had given her for Christmas. She was slicing onions. Beside her, with a music book propped against a milk bottle, Flora was playing slow, unlovely exercises on her flute.

Anna stopped slicing and offered Luke a cheek wet with onion tears.

'You missed the bus.'

'But not Mike Vinson.'

Luke gave Flora a mild cuff. She squealed.

'Where's Dad?'

'Not back yet,' Anna said.

Luke put his books on the table where they toppled sideways against the milk bottle which tipped over and spilled milk across Flora's music book. Anna took no notice. She picked the onions up between cupped hands and dropped them into the frying pan on the cooker. Luke began to mop clumsily at the pool of milk with a teacloth. Flora stood frozen, torn between wishing to scream and giggle. Her dilemma was solved by the telephone ringing.

'Do get it,' Anna said, 'I'm oniony. Say Daddy isn't back yet. Say don't ring till nine, after the meeting.'

'Say don't ring ever again,' Luke suggested.

'Hello, Ga,' Flora said with pleasure into the receiver. 'No, I've had an intolerable day. No, I'm not! I'm not! OK. I'll get her.' She held the receiver away from her with distaste. 'Ga says I'm a little tragedy queen.'

'It's not put on, you know,' Anna said to her mother, retrieving the telephone. 'She isn't making it up.'

'Is he back?' Laura Marchant hissed. 'Is Peter back?'

'No.'

'Hades. I left ringing till now because I was sure that he would be. Do you think his being so long is a good sign?'

'I simply don't know.'

'Oh, such wild celebrations there'll be! You can remove poor Flora from that sink of a school and send her to some nice nuns.'

'Tonight's celebration,' Anna said, 'is the Loxford PCC meeting in the dining-room. The secretary, who also organises the church flower rota, has just resigned in a huff, because she says the Sunday school has taken over some shelves in the vestry flower-vase cupboard without asking, so I have to take the minutes.'

'My poor darling. Shall I come down and bring a breath of life and urban decay?'

Anna shifted so that her shoulder was comfortably propped against the wall.

'I wish you would.'

'Next weekend – '

Luke dropped the sodden cloth back on to Flora's music book.

'Here's Dad, I heard the car – '

'Peter's back,' Anna said. 'I must go. I'll ring you.'

'Yes,' Laura said, 'yes. He must have it, he must. Or it's to hell in a handcart.'

Anna put down the telephone and waited. Luke and Flora waited too, by the table. They heard Peter slam the car door, then pull down the groaning metal garage door, then approach the house along the path of concrete slabs which were lethally glazed all year round with slippery green. He opened the kitchen door and came in and shut it before he turned to face them. He looked wholly unhappy.

'It seems – ' he said, and then he stopped. 'It seems I am not to be Archdeacon of Woodborough. The next Archdeacon of Woodborough is to be someone from the north, someone called Daniel Byrne.'

CHAPTER TWO

K neeling in the Rectory pew of Loxford church, Anna watched Peter preparing deftly for communion. He looked tired, in the bruised way that people who are physically slight do look tired, but not so much so that any of the congregation would notice. Anna was inclined to think that most of them would only notice if he looked disgustingly well, when they could say suspiciously to one another, The Rector looks all right, doesn't he, wonder what he's been up to? The rest of the time, they were not disposed to look at Peter as a human being, but only as a rector, a creature of whom standards of motive and conduct were expected that they did not expect of themselves. Anna's one great clerical friend, a woman deacon in Woodborough, said that it was being a village congregation. 'Towns are much more forgiving. Villages are crippled by people who can't bear to have the veil torn from their fantasy of idyllic retirement.'

Poor Peter. If anyone was crippled just now, it was Peter, by disappointment. In the three days since his interview with the Bishop he had scarcely been able to speak for the bitterness of his blighted hopes. He had lain wakeful beside Anna in the bed that had not been quite wide enough for twenty years and felt himself to be all at once boiling with misery and quite immobilised by it. A change of parish, the Bishop had suggested, a spell of team ministry, perhaps. He had not said, Frankly, Peter, you are not up to being Archdeacon, he had instead emphasised the need for someone from outside the diocese, for someone with ecumenical experience in urban work, for someone accustomed to ministerial care. Burble, burble. Peter lay in the dark and hated the Bishop. It was the only small luxury he could discover. He had telephoned the present Archdeacon of Woodborough, a valued friend, the friend who had indeed suggested and supported his application, and he had said that he simply did not know why Peter had been turned down, he had no idea. He was so sorry, he said, so very sorry. But then, he was going on to be a suffragan bishop in East Anglia and his sorrow and his support would go with him.

'I'm not moving,' Peter said to the Bishop. 'I'm not leaving Loxford.'

The Bishop waited.

'I am Rural Dean, after all,' Peter said, with a small defiance.

'Indeed you are.'

Peter looked round the Bishop's study, which was entirely lined with books. An academic, Peter thought with angry scorn. An academic! He's never even had a parish.

The Bishop, reading Peter's thoughts, would have liked to have put his arms around him, would have liked to have said, I cannot make you Archdeacon because you have insufficient judgement and experience, but you are a good priest, a conscientious priest, and I am wretched to disappoint you. Instead, he said gently, 'When you have thought it over, you must come straight to me if you would like a change.'

'I won't change,' Peter said.

The Bishop's wife had shown him out tenderly, as if he were ill. He imagined them putting the kettle on afterwards, making tea, saying, Oh dear, what an unfortunate business, so glad it's over. They did indeed put the kettle on, but then the Bishop took it off again and said he needed a drink more, oh, that poor fellow; and his wife said, 'And his poor wife.'

'It would have doubled his stipend,' the Bishop said, looking sadly at the remaining inch in the gin bottle.

'Don't,' said his wife. 'How old is he?'

'Forty-five.'

'And will he never go further?'

'I don't think so.'

'I'd share your gin,' the Bishop's wife said, 'except that it would make me further inclined to cry.'

Anna had not cried. It had all gone too deep for crying. She rather thought Luke had cried and Charlotte certainly did, on the telephone from Edinburgh. Peter did not think Anna should have told the children anything about it, but she was not, as she frequently said to him, that kind of mother. She hoped she had given Peter the chance to cry, if he had wanted to, but he had not taken it. Flora roared, without knowing why, just knowing something was violently the matter. Anna said to God, while she dug her prolific vegetable patch, 'I think You are a toad.' Now, kneeling on one of the Jubilee Year hassocks organised by the county Women's Institute, she was not inclined to think differently. She looked at Peter's back – she had not, she observed, done a perfect job this week on ironing his surplice and old Miss Dunstable, who was Mistress of the Robes at the Cathedral, but lived in Loxford, would both notice this, and point it out – and wondered what would become of him. Not in a career sense, because the leaden weight that lay on her heart told her that his career was now Loxford with Quindale, Church End, New End and Snead until relieved by the trumpets of Doomsday, but as a person. He would be changed by this; he couldn't avoid that. Even the gradual assimilation of his disappointment would leave scars and blights, like a landscape after fire. What a thing to do, Anna accused God, what a thing to do to someone who serves You. God said nothing. He held Himself aloof. Anna looked at Peter again and said to herself in a guilty whisper, 'Will he become even more difficult?'

She wondered if a stranger could tell that he was difficult, just by looking at him. Would such a person, watching Peter now, reading the prayers of Rite B in his level, pleasant voice, notice that resentment lay, like his blood, just under his skin, because the life he had chosen had not turned out as he had expected it to? Anxiously, Anna had sometimes wondered if Peter had lost his faith. As for herself, she was uncertain she had ever had any, and yet, for all that, she sometimes joyfully felt that she knew what it was about. She had tried to explain this fleeting instinctive comprehension to Peter, but he had said, 'I think you are confusing faith with emotion,' so she had not tried again. Peter had grown afraid of emotion; he considered it messy stuff that could lead one into a fatal labyrinth of self-forgetfulness. He had once said to Anna, in a touching burst of confidence, 'You know what's the matter with me? I'm just clever enough, and no more.'

Those limitations had been a great attraction to Anna, when they first met. The only child of parents whose steady outrage-ousness was only charming to outsiders – oh, the luck, Anna used to think as a child, oh, the sublime luck of being an outsider! – Anna, at university, sought out friends who seemed to be de-fiantly normal. Even the dullness of her room in a hall of residence possessed, for her first year at least, a kind of charm. Reality, in the form of banality, seemed very precious to Anna, a token of having stepped out of a nightmare into the sanity of the waking world. This overreaction was not to last, but, while it was still strong upon Anna, while she briefly favoured neat cardigans and regular library hours and institutional meals, she chanced upon Peter Bouverie.

She liked his name. She liked his quiet manner, his bookish looks, his thin hands emerging from the voluminous sleeves of jerseys knitted for him by his mother who plainly, in her mind's eye, saw him as a strapping youth of six foot two. He was reading theology, a subject which seemed to Anna both mysterious and sophisticated. He too was an only child, the son of a widow: his father had died of cancer when he was seven. Mr Bouverie was a solicitor, Peter said, but he had wanted to be a priest, had intended to try for ordination if cancer had not prevented it. His mother was called Kitty. He showed Anna photographs. Kitty Bouverie looked like an eager little lap dog, bright eyes hopeful under a curly fringe. 'My father adored her,' Peter said.

He made it plain, quite quickly, that he was poised to adore Anna. She rather liked it, not least because it was wonderful to have someone of her own, someone she could talk to. One of Peter's best qualities was his ability to listen. Anna told him about her childhood, about the house in West Kensington that re-sembled a gigantic, filthy theatrical props cupboard, smelling of face powder and cats and old ashtrays, where a five-foot plaster saint, dumped on the drawing-room sofa three years before, as a joke, by one of her mother's lovers, had subsequently never been

17

moved. The same lover had made palm trees out of Edwardian ostrich feathers and tied them to all the newel posts of the four-storey staircase. They were thick with dust, Anna said, but they too would never be removed. Peter said, 'My mother has never had a lover. I don't think she is interested in men now. I think there was only ever my father, for her.'

'But your father wasn't queer,' Anna said.

Peter, who was drinking coffee, stopped drinking. 'Is yours?'

'Yes,' Anna said loudly, full of pride and shame.

Peter looked at her speculatively.

'Then how – '

'Oh, he can do it with women,' Anna said. 'He'd just rather do it with men. So the house is always full of men. Men for my father and men for my mother.' She was suddenly overcome by the drama of her situation. 'Don't sit there like a stuffed owl!' she shouted at Peter. 'Say something! Do something!'

He put his arms round her. Then he kissed her. After a while he took off her cardigan and his jersey and then the rest of their clothes, and made love to her on the folk-weave bedspread of her university bed. Anna did not say that she was not a virgin, that she had been to bed with two of the men in West Kensington and had been, at seventeen, much inclined to suppose herself in love with one of them. She liked Peter's smooth, clean skin, and his childhood-smelling hair, and the way he gazed at her with huge eyes without his glasses.

'I'll look after you,' Peter Bouverie had said to Anna then. 'We'll do things together.'

He had wrapped her in a blanket off her bed and made her more coffee. 'Which saint is it,' he had said, 'the one on the drawing-room sofa?' And his question, making Anna laugh, drawing off the poison, sealed the success of his courtship of her.

Anna's mother loved him. She treated him as a malnourished curiosity, swooping down on him with tender cluckings, and se-ductive titbits – a crab claw, a lychee, a chocolate truffle – asking him to describe God, or Heaven, or sin, treating him as a con-fessional, trying to dress him up as a cardinal, showing him off to her friends. To Anna's amazement, Peter did not mind. He did not seem to like it very much either, but he was perfectly good-natured and only jibbed at the dressing up. He even showed a quiet courage.

'Say it,' Laura Marchant demanded of him. 'Go on, little padre, say it. Say this is the most toweringly revolting house in all Christendom. Don't just sit there and ooze the thought at me. Say it!'

'It's so disgusting,' Peter said calmly, 'that I'd rather not have meals here, and sometimes I have to put my shirt on my pillow.'

Laura adored that. She embraced him in a clash of bracelets and beads. He then, with equal calm, cleaned part of the kitchen. 'For Anna and me to use,' he said. Anna's father, an actor of no great distinction, said to Peter, 'Marry me. Marry me at once. You are wasted not being a wife.'

Peter made Anna, for the first time in her life, fond of home. Lifelong bogeys became jokes; the long tunnel of what had always seemed to her exaggerated behaviour and elaborate unorthodoxy had a light at the end of it, the light of a life with Peter. She was certain his faith would be infectious; that, like maternal love being born fiercely with the baby, her belief would spring to life with marriage. Her future mother-in-law, peering worriedly at her, said, 'You're sure you can cope with God? I mean, He's very full-time.'

'Oh yes,' Anna said, not understanding.

'You know best,' Kitty Bouverie said, fidgeting the flowers she was arranging. 'You know your own mind, a clever girl like you. But between you and me, I'm not sure I could have managed. With God, I mean. Perhaps it's a blessing – ' She broke off. 'There now. All that messing about and I've broken a lily.'

Little Kittykins, Laura called her. Anna's father called her Madame Bovary. She perched in the drawing-room beside the recumbent saint. 'Completely flat-chested, you see,' Anna's father said, indicating the saint, and offering a jaggedly opened tin of caviar and a kitchen spoon. 'So she must be St Agatha. Breasts sliced off – ' he held out a glistening spoonful; Kitty blenched – 'for refusing to submit to the lustful wishes of one Quintian. Eat up, Madame Bovary, eat up.' He licked his lips.

Kitty said, in her little voice, 'I'm afraid I can't bear caviar.'

Joyfully, the Marchants elected Kitty to the same category of quaint but endearing knick-knack which they had devised for her son. Like Peter, Kitty did not seem to mind. 'Your mother,' she said to Anna, 'thinks you are so clever to have found us.'

Anna said hastily, 'She doesn't mean to be patronising.'

'Of course not!' said Kitty in surprise. 'She is so kind.'

Anna stared.

'And brave,' said Kitty, taking out her needlepoint.

'Brave?'

Kitty unwound skeins of pink and beige wool.

'Brave. I'm not brave, so I always spot it in others.'

A fortnight before Anna and Peter were married, Anna's father was knocked down in the Fulham Road at two in the morning by a van driving without headlights. His companion managed to drag him into St Stephen's Hospital, where he died within the hour. Anna, neither knowing what she felt, nor what she would like to feel, went to her mother expecting to find Laura in a similar confusion of relief and distress, and treating her loss as occasion for a fine theatrical flourish.

But Laura was sad; deeply, quietly sad. She sat in the dishevelled shabby glamour of her bedroom and stared out of the window for hours at a time. Gently, Anna tried to suggest that a life free of an ageing queen had a great deal to recommend it. Laura said simply, in reply, 'But I loved him.'

Anna said, 'How – ' and stopped.

'If I had not loved him, I should have left him,' Laura said. 'But I did love him. And he loved me. He loved me more than anyone.'

In consequence of his death the wedding was very quiet. 'Barely audible, Kittykins,' Laura confided, putting on a brave show of a scarlet hat and a velvet coat stamped with heraldic signs in gold. Kitty wore powder-blue. Anna wore a short cream dress, from which her long legs emerged, seemingly, for ever.

After the service, Peter said, 'I wish we hadn't slept together. I wish tonight was the first night.'

'Are you being romantic or religious?' Anna asked, wanting to know.

He looked at her. 'You should know me better than to have to ask that.'

They had a peculiar little wedding breakfast in West Kensington. St Agatha was lifted from the sofa and stationed at the window in a bridal veil, to the electrification of passers-by. They sat, with some of the lovers, and with Peter's startled Uncle Roland, at an improvised round table draped in shawls, and ate seafood and drank Guinness and champagne. Anna felt, with a sudden pain, huge affection for her mother, for the house of her childhood, at last for her dead father. She looked at Peter, gravely answering the teasing of one of the lovers, and wondered if what she felt for him was the same quality of feeling that her parents had known and relied upon. Then Kitty kissed her, and gave her a pearl brooch, shaped like a lily of the valley, which had been her mother's, and they climbed into Peter's Morris Minor and drove away to Wales, for a honeymoon. They stayed in a pub, near Penmaen Pool, and walked for miles and miles each day. They only had a week. On the last day, Peter bought Anna a Welsh wool shawl she had craved, striped like the summer sea, and, when they packed to go home, she deliberately left all her cardigans behind, in the rickety chest of drawers of the pub bedroom.

At theological college, near Oxford, the docility of most of the wives of other students irritated Anna. She said to Peter, 'I won't be, in inverted commas, a "clergy wife".' She said sometimes to the other students' wives, 'I married the man, not the job.' Only the older ones, the ones whose husbands had been engineers and farmers and management consultants first, agreed with her. They often looked very strained to Anna, as if they were holding on to their loyalty for dear life. Loyalty was not yet a problem for Anna. She worked in a language school in Oxford, and returned home at night with coffee and flowers from the covered market, and a fine little air of independence. Peter admired her for it; he liked the way she stood out from the other wives. She made a friend at the language school, a fellow teacher called Eleanor Ramsay, who was married to a young don and wished to be a writer. In turn, Eleanor introduced her to someone else, a young woman named

Mary Hammond-Heath, who had been at Oxford with Eleanor, and who was not much interested in being married. She had read law as an undergraduate and was now reading for the Bar. She came home to Oxford at weekends, and she and Eleanor and Anna spent Saturdays together, and often the husbands joined them for supper. Peter called Mary and Eleanor The Friends. They were Anna's first women friends of significance.

When Peter was made curate in a northern suburb of Bristol, Anna celebrated the event by becoming pregnant. Eleanor Ramsay did not become pregnant until three years later. Anna and Peter had a small, yellow terraced house with a garden, and Anna worked part-time as a clerk in the almoner's office of a nearby hospital; the Ramsays had only a flat, off Norham Gardens in Oxford, and even less money than the Bouveries because they were supporting Eleanor's widowed mother-in-law, who had senile dementia. Mary Hammond-Heath, still not a qualified barrister, lived in a room in a house in Clapham, and came to see the Bouveries on the long-distance bus, because it was cheaper. They none of them had much money, but the Bouveries had a house, for which they did not have to pay rent. It was also a pleasant parish, and the vicar's wife was very kind to Anna and shielded her from exploitation.

'She is so young,' she said to her husband. 'And she's such an appealing girl. I don't quite know what it is, but it's more than looks. It's a kind of sparkle, and it would be such a shame to extinguish it with duty. She hasn't had time to have any freedom yet.'

That brief curacy was to be the best of her freedom. When Charlotte was born, Anna stopped working. The parish was very interested in Charlotte, and supportive, but Anna could no longer be independent. Her baby and the parish, like water flooding slowly across low-lying land, began to claim her, as did a new and unwelcome preoccupation with money. Without her earnings, and with the addition of Charlotte, money seemed to have dwindled to nothing. Anna was twenty-three.

It was the first occasion in her life that she had had to take stock of it. She had no idea whether she was early or late in doing so, and was inclined to chastise herself for self-indulgence. She wrote a long and intimate letter to Eleanor describing her state of mind and her new and disturbing sense of isolation, but Eleanor was working on the first draft of her first novel, and replied at length but not to the point. The lives of her characters were more pre-occupying to her than Anna's life. Anna read the letter with incomprehension, then put Charlotte into her secondhand pram – donated by the Young Wives' Group – and went out for a long and significant walk.

It was significant because during the course of it two things became very plain to Anna. The first was that, although several people recognised her and stopped her and peered into the pram saying 'Ah', to none of them could she have begun to say what was on her mind. In none of them, even in the young woman who was almost her age and who had a baby Peter had just christened, could she confide. They were friendly and nice, but she was the curate's wife and somehow, therefore, in a separate category of human being. If she had entrusted one of them with her secret thoughts, made one of them into a particular friend, it would have created immediate parochial difficulties, rifts and divisions and jealousies. There was, Anna saw with clarity, no possibility of intimate friendship within the parish, and never would be. Later, much later, when she had occasion to meet a policeman's wife, a woman who had been beaten up by her husband for taking a lover on the nights he was on duty, the wife said to her, 'Well, you ought to understand. You should know how lonely it is for us.'

The second thing that struck her was on a different plane, but was another restriction. She was suddenly hungry, being young and having pushed Charlotte for several miles on a cold October afternoon, and longed for a bar of chocolate. She had braked the pram outside a newsagent and was just stooping to pick up Charlotte and take her inside for the chocolate, when she thought: I mustn't. She had enough money with her and the chocolate wasn't going to be expensive, but chocolate was not what her money – Peter's money, their money – was for. She took her hands away from Charlotte and thought of the half-loaf at home. She must go back and eat that. She must get into the habit of using what she had, loaves instead of chocolate, herself instead of other people.

23

She was not, at twenty-three, in the least cast down by either of these realisations. Pushing Charlotte home in the dusk, she felt rather exhilarated, as if she had made a discovery. It did not cross her mind – and would not, for several years – that Peter could not supply a complete companionship and that she would intermittently always yearn for metaphorical chocolate. When she got home, she answered an advertisement in the parish magazine for a baby minder (how simple; why had she not thought of it before – she was at home minding Charlotte anyway, so why not several more?) and offered herself to the Vicar's wife for parish duties. The Vicar's wife gave her the magazine to edit and type up.

The moment she had settled to this, Peter was given his first parish, a little parish in a country town to the south of Bristol. The vicarage was half a huge Victorian house – once it had been the whole – and the parish was elderly and sedate. Within weeks, it became perfectly plain that the parish was in the inflexible grip of a powerful and intractable laity, who would not let go. Peter, unable to bear such a pedestrian first appointment (he saw himself in those days as a fervent worker priest), chafed almost from their arrival. He badgered his local rural dean, wrote letters to the nearest archdeacon and then to the Bishop, complaining of his frustration and begging he might be relieved of it.

Infected by his impatience, Anna grew restless too. There were no small industries around the town, so few working mothers, so no call for the baby minding she had grown accustomed to. There seemed to be nobody to teach, and the quiet, firm lay organisers of the parish were not about to allow a girl of twenty-four to interfere with the way things were done. They disliked having so young a couple in the vicarage and they made that plain. When Laura came to stay, and swept into church in an Easter bonnet of her own devising which quivered with artificial lilac, and laughed out loud at a tiny joke in Peter's sermon, to encourage him, one of the churchwardens wrote to the Bishop.

Bored and thwarted, Peter and Anna turned to one another. The result was Luke, born two weeks after Anna's twenty-fifth birthday, and almost called Benedict, whose Rule Peter was then enthusiastically studying. They argued contentedly about which saint emerged as the more attractive personality: St Benedict won on grounds of religious influence, St Luke on those of influence over secular life, because of his gospel. In the end, Anna won. Benedict Bouverie, she said, was affected in any case, because it alliterated. The day she brought Luke home from hospital Peter was offered a slum parish in another diocese, in Birmingham; sole charge, a mighty challenge. They celebrated in the cavernous vicarage kitchen with a shop pork pie and a bottle of local cider, both of which later gave five-day-old Luke colic.

To The Friends, Anna's life in a slum had radical chic. Eleanor's husband had secured his first lectureship, and her first novel had been acclaimed in literary circles. They had bought their first house and were expecting their first baby. They drove to Birmingham occasionally and were deeply, seriously interested in the problems of such a parish as St Andrew's. Mary Hammond-Heath had distinguished herself as junior to a QC in a fraud case that had made national headlines, and was inclined to regard the Bouveries' life as an excellent test case for some of her theories. She had also become agnostic, and could see no sense in expecting a God to take the slightest interest in St Andrew's. But she quoted the Bouveries in London, as the Ramsays quoted them in Oxford. Anna, knowing nothing of this, and battling to come to terms with the violence of her surroundings, while The Friends seemed to expand and achieve by the month, succumbed every so often to the demon envy.

It was also evident that St Andrew's was almost too much for Peter, even from the beginning. He took everything too seriously, and was apt to shoulder all burdens, all responsibilities, to initiate too many schemes for battered women, delinquent children, alcoholics, drug abusers, prostitutes, the old and the destitute. Anna, determined not to be able to reproach herself for not trying, took on the women and children. There was no peace. The kitchen and the one spare bedroom were constantly, noisily occupied, the doorbell rang at all hours, and once, answering it, a man she had never seen struck her on the side of the head with an empty bottle and told her to leave his wife alone.

They put a chain on the front door and bolts on the ground-floor windows. Anna only went to her meetings if she was accompanied, and never after dark because she trusted no one else to guard the children. One Guy Fawkes' night, she found the children's bedroom window shattered and a half-brick on the floor, so Peter tacked chicken wire across the frame inside. Anna was so frightened she grew furiously angry with Peter and screamed at him and accused him of putting God before herself and the children. He said, 'I am doing what I have to do.' Incoherent with rage and terror, she threw a dictionary at him and caught his temple. He bled copiously and went about the parish for a week adorned with a large piece of sticking plaster, like a clown. But he emptied the house of its demanding lodgers, some of whom subsequently abused him, when they saw him in the street. In the eyes of the more docile he read their unsurprised acceptance of the fact that even God would not help them. He wondered sadly aloud to Anna whether experience could finally make one more robust. Anna, worn through to her nerve ends, said she thought one would probably drop dead before one ever knew. 'I'm sorry,' he said. Anna put her hands over her face. 'Please don't be. I haven't the strength left to comfort you.'

One day, taking the children into central Birmingham, Anna saw from the bus window the name of the language school she had taught at, in Oxford, on a board outside a small office block. She got off the bus at the next stop, and went back to the building, pushing the children in a collapsible pushchair, which had a propensity only to collapse when occupied. Yes, it was the same school, just another branch. Yes, there was a vacancy for part-time work. Yes, Anna might apply for interview. Anna went home via St Andrew's Church, where she apologised to God and then thanked Him. She then went home – there was a man asleep on the doorstep whom she took care not to waken – and apologised to Peter. He said, 'It's hard, isn't it? I never knew it would be so hard.' They held each other soberly, and Anna noticed he was as thin as a ruler, all bone.

He's too thin now, Anna thought, kneeling in Loxford. St Andrew's nearly killed both of us, in various ways, but Peter couldn't say so. He had asked to be tested. Now, in a way, he has asked to be rewarded. He failed the test and the reward has gone to someone else and it is not, Anna said fiercely to herself, pressing her palms to her closed eyes, it is not fair that he should never know what he cannot do, that he should always set himself targets he can't achieve, that he should never be allowed to progress.

Around her the congregation rustled to its feet, indicating that she should go up to the communion rail first, as was fitting, as was customary. Peter did not look at her as she walked towards him up the chancel; he stood waiting, holding the paten, the first moonlike communion wafer ready between finger and thumb. She knelt in front of him and raised her crossed hands. There is no gaiety in Peter, she thought, bending her face to the wafer, no real pleasure in living, just an anxious shrinking from everything except duty; obligation has become his Rule, he clings to it, it stops him drowning. The communion wafer glued itself to the roof of her mouth. She pressed it with her tongue, as she had pressed hundreds, thousands now, over twenty years' worth of these papery discs stamped with crosses, made by nuns. I take communion too often, Anna thought, I take it to show the flag, Peter's flag, and I never think what I am doing.

'The Blood of Christ,' Peter said softly, stooping to her with the chalice. She took it in both hands. She loved the chalice, made in 1652, used in Loxford church for over three hundred years. She took a sip of wine, sweet and strong. Peter, with a square of folded white linen, laundered by Anna among all the Rectory sheets and pillowcases, wiped the place on the chalice that her lips had touched, and moved on.

27

CHAPTER THREE

Miss Dunstable decided to say nothing about the Rector's imperfectly ironed surplice. She decided this on Monday afternoon, having seen Anna digging manfully in the vegetable garden she had made behind the Rectory. The apple trees beside it, to Miss Dunstable's eye, also looked properly pruned. Miss Dunstable surveyed this evidence of – to her mind – most proper domestic industry, from a hundred yards away, on the footpath to her favourite walk, and made up her mind on the side of tolerance. So firmly did she make it up that she even waved her stout walking stick in the air, and hallooed at Anna.

Anna straightened up, looked round, and hallooed faintly back. Triumphant and satisfied, Miss Dunstable marched away. Anna returned to the task of removing the last, fibrous, old leeks of winter which would make, oh groan, yet more soup. She was proud of her ability to make things grow, a new skill, developed at Loxford, but a garden was a tyrant as well as a satisfaction, and this garden was regarded by her family as very much her business. Luke would mow, or sweep leaves, very occasionally, but with the air of one earning himself exemption from such tasks for months to come. Flora was only a nuisance, stopping after seconds of weeding to write her name in pebbles on the lawn (all ready for the tender teeth of the mower blades) or float daisy heads in a puddle, and Peter was never so galvanised by holy necessity calling from the far side of the parish as when the garden was mentioned. Anna thought he did not much notice the country, earth, growing things; but then he had not observed city things much, either.

'What are you thinking about?' Isobel Thompson said.

She had rung the doorbell, but as no one had come she had walked round the house to the garden. She wore a fawn mackintosh and a scarf patterned with neat flowers. Straightening up for a second time, Anna thought Isobel looked more like a librarian than a deacon. Was one of the problems with the public perception of women deacons the fact that they did, often, look so like librarians?

'Peter,' Anna said.

Isobel stepped on to the earth, and kissed her. 'That's why I've come.'

'It's really nice of you, but if you say one word about the Will of God, I shall hit you with my fork.'

Isobel said, 'Would you like me to dig too, or will you stop and make me a cup of coffee?'

'You can't dig,' Anna said. 'Not with your little white deacon's hands. And you've got trim little parish shoes on.'

Isobel Thompson took off her scarf and ruffled her grey curls. 'Goodness me. You are cross.'

'I'm angry. And miserable. Peter deserves better.'

'Shall I go away?'

'Please don't.'

Isobel said, 'I don't expect Peter minds as much as you do.'

'Why? Because of his vocation?'

'Exactly.'

Anna stuck her fork in the earth and scraped mud off her boots against it. 'I think you overestimate vocation.'

'How is Flora?'

'Much the same.'

'And Luke?'

'He wants to travel, this summer. Some friends have clubbed together to buy an old van and they think they are going to drive to India. I don't blame him, but we can't help him. I wouldn't mind driving to India.'

They began to walk back towards the house. Isobel put her hand on Anna's arm.

'I'm sorrier than I can say. Truly I am. But might it not draw you and Peter together?'

'Not so far.'

'Anna,' Isobel said pleadingly, 'Anna, don't so set your face against things – '

Anna whirled round.

'My face! My face is set against nothing! It's the damned Church, Isobel, that's what it is! Slammed doors, refusals, hierarchy, muddle, divisions, loneliness. I'm sick of it. And I'm sick of seeing what it's doing to Peter – ' She stopped and took a breath. 'It's a prison, you see,' she said in a calmer voice. 'It may not be spiritually so, if you are lucky, but socially it is a prison. I can't be myself. I can't be an individual, only someone relative to Peter, to the parish, to the Church. I'm forty-two and I don't expect I ever will be myself now. The parish has become the other woman in my life – our lives – I don't blame Peter for that, he has to believe in its importance in order not to feel he has wasted everything. I expect that for other clergy wives whose husbands are less disappointed than Peter God is the other woman. Do you understand me? Are you listening?'

'Oh yes,' Isobel said sadly.

They had reached the back door and the muddle of trugs and boot scrapers and milk-bottle crates that lay outside it.

'Of course I'm not tidy,' Anna said, following Isobel's gaze, 'of course I can't be. I'd go mad if I had to be tidy as well as everything else. Come in and I'll make you coffee.' She paused and opened the door. 'Actually, I think I shall go mad. It seems to me the only thing to do.'

When Isobel had gone – dear, patient, wise Isobel whom she loved and to whom she was often so unreasonable – Anna ran water into the empty coffee mugs and stood them in the sink. It was two o'clock. There was time to start on the parish magazines before the school bus came, a job which had reverted to Peter because he was not good at asking people to do things he did not like doing himself. So Anna did it, on foot, delivering the magazines to the twenty-seven households in Loxford who took it, chiefly, Anna suspected, for the useful directory on the back page of plumbers and decorators and taxi services. They also liked it – as did the other villages – for the spiteful inter-village competitiveness that lay under the seemingly innocent accounts of the Snead Women's Institute going on an Easter outing to Weston-super-Mare, while the Quindale branch could only muster a local dried-flower expert whose crisp and solid arrangements, adorned with bows of florist's ribbon, they could all have recognised in their sleep. There was also the monthly parish draw – top prize, £5 – a 'Children's Corner' (rabbits and a cross to colour in this month) and Peter's 'Letter from the Rector', which Anna had given up reading because she could not recognise the man in the message. 'Is it a myth that the Church is just for Sundays?' he had written. Exchanging her shoes once more for Wellington boots, Anna wondered if he found such phrases in a 'How to . . .' book.

She carried the magazines in a plastic bag from Pricewell's, the supermarket in Woodborough. It was the combination of the carrier bag and the boots and the voluminous purple cloak that had been a present from Laura that attracted the attention of the man at the first-floor windows of Loxford Old Rectory, the man who had decided to buy it.

Patrick O'Sullivan, whose Daimler stood at the elegant, twin-leaved front door below, turned to the present owner of the house and said, 'Who is that?'

Susie Smallwood peered out under the festoon blind. As was usual with Susie, she was being uprooted by her restless husband the moment the last blind was in place, this time to Oxfordshire. She didn't particularly mind leaving Loxford. At least the new house was close to the M40 and thus to London. She said, 'Oh, that's the Rector's wife.'

'Are you sure?'

Susie turned away from the window. 'She always dresses like that. Causes a lot of talk. Her mother's an actress.'

Patrick O'Sullivan went on watching as Anna walked along the lane.

'What is the Rector like?'

31

Susie had never been to church.

'He seems all right. Bit dreary.' She sighed. 'Do you want to see the main bedroom again?'

Anna walked on, swinging her bag. It was a dead time of day in Loxford, with only a handful of people out in their gardens – she would have to have the usual shouted conversation with Mr Biddle among his brassica stumps, and a whispered one with Mrs Eddoes, who treated life as a giant conspiracy – and nobody in the shop or on the green. She always began her delivery among the less picturesque group of cottages on the south side of the green. These cottage front doors were never used – some even had rows of flowerpots across the sill as a deterrent – and Anna had to go round to the back to find a resting place for the magazine. There was no sentimentality about these cottages. Their back doors were protected by makeshift porches of ribbed plastic, and the gardens grew as many derelict motor bikes as they did dahlias and cabbages. Only the windows had been modernised, with the old, many-paned windows replaced with blank sheets of glass through which Anna could see the inhabitants, burrowed deep in the comfortable fusty layers of their living-rooms, mindlessly absorbed in the relentless quacking of the television set. These were the people, Anna thought affectionately, who knew the rules of village living, as of old. She wedged their magazines between old paint tins and imperfectly washed milk bottles and towers of flowerpots, and crept away.

The north side of the green was another matter. The prettier cottages here faced south, and were divided from the green by a stream which necessitated a little stone bridge to every garden gate. Here the Vinsons lived, and the Partingtons, and the Dodswells, all newcomers to country life who had decided ideas, gleaned chiefly from magazines as to how to live it. Their cottages had scarcely survived their attentions. It gave Anna real pain to post magazines through one new front door hinged and studded so as to resemble part of the set for a pantomime of *Robin Hood*, and then another, moulded and classically pedimented, between half-pilasters made of fibreglass. The third had a goblin lantern, and stone frogs cemented (for fear of theft) to the little bridge and the nameplate which read 'The Nook'. Yet Elaine Dodswell, who inhabited The Nook, produced the annual Sunday-school Christmas Play, and organised the parish hospital-run for those visits to out-patients' departments at Woodborough so cherished by three-quarters of the population. 'You,' said Anna to herself, squeezing a magazine into The Nook's small and fancy wrought-iron mouth, 'are a snob. God is not a snob. God values Elaine Dodswell because she does what she does with a good grace. Which is more, my girl, than can be said for some.'

The Nook's door opened.

'I'm so glad to catch you,' Elaine Dodswell said. She wore a tracksuit and an expression of deep sympathy. 'I heard. I just heard. I'm ever so sorry for you both but of course I'm ever so relieved. We don't want to lose you.'

Anna stared.

'Colin heard in Woodborough. In the pub, he said. The Coach and Horses.'

Anna leaned weakly against the varnished door jamb.

'Nothing's private, is it? You can't breathe in a village – '

'Come in,' Elaine said. 'Come in and have a coffee.'

'I can't. I've got eighteen more houses before the school bus. But thank you.'

'Is Peter ever so upset?' Elaine asked cosily.

'Oh no,' Anna said, 'I think he's relieved. He was advised, you know, but he loves it here.' She stood upright again. 'It would have been an awful wrench.'

Elaine nodded.

'Yes. Yes, I'm sure it would. I'll tell Colin, then.' She began to push the door to. 'He'll be ever so glad. We were so worried, that Peter'd mind.'

The door closed and then Elaine pulled the magazine in, from inside, causing the letter box to snap shut smartly. Anna made a face at it before she turned away. Damn, damn, damn. No face to save, no place to hide. She crossed the bridge between the frogs and set off for the far end of the green, where the lane led up into the council estate. As she turned uphill, a dark-red Daimler slid by, and blew its horn at her. She stood and stared after it.

'It's the new chap!' Mr Biddle bellowed from his potato bed across the green. 'It's the chap that's bought the Old Rectory.'

Anna waved in acknowledgement. Poor Susie Smallwood, she had always said to herself, poor Susie, with her discontented little face and her sports car and her Rolex watch; but now enviable Susie who could, and would, albeit with a show of petulance, leave Loxford and begin again.

''E give four 'undred thousand!' Mr Biddle shouted. 'Bloody crackpot!'

Anna turned away from the green and climbed the hill towards the council houses, in whose gardens interminable lines of washing were guarded by yellow-eyed German shepherd dogs. She could not help reflecting, as she pushed a magazine into the first letter box, that a world in which Daimler drivers could pay four hundred thousand pounds for a country house while she could not even muster a couple of hundred for Luke's modest share of an old transit van had a certain imbalance to it.

The school bus was late, so Anna was on time. Someone said to her, 'Made it all right today, then, Mrs B?' and she said, 'I know. It's a bit of an achievement, isn't it?' and bravely smiled. They had watched her, in the council estate, they knew what she had been doing. They were not unkind people, not mean-minded, but it would never have occurred to them to offer to help. The parish magazines were Church business: Anna was the Rector's wife.

When the school bus pulled up, there was the usual avalanche of nine children, and then a pause. It was quite a long pause. Anna moved towards the bus steps and saw the driver looking behind him down the length of the bus, waiting. After several seconds, Flora came, as slow as a snail, bumping her bags down the steps, head bent.

'Flora,' Anna said. 'Darling – '

Flora raised her head a little. Her face was blotched and swollen with crying.

'Oh Flora,' Anna said, holding out her arms.

Flora stopped in front of her, and leaned tiredly against her, still holding her bags. The village mothers and children watched in uneasy silence. Flora said something. Anna could not hear it. 'What?' she said, stooping.

Flora whispered, 'I can't bear it any more.'

Holding her, Anna looked up at the others. They began to shift and move away. One of them, taking the lead, said loudly, 'It's a shame. Poor kid. You want to tell the headmaster, Mrs B. That's what you want to do.'

'I've got a deanery meeting,' Peter said.

He stood in the kitchen, half into his depressing mackintosh.

'Will you be late?'

'Nine-ish – '

'On the way to your meeting,' Anna said, piling supper plates, 'would you think about Flora?'

Peter shrugged on his second sleeve and began to button himself up, collar neat, belt buckled.

'Please – ' Anna said in exasperation. 'Please.'

'What?'

'Must you do yourself up so – so *trimly*? Must you look so utterly suburban?'

'I am suburban.'

'Flora,' Anna said. 'Just think about Flora.'

'I was. It was you – '

'I know. I know, I'm sorry. I'm on edge because of Flora.'

Peter finished buttoning and buckling.

'What do you suggest we do?'

'Take her away from Woodborough Junior and send her to St Saviour's.'

'But that's Catholic!'

'Same God.'

'No,' Peter said.

'So bullying is better?'

'Why St Saviour's?'

'Because it's the cheapest private alternative in Woodborough.'

'How cheap?' Peter said.

'Six hundred pounds a term.'

He let out a yelp. 'Six hundred!'

'Yes,' Anna said. 'Kind nuns. Small classes.'

Peter seized the black document-wallet he always took to meet-

35

ings. 'You must be mad. Where can we find six hundred pounds three times a year?'

'Borrow it,' Anna said, beside herself, not caring if the remark were a red rag to a bull.

Peter gasped. He glared at her, wrestling with himself, then he went out to the garage, banging the kitchen door behind him.

The telephone rang at once.

'Anna?'

'Yes – '

'Anna, it's Celia Hooper here. Just rang to remind Peter – '

'He's gone. Just left.'

'Oh good. Splendid. Just rang to make sure. You know.'

Celia Hooper, secretary to the Deanery Synod, one of what Anna thought of as Peter's groupies.

'Thank you, Celia.'

'Not at all. Must fly. Bye!'

If we haven't got the money, Anna thought, putting the telephone down, and we can't borrow it, we must make it. She visualised more hours at her red lacquer table. Well, if needs must, they must. She considered telephoning Laura, and Kitty, both of whom were long on sympathy and short on cash – so strange that Peter's orthodox solicitor father should have left his widow quite as poorly provided for as Anna's unconventional one had left Laura – and decided that it would be unfair. What could they do, except be made miserable by impotence?

She went upstairs. Flora was lying on her bedroom floor doing her homework. Through the wall came the thump of rock music which was Luke's required accompaniment to doing his.

'Flora,' Anna said.

Flora rolled over and peered up at her mother. She looked terribly tired. Anna sat on the edge of Flora's bed. 'Look,' she said, 'I think you've had enough.'

Flora waited.

'I don't quite know how we'll manage it,' Anna said, 'But we will, somehow. You won't have to stay at Woodborough Junior much longer. I promise.'

'St Saviour's?' Flora said. She had seen the nuns in Woodborough. They had appeared to her like grey gulls, mysterious and soothing.

'Is that where you would like to go?'

Flora considered. Girls at St Saviour's wore dark-green skirts and jerseys, not their own clothes.

'Could we afford the uniform?'

'I should think so. Secondhand, of course, but we're used to that.'

Flora, suddenly flooded with relief, said stoutly, 'But we always have new toothbrushes.' She got up from the floor and sat on Anna's knee. 'Soon?'

'I have to do a bit of planning. And talk to Sister Ignatia. You'll just have to bear it for a little while longer.'

Flora leaned back and Anna put her arms around her.

'Did you pray?'

'No,' Anna said.

'I did. I expect Daddy did. If you had, I might have gone to St Saviour's last term.'

'It isn't as simple as that.'

Flora wasn't listening. She began to play with the string of amber glass beads round Anna's neck (Oxfam Shop, Woodborough).

'Perhaps I'll have a best friend,' Flora said.

Laura came down from London on the long-distance bus. She had never learned to drive and disliked the train because, she said, you were too low in a train to see properly. A coach was just right; like being on a very tall horse, or even an elephant. And nowadays coaches had lavatories and armchairs and dear little hostesses whom Laura liked to induce to tell her their life stories.

'Do you know, Anna, my darling, that that poor child longed, only longed, to be a concert pianist but was literally forced by her ogrish father to nurse him while he died of drink and now her spirit is quite broken and all she can bring herself to do is dispense plastic cups of repellent coffee to OAPs going to Ferndown to see their married daughters?'

Laura travelled in style. She had a leather suitcase which bore the remains of labels from pre-war Oriental hotels, a hatbox and an immense carpet bag which sighed out little puffs of dust every time it was set on the ground. She also had a tattered travelling rug – 'Purest cashmere, darling, just feel, adorable little goat's tums' – and a string bag full of books and apples. As the bus came to a halt in Woodborough bus station, Laura slid open the window and lowered her string bag down to her son-in-law.

'Darling. Too thrilling. Take this, do. Reminds me of Port Said, and you're a little bumboy in a boat.'

The travelling rug followed the string bag, and then the driver came round the bus to release Laura's other luggage from the boot. She swept down the steps and embraced Peter warmly.

'Oh my darling, I've wept for you. I can't bear it.'

Leaning against her with an almost childish relief, Peter said, 'I'm not at all sure I can.'

'And Anna?'

'What do you think?' Peter said. 'What else can she feel but utterly let down?'

'Not by you.'

'Oh,' said Peter crossly, freeing himself and seizing Laura's luggage. 'Who else could it be but me?'

Laura opened her mouth to say, The Church, of course, and shut it again. Tact, as she often proudly said, was as alien to her as hygiene – 'The sign of a bourgeois mind' – but this was an occasion for affection above even a fine disregard for tact. If Peter were encouraged to despise and disbelieve the very authority he had given his life to, where would that leave him, but spinning in an abyss? So instead, Laura said, 'She's just desperate with disappointment for you.'

Peter, half hearing, said, 'Oh, I'm desperate all right,' and gave a little barking laugh, and set off across the bus station to the car park, grasping Laura's luggage.

Dear heaven, Laura thought, trotting after him with her string bag and her blanket. Dear merciful heaven, is this what happens to a thwarted man of God? She cast her eyes skywards, muttering soft curses. A man, passing her, took one startled look and reflected anew what a very unwise policy was the current one of closing nineteenth-century asylums and turning the inmates loose into an alarmed and inadequate society.

By bedtime, Laura was exhausted. She lay in Charlotte's bed and looked up at the ceiling that Charlotte had festooned with shawls and old curtains and Indian bedspreads (there was a definite small weight in one of those hammocks: what lay there? The body of a – mouse?) and considered the household now shut away around her in the spring darkness. They had all come to her, one by one, during the evening, an evening harried with telephone calls – 'I don't think,' Anna had said at one point, 'that we have eaten an uninterrupted meal in twenty-one years' – and they had all explained to her how awful they felt, and how guilty they felt about feeling awful, because it wasn't anybody's fault, and that made it worse, having nobody to blame.

'I know Mum and Dad can't help with the van,' Luke said. 'And I'd like to make the money myself, I mean, I could, easily, at the Quindale garage, but I haven't time because of A levels and the others are all going at the beginning of July.'

Laura, thinking privately that she would telephone Kitty and propose £100 each (St Agatha must be worth something, silly to hang on to her for sentiment, even though she had now become something of a friend, someone waiting when Laura came home to what was, to be honest, a deeply, darkly dire apology for a decent flat), patted Luke and said, 'Mmm.'

Luke said, 'I don't suppose you think it matters.'

She turned huge eyes on him. 'But I do! I'm plotting.'

'The thing is,' Luke said, encouraged, 'I don't want to give Mum a lot of grief about it, but you do get hacked off with being patient, a bit.'

'Wait!' Laura held up a forefinger burdened with an enormous cameo ring. 'Just wait! And trust!'

'Sounds like a bloody dog,' Luke said, grinning.

If Luke needed £200, Flora needed uniform. It had not crossed Flora's mind that St Saviour's might need payment for teaching her, only that her place there depended upon her ability to have

39

the right uniform, all the uniform, down to the last sock garter and science overall.

'They must be green,' Flora said to her grandmother, 'with my name here – ' she patted the left side of her nightie-clad chest – 'in chain stitch. Mummy can't do chain stitch.'

'Immaterial,' Laura said, gesturing. 'Chain stitch, satin stitch, feather stitch, stump work, back stitch, smocking, tacking – '

'Chain stitch,' Flora said loudly. She had been in the habit of anxiety and tension for so long that she could not stop now, merely because the menace was being taken away. 'Chain stitch, chain stitch,' Flora cried, bursting into tears. 'It has to be, I've seen one – '

Chain stitch, Laura thought, eyeing the weight in the ceiling cloth (had it moved?), chain stitch and £600 a term. She could only sell St Agatha once, and there was precious little left besides to sell.

'I don't mind more work,' Anna said, 'but I have to confess that my heart does rather quail and fail at the thought of three times as much French jacquard-weaving machinery specifications to translate as I have already.'

'Defy the village,' Laura said. 'Take pupils! Teach French!'

Anna, sitting on the side of Laura's bed wrapped in a bath towel, looked miserable.

'If it was just defying the village I wouldn't think twice. But if I defy the village – the parish – I automatically defy Peter. And truly I can't do that to him now, on top of everything.'

'I'll think,' Laura said, shutting her eyes. 'I'll cudgel my brains. Cudgel, cudgel.'

'Don't get me wrong,' Anna said, standing up, 'I'm not giving up. I'm just stuck. I can't think what to do next, except the same things. The same old rather fruitless things.'

Me too, Laura thought. Whither now, at sixty-five, with an agent who sends me postcards from abroad as conscience sops, but never telephones because what work is there for such a one as I (or is it me?)? And is it better to be poor Kittykins, in that dull ground-floor flat in the wrong part of Windsor, for whom life's highlights have dwindled to pension day and nature programmes on the telly box? Gnash teeth, thought Laura, roll eyes, tear hair.

She turned on her side so that, if the mouse on the ceiling began a stealthy movement, she would not see it. And then, as was her wont, she began to declaim 'The Lady of Shalott' to herself, to chant herself to sleep. 'God in his mercy, lend her grace,' she muttered, thinking of Anna, her Anna, who had grown from being such a dull child into a truly engaging woman, a woman so richly deserving of being lent a little of God's grace. And why, why in hell's name, didn't He?

On Saturday morning, Peter went off to do his rounds of parish patients at Woodborough Hospital. Luke went with him, to see schoolfriends and to get out of Loxford. Flora sat in the kitchen, laboriously practising chain stitch on a rag torn from an old shirt of Peter's, and Anna, who was in charge of the cleaning-rota, went off to the church to see if it actually had been cleaned. Being medieval, she thought it was unsuitable for the church to be visibly glittering, but, if the pews and the brass weren't polished, it quickly looked sad and Anna did not like it to look sad. She had an affection for the building, as if it were a sturdy and uncomplaining beast that had stood and endured human volatility and neglect since 1320. It demanded very little and gave a good deal in return. When she was alone in it, she would, in affection and gratitude, pat the squat stone pillars that held up the nave roof. Laundering its altar linen and hoovering its aisle carpet often seemed like the instinctive care she gave to anything dependent of which she was fond. Today, only the altar candlesticks had been forgotten (it was Elaine Dodswell and Trish Pardoe's week and they could at least be relied upon) so Anna gathered them up and took them home to polish. On the way back, she met Miss Dunstable with an armful of pussy willow intended for the church porch.

'Action, action!' cried Miss Dunstable, indicating the candlesticks. 'Good for you! Only way!'

'Only way to what?

'Get anything done!'

'I think,' Anna said a minute later, setting down her brass burden on the kitchen table, 'I think I have had a little revelation.'

'An angel!' Laura said.

'A tweed one,' Anna said, thinking of Miss Dunstable. 'A tweed one in a mackintosh hat. Action, she said, action. I've got to act – '

Flora, whose notions of acting were confined to the village nativity play, tugged in puzzlement at her sweaty chain stitch.

'As long as I do something *outside* the parish,' Anna said, 'does it matter what I do?'

'Teach again – '

'I can't. My qualifications aren't enough for state teaching, only for private language schools.'

Laura flung out her arms.

'Does it matter? Petrol pumps, shop assistant, filing clerk, who cares?'

Anna looked at her.

'I don't,' she said. 'Not any more.'

CHAPTER FOUR

The administration manager at Pricewell's seemed to Anna very young. He was slim and dark and he told her his name was Steve. (His office door – an office the size of a cupboard – had 'Mr S. Mulgrove' on it.) He said consolingly to Anna, 'The lack of experience isn't a problem. Most of our school leavers don't have any experience.'

It had been an impulse, appealing to Mr S. Mulgrove. Anna had been suddenly struck as she pushed open Pricewell's double glass doors, by the 'Vacancy' notice pasted to the inside of it. 'General staff wanted,' it said. 'Full- and Part-time. Stock and checkout assistants. Apply the Administration Manager.'

'May I take your name and address?' Mr Mulgrove said. Anna gave it. He did not flinch when she said 'the Rectory'. Perhaps he didn't even realise what the implication of living in a rectory was.

'I don't mind what I do,' Anna said.

He said delicately, 'Stock involves quite a lot of ladder work, in the warehouse . . .' as if Anna might not be up to such physical strenuousness.

'I think I'd rather climb ladders than sit at a checkout.'

Mr Mulgrove rather wanted to say that her voice and appearance would be an asset on the checkout, good for Pricewell's public image (a cause dear to his heart), but he was uncertain how to put this.

'I wouldn't like you to be in the wrong situation . . .'

Anna, emboldened by the energy of taking action, said, 'Would I be paid more for one than the other?'

He shook his head.

'What would I be paid?'

As Anna was the sort of person Mr Mulgrove associated with being a customer rather than a member of staff, he was suddenly embarrassed. He flicked, with much throat-clearing, through a plastic-sheeted folder.

'Three twenty-one an hour.'

'Three pounds and twenty-one pence – '

'Yes.'

'Heavens,' Anna said. 'You see, I need to make at least fifty pounds a week for thirty-six weeks a year.'

He could not look at her: he was overcome by her directness. He said, 'That would mean twenty hours a week as a part-time assistant. Four hours a day for five days.'

There was a little pause.

'You're on,' Anna said. She held her hand out to him. He took it doubtingly.

'You're sure?'

'Yes.' She smiled at him. 'Yes. It also means no Church and no village for twenty hours a week.'

He did not understand. He wondered if he were making a mistake. He said, 'Of course, there has to be a three-month trial – '

'Oh, of course.'

'And you will have to work under supervision for the length of that period – '

'Why do you think I might be difficult?'

Mr Mulgrove went scarlet. Give him a school leaver any day, or a nice, motherly woman going back to work once her children were grown-up, or an obliging pensioner, prepared to collect trolleys from the car parks . . .

'I won't be difficult,' Anna said gently, to comfort him. 'I need a job and I'd be really grateful if you would let me have one.'

He looked at her, for the first time. Why on earth did she need a job? What was she doing? Bravely he said, 'You're not having me on?'

44

'No,' Anna said, 'no. My youngest child is being bullied at school and I want to send her to St Saviour's. That's all.'

Mr Mulgrove relaxed. His sister had been to St Saviour's. He stood up.

'If you'd like to come this way, Mrs Bouverie, I'll show you the warehouse and the rest room.' He held the door for her to squeeze past. 'There's a bonus scheme, of course,' he said, 'for good work. Some people get awarded it before the trial period is up. It would mean an extra ten pence an hour.'

'I can go in on the morning bus with Flora,' Anna said, 'and home on the early-afternoon one to Quindale. It's perfectly simple. And they were so nice. They said I could work just in termtime as long as I give them notice of the definite weeks a month in advance.' She looked at Luke. They were sitting either side of the kitchen table, in the debris of supper. Peter had gone to the New End PCC meeting. 'I will wear a navy-blue overall with a checked collar and cuffs, and a little badge saying, "I'm Anna. Can I help you?"' She waited for Luke to laugh.

Luke did not laugh. People who are drowning in mortification do not find it easy to laugh. Luke would have said that politically he stood way to the left of his mother and way, way to the left of his father, but somehow he could not reconcile himself to the thought of his mother stocking shelves in Pricewell's. With a badge on. He had a lump in his throat and he felt his skin prickling with shame at the thought of his friends and his friends' mums going in to Pricewell's and seeing Anna unloading ketchup bottles with 'Can I help you?' pinned on her overall.

'Oh Luke,' Anna said. She used the tone of voice she had used when he was little and she caught him doing something he had been expressly forbidden to do. 'Won't your principles stand being acted upon?'

'Shut up!' Luke shouted. He glared at her. She'd promised him money for the van, which she would make wearing that bloody badge. He didn't want money made that way; he didn't want the humiliation.

'I'm sorry,' Anna said, 'I didn't mean to tease. But really you

45

must try to be a little consistent. And practical.' She stopped. She had been about to say, You're just like Daddy, but that, though true, would not have been fair, or kind. So she said, 'What's so different about my working in Pricewell's from your working at the garage?'

Luke squirmed. He could not say that the garage was macho and Pricewell's was naff, because she would tease him again. He was unable to imagine what she was after, why she had chosen this way out, why she seemed so bloody cheerful.

'I'm not qualified to do much else,' Anna said, in the gentle voice she had used to Peter. ('It's deliberate, isn't it?' Peter had said. 'Just rubbing my nose in it.') 'It won't be for ever.'

'Why can't you do something where people can't see?'

'Ah,' Anna said, 'I see. You do think like Daddy, don't you?'

'What's Dad think?'

'That I'm doing it to show off. That it's Ga coming out in me, a kind of exhibitionism. Why can't I go and be a clerk in the Council offices where no one can see, is that it? Well, I'd rather work in a shop, among people.'

'But –'

'Luke,' said Anna, leaning forward, looking intently at him, 'Luke. I want to be *normal*.'

He held her gaze for a couple of seconds, then dropped his own.

'Yeah.'

'This doesn't have to be a big deal. This has to be a practical way to rescue Flora and get you to India or wherever. You and Daddy seem to expect a freedom for yourselves you have no intention of awarding me.'

Jesus, Luke thought, I'm going to cry.

'If your friends' mothers despise me for working in a supermarket, then they are to be pitied. But they won't. They'll understand. Women do,' Anna said with vehemence.

Luke rubbed his hand across his eyes and nose.

'You ought to know,' Anna said more gently, 'you ought to know by now that things you want don't just fall off trees. There's Charlotte on the most basic grant, you dressed entirely from the Pakistani stalls in Woodborough market, Daddy miserable because he can't just magic up school fees for Flora. It's a struggle, isn't it? You know that.'

Luke nodded. He understood all right, but he had a dim feeling that dignity was all the same compromised by what Anna proposed to do. He thought he would not begin on all that, so he got up from the kitchen table.

'Well, Flora seems pretty happy – '

Anna smiled. 'Now she has cracked chain stitch, she's fine.'

'I liked Woodborough Junior.'

'You're a very different kettle of fish from Flora.' She paused, and then she said, 'And from me.'

Luke turned in the kitchen doorway and said suddenly, 'Mum, you OK?'

Anna nodded. Luke looked relieved. 'I'll go up then,' he said, and went.

On Anna's first morning at Pricewell's, she caught the early bus with Luke and Flora. Flora clung to her, like a limpet. As the bus swung slowly round Loxford green, Anna saw that two immense removal vans were parked in the drive of Loxford Old Rectory. The Smallwoods were off to Oxfordshire. Anna made a mental note to go in that evening and wish them well: Peter would like it; poor Peter, who had broken down in bed the night before, and wept that he had failed her, failed her as well as – but he couldn't actually articulate that.

'It's not your fault,' she had said, hardly knowing what she meant.

'It is, it is. I've failed everything I've attempted.'

'I don't think so,' Anna said. 'I think the goalposts have been moved. Godly goalposts.'

It was two in the morning. She had been downstairs to make tea.

'Are you lonely?' she said to Peter, handing him a mug.

He seemed reluctant to answer, doubtful. He said at last, 'I've got you,' in a slightly hearty voice. She waited for him to ask her if she was lonely, but he didn't, merely drank his tea obediently, like a child with hot milk.

47

'Do you want,' Anna said, embarking impulsively on the thinnest ice, 'do you want to reconsider everything? I mean *everything*? Our lives, where we live, even – even what you do?'

He stared at her.

'Heavens, no.'

'Sure?' she said, persisting. 'I wouldn't be afraid, you know.'

'No,' he said loudly. He set the mug on the tray. 'I can't just throw it in because I haven't succeeded yet. The test is part of it all.'

'Part?'

'Part of holiness,' Peter said rapidly. 'To be tested is to suffer. Suffering is part of spiritual progress. You know that, that's child's stuff.'

'So is listening.'

'Listening?'

'To me,' Anna said. She jerked a glance upwards. 'To Him.'

Peter made an impatient noise.

'So you think I don't pray?'

Inside herself, Anna shrank away. They had had this kind of conversation before and it always ended with her frustrated and him defiant.

'No,' Anna said tiredly, 'I don't think that. I was only trying to help spring you from a trap if you felt you were in one.'

'I'm not in a trap,' he said, 'I'm just in a dark bit of the wood.'

'Sure?' she said for a second time.

'Oh, quite.'

He'd slept then. In the morning he looked hollow-eyed, but he'd gone off, with dogged cheerfulness, to take prayers at Snead Hall, a sad, second-rate little girls' public school, where he was Chaplain, and the rest of them had caught the bus. He had not, Anna tried not to remember, wished her luck.

Flora had to be detached from Anna physically as the bus approached her school. Luke had to pull off her hands, one by one, and half carry her along the bus and down the steps. When he got her on to the pavement, she sagged against the school wall and would not move. Luke shouted up to Anna that he would take Flora in, and then walk on to the sixth-form college. 'You're a hero,' she mouthed back. She felt sick, and tearful at Luke's good-

48

ness. He waved and grinned at her and jerked a thumb upwards. The bus pulled away from her children and headed for the market-place.

'Anna,' said Mr Mulgrove with an effort (he would so much have preferred to call her Mrs Bouverie), 'this is your supervisor.'

'Hi,' said the supervisor. He looked about sixteen. He had red hair and a bad complexion and huge ears. But he was smiling broadly. 'I'm Tim.'

'I'm Anna,' Anna said, anxious to do what was expected of her.

'We're on grocery,' Tim said, 'we're doing bottled sauces and mustards this morning.' He waved a batch of papers at her. 'Stock reports,' he said enticingly.

Rustling in her stiff new overall – Mr Mulgrove's administrative eye had rested in disappointment on the extra foot of Anna's grey corduroy skirt that hung below it – Anna followed Tim out of the warehouse and down a grim cold staircase on to the shop floor. It was like coming on stage in a theatre, out of the dark wings into warmth and light. Tim loped off down an alleyway lined with pet food, and halted before a tier of shelves of bottles, brown and red bottles, ochre and copper and olive-green.

'Got to do your facings,' Tim said.

Anna nodded.

'Know about facings?'

Anna thought about the needlework classes of her schooldays, in which she had been such a conspicuous non-success. Facings had been something of a nightmare then, a closed book of mysterious rites that led, finally, her teacher assured her, to the temple of tailoring.

'No,' Anna said with complete honesty to Tim, her supervisor, who was certainly young enough to be Tim, her son, 'I know absolutely nothing about facings.'

Tim looked delighted. He turned behind him to a metal trolley where neat regiments of jars and bottles waited breathlessly under their sealing plastic. Tim considered them, glanced back at his shelves, noticed a gap and pounced upon a rectangular block of tikka masala sauce.

'Now,' he said. His ears glowed with satisfaction. 'Check your stock sheet. Column one: number of items in case.' He held out the block; this was a game for Anna to play with him. She counted obediently.

'Twelve.'

'No need to look. Stock sheet tells you that. Second column: shelf allocation?'

Anna peered.

'Two?'

'Right. Twelve jars to go two abreast. And the front two,' Tim said with emphasis, 'must touch the shelf rim exactly – that's called presenting – and,' he paused, 'they must all face the front. That's called facing up. Now you put them on the shelves, and I'll check you.'

It was not, Anna reflected, unlike doing the church flowers, except that Tim was being so much nicer to her than Miss Dunstable or Freda Partington ever were. He stood three feet behind her with his adolescent arms folded inside his blue overall sleeves and said, 'That's right. You're getting there. Cheers,' at intervals.

When Anna stepped back, she said, 'I think I'll go straight home and face and present the larder.'

Tim did not understand. He said, wagging a forefinger, 'No coffee break till ten-thirty-five!'

At ten-thirty-five, a stout woman in a blue overall with plain, pale-blue collar and cuffs to denote her seniority came up with a clipboard and said, 'Tim and Anna. Ten minutes coffee.'

Anna said, 'I'll just finish the teriyaki sauces.' They had a pretty label with almond blossom and a blue cone of oriental mountain printed on them. Tim and the stout woman looked astonished.

'It's coffee break,' Tim said reprovingly.

He led Anna back up the gaunt staircase to the dining-room Mr Mulgrove had shown her when she came for interview. 'Two-course lunch with fruit juice, ninety-five pence,' Mr Mulgrove had said, and then, indicating a brightly coloured graph on a notice board, 'Our wastage display. We try and beat it every week.' He had looked very grave at the thought of all those rotting star fruit, those superannuated pies and fizzing yoghurts.

'Smoke?' Tim said.

Anna shook her head. She was surprisingly pleased to sit down.

'Getting engaged, Easter,' Tim said, lighting up and drawing deeply.

'Are you? How are you going to ask her? Have you planned it?'

'I didn't ask,' Tim said. 'Her mum said why didn' we get engaged Easter so we said yeah.' He pulled a photograph out of his shirt pocket inside the overall, and held it out to Anna. 'She works at Crompton's, on the industrial estate. Wages clerk.'

Anna looked at a plump little person with a determined mouth. She wore jeans and a black leather jacket.

'Will you be married in church?'

'She wants it.'

'Don't you?'

'Bit old-fashioned, i'n'it?' Tim said.

'You could excuse God for thinking He was perhaps beyond fashion – '

'Come again?'

'Sorry,' Anna said, 'thinking aloud.'

Tim looked at the clock.

'Time's up.'

Later, silently passing each other little stone jars of French mustard, Tim said, 'I never heard anyone say God 'cept for swearing. Seems a bit rude to say it otherwise.'

'God and death,' Anna said, marshalling jars, 'two of the rudest words in the world.'

This was going too far. Tim said loudly, to quell her, 'We run six'n a half thousand lines in Pricewell's. Six'n a half thousand.'

He left her only once, to go to the lavatory. He was gone perhaps for five minutes. During those five minutes, while she was reading the history of the poppadom from the back of a packet, a female voice said to her, in a strangled way, 'Mrs Bouverie?'

She looked up. There, poised and trim in a camel jacket (probably Jaeger) and a plaid skirt (undoubtedly The Scotch House), stood Mrs Richardson. Mrs Richardson, wife of Colonel Richardson (churchwarden, Diocesan Board of Finance, Red Cross, Council for the Preservation of Rural England) of Quindale House. From her suavely coiffed pearl-grey head to her excellent shoes polished to the gloss of a new conker, Mrs Richardson radiated amazement.

'Mrs Bouverie. Anna.'

'Heavens, Marjorie,' Anna said, 'I quite forgot about you.'

'Forgot?'

'Forgot that, occasionally, you shop in Pricewell's.'

Mrs Richardson looked round.

'Are you an *employee*?'

'Yes.'

'With your husband's consent?'

'Only reluctant, I'm afraid,' Anna said. Tim was coming loping down the aisle. 'Needs must where the devil drives, Marjorie. This is my supervisor, Tim. Tim, this is Mrs Richardson, from Quindale.'

'Pleased to meet you,' Tim said cheerfully. 'Anna's first day.'

Marjorie Richardson swung her trolley in a neat, brisk semi-circle.

'I shall telephone you,' she said to Anna.

Tim watched her walk away from them, upright and outraged.

'She a friend?'

Anna checked her stocklist for the shelf allocation for the poppadoms (plain, spiced, garlic and chilli, ready-cooked) with all the slick professionalism of three hours' experience.

'Not any more, I'm afraid.'

'Was it very dull?' Kitty Bouverie asked her daughter-in-law, on the telephone.

'Yes. But quite peacefully so. I am instructed by a boy who is getting married because his girlfriend's mother has told him to.'

Kitty Bouverie was not really listening. Since hearing of Anna's job, she had been fired with restiveness, pacing round her small green-and-magnolia sitting-room, peering yearningly out of its single window at the narrow terrace which was all of the outside world that she owned.

'How old,' Kitty said, 'were the oldest people working at Pricewell's?'

'I should think in their sixties.'

'I'm in my sixties!' Kitty cried.

Anna waited.

'There's a branch of Pricewell's here,' Kitty said. The flat seemed suddenly as small and confining as a birdcage. 'Was it difficult, what you did today?'

'Oh no. And you are helped.'

The word help seemed like a balm to Kitty. Nobody helped her beyond the poor sad girl at the library to whom she was kind and who now bounded about the romantic fiction section for her, feverishly pulling down titles she thought Kitty would like. Neither of them cared for the sexually explicit – 'Rather like having an operation described to one, don't you think?'

'Do you suppose,' Kitty said now, 'do you suppose that there is even any point in my going to the manager and asking?'

Anna thought not, and could not say so.

'I would so like it,' Kitty said wistfully. 'I would so like to be with people.'

'Isn't there something gentler?'

'I'm tired of gentleness,' Kitty said crossly. 'I feel like an old Marie biscuit that someone's left under the sofa.'

'Then go to Pricewell's,' Anna said, closing her eyes at the thought of telling Peter. 'Go and good luck to you.'

She had hardly replaced the receiver, when the telephone shrilled again.

'Anna?'

'Yes.'

'My dear, it's Harry Richardson here. From Quindale. I wonder if I could just pop over. Have a quick word?'

On the second day, Tim showed Anna the system in the warehouse. On the third, he explained how to use the computer for reordering. On the fourth day he was off sick, and Mr Mulgrove asked Anna if she thought she could manage, and to ask Heather on flours and dried fruits if she wasn't sure of anything. She said she would be fine. Indeed, to have a whole morning undisturbed by any thoughts profounder than wondering why on earth the people of Woodborough should consume so much tandoori curry

53

powder, while ignoring pesto sauce, was quite luxurious. But Colonel Richardson came between Anna and the tandoori curry powder; personable, kindly, inflexible Colonel Richardson, who had sat in her insufficiently tidy sitting-room in his beautiful old tweed jacket, and had said to her that she was harming her husband, the community and the Church. She had explained to him about Flora, thinking that his undoubtedly benevolent heart would be touched. It was. Harry Richardson appalled Anna by offering to lend her Flora's school fees, interest-free, for as long as she needed them.

'Be glad to,' he said.

Anna sat dumbstruck.

'Marjorie mistook you,' Colonel Richardson said. 'Didn't understand. Thought it was defiance. No idea about Flora. Too bad. Poor girl. Frightful places, these great state schools can be. Such a pity. Noble experiment, state education. Like the welfare state.'

Anna said slowly, 'You are so kind. But – but I don't think I can accept.'

'Nonsense. Who's to know? You, me, Peter and Marjorie. Look,' he said, leaning forward and putting a warm, capable hand on her knee, 'I know what your financial situation is. Better than anyone. No joke. Don't blame you for earning a bit. Plucky stuff. Admire you for it. But it's out of the question. Completely, utterly. Not to be thought of.'

'I want to do it,' Anna said.

Colonel Richardson took his hand away.

''Course you do. Natural for a mother. Quite right. But you're a rector's wife before you're a mother. Church before children. Setting an example, if you like.'

'Oh no,' Anna said.

He stared.

In the phrase of twenty years before, Anna said, 'I married the man, not the job. I'm not an outboard motor, I'm another boat.'

'Don't follow you.'

'I am truly grateful to you. You're a kind, dear man. But you are so used to an unquestioned independence that you forget how many people don't have it, people who, in human terms, Christian terms even, have just as much right to it as you do. The Church doesn't understand it either. Lambeth has no idea in the world what it's like for people like us. I'm Peter's wife, not an unpaid curate. And I am Flora's mother, which I rate very highly indeed. I would rather, please, find her school fees myself. It is good for all of us, in this beleaguered little rectory, if I do.'

She could see she had made Colonel Richardson very sad indeed. It was not his way to speak sharply – that was his wife's department – but he could not conceal the fact that he thought Anna was both wrong and behaving badly. Her remarks about independence were totally incomprehensible to him. What did she mean? Good God, if you marry a parson, you marry all that goes with it! Like marrying a soldier, as Marjorie had, seventeen moves in twenty-four years of active service and never a bellyache out of her. She knew the terms even before he'd turned to her, by the water jump at a point-to-point in 1949, and said, 'I suppose you'd never marry me, would you?' So Anna should have known, indeed she should. What was the use, Colonel Richardson asked himself, what was the use of being such a splendid rector's wife all these years, and then chucking the whole lot out of the window, for a pig-headed whim?

'I suppose,' he said to Marjorie later, pouring whisky for them both, 'it's all this women's lib nonsense. Whatever that may mean.'

'Too old for that.' Privately, Marjorie Richardson had decided in favour of the menopause as the culprit, but not for the world would she say such a thing to Harry. Her own menstrual cycle, including its uncomfortable drawing to a close, had been strictly her own affair. Some things – love, sex, God, bodily functions – were simply not for discussion.

Am I being defiant, Anna thought now, pushing her metal cage of bottles down the aisle towards her allotted shelves, am I simply cocking a snook at Peter? At the Church? Is it because I am consumed with envy when I pass the Woodborough bookshop, and there is Eleanor's newest novel in a special display, and with resentment because I haven't heard from Mary for over a year because she is so busy now, commuting to Brussels being a

Euro-lawyer? Is it because I am forty-two? Or is it because I am worn out by passivity, by having to accept and bear and endure, and because I am quite clever and resourceful, I have just turned, like the proverbial worm? If I'm a worm, I'm a fairly angry worm, but then I did not like my interview with Colonel Richardson, and I did not like it because he wasn't angry, he was hurt. I could have coped with his anger, using mine, but not his pain. Colonel Richardson's pain is only the first pain to make me feel dreadful (why, oh why, do women take to guilt like ducks to water?) and most people won't be as nice as he was. It's only the beginning, this arranging of soy sauce, it's only a start. I wonder, she said to herself with a sudden lurch of her heart, I wonder if I'm embarking on something I shall not be able to stop?

'You there?'

Anna turned. Heather from flours and dried fruits was standing in the gap between two aisles. She was a small, rat-faced girl with a frizz of dry brown hair and a crucifix round her neck. ('They said to me in the shop,' she'd said to Anna, 'they said did I want the one with a little man on or not. 'Course I did! The plain ones look ever so bare.')

'Yes, of course.'

'There's a gentleman looking for you. I thought you were in the warehouse. I'll send him round.'

'Thank you – '

A gentleman? Round the corner came a perfectly strange man, a stocky middle-aged man with wire-rimmed spectacles and a shock of greying brown hair. He wore a grey tweed jacket and, oh, damn, Anna thought, a dog collar. Here he comes, sent by the Bishop, at the Richardsons' instigation, via all those labyrinths of diocesan checking-up they call ministerial review, ho ho, here he comes, the official ticker-off. He smiled at Anna. He had a sweet face.

'Yes?' Anna said, unhelpfully. She held a raft of glass jars between them.

'Mrs Bouverie?'

'Yes.'

'I'm so glad,' he said, 'I'm so glad. I was told I'd find you here.'

He looked at her burden. 'Vegetable ghee. How extraordinary that such a thing should sell in Woodborough.' He glanced at her. 'Mrs Bouverie, I am Daniel Byrne. I am to be the new Archdeacon here.'

CHAPTER FIVE

D aniel Byrne drove Anna home. He was not, she noticed, a good driver, nor was he at all car-proud. The back seat was strewn with books and newspapers, and the floor was littered with car-park tickets. If Laura had ever owned a car, Anna reflected, this is how it would have looked inside, with the addition of old shoes and chocolate wrappers and squashed hats. Indeed, their own car would probably look like this if left to Anna; but Peter tidied it, because of all the parishioners he gave lifts to. 'Oo,' they'd say at the merest smear of mud, 'you had a pig in here?'

'I saw your husband,' Daniel Byrne said. 'I found him at Church End. He said I was to talk to you first. He said you had been harder hit than anyone.'

Anna said nothing.

'I see,' said Daniel Byrne.

'I'm sure you don't.'

'But I will,' he said equably, 'in time.'

Anna looked out of the car window. The ploughed field they were passing was speckled with brilliant-green shoots. Damn Peter. Damn him for dissembling; for pretending to Daniel that he wasn't wounded to the core at being passed over, pretending that it was only Anna who was suffering, as if it were she who could not bear the lack of advancement, of increased prosperity. She glanced sideways at Daniel's profile. It looked sturdy and peaceful and good-humoured. Had Peter implied, or worse even, said, that Anna had rushed impetuously to take a job in a supermarket because anything was better than the prospect of an unchanged status quo? Had he – no. She must stop. She must not work herself up into a terrible temper on supposition.

'What are you bursting with?' Daniel Byrne asked.

Anna was so startled by his perception and directness that she said, 'I was worrying that you had got the wrong impression, that you – ' She stopped, silenced by loyalty.

He changed gear at precisely the wrong moment and the car bucked and complained.

'I'm a mass of impressions,' he said, taking no notice and merely raising his voice a little to be heard above the unhappy engine. 'I came down from Manchester two days ago, to meet my fellow archdeacons, and the Bishop told me of your husband's application and of course that made me wish to meet him, and to meet you. I had no idea.'

'Why should you have? It's hardly your fault.'

'That isn't the problem.'

'No,' Anna said.

'Which is why I came to find you. Why I am driving you home. Why I asked your husband if we could all three meet for a little when I got you home.' He swerved without warning to avoid a peaceable bicycle and was hooted at violently by an approaching car. He threw Anna a smile. 'If, that is, I do get you home – '

She did not mean to, but she laughed.

The sitting-room at Loxford Rectory was a surprise to Daniel Byrne. It had been a surprise to Loxford for ten years, previously accustomed, as rural communities are, to modesty and neatness in the pastoral dwelling-house. It contained the Knole sofa on which St Agatha had reclined in West Kensington (too large for Laura's tiny flat), several lowering pieces of reproduction Jacobean furniture donated by Kitty ('Your father loved it but I can't bear it, it's so threatening'), hundreds of books on shelves made by Peter out of bricks and planks and the unmistakable overlying detritus of family life. Anna, making room for Daniel on the sofa, moved a pile of sheet music, several seed catalogues, a jersey of Luke's and Flora's latest piece of chain stitch in which a huge needle glittered.

'How very nice,' said Daniel, sitting down. He looked round him. 'How comfortable. Tidiness makes me nervous.'

'When Peter married me, I was tidy,' Anna said, recalling her cardigans with a sudden pang; those emblems of an imagined and ordered future. 'I seem to have slumped, as time's gone on.'

'Me too,' Daniel said. He leaned back among the battered brocade and velvet cushions that the sofa had always owned. 'I was a monk until I was thirty-five. One would think that monastic orderliness would be ingrained in one as deep as heart's blood, by thirty-five, but it did not seem so, with me. Perhaps,' he said, turning as Peter came in with a tray of tea, 'perhaps being a monk is bad training for the handling of possessions. Not having any for fifteen years means I find them quite arbitrary now, impossible to control. It's as if they have a life of their own.'

Peter put the tea tray down with difficulty on a table already strewn with books and papers.

'You were – ' he said. His voice was tight with suppressed curiosity.

'A Benedictine,' Daniel said. 'I decided, when I was thirty-five, that I was more use out than in. Fifteen years on, I couldn't be sure of that intellectually, but the instinct still says I'm right. We none of us listen to instinct enough.'

'Hear, hear,' Anna said. She poured tea. Passing Peter to take a cup to Daniel, she tried to catch his eye, to give him a little loving glance, but his expression was withdrawn, his eyes and thoughts elsewhere.

Daniel watched them both. He drank his tea. He noticed how they took chairs at some distance from one another and from him. He debated, within himself, whether to be oblique or direct with Peter, whose face seemed to him both shuttered and vulnerable. He would clearly hate to be patronised; he would smell patronage in any apology, in any request for help made out of desire to soothe sore feelings. Daniel glanced at Anna, upright on her ugly dark chair, her gaze bent on the carpet. They don't talk, Daniel thought. They can't. I smell no honesty here. He sighed. He said, 'May I call you Peter?'

Peter jumped, 'Of course – '

'We are brothers in this.'

Anna wanted to say, I don't think Peter is brother material. That's part of the trouble, part of why he is so lonely, but she just looked at the carpet in silence, at the dark place where Luke had once spilled black coffee.

'I have never been in rural ministry,' Daniel said. 'I suppose I could learn without you, but I would so much rather learn with you.'

'Of course,' Peter said again, politely, without warmth.

'One of the useful things you learn, as a monk,' Daniel said, putting his empty teacup on the floor by his feet, 'is how to gauge character and mood without speaking. I am under no illusion about how difficult my presence here is for you.'

'Robert Neville will be a great loss to me,' Peter said rapidly, mentioning the last archdeacon.

'And I might be a gain,' Daniel said, 'if you would let me.'

He glanced at Anna. Her head was now so bent that her dark hair had swung forwards so as to obscure her expression. Daniel felt that she was willing Peter to respond, to show himself bruised and in need of comforting, to expose his wound so that it might be healed.

'Of course,' Peter said, yet again.

Daniel levered himself out of the sofa and stood up. He took off his spectacles and polished them thoughtfully with a red snuff-handkerchief. He seemed to be weighing up what he should say next when Peter exclaimed, 'It's so hard on Anna. And the children. She works too hard in any case, so much parish work, so much – ' He stood up. 'You should see her vegetables.'

'I don't mind,' Anna cried, flinging her hair back from her face.

Peter said, 'Of course you do.'

She said, 'I don't mind hard work. All I mind, all I really mind is – ' She caught Peter's eye and stopped.

Daniel said, 'May I go and see your church?'

'Certainly. Let me show you.'

Daniel put his hand on Peter's arm.

'Thank you, but no. I will go alone, if I may.' He turned to Anna. 'Thank you for tea.'

She looked up at him. Her eyes were miserable. 'And you, for the lift.'

61

Later she said to Peter, 'I think he's a lovely man,' and the moment she had spoken, she knew it was a mistake.

Sister Ignatia led Flora down a clean, polished corridor. On one side, the corridor was walled, but on the other it was glass, and through it, Flora could see a very orderly garden with a pink blossomed tree in the middle, and a bird bath. The corridor smelled of polish and Sister Ignatia smelled of cloth and soap. She wore a short grey habit and behind her glasses, her eyes were as bright and dark as a robin's.

They had left Anna sitting in Sister Ignatia's study, looking at the school prospectus. Sister Ignatia had said that Flora couldn't know whether she wanted to come or not until she had had a sniff of the place, seen some of the other girls.

'Convent schools aren't what they were,' Sister Ignatia had said to Anna, 'nothing like so enclosed. I like to think our academic standard's gone up, and we know what's what in the world. It wouldn't be much use a modern nun not knowing where to kick a troublesome man, now, would it?'

She led Flora by the hand. She said, 'And why aren't you getting on where you are?'

'I'm different,' Flora said. 'I don't know why, I just am.'

Like your mother, Sister Ignatia thought. She opened a cream-painted door and the smell of school lunch rushed out at them.

'Nobody'll be concentrating,' Sister Ignatia said. 'They never do, after twelve strikes, all thinking of their tummies. Now, in we go and you'll see the third form.'

She knocked on a second door and opened it to reveal twenty children of about Flora's age at old-fashioned desks with inkwells sunk into the top right-hand corners of the lids. There was a youngish nun by the blackboard, drawing a map of the River Nile. Everybody stood up.

'Good afternoon,' Sister Ignatia said, 'good afternoon, Sister Josephine. This is Flora, girls, this is Flora who may be coming to join us.'

Flora looked down. Twenty pairs of eyes stared at Flora. Sister

Josephine did, too, and so did Christ, sadly, from his crucifix above the teacher's desk.

'I know her,' someone said.

The eyes all swung to the speaker.

'Her father's a vicar,' the someone said. She was small and plump and her hair was tied in bunches like spaniel's ears. 'Her father's the Rector in our church.'

Flora raised her head. It was Emma Maxwell, from Snead. Flora waited, her heart like lead in her chest, for the inevitable reaction to her shameful and laughable parentage.

'Well now,' said Sister Ignatia, 'isn't Flora the lucky one?'

Emma Maxwell thought that actually Flora's luck lay more in having an older brother. She resolved to tell the others, over lunch, about Luke Bouverie, whose brooding adolescent glamour gave his parents a certain status in the eyes of the parish's girls.

Sister Josephine smiled at Flora. 'She is, indeed,' said Sister Josephine, with warmth.

'We'll leave you now,' Sister Ignatia said. 'We've the art room to see, and the music school. What about a kind goodbye to Flora?'

Amid an obedient chorus, Flora followed Sister Ignatia with a bursting heart.

'I don't think you'll feel so different here,' Sister Ignatia said. 'We're all different in ourselves, but we're all the same family. Now, who's family could that be?'

Back in the study, Flora turned a beseeching face upon Anna. Anna had no need to be besought, for she had done a quick sum on the back of her child benefit book, and had worked out that, if Flora could start at St Saviour's in the summer term, she would have earned enough to put down at least £100 towards the first term's fees. While she waited, she had rehearsed what she considered a dignified little speech for Sister Ignatia, explaining that, for this first term, it would not be possible for her to pay the fees in advance, as was customary, but that she would . . .

'If it helps to make up your mind,' Sister Ignatia said, 'I've four places a year to offer without fees. At my discretion. There are only two such girls in the present third year. I'd be happy to suggest such a place for Flora.'

Anna said, quite thrown, 'Oh, but you see, I can pay, and being Protestant – '

'Please,' Flora screeched, not comprehending Sister Ignatia's offer but terrified that Anna would somehow bungle her chance, 'please!'

'It's at my discretion,' Sister Ignatia said.

'How kind, how nice of you – '

'Talk it over with Flora's father. Talk it over. Then telephone me. I shall reserve a place for Flora from the end of April.'

Flora, heavy with adoration and gratitude, but uncertain of the etiquette involved in hugging nuns, stood and yearned towards Sister Ignatia.

'I will telephone,' Anna said. 'I am so grateful.'

Sister Ignatia put her hand on Flora's head.

'God bless you.'

Flora closed her eyes in ecstasy. Clearly quite a different and much more glamorous God than the Loxford one lived at St Saviour's.

Later, while sitting at the kitchen table making a special list of people to help with Easter flowers, and a subsidiary list of those who might be approached to donate Easter lilies, Anna and her conscience had a little tussle. Anna's conscience said that she must report the whole of her interview at St Saviour's faithfully to Peter, and then they could rejoice together that prayers had been answered, and that Pricewell's could be abandoned. But Anna found herself wholly disinclined to listen to her conscience. She discovered that she had no intention of making Sister Ignatia's offer plain to Peter, and no intention of giving up Pricewell's. Pricewell's, whatever its reality, represented the best taste of independence that Anna could remember since those far-off days in Oxford when Peter was a theology student. Twenty years was a long time to bear dependence if your spirit craved something stronger and your intelligence rebelled at continual submission to powers who neither, Anna felt, knew or cared how she and Peter lived. Pricewell's gave Anna that inch or two of dignity she had felt so sorely in need of and that she now felt she could never again surrender. What Eleanor and Mary took for granted in their lives Anna was just creeping towards, as a novice. If, she said to herself, writing Marjorie Richardson and Lady Mayhew and Miss Dunstable down for Easter lilies, if I do everything in the parish that I should do, and I keep the garden going and the meals and the house (sort of) and the translation, then where can be the harm in doing this other undeniably humble little thing that so curiously makes me feel strong and alive? And if I promise myself that, once Peter has calmed down, I will tell him of Flora's free place, where can be the danger of a little, temporary deception? She waited. Her conscience said nothing, it felt as if it were holding its breath. It was, of course, poor thing, out of practice at making decisions of the kind she had just put to it; it had, Anna considered, been given an easy ride for twenty years. She put her hands over her ears. 'That's settled then,' Anna said loudly, to whoever was listening.

Peter sat in Celia's Hooper's sitting-room in Quindale. Her house was a new one, built of bright reconstituted stone, and her sitting-room was full of blue Dralon armchairs, and occasional tables, each bearing a single china ornament, mostly whimsical animals. Celia Hooper's husband was a bank manager in Woodborough, and it was he who tended so ferociously the disciplined garden beyond the patio doors. Celia, who had trained as a physical education instructor, now ran the Loxford parish Guides, a swimming group for the disabled, and was Peter's Deanery Secretary. She was formidably efficient. Her minutes were works of precise art. She believed – and frequently declared – that the rural deaneries were the grassroots of the Church of England.

Peter sat in one of the blue chairs. At his elbow, a little table bore a cup of coffee and a piece of shortbread on a plate that matched the coffee cup. Celia Hooper – seated opposite him in just such a chair and situation, so that they resembled two bookends without intervening books – was suggesting that she should draw up a basic plan for the annual deanery party, which happened at Loxford Rectory after Easter, a get-together for all the priests of the deanery, eight of them, and their wives.

'If I do the planning, you see,' Celia said, turning to a clean page in her notebook, 'that will spare Anna.' Mindful of the proprieties, Celia was not going to mention Pricewell's.

Peter said quickly, 'Anna won't mind. She's so used to it – '

'I thought perhaps this year, if I just rustle up a few quiches, buy some French bread – '

'Very kind of you, Celia, but really I think Anna would like to do it.'

'She has so much on her plate. We all know that.'

'No more than usual,' Peter said loudly.

Celia looked at him. Her face was full of sympathy.

'I have no one to talk to,' Peter said suddenly, without meaning to.

'I don't think,' Celia said softly, 'I don't think you ought to assume that the laity doesn't notice. Or understand.'

He looked at her, at her neat, gleaming brown bob, at her clear outdoor skin and eyes, her new-looking, well-kept clothes. He said, 'Do you know, I sometimes think that the laity are the only people who do understand.'

Celia began to write in her notebook.

'Quiche, then. Several varieties. And some nice mixed salads. Mustn't forget, must we, that John Jacobs is a vegetarian – '

'Please,' Peter said protestingly, thinking of Anna.

'That's all right,' Celia said, thinking of her too, but differently, 'I'll ring Anna. Don't you worry.' She gave him a little glance of understanding. 'You've got enough to worry about. You leave what you can to me.'

On the way home, filled with an indigestible mixture of relief and regret, Peter observed that there were removal vans once again outside Loxford Old Rectory. The new owner – a man on his own, gossip said, a wealthy man – was plainly moving in. He would of course require a pastoral call even if he did not – and his car did not bode well – look like the kind of man Peter might hope for, as a breath of fresh air on the PCC; as a possible church-warden in place of old Sir Francis Mayhew who said he'd done fifteen years which was more than enough; or even as a par-ishioner willing to raise the £25,000 that the diocesan architect had said would have to be spent on Loxford church roof within the next three years. Peter drove slowly past the gates – the dignified gates through which most of his predecessors had stepped on their way to the church – and, as he did so, the new owner came out of the front door and clearly observed the dawdling and curious car.

Peter pulled up. He got out of the car and crossed the deep, luxurious gravel of the Loxford Old Rectory drive. He felt faintly foolish. The man on the steps was middle-aged and authoritative-looking, and wore well-pressed jeans and a brass-buttoned blazer. Peter said, 'This isn't really a visit. It's plainly no time for that. I was just passing – '

'Patrick O'Sullivan,' the man said, holding out his hand. He smiled.

'Peter Bouverie.'

'I've seen your wife.'

'Oh?'

'I'd ask you in – '

'No, no,' Peter said, 'not now. Just passing.'

'Lovely place, this,' Patrick O'Sullivan said.

'I hope you will be very happy here.'

'So do I.'

Peter backed away a little. Two removal men came past him carrying a huge painting shrouded in a blanket. 'Goodbye,' Peter said, 'and welcome. I mean, welcome to Loxford.'

Patrick O'Sullivan put his hands in his blazer pockets. He was still smiling.

'Thanks,' he said.

Peter got back into his car and started the engine. That had not been, on reflection, a successful impulse, nor a socially accomplished two minutes. He thought of his mother-in-law. 'What,' Laura had said, on her first visit to Loxford, 'what! Put you in that – that *kiosk* – and expect your parishioners to admire your humility? Why are you not where you should be? How can you retain any kind of status in that council house? I promise you, the village won't think you're one of them because you aren't in the proper rectory. They'll simply think you haven't any clout.'

Patrick O'Sullivan, standing easily on the steps of Loxford Old

Rectory, had looked to Peter a man on first-name terms with clout.

Patrick O'Sullivan went back into his house faintly amused. He was not conscious of having had any contact with a clergyman since school, where religion had been regarded as an unavoidable mixed dose of discipline, cissiness and mild buffoonery. In his address, the bishop who had confirmed Patrick and his year had urged compassion in sexual matters upon them, which had decided them all finally that the Church was a refuge for old women, and that Christianity was somehow neutering in its effect. When he left school, he forgot entirely about the whole business, forgot about it for a couple of decades, forgot until this thin, tired fellow, looking so very much like his old school chaplain, came and hovered in the drive, the epitome, it seemed to Patrick, of the doubting kind of modern Anglican clergyman.

He went into the kitchen where his housekeeper was filling cupboards with pans. 'I met the Rector!'

Ella Pringle, who was heavy with misgiving about the move from London, merely grunted. A rector was, in her view, part of the traditional and comic cast list she had expected to find in the country, along with the squire and the village idiot.

'Looks just as I expected,' Patrick said, plugging in the kettle. He sounded pleased. 'Shall I go to church?'

'You wouldn't know how to behave in church,' Ella said from inside her cupboard.

'I could learn.'

She came out abruptly. 'Learn? Whatever for?'

He was looking out of the window at his lovely new garden, at the exquisite magnolia just breaking into its goblet-like, glowing blooms which were, since Monday, also his. He had never owned a magnolia before nor a view. He said, 'Because my life is going to be different here. It is why I have come.'

Ella thought it was a fad, a passing and Toad-like enthusiasm for something novel. She had been Patrick's housekeeper for fourteen years, through his brief and disastrous marriage, through his long and complicated liaison with a woman who had left a year ago, telling Ella that there was no point in waiting any longer for Patrick to marry her. He never would, she said, because he didn't need to. He only ever did things he needed to do, and someone as economical with their emotions as that was not good lifetime material. Ella liked having Patrick to herself. She treated him as if she were his prep-school matron. When he said he was moving to Loxford to start another life before it was too late, she thought of abandoning him but she did not think it for long. He was, in any case, very persuasive. He needed Ella. He now said, 'Where's the tea?'

'Honestly,' she said, 'honestly. We move in seven hours ago and you expect everything to be in order.' She got up from her knees and made shooing gestures. 'Get out. Go into your garden. Come back in ten minutes, and there'll be tea.'

He went out through the glazed garden door at the back of the hall. There was a terrace outside, with a low balustrade and several graceful lead urns filled with early blue pansies – they don't look right, he thought. Wonder why – and then a great green carpet of lawn, and shrubs and trees, and, way beyond them, the far hills. He stood and breathed a bit, in and out, deeply. Then he went across his terrace and down on to his damp spring lawn.

It was a majestic lawn. It rolled away from the house for a couple of hundred yards, its length deceptively magnified by little outcrops of planting here and there which hid its true limits. To the right, as he walked down it, he could see nothing but the trees of his own orchard and, beyond them, the decorative ridge of a thatched roof, crowned with a squat brick chimney. To the left, he could only at first see his own garden, his tennis court, the old wall that screened his vegetables – to eat what one has grown, actually to eat that! – but then, across a low hedge and a fence that needed repair, he found he could see into the garden of the new Rectory, whose impersonal little back windows faced the same way as his own. He could see grass, and a long dug strip – vegetables, too? – and a few fruit trees. He could also see a line of washing, which included, he realised to his delight, the clerical undergarments. He must be the only person in the village with a view, if he chose to take it, of both vest and surplice. While he looked the back door opened, and a woman came out, calling over her shoulder to someone in the house, as she came. She wore a swirling dress with something bright wrapped round the waist, and she carried a laundry basket. Patrick leaned in satisfaction on a fence post. The Rector's wife.

He watched her. She went over to the vegetable patch and looked at the earth for a while. Then she carried the basket to the washing line and unpegged the clothes rapidly, chucking them down in a windblown tangle (Ella folded things as she took them out of the tumble drier. He would have to train her to a line. In his orchard? He thought of his Jermyn Street shirts blowing in the orchard, with pleasure) and then, for a second or two, she stood quite still, looking down, the back of her hand to her forehead under her dark fringe. When she stooped and retrieved her basket, and went rapidly back to the house with it, Patrick wished he had said something, that he had called out to her.

He went back to the kitchen.

'Now I've seen the Rector's wife. Again, actually.'

'Thrills and spills,' Ella said, pouring tea into a mug for him. 'Now see if you can find the gravedigger. Good game, this. Might even keep you quiet for an hour or two.'

Patrick took his tea and went up to the first floor, to the long landing window which looked over the village green. Smoke rose from several chimneys, straight blue columns in the still air, signs of habitation. All those cottages had people in them, Patrick realised, people and televisions and plates of fried fish and dogs and Wellington boots at the back door. He swallowed some tea. He was charmed by his thoughts, charmed by the look of his new village, like a doll's house with the front enticingly shut. And there, if he looked hard to the right, was the tower of the church, like a benevolent old watchdog, keeping an eye on things, protective, changeless. He looked down at his clothes, on an impulse. They looked wrong, suddenly, too blue, too urban. He must buy some corduroys.

CHAPTER SIX

I sobel Thompson had been a missionary in West Africa for seventeen years before she became a deacon. She had loved it. She had loved the sense of purpose and the freedom and most of the Africans, and she had always supposed that she would stay there all her life, and finally die there, and be buried, like David Livingstone's wife, under a baobab tree. She prayed steadily, all those seventeen years, for guidance, for confirmation that she was still fulfilling divine purpose, and was only interrupted at last by her mother's voice, demanding in a querulous letter that Isobel should come home and nurse her while she died – as she had been told she soon would – of cancer.

She took five years to do it, five years of remissions and declines and suffering borne with no patience whatever. She was furious with Isobel for preferring God to any man, and thus denying her the status of grandparenthood, and furious with her husband for dying before her. She lay in her carefully, fustily feminine bedroom in her little house in Woodborough, and tormented Isobel. Nothing was right, from her physical misfortune through Isobel's appearance to the strength of her early-morning tea. Isobel began to feel that her life had been the wrong way round, that Africa had been no training at all, with its comparatively easy, impersonal requirement of Christian love, for these savagely difficult demands for daughterly love. Praying was ten times as hard as it had ever been in Africa, so was steering clear of hatred, a problem

Isobel had never encountered before. She told herself that she must confine herself to anger only, but it was easier said than done. Standing at last in Woodborough parish church – dedicated to St Paul – watching her mother's coffin being lowered on to trestles below the chancel steps, Isobel was so riven with thankfulness she could hardly keep upright. Her dedication would now be complete, an offering made from a full heart and an intimate knowledge of mental pain. There was to be no more Africa, however much it beckoned. Isobel would enter the Church as a deacon, would tackle the domestic problems of Woodborough. If she had failed to love her mother, she the missionary, what must it be like for people who, without God, had not even got a Christian obligation to try?

Sometimes, in the years that followed, she longed for Africa, like a lost love affair. Yet she also knew that if she had succumbed to her longing she would not have been satisfied, knowing what she now knew of the terrible difficulties of love. She also came to see that, as a woman, she understood the psychology of this difficulty of human love better than most of her male colleagues who were often, she considered, almost callous in their disinclination to feel the emotional agonies in which some people laboured, shackled to delinquent children or senile parents or destructive marriages. You could not just say, Christ will help you bear it. That was opting out. You had to show that you understood the suffering, knew the price it exacted, as a fellow human being, before you even thought of bringing Christ into it.

It was such a discussion that had first brought Isobel and Anna together. The last Archdeacon of Woodborough, a genial and easy man, had invited all the priests of his eight deaneries to a fork supper, laid on with great relish by his wife, a woman whose every fibre rejoiced at being a clergy wife. In the Victorian Woodborough Vicarage, the priests and their wives milled through the ground-floor rooms with plates of cold chicken and ham, and glasses of encouraging German wine. The atmosphere was of an end-of-term party given by a headmaster in his study for the prefects. Anna and Isobel, finding themselves together in front of a bright watercolour of a Cornish harbour painted by Archdeacon Neville on one of his walking holidays, fell into conversation.

It was an easy conversation from the beginning. After a while, they left the watercolour ('Not a very adventurous subject,' Isobel said) and found two chairs in a corner. Isobel, who had told nobody about her mother, found herself telling Anna. From there, they progressed to the enthralling problem of human and divine love. Isobel said that, personally, she found the latter much easier, but that she felt that the former was, in every sense, her job.

Anna said, looking round the crowded room whose noise-level had risen considerably with alcohol-released confidence, 'Do you think most of the men here feel like that?'

'I do. And what is more, I think most of them give in. How much easier and publicly commendable it is to devote yourself to the parish, however demanding, than to a wife having a nervous breakdown at home.'

'Oh Isobel,' Anna said. They looked at each other. 'You don't even need to be having a nervous breakdown to become a burden to a priest husband, you know. You simply need to ask to be visible, to be seen as a human being, not an unpaid curate. That's all the amount of nuisance you have to be to drive a man into the arms of his parish.'

Isobel said, 'Are you speaking personally?'

Anna felt herself colouring. She had gone too far. 'Some husbands,' she said, pulling herself together, finishing her wine, 'get very disheartened. There are so many demands, so little help. Were you lonely as a missionary?'

'Oh no,' Isobel said. 'Never. I felt like the nineteenth-century missionary, Annie Besant, who wrote in her diary on Christmas Day, in a blizzard on a Tibetan mountain surrounded by absolutely untrustworthy tribesmen, "Quite safe here with Jesus." Africa was wonderful. It was in every way so much easier than here, but then the love required was simpler, more childlike. It was, looking back, a kind of holiday at times.'

Anna stood up. 'Come and see me,' she said, 'any time. Just come. I could do with a friend.'

Isobel smiled up at her. 'So could I.'

It was not a friendship Peter understood. He liked Isobel well enough but she seemed to him to bring, as did most of the other women deacons in the diocese, a fussy, housekeeping approach to Christianity, a domestic preoccupation with women and children and primary schools, that irked him. She did not, in his view, understand ritual and language, she did not speculate about theology, she used her heart too much without her head. He could not see why Anna did not find her dull. But he could not complain of the unsuitability of the friendship between his wife and Isobel, and at times it was extremely useful. Isobel could be, occasionally, a channel to communicate through, with Anna. It was obvious now that Isobel should be the person to talk to Anna about this job in Pricewell's.

Isobel objected at first. 'It seems harmless enough to me.'

'In itself, of course it is,' Peter said. They were in the sitting-room of Isobel's little house, the house she had inherited from her mother. It looked across the street at one of Woodborough's dental practices, so that people passed the windows all day in various stages of apprehension and relief. 'The job itself is innocent. It's the motive, and the effect.'

'Ah,' said Isobel.

'Anna was terribly shaken by Daniel Byrne's appointment. She couldn't bear to feel helpless, to be passive. But there is nothing I can do, we can do. She has relieved her most understandable feelings by taking this job.'

'Do you think she is defying you?'

'Yes,' said Peter.

'Oh dear.'

'And possibly the parish, too.'

'I don't mind so much about them.'

'They mind,' Peter said. 'I can't go anywhere without falling over references to it. I've even had a letter from Lady Mayhew who before she realised who it was, found herself asking Anna for the whereabouts of Dijon mustard.'

Isobel said, 'Bother Lady Mayhew.'

'She is my parishioner. I have to live in such a community. You may think Loxford light years behind Woodborough, but it is my patch, where I live and work, however anachronistic. I've just got all the apples into the cart, and it looks as if Anna has upset the lot.'

'Why have you come to me? Why don't you go to our nice new archdeacon?'

'I don't know him. He doesn't know Anna. He doesn't know this area. He said he knows nothing of rural ministry.'

'Typical,' Isobel said. 'All right. I'll try.'

In the Loxford Rectory garden Anna was in tears. In front of her, close to tears also, stood Luke with his chin thrust out mulishly. She had taken him out into the garden to show him various easy spring tasks that must be done, and for which she would pay him, and he had refused. He didn't want to garden and he didn't want her money. Anna, exhausted by all she was trying to do, plummeted from fury to weeping.

'Don't you understand, you stupid child!' she screamed at Luke. 'Can't you see? I'm earning to pay you to help me! To save your blasted dignity since you think a supermarket beneath you!'

Luke muttered, 'I don't think that.'

'What then? What do you think?'

Luke shuffled. He put his hands in his jeans pockets and hunched his shoulders.

'You're making Dad look a fool. And me. And Flora. You're making us look pathetic.'

Anna said tiredly, sniffing, 'We are pathetic.'

'Well, you don't have to broadcast it,' Luke said, gaining courage from her ceasing to shout. 'You don't have to advertise it, do you? Other vicars' families manage, don't they?'

'We aren't other families. We are us.'

Luke said in relief, 'Here's Isobel.'

Anna looked up. There was Isobel, coming up the path in her fawn mackintosh. She waved.

Isobel waved back, all smiles, then saw their faces and said, 'Oh dear. I thought I heard shouting.'

'You did.'

'Will you tell me why?'

'Luke will,' Anna said unfairly, turning away and looking at her beautifully dug earth, and thinking how much she would just like to lie down on it and sleep.

Isobel looked at Luke. He wore an expression of the deepest misery. 'No,' Isobel said, 'you will. And Luke can correct you if he needs to.'

There was a silence. Then Luke said, 'I do want to help. Just not this way.'

Anna put a hand out to him. He took it awkwardly. She said, 'I'm so sick of being limited, tyrannised. Whenever I turn to try and get out of the cage, someone is offended or upset, says I'm defying them or humiliating them. I have a space to occupy on this earth, you know, I have a space with just as much validity to it as yours or Dad's or – or the Archbishop of Canterbury's. But I don't hedge you about with my objections or complaints, do I? I don't criticise you for enterprise or initiative. Do I? Do I?'

Tears slid down Luke's face. He said with difficulty, 'But you've still got the power – '

Anna dropped his hand. 'How mistaken you are.'

Luke turned and fled. Isobel came over to Anna and said, 'I suppose this is all about Pricewell's.'

'Of course.'

'Peter came to see me.'

Anna fumbled about in her pockets for a handkerchief.

'So this is a little pastoral call to dissuade me.'

'If it's defiance, yes.'

Anna's eyes, visible over the top of her handkerchief, were enormous. 'Defiance?'

Isobel said steadily, 'If you are aiming somehow to shame the Church establishment for what you see as its treatment of clergy families, and you imagine that this might be achieved by humiliating Peter, then yes, defiance.'

Anna blew her nose ferociously.

'Go away.'

'So I am somewhere near the truth?'

'Isobel,' Anna said. Her voice was not at all steady. 'Isobel, would you please stop being a deacon and be a human being for a moment? If I don't do something, take some action, in our present situation, then I shall not have one atom of strength left to support Peter. I want to support him, I am doing so, even if he refuses to acknowledge that just now because it's easier for him to bear what

76

has happened if he pretends it is me who is more broken than he. But I can't just play the pawn any more. I can't just bear and endure. And don't,' she said with sudden vehemence, 'don't tell me that suffering is part of the Almighty package.'

'But marriage – '

'What would you know about marriage?'

Isobel turned and began to walk back towards the house. Anna watched her, tense with the impulse to run after her, say sorry, throw her arms round her, make up, be friends again. Isobel did not turn. Anna did not move. Isobel vanished round the house and after a while Anna heard the engine of her little car start up and putter away down the drive.

Ella Pringle only let Luke into the Old Rectory because he said he was the Rector's son. He had knocked on the back door while she was kneading the first batch of bread dough she had ever made in her life – something to do, she thought crossly, with coming to the country – and she had gone to answer him with floury hands and a frown. He said could he speak to Mr O'Sullivan and she said no. He said please, he was Luke Bouverie, he was the Rector's son, and Ella, uncertain of village etiquette, acted out of character on the safe side, and allowed him in. She left him in the kitchen examining the espresso coffee machine with wonder, while she went to Patrick's office.

Patrick had made it a rule that he was never to be disturbed in the mornings, but that she might bring him urgent interruptions in the afternoon. Ella was doubtful of Luke's urgency. She knocked and opened the door and saw Patrick asleep in his wing chair. Ella considered daytime sleeping decadent. She said loudly, 'You have a visitor.'

He woke calmly. 'I do?'

'The Rector's son. Shall I send him in?'

'Of course!'

A minute later, Luke said diffidently, 'In here?' His face came round the door.

'The Rector's *big* son, I see. I thought you might be conker-age.'

77

Luke came in and looked round him. 'Wow.'

'How to run a business at arm's length.'

'We do computer courses at school – '

'Would you like tea?' Patrick said. The boy's face looked faintly smeared, as if he had been crying. But of course, boys that size did not cry.

'Oh,' Luke said, his face lighting up. 'Yeah. I mean, please – '

Patrick went out to the kitchen.

'A vast tea,' he said to Ella. 'Everything you can think of. Bunter-style.'

She looked pointedly at the front curve of his new olive-green Shetland jersey.

'For my guest,' Patrick said.

'I see.'

Back in the office, Luke was standing in an attitude of longing in front of Patrick's computer.

'Suppose you tell me why you've come, and then we'll enjoy ourselves.'

Luke said, going scarlet and looking out of the window, 'I wondered if, I mean, do you need, I mean, would you have any job you could give me? Anything, I mean, I don't mind what, logs, digging, you know – '

'A job.'

Luke nodded.

'What,' said Patrick, 'is the basic industrial wage?'

Luke swallowed. 'If you're over eighteen, two seventy-five an hour.'

'And you?'

'Seventeen,' Luke said.

Patrick, who was enjoying himself, eyed his visitor. 'And what experience have you?'

'I help Mum and stuff – '

'Yes.'

'Garden, firewood – '

There was a pause. Luke spent it wishing he had never come, dreading tea, dreading having to say he didn't mind, that it was quite OK, he quite saw, shouldn't have asked . . .

'All right,' Patrick said. 'I'll pay you two fifty an hour for as many hours as you can put in these holidays. Does your mother know you are here?'

Luke gaped.

'I see. Then should we ask her? When we have had tea, I think we should go home together and ask her. Don't you?'

Luke said, 'She won't mind – '

'But I might. I'm a newcomer here. Don't know the rules, don't want to tread on any toes. Now, while we wait for tea how would you like to send a fax to New York?'

'It's four afternoons a week,' Kitty Bouverie said down the telephone to Anna. 'Four, and sometimes five if the owner's busy.'

She sounded full of triumph. She had combed the shops of Windsor looking for work, and at last had found some.

'I suppose it's a gift shop really. Birthday cards and little ashtrays with pictures of the castle on them and necklaces and keyrings. That sort of thing.'

'Kitty. You're so clever!'

'I know,' Kitty said, 'but I'd never have thought of it without you, it just wouldn't have crossed my mind. The owner's so nice, another widow. She has a Pekinese. She wants to open a coffee shop next door. If she does, I could make cakes for it, couldn't I, and jam – '

'What about the adding up?'

'I have a calculator,' Kitty said proudly, 'made in Japan.'

'Oh Kitty, I think it's wonderful. I'd get Peter, so you could tell him, but he's out – '

'There's no point telling him, is there? He'll only sniff. No, it was you I wanted to tell. How's Flora?'

'On the verge of seventh heaven. St Saviour's next term. She's practising for Catholicism. Draws pictures of the Virgin Mary and writes, "Our Lady" underneath – ' Anna broke off. Through the window, she could see Luke coming up the drive accompanied by a strange man to whom he seemed to be talking animatedly. She said, 'Kitty, I think I have to go. Luke seems to be bringing a visitor. I'm so pleased for you. And admiring. I'll ring you in a day or two.'

'I'm admiring too,' Kitty said. 'I'm so pleased with myself, you can't think.'

The back door opened, and Luke ushered in his companion.

'Mum, this is Mr O'Sullivan – '

Anna held out her hand.

'Anna Bouverie.'

'Yes. I know.'

'Welcome to Loxford.'

'Thank you.'

Anna said, 'Come through. Come into the sitting-room. Luke, put the kettle on.'

'No. No thank you. We are groaning with tea. Aren't we, Luke?'

Luke looked tremendously happy. 'It was brilliant.'

Anna looked at them both.

'I don't understand – '

'We have just had tea together,' Patrick said. 'Luke came to me looking for work, and we sealed the bargain with egg sandwiches. Now we have come to ask if that's all right.'

Anna said, startled, 'Yes, of course, what kind of work?'

'Gardening, logs, that kind of thing.'

Anna looked at Luke. 'Gardening?' He blushed.

'Is he no good?'

'Oh, I think he's perfectly good. His goodness seems to depend upon who asks him.'

Luke said hurriedly, 'I'll go and see to the sitting-room fire.'

When he had gone, Patrick said, 'Is this all out of order?'

'Not at all. It's very kind of you.'

'I felt I should come and ask you – '

'Thank you.'

' – but what I really wanted to ask you,' said Patrick O'Sullivan, putting his hands in his jacket pockets, 'is what is a woman like you doing in a place like this?'

And then Luke came in and said the fire was fine and that he'd bashed the cushions up a bit, to make it all OK for them.

★

80

Woodborough Vicarage was the largest space Daniel Byrne had ever occupied. In Manchester, he had shared a simple, newish little house with a succession of curates, and he rather thought, pacing his new Victorian Gothic halls, that he would like a whole army of curates with him now. The last three archdeacons had had sizeable families so that the Vicarage, though impractical to run, had at least been filled. Yet even though Daniel had spread himself as far as he could, including making himself a primitive chapel out of an east-facing bedroom, there was still a good deal of vicarage left over.

The diocese had found him a housekeeper, a Miss Lambe, who was as small and anxious as a hamster, and who had taken a tiny, remote bedroom as her burrow, and already filled it with crocheted mats and pictures of the Royal Family. Daniel had explained to her that he liked very simple food that he could eat with one hand, because of his inability to eat without reading, and so, for supper his first night, she had brought him scrambled egg on a piece of toast that she had already cut up into precise and helpful squares. He thought, eating it, that he must be careful not to be too metaphorical in his instructions, since, in her anxiety to obey him to the letter, she might feed him a diet of unrelieved soup and rice pudding.

Miss Lambe helped him to unpack his books, holding each one with as much reverence as if it had been the Sacrament. It took for ever. In the middle, she went away to make tea, and brought it back with digestive biscuits she had broken into quarters.

'You will have to get used to my peculiar sense of humour,' Daniel said.

Miss Lambe blinked at him. 'I quite like a joke,' she said bravely.

He pinned a huge map of the diocese on his study wall, and then outlined his own archdeaconry in red. Eight deaneries lay within it, of which only one – Woodborough itself – had any kind of urban character. The rest were a maze of villages with names that sounded like the refrain for a pantomime song, villages whose lives were as far removed from those Manchester lives he had known for so long that it was as if they inhabited another planet. He had wanted this change, not least because he felt that the rural

Church was being neglected, that progressive Church thinking was forgetting to take into account that huge section of the population whose rhythms were dictated by quite other influences than urban ones. He had also felt that, contrary to popular supposition, a dangerous loneliness might afflict priests living and working in rural places, however lovely. Looking at his map, and thinking of such men – men who were much less resilient than those to whom a more evangelical and dogmatic faith appealed – Daniel Byrne thought of Peter Bouverie. No doubt, it was for such men as Peter Bouverie that he felt he had been called to come south.

Peter himself, robing in the vestry at Quindale for the last of the special Lent evening services – theme: 'Can there be change without sacrifice in a Christian world?' – was not thinking of Daniel Byrne. He was thinking instead of the twenty minutes he had spent at home between a difficult hour persuading the voluntary organist at New End (a retired primary-school headmistress who felt she was being taken for granted) to continue, at least temporarily, and this service of compline at Quindale. In those twenty minutes, Luke had told him that he had found part-time employment at the Old Rectory, Anna had told him that his mother had found employment at a Windsor gift shop, and his mother-in-law, Laura, had telephoned to say she had landed three lines in a television commercial for an Irish stout, dressed as a pearly queen.

Peter had heard all this, sitting at the kitchen table with a cup of tea, and a sandwich made for him by Anna to sustain him to the far side of compline. While he ate and listened, the telephone rang three times on minor parish business and Flora badgered him to read a pious poem she had just written which began:

> I love Jesus,
> He's my baby brother
> I love Mary
> She's my Holy Mother.

('Yuk,' said Luke with vehemence, 'and you aren't even at St Saviour's yet.')

Peter noticed that Luke and Flora both looked extremely happy, and that Anna looked desperately tired. She had said that Isobel had been to see her, and that she, Anna, had been horrible to her. Peter said nothing. He said nothing for almost the whole of the twenty minutes, until he got up and carried his plate and cup to the sink and then said, as he left the room, 'I see. So I am now the only one in the entire family without a job in the real sense. So you can all do without me.'

Now, in Quindale vestry, putting on his Lenten stole (regarded as unacceptably High Church by some of his deanery) Peter was full of remorse for his petulance. Yet, at the same time, he could not bear the feeling that, if the career tides were receding from him, then his family's response of withdrawing too, into their own remedies and inevitable independence, might leave him quite beached like an old wreck on the shore.

Celia Hooper's husband, Denis, had fixed up a little mirror for Peter to examine himself in before he emerged into the church. Peering in it now, he thought: How grudging I look, how pinched, how disappointed. He straightened up. I am disappointed, he told himself, and I am quite trapped in it. I can't think what to do next.

He went quietly out through the little vestry door – ancient, ogee, poignant – into the chancel. There were seven people waiting for him, the Richardsons, the Hoopers, two parishioners from Snead, and Miss Dunstable from Loxford. As he passed her, Celia Hooper raised her head and gave him a look of steady encouragement.

CHAPTER SEVEN

At the beginning of Holy Week, Charlotte Bouverie came home. Term at Edinburgh University had ended weeks before, but Charlotte had stayed on in order to try and resuscitate an ailing love affair with a boy in her year. The attempt had failed, largely because Charlotte had discovered that she was so annoyed by Giles's apathy and introspection that she could hardly remember how wildly attractive she had found him only a month before. She gave him a lecture on his immature shortcomings, during which he lay on his bed with his back to her and emanated suffering, and then she packed her black kitbag with the possessions necessary for Easter at home – Simone de Beauvoir, cigarettes, black socks, Texas Camp Fire tapes and scent – and caught the overnight bus south.

Like her grandmother, Charlotte was good at bus travel, making friends and ignoring tedium. She changed buses in London, and telephoned Loxford to say what time she would be getting to Woodborough. The telephone wasn't answered. Charlotte, assuming her mother to be about the parish somewhere with Flora, and Luke to be in his room working with the music turned up so loud that no telephone stood a chance against it, caught her intended bus anyway. She would ring again from Woodborough.

Now that the Giles question was settled – as much a relief, curiously, as a disappointment – Charlotte was pleased to be going home. She was staunchly fond of her family but, being the eldest, guarded her pioneering independence fiercely, and therefore stayed away from home a good deal in order to train her family to detachment as much as herself. For the same reason, she seldom wrote letters, and for financial reasons, seldom telephoned. But she thought about the Rectory at Loxford a good deal more than its inhabitants supposed, even if being a clergyman's daughter was not something she actually advertised in her socially and politically dogmatic student circles. Being agnostic, as she was, Charlotte couldn't exactly empathise with her father's faith, but she could envisage a time in the future, when she was famous – and she fully intended to be – when admitting to her parentage would be something that could only benefit her image; something indeed rather stylish.

When the bus reached Woodborough, Charlotte again tried to telephone. Again there was no reply. She crossed the bus station to read the timetables – remembering, she thought, an early-afternoon bus to Loxford – and met her mother, burdened with Pricewell's bags and looking quite exhausted, coming towards her. Dropping everything, they embraced each other with enthusiasm, and the lady driver waiting to drive the next Loxford service remarked to her friend, the bus station manager, that there was no mistaking those two being mother and daughter.

'But why didn't you ring?' Anna said. 'I'm absolutely enchanted but I'd have hated you to get home and find nobody – '

'Nobody?'

'Oh darling, we're such a hive of industry. Luke is working for the tycoon who's taken the Old Rectory and Flora's gone to play with Emma Maxwell at Snead in the mornings while I work, so that she will have a thorough friend to start St Saviour's with.'

'What?' said Charlotte.

'I wrote. I wrote and told you. About Flora being so miserable and my job and Luke wanting to go to India.'

Out of the mists of recollection swam a dim memory of such a letter. Indeed, Charlotte could almost visualise it, on her table, among the dye pots and coffee mugs and edifices of books, most of which she never opened.

'Oh Ma. Sorry, but I've been absolutely frantic – '

'It doesn't matter,' Anna said, stooping to pick up the bags again.

It clearly did. Charlotte said, 'I really am sorry. I get sort of caught up – '

'I know.'

'Remind me about your job,' Charlotte said in a small voice.

Anna swung an armful of bags. 'Pricewell's.'

Charlotte remembered. ''Course.'

'Your turn now,' Anna said.

'My turn for what?'

'Your turn to say that I am defying Daddy and humiliating us all and failing the parish.'

'Who says that?'

'Everyone. Everyone except the grannies, who are wonderful.'

Charlotte said, 'I join the grannies.'

Anna looked at her. Charlotte's expression was determined.

'Darling. Do you?'

'Of course. It's great of you. I just wish – '

'What do you wish?'

'I just wish,' said Charlotte, 'that you could do something that exercised your intelligence more.'

Loxford church was in a ferment. The new Archdeacon had elected to celebrate an Easter eucharist there, before driving back to St Paul's, Woodborough, for family mattins. This had thrown the flower ladies into a competitive frenzy. Loxford must surely outdo St Paul's in Paschal floral glory, so that the Archdeacon would have his eyes quite dazzled by their achievements and in consequence be almost blind to anyone else's, all Easter Day. To Loxford's intense satisfaction it started with two tremendous advantages, Loxford church was stone, and fourteenth century, St Paul's was brick, and Victorian. In Miss Dunstable and Lady Mayhew, Loxford possessed flower arrangers of an almost poetic ability. St Paul's, dominated as it was by the diocesan Mothers' Union, could hope for nothing so elevated.

The only drawback was that no plans could be put into action until after the three-hour service on Good Friday, when Peter liked the church quite unadorned, with the crucifix above the altar shrouded in black. Even so, on Maundy Thursday evening, special long-spouted watering cans appeared in the vestry, along with new rolls of wire netting and blocks of flower arranger's foam.

Anna, who had had a grim time persuading anyone to give Easter lilies – 'Considering what she is doing to the parish,' Lady Mayhew had remarked to Miss Dunstable, 'I think she has a nerve to ask' – found herself suddenly inundated with offers. What might not be given to God in the name of His risen Son most certainly could be given to the Archdeacon in the cause of snubbing St Paul's. The flower ladies, those obliging people like Elaine Dodswell, found themselves issued with instructions, in Miss Dunstable's large, old-fashioned hand, run off on the copier in the village post office. Anna said to Elaine Dodswell, in the shop, 'I'm so sorry. It all seems to have got out of hand,' and Elaine, who had spent the last weeks quite stunned with horrified pity that Anna should be reduced to taking a job in a supermarket, said quickly oh, it didn't matter, you just had to humour people sometimes, didn't you?

There was, Anna discovered, to be no place for her in these arrangements. She had done twenty-two Easters at Peter's side, but she was plainly not going to be allowed to do this one. Whether the parish wished to punish her or cherish her – and she strongly inclined to the former view – hardly mattered; the exclusion was frightfully annoying.

'The small-mindedness of the Christian community when seen at close quarters,' she said angrily to Peter, 'beggars belief.'

Peter thought he would not mention Celia Hooper's competent plans for the deanery supper. He thought also that he was not, just now, very sympathetic to Anna's temper. He had even allowed Lady Mayhew to be loudly sorry for him in front of Marjorie Richardson, and although he was later ashamed, he knew he was not ashamed enough.

Anna went down to the church alone on the evening of Good Friday. Flora had wanted to come – 'I must *practise* my prayers!' – but had been deflected by the lure of being allowed to dress up in Charlotte's clothes. Luke was, as usual, over at the Old Rectory, and would return at supper-time with the air of small

superiority he had adopted for his family after ten days' associ-
ation with the way of life of Patrick O'Sullivan. Peter was at
Snead, taking evening prayer. The flower ladies, Anna thought
with some savagery, would be at home, down on their marks for
an early night before the onslaught on the church in the morning.
But for now, in the quiet early evening, the church was to be hers
and she could explain to it how the unseemly exhibitionism that
was about to overtake it was nothing to do with her and that she
quite understood its distaste.

The church, however, was not empty. Standing in front of the
altar and looking up at the west window – the original glass re-
grettably replaced by a Victorian riot of red and blue with a voluminously robed Christ presiding in the centre – was Daniel
Byrne. He was dressed as he had been dressed on the day she met
him, and he had his hands in his pockets.

He glanced round at Anna's step, and said, 'I suppose it's un-
realistic of me to expect a late-nineteenth-century craftsman to
have any understanding of humility.'

Anna came to stand beside him. She regarded the glassy Christ.
'Wouldn't you say He looked serene?'

'No,' said Daniel Byrne, 'I'd say He looked smug.'

Anna laughed. 'I've come in here to work off temper.'

'And I've come in to make sure I know the lie of the land before
Sunday. I'm always thrown by strange churches. Can't concentrate if I think I'm going to miss steps.'

'Are you settling in?' Anna said politely.

'Ask me in six months.'

'Mr Byrne – '

'Daniel.'

'Daniel,' Anna said. She paused. 'May I tell you something?'

'I wish you would.'

'I have been given a pay-rise.'

He said gravely, 'At your supermarket.'

'Yes. And a recommendation to apply for a management
course. I shan't, of course.'

'No?'

She looked at him. He said, still gazing up at the window, 'I
congratulate you.'

'Heavens!'

'I expect you haven't told your family.'

'Oh no.'

He looked at her. 'Won't you try?'

'No,' she said, 'I don't think so.'

He turned to face her. His eyes, enlarged by his spectacles, were the same grey as the tweed of his jacket.

'If you have the courage to do what you are doing, why don't you have the courage to speak to them?'

'Courage!' Anna said, 'courage! Round here it's called defiance.'

'Then round here is wrong.'

She would, she suddenly discovered, have given a good deal to step forward and put her head down on his sturdy shoulder. Had anyone ever done that? Did monks, even ex-monks, get touched?

'I think,' Daniel said, taking her hand in a firm grasp, 'I think we will sit down and talk.'

He led her to one of the front pews, to the carved and throne-like seat where Sir Frances Mayhew led his lady with no small pomp and circumstance on Sundays.

'You can't do this,' Anna said. 'You can't give time to this. You're an archdeacon, you've got rectories and churchwardens and bridges to build to Methodism to think of, you can't – '

'Yes, I can.'

He sat down beside her on the flat, red-velvet cushions.

'If I hadn't liked humanity, I'd still be a monk. My brother says I am still a monk, only now in high-street clothing; a voyeur monk, he says. You will meet him on Sunday. He's coming to church here. He is younger than me and very clever and difficult. I suppose,' Daniel said thoughtfully, 'I suppose Jonathan is really my private life. And of course you,' he turned to Anna, 'you can't have one. Can you?'

She gazed at him.

'Or is it more accurate to say that you could have a private life, but that you don't happen to?'

'I truly don't know, I've changed so, things haven't turned out as we hoped. Everyone underestimates the effect of disappointment, of prolonged disappointment. Poor Peter,' Anna said suddenly, putting her hands over her face.

'The parish needs him for what they need – '

'Yes.'

'And you, similarly.'

'Yes.'

'Odd,' said Daniel reflectively, 'so odd that humanity declines, on the whole, to think that other people are as human as itself.' He was silent for a moment. 'I don't know what I can do to help you. If anything. Is it enough to know for the moment that I understand?'

She nodded. He stood up. 'I must get back. Jonathan is arriving, and I'm afraid he will alarm Miss Lambe if I'm not there to restrain him.'

'Is your brother a priest?'

'No indeed. He's an academic, a philosopher. He is taking a sabbatical term and will live with me while he writes a book.'

'Does he – ' Anna began doubtfully, uncertain as to how to ask if Jonathan Byrne shared his brother's faith.

'Lord, no,' Daniel said. 'Thinks the whole thing is a fairy story devised to keep the peasants quiet.'

'A plot?'

'Yes – '

'I shall like your brother,' Anna said robustly. 'I think a lot of it's a plot, too.'

'We played nuns at Emma's,' Flora said. She threaded tubes of macaroni cheese on to her fork. 'I was Mother Superior.'

Everyone ignored her.

'I did chanting. I went, "Ho-o-o-oly, ho-o-oly, ho-o-oly is His Na-a-ame."'

'Shut up.'

'I did it in the bathroom, because it echoes. They've got a shower curtain with flowers on. I sent Emma behind it to confess. She had to confess her sins.'

'What sins?'

'She lied,' Flora said complacently.

'Flora!'

'She did. She told her mother she hadn't had a biscuit when there was one in her hand.'

'Flora,' Peter said, 'any more of this and you will not go to St Saviour's.'

Flora, secure in the knowledge of the division between her parents on this subject, merely looked smug. She had made Emma wail, 'Oh woe, oh woe, oh woe is me,' behind the shower curtain, and tug at her fat bunches of hair in an agony of remorse. The memory of this was very satisfying.

'I do hope,' Charlotte said seriously, 'that St Saviour's is going to be intellectually up to Flora.'

Luke said, 'God, don't egg her on – '

'Don't say God like that.'

'Charlotte, must you put spanners in the works?'

'In my view, Anna, Charlotte has a perfect right to ask, and I think has a very valid point.'

'But you are actually trying to make quite a different point.'

'This,' Peter said repressively, 'is no moment for such a discussion.'

Anna leaned forward. The children stopped eating and waited. 'Look,' Anna said to Peter, trying to make him meet her eyes. The telephone rang. 'Damn,' Anna said.

Luke got up. 'I'll go.'

Anna hissed at Peter, 'If you think I'm going to dodge crucial issues because of your notions of what is seemly and what – '

'It's for you,' Luke said, holding out the telephone. 'It's Celia Hooper.'

Anna got up. Peter's heart sank. He pushed his macaroni to the side of his plate and looked without much hope at Charlotte. She was gazing away from him at some spot on the kitchen floor, and her mind had left Flora and her family and had alighted upon Patrick O'Sullivan, whom she had met that afternoon. He represented, Charlotte reflected, absolutely everything she despised, and she had found him hugely attractive. He had been dressed in that terrible affluent middle-class uniform of corduroy trousers and striped shirt and heavy jersey, and he had simply exuded confidence. Charlotte very much hoped she hadn't flirted with him, but she was anxiously afraid that she had.

'No,' Anna said loudly into the telephone. 'No, thank you. Of course I can't forbid you, Celia, I wouldn't be so stupid, but I can make it plain that I would so much rather you didn't. When I want help, I'll ask for it. What do you mean? What do you mean, I need it? Need what? To be bossed about and organised by people who think they can do my job for me better than I can? Celia, I am sure you mean well – or am I? – but I will organise the deanery supper as I have done, thank you, in the past. And I won't be patronised. Do you hear me? Thank you for ringing. Not at all. Good night.'

She put the telephone down and turned to Peter.

'You knew about this.'

He said nothing.

'You not only knew, you encouraged her.'

'I tried to stop her –'

'Huh!' Anna shouted. Flora wondered whether to cry and decided not yet.

Peter stood up. 'You drove me to this,' he said furiously, 'and Celia. You are deliberately pushing the whole parish to take stands against you so that you can be the victim, you can feel you are in no way to blame. If you refuse to do what it is your duty to do, then no one is to be blamed for generously doing it for you.'

Anna stared. Luke and Charlotte watched, breaths held. Flora let out a loud wail and rushed to her father, and over the top of her head, Peter glared accusingly at Anna. She said nothing. Her anger had died out of her like a blown flame. She made some small clumsy gesture with her hands towards Peter, and then she turned and went out of the kitchen door into the garden.

It was dusk-dark. The black silhouettes of trees stood against a sky still lit by a dramatic glow from the western horizon, and faint mutterings from the branches indicated that it was not quite yet night. Anna walked carefully along the slippery path to the garage and unhooked, from a nail inside the door, the elderly mackintosh she used for winter gardening. Like so much they possessed, it had been left behind at the end of a jumble sale, a waif and stray nobody wanted, despite the faded Burberry label at the back of the neck. Anna put it on. It smelled of earth and its pockets rustled with garden tags and toffee papers and torn seed packets. Anna put her hands down into the comforting rubbish and simply let the tears slide.

It was easier to cry if she walked. She went across the patch of lawn in front of the house, and down the drive beside the church-yard wall. The sight of the bulk of the church was comforting, and for a moment she thought of going in and sitting where she had sat, only hours before, with Daniel, and talking to his imaginary presence. But then she remembered that Peter would have locked the church on his way home from Snead, because he was afraid that the chalice would be stolen from its safe in the vestry, or that vandals would deface the altar, or the huge bible that rested on a lectern carved into an eagle with its wings outspread. So she turned into the lane, and walked slowly past the high garden wall of the Old Rectory, blowing her nose fiercely on a crumpled paper handkerchief from one of the pockets of the Burberry.

From behind the wall, Patrick O'Sullivan heard her. He had been lured out by the gleaming spring night to see if – as one of his newly acquired gardening books promised him – his *Magnolia stellata* actually glowed in the dim light. It didn't; but, while he peered at it, willing it to enchant him all the same, he heard the sound of someone coming crying along the lane; and then he heard them stop, and sigh, and then whoever it was blew their nose, and he could tell that it was a woman. He straightened up. He thought of rural tragedy, of abandoned girls in ballads. Then he thought of Anna Bouverie. He moved quietly away from the magnolia, on to the rim of grass that edged the gravel of the drive, and, as Anna's figure passed the open gateway, he said, 'Good evening.'

She gave a little cry.

'I'm so sorry to startle you,' Patrick said, 'but I couldn't help hearing. And having heard, I couldn't ignore you.'

Anna did not turn. She simply said, 'I think you'd better.'

'Ignore you? Certainly not. Unless of course you want me to.'

She stopped walking. He couldn't see her face in the darkness, but he could tell she had also stopped crying. She said, 'I wish you hadn't heard me, of course, but now that you have it would be melodramatic to demand that you pretend you never heard a thing.'

He stepped on to the gravel.

'Will you come in?'

She hesitated.

'Please,' he said, 'I'd like to give you some brandy.'

The thought of brandy suddenly seemed heaven-sent. Anna said, 'Oh! Oh, thank you,' and moved forward. He grasped her arm firmly and led her up the steps into what seemed the exaggerated brilliance of his lighted hall. He looked at her. She was wearing a tramp's mackintosh and her face was absolutely forlorn. He said gently, 'This is rather an honour. For me.'

She gave a little smile. She let him take off the Burberry and lay it on a chair, and then lead her into the room that Susie Smallwood had painted dull red, and then hated, and which Patrick had lined with handsome books and careful pictures. There was a blazing fire. Patrick put Anna into a fat chair. He said, 'Perhaps you'd rather have whisky?'

She shut her eyes and put her head back into the cushions. She said, 'I think brandy. I don't know. I'm hopeless at drink. Not enough practice.'

He went across the room to a tray of decanters and bottles on a table made of beautiful, rich, red-brown wood. The cushion under Anna's head was beautiful and rich too, and so was the carpet in which her feet were now sunk, feet encased in shoes that had no business, she dreamily felt, to consort with such a carpet.

'I don't quite know,' Patrick said, coming back with a tumbler and a dark bottle, 'having had so little practice myself, if there are special rules of conduct for talking to rectors' wives.'

'Oh, please,' Anna said faintly.

'Please what?'

'Don't make a category. I live in one all the time. You're a newcomer. You start new.'

'Right,' he said. He poured brandy into the tumbler, a lot of brandy.

She eyed it. 'I think you should dilute that. And halve it.'

'If I dilute it, you'll feel drunker quicker.'

She looked pleased. 'Will I?'

He put the tumbler on the shining wood at her elbow, beside a small bronze racehorse on a little podium.

'Everything here is so new – '

'I know. Nothing I can do about it. You can't hurry ageing, except in people, where you don't want to.'

He sat down opposite her and crossed his legs. His shoes were suede. Anna took a swallow of her brandy and said, 'I wonder if anyone saw me come in.'

'Does it matter?'

'Yes.'

'Is that why you were crying?'

'Among other things.'

'Such as?'

Anna said primly, 'I don't know you well enough for this kind of conversation.'

'You won't get to know me better any other way. Nor I you.'

'Does that matter?'

'The very fact,' Patrick said, 'that you made that last remark a question not a statement shows that you are enjoying yourself.'

'Oh dear,' Anna said, bending her head to hide her smile.

He watched her. She was staring down into the brandy glass she held between her hands, in her lap, and she was plainly doing a lot of thinking. He realised, with no small *frisson* of pleasure, that she was not used to being flirted with, that men did not flirt with priests' wives, whom they put into a special social category that made them, in the public view, virtually sexless. Patrick looked at Anna's legs. Nothing wrong with those. He saw her suddenly at twenty, at the age of the pretty daughter he had met that afternoon, full of promise and enthusiasm. He was very touched – touched and excited.

He said, 'There's no need to be so lonely, you know.'

She put her brandy glass down with a bang.

'I don't want this kind of thing,' Anna said, struggling out of her chair.

He stood up to help her, but she shook him off.

'I'm so sorry. Clumsy – '

'I'm not a toy,' Anna said. 'I may be naïve but I am not a plaything.'

'I wouldn't dream – '

'People assume,' Anna said angrily, 'that priests are quite inexperienced, that they know nothing of the world. It's so patronising and ignorant. Who else, if not priests, see humanity at its very worst?'

Patrick put his hand on her arm. With her free hand, Anna picked it off.

'Won't you even let me apologise?'

She looked at him.

'Of course.'

'I am really sorry,' Patrick said, 'to have behaved like a bad cliché, to have been so arrogant.'

She managed a faint smile.

'But I would like us to make friends.'

Her smile faded. She said, 'You'll see, after a month or two, how difficult that would be.'

He opened his mouth to say that he would like a challenge, then shut it again prudently. Her expression was not encouraging. She crossed the creamy carpet to the door.

'Won't you even finish your brandy?'

'No, thank you.'

'When will I see you – '

'In church. On Easter Day.'

He reached in front of her to prevent her turning the door handle.

'Look. You are a prisoner and you hate it but you refuse to be released!'

Anna looked at him again. She said, 'It isn't as simple as that,' and then she looked pointedly at the door handle.

When she had gone – she declined to let him see her home – he poured his remaining brandy into hers and took her tumbler back to his armchair. He held it up. There was no trace of lipstick on the glass, no fingerprints, nothing. Her hands must have been very cold. He closed his eyes and thought of them, of warming them. He said to himself sternly, 'This must not be a game.' It did not strike him that there was any doubt of his both having and keeping the upper hand.

'Where've you been?' Luke demanded. He was making himself a mug of hot chocolate.

'Drinking brandy with your boss,' Anna said.

Luke whirled round from the cooker. 'You can't mean you just went and asked – '

'Of course not. He was skulking about in the garden as I went by, and then he asked me in.'

'Brandy!' Luke said.

'Yes. All of three swallows.'

'What was he doing in the garden?' Luke was aggrieved. Patrick was his. It was bad enough having to introduce him to Charlotte who had, of course, gone straight into the blatant routine Luke knew she would, but Mum . . .

'I couldn't tell you. Where's Flora? In bed?'

'Watching telly. Dad's in his study.'

'I'll go in to him.'

Peter was at his desk, bent over the foolscap pad in which he wrote his sermons. He said, without looking up, 'Celia telephoned. To apologise for upsetting you.'

'That was nice of her,' Anna said, 'but she doesn't understand.'

Peter ruled a neat underlining.

'Nor do I.'

'I think you do,' Anna said, 'if you really think about it. If you're honest. As honest as you once were.'

'Thank you.'

'Please – '

Peter said, 'We are committed to God. Both of us. With all that that entails.'

She came and sat in a chair beside the desk so that she could see his face.

'Are you saying, or implying, that only sacrifice counts? That unless we sort – sort of immolate ourselves, there's no point in it?'

'You are so melodramatic.'

She put a hand out to him. He ignored her.

'Do you love me?'

'Of course,' he said, not turning.

'That's no answer.'

'There isn't an answer that would satisfy you. Not in your present frame of mind.'

'Peter,' Anna said desperately, 'Peter, what do you want of me?'

He turned then. He looked at her gravely.

'You know perfectly well.'

'Can we talk about it? Can I tell you how I feel?'

The telephone rang. Peter picked it up at once, and then handed it to Anna.

'Trish Pardoe. For you.'

'Yes,' Anna said. She took the receiver. 'Trish. Yes. No, I haven't forgotten. I'll be there. Two o'clock. Yes. Goodbye.' She put the telephone back on its cradle. 'The Brownies' Easter Cake Bake. I had forgotten, actually.' She stood up. 'I'd better make something now.'

'Right.'

'Could we talk? Will you come into the kitchen while I make a cake?'

Peter said doggedly, 'There is no more to say. You know what the situation is as well as I do. And Sunday is Easter Sunday and I have a sermon – '

'But Daniel Byrne is coming!'

Peter put down his pencil. His shoulders sagged.

'Of course,' he said, 'of course. He will preach, not me. I forgot,' and then he turned away from her completely, so that he might not be comforted.

CHAPTER EIGHT

Colonel and Mrs Richardson came to Loxford church on Easter morning, on account of the Archdeacon. Colonel Richardson always made a point of saying that he did not like to worship outside his own parish, which remark roughly translated as meaning that he did not like to be upstaged at Loxford by Sir Francis and Lady Mayhew who had an unwritten tenancy of the best pew (front, left-hand side). Also, if you were churchwarden on your own territory, it was hard, he found, to submit to someone sitting in a pew which wasn't guarded by his official wand. All these feelings, which he would not have dreamt of revealing to Marjorie, made him gruff at breakfast, sharp with the dogs and moved to say, as he entered Loxford church in all its floral abundance, 'Good God. Looks like the flower tent at the County Show.'

Marjorie Richardson, who knew exactly what he was thinking, moved ahead of him up the aisle, graciously greeting people. She made a point of not discriminating socially. She could see Anna's back, upright in the Rectory pew, beside her untidy children, and she planned, if Anna turned, to give her just a little nod of greeting, a nod that acknowledged her – as was proper – and no more. But, before she reached the pew they had decided upon, the Archdeacon himself, still simply in his cassock, and accompanied by Peter, came out from the vestry and walked briskly across to the Rectory pew and shook hands warmly with them all, smiling down at them as he did so.

99

Thrown, Marjorie Richardson halted. The Archdeacon was stooping over Flora, who had been allowed to come to church with her hair apparently screwed up in coloured rags.

Behind her, Harry hissed, 'Sit down! We'll miss him.'

Startled, Marjorie shot into the pew and dropped her immaculate navy-blue handbag. Somebody sniggered. By the time she had retrieved it, and briefly and uncharacteristically hovered over the choice between a quick mannerly prayer or immediately standing up again, Peter Bouverie was by their pew saying, 'And this is Colonel and Mrs Richardson of Quindale. Colonel Richardson is churchwarden.'

'How do you do,' Daniel said, taking Marjorie's hand in a firm grasp.

She could not think of a fitting reply. She opened her mouth, but no sound came.

Daniel looked at her for a second, and then shook Harry's hand and said, 'Ah. Diocesan Board of Finance couldn't do without you, I hear, Colonel Richardson,' and Harry said, as she knew he would, 'It's nothing. Nothing at all. Like to do my bit.'

Then the Archdeacon smiled, and moved on, and Marjorie fell to her knees, ignoring Harry's pleased whisper of, 'Very civil. Wonder how he knew? Like a chap who does his homework.'

Marjorie was uncertain she liked this chap at all. She was ever more uncertain when, at the end of his thorough and genial circuit, he paused by the Rectory pew for a second time and definitely, quite definitely, said something more to Anna.

What he said was, 'I have persuaded my brother to come. Quite an achievement.' He did not add that Jonathan had come purely to escort Miss Lambe, for whom he had conceived an arcane enthusiasm – an enthusiasm Daniel suspected. 'You must not make a fool of Miss Lambe,' Daniel had said to Jonathan. 'She is easily alarmed.' Jonathan had looked mildly affronted. Miss Lambe had dressed for Easter Sunday at church in a grey-flannel spring coat and a matching beret to which she had rakishly pinned a bunch of artificial daisies. Kneeling beside Jonathan, the flamboyance of the daisies troubled her sense of what was fitting. She was glad that they were on the opposite side of her head to Mr Byrne.

Jonathan Byrne was not thinking about Miss Lambe or her daisies. He was contemplating, all around him, the seemly manifestations of the rural Church of England; the well-groomed plaster and stone of the church, the flowers, the brushed heads and shoulders ahead of him, the decent sunlight falling through old glass on to the decorous whole. He remembered Daniel's Manchester parish, the church of red- and blue- and yellow-diapered Victorian brick, the energetic and disparate congregation, the bursts of rowdy evangelism. Of course, the Church itself had been ever thus, traditional, tolerant and restrained on the one hand, sectarian, noisy and doctrinaire on the other, and Daniel was, by temperament, the kind of man who could understand both. He was, Jonathan thought with the strong affection for his brother that he seldom gave voice to, the kind of man who might, by this very perceptive intelligence, thoroughly disconcert such a congregation as now knelt before him, intoning the confession without, Jonathan observed, much anguish of guilt. 'We have left undone those things which we ought to have done, and we have done those things which we ought not to have done, and there is no health in us.' Sins of omission and commission. What exactly did such sins consist of in a place like this?

Beside him, Miss Lambe and her daisies trembled a little. The general confession, with its dark hints at the opportunities for sin, always made her flinch.

After the service, Anna was amazed to find herself greeted with smiles. Bruised by a difficult weekend with Peter and excluded from the decoration of the church, she turned from her pew, chin high, keeping the children close to her, and expected to be confronted with no more than formality from the congregation. But she had not reckoned on Daniel's influence, his deliberate friendliness to the Rectory pew.

'I must congratulate you on the flowers,' Marjorie Richardson said.

'Oh, not me, Lady Mayhew – '

'A Happy Easter, my dear.'

'Oh Harry. Thank you.'

'Nice to see the children in church, Mrs B.'

'Yes – '

'What a lovely morning, Anna, so perfect for Easter.'

'Isn't it – '

'My dear, you look tired. So does Peter. Of course Easter is such a thing – '

'Rather – '

'I wonder if we could have a quick word about the Evergreen Club's spring outing?'

'Oh Elaine, of course, could you ring me?'

'Ah. Little Flora. I hear we are going to a lovely new school?'

'Yes, she is. (Don't scowl, Flora.) Next term – '

'Mrs Bouverie. Good morning. We seem to have struck lucky with our new Archdeacon, don't you think?'

'Oh, I do – '

'Anna,' Daniel Byrne said as the press bearing her along bore her to him where he stood shaking hands in the porch, 'Anna, I would like you to meet my brother, Jonathan.'

Jonathan Byrne was taller than his brother, less sturdy, and without spectacles. He held out his hand to Anna. 'How do you do.'

'Welcome to Loxford,' she said automatically.

'Your brother took the service beautifully,' Anna continued in her parish voice.

'Did he? Should that matter? Is it like comparative performances of *Hamlet*?'

The children, who detested their visibility at such moments, hissed at Anna that they were going, *now*, and went, ostentatiously.

'Yours?' Jonathan Byrne said.

Anna watched them. Charlotte was actually running, which seemed exaggerated of her.

'Mine.'

'What is it like, being a rectory child?'

Anna gave him a quick glance.

'I expect you can imagine it. What is it like, being an archdeacon's brother?'

'*Touché*,' he said.

'Forgive me, Mr Byrne, but I ought to – speak to people.'

He stood aside and sketched a little bow.

'Of course.'

She hesitated. She wanted to say something grateful about Daniel, something that his brother could pass on over the fraternal lunch-table, but could think of nothing quite right. So she simply said, rather uncertainly, 'Goodbye then,' and felt foolish.

By the lich-gate a few minutes later, she met Patrick O'Sullivan. He wore a blue blazer with brass buttons and a boldly striped shirt which had been ironed with visibly professional skill. He said, 'I hope I look quite different. That's the first time I have darkened church doors except for weddings and funerals since I was at school.'

Anna resisted saying, but do you feel different? and merely said, 'Well, you were lucky. Because of the Archdeacon, I mean,' and then hurried away from him to catch up with Trish Pardoe and ask how much the Brownies' Easter Cake Bake had made.

'Twenty-three pounds! But that's marvellous!' It was necessary to say that, whatever the sum. Brownies, like rectors and mothers-in-law and Flora, and probably archbishops as well, always needed encouragement.

'They were ever so disappointed,' Trish Pardoe said, ignoring her, 'broke their hearts, really. The Quindale troop made twenty-seven pounds and forty pence.' She looked round her. 'But what can you expect, from this village?'

On Easter Monday, Patrick O'Sullivan took Charlotte and Luke to a point-to-point. Charlotte, disapproving of such events on social grounds, was poised to decline the invitation, even to the extent of preparing a little speech in her mind, to that effect, to make to Patrick; but Anna and Peter had a quarrel at breakfast, and Charlotte's antipathy to seeing the braying classes at play was dwarfed by her antipathy to the atmosphere in the Rectory. When Patrick manoeuvred his gleaming car up the Rectory drive, both Luke and Charlotte – carefully attired to stand out from the green-gumbooted crowd – were actually ready and waiting.

Patrick got out of the car and looked hopefully about for Anna. He was pleased to be taking these attractive children out, but the splendid picnic that lay shrouded in napkins in the boot had unquestionably been ordered with a view to good reports being made of it later. He said, 'Right then. Should you sign off before we go?'

'She's gardening,' Luke said. She was, furiously, digging the main-crop potato bed as if her life depended upon it.

'Shouldn't you – '

'No,' Charlotte said. She eyed the car. The windows had mysteriously tinted glass.

'Sorry,' Patrick said, opening the door for her, 'habit. I have to tell Ella if I'm even going to post a letter – '

'Hang on,' Luke said. He turned and dashed round the house to the vegetable garden. Anna had her back to him, her hair held off her face with a red handkerchief.

'Mum – '

She stopped digging, and turned.

'We're off,' Luke said lamely.

'Have a good day. Win lots of money.'

'Mum – '

Anna waited.

'Sorry,' Luke said. He gestured at the potato bed. 'I mean, sorry to go out, not to – '

'You go,' Anna said. 'I'm not fit for anything but digging, not today.'

Luke hovered. He wished very much to make it plain that he loved her, but found himself quite unable to think how. After a long pause he said, 'OK then,' and she said, 'Go on. Don't keep Mr O'Sullivan waiting,' so he went. When he reached the car, Patrick and Charlotte were sitting in the front together, and laughing.

Anna stuck her spade in the earth and went down to the end of the garden, to the rough patch where cow parsley bloomed profusely in May and dandelions flourished their downy clocks about, unchecked. In one corner of this little wilderness was Anna's compost heap and beside it was a low wooden gate, leading into the pasture beyond, a gate Anna had imagined herself using every day for regular, healing country walks. Reality had, of course, proved quite the opposite. She had scarcely opened the gate in ten years and an annual growth of convolvulus knitted itself round the latch. The nearest she ever got to a walk was – as now – to lean briefly on the gate's splintering top bar and gaze at the dark copse on the furthest hill and try to recapture that feeling of combined serenity and adventure that the view had first inspired in her.

Today, however, it inspired nothing. The view lay in all its pretty layers of green like some ingenious tapestry done by the Women's Institute – decorative, controlled, passionless – and had no message. Above it, the sky hung in a tranquil perfection of pale-blue and white. Around her, birds sang casually of this and that, and from the village came the occasional and distant shout of a child. It was all in order and quite remote.

In the house behind her, she had left Flora inventing a newspaper at the kitchen table – *The Loxford Post*; editor, Flora Bouverie; reporter, Flora Bouverie; cartoonist, Flora Bouverie; nature notes, Flora Bouverie; assistant, Emma Maxwell – and in his study, Peter and his sore feelings would be plunged in deanery files. Even if, by going in to him and putting her arms round him and suggesting that they were reconciled, she might have made things better, Anna had no heart for it. She had felt not just anger at breakfast, but dislike; sudden, fierce dislike for Peter's unsmiling, shuttered face, his refusal to look at her, his adamant insistence that, while he was not free to choose how to act, she was – and had chosen to oppose him.

He had, it seemed to her now, leaning on her gate, rejected her. All those years of defending him, of understanding him, of trying to interpose herself as an insulating layer between him and his disappointment, appeared to have gone for nothing. He had made it plain over the debris of breakfast that not only did he feel betrayed by her – and after all she'd done! – but that he did not really want her near him. She had tried to touch him at the end of the quarrel, but he had shied away from her, folding himself into himself like the spines of a rolled umbrella.

I am lonely, Anna thought. An exploring tendril of ivy was growing along the gate, and she began to rip it up, in little bursts, tearing its dry brown suckers from the wood. I am, in all essential senses, alone, because it would be wrong, or unfair, to burden anyone close to me with my isolation and my frustration. And it is more than that; it is that Mrs Bouverie is taking over from Anna, and, if even Peter does not want Anna any more, then what is to become of her? Is she to become just a competent Pricewell's worker with a blue overall and a jolly plastic badge? Is that to be Anna? She looked up at the innocent sky. 'Do you want Anna?' she demanded. The sky smiled on, not heeding her. God was probably as little inclined to indulge such silliness as Peter had been. Why was it that she was made to feel that her claims had no validity, that her existence was only permitted by everyone as long as it remained relative? How did people, Anna cried to herself, how did people get to be primary people – the ones who made others relative? And why, if you picked up a difficult burden, was it then assumed that you loved your burden and would gladly carry it for ever and ever . . .

'Anna!'

She turned. Peter was standing by the potato bed.

'Yes?'

He made no move to come forward. He called, 'You have visitors.'

'Who?'

He called again, without answering her, 'I think you should come,' and then he turned and went back to the house. Glaring at his grey-wool back with something approaching loathing, Anna followed him.

In the sitting-room, Celia Hooper and Elaine Dodswell were standing together on the hearthrug. Peter had invited them to sit down, but had not observed that, unless he did some preliminary clearance, there was nowhere for them to sit. Five people over the Easter weekend had left the Rectory deep in the litter of family living.

Anna appeared shoeless in the doorway.

'Do forgive us, Anna, on a Bank Holiday Monday too, but we knew we'd find you in – '

Anna said, 'That's perfectly all right.' She moved to the sofa and began to subdue billows of discarded Sunday newspapers. 'Would you like coffee?'

'We'd hate to put you to any trouble,' Elaine said.

Anna said briefly, 'No trouble.' She collected Charlotte's ostentatious scatter of books from an armchair. 'Please sit down.'

'So naughty to interrupt your gardening.'

'I'd stopped.'

'Robert's hard at it too,' Celia said cosily. 'First cut of the year. He's fanatical about his edges.'

Anna went out to the kitchen.

'Ought my cartoon to be political?' Flora said.

'I think that would be terribly difficult. A political joke – '

'Perhaps I could do something a little bit rude about the Queen – '

'She's certainly easier. If I put all these things on a tray, will you make coffee when the kettle's boiled and bring it in?'

Flora didn't look up. 'Who's there?'

'Mrs Hooper and Mrs Dodswell.'

'Pooper and Plodswell.'

'Yes. Shh.'

'Mummy,' Flora said, 'Emma's mother plays golf.'

'Does she?'

'Lots of mothers do. Emma's mother said would you like to but I said you spent all your time doing Pricewell's or the garden or German.'

'What a help to my image you are,' Anna said. 'Don't forget the kettle.'

In the sitting-room, Celia and Elaine were having a carefully anodyne conversation about the church fête. When Anna came in, Elaine was saying, 'Well, you can't ask Mrs Berridge to do teas again, not after last year, with the tea stone cold and flies on the rock buns – '

'Flora's bringing coffee in a minute,' Anna said. She sat down on the sofa and looked at Celia. 'How can I help you?'

Celia leaned forward. 'Oh no. It's quite the other way about. We've come to ask how we can help you.'

Anna stared at her. She stared at her blue-and-white weekend jersey and her matching blue weekend trousers.

Elaine, who was genuinely fond of Anna and was disconcerted

by her expression, said hastily, 'It isn't interference, Anna, really it isn't. It's a Christian helping hand.'

Anna turned. 'In what way?'

'There's so much for you to do, you see – '

'The cleaning rota, the flower rota – '

'Attending all the parish clubs and services – '

'The parish magazine – '

'And I expect the telephone never stops!'

'And then, of course, the deanery entertaining responsibilities – '

'And your own life – '

'Oh yes, Anna, your own life.'

'We just thought,' Celia said, never allowing her smile to slip, 'we just thought it was all too much for one – for one *busy* person like yourself, so we have come to offer ourselves as – as your deputies.'

The door opened uncertainly and Flora wavered in with the coffee tray. Anna got up.

'Thank you, darling.'

'I spilled a bit – '

'It doesn't matter.'

'Thank you, dear,' said Celia Hooper. 'What a helpful girl.'

Flora, who had abandoned the Loxford Brownie troop after two sessions because of what she termed all that icky *helping*, looked lofty.

'You will excuse me,' Flora said firmly, and returned to the kitchen.

Anna, whose hands did not seem as steady as she could have wished them, handed round the cups of coffee. She said, offering Elaine sugar, 'Did I hear you right? Are you offering yourselves as deputy rector's wives?'

Elaine looked at her with great earnestness. 'Yes.'

A mild hysteria seized Anna. She fought with the urge to say, In every sense? and won, by the simple expedient of remembering that, for the last eighteen months, her and Peter's nights had been purely for sleeping.

'Have you spoken to Peter of this?'

Celia looked shocked, largely because she had wished to, and Elaine had prevented her. 'Of course not.'

Anna returned to the sofa. A dull misery was settling on her like fog. 'What exactly do you propose?'

'Well,' Celia said. She leaned forward and looked very, very caring. 'We thought we could relieve you of all the mundane things – cleaning, flowers, magazines, etc – and perhaps some organisational things too, like the nuts and bolts of deanery entertaining, and leave you, as is only proper, the public roles. Being in church, visitors, attending functions. That sort of thing. We have a little team in mind, seven ladies – '

Anna closed her eyes.

'Are you all right?' Elaine said anxiously.

'Yes. Yes, I'm fine – '

'There you are. Worn out – '

'Please,' Anna said.

Elaine stood up. 'I think we should go. You think about it.'

When they had gone, Anna went back to the sofa and lay on it, in a stupor.

After a while, Flora came in and said, 'Why are you lying down?'

'Because I'm tired.'

'Why are you tired?'

'Because I think I'm vanishing,' Anna said.

Flora looked at her, up and down. 'Emma's mother,' Flora said, 'would think that was a very silly way to talk.'

Later that day, Anna tried to explain to Charlotte. Charlotte had enjoyed the point-to-point, to her amazement, and had won £6. Luke had been allowed to drive the Daimler on a quiet side road, and they were both rather anxious everyone should know that they had been given smoked salmon sandwiches, and then sloe gin to wash down fruit cake. After supper at the Rectory, Luke returned to the Old Rectory to sluice the day's mud off the Daimler, and Charlotte said she would wash up. Anna said they would do it together then, and, when Charlotte protested, explained that she wanted to talk.

Charlotte, however, did not want to talk – or at least, not in the way Anna wanted to. Anna wanted to describe the morning, and her visit, and to attempt to decide, by thinking out loud, why this offer of apparent help should seem to her so deeply depressing, almost offensive. The two women had, after all, proposed to lift chores from her shoulders, but they were chores which, in a curious way, gave her an identity, and at the moment she was truly afraid of having no identity at all. She tried to explain this to Charlotte, to explain her sense of isolation and of losing what little control was left to her. She said, 'You see, being married to a priest means such a different kind of marriage to a secular one. It is rather like having a crucial relationship with someone who is always half turned away from you.'

Charlotte listened, sloshing soapy water about the sink, but she didn't reply. It seemed to her that her mother was being relieved of all the most demeaning parish duties and that she ought to be absolutely thankful, and accept at once, and go out and find a decent teaching job instead of this obscene supermarket one. She had quite a lot of sympathy for her mother – she found her father impossible just now, quite unapproachable – but she couldn't see why Anna clung to just that society-enforced female stereotyping that Charlotte and her friends were staking their lives upon overturning. She also, at bottom, was not deeply interested. After two weeks at home, she was beginning to feel stifled, and to need the reassurance of her friends that she was independent and free-thinking. She lifted a bunch of knives and forks out of the water and dumped them, clattering, on the draining board.

'You must just do what you want, Mum. You're in charge.'

Anna said, 'Luke says that. But it isn't true. The constraints may be invisible, but they are very strong.'

Charlotte began to dry her hands very carefully, before fitting back on to her fingers her armoury of Indian silver rings. 'It's no good, being passive – '

'I know that. But being trapped is different.'

'Look, Mum,' Charlotte said, 'I'd accept if I were you. And get a decent job. What's going on just now is pretty silly – '

'Silly?'

'In all honesty,' Charlotte said, 'I can't support this super-market.'

Anna turned away and began to stack the clean plates in cup-boards. Charlotte watched her for a while and then she said, almost without meaning to, 'Sorry – '

'That's all right,' Anna said. They did not look at one another. 'You go off now – '

Charlotte sidled round to the back door.

'Patrick said to join him and Luke for a drink after Luke had washed the car – '

''Course – '

'Won't be late.'

'Doesn't matter.'

Cold air rushed in with the opening door. ''Night,' Charlotte said, in a voice rich with relief, and vanished.

On the first morning of the summer term, Peter elected to take Flora to St Saviour's. This meant that they all drove into Wood-borough together, and, after Luke had been dropped at the sixth-form college gates, Anna was let out, with elaborate lack of comment, at the staff door of Pricewell's. Peter then escorted an extremely overexcited Flora to St Saviour's.

He was slightly defiant about doing this. He was genuinely abashed at his opposition to a move which was very likely to benefit Flora, while at the same time feeling that Anna, by taking charge, had not only made him look weak, but had meant to. She had also said that morning, while they were dressing, 'I suppose you aren't trying to impress the nuns, are you? Taking Flora on her first morning when I can't remember you ever taking any of them to school before – '

He said, 'I'm trying to make amends.'

She had looked at him, with a look that wasn't unkind but wasn't particularly loving either, and then had gone downstairs to find that a radiant Flora, flawless in her new uniform, had already laid breakfast (unheard of) and was slicing bread for toast with a fine disregard for symmetry. Breakfast had been quite cheerful, with Flora so exuberant and Luke able to face a new term and old friends with the dignity of actually, for the first time in his life, being in funds. Charlotte had gone back to Edinburgh on her bus three days before, kissing everyone goodbye with a fervour born of relief. She had left Anna a postcard on her pillow, a reproduction of a Klimt, with, written on the back, 'Dearest Mum. Women are no longer victims of circumstance. You have to believe that. Love, Charlotte.' Anna had been very touched. The card – an erotic, exotic painting of Judith – was in her bag now.

When he had dropped Flora – 'Ah,' Sister Ignatia had said, clasping his hands in both her faintly damp ones, 'now here's a very special little newcomer' – Peter drove back into the market-place, and managed to park in the double file of spaces in the centre. He got out, locked the car carefully, and crossed to the pavement that led down to Pricewell's, at the point where the market-place narrowed into the High Street. He walked against the buildings, slightly sideways as if trying not to be conspicuous, and, when he reached the great blank windows of the super-market, he stopped, and peered in at an angle. The inside was brightly lit, but his view was half obscured by the row of tills against the window. He began to sidle along the glass, gazing up the aisles between the rows of tins and packets and bottles. From half-way along one, standing on a small stepladder, Anna watched him. She watched him reach the door, hesitate, and turn away. He walked back, more briskly, the way he had come. Anna looked for a while at the point at which he had vanished and then shook herself, and turned back to her shelves.

CHAPTER NINE

Jonathan Byrne made himself a study in Woodborough Vicarage. He spent a happy afternoon roaming through the unused upper rooms, and chose one with an elaborate stone-mullioned Gothic window surmounted by trefoils filled with coloured glass. The diocese was, of course, agitating to sell the Vicarage and erect the usual sensible, faceless, mediocre building instead, so perhaps within years this room and its splendid window would be taken over as a dormitory by boys from The Kings' School, an undistinguished private establishment currently benefiting from parental anxiety about the unreliability of state education, and needing to expand.

In the meantime, Jonathan decided, it would serve him excellently. He retrieved various pieces of furniture from around the Vicarage – a table, some tremendously heavy pitch-pine shelves, several chairs and a spectacularly morbid Piranesi print of dungeons – and arranged these to his satisfaction. Miss Lambe, luckily, had no notion of how to interfere or domesticate, so he was not burdened with curtains or cushions or unwanted strips of comforting carpet. The uncompromising angularity of the room, when he had finished, pleased him very much. He went down to Daniel's study to summon him on a little tour of appreciation, but Daniel was not there. He was, said Miss Lambe, out in the combined parish of Great and Little Blessington with Mumford Orchus, swearing in a new churchwarden.

Jonathan felt the need of company. Miss Lambe, for all her hamster-like charm, was not much good for conversation on account of her powerful sense of anxious inadequacy, and in any case, she was doing the ironing and, whenever addressed, gave a little start and put the iron down in order to attend respectfully to whatever was being said to her. It was clearly both kinder and more practical not to say anything. Jonathan collected his jacket and a handful of change and said he was going out for an hour. Miss Lambe stopped ironing to say it looked like rain.

Woodborough Vicarage opened straight on to a cobbled lane that ran down to the High Street. It was a neglected lane, too narrow for all but the smallest cars, and dank weeds and mosses grew sadly between the cobbles. It was closed at one end by a small lich-gate to the churchyard intended by the Victorians for the Vicar's private access, and opened at the other on to the pavement opposite Woolworth's. As Jonathan turned away from the church, its clock announced that it was five – time, he considered, for a cup of something to reward his scene-shifting efforts.

The pavements were quite full. Jonathan threaded his way along, thinking how aggressive and proprietorial of pavement space the possession of a pushchair made most women. He passed a newsagent and an electrical goods shop and a window full of women's clothes – Jonathan had never known how to look at their clothes, but this riotous assembly of floral patterns struck him as quite inappropriate (except, of course, if you were a flower) – and then he came to Pricewell's. Pricewell's. He remembered. He stopped. In Pricewell's worked the interesting Mrs Bouverie who had, Daniel said, caused such fluttering in her parish hen coop by her small, brave show of independence. Jonathan had seen her on Easter Sunday, but she had been harassed and tense, in no mood to be interesting. He thought he would go in and spy on her, just briefly. He pushed open the door.

Pricewell's was almost empty. In ten minutes, it would be full of people released from their offices, but for now it felt calm and spacious. Jonathan walked up and down the aisles, marvelling at the extraordinary things the public seemed to have a taste for, and looking for Anna. She was nowhere to be seen. Perhaps Thursday was not her day. He stopped a plump woman patting packets of paper towels into order and asked her where Anna was. In the warehouse, she said. Could you – she looked at him. He smiled. 'All right,' she said, but she sighed.

He waited for what seemed a long time among the quiet columns of lavatory paper. When she came down, Anna was wearing a blue overall over much longer clothes, and looked anxious.

'Mr Byrne, is anything the matter, has your brother – '

'No,' Jonathan said, 'I just wanted someone to have some coffee with. To talk to. I came in here to have a snoop at you going about your tasks, but then I thought I'd much rather take you out and talk to you.'

She looked flustered. 'I can't leave until five-thirty – '

He held out his wrist. 'Twenty minutes.'

'Then I catch the bus to Loxford – '

'I'll drive you.'

'Mr Byrne – '

'Jonathan.'

'I'm afraid,' Anna said primly, 'that my life doesn't allow for impulses.'

He stared at her. She looked down.

'Tomorrow,' he said, 'what hours do you work tomorrow?'

'Until three. Then I collect Flora at four.'

'Three o'clock tomorrow then.'

She looked up again. 'Is there something specific? That you want to talk about?'

'No,' he said, 'should there be?' Then he said, to help her, 'I'm a total stranger here, you see. Daniel's very busy.'

'But you are writing a book – '

'Not all the time.'

She seemed to give herself a little shake. 'Tomorrow then. Thank you.'

He nodded and turned away and, on the way out, bought himself a loaf which called itself Lincolnshire Plum Bread, from the bakery section, because it reminded him of the poacher's song he had so loved when he was small.

★

Long before, Jonathan Byrne had married a fellow undergraduate, the moment he came down from Cambridge. She was ferociously clever, cleverer, he knew, than he, and with a singleness of purpose that he had imagined would give them both freedom. In fact, it gave them no shared goal since Jonathan was not sufficiently emotionally mature to understand the necessity for his own contribution. They had stayed married for three years, and had divorced with brisk friendliness, acknowledging that there was no point to their shared existence because they did not, in fact, share it or wish to. Stephanie had gone to America and a distinguished academic life which now included, Jonathan heard, a veteran Hollywood actor old enough to be virtually her grandfather. After a few cursory and reactive affairs, Jonathan grew out of the habit of full-time women, assuming, with a certain resignation, that he had not much aptitude for them. When Daniel came out of his monastery and looked about at life, he had asked Jonathan why he hadn't married again and Jonathan had said because he hadn't wanted to. Now, both brothers were conscious of the unmistakable companionable warmth of having one another in Woodborough Vicarage.

Miss Lambe laid supper for them each night at the inadequate dining-room table – inadequate, that is, for the proportions of the room. They ate early, to allow her to escape to her burrow and her wireless – she was disconcerted by television. She left covered dishes and plates on the sideboard, and then hovered in the kitchen until they had eaten because it would have distressed her immeasurably to think of an archdeacon – even a modern archdeacon – washing up. She cooked safe, dull food, but at least Jonathan's presence had broken her habit of cutting up Daniel's meals as if he were a toothless invalid. To be obliging, they ate their chops or ham or sausages at breakneck speed, and then took cups of coffee into Daniel's study. Behind them, in the dining-room, Miss Lambe mourned over an abandoned potato, a half-finished apple crumble. Anything left could only mean that there had been something the matter with it.

The telephone in Daniel's study constantly interrupted them. Jonathan wondered if the Church of England and City of London foreign-exchange dealers had almost comparable telephone bills.

The interruptions made sustained conversation difficult, but there was at least time to tell Daniel about his foray into Pricewell's and his stiff little interview with Anna.

'She was very disapproving. I felt I was behaving improperly. It was only an impulse.'

Daniel said, spooning far too much sugar into his coffee, 'It was improper. For her, I mean. It isn't the kind of thing that happens to her.'

'Why not?'

'Because almost no one treats clergy wives as if they were human beings.'

'Rubbish.'

'Not at all rubbish. I didn't see it so much in Manchester because I think cities are much more socially liberal and the hierarchy doesn't exist to the same extent. But out in the country, the vicar's wife is the vicar's wife, and she is required to remember that.'

'That's status – '

'No,' Daniel said, 'it is not. It is an assumption – and not a generous assumption – that not only is a clergy wife expected to live by almost exaggerated standards of rectitude, but that she is somehow immune to the devices and desires of all other human hearts. It isn't just Anna Bouverie. The wife of the priest out at Mumford Orchus was shut in her sitting-room this afternoon with the curtains drawn and the television on. The husband made me a cup of tea in the kitchen and I couldn't help noticing a whole basket of pill bottles on the table. Nice fellow, bit smug, but I don't suppose he knows what on earth is the matter, or why it has come to be the matter.'

'Doesn't all this apply to men?'

Daniel drank his coffee.

'Oh yes.'

'Well then?'

'The men have chosen God.'

'Haven't their wives?'

'A great many of them have. They aren't the problem. The problem lies with the wives who discover, quite legitimately, that, although bowing to the will of God of your own free will is one thing, bowing to it as translated to you by your husband, who has somehow assumed a monopoly on the first place with God, is quite another. This is not pure Christianity, I know, but it is pure human observation.'

The telephone began. Jonathan got up to answer it. 'Yes? I think so. Who is it speaking?' He put his hand over the mouthpiece. 'Terry Bailey. From Dummerford.'

Daniel looked pleased. 'Ah,' he said, 'my pet misfit. A full-blooded evangelical who preaches like a Welsh Baptist, stuck in a village made up entirely of retired admirals and genteel widows.' He seized the receiver. 'Terry? What can I do for you?'

Jonathan went out of the room and quietly closed the door. He crossed the hall, and climbed the stairs, past Miss Lambe's shut door through which the wireless clucked comfortingly, and up to his new study. Before he went to bed, he would fill the shelves with books.

Anna led Jonathan to a coffee shop attached to a delicatessen whose window was full of ostentatious Italian machines for making pasta. This was not because it crossed her mind as being more suitable for his mildly eccentric appearance, but because she knew that the inhabitants of Loxford, when they came into Woodborough to shop, preferred their refreshment (according to class) at either the jolly red plastic hamburger joint in the market-place, or the Country Kitchen, whose décor was refined rural and whose motto was 'home-made'. The delicatessen coffee shop was used chiefly by the young bookbinders and jewellers and leathersmiths who rented workshops in Woodborough's former brewery. It was evident at once that Jonathan only noticed his surroundings if that was what he happened to be concentrating on at the time, which was not, at this moment, the case. He collected coffee for Anna and himself, and then pulled an ancient paperback copy of André Maurois' *Ariel* out of his pocket and laid it beside her cup.

'Have you read that? It's about Shelley.'

'No.'

'Do. It's dated, but there's something there. And it's relevant. To what I want to talk to you about.'

'Oh,' Anna said, relieved. 'So there is something.'

'I want to talk to you about subversion.'

'Heavens – '

'Does that interest you?'

She spread her hands. 'I don't know. I'm not quite sure of the rules of this kind of conversation – '

'You mean because it isn't orthodox. Or shows signs of becoming unorthodox.'

She said, looking straight at him, 'I imagine, I can't be sure, being rather out of practice at talking like this, but I imagine it is perfectly possible to long for and dread the same thing.'

'Like unorthodoxy?'

'Yes.'

'Oh good,' he said, 'this is exactly what I was hoping for. Are you hungry?'

'No,' she said.

He settled himself over his coffee cup. 'Don't you think,' he said, 'that it would be exhilarating to feel a rush of liberating energy?'

'What has that to do with subversion?'

'Aren't they linked? Isn't the desire to undermine the status quo and to mock pretension and apparent unassailability tied up with feeling that after they are overthrown there will be a wonderful, energetic freedom?'

She drank her coffee. She looked at him. She said boldly, 'Are we – you – talking about me?'

He smiled. Like his brother, he had a charming smile. 'I am absolutely fascinated by your situation.' He waited for her to reply that he wouldn't be if he was in it but she said, without heat, 'I'm not up for discussion, Mr Byrne.'

'Jonathan. Haven't you talked to Daniel?'

She looked indignant but said, 'That's quite different.'

'Because he's a priest?'

'Because,' she said, her face softening, 'because he really does understand the dilemma.'

'How do you know I don't?'

Anna thought, briefly, of Patrick O'Sullivan. 'You are a man, but not a priest, so I don't trust you.'

'What!'

'I can't,' she said candidly. 'You can't imagine how little chance I have had to form close relationships outside my family. I have seen how people behave, but I haven't experienced it. I've experienced a lot of very unpleasant things that I don't suppose will ever come your way, but I haven't, personally, intimately, been in the thick of human things because, as a priest's wife, I can't be. Are you married?'

'Not now,' he said. He wanted to look at her with admiration, but controlled himself.

'In that case,' she said unexpectedly, 'I assume you know a good deal more at first-hand about women than I know about men. You've probably noticed that there is often a kind of aura of – of unworldliness, almost innocence, about clergymen and their wives. I suppose it is partly lack of money but I think it's partly what I've been saying, too.' She stopped.

'Go on,' he said.

She shook her head. 'I never talk like this,' she said severely.

'I want to know more about this detachment, this sensation of being in a separate category – '

'I have to go. I have to collect Flora.'

'Don't you like this? Don't you like a little mental exercise? Don't you want to be talked to as if you had never heard of the Church of England?'

She looked up again. She looked quite distraught. He was horrified, remorseful.

'Oh my dear girl, I'm so sorry, I'm so clumsy – ' He pulled a huge navy-blue handkerchief out of his pocket and proffered it. 'I meant to be sympathetic, not challenging, I meant to be generous, if that doesn't sound patronising.'

She nodded, round the handkerchief. 'I know – '

He said, 'I was too sudden.'

'I think I was rather priggish – '

He leaned across the table towards her. 'Is it very imprudent to ask if you believe in God?'

'I think I do. Very occasionally I am almost sure I do. But it is not a God who seems to bear much relation to – ' She stopped. She had been going to say, Peter's God.

Jonathan stood up and came round the little white table to help her up, as if she was ill.

'If I'm very careful, will you talk to me again?'

'Of course,' she said crossly. 'I don't have to be humoured.'

'I didn't mean that. I meant if I wasn't so rough and unimaginative.'

She said, 'I'll wash your handkerchief.'

'And read the Maurois?'

'Why?'

'For a portrait of a particular kind of rebelliousness. Just for discussion.'

'I see.' She smiled at him.

He said, 'Until the next time then,' and they went out into the street.

'You're late,' Flora said.

'Darling, only five minutes – '

'Five minutes late. That was all very well at Woodborough Junior but here, I can tell you, the mothers are a very different kettle of fish. Where have you been anyway?'

'Sitting in a coffee shop talking about myself with the Archdeacon's brother.'

Flora wasn't interested. 'I got *another* merit star. In English.'

Anna took her hand to draw her down the steps on the way to the bus stop. 'Well done. What for?'

'A self-portrait in fifty words. Mine began, "I am not strong but I am tall and sensitive".'

Anna suppressed a smile. 'I see.'

'Sister Josephine thinks I might be quite a spiritual child.'

'Oh?'

'But I'm not sure I'd have the *patience* for it.'

'Flora,' Anna said, suddenly glowing with delayed benevolence from her conversation with Jonathan Byrne, 'Flora, do you like St Saviour's?'

Flora said seriously, 'I am absolutely blissful.'

'Oh, good,' Anna said, squeezing Flora's hand too hard in her emotion. 'Oh darling, I'm so pleased.'

'But it is *not* blissful,' said Flora, seizing her opportunity, 'to be the only child at St Saviour's with a mother who is *late*.'

A miasma of elaborate tactfulness hung over Loxford on the subject of the deanery supper. It was known throughout the parish – Celia Hooper felt it was her duty in supporting Anna to disseminate this knowledge – that Anna would be very upset if it was even hinted at that she could not manage it this year. It was not, Celia said seriously to people, as if it was a parish affair involving the laity: no, it was strictly Church business, a little party for the deanery priests and their wives, and Anna must not be made to feel that the laity was in any way butting in. Talking about the deanery supper gave Celia Hooper an excellent chance to moot her idea of a little parish support-group for Anna. Most people were very sympathetic, and eager to help; only Lady Mayhew and Marjorie Richardson indicated that they thought Anna needed a spank rather than support. Celia had said to Elaine that they wouldn't push the matter any further just now, they'd let Anna get her party over.

The pattern of the deanery supper had set itself in amber some years before, not particularly by Anna's wish, but more by the prevailing wish of her guests, most of whom knew what they expected of a rural dean. They knew, for instance, that he had no extra income from the position, and only a small entertainment allowance. This meant that they wished to be entertained with a delicate balance between modesty and generosity. Cider would be an insult, but anything better than *vin de table* would be improper. The food Anna had learned to provide – cheeses and salads, cold meats and rolls, followed by slightly childish puddings – was always much appreciated. They all ate with an old-fashioned gusto. It was one of the aspects Anna liked best, this unaffected, unspoiled pleasure at greedy eating in a party atmosphere.

The day of the party, she got up at six and moved the furniture in the sitting-room back against the walls. She then collected all the chairs round the house and arranged them in conversational groups. After that, she made three pints of custard for the trifles, washed four lettuces, counted out seventeen plates (mostly odd), seventeen pudding bowls, and arranged them in the sitting-room between fans of paper napkins. When it was properly light, she went out into the garden and brought in armfuls of the last daffodils, and some branches of new willow. Then she got breakfast. In the middle of breakfast Peter said had she remembered that John Jacobs from Dinsbury was a vegetarian and she said thank you, she'd remembered everything. Should he pick up the wine? No need, thank you, she had asked Mike Vinson to bring it home with him. And glasses? We don't need them, there are enough at the village hall.

'Then,' said Peter, 'what is there I can do to help?'

Anna began marshalling jars and cereal boxes on the table prior to putting them away. 'I don't honestly know.'

Luke tried to catch his father's eye for a wink of complicity, but it was not to be done. Peter folded up the newspaper with elaborate precision and carried it out of the kitchen.

'No need, really, Mum,' Luke said, 'to give him a hard time. He was only offering – '

'He doesn't want me to do it. He doesn't think I can do it.'

'I think he just feels a bit guilty that you have to do it.'

Anna turned from the cupboard where she was stowing things away. 'Do you?'

Luke nodded. Anna looked at the clock. 'Oh Lord. Ten to. I haven't time to sort it out now. Get your stuff, will you? And shout for Flora.' She ran out of the room and up the stairs. Peter was locked in the lavatory. She called, 'I'm sorry. Sorry to be disagreeable.' He said nothing. 'I'll see you later,' Anna called. 'Will you open some beans for lunch?' She stopped herself from apologising for the beans. Flora came out of her bedroom.

'Come on,' Flora said, sensing drama. 'Come on, come on, come on or we'll miss the bus and it will be *utter* disaster.'

The guests arrived exactly when they had been asked, at seven-fifteen. Anna felt relief at the sight of them, at their familiarity, reassured by their kind little questions as they came in and by their exclamations of enthusiasm at the sight of the daffodils, of Flora in her green school uniform, of the sherry trifle. They would remain docilely in their couples until, emboldened by a glass or two of wine, they would bravely separate into sexes and get down to the business of the evening which was, of course, diocesan gossip. The priests would compare the impossibleness of their parishes and speak of job opportunities; their wives would talk personalities. Two of them had recently had tea with the Bishop's wife: the rest were burning to hear about it.

The last to come was Isobel Thompson. She had taken to coming several years before, to help Anna dole out supper, and then to wash up. This year she came with a certain amount of trepidation, but Anna seemed only pleased to see her, not surprised and not touchy. She looked, Isobel thought, strained and tired, but she was smiling, and the house and the supper-table looked lovely. Accepting a glass of white wine, Isobel decided that Anna must have come to some kind of reconciliation with herself, and her role, and that the effort she had clearly made for the party was the first step in a new determination. She said to Daphne Jacobs, 'Hasn't Anna done us proud?'

Daphne Jacobs had brought up five children in three rectories and, in between, had taken a quiet pride in her parish work. She had seen Anna in Pricewell's, and had heard from Mary Marshall at Crowthorne End that she had taken the job out of disappointment when Peter failed to get his promotion. Later in the evening, she intended to discuss it further (covertly) with Mary who was busy, just now, putting something of everything available on to her plate. In the meantime, she said quellingly to Isobel, 'Lovely daffodils. Ours are all over.'

Sighing, Isobel went across the room to talk to Marion Taylor from Mumford Orchus, whose husband had become a priest when he was fifty-five, to her abiding dismay. He had been an accountant before; they'd had a nice house in Lichfield and she had never wanted life to be any different from the uneventful regularity she had known then. Her secret afternoons with old movies on television were not so much a consolation as a lifeline. She told her daughter that the pills she took were vitamin supplements and iron, for her anaemia. She made a place for Isobel beside her on the Knole sofa.

'Anna looks tired.'

'She's made such an effort for us,' Isobel said. 'How's your Sunday school?'

'Folded. Hopeless. They all just used it as somewhere to dump the children for an hour. And I'm no teacher.'

'You should learn to play the guitar. It's such a help, a little music, with children.'

Marion Taylor leaned closer. 'I don't blame Anna, you know. I admire her. I seem to have lost the will to do much, but it doesn't mean I don't sympathise.'

Isobel said stoutly, 'We have all been praying for her.'

Marion Taylor gave a little snort and her wineglass shook in her hand, spilling some into her beige, pin-spotted lap. She mopped at it fiercely with a paper napkin. 'Prayer!' she said. 'I don't know I've much use for it. But I do know that, if anyone mentions waves of prayer to me again in that awful sanctimonious way they have, I shall be sick.'

The party swelled steadily in volume. An animated discussion of Daniel Byrne in one corner was balanced by a debate on the ineffectiveness of synods in another, while in between the subjects of children and villages and the Bishop's wife (a dear, but not really in touch, somehow) ebbed and flowed. Peter toured the clumps of people dutifully with bottles of *vin de pays* and tried to look as he had felt at all previous deanery suppers – like a man with something of a future. They were all extremely nice to him, a little hearty, a shade solicitous, and he began to feel a revived gratitude towards Anna, mixed with a new relief that she might be, somehow, coming through a difficult phase (most natural after such a blow, after all) and that this party was a token of a new leaf turned. He emptied the last of the bottles he had in either hand into the glasses held out to him by Colin Taylor and John Jacobs (vegetarianism, he couldn't help noticing, seemed to be no dampener of enthusiasm for drink) and went out to the kitchen in search of what he was afraid was probably the last of the wine.

Anna was sitting at the kitchen table with her face in her hands, racked with sobs. He said, '*Anna.*'

She did not look at him. He put the empty bottles down among the piles of dirty plates and bent over her, putting his arm around her shoulders.

'What is it? Anna, tell me, what is it?'

She hardly could. She said something incoherent, something about its being no good, it all being a sham, and then the tears took over again.

Peter said, 'Hold on. Wait a minute,' and went back into the sitting-room. Isobel was in the middle of the synod debate, saying with some firmness that the laity didn't contribute more because they were never allowed to know better than the Church. Peter went up to her and whispered, 'Can you come? Anna's in the kitchen in an awful state and I can't tell what's the matter.'

When Isobel reached the kitchen, Anna was stooped over the sink splashing cold water on to her face.

'My dear, Peter said you were terribly upset – '

Anna turned round, reaching blindly for something to dry her face on. Isobel handed her a tea towel.

'Thank you. Yes. I'm sorry he found me.'

'What is it? What *is* the matter?'

'I don't belong, Isobel. I'm out of it, apart.'

'Oh my dear – '

'Don't talk Church to me, Isobel,' Anna said, interrupting. 'Don't talk about Christian love, I beg of you. It isn't just that I don't belong, but I don't *want* to belong. I feel as if I've been in some school crocodile for twenty years and if I don't break ranks I'll suffocate.'

Isobel regarded her. Words like tired and overwrought presented themselves to her. In Isobel's experience, a change of scene was often the best possible medicine for such cases as these. She wondered where Anna could go? She would ask Peter. She went across to Anna and took the tea towel away gently.

'I'm going to get you up to bed. Cup of tea and some aspirin. You're worn out.'

'I'm sorry,' Anna said, 'I'm sorry.'

'For what?'

'Breaking down, not being able to cope – '

'Once,' Isobel said, 'when I suddenly felt I couldn't cope another moment with my mother, I hit her with *The Oxford Companion to Music*. It was lying on the floor, propping the door open.'

Anna began to giggle weakly.

126

'And then,' said Isobel, 'realising I had given her a lifelong stick to beat me with morally, I thought I hadn't hit her nearly hard enough. Come on, upstairs with you.'

'The party – '

'It's running itself. I'll tell them you've got a blinding headache. It was a splendid supper.'

'I bought nearly all of it. I only made the trifles.'

'So?'

'Oh Isobel,' Anna said, 'you know. Could I buy things if I wasn't earning?'

'Up,' Isobel said, 'shoo. I'll bring you tea in two ticks.'

In the morning, Patrick O'Sullivan went into the Loxford shop to buy tonic water and peppermints, and heard that Mrs Bouverie had been taken very ill in the middle of a big function, and although she wasn't in hospital, it was touch and go. So he drove into Woodborough and ordered her a basket of lily of the valley, and wrote a card to be dispatched with it.

The flowers arrived and were brought up to Anna by Luke who had decided on a day off school to look after her and/or revise.

'Heavens,' Anna said.

'D'you like them?'

'I like the *flowers* – '

'Yeah,' Luke said, 'you can't blame the flowers. But doesn't sending them strike you as pretty obscene?'

CHAPTER TEN

Eleanor Ramsay, alerted by Peter, telephoned Anna and asked her to come and stay in Oxford. Anna demurred, thinking of the administrative complications. Isobel, however, was ahead of her in this, and said that she would have Flora to stay for a week, and that Luke could spend the week with his friend Barnaby whose mother liked Luke because she believed he was a sobering influence.

'Don't you want to go?' Peter said.

She was stirring a cup of tea, round and round, pointlessly, since she never had sugar. 'Yes, I want to go. But I don't want to have to go.'

'Things have got too much for you before, you know,' he said, unwisely, thinking of her frantic outbursts at St Andrew's, all those years before.

She glared at him. 'You too,' she said, quick as a flash.

He got up and poured more hot water into the teapot.

'I suppose I might get some translation done in Oxford. I've neglected it. I couldn't somehow face it recently, it seemed both inexorable and insultingly second-rate.'

'Even compared with loading shelves in a supermarket?'

'Even,' said Anna in a dead level voice, 'with that.'

'Perhaps now's the moment to give that up – '

'And perhaps it isn't. I'm only away a week. You forget I'm a star employee. Nice Mr S. Mulgrove is a man of sympathy and flexibility. I'll work longer hours the week after.'

'And collapse again.'

'I expect so,' she said. She was beginning to seethe with rage. 'You would like that, wouldn't you?'

'No,' he said maddeningly, 'it is a great inconvenience to me.'

She closed her eyes. She heard him refill her cup. She did not want her cup refilled. She said, hardly caring, 'Will you be all right on your own?'

'Oh yes,' he said. His voice was faintly complacent.

'The groupies. Of course.'

'Don't be cheap, Anna.'

She picked up her teacup and flung the contents at him. They hit his chest, just below his dog collar, across the triangle of grey-polyester clerical shirt-front that showed above the V-neck of his grey clerical jersey. Then she got up and walked out of the kitchen into the garden, closing the back door behind her with tremendous care.

Eleanor's husband, Robert, met her at Oxford station. It was, he said, perfect timing for an arrival, just after the afternoon batch of tutorials, and before a senior common-room meeting. He was a tall, thin, awkward man with the face of a kindly rabbit. He seized Anna's case and took her arm solicitously.

'Eleanor and I were saying we don't think we've seen you, actually seen you, for over ten years. Certainly not since Ptolemy was born. These parenthood years are simply extraordinary, aren't they? One spends all this time and emotional energy developing a great supporting muscle, and then at sixteen they turn round and say they are living their own lives now, thank you, and simply hack it through. I'm afraid Eleanor has spoiled Ptolemy, being the youngest and unquestionably our most able child. That's why she couldn't meet you. Your train didn't tie in with his violin lesson.'

He stowed Anna away in an estate car consolingly strewn with crumbs and discarded lists, and drove her round the city centre, past the Ashmolean Museum, to a large and startling house off Norham Gardens. It was redbrick, its rearing walls irregularly pierced by fantastic windows, and it was crowned at its two front

corners with turrets capped in pinnacles of green copper surmounted by Maltese crosses. It was clearly, from the state of the
gardens, and the condition of the paintwork, divided into two.
Robert Ramsay pulled into the tidier half. His rabbity face
glowed with pride.

'Bought this six years ago. After Eleanor won that great prize
for *No Joking Matter*. Wonderful family house. We love it.'

He took Anna up the steep front steps to a tall door under a
fretted canopy. The hall inside was floored with lozenges of black
and ochre and russet. Doors were open everywhere and the
glimpses of the rooms beyond them gave an impression of vigorous life – tables piled with books, musical instruments propped
against armchairs full of papers and cats, wine bottles and bowls of
fruit, shawls and jackets thrown about, strong colours, cascading
curtains. Robert led Anna up a great wide red wooden staircase,
past long windows with occasional idiosyncratic patches of
chequered glass in blue and yellow, to an immense landing where
huge brass and china pots stood about filled with enormous thirsty
plants, and books and laundry lay in amicable disorder together
on the polished wooden floor.

'In here,' Robert said. He flung open a door and showed Anna
into a tall, dramatic room looking out at the back of the house. It
contained a brass bed – a very big brass bed – several wardrobes
and tables, two armchairs, a black-marble fireplace, a hatstand, a
crowded bookcase and curtains of maroon plush.

'Make yourself comfortable,' Robert said, 'bathroom straight
opposite. Hang on to the chain and count seven before letting go.
I'll make some tea. Eleanor will be back in five minutes.'

He closed the door. Anna looked about her. There was a copy
of *The Times Literary Supplement* by her bed, and the nearest book
she could see in the bookcase was called *The Ethics of Ecology*. Her
bed had an orange cover on it and a pile of riotously embroidered
cushions. The room smelled faintly of incense. Anna put her
handbag down on an armchair, and felt suddenly very shy.

Eleanor, she discovered, had not so much changed as solidified.
She was everything she had been as a young woman, but more

intensely so – more articulate, more decided, more culturally avid, more impersonal. She was also fatter. Her averagely shaped body had swelled at the hips to fill her capacious jeans and large, jolly jerseys. She was not only now a very successful novelist, but also a voracious committee woman. She was, she told Anna, a campaigner, and as soon as Ptolemy was ten – the age that he had been assured would allow him to bicycle to school alone – she intended to throw herself into yet more activity. She told Anna that England had become shockingly philistine and repressive; she intended to promote the freedom of the pen.

Ptolemy was a quiet, snuffling child who gave the impression of having a profound inner life that he was protecting from his mother. His two elder brothers, both day-boys at a city school, had the lugubrious sartorial appearance of impoverished Victorian undertakers, and sloped sullenly about the house, slopping endless bowls of cornflakes and muttering for hours into the telephone. They were kept deliberately short of money by Eleanor – 'The only practical answer, I'm afraid, to Oxford's drug problem' – and so were to be constantly caught unabashedly combing cupboards and drawers for the latest hiding-place of her purse. She seemed to think that this was perfectly normal behaviour and as much an inevitable part of the messiness of adolescence as spots (which they both had) and wet dreams. She informed Anna a great deal about her life, her children's lives and life in general, and after two days had not asked her a single question in return. Anna, who had read *No Joking Matter*, all the first night when she couldn't sleep, began to feel that she was in every way in uncharted country.

The pattern of the day was very decided, and fraught with argument since Eleanor and Robert believed in the right of every member of the family to discuss every topic from the threat to the environment down to whether Ptolemy or Gideon should be allowed the last helping out of a box of Ricicles. Breakfast happened about eight in an atmosphere of steady acrimony, and then Robert herded the older boys into the car for school – this provided a wonderful chance for prolonged defiance – before he went on to college, and Eleanor walked Ptolemy to his school. Anna offered to do this (Ptolemy's eyes gleamed dully at the prospect) but Eleanor said no, because she and Ptolemy had a weekly discussion programme worked out for each term which they got through in fifteen-minute bursts, as they walked. Anna asked what this week's topic was, and Eleanor said, 'Racism,' and Ptolemy said, 'Boring.'

When Eleanor returned from the walk to school, she shut herself in her study until lunchtime, and sometimes teatime, and someone called Mrs Lemon, who bicycled in from Marston, let herself in through the front door and scattered dusters and tins of polish about to create a good impression while she went to make herself coffee in the kitchen and have a good read of the paper.

Anna felt she must be quiet. She explained to Eleanor about her translation and Eleanor said, 'Splendid,' without taking in what she was being told. Anna spread her papers and machinery manuals out on one of the tables in her bedroom, and could progress no further. She tried lying on her bed and reading – every modern novel of any significance was in the house, mostly inscribed by the authors to Eleanor – but unease and a sensation of pointlessness cut her concentration to ribbons. She tried being nice to Mrs Lemon, but Mrs Lemon came to work almost exclusively to get away from her mother's ceaseless talk, and said she was afraid she hadn't time to chat, not with a house this size (she was sitting down at the time, with her feet on a second chair, filling in a competition to win a holiday in Greece with the companion of her choice). So Anna went out, and walked. She walked all through Oxford, and the Parks, and the Botanical Gardens and Christchurch Meadows. She went up the spire of St Mary's, into all the colleges that would admit her, and several times to the Ashmolean Museum. She looked at things of great beauty and great antiquity and great curiousness, and she spoke politely to people who addressed her, and smiled at porters in lodges, and at girls in coffee shops who brought her coffee. And all the time, she felt with a gathering strength that she had, to all intents and purposes, simply ceased to be.

To cheer her up, the Ramsays gave a dinner party. Anna, who only ever went to dinner parties as the Rural Dean's wife, and that most infrequently, was mildly apprehensive. Eleanor did not seem to notice this, but firmly said that Anna would find the people coming most refreshing – a poet, three academics, a flautist and a psychiatrist specialising in paedophilia. Anna would have much preferred to spend the evening playing snakes and ladders with Ptolemy, a game which was his furtive passion and of which Eleanor disapproved.

There were no preparations for the dinner party until about an hour before everyone was due to arrive. Eleanor said how sweet of Anna to offer to help, but really she did so prefer spontaneity, both for the atmosphere and the taste of the food. In practice, spontaneity meant that the kitchen suddenly became an inferno of chaos and screams, loudly scented with garlic and olive oil and roasting peppers, and Eleanor grew scarlet in the face and yelled that she didn't bloody well see why she should have to work so hard to keep them all so fucking comfortable and *still* be condemned to this sodding domestic slavery.

Robert gave Anna a glass of wine and indicated that they should both leave Eleanor to it. With elaborate quietness, he drew Anna across the kitchen – Eleanor's back was briefly turned while she shrieked and hurled chilli powder into a bubbling pot – and out into the hall, where he closed the door behind them. They sat on the stairs.

'It's always like this,' he said. He sounded perfectly relaxed. 'I don't think a creative temperament can successfully be otherwise. She becomes absolutely Wagnerian at Christmas. Wonderful woman.'

'I wish she'd let me help, I feel such a drone – '

'Fatal, dear girl, fatal. It has to be her creation as much as her novels do. She needs, craves, the achievement as much as the applause.'

'I see,' said Anna. 'So my role will be the washing-up.'

'Exactly so,' said Robert, beaming.

Anna went up to her bedroom and looked at her clothes. At least, with a mother like Laura, some of them had a raffish distinction not usually associated with the wardrobes of the Church of England. Ptolemy came in with his snakes and ladders board.

'You'll hate dinner,' he said gloomily, 'it'll be all red and pongy and your mouth will simply blaze.'

Anna indicated the clothes on her bed. 'What do you think I should wear?'

Ptolemy looked, without enthusiasm. After a while he said, 'Oh that,' in a bored voice, pointing to a voluminously skirted black dress, and then added, 'No one'll see, anyway. Will you play with me?'

They sat on Anna's bedroom floor and played three games. Ptolemy won them all. Then Anna said she must dress and Ptolemy said he might as well stay – he always saw Eleanor in the bath so there were no surprises for *him*. Anna put on the black dress and tied a golden yellow Paisley scarf round the waist, and Ptolemy said he was thankful he wasn't a girl. He picked up his snakes and ladders board and went out of the room saying, 'You can always come and play some more if it's too ghastly,' and trailed up to his bedroom on the top floor.

Anna went out on to the landing and listened. It was not only calm, but an aria from *Don Giovanni* was floating out of the sitting-room. As she stood there, Eleanor's bedroom door opened, and Eleanor emerged in an evening pyjama suit of purple-patterned silk with barbaric golden jewellery. She smelled of scent and garlic. She was smiling.

'Anna. Perfect timing. As always at these moments, I ask myself, why *does* one do it?'

It was an evening of extreme difficulty for Anna, because, when asked about herself, she could only say truthfully that she was a parson's wife, it being clearly out of the question to embark on a long description of her relationship with Eleanor, and how that had once been, and how it had changed. It was not, she found, in this enlightened and intellectually fashionable company, at all socially helpful to say that one was a parson's wife. It froze conversation. Eleanor tried to get her to talk about St Andrews, but she said firmly that, as that was ten years ago, it wasn't now relevant. Eleanor persisted, demanding that she recount finding the half-brick through the children's broken bedroom window.

Anna took a deep breath and said very clearly, 'Eleanor, I may be a clergyman's wife, but I am not a party turn.'

134

There was a silence. It was a very complete silence, and it seemed to go on for an unnaturally long time. Anna did not look at Eleanor because she did not wish to see the expression of fury she knew she would be wearing.

Robert gave several little bleats that refused to develop into sentences and then the poet, who was sitting next to Anna, said, 'You must make allowances for us. It is a long time since religion had any real relevance in Oxford.'

Anna turned and stared at him. He stared back for a little while but he was shorter than she, and staring upwards (unless you are a cat) puts you at a disadvantage.

One of the academics – an appealing, ugly, elderly woman with a deep voice – leant across the table and said, 'Do be careful, Fergus, or Mrs Bouverie will think us so very ignorant,' and then she winked at Anna and brandished her wineglass. 'Now look at that. Empty again. Extraordinary,' and there was relieved laughter.

After that, Eleanor took no chances. Anna had been graciously, *generously*, invited to shine and had been most churlish in her refusal: she would not – Eleanor intended to see to it – get a second opportunity. Conversation could now safely exclude her and follow the pattern they all preferred – a little mild intellectual showing-off to warm up with followed by the most excellent Oxford gossip.

Anna and Robert washed up. While they did this, Eleanor sat at the kitchen table analysing the evening, and smoking a Turkish cigarette: 'My absolutely only self-indulgence.'

When the last plate and fork and glass were dried – Eleanor had not moved – Robert said, 'Come on, dear girl. Bedtime.'

Unexpectedly, Eleanor said, 'You go up. I want to talk to Anna.'

Anna and Robert exchanged glances of surprise. He mouthed, 'Better stay,' at her. She looked at Eleanor.

'As a novelist,' Eleanor said, lighting another cigarette, 'I am, as it were, helplessly observant. I am programmed to it. I've noticed far more this week than you might think.'

Robert went stealthily to the door. Anna was beginning to despise his kindness to her which was, she saw, only part of his voluntary subservience to Eleanor. She said, 'Good night,' loudly, to his vanishing back.

Eleanor took no notice. She waited until Anna sat down and then she said, 'Of course, my dear, the time has come for you to leave Peter.'

Anna said nothing.

'Do I read your mind?'

Anna said warily, 'I have a strange diffidence – '

'About what?'

'About abandoning a situation which I have been part of for so long. About being sure that changes in me are permanent changes. About how much confidence I have, real confidence, not just bursts of temper – '

'You weren't ever in love with Peter,' Eleanor said, in a voice suddenly much more like her youthful voice, 'were you?'

'Not *in* love, I don't think, but I believe I loved him – '

Eleanor leaned forward. 'I believed I loved Robert. I was desperate to stay in Oxford and I thought he was clever and he was so admiring of my ideas and ambitions.' She reached across the table for a half-empty bottle of wine and poured some into two glasses still warm from Anna's washing-up. 'Of course, he isn't clever in the least, and I could in fact have stayed in Oxford anyway, and his slavishness drives me absolutely insane.' She took a gulp of wine. 'He's simply hopeless with the boys, no kind of notion of discipline, and the moment there's any question of a decision to be made, he vanishes to college muttering about his commitments. As a lover, he's as much fun as an old sock, and he's perfectly idiotic with money, going into a maddening sort of goofy helpless routine when the bills come in. But you see, Anna, the thing is, I've *pretended*. I'm not just someone of significance in Oxford, I'm beginning to be so nationally – actually, there's talk, too, of an American promotional tour – and I've said to everyone, over and over again, that I am succeeding, that I have life taped. I'd give my eyeteeth for a lover, but who's going to ever think of tackling me with my loudly trumpeted perfect life? Oh Anna,' said Eleanor, reaching out for Anna's hand and bursting into tremendous tears. 'Oh Anna, it's so wonderful to have you here with all your wealth of knowledge of the human dilemma. I never thought I'd say it, but thank heavens for your connection with the Church. It's such a relief to have someone who understands to confide in, you can't imagine.'

When Anna climbed off her homebound train, she found Patrick O'Sullivan waiting for her.

'I offered,' he said, 'and I won. I offered and so did Elaine Dodswell, but I won because I hadn't also promised to take Mrs Eddoes in to the arthritis clinic this morning. Though if I live here much longer it may come to that.'

Anna said, 'But where is Peter?'

'Busy. What does he usually do on Thursdays?'

'They vary,' she said. She had promised herself, all the journey home, that she would arrive in a mood of generosity and optimism, that she would greet Peter with affection, that she would . . .

'Are you all right?'

She lifted her chin. 'Fine, thank you. Rather a late night, last night; a grand finale – '

Eleanor had talked and cried until almost three in the morning. She talked herself through leaving Robert to staying with him after all to leaving him once again for a life founded upon honesty. When she finally allowed Anna to go to bed, she had embraced her warmly and said that she was absolutely thankful Anna had come and been able to make her see what, simply, had to be done, and that more self-respect was to be gained that way than via any kind of self-sacrifice. Anna, who had scarcely uttered, and was entirely uncertain which conclusion Eleanor had finally lurched to, returned her embrace, and then lay exhausted and wakeful until Ptolemy came in at seven-thirty and said Eleanor had relented, and Anna was allowed to walk him to school because it was her last morning, but that they were not going to converse because he was going to tell her jokes out of his *Hundred Worst Jokes Book*. Briefly, she considered relaying the one about a gooseberry in a lift to Patrick O'Sullivan, but decided to save it for Flora.

'I don't wish to be ungrateful,' Anna said, getting into the car, 'but I thought you were a very busy man. After all, this is a very domestic kind of errand.'

Ella had in fact offered to come in Patrick's place, but he had declined. He said he was picking up some wine on the same journey. She had said, 'Oh yes,' in a voice loaded with sarcasm.

Patrick shut Anna into the car and came round to the driver's side.

'Don't sound so suspicious,' he said, starting the engine. 'I am merely learning to be a good villager. Doing my bit, as it were, for the Rector's support-group.'

'The what?'

'It's in its first week. Can't remember whose idea it was. But we have all received an earnest circular about doing our bit for our overworked Rector and his lady, for which the accepted term seems to be lay involvement.' He looked sideways at Anna. 'I wouldn't mind,' he said softly, 'a little lay involvement myself.'

Anna wasn't listening. 'A group? Started last week?'

'Humming along. Beavering about going on all over the place. I expect you'll get home and find there isn't a thing left for you to do.' He glanced at her. 'Did you like my flowers?'

On the kitchen table sat a mauve-pink African violet with a little card propped against it. The card read, 'Welcome home. Celia, Elaine and the parish group.' There was also a note from Peter on the back of a brown envelope, saying that he would be back at twelve-thirty and that Celia had left something in the fridge. Anna opened the refrigerator door. Two perfect, technicolour salads lay on two matching plates (not Rectory plates) under plastic film. Anna banged the door shut. The kitchen smelled violently hygienic. The floor shone; the sink gleamed. 'Be *thankful*,' Anna instructed herself, fighting with rage.

She went upstairs; the staircarpet had been brushed. In her bedroom the air was fragrant with polish, and the dying lilies of the valley had been ostentatiously left in a bowl of clean water. Someone strange, Anna noticed with a spurt of fury, had made their bed, since the cover was arranged with hotel-like precision, tucked trimly in under the pillows, smooth and neat. Peter's slippers lay smugly together by the wardrobe, and the piles of books on their bedside tables had been graded into pyramids.

She ran into the bathroom. All was shining and regimented. The toothbrushes stood in a sparkling tumbler, the towels hung in ordered oblongs. She sat down on the edge of the bath, suddenly winded by the effrontery of it, the intrusiveness, the heavily implied criticism of everything she had previously done, from her behaviour in the parish to the way she did (or didn't) polish the taps.

She found she was shaking. Had these unseen hands also been through her drawers, her medicine cupboard, her linen shelves, looking for letters and tranquillisers and compromising underclothes? She went back unsteadily to her bedroom. Her translation table – oh, the guilt about that, weeks and weeks behind and the silence from the publishers so ominous – had been discreetly but definitely tidied. Whoever had done it now knew about it, just as whoever had ordered their books knew what they were reading. A new thought came to her. She sat heavily on the edge of the bed, too stunned even to take pleasure in creasing its smoothly plump surface. Peter must not only know about all this, but have sanctioned it, given permission for his pyjamas to be folded, his toothglass polished, his wife's sad little collection of cosmetic jars marshalled, to – whom?

The doorbell rang. Anna got up off the bed and went slowly downstairs. She opened the door to Elaine Dodswell, whose face, above one of her weekday tracksuits in jade-green with a white stripe, wore an expression of mixed welcome and apprehension.

'I just came – '

Anna held the door a little wider. 'Come in.'

'You're only just back, I know, I saw Patrick's car. I just wanted to say welcome home, you know. Did you have a nice rest?'

'No,' Anna said.

She led the way into the sitting-room. The furniture looked as if it were standing to attention. The cushions were bosomy; there were no newspapers.

Elaine said, almost in a whisper, 'Oh Anna, I'm so sorry – '

'I ought to be grateful,' Anna said, softening at her evident distress. 'I should be, but – '

'I wasn't at all certain we should do it, I mean, I said, look it's her *home*, but when Peter – ' She stopped.

Anna sat down on the sofa. She patted the cushion beside her for Elaine to sit down too.

'Was it Celia?'

Elaine said, loyally, 'It was the group, the new parish group.'

'And what has the new parish group left for me to do?'

'Anna,' Elaine said pleadingly, 'we were *worried*. You must see that, what with your taking a job that's, well, that's beneath you and looking so tired, and having to put a brave face on your disappointment over Peter, we wanted to *help*, we wanted to show we *understand*, I mean, we're women too – '

Anna took her hand. 'I know. I believe you. I think you are a kind woman, Elaine. But – and this will seem harsh and ungrateful to you – I need the sort of kindness that is tailored for me, not just the unimaginative sort that it suits other people to give. Do you understand me?'

'No,' Elaine said. She took her hand away. 'It took three of us all yesterday and two hours this morning. Celia and me and Trish Pardoe. We haven't moved anything.' She got up and said in a voice now tinged with resentment because Anna had failed to soothe her anxiety with comforting, understanding gratitude, 'Peter was ever so pleased. He said the house hadn't looked like this in years.'

Anna stood up too. 'And if Colin said that about your house, after someone else had cleaned it, and the cleaning of it was usually your responsibility, what would you feel?'

Elaine stared at her for a moment. Then she went bright-pink. 'He'd never say it!' she almost shouted, 'he'd never have cause to! I keep my home like a new pin!' and then she ran from the house.

Anna and Peter ate lunch almost in silence. Peter, Anna observed, looked much better for her absence, not so bony and with even a little colour. He ate Celia's brilliant salad with relish, wiping his mouth at the end with the little scallop-edged paper napkin she had so daintily provided. Anna blew her nose on hers.

By the time Peter had come home, Anna had had a private tantrum in the garden, and had washed her face and prepared herself to be calm but not particularly friendly. Peter clearly felt the same. She did not mention the spotless Rectory, so neither did he. Nor did she broach the subject of the parish group, a sleeping tiger he was clearly not going to poke awake. Instead he told her of uncontroversial parish matters and she told him of Eleanor's troubles and neither commented upon the other's information. When lunch was over, Peter gave Anna a brief kiss, said it was good to have her back and that he must go, to take prayers for the Thursday Club at Snead. As he went out of the back door, he was humming. He sounded almost jaunty.

CHAPTER ELEVEN

When he had gone, Anna washed up, brushed her hair, found the quilted Indian jacket that Charlotte had discarded as being reminiscent of a sixties earth mother, and locked the house. There were no afternoon buses from Loxford into Woodborough, so she walked the mile and a half to the main road, and caught a bus there. She had brought shopping bags because she told herself that she was going to buy supper before she collected Flora, but she had also brought the paperback copy of *Ariel*, which she had not read, because she knew she was really going straight round to the Vicarage. She did not, as she sat on the bus and stared out of the window at the prosperous fields of wheat and barley, and the blazing fields of rape, allow herself to articulate why she would go to the Vicarage. Instead, she permitted herself half an hour of mindless luxury of having a purpose that would also be a pleasure.

The door of the Vicarage was opened by Miss Lambe. She stood, as she always did, holding it only six inches open and peering up at Anna in an anxious and mouse-like way. Anna stooped a little and asked in a very kind voice for Mr Jonathan Byrne. Miss Lambe whispered that he was working and wasn't to be disturbed until teatime.

'In that case,' Anna said sadly, 'would you give him this? Say that I'm returning it. With many thanks.'

Miss Lambe nodded and shot out a paw for the book. Behind

her, in the cavernous hall, a door opened and Daniel Byrne ushered someone out of his study. He was saying, 'I do agree with you, but I don't want to do it so delicately that it ends up looking apologetic,' and then he saw Anna and said, 'Mrs Bouverie! How extremely nice. Come in, come in.'

'I was just returning a book – '

'Can't you just come in, too? Mrs Bouverie, this is our new Methodist minister, here in Woodborough. We were having an ecumenical discussion about a joint confirmation service.'

The Methodist minister looked as if he thought the subject of their discussion ought to be strictly private. He nodded stiffly to Anna.

'Miss Lambe,' Daniel said, 'could you rustle up yet more coffee?' He shook the minister warmly by the hand. 'It's been such a useful discussion. Thank you so very much for coming.'

When the front door had closed, he said, 'A good man but he swallowed a poker.' He took Anna by the arm. 'How very nice it is to see you. Come in, come in.'

She allowed herself to be led into his study and installed in a wing chair upholstered in faded tobacco-coloured corduroy. Daniel seemed entirely at ease, pottering round her, moving books off a stool for her coffee cup, stuffing papers into a cardboard folder, talking comfortably. He talked about Methodism for a little, and then about a Christian therapy group he had been asked to lead – 'They all complained of the sensation of being lost, of not knowing where they were going but I said what about starting with the notion that you can only be lost if you have no destinations, and if you are Christians, as you say you are, then surely you *do* have destinations?' – and then about Miss Lambe – 'A rare little bird, indeed, but her innocence is such a responsibility' – and then he settled himself in a chair opposite Anna's and said, 'Now. Let's get down to business and talk about you.'

She said, 'I might behave just like your therapy group.'

'You have a sense of humour – '

She looked down. 'And a sense of shame.'

'My dear girl – ' He leaned forward. He waited.

She said reluctantly, 'I'm very much afraid of sounding self-pitying. Self-pity is so absolutely disgusting.'

'I think you should simply *speak*.'

She looked up. He was watching her, his head on one side. She would very much have liked to cross the room and sit on his knee, and her eyes widened involuntarily in horror at herself.

'Anna,' Daniel Byrne said, 'concentrate.'

She blinked. She said, in a sudden rush, 'I've been away for a week in Oxford, staying with a friend. It should have been a release but somehow it wasn't, it was simply quite foreign. And I came home this morning glowing with good intentions, and found that a newly formed parish support-group, with Peter's blessing, had scoured my house from top to bottom. All very well meant and yet absolutely outrageous. I am so offended, I hardly know how to express it, and yet I know any outsider would think me an ungrateful *cow*.' She paused, took a breath, and hurried on. 'The thing is that the validity I am assured, almost commanded, that I have as a Christian, seems not to be carried out in my human life. I seem to have less significance not only than my husband but than most of the parish. I'm not a person, I'm simply a sort of function, and a pretty lonely sort of function at that. And when I think about love,' Anna said, warming up, leaning forward, 'which I know to be absolutely vital, I can only think, except for what I feel for my children, of something rather monochrome and tired and dutiful. It isn't that I don't try, I try like mad, and then of course the lack of result seems even harder to bear. Sometimes, I've been known to yell at the sky just trying to get an answer.' She stopped, wondering if she had overstepped the mark. She shot him a little glance. He looked exactly the same.

'Go on,' he said.

She took a breath. 'Have you ever felt like this?'

'Of course. The dark night of the soul.'

'I suppose, though, if you were a monk – '

'If you mean sex,' Daniel Byrne said comfortably, 'it stopped mattering quite simply when – and because – other things of much greater importance came to fill its place. But it was a shocking trouble before that.' He put his hands behind his head. 'I wonder if you are confused about love? You are so determined to strive and struggle, to bash away. But divine love – don't look away

– is about receiving, not giving. That's why it's so different, so instinctive, also why it's the easiest.'

The door opened. Jonathan put his head in. His face lit up.

'Anna!'

Daniel said, 'That was a tactless bit of Porlocking. Haven't you the discretion to knock?'

Jonathan came right in. He was wearing jeans and an enormous dark-blue jersey and his hair was tousled. He said, 'In case you have a choirboy in here?'

Daniel ignored him. He said to Anna, 'I find you very brave. It's so wrong to think that spectacular courage is the best bravery. The noblest bravery is battling against these dreadful daily assaults, often very minor, on one's spirit.'

Jonathan came to sit next to Anna. 'Can I join in?'

Anna looked up at him. Her eyes were shining. Sitting here in this shabby, untidy, human room with the Byrne brothers suddenly seemed perfection, a happiness she could hardly bear to abandon. She said sadly, 'I have to get Flora.'

Jonathan said, 'Then I'll drive you back to Loxford.'

'The bus – '

'No,' Jonathan said with vehemence, 'no. Don't always object to everything. Don't be so bloody difficult.'

'She's not difficult,' Daniel said.

'I know that. I know that really. She's lovely.'

'Stop it!' Anna said, 'stop it!' She was laughing.

Daniel got up. 'You just hold out your cup,' he said to her, 'just hold it out and let it be filled.'

'Like letting me drive you home – '

'Only if that's what she *wants*.'

'Do you?' Jonathan said, turning. She nodded. 'Good,' he said, smiling at her, 'I'll go and find the keys.'

When he had gone, she said to Daniel, 'I thought it was a requirement of maturity, and of grace, to be very hard on yourself, as hard as you were generous to everyone else.'

He put his hand briefly on her shoulder. 'It's all a deal, a two-way business, if it's man to man. That's what makes us undivine. But you try a little taking from God. Just relax into it. And in a

145

while, we'll talk some more.' He moved away, back to his desk. 'We aren't all the same, you know. We all need something different, we all hear different messages.' He paused and then he said softly, 'So many people just lack the capacity to live richly, at any level. You aren't one of them. It's too easy to defend a castle that's never been attacked. Don't be afraid. And now here is your chauffeur.'

It was a strange drive home. Flora had begun to write a play in her English lesson, and was so absorbed in her second scene (an encounter between her orphan heroine and a mysterious cloaked stranger) that she actually elected to sit in the back of the car and scribble furiously in her notebook. Jonathan had pleased her by saying seriously, 'Ah, the second scene. Of course, it's the second act that is always notoriously so difficult,' to which she had gravely nodded. From the back seat, she watched the back of his head and wondered if he would serve as a model for her stranger, when he removed his cloak and shed his mystery.

Jonathan talked most of the time. He drove better than Daniel with an instinctive ease that freed him for talking. He talked with energy and fluency, mostly about the education of the feelings, and how important it was, and how feelings make or break men and women and give them their best capacity to understand other people. He told Anna that Stendhal had declared that you had to look into your own heart to discover who you were. He said that one of the messages of literature is that everything is different in the grip of strong feelings, and that is why passion is dangerous as well as wonderful.

Anna listened. She simply lay back in her seat and watched the sky swoop past through the windscreen, and listened. There was no need to say anything.

Jonathan said, 'We all overlay our feelings with too much thinking. We are afraid of our feelings because they are arbitrary and volatile, and we often need literature to make our feelings intelligible to us, to make us see that our reaction to what we can't choose and what we can is what shapes our lives.'

The journey was over too soon for Anna; she saw the village

green slide by with apprehension. She said, 'It's so nice of you. Just drop us by the church.'

The car stopped. Jonathan said, 'You see, it is so terribly important to stay *alive*,' and then, without warning, he picked Anna's hand from her lap, and kissed it.

Later, Flora said, 'Why did he do that?'

'Because it's awkward to shake hands sitting side by side in a car.' (Well done. Quick thinking.)

'You couldn't,' Flora said clearly, 'do that to a *man* – '

'But I'm not a man.'

Flora regarded her. At the end of scene two, the mysterious stranger might take the heroine's small cold hand in his great gloved one and kiss it. 'Telling me,' Flora said.

In Woodborough Vicarage, Jonathan looked without enthusiasm at the slab of pork pie lying palely on his plate and said, 'Can I ask what Anna came to see you about this afternoon?'

'Not really.'

'Was it to tell you that she didn't love her husband any more and to ask you what to do about it?'

'If you knew what she came for,' Daniel said, putting down his knife and fork, 'why do you ask me?'

The evening passed with rigorous politeness. Luke had much enjoyed his week living in Woodborough and listened enviously to Anna's account of Eleanor's sons' lives in the wild paradise of Oxford. Flora explained about her play – 'It's a tragedy so of course the end will be awful' – and Peter and Anna avoided looking at one another. After supper, Peter said he would wash up, but the telephone rang and a young woman from Church End said her father had died that afternoon and she couldn't do a thing with her mother, so he had put down the washing-up brush, and put on his jacket, and gone. Luke and Anna washed up instead, and Luke sensed that Anna didn't want to be back at home any more

than he did, but he didn't wish this to be the case, so said nothing.
Instead, Anna told him about coming home to find her gleaming,
burnished house, and Luke said, 'Interfering old cows. At least
my room defeated them,' and they laughed. Then he said, 'I've
got two hundred and eighty pounds towards India,' and she said,
'Wonderful. Well done,' and he nodded, and the doorbell
rang.

It was Elaine Dodswell. She was holding a pile of parish magazines for May. Luke looked at them. Elaine said breathlessly,
'Would you give these to your mum? We thought perhaps – I
mean, we know she likes to do them herself, so after all we
thought – ' She stopped.

'OK,' said Luke, after a while, 'if you want.' He took the magazines.

Elaine stepped back a little. 'Tell her – ' Luke waited. 'Say I
called,' Elaine said. 'No hard feelings.' She turned and hurried
down the path.

Luke shut the door and went back to the kitchen.

'What are those?'

'Guess.'

'Who brought them?'

'Elaine Whatsit. From that house with those gross frogs. She
said no hard feelings.'

Anna sat down. 'Do you know, I think they believe that by
handing back the magazine round they are somehow restoring my
raison d'être.'

'Don't do it, then.'

'I have to,' Anna said. Luke was suddenly afraid she was going
to cry. 'I have to. I've painted myself into a corner.'

Three days later, in the early evening, as Anna pushed a folded
magazine into the gleaming brass letter box of the Old Rectory,
the door was opened from the inside.

'Come in,' Patrick said.

Anna shook her head. 'Thank you, but I can't – '.

'Just for a moment. I want to talk about Luke.'

'Luke? Why, has he – '

'Don't look worried. He's wonderful, a real asset. No, it's a scheme I have.'

Cautiously, Anna followed him into the hall.

'Come and sit down.' He opened the door to the room where he had taken her before, and given her brandy. The fat chairs beckoned like pillows. She longed to sit in one.

'Drink?'

'No, thank you.'

'Just innocent tonic water, then. Why do you treat me like Bluebeard?'

Anna did not want to encourage him by saying that all conversations with him immediately seemed to flicker with danger, so she simply said primly, 'I treat you like any other parishioner.'

He grunted. He poured tonic water into one of his extravagantly cut tumblers and added ice and lemon. 'About Luke.' He handed her the glass.

'Yes?'

'I want to help him.'

'I believe you already are – '

'No. More than that. I want to get a bit involved in this fearsome trip they're all planning, see they have a roadworthy vehicle and so forth, and then, if you'll agree, help him with the next stage of his life, the right art school, that sort of thing.'

Anna said with distaste, 'A patron.'

'If you like. Why should that matter? I'm rich and childless and I like Luke. There wouldn't be any sinister strings.'

Anna shook her hair back. 'I'm terribly sorry. I was disagreeable and rude. It's exceedingly kind of you to want to help and heaven knows, Luke could do with a guardian angel like you. May I mention it to Peter? And then – and then, perhaps talk some more?'

'Anna,' Patrick said, 'I do genuinely want to help Luke. But I must confess, I'd do anything on earth to get you to talk to me some more.'

She stared at him. He took a swallow of the drink he had poured himself and then put the tumbler down on the tray where all the bottles stood. Then he crossed the few feet of carpet between them, removed her glass from her hand, set it down, put his arms firmly about her and kissed her. He kissed her hard and competently. Anna, who had been kissed by no man but Peter for over twenty years and had come to assume that she was surrounded by some *cordon sanitaire*, was so entirely startled that at first she did nothing. She simply stood in his embrace. Then panic set in; not the indignant panic of outrage at being kissed but the hysterical panic of realising that she did not dislike it. She brought her arms up sharply and shoved hard against his chest.

He said, 'And now you can say, "How dare you!"'

She stepped away from him crying, 'But I don't want to be seduced!'

He said, 'Do you know, for a second I could have sworn you did?'

She ran for the door. He ran after her, and seized her wrist. 'Don't go!'

'What I hate,' Anna said, swinging on him, eyes blazing, 'is this assumption that I'm easy game, that I'm some sort of imprisoned innocent who will be grateful to you for releasing me. You are a stupid, arrogant, insensitive man.' She wrenched her wrist free. It hurt. She cradled it with the other hand. 'Just because I'm inexperienced,' she said furiously, 'doesn't mean that I lack perception or native wit. I'm not a *fool*,' and then she flung the door open and vanished across the hall and through the outer door, letting it crash shudderingly behind her.

Slowly, Patrick moved to the hall in her wake. Ella came out of the kitchen, holding an oven glove. She looked at Patrick. Without uttering a word, she communicated to him that she was pleased to see he had at last met his Waterloo. He said, without returning her look, 'I haven't finished yet.'

CHAPTER TWELVE

I n the sixth-form college's boys' lavatory, companionably pee-
ing side by side, Luke said to Barnaby that home was really
weird just now. Barnaby, who had always hankered after more
weirdness than his mother's strong sense of order could stand,
said how come? Shaking himself and then zipping up his jeans,
Luke said kind of furtive.

'Furtive?' Barnaby said. 'Like hassle?'

No, Luke said, not like hassle, in fact no one was hassling him
at all. It was more a sort of atmosphere, people not saying things
when they were dying to, Mum and Dad kind of pretending the
other wasn't there.

Barnaby considered this very briefly and abruptly lost interest
in the whole topic. 'Want a smoke?'

Later, on the last bus to Loxford, Luke's mind returned reluctantly
to the subject. He wasn't much surprised, since his mind, just at
present, lurched between the disagreeableness of home, and sex.
Sex usually won. Luke was horrified and fascinated to find how
much he thought about it and longed for it and was afraid of it.
He couldn't see, usually, how he was actually going to *do* it for
the first time but he feared that if that first time wasn't soon he'd
probably explode. This state of affairs had come upon him quite
suddenly and he was entirely at its mercy. He got erections all the

time, without warning, and had fantasies of a slightly brutal kind about a girl in his art-history set, a girl called Alison with long, rough red hair and sneering eyes, like a cat. She was reputed to have slept around since she was fifteen. Luke's imagination returned constantly to what, if this were true, she might know that he did not. The power that she would have in possessing such knowledge made him almost sick with excitement. It also made this daily departure from Woodborough, where Alison lived and where she lounged about in the evening with Barnaby and a group of others, almost unbearable. Add to that the atmosphere in the Rectory, and Luke sometimes thought he couldn't take any more.

And yet . . . There was some little haunting thing about his mother that sang in Luke's mind. Ever since she'd come back from Oxford, she'd seemed secret, shut away, but the secret clearly wasn't a thrill like the secret of Alison, it was something sad, as if something had got broken. Luke didn't want to talk about it because he didn't really think he could cope with being confided in, but the look of her made him uneasy and sorry. His conscience drove him home, and then his feelings of being helpless and disconcerted drove him out again, to the Old Rectory, to cut the edges of Patrick's lawn, and polish Patrick's car and rake Patrick's gravel and to feel, as he did so, the healing balm of Patrick's prosperity and assurance.

When the bus got to Loxford, Luke found that he simply could not face the Rectory yet. He got off at the far side of the green, and was immediately ambushed by old Mr Biddle from behind his garden wall.

' 'Ere,' Mr Biddle said. He beckoned Luke over. He wore a cap, winter and summer, and a sagging tweed jacket, and he had filthy fingernails and bright, sharp old countryman's eyes. 'What about 'im?' said Mr Biddle in a conspiratorial, screaming whisper.

'Who?' Luke said.

Mr Biddle seized Luke's sleeve. He gestured at the Old Rectory. ' 'Im. O'Sullivan. Does he 'ave wimmin there?'

'All the time.'

Mr Biddle licked his lips. 'Wimmin from *London*?'

Luke nodded. 'Belly dancers.'

'Cor,' Mr Biddle said. He let Luke go. He sketched huge breasts on the front of his jacket and grinned. 'In the war – ' began Mr Biddle.

'I'm late,' Luke said. 'I'm supposed to be working for him. Got to get the spuds in.'

'Spuds?' Mr Biddle said. He gave a little cackle.

Luke did not, despite lurking thoughts of Alison, want to know what spuds reminded Mr Biddle of. 'Gotta go,' he said.

Mr Biddle nodded. He took a step back, his glance suddenly clouded. Belly dancers! In Cairo, in 1942, he'd been offered a little girl, she couldn't have been more than ten. He hadn't remembered that for twenty years; he wished he hadn't remembered it now. He squinted at Luke. 'You take care.' His voice wavered a little. 'You take care around that O'Sullivan. Money ain't to be trusted.'

Luke walked briskly away across the green, hoping that his air of purpose would prevent anyone else from accosting him. Patrick had not in fact asked him to come in this evening, but, as there was always things to do, Luke assumed it wouldn't matter. He went round, as usual, to the kitchen door and knocked. No one came. He opened the door cautiously. The kitchen was empty and tidy and faintly fragrant with baking. A row of Ella's loaves – she was now highly proficient at bread-making and, to her scornful pleasure, in demand for demonstrations to local women's groups – stood on racks on the table under blue-and-white cloths. Luke's mouth watered.

He crossed the kitchen and knocked on her sitting-room door. No reply. He opened the door. Like the kitchen, the room was empty and orderly. Luke went back through the kitchen and out into the hall and listened. It was very quiet, but clearly someone was at home because the back door had been unlocked. He knocked softly on the door to Patrick's study.

There was a pause, and then Patrick called, rather absently, 'Come!'

Luke put his head in. Patrick was sitting at his enormous desk, writing. This was most peculiar. Patrick never wrote, he only signed things. But now, he was writing what looked like a letter, in a very neat black hand on the stiff white paper he had had specially printed for the Old Rectory. He looked startled to see Luke, as if Luke had woken him up.

'Luke!'

'Sorry,' Luke said, 'I just wondered, I mean, d'you want anything done?'

'It's Wednesday.'

'I know. I just wondered – '

'No,' Patrick said, 'no. Nothing. Tomorrow, as usual.' He looked down at the half-filled sheet of writing paper, and then at the hand holding his pen which seemed to hover with eagerness to get back to writing.

'Sorry,' Luke muttered. He withdrew his head and shut the door. Patrick hadn't even smiled. There was nothing for it but to go home.

Only his father was at home. Flora had gone to tea with the Maxwells, which she liked to do because she was conscious of adding glamour and colour to their tidy lives, and Anna, said Peter, had gone to Brownies.

'But she doesn't do Brownies.'

'Trish Pardoe is ill. Mum said she would step in.'

A sudden childish misery settled on Luke. He wanted Anna to be there, as he had wanted Patrick to welcome him. 'I'm hungry,' he said, 'starving – '

Peter looked at him. He said, 'You know where the bread is.' Luke's face was sullen. Peter felt, as he often now did, that he was too tired for his children, that he was so worn out by inner emptiness and the need to show outer confidence that he had nothing left over. He had never quite known what to say to Luke, had come to regard communication with Luke as Anna's business; now, he was bored by Luke, bored by his age, his unfinishedness, his mixture of obstinacy and apathy. Flora, luckily, was both more outgoing, and still a child. Peter said, 'Make yourself a sandwich.' He tried to sound helpful.

Luke sighed. He let his bag fall with a thud. He would have liked, with a sudden mindlessness, to have lashed out, to have slammed his fist into something – the wall, the closed sitting-room door, his father's face. Muttering, he turned away, and slouched into the kitchen, where he made himself a heavy crude sandwich, not bothering to put away the bread, and leaving the knife stuck in the butter. Then he went upstairs and shut himself into his bedroom, and turned his music on so loudly that downstairs in the study objects danced on Peter's desk and the furniture shuddered. Peter, writing a piece on 'The Church in the Nineties' for the diocesan magazine, put his hands over his face, and despaired.

Two days later, Anna found a stiff white envelope in one of her Wellington boots. It was long and smooth, and it had 'Anna' written on it in black ink. She took it down the garden with her, on her way to unpeg the washing, and opened it the far side of a screen of several sheets, two towels and a surplice.

It said, 'Anna, I have to write because you will never allow me to speak. You are determined that I am unscrupulous, that I am amusing myself, that I am playing a seduction game. You are so wrong. I am in earnest.' The 'earnest' was underlined.

Anna's mouth was dry. What she held in her hand was a love letter. A *love* letter! Extraordinary. Being kissed had been strange enough – though not, she had told herself with rigorous insistence on the truth, unexpected – but a letter was even more unmanageable, because it prolonged what might have been just a mad moment into a mad situation.

'You accuse me,' Patrick wrote, 'of wanting to release you. Of course I do. Of course, because of admiring you as well as being in love with you (in love with me, Anna thought, in love with me. Dear heaven! What is *happening*?), I wish to rescue you from a life where you are neither valued nor fulfilled. If you were less determined to write me off as a bastard, you'd see that my intentions are gallant, not patronising. I want to give you clothes and books and travel. I want to give you comfort, even luxury. I want to give you money. I want to take you among people who will appreciate you – not as my possession, but because I absolutely cannot stand to see you wasted here. You aren't just wasted as a person, you are wasted as a *woman*.'

The letter was signed simply 'Patrick'. Anna folded it and put it back in its envelope and put that in her pocket. A few heralding drops of rain were beginning to fall. Anna turned to the washing line and began to tear the laundry down rapidly, thankful for any action that might calm her incipient hysteria. A man I hardly know, she thought, holding pegs between her teeth while she folded a sheet, a man I hardly know has asked me to leave Peter and come away with him so that he can shower me with glittering things and company. It's daft. It's not just daft, it's silly and ludicrous and not what happens in life. It's a stupid fairy story. It might even be a particularly disagreeable joke. She touched her pocket. She thought of Patrick's armchairs, his carpets and decanters, his hair, his clothes, his voice saying, in her own kitchen, 'Now, what is a woman like you doing in a place like this?' If this was temptation, Anna thought, holding Peter's surplice against her unheedingly, then it had all the subtlety of a charging bull. Yet it also, undeniably, sang a soft and siren song. To exchange what she had for what she might have! She blushed for herself. 'You must never,' she told herself sternly, picking up the laundry basket, 'make the mistake of underestimating what you don't have. Thinking that way shrivels the soul. But, oh – '

Back in the kitchen, Luke was sitting on a tilted back chair talking to Barnaby on the telephone. When Anna came in, he dropped his voice to a mutter. He waited for her to say don't be long – the parish paid only half the telephone bill, as he was sick and tired of being told – but she didn't. She didn't really seem to take him in at all, just put the clothes basket down on the table in a dreamy kind of way, and then went over to unplug the kettle before filling it. Luke watched her. She was wearing an Indian skirt Laura had given her, of rough russet cotton with big pockets, and round the hem darker russet embroidery encircling tiny moons of mirror. Something stuck out of the top of one of the pockets, something white and oblong. Anna turned from the sink. Luke could see it was an envelope. For no reason he could think of, Luke felt abruptly horrible; sick and sweaty. 'Yeah,' he said to Barnaby, gripping the receiver tightly, 'Yeah.'

Ella had several broken nights. Being a person who prided herself on competence, this was annoying enough in itself (when you are flat in bed, my girl, you are there to *sleep*) but was made worse by anxiety. Patrick had accustomed her over the years to what she termed his scrapes, but this present business was another matter altogether. Ella was a fast learner. She might not have cared for the look of village life at first glance, but as it appeared to be her future she had decided to accept it. It had not taken her long to realise that what could pass invisibly in Fulham or Notting Hill Gate was laid bare for all to see in such a place as Loxford. In Ella's view, it was only a matter of days, rather than weeks, before all five villages knew that Patrick O'Sullivan was laying siege to the Rector's wife.

Ella had made friends. She had found in Celia Hooper and Sheila Vinson and Elaine Dodswell just that practicality that she rejoiced in in herself. They shared with her, too, a small but steady resentment of the upper classes as represented by the Mayhews, the Richardsons and Miss Dunstable – Patrick was exempt from this social disapproval because he was a bachelor, and approachable, and had clearly made his money himself, quite recently. Conversations between the four women fell only just on the right side of bitching. They were very confidential with one another, but Ella felt instinctively that Patrick's current adventure had to be kept to herself. This was hard, with her new-found companionship.

What troubled Ella was not only that Patrick was about to create a scandal, but that Anna Bouverie might help him. Ella quite sympathised with her new friends' view that Anna didn't pull her weight and that she was guilty of wearing an expression of separateness – almost of superiority. Country parishes, they were all agreed, were very different from urban ones, and most priests' wives would think it a privilege to live somewhere as friendly as Loxford. Anna's job at Pricewell's was, Ella considered, pure exhibitionism. It was this element in Anna that Ella feared might make her revel in the limelight of an affair with Patrick. It was all of a piece with that terrible purple cloak.

Then there was Luke. Ella, who did not like boys, liked Luke. Whatever Anna's failings in other directions, she had done a good job on Luke. He had nice manners, worked hard, and was clearly very fond of his mother. Ella showed her approval by treating him as she did Patrick, and by feeding him. He ate relentlessly. It was almost a luxury, Ella thought, to watch her excellent loaves and fruit cakes and scones disappear into Luke like coal into a furnace. She found that she felt very troubled indeed about Luke when she thought of Patrick and Anna Bouverie.

There was nothing to be gained by speaking to Patrick. He knew without question that she thought his behaviour both stupid and wrong. He believed himself to be thoroughly in love this time and was, as he had become accustomed, determined to have his own way. Ella had nothing to threaten him with. If she told him she was leaving, he would simply ring up an agency for a temporary housekeeper. Putting a kipper down in front of Patrick one breakfast, she said, 'Well, if you haven't the sense to think of yourself, at least think of that poor boy,' and Patrick had replied, in his genial way that contained just a hint of menace, 'Mind your own business, my dear.'

There was nothing Ella could do except get on with her job. Practicality, she discovered, was no match for power.

Luke burned with an inarticulate rage. He was haunted by suspicion and could not bring himself to hunt through Anna's drawers to find that envelope and have his suspicions confirmed. Instead, he was surly and oafish. He came home on the last possible bus, avoided going round to the Old Rectory and then announced that he was spending a few nights in Woodborough with Barnaby. Neither of his parents seemed to mind at all. Flora said, 'Oh, *good.*' During one of those Woodborough evenings, he got drunk and aggressive, and then tearful, and Alison took him home with her. She lived with her divorced father, who was a salesman and often away. She made it very plain that she would allow Luke to fuck her, but only after he had done to her all the things she required for her own pleasure. This had never struck him as constituting part of the sex deal. He didn't like it very much. Parts of her tasted soapy and other parts salty or fishy. He came several times, helplessly, during the course of this, and, when he was finally allowed inside her, it was over almost before it had begun. He had slept afterwards as if poleaxed and woken feeling absolutely terrible. Over mugs of instant coffee before school, Alison said that, now he'd had what he wanted, perhaps he'd kindly leave her alone; he was too young for her anyway.

The day passed in a furious, nauseous daze. Barnaby, who of course knew where Luke had spent the night, behaved with rare tact and simply left him alone. After the lunch break Luke, impelled by instinct rather than conscious thought, cut an English literature class (*Hamlet* – a discussion of the relative significance of action and inaction in the play) and caught the early afternoon bus to Loxford. Sometimes, after a morning shift at Pricewell's, Anna caught that bus too. Luke looked furtively round. She wasn't there; no one he knew was there.

He sat slumped across the seat, staring out at the landscape. He knew every tree and hedge, every house and barn. All the things that usually pleased him – a gaunt dead tree alone in a shallow valley, a spire rising above a beech hanger, a secret lane that suddenly plunged downhill off the main road like a rabbit hole – looked as interesting as grey cardboard today. After a while his eyes grew gritty and strained with staring so he shut them. It made him feel slightly sick, but at least that was a diversion. He kept them shut until the bus stopped on Loxford green.

He went slowly, steadily, across it to the Old Rectory. This time, Ella was in the kitchen, doing household accounts at the table with the bills spread round her in little piles.

'Luke!'

He shut the door and leaned against it.

'You should be at school – '

'I've come to see Patrick.'

Ella rose. 'We thought you'd given us up. Revision, I said to Patrick, with A levels only a month away – '

'Sorry,' Luke said. He dropped his bag.

Ella came nearer. 'You look dreadful.'

'Feel it.'

'Luke,' Ella said, 'where have you been? What have you been up to?'

Luke made drinking movements with one arm. 'I stayed in Woodborough last night.'

'So you've come here for me to make you respectable to go home to your mother.' Ella sounded pleased.

Luke looked at her. 'I've come to see Patrick.'

Ella's expression changed. 'I don't think that's wise. Really I don't. I'll make you a sandwich and we'll chat – '

'*No*,' Luke said loudly. 'I've got to see him. Please.'

'But what will it achieve? Just think a moment – '

'It'll stop it,' Luke said, 'that's what.'

They stared at each other. Then Ella said uncertainly, 'He's in his study. As usual.'

Patrick laughed. He came round his desk and tried to put his arm round Luke's shoulders. Luke flinched away. 'Come on,' Patrick said easily, 'no melodramatics.'

Luke was trembling. He said, 'Don't lie, don't lie, I *know* – '

Patrick laughed again. 'My dear old fellow, you know nothing. How could you? You're only seventeen.' He put his hands in his pockets. 'I like it. Really I do. I like your loyalty, your protectiveness towards your mother. You're a good lad. I don't blame you for coming, it does you credit. But you have to believe me when I tell you that you don't actually understand what you've come for.'

Luke yelled, 'You're making a fool of my mother!'

Patrick stopped laughing. He looked grave and sad. 'Oh no,' he said, 'that is the last thing I would do to someone who means as much to me as your mother does.'

Luke lunged forward. Patrick caught him easily and pinned him against a bookcase.

'Don't be such a bloody fool.'

'You're a shit,' Luke tried to say, 'a shit, a shit,' but tears were flooding down his face and he could not speak for rising sobs. Patrick propelled him out of the door. Ella was waiting in the hall. She took Luke from him and led him into the kitchen.

Isobel Thompson had had a trying afternoon. Her car had broken down on the way to her weekly session with the girls at a remand home some ten miles outside Woodborough, so that she was over an hour late and the girls, difficult and truculent at the best of times, were impossible. She felt out of touch and useless, with no spirit even to ignore the repulsive language they were deliberately using for her benefit, let alone rise above it. There was no question of love that afternoon, only of endurance. Isobel endured until four-thirty, and then nursed her complaining car slowly back to Woodborough. The garage had told her they would probably find her a reconditioned engine for five hundred or so, which would give the car another few years of life. Five hundred! And on something so dull. For three years, Isobel had been promising herself a trip to India, a walking trip in the foothills of the Himalayas before she was too old to take it on. She had £700 saved towards it. Isobel set her jaw and drove tensely on.

At home, the telephone-answering machine was loaded with querulous messages. Unmarried women deacons were, Isobel thought, assumed to have no life of their own worth having, and were therefore bound to be terribly grateful for all the unpleasant bits of other people's. She wrote down the messages in her notebook, and went out to the kitchen. If she had a pound for every time she put a kettle on each day, either in her own house or anyone else's, she'd have enough money in six months to go to India *and* buy the car a new engine.

She made herself tea. She longed for a biscuit, but she was steadily putting on that kind of solid, middle-aged weight there is no shifting, and was trying to resist all the sweet and comforting things, that, if taste were anything to go by, were her natural foods. Her mother, who despised sugar, had always been contemptuous of Isobel's preference for sweet rather than dry sherry, milk chocolate to plain, a bun instead of a cheese sandwich. In Africa, Isobel had never thought about sugar; in England, if she was honest, she thought about little else.

She took her shoes off and sat down with her cup and saucer. She looked at her stockinged feet. Serviceable things, no more. When she was a girl, she had been rather proud of her high arches, but these had dropped long since, padding about sandalled in Africa. Oh, she thought, closing her eyes, how much I left in Africa!

The doorbell rang. Isobel found she would rather have liked to say several of the things those girls on remand had said this afternoon. She put down her cup, found her shoes, and went stiffly and wearily into her little front hall. There was a telescopic spy hole in her front door. She put her eye to it and gave a little gasp. She flung the door open, and there stood Luke Bouverie, looking on the point of collapse.

When she had put him to bed – 'I'm not discussing anything more, dear, until you've had some sleep' – Isobel rang Anna.

'He's quite safe. He's had a bath and he's asleep. I'm afraid he went drinking with Barnaby last night, and then cut classes this afternoon. He'll be fine in the morning.'

'Oh Isobel,' Anna said, 'I'm so grateful. But I'm sorry too, it shouldn't have to be you – '

'I'd rather Luke than most of the people who end up in my spare room.'

'He's having a bit of a phase, poor fellow. I don't think the atmosphere here is good for him at the moment.' She stopped, just before she said, Any more than it is for any of us.

'I'm always here,' Isobel said. 'You know that.'

'I do. Bless you. And bless you for having Luke. Did he confess to you?'

'About the drinking,' Isobel said firmly.

She put the telephone down, and went upstairs. Luke slept on his side, his dark head deep in the pillow. Isobel stooped and picked up his clothes which he had simply dropped on the floor. When she had put them into her twin-tub washing machine, she thought she would telephone the Archdeacon.

'I think it's just a bit of nonsense,' Isobel said to Daniel. 'Instead of a woman parishioner getting a crush on the priest, it's a male one on the priest's wife. But it's upset the boy a lot and he says he can't talk to his parents.'

Daniel was scribbling with his free hand. The other was occupied with the telephone receiver. 'Do you know the man?'

'Only by sight. He hasn't been there long. He came from London. And, of course, Anna's so attractive.'

'Hasn't she put a stop to it? It isn't difficult, for a clever woman.'

Isobel hesitated.

'Oh dear,' Daniel said.

Isobel said hurriedly, 'Things have been so difficult at Loxford recently – ' She wanted to say, Since you got the job Peter wanted, but contented herself with, 'It's often the way after ten years in a parish. And the children are growing up – '

'I understand you perfectly,' Daniel said. 'I've spoken to Anna recently and I know something of her situation. If I speak to her again,' he said musingly, 'I'm taking her into a confidence her husband isn't sharing, and I think he is even more isolated than she, just now. Do you agree?'

Isobel said, 'He's a very difficult man. He knows he is, which makes it worse.'

Daniel made a resolution. 'I will go and speak to them together. This is, after all, a difficulty for them both.'

'I never listen to rumours,' Peter said, 'I never have. You can't afford to in the country.'

'But, if your son is distressed – '

'Luke is taking A levels and is not at an age where anything is easy. He gets overwrought.'

'All the same,' Daniel said patiently, 'I should like to come out to Loxford and talk to you and to Anna.'

'No, thank you,' Peter said. He sounded as if he were holding the telephone receiver well away from his mouth. 'I appreciate your concern but there's nothing the matter. Temporary tittle-tattle. I'm afraid Luke got led astray by friends and overreacted. Isobel Thompson has known him since we came here, so it was natural he should go to her. 'Perhaps she – she gave more weight to things Luke said than she ought.'

'Peter, may I not suggest even that you and I might meet, just briefly – '

There was a pause. Then Peter said, 'Perhaps, when I'm not so

163

committed. In a few months. Thank you for ringing. Goodbye.'

Daniel replaced the receiver and sighed. He looked out of his study window at the white clouds sailing briskly across a cool May sky.

'Over to You,' Daniel said, out loud.

CHAPTER THIRTEEN

L aura Marchant's television commercial had proved rather a success. Although it hadn't reached the screens of the nation yet, it was much talked of in the offices of the company that had made it. There was a strong sense that Laura was something of a find. She was put on a retaining fee not to accept work from any rival until the effect of the original commercial could be assessed.

This made her more comfortable, but it was boring. Like an old hound scenting the chase, the relief and pleasure of acting again had given her a renewed taste for it. While she waited to see whether she and the Irish stout proved to be something – or nothing – of a triumph, she auditioned down at Chiswick for a small part in a new play, and got it. The part was a seaside-hotel landlady and, although she hadn't many lines, she was on stage a good deal and she intended to make the most of that. Given her dimensions and the exuberance of her personality, she thought her mere presence on stage might be one of those things the audience found they could not ignore.

She adored rehearsals. She loved the purposeful travelling to them, the gossip and coffee breaks, the reborn contact with the theatre and its people. She became the auntie of the company, the source of consolation and liquorice allsorts. All thoughts of selling St Agatha vanished from her mind since not only could she now squirrel away weekly sums to help Luke and Flora, but St Agatha was clearly the cause of her new-found success. All those years of confiding in the saint, of treating her as a true companion, had reaped their reward. On St Agatha's painted plaster face, despite the scars and chips of her arduous life, Laura was now sure she could detect a faint but unmistakable animation.

The play in Chiswick was not admired by the critics or by the public; the only person to get even reasonable notices was Laura. After its allotted three weeks it closed, with no mention of a West End transfer, and Laura went back to St Agatha, determined to audition for something else as soon as possible. Mutely and powerfully, St Agatha indicated that, perhaps, before she started to badger her agent once more, Laura should pay a little attention to matters closer to home. The word 'Loxford' emanated from St Agatha as powerfully as if she had spoken it.

'My dear girl,' Laura said, 'you are perfectly right.'

St Agatha made it very plain that that was what saints were for.

Laura telephoned Loxford. Peter answered. He sounded polite and a little formal. He said that Anna was out – in such a way as to make it plain that Anna was always out – and that Flora and Luke were at school. Laura proposed herself for the weekend. Peter said he was sure that would be fine and that he would get Anna to confirm the arrangement that evening.

'Darling boy,' Laura said, 'I don't like the sound of you. What is the matter?'

Peter said he had rather a cold, thanked her for telephoning and rang off. Laura dialled Kitty, in Windsor. Kitty's employer had started a tea shop for the summer months and Kitty's duties now included making scones and showing people to their tables, as well as selling souvenirs in the shop, and taking the Pekinese out to spend constant, minute, senile pennies. She'd had a pay-rise too, and had booked herself a holiday in Jersey, a week in October, her first holiday in years. She was going with her employer who knew a lovely hotel where they did all their own baking . . .

'And have you heard from the family, Kittykins?'

'The – '

'Do concentrate, darling. Life isn't all lardy cakes. Have you heard from Loxford?'

'I ring every week, dear. Just for a little word. Flora loves her school – '

'Kitty,' Laura said, 'I spoke to Peter just now and he sounded perfectly morbid.'

'He never could rise above knocks, not even as a little boy. I remember – '

'No,' Laura said, 'no reminiscences. Have you spoken to Anna?'

Kitty rather thought Anna was overtired. Of course, shop-work was terribly tiring, she ought to know, and Anna's standards were so high, always had been, whereas hers had got lower and lower until she realised, before her job came along, that she was simply never cleaning the bath, because no one saw it but her, and she didn't care . . .

'I am worried,' Laura said emphatically.

'Are you, dear?'

'I don't like the atmosphere. I shall go down this weekend.'

'You're so decisive,' Kitty said. 'I do admire it. I've found that if you dust the tops of scones with flour before you put them in the oven they come out as light as air.'

Laura put the receiver down sadly. As light as air. As light as Kitty's heart and head. Scones! Laura dialled the number of a na-tional, long-distance bus company and, in an exaggerated German accent for her own amusement, asked the times of the service to Woodborough, on Friday afternoons.

In the garden of Woodborough Vicarage, Anna and Jonathan Byrne sat on a bench in the sun. It was a wooden bench, on whose back had been carved 'Our God Himself is Moon and Sun'. Jona-than said it was a quotation from Tennyson. Above the bench hung a few branches of white lilac, and in front of it a lawn stretched in a neat oblong to a solid border of hostas beneath the boundary wall. Anna thought it a dull garden, but she was very contented to be sitting in it, in the late May sunshine, with Jona-than Byrne.

He had come into Pricewell's at the end of her shift, and dis-suaded her from the errands she was then intending to do. She had said, automatically, 'Why?' and he had said, 'Because I need to see you.' In Anna's present bemused state of mind, this had seemed as good a reason as any for obliging him. Daniel had gone to London for the day, Miss Lambe was having her weekly afternoon off at the Wednesday Club (an outing, this week, to nearby water gardens followed by tea in St Paul's Parish Room) and the Vicarage was empty and quiet. Anna followed Jonathan docilely out into the garden, as she had followed him from Pricewell's. He sat her on the bench, and then he went back into the house and returned with a tray bearing a loaf, a piece of cheese, two apples and a jug of cider. Anna took off her shoes and sank her grateful bare feet into the grass.

While they ate, Jonathan told Anna about his and Daniel's childhood. They had been brought up in York. Their mother had been a Baptist, simple and stern, and their father a most unlikely mate for her, a ranting and eloquent Scot who ran a timber yard. Daniel was born ten years before Jonathan and had, from his birth, treated his younger brother with peculiar tenderness.

'So how old is Daniel now?'

'Fifty.'

'So you are younger than I am.'

Jonathan looked at her. 'Not by much. And not to judge by appearances.'

Anna surveyed her feet. She said calmly, 'I love Daniel.'

'Yes,' he said, 'I know.' He waited for her to say something more, but she didn't, only sat and stared at her feet in the grass. So he said, 'Could you love me?'

Very slowly, she turned to look at him. After what seemed like a very long time, she said, 'I think so.'

'Only think?'

She said seriously, 'I have to be honest. I love Daniel and that's one kind of love. I believe I love Peter, and that's another. I'm being besieged by a parishioner with yet another brand. But when I'm with you I feel that, in a way I can relax best, I've come home.'

He didn't touch her. He bent down to the tray and refilled their glasses. He held Anna's out to her. She said, 'I'll go straight to sleep.'

'Not straight –'

The hand she had stretched out for the glass shook a little. She withdrew it. He said, 'I'm in love with you. I had thought I wouldn't say it because the words are so weary, so overused. But I want to be quite plain with you, I want you to be quite sure of what I'm saying.' He leaned towards her and kissed her mouth lightly. Her eyes were full of tears.

'Oh Anna. What is it?'

She gave herself a little shake. 'Relief,' she said.

Jonathan stood up. Then he bent and took Anna's hand and led her after him back into the house. She felt heavy and peaceful. They crossed the cavernous hall – the Victorian tiles, patterned with crude imitations of medieval designs, were cold and smooth under Anna's bare feet – and climbed the gaunt staircase to the first-floor landing where narrow strips of brown carpet led off down various dark passages, like arrows. Jonathan led Anna along one of these to his study, to which he had now become so attached that he had moved a divan in, and started sleeping there. He opened the door. Anna burst out laughing.

'What a funny room!'

'Is it?'

'Yes,' she said, 'yes.' She was enchanted by it. 'So mad and so exuberant and so grim – '

He seized her. 'Too grim to be seduced in?'

She stopped laughing. 'Oh no,' she said, 'and anyway it isn't a seduction.'

'What?'

'It would only be a seduction,' Anna said, leaning into his embrace, 'if I wasn't as willing as you are. Which isn't, as it happens, the case.'

When Anna got home, there were, as usual, several telephone messages (Peter had said that the parish group were going to raise money to give them an answering machine and Anna had said, 'Are you sure Celia wouldn't rather just sit here and take the messages herself?'). There was one from Sir Francis Mayhew about the honey rot he had spotted in two beech trees in the churchyard, one for Luke from Barnaby, and one from Laura. At the bottom of the list, Peter had written, 'Out until 6.30. P.'

Flora said, 'Sarah Simpson at school says Barnaby takes drugs.'

Anna put her arms round Flora. She wanted to hold her, to feel the great warmth she was full of spreading into Flora. Flora squirmed.

'Do you mean he smokes pot?'

Flora wriggled free. '*Much* worse.'

'Barnaby's mother is a pillar of rectitude. And his father likewise. What do you know about drugs, anyway, Flora Bouverie?'

'Heaps,' Flora said.

Anna wrapped her happy arms about herself instead. 'I think you just like gossip.'

'I do not like Barnaby Weston.'

'I see,' said Anna.

Flora went pink. 'I don't!'

'No, darling. Are you hungry?'

'Starving – '

Anna unwrapped herself, and delved into a carrier bag. 'There.'

Flora's eyes bulged. 'Chocolate hazelnut spread! We *never* have that!'

'We do now.'

Flora looked at her. She appeared to Flora to be sort of – *shining*. Flora said fervently, 'Thank you.'

Anna smiled, 'Not at all. Don't eat too much at once. It's for sandwiches, not spooning. I'm going to telephone Ga.'

'Is she coming?'

'For the weekend,' Anna said, turning to the telephone. Behind her back, with infinite stealth, Flora extracted a teaspoon from a drawer and unscrewed the lid of the chocolate jar. What, after all, was the point of a treat in half-measures?

Laura decided at once that she didn't like the look of any of them. Peter looked withdrawn and offended, Luke looked ill and Flora was thoroughly out of hand. As for Anna . . . What was the matter with Anna? She looked fine really, better than Laura had expected, but it wasn't somehow a reassuring fineness. Her eyes were full of energy, a quick, restless energy. It was, Laura decided, as if some bright inner life were both firing and alienating her. Was her behaviour, Laura wondered, just a little mad?

She tried to corner Anna. Saturday was hopeless. 'You know Saturdays here,' Anna said, 'almost worse than Sundays. Definitely Rabbit's Busy Day.'

In the afternoon there was a sad, amateur, little fête at Snead Hall, where the headmistress prided herself on insisting that the girls use their own initiative. As they were aged between eleven and sixteen, and were spending these precious years of their adolescence being irrationally disciplined and indifferently taught, most of the pupils at Snead Hall either had no initiative or were damned if they were going to use any. Under a lowering sky, a scattering of stalls had been set out on the ruined lawn of what had once been a beautiful garden. The five villages, drawn to the fête by the same instinct that drew them to jumble sales and carboot fairs, poked about among the secondhand paperbacks and lopsided offerings from the cookery room, and obligingly guessed the name of a giant, pink, plush teddy bear, donated by the husband of the school secretary, who was a traveller in soft toys. Laura said, 'Satan.' The child detailed to write down the suggestions (10p a time) wrote the name down without a glimmer of comprehension.

It was obligatory for Anna and Peter to visit every stall. Laura, discouraged by her anxiety out of almost all her natural ebullience, trailed after them. She bought a gloomy little bag of melted-together fudge, a paperback of a historical novel about Joan of Arc and a pair of curiously lumpy oven gloves from a craft stall, whose holder explained breathlessly that she'd had to use old tights in them as their needlework teacher had run out of wadding. Flora brought a stout pink child with spaniel's ears of brown curls to meet her, a child called Emma something, but they didn't stay, being too much occupied with showing off to the poor prisoners of Snead Hall. Clutching her purchases, and feeling the fudge soften unattractively under her fingers, Laura resolved that, before night fell, she would tackle Anna.

However, Luke got to her first. He came into Charlotte's bedroom which she was as usual occupying, while she was repinning

171

up her luxuriant dark-grey hair before supper. First he said it
was great of her to have given him the money for India but he
didn't know if they'd be going now, it was all a bit difficult
and Barnaby's mum was anti the whole thing, he'd have to see.
Laura said did he have to go with Barnaby and Luke looked
shocked and said there wouldn't be any point otherwise. Then
Laura said, 'Is that why you look so awful, darling? Or is it
looming exams?' and Luke ducked his head and muttered that
it was Mum.

'Mum?'

Luke said, 'Well, not Mum, really, her and Dad. And this
bloke – '

'*What* bloke?'

'The one I worked for, the one with the Daimler.'

Laura put down her combs and pins. She came over to the bed
where Luke had slumped and sat down beside him. He smelled
sad and unwashed.

'Darling, tell me all you know.'

'I don't *know* anything – '

'Then – '

Luke turned on her. 'That's just it, I don't know anything, nobody says anything, but the atmosphere's awful, I hate it, they're
hardly speaking – '

'I noticed.'

'Ga,' Luke said, 'Dad makes it hard, you know, hard for all of
us. And Mum . . . This bloke fancies her.'

'The Daimler bloke?'

'Yeah. He wrote to her. This letter – '

'You never saw it – '

'Not the words.'

'And Mum. What does Mum think of Signor Daimler?'

'Dunno.'

'Then what does it matter?'

'I don't like it!' Luke shouted suddenly.

'Why?'

He glared at her. Couldn't she see? Couldn't she see that he was
full of love and loyalty and confusion, none of which could possibly be explained? Could she not also see that, by doing something

172

wrong, or clumsy, he might unwittingly break some magic rule and lose the thing he loved?

'Sorry,' Laura said, 'sorry, darling. I shouldn't have asked. I'll talk to her, I'll talk to Mum.'

'No! No!'

'Why not?'

'I don't want to squeal on her,' Luke said, 'not on her.'

'No. Of course not. Though I don't see how I can help if I stay silent.'

Luke looked at her. 'That's the problem,' he said in exasperation.

On Sunday, Laura accompanied Anna to church. It was a sung eucharist. The church looked very bright and clean and there were horrible stiff triangular flower arrangements on the altar and by the chancel steps. 'Freda Partington,' Anna hissed. 'Fields full of cow parsley just now and she buys, actually buys, chrysanthemums.' There were not many communicants. Sir Francis Mayhew limped round with the collection bag, having first put in his own five-pound note, in full view of the congregation. Laura watched her son-in-law and reflected that, however difficult and unapproachable he was in real life, he still took services with grace and dignity. Beside her, Anna thought much the same thing.

Anna also thought about Jonathan. What astonished her was not so much that she had been to bed with him – and was now an adulteress – but that it should have been so natural to do so, and even more, so natural in its doing. Her every dealing with the Byrne brothers had been characterised by sheer ease, from that first drive to Loxford with Daniel, to Jonathan saying into her shivering skin, 'And do you like this? And this? But not that?' She had slipped along in her relationship with them like a fish in a stream, seeing at last, because of them, her passage clear to the sea. She was perfectly certain that she would continue to go to bed with Jonathan and that her love for him would grow until – she looked at Peter's surpliced back before the altar – until she saw unquestionably what she should do next. For the moment, she would just gratefully draw strength from this astonishing new

173

source. A thought shot into her mind like a bolt from the blue. Had Jonathan actually been *offered* to her?

Going out of church, she and Laura were accosted by Patrick. He shook hands fervently.

'I'd adore you,' he said to Laura, 'to see my garden.'

'Dear boy, I'm hopeless at gardens.'

He said, 'Hopeless?'

'Can't see the point of them. But mountains! Ah now, *mountains –* '

Patrick, sensing he might be being made fun of, stepped back a little. 'Can't offer you those, I'm afraid.'

Anna hadn't looked at him. Nor had she replied to his letter. Both omissions gave him heart. He said, rallying, 'Perhaps I can manage a mountain for your next visit – '

Laura smiled at him. He was very attractive. 'Do try.'

At the lich-gate, Miss Dunstable paused to say, 'Terrible flowers,' to Anna.

'I quite agree. But you'll have to complain to the parish group about them. They've taken over the rota.'

'Let them try taking over my altar frontal!'

Later, in the Rectory kitchen, making coffee, Anna said with no self-consciousness, 'I'm being besieged by Patrick.'

Laura affected outrageous surprise. 'Darling!'

'I expect Luke told you.'

Laura deflated. 'Actually – '

'Poor Luke. There's nothing for him to worry about. I feel nothing for Patrick except temper.'

'Sure?'

Tiny pause.

'Sure.'

'You must make that plain to Luke.'

'Does he think – '

'He's afraid to think. Anna, I had one golden rule for affairs. No teasing.'

'I'm not having an affair,' said Anna with her back to her mother.

'But Patrick thinks you soon will. He's blazing with that caveman certainty of incipient conquest, simply blazing. You must tell

174

him once and for all. It's perfectly easy to make yourself quite plain.'

There was a silence.

'For Luke,' Laura said.

'Of course.'

'One last meeting. Face to face. Finish.'

'There's nothing to finish.'

'Oh yes, there is,' Laura said. 'In Patrick's mind, at least.' She looked at Anna, leaning against the sink, her dark head bent. Poor darling, Laura thought, poor wasted darling. What a life! And Peter. What had withered Peter? 'Anna,' Laura said, holding a hand out to her daughter, 'Oh darling,' and felt as if her heart would burst.

That night, Anna attempted to comfort Luke. She explained that Patrick had developed an infatuation which she didn't in the least return, and that she was angry and sorry that such adult foolishness had spoiled his own relationship with Patrick. She said she was going to put a stop to everything. It was, she said, very easy for a woman to make sure a man never tried anything again. (Remembering Alison, Luke could at least believe that part.) She said he was not to worry any more and that she felt most remorseful that he should have worried in the past over something so silly and fantastic. He allowed her to kiss him. He wanted her to stay a bit, but not to talk any more, but he didn't say so, so she went. When she had gone, he lay on his bed and felt worse than he had done before she came in.

Two days later, she caught the early afternoon bus back to Quindale. Jonathan had put her on it, having walked with her from Pricewell's to the bus station. He said he was in such a frame of mind and heart at the moment that he was inclined to walk into walls. When he had found her a seat on the bus, he put an envelope in her lap and said, 'I'm afraid there'll be a lot of this. Letters and poems. I'm bursting with the need to communicate with you.'

She read the letter in the bus. It described Jonathan's sense of joyful recognition at meeting her. She read it several times. Then she put it away in her skirt pocket and leaned her head against the shaking glass of the bus window, and uttered a mute and fervent prayer of thankfulness.

It took a quarter of an hour to walk from Quindale to Loxford. The lane between the two villages was only travelled by local people, and ran between peaceful fields used for grazing cattle and sheep. They were, at the moment, full of lambs, as raucous as a primary-school playground. Anna walked along the verge – the lane twisted a good deal and the hedges made visibility difficult – and looked at the lambs and the new, soft, bright growth on the trees and thought of her letter and her good fortune. One field, brilliant with buttercups, seemed to her to be almost a symbol. She stopped in the gateway to gaze.

When, half a minute later, Patrick drew his car into the gateway behind her, she felt a mixture of irritation and relief. It was exasperating to have her reverie broken, and yet this was clearly an excellent chance to say what she had to say, a chance that avoided all kinds of disagreeable contrivings. All the same, as he got out of the car and came round it towards her, she felt suddenly nervous.

'Anna.'

'Hello.'

'What a chance. I was going to pick up some new greenhouse glass.' He leaned on the gate beside her. 'Why haven't you replied to my letter?'

'There is no reply,' Anna said.

'Oh yes,' he said, 'there is. And you know it.'

She was silent, resolving exactly what she would say.

'I asked you to come away with me. I'm asking you again now. I'll ask you until you come because I know it is what you want.'

A car was coming along the lane. Instinctively, Anna moved away from the gate to put a prudent distance between herself and Patrick, but he leaned forward and seized her wrist.

'I love you,' Patrick said.

The car passed. Anna dared not look at it. She said, as contemptuously as she could, 'Let go.'

He dropped her wrist. 'Please,' he said.

'This is the last time we shall have anything to say to one another.'

'Why, what do you mean – '

'I despise you,' Anna said. 'I despise your arrogance and your insensitivity. I was a fool to believe you wanted to help Luke.' She turned and began to walk hurriedly along the lane towards Loxford. After her, Patrick called, 'But I did! I do.' She didn't hear him. She began to run, dreading to hear the Daimler's sleek purr behind her, catching her up. But it didn't come, nobody came, except Mr Biddle, pedalling slowly on his creaking bicycle, never looking at her but simply shouting at her as he went by.

'Want to get yourself a bike, Mrs B!' Mr Biddle bellowed. 'Want to get yourself modernised, you do!'

'It's true,' Trish Pardoe said. She stood in the Old Rectory kitchen, confronting Ella. She had driven straight to Ella even though it would make her late for picking up her mother at the Woodborough Pop-In Club.

Ella, who knew all too well it was true, simply nodded.

'They were holding hands,' Trish said. Her voice shook. 'In a gateway. Broad daylight. I nearly crashed the car.'

Ella said, 'It's been going on some time. He got a bee in his bonnet about her the minute he got here. I thought it was just a fad. He's like that.' Unaccountably, she found she wanted to defend him, to say that he was a romantic, that he saw himself rescuing a princess from a tower, that he wanted to give her all the things she had plainly never had. But Trish Pardoe's expression was not conducive to any defence of Patrick.

'It's disgusting. That poor vicar.'

'I suppose she's a human being, like the rest of us – '

'Ella!'

Ella said sadly, 'Perhaps it's a good thing it's come to a head. That you've seen them – '

'I saw them all right.' Trish peered at Ella. 'What'll we do?'

Ella sighed. 'I suppose I have to go and talk to the Rector.'

'I'll come – '

'No.'

'Why not? I saw them – '

'Because it will be easier for Peter if he thinks only I know. If he doesn't think it's general village gossip.'

'Soon will be – '

'It needn't be,' Ella said with emphasis.

Trish hesitated. 'Of course, I wouldn't say a word – '

'No.'

'What's she got to complain of? Tell me that. How many vicars' wives get the help she gets, I'd like to know? Gives her all the time in the world to mess about with her fancy man – '

'Shut up,' Ella said.

'I beg your pardon – '

'Go away,' Ella said, 'I've got to think. And keep your mouth shut. If I hear any rumours, I'll know where they started.'

'Whose side are you on?'

Ella looked at her. 'Peter's.'

'Me too,' Trish said.

Flora brought a note home with her from school. It was from Luke. He had delivered it to St Saviour's at lunch-time. It said, 'Dear Mum, I'm going to live at Barney's for a while. Till the exams are over. Mrs Weston says it's fine. I can give her a bit out of my savings to help with food. Take care. Love, Luke.'

CHAPTER FOURTEEN

P eter sat alone in Snead church. He had gone to take the mid-
morning Thursday communion service to which almost nobody came, but which was clamorously defended whenever he
suggested dropping it. He liked Snead church. It was the simplest of
his five churches, a Norman nave with a single shallow transept in
which the wheezing organ lived. There was no coloured glass in the
windows and the Parochial Church Council of Snead preferred sisal
matting in the aisle to the red carpeting favoured by the other four
churches. The restraint appealed to him.

He sat in the north side of the choir stalls and looked out at the
waving plumes of a willow tree in the churchyard. He did not
really see it, any more than he saw the sky beyond it, or the grey-
ish stone window that framed it. He was conscious of very little
except the quiet and his unhappiness, which filled his whole being
like cold, still water. It was water he was afraid to disturb, to dive
into, because he couldn't bear even to begin to analyse why he felt
as he did. He shrank from his thoughts, just as, these days, he
shrank from Anna. If their limbs brushed each other in bed, he
could feel his withdrawing, flinching. In the same way, his eyes
turned away from meeting hers when they spoke. He was terribly
afraid that he was going mad. Long ago, as a theology student,
he had had a crisis about prayer, a period of alarming doubt. His
tutor, a man of enormous experience in ministerial matters, had
simply counselled him not to struggle. Throw out the idea of

God, he had said, just forget it. Think instead about something about which there can't be personal anguish, something more abstract, like a desire to be good or kind, or the wish to love, and voice that wish in your mind, over and over. After a while, try saying it to Christ, but only when you feel you want to. This had been sound advice. When things were difficult, he had thought about the qualities necessary to ease those difficulties; but of late, he had only thought of how to endure. All softness in him seemed imperceptibly, involuntarily, to have hardened. He didn't feel in the least interested in love or goodness or kindness; the only thing that stirred him was a determination not to give in.

He sighed, and slipped automatically to his knees. Footsteps sounded in the porch, and the heavy iron latch on the door was lifted. A slice of sunlight fell in and a woman said, 'Oh, I'm ever so sorry, Mr Bouverie, I'd no idea – '

He looked up. It was Emma Maxwell's mother, clutching a dustsheet.

'I just came to clear away last week's flowers. But I can easily come later – '

He got stiffly to his feet. 'No, no, please come in, I was just going.'

'You sure?'

'Quite,' Peter said. He smiled at her. She was plump and pink and her hair curled cheerfully, exactly like her daughter's.

'We're so pleased Emma and Flora are such friends,' Mrs Maxwell said, encouraged. She advanced up the aisle. 'St Saviour's is a lovely school. So kind.'

'Flora seems very happy.'

'She makes us laugh. What an imagination!'

'Too vivid, sometimes.'

'Oh, I don't know. Most children never use theirs, because of television, so it's lovely to see a child like Flora. The nuns are dears.'

'I only – '

'So tactful,' Mrs Maxwell said, rushing on, pressing her dustsheet to her bosom in her enthusiasm. 'I mean, if you don't mind my mentioning it, they make no distinction between the fee-paying children and the free-place ones. I shouldn't think the other children even know. Emma certainly doesn't know about Flora.'

Peter came out of the choir stalls. 'I beg your pardon?'

Mrs Maxwell blushed. How clumsy and stupid to bring it up! Probably little Flora didn't even know herself.

'I'm so sorry. I've no tact. Please forget I ever said such a thing.'

A small light was dawning in Peter's comprehension. He said quietly to Mrs Maxwell, 'Please don't worry. Don't think of it.'

She nodded. She said quickly, wishing to make amends, 'I hope you know that Flora is welcome any time, at our house. Very welcome.'

'Thank you,' Peter said, 'thank you.' He smiled again. 'And now I'll leave you to your flowers.'

He drove home in a very different mood. The paralysis of unhappiness had abruptly given way to the energy of anger. He left the car in the drive and hurried into the house. The telephone number for St Saviour's was written up, in red, on the emergency list that Anna had stuck to the wall. Peter dialled it. He stood up straight by the telephone, almost to attention, looking out of the window. The school secretary answered.

'This is Peter Bouverie speaking, the Reverend Peter Bouverie, Flora's father. I wonder if I might speak to Sister Ignatia?

At lunchtime, Peter made himself a sandwich and a cup of coffee. After he had eaten, he washed up his cup and plate, and then he had a good look in all the cupboards. There was nothing in any of them that wasn't familiar, nothing new, or exotic, only a virgin cheese-grater still in its plastic film and an untouched, sealed tin of shortbread.

He went upstairs, quietly, as if he were a burglar. He looked in the bathroom; same towels, same toothglass that the Quindale garage had given away at Christmas with every twenty gallons of petrol, same cracked and charming Victorian soap dish. He crossed the landing to his and Anna's bedroom. Methodically, one by one, he slid out drawers and opened cupboards. Anna's colourful and wayward clothes lay and hung there in absolute familiarity; her shoes were in the tumble on her wardrobe floor that had always so exasperated him and were all, in any case, unquestionably well worn. There were no new books beside her bed, no scent bottles on the chest of drawers, no evidence anywhere that Anna had spent a single penny of her earnings on herself or her house.

So where were those earnings? They wouldn't be much, but there would be, Peter reckoned, at least £500. Why had she concealed Flora's free place? Why was she hoarding? In all their married life, anything she had earned he had thought of as pin money, holiday money, money for violin lessons for Charlotte (a failure) or a school trip to Venice for Luke (a success). He believed she had thought of it in the same way, that they were well-suited in their approach to money, that she had grown accustomed to frugality, adjusted to it. Of course, being an archdeacon would have brought in substantially more and of course it was only human to regret that; but why deceive him? Why take this attitude of secrecy and defiance?

He went downstairs again, and into his study. He was not going to conduct this war Anna had started using her own guerrilla tactics; he was going to act decisively and openly. Sister Ignatia had, unsurprisingly, been much startled to hear Peter's question, and, although she had said nothing even faintly condemning of Anna, her tone of voice had been unmistakable. Sister Ignatia was the first step. The next two seemed to him perfectly plain. When he had taken those, Anna could not but confront the reality of her actions. What would happen after that, Peter chose not to think.

Peter said to the supervisor on the checkout that he would like to see the administration manager. The supervisor hesitated. Peter had no appointment, and there were rules in Pricewell's about appointments, but he had a dog collar and was therefore in an unusual category of visitor. After a moment, she asked Peter to follow her and led him up the aisle between pet foods and washing powders to the staircase to the office.

Even though he knew Anna's shift was over, and that she was on the bus back to Loxford, Peter kept his eyes on the supervisor's back. He followed her up the gaunt staircase and along a corridor to Mr Mulgrove's office. Mr Mulgrove was very startled. The sight of Peter gave him the same sensation as being visited by the police.

He offered Peter a chair in his tiny office. When he resumed his own seat, their knees almost touched, which horrified him as it seemed so disrespectful. He thought Peter had probably come to ask Pricewell's to make a donation to some local cause, and, as Pricewell's had a charities policy, he had his patter all ready for that. But Peter said nothing of the sort. He said that his name was Peter Bouverie, the Reverend Peter Bouverie, and that he believed that his wife worked part-time in the shop.

Mr Mulgrove stared. 'Anna!'

'Yes,' Peter said, 'my wife.'

Mr Mulgrove's eyes strayed to Peter's dog collar. A vicar's wife! Anna, a vicar's wife! He started to say that Anna was one of their best staff but of course she was really management calibre only he couldn't persuade her – but stopped himself. It didn't seem, somehow, an appropriate observation to make in the circumstances, with Peter turning out to be a vicar, sitting there almost in Mr Mulgrove's lap.

'Were you unaware that she came from a rectory?'

'Why, yes, I mean, I knew her address, of course, but so many people now live in old rectories I didn't think. I knew she was, well, not exactly what we usually – ' He stopped.

'No,' Peter said. He wasn't smiling.

Mr Mulgrove had a flash of loyalty for Anna. 'She wanted the job to send her daughter to St Saviour's. My sister went to St Saviour's.'

'My daughter has won a free place at St Saviour's.'

They looked at each other in silence.

'She's a good worker,' Mr Mulgrove said, and then, 'This is a good company to work for.'

'I don't doubt it. But there isn't any need for her to work here any more.' Peter had a brief battle with the precise truth, and lost it. 'Not now that St Saviour's has given Flora a free place.'

'I see.'

'So from the end of this month, my wife won't be working for you any longer.'

183

Mr Mulgrove hesitated. When he had first begun at Pricewell's, as a school leaver of sixteen, it was quite common for the husbands of women with jobs in the store to organise their wives' working lives for them, accompanying them to interviews, complaining to the manager about poor working conditions or low pay. But things had changed now. Mr Mulgrove doubted that any of his female workforce even consulted their husbands about where or when they should work. He supposed that vicars were a bit old-fashioned. He said, 'She's said nothing to me.'

'No. I think she preferred it that I should speak to you.'

'I'll have to confirm it with her – '

'Of course.' Peter got up with difficulty.

Mr Mulgrove stood too. He was taller than Peter, and younger, and it struck him that Peter was not just old-fashioned but stuffy. He couldn't somehow see Anna as Peter's wife. Looking down at Peter before he performed the necessary contortion to open the door, he said, 'We'll be sorry to lose her. She's very popular.' He paused and then he said, with just the faintest hint of aggression, 'We're proud to work here, you know. We're proud of this company.'

Anna was not on the bus to Loxford. Anna was lying on the headland of a sweet-scented bean field in flower, five miles out of Woodborough, with Jonathan. They had started to make love but it had been terminated by Anna's sudden violent distress at recalling Luke's going off to live with the Westons. It had shaken her dreadfully. She had been to see Mrs Weston, who had been kind and ordinary and talked sensibly about exam pressures. She said she'd fill Luke up with bread, and in any case she was glad to have him; his presence made Barnaby less truculent. Luke would clearly be safe and well provided for with the Westons, which was bearable, but the probability that he would also be happier was hardly bearable at all.

Jonathan was very comforting. Anna said sternly to him that he mustn't feel he had to comfort her because her family troubles were hers and she certainly wasn't about to offload them on to him. He held her in his arms and told her she was a perfect fool;

didn't she realise that he loved the whole package of her, not just the bits and pieces that related directly to him? He said he would go and visit Luke, that he would like to.

'To my amazement, I like adolescents. You'd think, after fifteen years of teaching them, that I'd have developed a violent antipathy. But I really like them. They interest me. I don't at all mind that they haven't got their acts together, I like all that passion and confusion.'

'Luke has all that,' Anna said, sniffing, 'and he's so loving.' Her voice shook.

Jonathan began to kiss her face. 'So am I.'

'Jonathan – have you told Daniel?'

'About us? No.'

'Will you?'

'In time. Have you told Peter?'

'No.'

They looked at each other. Jonathan traced the outline of her mouth with his finger.

'All that'll come soon enough, you know.'

She caught his finger in her teeth. 'I quite want it to. I want action – '

He burst out laughing. Then he swooped down on her. 'Then you shall have some!'

Flora lay in bed. It was late, but it wasn't dark. She hadn't pulled her curtains because there was, tonight, a romantic view of a new, pale moon which would do very well as the subject of a poem for her newspaper. (This was not going well. Emma was becoming restive at the lowliness of her role, but anyone with half an eye could see that Emma had no *vision*.) 'Oh moon of May,' Flora began. She didn't seem to feel like poetry. She wished Luke was there, through the wall, with his thudding music. She'd thought she'd love to be at home without him, but she found that she didn't at all. She felt lonely, and it was dull.

She got out of bed and peered out of her window. The garden was all shadowy and mysterious in the gleaming, dark-blue light. She could see the line of sticks Anna had put up for the sweet peas, and the neat clumps of the new-potato leaves. It was very quiet. She tiptoed across the room and out on to the landing. She thought she would just go into Luke's room and smell his smell for a bit. He might even have left a Twix bar somewhere.

The landing, however, was not quiet. From downstairs came the sound of voices, cross voices, behind a closed door. Flora went to the banisters and peered over. The hall was dark, but there was a line of light under Peter's study door. Behind it, her parents were quarrelling.

'You can have it,' Anna said, 'take it. I don't want it.'

'I don't *want* it,' Peter said. He sat at his desk, staring down at his green blotter, furiously rolling two pencils.

'I was going to tell you about Flora's place. When – when you seemed a little more approachable. But I knew if I did you would insist on my leaving Pricewell's, which I didn't want to do because I like it. I like the people, I like the ordinariness, I like being out of Loxford. The money isn't for myself, anyway. I've bought a few things, a few wickedly, sensationally extravagant things like a jar of chocolate spread for Flora – '

'There's no need to be sarcastic.'

'But you are implying that I'm hoarding for myself. The money was for the children, for you if you wanted it. It's sitting tamely in a building-society account. Take it. I said so.'

'And give you the evidence you want that I don't provide adequately for you?'

'Peter!'

'Well, what else is all this about?'

Anna took a controlling breath. 'It's about my not telling you that Flora had a free place at St Saviour's.'

'About your *concealing* from me – '

'God!' Anna said, 'you'd try the patience of a *saint*! Well, you know now, so that's all over. I'm going to make some tea.'

'One more thing – '

'What?'

'I am not remotely interested in how much money you have or

186

what you've done with it or do with it. But there won't be any more from Pricewell's.'

Anna leaned towards him. 'Oh my dear, don't always kick me when I'm down. If it upsets you so much I will try and get a more prestigious job, but not yet. Just let it ride a bit, just let me get Luke a little launched . . .'

He did not look at her. 'I went to see the administration manager today. There will be no more work for you from the end of this month.'

Anna stood up and leaned against the end of his desk. She closed her eyes for a moment but the swirling angry darkness behind them made her feel dizzy, so she opened them again and looked at Peter. He seemed to her all at once as familiar as herself and an absolute stranger.

'You went into Pricewell's and you cancelled my job.'

'Yes.'

'After you had spoken to Sister Ignatia.'

'Yes.'

'But you didn't think of speaking to me.'

'You would have refused.'

'I do refuse,' Anna said. She held the rim of the desk in both hands. She was so angry she was afraid.

Peter said, 'So you will make our – difference – plain to Mr Mulgrove?'

There was a pause while Anna struggled with herself. Peter didn't look at her. She said at last, 'Peter, I've asked you this before but I'll try once more. What is it that you want of me?'

He thought. Even six months ago he would have said he wanted her to be a loving wife, a helpmeet, an ally. Now all he wanted was to have her out of his study. He said in a voice that shook with the impact of this realisation, 'If you can't see that, I can't possibly explain it to you.'

'Mummy.'

Anna looked up. Flora's nightied figure was dark against the dim landing.

187

'Flora! You should be in bed.'

'I hate it when you cry – '

Anna came up the stairs. 'I'm not crying, darling.'

'All that shouting,' Flora said, 'I hate it. Why are you quarrelling?'

'Money,' Anna said.

Flora's chest contracted. 'About St Saviour's?'

'No, no. St Saviour's is quite safe. It was a very dull adult quarrel. Nothing to worry about.' She reached the landing and put her arms around Flora. 'Isn't it quiet without Luke?'

'Horrid,' Flora said.

'He'll be back soon.'

Flora said into Anna's shoulder, 'I don't want to be Emma's friend any more. I want to be Verity's.'

'Can't you be both?'

''Course not,' Flora said scornfully.

'No unkindness to Emma, Flora.'

Flora tensed a little. 'No unkindness to Daddy then.' She withdrew from Anna's embrace. 'I'm going to sleep in Luke's room.'

'All right.'

Flora marched across the landing. She put her hand on Luke's door and pushed it open. Anna didn't move. Suddenly, Flora didn't like her little victory. She turned and scuttled back to Anna, dissolved in tears, and Anna, soothing her, thought that all these years of her own self-sufficiency seemed to have conditioned her for nothing, since all she now longed to do was to telephone Jonathan. Which, of course, she couldn't.

Patrick told Ella he was going away. In the past, this would have meant nothing, Patrick was always going away, but since coming to Loxford he had hardly stirred. His business, those mysterious companies in which he played an unspecified but clearly significant part, had taken him to Germany a good deal, to Frankfurt, and Munich, and also to America. He always brought Ella something if he was away for more than a week. She couldn't help noticing that, after the past months of rural life, she was running

188

low on duty-free scent. She had always liked the fact that Patrick bought her scent.

When he announced he was going away, Ella felt a huge relief. She had put off going to see Peter because she found she could hardly face it. It wasn't just the errand itself, but having to confront, because of it, the fact that Patrick was wildly attracted to Anna. His long-term mistress had been someone Ella could assimilate, an idle, witty, impractical creature with none of the qualities Ella thought important, because she possessed them herself. But Anna was different. Anna was original and attractive, with a suppressed wildness about her, like something caged. Ella herself had no wildness; as a quality it alarmed her and so she disapproved of it.

Her sister, Rachel, had prophesied that Ella would fall for Patrick if she went to work for him, but Ella had snorted and produced her good sense, her age and her pragmatism as evidence that she was proof against a thousand Patricks. So it had been, and a relationship had developed that had never overstepped the mark into either formality or informality, its tone dictated, Ella was sure, by her own cool head. Patrick could be such a boy . . . But he was a man, too, and the man in him had clearly now got the upper hand and was bearing him away to Germany to collect his wits.

'He's going to Germany,' she told Trish Pardoe in the Loxford shop. 'For three weeks.' The shop was full, it being a Friday, but she lowered her voice all the same. 'I think he's come to his senses.'

'She looks terrible,' Trish said. 'I saw her getting on the early bus. White as a sheet.'

'Perhaps he said something.'

Trish rootled in a box of crisp packets for the cheese-and-onion-flavoured ones. 'Will you go and see Peter, all the same?'

'I don't know. Not if – '

'Leave well alone, I think.'

'But you thought – '

'I was upset,' Trish said, 'wasn't I? It was a shock, seeing them. But I've got enough to worry about, what with Mum and the Brownies being threatened with amalgamation with Quindale. I ask you! Poor little mites. Might as well send them into Woodborough and have done with it. There now. I always put these on top, because they're the most popular.'

'Then why,' said Ella, nettled, 'don't you put them at the bottom?'

She packed for Patrick with exaggerated care, feeling that this trip was of great significance. He seemed, she had to admit, very cheerful, almost jaunty, and not in the least like a sober adult taking a blow bravely. But then, Patrick was resilient. When his mistress had left, Ella had heard him whistling while he shaved less than a week later.

He surveyed his suitcase. 'You're a pearl.'

'Nonsense,' she said, 'I'm paid for it.'

He grinned. He said, 'I may not be a whole three weeks, of course. Why don't you go away, go to your sister? You don't want to be stuck here – '

'To my great chagrin, I like it here.'

'Me too.'

She set her mouth. 'Time you got away, though.'

'And what is that supposed to mean?'

'You know perfectly well.'

He laughed. He picked up his case and started across the hall.

'I read your mind like an open book, Ella. Keep an eye on the Rectory for me, while I'm gone.'

She said grimly, 'There'll be nothing to see.'

He stopped at the front door and turned to her. 'Oh, I hope there will. That's the chief reason I'm going. Absence, as they say, makes the heart grow fonder.' And then he let himself out into the sunshine.

Anna read the letter several times. It was quite a courteous letter, but it was firm as well. It was from the publishers of her translations, a firm in Bristol. They were sorry, they said, to have received no work from her for some months now, despite frequent reminders (oh, help, those envelopes pushed into the kitchen-dresser drawer in the hope of their just vanishing) and assumed that she was no longer in a position to work regularly for them. As they themselves were now under increasing pressure from European manufacturers extending into the British Isles, and vice versa, they had to be certain of the reliability of their translators. They therefore thanked her for past work, requested the return of anything unfinished and begged her to regard this letter as the termination of any arrangement between them.

It should be a relief, Anna thought, and it's the reverse. She felt a sudden, irrational affection for that mad Oriental table upstairs at which she had sat for so many resentful, disciplined hours, coupled with a sharp nostalgia for those past times when things had seemed under her control. She might not want to translate another word, but she might not want to see it go from her either. This was not in the least logical, she knew, but sometimes the least logical things were the ones that twisted a slow knife in you until you cried out.

She went upstairs and looked at her books and papers. The last manual – of which she had only done twenty pages – was the German specifications for a machine that laminated plastic. She closed it sadly, and made a little pile of it, and her few typed pages of translation, and another manual, in French, that she hadn't even opened. Then she typed a letter to the publishers, saying that she was sorry, and took everything downstairs to make a parcel.

Later, she showed the letter to Peter. He read it without comment, and handed it back to her.

'Aren't you pleased?'

'I assumed this would happen.'

The parcel, ready for posting, lay on the kitchen table between them. She longed to pick it up and hurl it at him.

'Aren't you triumphant? Isn't this what you wanted? I've got no job now, nothing. You can disband the parish group, if you want. Here I am, Peter, here I am. Just the Rector's wife.'

He looked at her. After a pause he said, not unkindly, 'I'm afraid, Anna, that simply saying it doesn't make it so.'

The telephone rang. Peter made no move to answer it. Anna picked up the receiver.

'Anna? This is Celia. How are you? Good, good. Now, I hardly

like to trouble you, knowing how busy you are, but what I'm
going to ask won't take much time – '

'Celia,' Anna said, interrupting, 'just ask away. I've got all the
time in the world.'

CHAPTER FIFTEEN

O n Anna's last day at Pricewell's, she was presented with a
double begonia in a china pot and Mr Mulgrove said to all
the staff who were assembled for their lunch break that it had been
a pleasure to have Anna working with them, and that they would
miss her. Anna, clutching the curious and unEnglish flower, felt
slightly tearful and said she would miss them too. Only Tim, her
erstwhile supervisor, who clearly felt a personal betrayal at her
departure, asked her why she was going, just when she'd got used
to it. Anna, shackled for new reasons by old habits of loyalty,
said, 'Because I ought to be at home more.'

Tim looked unconvinced. In his world, the women were
always out, took all kinds of jobs, seemed to feel no obligation to
do anything they weren't inclined to do. His own mother had
weekly rows with his father over both her job at a launderette and
her regular expeditions with girlfriends to watch the male stripper
down at The Royal George. Tim was used to seeing his father's
apoplectic flailings at his mother's independence; he thought it was
something that probably afflicted you as you got older. Perhaps it
had hit Anna's old man, perhaps he'd said she'd got to stay at
home and visit the sick or whatever vicars' wives did. But then
Anna didn't seem to Tim like the kind of wife who took orders,
even from a vicar.

He said, truthfully, 'I'll miss you. I don't know anyone like
you.'

Mr Mulgrove said, 'I'm really sorry about this. We hoped you'd have a future with us.'

Heather from flours and dried fruits said, 'Don't blame you. Who wants to spend their life stacking bleeding sultanas?'

Anna took her last pay envelope, drank her last cup of subsidised canteen coffee, hung up her blue overall and went out into the market-place. In her bag, she carried the plastic badge she had worn, the badge which said, 'I'm Anna. Can I help you?' Glancing up at the sky; behind whose high summer clouds dwelt that inscrutable power whose presence she could not quite get out of her mind, she thought of her badge and its slogan, and said to herself: It wouldn't hurt *You* to wear one . . .

Being market day, Woodborough was full. The country buses brought people in after breakfast and took them away before lunch, their carrier bags bulging with fish from the woman who travelled up from Devon, jeans and T-shirts from the Pakistanis who travelled down from Birmingham and cheese from the man who made his own from herds kept in pastures not five miles from Woodborough. Threading her way among the stalls, Anna bought some vacuum-cleaner bags, a bargain box of soap powder and a punnet of strawberries for Flora, who had crept into her bed at dawn that morning and said uncharacteristically, 'I'm worried about you.'

'Don't be. I'm fine.'

'Mothers always say that. Verity says when her mother says it, it means she's got a migraine.'

Flora couldn't cuddle, never had been able to. She lay awkwardly against Anna for a few minutes, then bumped a clumsy kiss on her, climbed out of bed again and padded back to her room. Peter didn't stir. Missing Flora, Anna took revenge upon his stillness by wishing the bed was just hers.

Now she looked at the strawberries. Should she buy another punnet for Peter? Would he notice? Was he remotely concerned as to whether she gave him strawberries or a banana? Or a black eye? She glanced at her watch. Half an hour before she collected Flora, half an hour in which to dawdle about Woodborough while her mind scurried round and round its new trap, like a mouse on a wheel.

She left the market-place and turned down Sheep Street, a narrow street forbidden to traffic which Woodborough Council had dotted with tree-shaded benches usually occupied by clumps of dismal teenagers waiting, without much hope, for action. Ahead of Anna, a tall young woman was pushing a pram. She stopped the pram outside a newsagent, stooped to pick up the baby (it was new, Anna could see, from its size and the swaddled oblivion of its tiny head), and then, as if recollecting something, abruptly put the baby back, tucked it in decisively and pushed the pram onwards. Anna who had not thought of it for years, suddenly remembered her twenty-three-year-old self outside a newsagent in a Bristol suburb, making the abrupt decision not to buy chocolate. She had half lifted Charlotte from the pram, even, just as that young woman had done. She could see Charlotte clearly, a neat, small baby with a dark, downy head, and her own hands holding her, hands emerging from the sleeves of a scarlet duffel coat Laura had given her, a stiff, thick coat with a hood and black-lacquered toggles. That was twenty years ago, that October afternoon, twenty years, nearly half my life . . .

Anna crept to one of the benches and sat down. There was a gloomy girl at the far end, her feet thrust into huge, black shoes, smoking ferociously. She didn't look at Anna. Anna sat cradling her parcels, inhaling the peculiar, synthetic, red smell of the strawberries, grappling with herself. Where had she come, in the last twenty years, but round in a huge, slow circle? Even the children, even now Jonathan, were they enough, was he? Should she now just break cover and run for dear life, literally for her dear life? But it wouldn't do to run to Jonathan, she could only do that if she was running a hundred per cent towards him, for his sake alone, not seventy-five per cent away from something else. All the same, thank heavens for Jonathan. She thought she could hear him, she was sure she could hear his voice. She looked round, enchanted, and there he was, coming leisurely up Sheep Street, accompanied by Luke. Luke looked just as usual, in jeans and a T-shirt, his denim jacket slung over one shoulder. He was listening intently to Jonathan, slightly turning his head towards him.

Jonathan was deep in explanation, gesturing for emphasis. They walked slowly past Anna, quite absorbed, not seeing her. As for her, after a first, quick, involuntary gesture of greeting, she didn't move, simply sat there and watched them drift obliviously by.

The girl on the bench had watched them too, particularly Luke, with resentful interest. Anna said, on impulse, to her, 'That's my son.'

The girl stared. Then she shrugged. 'Yeah,' she said, 'and I'm the Queen of England,' and slouched away.

Flora ate her strawberries on the bus, throwing the hulls out of the window. Anna told her about seeing Luke, and Flora said Luke had been to St Saviour's and seen her, too, and he'd said living in Woodborough was great and she thought she'd like to stay with Verity for a few nights and live in Woodborough as well.

'Suppose,' Anna said, 'just suppose I wanted to live in Wood-borough?'

'You couldn't. You have to stay in Loxford.'

'Do I?'

Flora ate the last strawberry. 'You know you do. That's what happens.'

The village green was already showing signs of summer wear. The mothers, waiting for the bus, had trampled their habitual spot into a depressed, yellowing circle, and there were bare patches in front of the two benches and the litter bin. Anna and Flora climbed down the steps of the bus and the mothers said, 'Warm enough for you, Mrs B?' and, 'Like your hat,' to Flora, who scowled and put her convent Panama behind her back. They trailed together across the green, Flora bumping her school bag behind her like a recalcitrant dog, and Anna holding her begonia tightly, as if it were a talisman.

From the landing windows of the Old Rectory, Ella watched them. She hardly knew Flora, who seemed to her a precocious and unattractive child with none of Luke's undoubted warmth of heart. She glanced at Flora, in her striped St Saviour's summer dress, red and white, and thought, for a brief and disquieting moment, of motherhood, a state she could hardly even visualise. Anna was a mother, and Anna interested Ella far more. Walking beside Flora in a long, full-skirted, dark-blue dress sashed in buttercup yellow – why, Ella thought crossly, why were Anna's clothes so irritating? – she looked as if she belonged to Flora, and was, at the same time, separate. She looked too, thoroughly despondent. Ella studied her. Her shoulders drooped a little, her head was slightly bent, both noticeable in a woman who usually carried herself with assurance. She seemed to be bent over some lurid, pink-flowered plant she was carrying, as if she were protecting it. Ella took a breath. It couldn't be a plant Patrick had sent. Could it? It didn't look Patrick's style; he would send lilies or an orchid, something exotic and showy. She thought of Patrick. 'Absence makes the heart grow fonder,' he'd said as he left. Looking at Anna, Ella now thought, with a sinking heart, that perhaps he might have been right.

Anna put the begonia on the kitchen table.

'It's an awful colour,' Flora said.

'I know. But I feel very fond of it.'

Flora began to rummage for biscuits. 'What job'll you do now?'

'Celia has given me a piece to write for the parish magazine. To try and encourage people to help clean the church. I think you should have bread before a biscuit.'

'That won't take long,' Flora said, finding two digestives and ignoring the bread bin, 'that's not a job.'

'No. I'll find something else. Don't worry.'

'You keep saying that. You said that to Luke.'

'I mean it.'

'You can't just switch off worry,' Flora said. 'You can't just take an aspirin.'

Anna ran water into the kettle. 'What exactly worries you?'

Flora spread her arms, showering crumbs. 'The feeling here.'

Anna said nothing. She put the lid on the kettle and plugged it in.

'When I grow up,' Flora said to her mother's back, 'I'm never, ever going to marry a vicar.'

Daniel and Jonathan Byrne sat in Daniel's study. They had not put any lamps on, because the light was fading so beautifully outside the window that it seemed a pity to outshine it. Miss Lambe had given them coleslaw for supper, and Daniel was revolving in his mind how to tell her tactfully that he found coleslaw disgusting. He thought he might say that it gave him indigestion (it didn't; nothing did) because that would let them both out so easily. Caring for the tenderness of Miss Lambe's feelings – as small and vulnerable as seedlings – was becoming an exhausting and full-time job.

Jonathan was not thinking about coleslaw. He was less chivalrous towards Miss Lambe – perversely, she adored his mild carelessness towards her – and simply hadn't eaten his, pushing the pale, glistening heap to the side of his plate, and leaving it there. He was thinking about Anna, and about Luke, whom he was getting to know and getting to like. Luke's conscience was deeply troubled at leaving home, at abandoning his mother, but, as he could see no way to improve anything, and was being driven demented by the atmosphere, getting out had seemed the only course. He had said this quite directly to Jonathan, on their second meeting, and Jonathan had said there was only point and merit to sacrifice as long as it achieved something. The next natural step would have been to talk about Anna, but both avoided it. Jonathan had talked to no one about Anna; he simply thought about her.

He said to Daniel now, 'I want to tell you something.'

Daniel's mind, which had abandoned coleslaw for tomorrow's meeting with the Bishop, came swiftly back. 'Of course.'

'I'm in love with Anna Bouverie.'

There was a fractional pause and then Daniel said, 'Yes, I know.'

'How do you know?'

'Little things. Remarks. The look of you.'

'And?'

'What do you mean?'

'Does a sermon follow? Will you try and stop me?'

'Have I ever,' Daniel said, 'tried to stop you doing anything?'

'But what about Peter Bouverie? He's a priest of yours – '

'Are you asking me to make up your mind?'

'Oh no,' Jonathan said, 'I've done that. I want to marry her.'

'She is married.'

'Daniel – '

'I can't encourage you. I may understand why you feel as you do, but I can't encourage you to act on it. Marriage is difficult enough, these days; for one thing it tends to go on for so long, but it mustn't be attacked, undermined, by people who have the power to withhold themselves, even if they haven't the inclination.'

'And Anna?'

Jonathan couldn't see Daniel's face in the dark, but he could hear that his voice had softened.

'Ah. Anna.'

'Throw Anna to the wolves in the name of orthodoxy? Is that what you think?'

'I think individuality of choice and personal convenience are inadequate as moral principles.'

'Choice and convenience! Is that what you think has brought about Anna's situation?'

Daniel swung round in his chair. 'Don't cheapen what I say. For wisdom and balance, humanity must give its unequivocal support to the defence of human life and to Christian institutions such as marriage.'

Jonathan got up. He crossed the room to stand over Daniel.

'There speaks the natural celibate. Sacrifice of the spirit, however futile and destructive to the individual, is to be encouraged as long as appearances are maintained for the comfort of your *Christian* society.'

'Not comfort. For morality.'

'Morality! And is it moral for Peter Bouverie to starve his wife and parish of everything but pure form?'

'He's a sick man,' Daniel said.

Jonathan shouted, 'Well, do something about him! And leave his wife to me!'

Daniel bent his head. 'Has she said she would like this?'

'Not in so many words.'

'Then your love isn't returned?'

'Oh yes. But she's encumbered. She can't rush forward freely as I can. There's her husband and children. And there's your damned Church. Where's its tolerance and intellectual subtlety? Where, for God's sake, is its vision?'

Daniel rose too. He said sadly, 'You know what I think. You know I think the modern Church lacks holiness because we've played about with the truth. I hate its narrowness of spirit.'

'Yes. So you say. But may Anna not be allowed to hate it too and to try to escape from it?'

Daniel turned and put his hands on his brother's shoulders. 'Give me a day or two. Let me talk to the Bishop.'

'What good will that do? What bishop can ever decide anything? And what has the Bishop got to do with it, anyway?'

'I must,' Daniel said, 'for Christian and Church reasons. For you and Anna. And for poor Peter Bouverie.'

It was the first time for weeks that Anna had been at home at lunchtime. She made Peter a salad and called him to the kitchen. He said that he was terribly busy and would like to have it on a tray in his study. Anna carried it in, in silence.

'You are very kind,' said Peter, as if speaking to someone he hardly knew.

'Not at all.'

'Have you had a good morning?'

'No.'

'I'm sorry to hear it.'

'I spent the morning being congratulated by the village. Celia Hooper even stopped her car to say with a merry laugh that I'd now put them all out of a job. She sounded quite resentful.'

Peter turned his head away. Would she never stop? Would she never admit defeat, but make a grievance, a point of discord, out of everything? He had never thought, until recently, that Anna was a greedy woman. He didn't look at her; he didn't want to. He looked instead at his salad, at the slices of cold chicken, at the lettuce leaves sprinkled with herbs. He said, 'Thank you for this.'

Anna paused by the door. 'I'm going into Woodborough. To collect Flora.'

'I thought she came on the bus.'

'She does. I want to go with her. I need the occupation. I suppose I mayn't have the car?'

'I'm afraid not.'

'And I suppose we couldn't have a walk together. Instead?'

He sighed. He said, 'I have parishioners coming.' Patrick O'Sullivan's housekeeper had asked to come, he couldn't imagine why.

'Please,' Anna said.

Peter didn't reply. After a second or two, she went out and closed the door gently behind her.

In the kitchen, her own salad lay on the table. She felt tremendously unhungry and put it in the fridge, thinking: Never mind, Luke can make it into a sandwich later. But Luke wouldn't be here later. No one would be, except herself and Peter and poor Flora who didn't like the feeling in the house. Who could blame her? Who *could* like the feeling? Standing by the refrigerator and gazing out of the window at those orderly, green rows of vegetables she had planted, Anna felt that, almost without realising it, she had turned some kind of corner. There was nothing to be gained any more from steeling herself and ploughing on – and there was plenty to lose. I've given him every chance, she told herself, every chance to come close to me, and every olive branch I offer he breaks across his knee.

She glanced at the clock. It said five past one. Over three hours until Flora returned, three hours in which she had more than half intended that she would go and see Jonathan. But on reflection, she decided she would not do that. She would instead walk down her garden past her beans and peas, past her washing blowing on the line and through the neglected gate at the bottom. Then she would make her way to the hills beyond the river, just going straight across country like a wild animal, and climb the slopes to that mysterious copse. When she got there, she knew she would have decided, she knew she would be sure what she would do.

She opened the back door, her spirits suddenly lifting, and closed it firmly behind her. The few clouds were high in a clear sky and the air smelled clean, full of the scents of grass and earth. Then she paused, checked by an impulse to go back into the house to say goodbye to Peter. Why? He thought she was going to Woodborough; he expected her to be out. She shook her head at the thought of him. Does one ever know, she asked herself, the difference between love and habit? Above her, a blackbird sang, and then another answered it from yards away, quite sharply, as if in reprimand. Thrusting her hands into her pockets, Anna stepped out along her garden path towards the distant hills.

When Ella got up to go, Peter rose and showed her courteously out of the house. He seemed perfectly calm. He had been perfectly calm all the way through their interview, so that it was impossible for Ella to tell whether he knew the whole story already. At least his apparent tranquillity had made it much easier for Ella, who had been able to relate what she knew unemotionally, as if she were reciting facts to a police sergeant. Peter had nodded once or twice, and glanced at her occasionally, but mostly he had looked past her, at a picture hanging just behind her which she saw, when she got up, was a seascape, a watercolour of waves and foam and sky and, in the foreground, a little wooden dinghy beached on shingle.

On the Rectory doorstep, she said, 'Goodbye. And thank you for seeing me.'

Peter said, 'Goodbye.' Ella waited for him to thank her for coming, but he didn't, so she turned, a little clumsily, and went down the drive beside the churchyard wall. She felt tremendously depressed and not at all relieved. It was certainly the right thing to have done, and it was equally certainly a most unpleasant thing to have done. Her sister Rachel would have said she should have done it weeks ago, nipped the whole nasty business in the bud.

She reached the lane and squared her shoulders. Across the village green, Elaine Dodswell was planting petunias in two urns that guarded her little bridge in summer, in addition to the frogs.

A pang of envy seized Ella. What wouldn't she give, at that moment, for a cottage of her own, with her own untroublesome petunias, instead of this ill-defined life, half prefect, half parasite, on the coat tails of Patrick O'Sullivan's wishes and whims? She quickened her steps and Elaine, seeing her, brandished a trowel at her and called out the offer of a cup of tea. Thankful for the distraction, Ella nodded, and hurried towards her.

After Ella had gone, Peter went into the sitting-room and sat carefully on the sofa. He sat there for a long time, slipping his thoughts through his mind like the beads on a rosary. One thing was very plain and that was that he wasn't at all surprised; indeed, he felt almost relieved to know the key to Anna's extraordinary behaviour recently. What was more, knowing the key, being in power by possessing his new knowledge, made him feel, for the first time in months, curiously elated. He looked around the room, reduced once more to its habitual untidiness, and found he even wanted to smile. It was such a relief, such a violent, savage, unspeakable relief to know that he hadn't imagined things after all, that his revulsion from Anna had been instinctive – rightly instinctive – and that he wasn't, oh, joy of joys, going off his head. His unconscious mind had known what his conscious mind had refused to know. In a curious way, he felt himself to be free, as if shackles had fallen from him. He found that he was trembling.

He got up and began to pace the room, rhythmically banging one closed fist into the other open hand. His father used to do that, and it always, Peter remembered, made Kitty nervous because she never knew how to react to her husband's perturbations of spirit, being incapable of either dealing with them or leaving them alone. Peter thought of Kitty with great affection. There was a loyal woman! A selfless, devoted, faithful woman! He forgot that most of his life she had almost driven him mad with her indecisiveness, her fluttering mind, and that it was Anna who had kept up communication with her. Now, pacing his sitting-room, Peter thought of his mother as someone almost noble. Even so, he did not contemplate telephoning her. He simply pictured her in his mind as a symbol of good womanhood and as a contrast to Anna with her perversity, her rebelliousness, her seething dissatisfaction.

He paused by the window and looked at the church, across the drive and the churchyard wall. He felt no urge at all to go and sit in it, no flicker of desire to pray. He felt he could never forgive Anna for having perceived in him this growing hollowness, and the fear that accompanied it. Oh, her behaviour had been so calculated, almost cynical, a carefully orchestrated campaign against him, culminating in this offensive revelation of a liaison with Patrick O'Sullivan! Well, at least this was a culmination. It had made up his mind for him. Either Anna repented and made amends for what she had done, or he would divorce her. Simple.

He left the sitting-room and went upstairs to wash. He combed his hair, looked at himself without affection in the bathroom mirror, and exchanged his cardigan for a jacket. Distasteful though it was, his first obligation, as a clergyman, was to confide the details of his troubles to his superior, the Archdeacon of Woodborough. He thought he would simply call, on the off-chance, so that by the time he faced Anna with her choice of futures the facts would already lie safely in official hands and she could not distort them. If Daniel Byrne wasn't in, Peter thought, he would just wait.

He left Anna a note on the kitchen table. It said, 'Back later, P,' and he wrote the time, '3.10,' underneath, and the date. Then he locked the back door and put the key under the brick which was, he had been telling Anna for ten years, the most blindingly obvious place to put it, and went out to the garage.

He drove slowly through Loxford, raising his hand in response to the few people who waved to him. He was conscious of his hand going up and down steadily, regally. How calm I am, he thought, how released, how free. Lady Mayhew was crossing the green with her dogs and she began to gesture towards him, as if she wanted to speak to him, but he felt that he had no obligation to anyone that afternoon because he was, serenely and composedly, bound upon something that was almost a mission. As he turned away from the green towards the main Woodborough road, he could see, in his driving mirror, Lady Mayhew's obvious exasperation. He almost smiled because it mattered to him so little.

He drove on between the still green wheatfields. He observed that the barn on the right which had been so damaged in the winter gales was having a new roof put on, and beyond it, a field of linseed was in full, blue flower. He saw scraps of litter in the verge and wild, purplish cranesbill in the hedge, and ahead of him, swerving blackly across the tarmac, the tyre marks of a skidding car. He felt acutely observant, as if the world had come into a sharp, clear, new focus now that he possessed the key to what had been the matter. It wasn't just relief either; it was something more akin to triumph.

The lane turned sharply just before the main road. Peter braked, as he always did, changed gear, and drove smoothly round. The main road was quiet ahead of him. He pushed his foot forward to step on the brake, and as he did so a bright, detailed, unwanted, unbearable picture came into his mind of Anna, naked, in the arms of Patrick O'Sullivan. Peter gave a little cry, which turned into a much greater cry, and the car sprang forward of its own accord and as if in response to his sudden agony. Blinded by tears, Peter simply let it go.

At the inquest, the bus driver said he had had no chance. He'd been coming along, all slowed down and ready to turn down the Loxford lane, when the Reverend's car had shot out, without any warning, and headed for him, straight for him. It was all over in seconds. He'd braked, of course, braked as hard as he could, but there was no avoiding it. He said that, if it was all right, he'd like to express his real sympathy for the Reverend's family and tell them he'd be haunted by those ten seconds the rest of his life. Then he broke down and had to be comforted by a constable.

Chapter sixteen

Loxford church was packed for Peter's funeral. Anna had said she would like it to be full of flowers, and it was, most touchingly, with all the fragile, impractical flowers that she loved, like delphiniums, already shedding petals, and cow parsley, distributing its peppery dust. The Bishop came, with his wife, and he and Daniel officiated together, and Peter lay before them in his coffin, below the chancel steps.

Anna sat in her usual pew, with the children and the grandmothers beside her. Charlotte had come down from Edinburgh on an overnight bus and, despite having hardly slept, was composed and controlled. At one point, she even briefly took Anna's hand. On her other side, Luke and Flora wept and wept, Flora out of fear and Luke out of anguish.

'I didn't love him,' Luke had hissed to Charlotte in the few moments they had had alone together. 'Don't you see? I'm a bastard. I feel so guilty.'

'You did love him,' Charlotte said, who had had all night in a bus to think about this. 'You did. You just didn't like him much recently. He didn't like himself.'

They neither of them said anything of this to Anna. She was most affectionate to them, but nothing she said invited a confidential conversation.

'She's working it out herself,' Charlotte said. She felt extremely old suddenly, tired and experienced. 'None of it's straightforward for her.'

'It's shock,' everyone else was saying. How could it be otherwise? What would you feel, they said to each other, if you came back from a country walk and found a policeman in your garden with such news as that? Of course, Peter and Anna hadn't seen eye to eye just recently, but what marriage is ever all plain sailing? You had to admire her dignity. Really, her dignity was perfect. So brave; too brave, of course, there'd be a reaction soon, a breakdown. Most of the congregation, craning round each other to look at the occupants of the Rectory pew, speculated with an uneasy excitement about Anna's precarious future.

So, without excitement, did Laura. She stood beside Charlotte in a hat waving with funereal plumes, and felt anxiety almost obliterate her grief. She thought intermittently of Peter, of young, student Peter painstakingly scrubbing a corner of her kitchen table to make it fit to eat off, but she thought predominantly of Anna. Her heart sank when she thought of Anna, because it seemed to her that Anna was about to embark, and not out of choice, upon exactly the shapeless, unstructured, struggling life that she had had herself, and that she knew to be such a weary battle for the spirit. She had believed Anna wasted in her marriage to Peter; now that he was dead, the uncertainty of the future seemed more destructive than the waste of the past. Laura heaved a gargantuan sigh and a shred of feather detached itself from her hat and floated down on to Kitty's prayer book.

Kitty couldn't see her prayer book for tears. She couldn't believe that she was not simply a widow now, but childless too. What have I been for? she asked herself over and over again. When the fragment of feather alighted on her book, she thought it was a spider for a moment and gave a little shriek. Behind her, the congregation murmured in sympathy. Poor little woman, and Peter her only child! Poor little me, Kitty thought, and Peter my only child. She mopped and blew, and around her feet crumpled paper handkerchiefs gathered like fallen petals. Must pull myself together, she told herself, stand up like Laura. It won't help Anna if I give way, or the children, it won't help anybody. She heard her father's voice of half a century before saying, 'Tears,

Katherine, should only be shed for others.' But I can't, Kitty thought desperately. I can't, I can't; I only know how to cry for myself. Silently, majestically, Laura passed her an enormous handkerchief of plum-coloured silk.

As the priest who had known Peter the longest, John Jacobs climbed into the pulpit to give the address. He said how sad he was to be in Peter's pulpit on such an occasion. He said how his heart went out to Peter's family. He described Peter's great spirituality and his devotion to duty and his kindness and his work for the diocese. He spoke of a man of God who had understood the needs of the rural church. He spoke of a priest who had never, for all his faith, compromised his family. He spoke for a long time and illustrated his address with anecdotes about Peter that seemed appropriate to almost any clergyman in the diocese except Peter. He concluded by saying that, if ever a priest had been a square peg in a square hole, that priest was Peter in Loxford. The congregation listened politely. The Bishop looked out of the south chancel window. Anna looked mostly at the floor.

Then they all filed out into the churchyard for the burial. It was a proper burial, in an old-fashioned grave, as Peter had wished, his father having had a full burial before him. Luke led Flora away from the graveside and sat on a tombstone, holding her on his knee. Charlotte took Anna's arm. Kitty took Laura's hand. When the coffin had been lowered in, they all threw flowers down after it.

'You OK?' Charlotte hissed. Her arm clamped Anna's to her side.

Anna nodded.

'What?' Charlotte demanded, 'what, what?'

Anna turned and kissed her.

'I'm so relieved,' she said, 'so relieved. For him almost more than for me.'

There was tea afterwards at the Rectory. The parish group had made it, plates and plates of sandwiches and scones and ginger biscuits and slices of fruit cake. They had set up the Mothers' Union tea urn in the kitchen, and borrowed the Loxford village-hall teacups, all six dozen of them, and it looked as if they would all be used. Anna, feeling tea was somehow not sufficiently encouraging, had bought some bottles of sherry from Pricewell's, and Luke was detailed to be butler. He came upon Anna, with his tray of glasses, and said to her, 'I'm sorry, Mum, I'm sorry, I'm sorry.'

She looked at him. She wanted, violently, to embrace him, tray and all. She said, 'You drink one of those. Straight down. We'll talk later.'

The atmosphere in the sitting-room was heady with relief. It was full of people holding plates and the plates were full of food. The Bishop was slowly eating sandwiches, one after another, almost absently. He said to Anna, 'You are all so much in our prayers.'

'Yes, indeed,' his wife said. She looked keenly at Anna. Anna was very interesting to her.

'I want to talk to you,' Anna said.

The Bishop looked mildly alarmed.

'Not about the past,' Anna said, 'about the future.'

The Bishop thought of housing, of the three Bouverie children. His brow cleared. 'Of course.'

'No,' Anna said, reading his mind. 'About my future, what I should do.'

He peered at her. His wife watched.

'I'm not putting this well,' Anna said, 'and I don't suppose now is the time. But I have a plan, you see, a plan that will involve the diocese. At least, it ought to involve the diocese.'

The Bishop said, 'Come and see me. In a week or so. Just ring my secretary and come and see me.'

'Thank you.' She smiled up at him. Celia Hooper appeared with a plate of sandwiches, flagged 'cucumber', smiling too, but in a hostessly way.

'I say,' said the Bishop, taking two.

'His favourite,' said his wife. She looked after Anna, who had moved away. 'Wonderful, really. So composed.'

'One always hopes there won't be a reaction,' Celia said.

The Bishop's wife looked at her. 'There's usually a reaction,' she said crisply, 'if there's guilt. Guilt is much harder to live with than grief.' She thought of Peter Bouverie coming out of her husband's study when he knew he would not be Archdeacon. 'I wish,' she said with some vehemence, 'I wish I had taken the trouble to get to know Anna Bouverie months, years, ago. I wish – ' She stopped. Celia and the Bishop looked at her.

'Have some of Mrs Pardoe's fruit cake,' Celia said.

'I say,' said the Bishop.

Daniel found Anna in the kitchen. She was refilling the urn with kettles of boiling water, her hand muffled in a tea towel.

'My dear.'

She put the kettle down. Daniel took her in his arms. She said, 'I've only said this to Charlotte, but I'm so relieved – '

'I know.'

'The service was terrible, so false, except for the lovely bit by the grave.'

Daniel let her go, and she picked up the kettle again. 'The burial service,' Daniel said, 'is the most triumphant, the most exhilarating of all the services. I know no music as resoundingly confident as the English of the burial service. Perhaps that very confidence is what people shrink from now.'

'I don't,' Anna said, pouring. 'I'm thankful for it. I'm desperately sad that Peter got so empty and that we grew so far apart, but there wasn't a remedy. It was all too deep in him and in us, and too complicated.'

'Did he know about Jonathan?'

Anna looked straight at him. 'No.'

'Oh Anna – '

'Why?' Anna said. 'Why, "Oh Anna"?' Her gaze was candid. 'Why should I feel guilty? I'm not guilty. While he was alive, I was always wracked with guilt, but now he's dead it's stopped. I know I was a good wife to him. I was a good wife until he didn't want me any more.'

She turned away to fill the kettle again and plug it in.

'You had an affair with Jonathan.'

'And is that morally worse than having an affair with duty? The withdrawing of the essence of yourself, of your emotional and imaginative generosity, is what kills relationships. I never withdrew mine. Look,' Anna said turning back, 'I've come to love you dearly, and to admire you, but there are things about men and women that I now know better than you.'

Daniel bowed his head. Anna watched him and thought of the previous evening when poor distraught Ella Pringle had come round and had told Anna that she had been the cause of Peter's car crash. Anna, who had never liked Ella much, had found herself being genuinely tremendously sorry for her. She had taken her into the sitting-room, and had sat beside her on the sofa, soothing and patting. Ella's story seemed to her a sad and scruffy little business, and not significant.

'It was pure coincidence,' Anna said, over and over again. 'You are not to blame. He was in a very sad state, very wound up.'

'I'm leaving Patrick,' Ella said. 'I can't stand his attitude any more. I believed him. I believed he had a relationship with you.'

'No,' Anna said, 'he was playing a game.' She looked at Ella. 'Are you in love with him?'

'No,' Ella said. 'Yes.'

'It's harder to leave than to stay,' Anna said. 'If it's any comfort to you, I had decided to leave, the very afternoon Peter was killed. I came down from the copse to tell him that, and found the policeman. I've been given freedom, but I would have left. You must, too. Patrick is too arbitrary to live with, too tyrannical.'

And Ella, who disliked touching women, leaned across and kissed her.

'I've learned so much in a week,' Anna said now to Daniel, 'that I'm quite exhausted.'

He smiled. 'Life certainly never gets any easier. Or simpler.'

The kitchen door opened. Elaine Dodswell came in, followed by Trish Pardoe. They were carrying piles of empty plates.

'I'm ever so sorry,' Elaine said, looking from Daniel to Anna, 'I'd no idea – '

'You weren't interrupting,' Daniel said. 'Nothing that can't be resumed.'

Elaine said to Anna, 'Oh, I do hope you've eaten, you must eat, you know, it doesn't help not to eat. Oh Anna, I'm so sorry, I'm so terribly sorry. What are you going to do?'

'Do?'

'Yes,' Elaine said. She put the plates down and gestured at the kitchen, at the table and the cream-painted units and the blue-checked curtains overprinted with vegetables that had been a present from Kitty. 'What are you going to do, poor Anna, now that you aren't the Rector's wife any more?'

Anna stood by the front door so that they could all say good-bye. Most people, particularly those she hardly knew, kissed her with fervour. The sherry had clearly been a good idea. Flora came and leaned tiredly against her, and so got kissed as well. Her eyes, behind her glasses, were swollen and tender from crying.

Isobel Thompson kissed Anna warmly. 'Come and stay. Don't be alone. Don't hesitate to ask for anything.'

'I won't,' Anna said.

'Sometimes it's so much easier to talk to a woman – '

'I'll talk to you because you're Isobel. Not because you're a woman or a priest.'

'Oh Anna,' Isobel said. 'You don't change – '

'Oh, but I have. I've stopped pretending.'

'Yes,' Isobel said uncertainly, moving back a little. 'Yes.'

Colonel Richardson embraced Anna with relief. 'My dear,' he said. He knew what to do with her now; she had stepped back into a category he could manage, the plucky little widow putting on a wonderful front. Damned good-looking, too, good carriage, great dignity, never a public tear. 'Don't forget,' he said, 'Marjorie and I are always there. Anything you want. Only have to ask. Anything. Frightful business.' He wrung her hand.

Marjorie Richardson brushed her face with a powdered cheek. She looked at Anna oddly, as if about to speak, but said nothing.

'Mummy,' Flora said.

Anna bent. 'Yes, darling.'

'Where,' said Flora, her eyes widening in alarm, 'where exactly did Daddy go?'

Several people were waiting. Anna looked round at them; Lady Mayhew, Miss Dunstable, that poor deaf man from Snead, even

Mr Biddle in a bursting, decent, dark suit. She said, quite clearly, to Flora, 'To paradise.'

Ella put Patrick's chicken casserole for supper into the Aga, and went upstairs to brush her hair. She also put on some scent, her new lipstick and her pearl ear-rings. She felt she must be armoured.

Patrick was in his small sitting-room, in the armchair Anna had briefly occupied on the night he had heard her crying in the lane, with a tumbler of whisky and a financial newspaper. He had not been to the funeral; he had not commented, even, on Peter's death, beyond saying to Ella in a tone she didn't at all care for, 'I wonder what triggered him off?'

She said now, 'May I speak to you for a moment?'

'Of course,' he said. He got up and indicated a chair. 'Drink?'

'No, thank you.'

'I see. So I'm in for some kind of wigging.'

'No,' Ella said. She sat down and crossed her legs. He surveyed her with approval.

'How was the funeral?'

'Sad,' Ella said. She waited for him to ask her about Anna, but he didn't, he simply went on watching her.

'I've come down to say that I am leaving at the end of the month.' She paused.

'And?'

'And?'

'And why you are going and what are you going to do?'

'I've applied to be matron at Snead Hall.'

He laughed. He stared at her and he laughed. Then he sat down again.

'My dear Ella, they'll pay you half what I do and you'll moulder – '

'Anything,' Ella said, 'anything is better than staying with a man who plays games with other people's feelings.'

'Who have you been talking to?'

'It doesn't matter.'

'I can guess,' Patrick said. 'She doesn't matter either. Not now.'

He looked at Ella with a queer sideways glance. 'I didn't play games with Anna Bouverie, you know. She played them with me. She used me. It's never happened to me before and I don't like it.'

'I don't want to talk about it,' Ella said.

'I've had everything generous I've done thrown back in my face. Luke, Anna, now you. Can you imagine how I feel?'

'Oh yes – '

Patrick leaned forward. 'Please stay. All the usual inducements, of course, more money, more time off, but really because I need you to. I want you to.'

Ella stood up. 'So sorry, but no. I'll stay until the end of August. Then I shall go. You'd be better off with a couple to look after you, in any case. There are so many jobs for a man.'

'I may not even stay here – '

'I didn't think it would last long.'

Patrick looked up at her. 'I believed in it all, you know.'

'All I know,' said Ella briskly in her usual voice, 'is that now Anna Bouverie is free for the having, you don't want her any more. And that you are furious with her for that.' She marched to the door. 'If I ever marry, Patrick O'Sullivan, I shall make sure that my mate for life is a decent woman, or even, maybe, a book.' And then she went out quickly before he had time to collect his wits to reply.

Anna lay in the centre of her and Peter's bed and gazed up into the pale summer darkness. The doctor had left sleeping pills, but she thought she wouldn't take one until it was perfectly plain that she wouldn't sleep naturally. All around her in the Rectory's other bedrooms lay her relations, also probably, except for Flora, staring into nothing. Anna had climbed into bed with Flora and held her until she slept. On the floor beside her bed lay the dictionary, where Flora had wanted to look up 'paradise'. The dictionary had said that it was an ancient Persian pleasure ground and a place of bliss and the final abode of the blessed dead. It went on to describe paradise fish and paradise birds, gorgeous in colouring and plumage, and Flora's brow had cleared a little. She looked very small, to Anna, small and childish. It was a relief when her body relaxed and Anna could see she was truly asleep.

Then there had been Kitty. Kitty was not to be comforted with descriptions of Persian pleasure grounds. Kitty sat and nursed a tiny glass of sherry and said that her human landscape had quite fallen away and that she was not only desolate but absolutely no bloody use to anyone. No one had ever heard Kitty swear before. They looked at her with new respect. She blushed and tossed off her sherry and said loudly that she'd do her best to die soon, too, so that Anna could have her savings and her amethysts, and then she burst into tears again.

Laura said why didn't they have a suicide pact? She thought they might dress in black velvet and do it with poison at midnight. She meant to make Kitty laugh, but Kitty cried harder. Laura took Charlotte into the kitchen and they fried bacon and eggs and discussed the future. Laura said she was going to sell her flat and offer the money to Anna, and Charlotte said she was going to leave Edinburgh and get a job, any job. They took the bacon and eggs into the sitting-room and distributed the plates around to Anna and Kitty and Luke. Kitty said she couldn't face it, so Anna fed her little bits, like a baby, and after a while she stopped crying and ate by herself, until her plate was empty.

After supper, Laura took Kitty up to Charlotte's room, which they were sharing, and Charlotte said was it all right if she made a phone call.

'She's got a new bloke,' Luke said, when she had left the room.

'Oh? What sort of bloke?'

'He's called Adam. He's reading engineering.' He looked across at Anna. 'Mum – '

'Yes,' she said. She was so tired she felt as if she was floating, as if her mind was hovering some distance above her body like a little spotter plane.

'It wasn't Patrick, was it?'

'No.'

'It was Jonathan.'

'Yes.'

Luke dug himself out of his armchair to come and collapse on the floor by the sofa where Anna lay.

'I'm not going to India.'

'Oh Luke – '

'I don't want to.'

'Don't decide anything,' Anna said. 'Not yet. It's too soon. One longs to decide everything, it's a kind of reaction, but we mustn't. We'll decide the wrong things.'

'Are you going to decide about Jonathan?'

Anna turned her head to look at Luke. 'I decided that before Daddy died.'

'He's a great bloke.'

'Yes.'

'Are you going to marry him?'

Anna put out a hand and ruffled Luke's hair. 'I'll tell you that the minute I've told him. Promise.'

'And Dad?' Luke said.

'The funny thing is,' Anna said, 'that now he's dead I feel I can be fond of him in peace.'

Luke rolled over so that his face was buried against Anna. 'I want to love someone.'

'You will.'

He gripped her hand. 'It's the waiting,' he said. 'That's what I can't stand, the waiting.'

When Charlotte had come back into the room, she carried a little private glow with her. She sat down beside Luke and described Adam the engineer. He was six foot two and his parents lived in Cheadle Hulme. He played the clarinet and she had known him three weeks, at least, three weeks seriously, although of course he'd been around all her time at Edinburgh. She said he'd offered to come down and sort of be around, if it would help.

'Of course,' Anna said. It would clearly help Charlotte.

They sat there for a long time in the growing dark. The telephone rang several times and solicitous people asked if they were all right and did they need anything. To all of them, Anna said they were fine, thank you, and that all they needed was time. Then they took the telephone off the hook, and went upstairs together.

Charlotte went into Flora's room, where she was sleeping on a mattress on the floor. Luke paused before going into his room, just long enough to say, 'Will you be lonely?'

Anna said carefully, 'I don't think so.'

Now, lying awake, she wondered about it. What exactly did lonely mean? What had she meant by it, in the past, when she had declared herself to be so lonely within inches of Peter's living, breathing self? She switched the light on again, and picked up the dictionary from the floor. 'Alone,' it said, 'solitary, standing by oneself.' Yes, Anna thought, yes, I am all those things. 'Abandoned,' the dictionary went on, 'uncomfortably conscious of being alone.' She closed the book emphatically. She was neither of those last two things. She reached out and switched off the light. Those two things had been the loneliness of the past.

Miss Lambe was polishing the brass in Woodborough Vicarage. It was a huge task, involving over thirty pairs of door knobs, not to mention the front-door knocker and the letter box and the Archdeacon's study fender. Miss Lambe had chosen it deliberately, because it took her mind off things. The thing she wanted her mind particularly taken off was Jonathan's leaving the Vicarage. At the end of the week, he'd said to her in the kitchen that morning, at the end of the week he'd be going back to his university and then to Greece. Miss Lambe had little enough idea of the whereabouts of his university, and none at all about Greece, but they both sounded a long way off. He said he'd be back, of course, but Miss Lambe knew that that would not be the same as knowing, on a daily basis, that she'd find his blue shirts in the linen basket to be washed, along with the Archdeacon's grey ones.

She knew that he and the Archdeacon had had a long talk the night of Mr Bouverie's funeral. She hadn't been able to sleep, and had pattered downstairs, anxious not to be seen in the intimacy of her all-enveloping pink woolly dressing gown, and had noticed a line of light under the Archdeacon's study door, and heard their voices, just as the clock struck midnight. It did not occur to her to listen, but, as she scurried by, she could feel through the closed door that the atmosphere of the conversation was grave. It was, in consequence, no surprise to her to hear that Jonathan was going, but it made her feel most peculiar all the same, shaken and unsteady, and prone to snuffle. Polishing was a good antidote to snuffling.

She was painstakingly rubbing polish into the front-door knocker with a toothbrush when Anna appeared. Miss Lambe did not like Anna, who seemed to her not a good churchwoman, not properly modest and unassuming. Anna smiled at Miss Lambe. Miss Lambe clutched her toothbrush.

'I wonder if Mr Byrne is in,' Anna said.

Miss Lambe gave a tiny toss of her head.

'Mr Byrne is working.'

'Do you think I might interrupt him very briefly?'

'No,' said Miss Lambe.

'I think,' Anna said, putting her hand on the door, 'I think I just will, all the same.' She gave the door a little push.

'Stop!' said Miss Lambe.

'No,' said Anna. She pushed the door again and it swung open. The tiles of the hall were still damp from Miss Lambe's morning mopping. She stepped forward. Miss Lambe sped after her.

'He's private!' Miss Lambe cried, prodding Anna with her polishing toothbrush.

'Oh Miss Lambe,' Anna said turning. She was laughing.

Miss Lambe was full of sudden hatred. 'Stop that!' shrieked Miss Lambe.

A door opened on the landing and Jonathan appeared. They looked up at him.

'She wouldn't stop!' Miss Lambe cried to him. 'She wouldn't, she wouldn't!'

He began to descend the stairs. Anna could see he was fighting laughter. She said, 'Miss Lambe was very properly defending your working privacy. But I'll only be a moment.'

'I hope not,' Jonathan said. He put his hand under Anna's elbow. 'Thank you,' he said to Miss Lambe, leading Anna away. Miss Lambe watched them go up the stairs together, his hand still under her elbow. She would not, she decided, make them any coffee.

'Now,' Jonathan said, holding Anna hard against him. 'Now, my darling. At last, at last. Are you all right?'

'I think so.'

'I love you.' He led her to the divan and sat down on it, drawing her down close to him. 'Daniel has dismissed me. Very kindly and nicely and inevitably. To do me justice, I think I should probably have dismissed myself, to make things easier for you. For us.'

Anna leaned against him.

'I came to dismiss you too.'

'Did you?' His voice was indulgent. 'How comfortable, that we should all be in unison. I shall go back next week and set things in motion.'

'Things – '

'For you to join me. For you, after a decent interval, to become a don's wife and thus exchange one set of stereotypes for another.' He was laughing again.

'Not that,' Anna said softly.

'Not quite that, of course, but I fear not so different – '

'Jonathan,' Anna said, 'I love you and you saved my sanity and I want to be in bed with you. But I'm not marrying you.'

'I'm sorry,' he said, 'I'm so clumsy. Peter's only been dead a fortnight.'

Anna picked up his hand and separated the fingers. 'You aren't clumsy at all. And it isn't Peter. It's two other things. One is that I don't want another relationship just now, I don't want the involvement again yet. The other is that I have things to do.'

'What things? I'd never stop you – '

'Things,' Anna said, 'that I haven't done for too long, for twenty years. Things I can do for their own sake, not in relation to other people. I have to learn, you see, to live with myself, I have to learn what I can do. It's so trite to talk about being oneself, but it's what I feel, what I truly feel.'

'Why should marriage stop that? I'm the least possessive of men.'

Anna turned to look at him. 'To be perfectly honest with you, I am desperate for a rest from marriage.'

'But – '

'I know marriage to you would be unrecognisably different from marriage to Peter, but I still don't want it just now.'

'Darling Anna,' Jonathan said, putting his arms around her and pulling her down to lie beside him. 'You are very difficult to follow. Could you please tell me what exactly it is that you do want?'

'Yes,' Anna said. She looked straight at him. 'I want a lover.'

CHAPTER SEVENTEEN

The Bishop's study was a modest room. It was painted pale green and it looked out on to a long lawn lined with herbaceous borders that ended with a fine view of the Cathedral's Chapter House. It contained comfortable, ugly furniture, a great many dark, grave books and several photographs of the Bishop's grandchildren, all of whom appeared to have spent many, many years without any front teeth. There was a vase of yellow roses on his desk, and a very old mongrel asleep on the hearthrug.

When Anna arrived, the Bishop said he was so sorry, his wife was out, so they would have to make coffee for themselves. Anna said she would be delighted, and they spent a long time in the kitchen while the Bishop opened cupboards full of saucepans, and bags of flour, looking for cups. Once he said, 'Ah, biscuits,' in a pleased voice, and put a tin on the table. Then, in the midst of these explorations, his secretary came in, and looked crossly at Anna, and shooed them both into his study. Ten minutes later, she appeared with coffee on a tray laid with a tray cloth, and biscuits arranged in a fan on a flowered plate. The Bishop, who was deep in thought over what Anna had just said to him, failed to acknowledge her arrival, or her indignant departure.

Anna took a cup of coffee and the sugar bowl over to the Bishop. He said, spooning sugar, 'So what you are suggesting is a series of local support-groups for clergy wives?'

'Not exactly,' Anna said. 'That could turn into precisely the sort of bossy, ill-defined, do-gooding group that makes parish life so difficult. I think it ought to be a diocesan project. Like the ministerial review, or whatever you call your care-of-priests scheme. What's wrong is that the top administrative end of the Church doesn't know what it's like to live out in a rural parish. And I have to say that it often feels as if they don't much care, either.'

'You'd be quite wrong about *that*,' the Bishop said with some energy.

Anna said nothing. The Bishop stirred his coffee. He cleared his throat. 'Would you wish to be part of this scheme? In this diocese?'

'Oh yes,' Anna said, 'of course. After all, I know the other side. Trying to live with someone with a strong sense of service is taxing enough, so what must it be like being married to a vocation?'

The Bishop looked at her. 'What about a wife's sense of service?'

Anna looked back. 'A sense of service to God is one thing. It's independent, you chose it, you choose how you fulfil it. A sense of service to a husband who has chosen God is quite another. Handmaidens of the Lord have a much better time of it than handmaidens of husbands.'

The Bishop began to feel relieved that his wife was out. He had felt a little uneasy at seeing Anna and had wished for his wife's presence, but, now that he knew her errand, it seemed to him that his wife might not altogether have taken his part. He could not fault his wife's loyalty, but he had felt, in the last few weeks, a certain steel in her that he had not observed before.

'A clergy marriage,' Anna said, 'isn't immune to anything a lay marriage is vulnerable to.'

The Bishop leaned forward. 'I shall talk to my council.'

'Will you?'

'Can you think of any specific examples – '

'Yes,' Anna said. She got up. She was suddenly weary.

'I doubt we could pay for your help. I imagine such advice as you might give would have to be voluntary.'

'I never imagined otherwise.'

'My dear Mrs Bouverie,' the Bishop said abruptly, getting up too, 'how are you managing? What is your future?'

'We have to leave the Rectory, of course. But I have plans – '

He peered at her. 'Do you? Are you getting help? From the Archdeacon?'

'I am inundated with help,' Anna said, 'which I don't at all seem to want to accept.'

'Don't you?'

She regarded him. 'Would you? In my position? Or, for that matter, at any time in your life? Would you like to be beholden?'

The Bishop smiled. He put out his hand and grasped hers. 'I should absolutely loathe it,' he said.

Everybody had made offers. Laura and Kitty had offered to sell their flats; Sir Francis Mayhew had suggested the old coachman's rooms over his stables; Eleanor had telephoned from Oxford saying that she had finally decided to leave Robert and – this was added rather perfunctorily – she was so very sorry to hear about Peter, so why didn't they join forces and set up house together in Oxford? No sooner had she declined all these, than Daniel came out to Loxford to suggest, rather diffidently, that they might all move into the Vicarage, which needed people as he did, and to be quite honest, Miss Lambe . . .

'No,' Anna said gently. 'No. But thank you very much.'

'Because of Jonathan?'

'Because of independence.'

'But I would regard you as being wholly independent – '

'Daniel,' Anna said, putting her hands on his shoulders, 'I think I believe in God now more than I ever have, but at the moment, I simply can't stand the Church.'

Soon after Daniel had gone, the telephone had rung. Luke had answered it and came to find Anna, who was pulling early carrots, saying that it was the Diocesan Secretary. Anna looked amazed.

'Who's he?'

'I dunno. Said his name was Warbash. Brilliant.'

'Mr Warbash?' Anna said into the telephone.

'Commander Warbash, actually. Mrs Bouverie, could you run into Church House this week for a moment?'

'Is it about my idea?'

'No,' said Commander Warbash, who regarded clergy wives as a pretty low priority in his scheme of things. 'No. It's about something much more to your advantage. Something practical.'

'Can't you tell me on the telephone?'

'No,' said Commander Warbash.

Three days later, across his well-marshalled desk, he offered Anna a house. It was a cottage on glebe land the far side of the diocese. It had three bedrooms and an orchard and it was on a bus route. Anna might have it rent-free for five years.

Anna explained that Flora was at school in Woodborough and that Luke was probably going to do a foundation art course at the polytechnic. Commander Warbash said that both those facts might be regarded as details.

'I don't think so,' Anna said.

Commander Warbash said that the suggestion of a house had been made by a well-wisher of Anna's on the Diocesan Board of Finance, and that he, Commander Warbash, had assumed that, in her position, she would leap at the offer.

'I think,' Anna said boldly, 'that the test of true kindness is whether it benefits the recipient more than the donor.'

'So you decline Glebe Cottage?'

'I'm afraid so. I'm very grateful for the offer, but I can't disrupt all our lives by moving twenty-five miles away. Also – '

'Yes?' said Commander Warbash.

'Let's just say that the Church doesn't owe me anything any more. I'm – ' She paused. She wanted to say 'free' but thought it would sound aggressive, so she said instead, 'Separate now.'

'So how will you live?'

'I don't quite know yet.'

'You have your children to consider.'

She wanted nothing so much as to lean across the desk and slap him. She looked at his healthy, cleanly shaven, decent, insensitive, English face and imagined how it would feel under her hand. To restrain herself, she put her hands in her pockets.

'I imagine,' Commander Warbash said, 'that we have nothing more to say to one another.'

'Nothing.'

He rose and held out a hand. 'Then I will bid you good morning.'

Anna smiled. 'Good morning. And thank you for your time. I do hope,' she said with great warmth, 'that you will find a nice, amenable, *grateful* tenant for Glebe Cottage.'

'So do I,' he said. But when she had gone, and he reflected upon Glebe Cottage's dismal downstairs bathroom and front windows only a few feet from a main road, he rather doubted it. He began to hum. Confrontations always stimulated him a little, particularly with pretty women.

Anna said, 'I'll have to go and thank Colonel Richardson. It was his idea, clearly, and at least he really meant to be kind.'

Flora was drawing at the kitchen table. She wanted to live in a house like her new friend Verity's, with a conservatory and a double garage. She hadn't chosen to grasp the fact that there was even less money than before, only the fact that she was no longer committed to living in a Rectory. She said, 'It would be kind to me to live in a real house.'

'It would be quite kind to me, too,' Anna said.

Flora drew a blobby tree and began to add apples. 'If you died now, I'd be an orphan.'

'Would you like that?'

'No!' Flora said in terror.

'Then why say such things?'

Flora drew a rabbit under the tree. 'To scare you. To *make* you stay alive.'

Anna bent and kissed her. 'I'm going to see Colonel Richardson. Luke's upstairs if you want him.'

'Yes,' Flora said. She drew a second, smaller rabbit. 'Drive carefully.'

It was curious and exciting to drive so much, to feel that the car was hers to drive. She reversed slowly and drove down to the lane. She passed the Old Rectory without looking at it; the thought of Patrick O'Sullivan filled her with a dull rage mixed with shame. She drove across the green, waving to Mrs Eddoes who was tying up her sweet peas with raffia, and to Sheila Vinson who was washing her front-door paintwork, and turned down the lane to Quindale. She decided, as she drove, that she would not attempt to rehearse her explanation for turning down Glebe Cottage. She would simply, when confronted with Harry Richardson, tell the spontaneous truth.

But Harry Richardson was not at home. It was Marjorie, in a blue-and-white-patterned summer dress of immaculate cut, who opened the impressive front door of Quindale House. Anna was rather thrown.

'Marjorie. I'm so sorry to disturb you, but I wondered if I might have a word with Harry, he's been so kind – '

'I'm afraid he's out,' Marjorie Richardson said. 'Regimental re-union in London.' The hand that was not holding the front door crept to her double row of pearls. 'Come in,' she said unexpectedly.

Anna came. She followed Marjorie across the beautiful old rugs on the hall floor to a pretty back sitting-room with a door open to the garden. Out on the lawn beyond, the Richardson Labradors lay stoutly in the sun.

'Coffee?' Marjorie said, 'or gin?'

Anna said, startled, 'I suppose it better be coffee – '

'Why? Wouldn't you rather have gin?'

'I've almost never drunk it – '

'I've drunk it all my life,' Marjorie said. 'All my generation have. We're nothing like so fond of wine, but we all grew up on gin. I'll make you a weak one.'

Anna sat down, slightly dazed, on a fat, chintz-covered chair. Marjorie went over to a lacquered tray full of bottles and began some competent mixing. She came back to Anna with a small stemmed glass full of ice and lemon.

'That's a dry Martini. There's no pick-me-up like it.'

'Heavens,' Anna said. She took the glass gingerly.

Marjorie Richardson sat down opposite with her own much fuller glass. She waved it. 'Cheers,' she said.

Anna took a tiny, electrifying sip. She said, after a moment, 'Harry did something very kind. He got the diocese to offer me a cottage for five years. I'm terribly touched, but I'm afraid I've turned it down. It was such a kind idea.'

'It was mine,' Marjorie said.

Anna stared.

'Yours?'

'Yes. I thought it would be easier to accept from them than from any of us.'

Anna put her glass down. 'Then I'm even sorrier I turned it down – '

'Don't be,' Marjorie said. She crossed her handsome legs. 'I'm not surprised. I'd have turned it down too.'

'What – '

'You've had enough, haven't you? You've had an absolute basinful of being towed along behind some male institution, haven't you? I think you want out.' She paused and took a swallow. 'I think this because I think it too. Church or Army, what does it matter, they're all the same. Fill a man with notions of duty and obligation and then expect the wife to feel privileged to fall in with him. Makes me sick.'

Anna leaned forward. She wondered briefly if Marjorie had begun on the gin some time before her arrival.

'But you've always disapproved of me being a maverick! You were furious over Pricewell's – '

'Fury born of envy and admiration. I never had your guts, you see, I never had the guts to rebel. I went along with Harry and the Army for forty-three years, while everyone told me what a brick I was and ideal for an Army wife. Even Harry began to believe it. I don't think it's crossed his mind to wonder if I can look back on my life with even a fraction of the satisfaction he can look back on his. These male institutions – ' She paused, took another swallow and went on. 'I'll tell you something. Our elder daughter, Julia, was married to a sailor. He's a bit older than her, and he was a captain during the Falklands War. While he was away, Julia became responsible for all the wives and mothers and girlfriends of the men on his ship. They rang at all hours, all the time. She travelled all over England seeing these women, in her own time, at her own expense. When the Task Force returned, her husband was promoted, went off with a WRNS officer and the Navy never even said thank you. Not a postcard. Nothing. As a service wife she was expected to do all that and feel honoured to do it. You should hear Julia on the subject. You'd like Julia.'

'Marjorie,' Anna said, 'you've absolutely taken my breath away.'

'I owe you an apology, really,' Marjorie said. 'I've been pretty hard on you. I suppose suggesting the cottage was part of a wish to make amends. I'm glad you've turned it down. Now you're free, stay free. Would you let me lend you some money?'

'No,' Anna said gently, 'I wouldn't.'

'Damn. Though I don't see why you should take it just to make me feel better. You aren't drinking your drink.'

Anna picked up her glass. 'I'm rather startled by it. The combination of it and you has made me feel as if I'd already drunk several – '

'Where are you going to live?'

'Woodborough,' Anna said.

'Good. So I can come and see you? You'll accept veg and stuff – '

'Oh yes. I'd love to see you.'

'I'll bring Julia.'

'I'd love to meet Julia. Marjorie,' Anna said, 'will you tell Harry about the cottage? Will you explain that I'm so grateful but that I must be independent now? I'm afraid – I'm afraid that the cottage I was offered sounded rather – '

'Grim? I bet it did. Of course I'll tell Harry.' She looked at Anna and then tossed off her drink. 'Funny old fellow. Terribly protective, without one clue as to how we tick. Not one. I hope you'll keep in touch, let me know where you are, what's going on. I'm stuck now, of course, but I don't half get a kick out of watching you throw over the traces.' She brandished her glass. 'Want the other half?'

Anna hadn't been in Sister Ignatia's study since the day of Flora's interview. Sister Ignatia seemed quite unsurprised to see her, but then, she reflected, nuns did not seem to go in for visible surprise about anything. Anna sat down and let Sister Ignatia tell her all that St Saviour's was doing to comfort Flora over the loss of her father. Anna felt that the expression in Sister Ignatia's sharp eyes did not quite match the gentle platitudes of her speech. She said how grateful she was, what a difference the school's sympathy made to Flora. Then she waited. Sister Ignatia waited too, for a few seconds, to allow her a decent transition of mood, and then she said, in quite a different tone, 'And how can we help you?'

'I need a job,' Anna said.

Sister Ignatia nodded.

'I'm qualified to teach French and German in language schools, but not in the state system. I have also taught English as a foreign language.'

'And why have you come to me?'

'Because you don't have the same requirements as a state school, and because I know you a little and because I saw your advertisement in the *Woodborough Echo* for a languages teacher.'

'It might not benefit Flora.'

'It would do her no harm to learn to accept it.'

They looked at one another. Sister Ignatia remembered that Mrs Bouverie had concealed Flora's free place from her husband. She also remembered that, after her initial surprise, she had remarked to herself that Mrs Bouverie doubtless had her reasons.

'You are my first attempt at getting a job,' Anna said. 'I won't be surprised if you turn me down. But I'd like to teach here, I think.'

Sister Ignatia folded her hands under her scapular.

'I thought you might come to me.'

'And did you think what you might say to me when I did?'

'I thought I might agree. At least to a term's trial.'

'I'd be very grateful.' Anna leaned forward. 'How did you know I'd come?'

'You've a very ecumenical archdeacon here in Woodborough.'

'No!' Anna said. 'Not Daniel! This isn't a plot, is it, between you and Daniel Byrne? Will I never be free of the Church?'

Sister Ignatia gave a tiny, ironic smile.

'Oh Mrs Bouverie,' she said, 'it's not the Church you'll never be free of – '

★

When she left St Saviour's, Anna made her way to the market-place. It was market day, and busy, and the busyness added to Anna's sense of elation. Sister Ignatia had offered her a term's trial of full-time French and German teaching, a position to be reviewed at Christmas. It was, Anna could not help realising, exactly the kind of job that would have earned Peter's approbation. It was also, she could not avoid admitting, exactly the kind of job she would not take while he was alive. Flora would, of course, be most indignant. Anna's presence at St Saviour's would unquestionably cramp her style.

'A most imaginative child,' Sister Ignatia had said.

'Do you mean not strictly truthful?'

Sister Ignatia hadn't smiled. 'I simply mean what I said.'

Anna's goal in the market-place was the clutch of estate agents' offices, which huddled together for safety, rather as building societies and antique shops tend to do. Her errand was, she thought, quite simple; she wanted a house to rent with a minimum of three bedrooms. A garden would be nice. A garage didn't much matter. The first two agents she visited said they had nothing to rent whatsoever and the third offered her a sad-looking bungalow be hind the fire station. All three said she would find rented property very scarce; very scarce indeed. They shook their heads. They tried to interest Anna in small houses they had for sale, dull little houses on residential estates. Anna said she had no capital and could thus make no down payment. They looked at her pityingly, but made it plain that it was not their business to do any more for her.

The fourth agency produced two houses. One was a sturdy villa in a suburb of Woodborough, the property of a businessman currently living in the Far East, the second a narrow slice in a Victorian terrace. Anna said she would like to look at it. The agent urged the villa.

'But I'd rather be in the middle. And it's cheaper – '

'Nothing like so pleasant, though. And only three bedrooms.'

'May I see it? May I?'

The agent sighed. He knew it would be a waste of time. The house had been on his books a year. He called a girl from a back office where she was photocopying particulars.

'Debbie. Take Mrs Bouverie to 67 Nelson Street, would you?'

'You won't like it,' Debbie said to Anna, on the pavement.

'Won't I? Why won't I?'

'It's ever so dark. Creepy.'

'Is this a very good way to do business, do you think, putting clients off before they even get there?'

'Only trying to help,' Debbie said. It might be a stupid errand, but anything was better than the photocopier. 'You're the ninth person I've taken. That's all.'

Nelson Street was five minutes from the market-place. It was too narrow, and it lacked front gardens, but the far end of it opened into the old abbey grounds, an eighteenth-century park designed picturesquely round the ruins of Woodborough's medieval abbey. Number 67 was exactly like its neighbours; flat-fronted, built of brick, with a window beside the front door, two above it, and one in the top-floor gable, under cuckoo-clock eaves of painted wood.

'Terrible, isn't it?' Debbie said.

Anna did not think so. She took the key firmly from Debbie and opened the front door. A smell of old, damp newspapers greeted her. The hall was narrow and dark, with a sharply rearing staircase, but beyond it Anna could see sunlight through a back window and something green further off. She turned to Debbie.

'Why don't you go off for ten minutes, and I'll explore on my own?'

'I'm not allowed to do that. I'm not allowed to leave the client.'

'Even if the client refuses to look at the property with you standing scowling at her?'

Debbie gaped.

'Go away,' Anna said. 'Go away and come back in a quarter of an hour.'

'Mr Rickston – '

'I'll deal with Mr Rickston.'

'Barmy,' Debbie said. But she backed away through the front door. Anna shut it behind her.

'Now,' she said to 67 Nelson Street.

It waited. It allowed her to open doors and windows and climb the staircase and investigate cupboards and trap doors. It let her look into the bathroom (very bad) and the kitchen (worse) and observe the discouraging boarding-house décor. Not until she had looked out through the back windows and seen the wholly neglected little garden surrounded by old brick walls, in which an apple tree was growing (an apple tree laden with infant fruit), did it begin, tentatively, to defend itself. Coming away from the window – the garden was full of sunlight – Anna saw that, although the walls were covered in embossed and terrible papers, and the paintwork was ochre and lime-green, the fireplaces and mantelpieces were still original, there were proper cornices and deep skirting boards, and, above all, an unmistakable atmosphere of profound benevolence.

'I don't think you're dark or creepy,' Anna said out loud. 'Nobody could hope to look their best under salmon-pink gloss paint.'

The doorbell rang hoarsely. Anna went down the stairs and opened the door saying, 'That wasn't quarter of an hour – '

'What wasn't?' Jonathan said.

'Jonathan!'

'I followed you. I saw you in the market-place. Are you going to live here?'

She drew him in. 'I might. I think I like it.'

He looked round. 'I have no eye at all. Never know what I like in houses.' He looked at her. 'Only in people.'

She took his hand. 'Come and see. There's room for all the children and a garden.'

'Is there room for a lover?'

'Not as well as the children.'

He kissed her.

'Worth a try – '

She led him into the kitchen and pointed out through the window. 'Look. An apple tree. And lovely walls. I'm going to teach at St Saviour's.'

He put his face into the back of her neck. 'Try not to be too self-sufficient. Try to need me a little. There are my feelings to consider after all.'

She said, 'It was you who said seize the moment.'

'That was before I was as deep in as I am now.'

She turned and put her arms round him. 'I'm in love too, you

232

know. It's just taken me in rather a different way. Just as Peter's death has taken me in a way I never dreamed of.'

He regarded her for some time. Then he smiled and said, 'I understand, you know. And you thrill me, the way you're behaving, you really do. Now, show me your house.'

CHAPTER EIGHTEEN

The new Rector of Loxford had not been ordained until he was forty-five. He'd been an insurance agent before that. He was called Philip Farmer and he had a wife called Dorothy and two grown-up sons in the computer industry. He was a big, solid man with a genial expression and spectacles, and he told the Parochial Church Councils of the five parishes that it had been his and Dorothy's dream for ten years to come to a rural living, and that they felt very privileged to have been accepted.

Dorothy Farmer was evidently capable. Within weeks of her arrival, new curtains of her own making blew out of the constantly, healthily, open Rectory windows and the WI Friday market had benefited from jars of her excellent chutney. The parish group found themselves somewhat disconcerted. Celia Hooper, Trish Pardoe and Elaine Dodswell had all paid an eager early visit to the Rectory, to explain their willingness. Dorothy Farmer had shown them into the newly painted, trimly furnished, almost unrecognisable sitting-room, with a single picture (a quiet landscape) hanging dead centre over the fireplace, and a row of African violets in copper pots on the gleaming windowsill.

'Now then,' said Dorothy Farmer, bringing in a tray of coffee and home-made biscuits, 'tell me about yourselves.'

They tried. They told her about the Brownies and the old people and the Sunday school Christmas play and the difficulty of finding volunteers for the church-cleaning rotas. They attempted to explain delicately about their efforts to help Anna. They pointed out what a lot of work five parishes gave a priest, and how they knew that clergymen and their wives were under a lot of stress these days and that it was their fervent wish to help to alleviate this.

Dorothy Farmer listened. She made notes in a notebook. She smiled a good deal, and nodded, and looked at them through her well-polished spectacles. When they had finished, she let a little pause fall, and then she picked up the coffee pot, and went round their cups with it saying, 'I can see you've had a very difficult time. I'm so pleased Philip and I are here. I shall of course, being a trained physiotherapist, do a bit of work at the hospital to keep my hand in, but the rest of the time I shall be here, in the parish.' She paused and smiled again. 'Very much so, in fact.'

They watched her. She sat down again in her neat oatmeal chair.

'Between you and me,' Dorothy said confidingly, 'I think there's a lot of nonsense talked about clergy stress. It's a question of attitude, to my mind. If you ask me, most clergy wives these days are a lot of moaning minnies.'

Anna was invited to Philip Farmer's induction service. Laura was staying with her at the time, and so she came too, in the gilded velvet coat she had worn for Anna's wedding. As she had just signed a contract for a new series of Irish stout advertisements – the first batch having become a cult success – she bought a new hat. It was a straw cartwheel with the crown swathed in golden satin. Laura added artificial flowers and ears of corn and a huge glistening brooch shaped like a dragonfly. Her final appearance made Anna feel very affectionate.

Apart from regular visits to Peter's grave (it had no headstone yet because there were arguments over the lettering), Anna had not lingered recently in Loxford. She had not, for one thing, had time, and for another, it seemed only fair to stay out of Dorothy Farmer's way. She had paid a single, brief courtesy visit to the Rectory and come away astounded. 'You wouldn't believe,' she said to Luke, 'that it was the same house.' Luke, who had contentedly painted his attic room in Nelson Street black all over, merely grinned. Life in Loxford seemed to him, at times, already as remote as the moon.

Loxford church was not as full as it had been for Peter's funeral. It looked tremendously clean – almost too clean, Anna thought – and there were the usual lovely flowers which bore the mark of the skilled hands of Lady Mayhew and Miss Dunstable. In the Rectory pew sat Dorothy Farmer in a fawn-checked two-piece, and beside her, two large sons and one small daughter-in-law. They were, from head to foot, impeccably brushed and polished.

Anna and Laura sat at the back. Several people turned round and made welcoming faces and grimaced at them to come further up the church. Anna shook her head. She wished Kitty was there, but Kitty had refused to come. She had sent Anna her amethysts, with a note saying that, as she might as well be dead, why didn't Anna have them now? Anna had sent them back, saying that (a) nobody could enjoy a present sent in such a spirit and (b) she wanted, please, Kitty to stay alive as long as possible. Kitty had sulked after that, and refusing to come to the induction was part of the sulking. 'Poor Kittykins,' Laura said, 'she thinks it makes her glamorous.'

The Bishop conducted the service. Daniel was there too. Philip Farmer looked very pleased at the whole proceeding and beamed confidently at his new flock. He had plans for them, evangelical plans, plans that he had been shrewd enough not to reveal in front of the likes of Sir Francis Mayhew and Harry Richardson, before they had finally accepted him. He thought he would start with the music; a good modern song book, some young mothers with guitars, a few Taisé choruses. Then he would turn to the services and replace Rite B with Rite A. It would be nice to encourage the congregation to participate in the services; some personal confessions, perhaps (surely even Loxford had a reformed alcoholic or two – even perhaps a drug addict?), and the warm exchanging of signs of peace. Loxford needed bringing to God, he could see that, plain as the nose on your face. It had got fossilised, poor old Loxford, fossilised by notions of 'the Church'. Well, Philip didn't call it 'the Church', and nor did Dorothy. They called it 'the Jesus

Movement'. Dorothy had played the recorder at services in their last parish and she would undoubtedly do it again here; it was a wonderful ice-breaker, a wonderful way to bear witness to the Lord. Philip Farmer's smile grew and grew. He looked upon his unsuspecting parishioners with love. He had so much to share with them.

In the churchyard afterwards, Celia Hooper came up to Anna. She said, 'Oh, I'm ever so pleased to see you,' and then to Anna's amazement, she kissed her. 'Are you all right?' she said. 'Are you settled?'

'Yes,' Anna said, recovering. 'Yes, I am. We all are. It's a funny little house but we like it.'

'Oh Anna,' Celia said. Her eyes were unnaturally bright. 'We miss you – '

'I expect it's just the change – '

'No. No, it's more than that. You ask Elaine.'

Anna looked across the churchyard. Dorothy Farmer was saying something to Daniel. Even from this distance, her demeanour looked arch.

'She seems terribly efficient – '

'Oh yes, she's efficient all right. I suppose I shouldn't say this, but I feel, we all feel, that there isn't the same humanity, somehow. We've lost the colour.'

'It's very early days,' Anna said, battling for the right platitudes.

Two precise tears spilled from Celia's eyes. 'We miss Peter – '

'Of course.'

'I shouldn't say this, to you of all people, but you felt you could get close to Peter, that he needed you in some way – '

'I'm so glad.'

'Am I offending you? I'd do anything rather than offend you.'

'Don't you think,' Anna said, 'that you and I have got quite beyond this kind of conversation? You did offend me, in the past, quite tremendously, but then, in a sense, I offended you by not being what you thought I should be. It's all over now, all of that.' She glanced round the churchyard. 'This isn't my parish any

237

more, this isn't my patch. I'm not part of the Church now, not the way I was.'

Celia looked at her. 'You seem so controlled – '

'I know.'

'Don't you feel sad, being back here? Don't you hate seeing her being what you were? And what about Peter – '

'What about him?'

Celia looked suddenly nervous. She said, 'I didn't mean to suggest – '

'Shall we leave it?' Anna said. 'Shall we just leave it there?'

'Except – '

'Except what?'

'I'd love to do something to help. Really I would. Make curtains for you or something.'

Anna stared at her. Would she never understand? Then she touched her arm briefly. 'Thank you so much, but I'm making my own. Not very well, but I don't seem to mind that.'

And then Laura came up, and said that the Bishop had told her that her fleeting appearances on television were about the only reason he ever turned the thing on these days. She glanced roguishly at Celia. 'Rather a feather in one's pagan cap. Don't you think?'

Patrick O'Sullivan had seen Anna arrive in Loxford. He had told himself that he wasn't looking out for her, but that he would have been reading the paper in that particular chair by that particular window just then, in any case. It was chance that he should happen to look up and see her helping Laura out of the car, followed by a brief pantomime with the wind and Laura's hat. He had craned forward. Anna looked very well, he thought. She wore clothes he didn't recognise. She was a schoolmistress now, he told himself. He tried to smile.

He did not go across to the church. He wasn't particularly interested in this new Rector and even less so in his purposeful, bolster-shaped wife. Ella, who came to see him sometimes on her half-days off from Snead Hall, said that there was a lot of muttering in the parishes about Dorothy Farmer. As a leaving present,

Patrick had given Ella the deposit on a bungalow at Church End, which she would use in the holidays, and when she retired. She seemed to like Snead Hall. She said it was a relief to work with other people.

In her place, Patrick had hired a Spanish couple. They had lasted three weeks, and then the wife had said that the country gave her allergies, and they had gone back to London. The agency Patrick used had replaced them with a quiet Scottish pair. Patrick had the feeling that the husband – courteous, unobjectionable, industrious – had once been in prison. It was something to do with his self-effacement and his wife's watchful protectiveness. The wife cooked better than Ella, but she had no sense of humour. Patrick missed Ella.

He looked out of the window again. Below him, in the shrubberies around the front drive, his silent Scots manservant was pulling out bindweed. Everyone was coming out of church, and the privileged few were straying off in the direction of the Rectory. Another tea party. Was the Church of England wholly sustained on tea and coffee and custard creams? He saw Anna from a distance. There was quite a crowd round her, an eager-looking crowd; he could even see Miss Dunstable in it, and Lady Mayhew, of all unlikely people. The crowd moved slowly out of the churchyard and across the green to where the cars were parked. Anna stopped by hers, unlocking the passenger door for Laura. Then she turned and said something, laughing, to Sheila Vinson, who was standing quite close to her, and for a moment Patrick could see her face very clearly, and she looked suddenly very young, and very like Luke. Patrick gripped his newspaper. It wasn't just Ella he missed. He missed Luke. And Anna.

67 Nelson Street was much improved. Charlotte had brought Adam, the engineer, to stay for a fortnight – this had caused great complication in sleeping arrangements, with Anna and Flora ending up quarrelsomely sharing Anna's bed – and he had steadily, good-humouredly, obliterated most of the fearful wallpapers under coats of bargain emulsion, bought from a stall in the market. Then he had taken Charlotte off to Italy, with backpacks,

and Luke and his friend Barnaby had, to Anna's amazement, offered to clear the garden. They did it with enormous gusto and lack of finesse, lighting vast belching bonfires that brought Anna's new neighbours round at once in high states of indignation and leaving the garden looking like a lunar landscape. 'There,' Luke said with evident pride. 'Now that'll give you a really clear start.'

Luke, she observed, was very happy. He had acquired a girl-friend – a small, dull, sweet thing with huge brown eyes and a perfect rosebud mouth she hardly ever opened – and a holiday job collecting trolleys for Pricewell's. (It took some self-control for Anna not to tease him about Pricewell's.) Above his bed in his blackened eyrie, Luke had pinned reproductions of paintings he admired, a poster Barnaby had given him advertising a new political group at Leningrad University (in Russian which he did not speak or read), and a photograph of Peter. It was an official photograph taken for the Woodborough paper when Peter became Rector of Loxford. He was in his cassock, and a surplice, and he stood gravely in front of the south porch of Loxford church. It was not the one Anna had on her dressing table. That one had been taken when Luke was born, and Peter was standing by a gate to a field holding the baby, and looking at the camera, and laughing. Flora didn't like that photograph. She didn't like the fact that the baby Peter was holding was Luke and not her.

People began to come, quite soon, to Nelson Street. Daniel came, and Isobel Thompson, and a fellow teacher from St Saviour's. Flora brought friends home; so did Luke. Marjorie Richardson brought her magnificently outspoken daughter, Julia, who stayed to supper and then put herself to bed on the sofa. And then, quite unheralded, Patrick came. Anna opened the front door, expecting Isobel, and there he was, standing on the pavement, looking up at her. Her heart sank a little at the sight of him.

She said, quite truthfully, 'You are the last person I expected.'

He followed her into her sitting-room. He said, 'This room could belong to nobody but you.' He looked odd in it, so ordered and expensive amid Anna's possessions which seemed to crowd round him in this little room with almost an air of eagerness. He held out a paper-wrapped bottle. 'Something for you. To christen the house.'

240

She knew it would be champagne even before she opened it. She said, 'How very kind,' and put the bottle down carefully on a little table by the fireplace. Then she waited.

Patrick sat down on the Knole sofa, which now dominated Nelson Street like a dead mammoth.

'Are you happy here? Not cramped?'

'Oh yes, we're cramped. But it doesn't matter, it isn't important.'

'I've wanted to come, for weeks,' Patrick said, 'but I've managed to restrain myself. I wish you'd sit down.'

She sat, on a low chair across the room from him.

'Ella accused me of playing games with you. She nearly admitted that you had said so to her. And then she accused me of losing interest in you the moment Peter died, the moment you were free. I simply can't rest until I've told you that neither are true.'

'I've got some deeply ordinary wine,' Anna said. 'Would you like some?'

'I'd rather you listened to me.'

'I was only trying to lubricate the occasion – '

Patrick shouted, 'Don't mock me!'

'I don't have to listen to you,' Anna said. 'I certainly don't have to if you shout.'

He leaned forward, his elbows on his knees, staring at her. 'I suppose this is some kind of revenge.'

'Revenge?'

'Once I had the upper hand. Now you do. And you're enjoying it.'

'Patrick,' Anna said, 'you don't have a clue, do you?'

'I have more than – '

'No,' she said, interrupting, leaning forward herself, 'no. You don't. You talk of revenge. Revenge has never crossed my mind. All that I'm interested in just now is independence.'

He smiled. 'That's just this modern woman thing.'

'It has nothing to do with gender. It's to do with humanity. Do you know what independence means?' Anna said. 'It means not being subordinate. It means thinking and acting for yourself. It means not depending on anyone else for your sense of value. Wouldn't that describe you?'

'I'd like to think so – '

'Well, I'd like to think it described me, too, now.'

'But have you enough money?'

'Yes,' she said, suddenly furious. 'Yes. Heaps. Billions. More than I know how to spend.'

He sighed. 'If I can't help you, and clearly I can't, is there any way we could have some kind of relationship?' He looked at her. 'Would you come to bed with me?'

She said, 'I do have to admire your continuing nerve – '

'But you responded when I kissed you.'

'I did.'

'So you liked it.'

'I did.'

'So you would like some more.'

'No, I wouldn't.'

'There's another man,' Patrick said.

'Correct.'

'Anna,' Patrick said, holding his hands out to her, 'why not me?'

She stood up. She was weary of him. 'Because you're a bully,' she said, 'and I'm tired of bullies.'

The Farmers were eating an early supper in Loxford Rectory. It was the evening of a Parochial Church Council meeting at Quindale. Celia had just resigned as secretary. Philip Farmer proposed to suggest that Dorothy should take her place. Dorothy had always been excellent at that sort of thing.

They ate their supper in the kitchen. It was newly painted in lemon-yellow and looked out on to the beginning of the patio with which the Farmers intended to replace Anna's vegetable garden. They would certainly go on growing vegetables, but at the far end of the garden where there was that terrible wilderness. It would be a good spot for Dorothy's rotary clothes-dryer too, out of sight of prying eyes.

Between them, on the table, by the salt and pepper mills, lay a letter from the Archdeacon. It was about a new diocesan project to help the wives of clergymen who got into difficulties. The help would cover a whole spectrum of domestic problems – lack of money, loneliness, marital misery. The Archdeacon asked all the priests in his area to think of anyone they knew who might be in trouble of this kind. The names of such people, and the source from which they came, would be treated, of course, with the utmost confidentiality.

Philip said cheerfully, reaching for the water jug, 'Well, we needn't put you forward, dear.'

Dorothy reread the letter. She said, 'You know, I think it's shutting the stable door after the horse has bolted. I think they all got their fingers burned over Anna Bouverie and now they're trying to stop anything like that happening again. Though I must say, I'm amazed he's got the nerve to send out a letter about it himself.'

'The Archdeacon? Why?'

Dorothy folded and rolled her seersucker napkin and pushed it through her napkin ring.

'You know how I am about gossip – '

'Yes,' said Philip, who did. He went on eating, as if he didn't care.

'Of course, one must be terribly careful in villages.'

'Certainly.'

'I think I wouldn't have given this tale any credence if it hadn't tied up with so much evidence.'

'Of course not.'

Dorothy folded her hands on the table. 'The rumour is,' she said, 'and mind you, I can hardly believe it – but the rumour is that Anna Bouverie formed a liaison with the Archdeacon of Woodborough.'

'Polyester!' Miss Dunstable shouted.

Anna held the telephone a little away from her ear.

'Modern!' Miss Dunstable bellowed. 'That's what she said to me! "This is the modern Church," she said to me! "We need easy-care altar linen." Easycare!'

'Oh dear,' Anna said, 'I'm so sorry – '

'It's blasphemy!'

'Perhaps she really wants to save trouble – '

'Don't you start,' Miss Dunstable said. 'What's trouble beside standards, I'd like to know? She's a frightful woman.'

'Are you sure,' Anna said, leaning against the wall of her tiny hall and smiling, 'that she isn't just different?'

'Vulgar,' Miss Dunstable said. 'Wants dried flowers in the Lady Chapel. It'll be plastic poinsettias at Christmas next.'

'I'm so sorry. Really I am. But I don't think I can do anything.'

'No. No, no. Of course you can't. I just had to let off steam. You know.'

'Of course I do – '

'I've saved you some of my Californian poppy seed,' Miss Dunstable said, in a different tone.

'How nice of you – '

'I'll give you some pinks when I divide them.'

'That would be lovely.'

There was a little pause and then Miss Dunstable snorted, 'Easycare, indeed,' and banged down the telephone.

Luke was in the kitchen, cooking pasta. This week, he thought he would probably be a sculptor. Last week he had toyed with photography. He called out, 'Who was that?'

'Miss Dunstable.'

'What did she want, for heaven's sake?'

'I think,' Anna said, 'that that was yet another apology.'

Luke twirled long, pale lengths of tagliatelle out of the saucepan on a wooden spoon. 'Weird,' he said.

Seventy miles away, in his unremarkable university rooms, Jonathan was writing to Anna. He wrote to her a great deal, long, discursive, loving letters which were, he found, small but vital compensation for not seeing her as much as he would have liked to. His need to see her troubled him considerably, because it was a need that was new to him, and because it interfered with the self-sufficiency he had grown accustomed to, and dependent upon. He was also troubled by thinking that not only did Anna not seem to need him as reciprocally as he needed her but also that part of her remained elusive. Another part of her, which he also found difficult to come to terms with, seemed to be particularly attached to Daniel. It didn't, in Jonathan's mind, make all of a piece, it didn't seem to be consistent. When he looked back on his relationship with Anna, he saw an image of her, standing in a cage surrounded by people who were either longing to rescue her or determined that she should not escape. And then suddenly, it seemed to him, the cage was empty and Anna had eluded all those people and had run ahead of them, away from them. It was almost, now, as if she were in hiding, and they were all looking for her, guided only by bursts of slightly mocking laughter from her hiding-place. The tables were turned – but how had she done it?

For the first time in his life, Jonathan thought a good deal about the future. He thought about it because it had begun to matter. He found he wanted to plan. He had to stop himself from saying to Anna, In two years' time, will you – or even, Next Christmas, can I – because he wasn't inclined to tempt providence. Her life looked predictable enough, but its essence was so changed from her former life that it hardly seemed to belong to the same person. She had said to him once, seeing his anxiety, 'I will need someone else one day. I think I will. When I've got used to myself.' He had to be content with that.

Yet her growing degree of self-government disturbed him. You could see it reflected in her children, in her appearance, in her actions, which seemed to him sometimes arbitrary, because they weren't predictable. She excited him terribly, her personality quite as much as her body. He felt he was on some marvellous quest, at the best of times, and utterly lost in a hostile maze, at the worst. He was more deeply interested than he had ever been in his life before, more committed, more afraid.

He wrote, 'I am afraid.' He looked at it. He didn't like the look of it, so he crossed it out blackly and wrote, 'Damn, damn. Mustn't whine. Won't whine,' instead. He put his pen down. What was there, after all, to be afraid of? What was there to fear in placing his hopes and fears in Anna's hands? Of all the people Jonathan had ever known, besides his brother Daniel, Anna had a faithful heart, that commodity he had never thought to value before and which he now knew to be more precious than pearls. Smiling to himself, Jonathan seized his pen again and began to write rapidly.

CHAPTER NINETEEN

Anna sat on Peter's grave. When it had been covered over, the turfs had been put back, like a roughly torn green rug, and they were at last slowly beginning to knit together once more. The mound of earth had subsided as well. It was starting to look, Anna thought, much more harmonious with the surrounding churchyard.

It was November, a soft, dove-grey day with no wind. Beside Anna lay a spade and an empty black plastic flowerpot which had contained the old shrub rose she had just planted at Peter's feet. At his head, there was nothing. There should have been a head-stone, a simple upright slab of local stone from the quarry beyond New End, but Anna had only just won the battle over the letter-ing; her last battle, she sometimes thought, of the whole long business.

'Are you listening?' Anna said. She looked round. The church-yard was empty, and so was the lane beyond it. If anyone was watching from behind the shining Rectory windows, Anna thought, well, let them.

'Peter,' Anna said, 'I have to talk to you.' It was easy to talk to him, sitting on his grave in the mild, still afternoon, with her arms wrapped round her knees. 'We needn't pretend now, need we? We needn't avoid the fact any longer that we had come to the end of our happy times together. Do you get the feeling that we were, in some way, rescued? I wish you hadn't been the one to pay the price, I violently wish that, but I can't help wondering what would have become of us, with my growing appetite for life, and your increasing distaste for it.'

A little, diffident gust of wind blew a few yellow leaves across the grass towards her. She picked them up. They came, she noticed, from the silver birch by the Rectory garage that she had so despised as suburban when she first came to Loxford, and had then grown to love for its grace and colouring.

'It's lovely now,' Anna said, laying the leaves down Peter's mound like a row of buttons. 'I can love you in peace, I can remember things without bitterness. I think you can understand that now, can't you? If you can't, if you still feel I ought to be doubled up in self-abasement, then you haven't been in paradise long enough. But I don't think you do. I don't feel you haunt me.'

She looked at the space at the head of the grave.

'I want to talk to you about this headstone. You know what the parish wanted? They wanted "Peter Bouverie" and then your dates, and then "Rector of this parish from thing to thing", and then "Beloved husband, father and friend". Well, I struck. I mean, you don't want that kind of meaningless, sentimental claptrap, do you? I struck and I've won. I'll tell you what you're getting and it's from me to you, Peter, from me to you.'

She turned and put her hands on the grave, as if on his chest.

'In very simple letters, we will put your name and your dates. And then underneath, this will be carved. Listen: "Pray for me, as I will for thee, that we may merrily meet in heaven." And the emphasis, Peter, is on the "merrily".'

'Oy!' someone shouted.

Anna looked up. Mr Biddle, unchanged in every degree, was leaning on the churchyard wall. He took off his hat and shook it at Anna.

'Waste of time!' he bawled. 'Waste of time, Mrs B! 'E can't 'ear you!'

He cackled with mirth. Anna got up off the grave and stood

looking down at it, calmly, dusting her hands together. Then she waved at Mr Biddle, smiling.

'Oh yes, he can!'

She glanced down at Peter. She said again, so softly that only he could hear, 'Oh yes, he can.'

A NOTE ON THE AUTHOR

Joanna Trollope is the author of a number of historical novels, and *Britannia's Daughters*, a study of women in the British Empire. *The Rector's Wife* is her fourth contemporary novel, following *The Choir*, *A Village Affair* and *A Passionate Man*. She was born and lives in Gloucestershire.